D0874872

Anita Burgh was born in Gillingham, Kent, but spent her early years at Lanhydrock House in Cornwall. Returning to the Medway Towns, she attended Chatham Grammar School, and became a student nurse at UCH in London. She gave up nursing upon marrying into the aristocracy. Subsequently divorced, she pursued various careers – secretarial work, as a laboratory technician in cancer research and as an hotelier. She divides her time between Gloucestershire and the Auvergne in France, where she shares her life with her partner, Billy, a Cairn terrier, three mixed-breed dogs, three cats and a bulldog puppy. The visits of a constantly changing mix of her four children, two stepchildren and six grandchildren keep her busy, happy, entertained and poor! Anita Burgh is the author of many bestsellers, including *Distinctions of Class*, which was shortlisted for the Parker Romantic Novel of the Year Award. Visit Anita Burgh at her website: www.anitaburgh.com.

By Anita Burgh

Daughters of a Granite Land 1: The Azure Bowl
Daughters of a Granite Land 2: The Golden Butterfly
Daughters of a Granite Land 3: The Stone Mistress

Distinctions of Class
Love the Bright Foreigner
Advances
Overtures
Avarice
Lottery
Breeders
The Cult
On Call
The Family
Clare's War
Exiles
The House at Harcourt

Tales from Sarson Magna: Molly's Flashings
Tales from Sarson Magna: Hector's Hobbies

THE GOLDEN BUTTERFLY

Daughters of a Granite Land

BOOK TWO

Anita Burgh

ORION

The author would like to thank Romi Earle
for her generosity in sharing her reminiscences
of France in 1940.

An Orion paperback

First published in Great Britain in 1990
by Chatto & Windus Ltd
This paperback edition published in 2001
by Orion Books Ltd,
Orion House, 5 Upper St Martin's Lane,
London WC2H 9EA

Second impression 2002

A CIP catalogue record for this book
is available from the British Library.

ISBN 0 75283 758 3

Typeset at The Spartan Press Ltd,
Lymington, Hants

Printed and bound in Great Britain by
Clays Ltd, St Ives plc

For Alison Samuel,
my editor and friend

And all about her wheeled and shone,
Butterflies, all golden.

John Davidson

Chapter One

1

'If there's going to be a war then I want to be part of it.' That's what she had said and that's what she had meant – then. Two years later she frequently regretted that she had won the argument.

It seemed a lifetime ago, not a mere two years, since she had stood in her parents' New York drawing room and defied them. It was easy to get her own way – as it had always been easy. At nineteen, Grace had had years of experience in dealing with her parents, of knowing when to persuade, when to cajole or sulk, and when to throw a tantrum to get exactly what she wanted.

She sat at the desk, the oil lamp, partly shaded, hissing beside her – an oasis of light in the centre of the long, darkened room. She sat still – an island of silence surrounded by the snuffling, sighing, tossing rows of restless men in their black iron beds. She pulled her blood-red cloak about her against the early morning chill, making a gash of colour in the monochrome of night.

A noise, half sigh, half strangled groan made her look up. Her ears were trained to differentiate such signs of distress from the customary sounds of sleeping men. She stood and peered at those beds closest to her desk which held the men whom only hope was now sustaining. They slept. She listened carefully. The groan was not repeated.

She was the only nurse in the ward, the others having gone to take a quick bite to eat in this unexpected lull. Since the new offensive started they had been grabbing food and sleep as and when they could. The days of the week or hours of the day were no longer clearly defined.

Now the passage of time was marked by how many operations were performed, how many more were to be done, the number of dressings to attend to, and how many hands of dying men there were to hold. Where the nurses found the energy was a continuing mystery. Time without number, when they seemed near to collapsing with fatigue, from somewhere had come sufficient strength to tend a new wave of men unloaded from the ambulances and placed in their care. Through pain-blurred eyes the men looked at them with hope and gratitude and instantly the women's tiredness vanished, the aching feet were forgotten and work and healing began again.

She looked down at the note pad on her desk and frowned at the letter she was trying to write. As the carnage worsened she found there was nothing to write home about. She did not have enough skill to tell them effectively of the sights she saw, but in any case she no longer had the inclination to let her parents know. For what was happening here was her world, belonging only to her and the patients and the other members of staff. That other cosy world in which her parents lived had no relevance to her any more. How could she tell them of the suffering, the stinking horror of it all? What could be their reaction as they sat in the luxury of their drawing room, in clean laundered clothes, after a fine dinner with a good claret? – incomprehension.

She read what she had written, that it was night time, that she was alone, that a man had just groaned . . . To survive with her sanity intact, Grace had found it was best if she concentrated only on this one minute within this one hour. It was better not to think of what had gone before, or what the long line of ambulance trains might bring here tonight.

She heard the barrage echoing in the distance. That was the backdrop of her life now. She had almost forgotten what it was like to hear birdsong, for there were no birds left to sing, just the booming of the great guns on the Somme raining down death and destruction.

2

Just recently she had begun to think that she had no past and that there was no future for her outside this base hospital in France. If she tried to remember her home, the warmth and comfort, she found she could not. There were times when she was convinced that life was a dream, that all her life she had been here, in this hell.

The groan rang out again. This time there was no mistaking it. She picked up her lamp and moved silently between the beds. When she held the lamp aloft and watched its light falling on the long rows of beds, she knew full well that when she had made her brave statement this was how she had imagined it would be – herself as a modern Florence Nightingale. No one had warned her of the blood, the pus, the gangrene, the stench and the tangible terror of the patients that filled the large room.

'Is the pain too bad, Captain?' she whispered to the patient brought in two days ago with a shattered leg and no vision. She leant across him, straightened his sheet, and gently lifted his head to turn his pillow on to the cooler side. He was a large muscular man and she wondered what he looked like beneath the bandages wound round his sightless eyes. Her breast brushed against him. He grabbed her hand.

'I'm so frightened, Nurse. Where am I?'

'You're safe, Captain. There's no need to be afraid, I'm here,' she comforted him, a young girl of just twenty-one, so full of her own fear that sleep was difficult to find. And so near to breaking that she frequently shook uncontrollably before she came on duty. 'I'll care for you,' she said, automatically.

'He was one of ours. I made him die.'

'There, there, I'm sure you didn't,' she said in the automatic, soothing tones of her profession.

Marshall had changed. Before he had only flirted with hedonism, now he was determined to pitch himself head-long into a life of self-indulgence – once he had recovered.

3

In the weeks since he had been wounded his life had been a series of fragments, some bright and clear, others dim and barely remembered. At the beginning he had struggled to remember, desperate to join the fragments into a cohesive sequence that made sense. But now he was resigned to the idea of spending the rest of his life with this unmade jigsaw inside his head.

He wondered if it would be better when he could see – if he *would* see – he added to his thoughts like a talisman, like touching wood. Stupid really, as if a thought could alter the surgeons' skill, could lessen the damage to his tissues.

He had always hated the dark. Now he was in a darkened world living with the threat that it might be permanent. He had decided right at the start what he would do if that was the case – a bullet through the temple, quick and clean. No white stick for him, no shuffling through life. If he could not see a pretty woman, if he couldn't admire the claret in his glass, watch his retriever work, admire a spider's web with the dew on it – then he didn't want to live.

'Time for medicine, Captain Boscar.' The nurse touched his arm to let him know she was there. He hauled himself up in the bed cursing the pain that shot through his shattered leg.

'Naughty, naughty, Captain. No bad language on such a lovely day,' the nurse said in a sing-song voice, for all the world as if she were talking to a child. He could quite happily murder them when they spoke like that. What made the women in this profession assume that patients did not mind being spoken to like imbeciles?

He hated the thought that 'Beautiful Breasts' might talk to him like that. That was one of the happiest fragments of memory, the wonderful, soft yielding feel of a young breast brushing against him as she leant over to straighten his bedding. Surely a woman with breasts like that would not talk to him like an idiot? But he had no idea which nurse it was or in which hospital it had happened, there had been so many. That was the problem with the fragments, they were never in any sequence.

He lay quietly allowing the morphine to work. Four times a day they gave it to him – the bliss for the next couple of hours when the drug's power was at its height and the pain became only a dull ache.

He knew about his leg. He knew they had saved it – just; that it would be another month before he could stand; that he would always have a limp. All this he could accept, if only the pain would go away. But none of them could tell him if it would.

As he relaxed on his pillows he knew before it happened that it was coming. It was as if leaves were rustling in his brain and then, as always, from nowhere he could hear it – '*Rosemary!*' the voice in his mind called. He winced. He hated this fragment of memory worst of all. The voice was as clear as if the man were in the room with him. Would he never go away, would he never leave him alone? For the man who had called Rosemary out there in the mud was the shame of his life. He'd like to have shaken his head to rid it of this fragment, but they'd warned him not to for the sake of his eyes. So he braced himself, for he knew there was no escaping the memory . . .

'*Rosemary*,' it was not a call but a scream. It came from half-way across the crater. He twisted towards it.

'Who's that?' he called.

'Help me! For the love of God help me!'

The pain in his leg made stars form in front of his eyes as he laboriously dragged himself through the mud and slime, mercifully unaware that some of the slime was the remains of comrades. It took him an hour to make his way to the screaming voice.

When he got there he wished he hadn't. The man had half a head and no legs. He should have been dead, not clinging on to life like this screaming for some woman.

'You're supposed to be calling "mother", not some

other woman's name. That's what we're supposed to do,' he said, sharply.

'She *is* my mother,' the half-head gasped in reply, blood oozing out of his mouth.

The captain unwrapped the field dressing he carried with him, muttering an apology as he clumsily wrapped it round the poor head as best he could in the dark.

'*Rosemary,*' the man screamed and then kept screaming for hours, just that one word which bored into Marshall's head as he lay slumped in the mud beside him too exhausted to crawl away. God, he thought, when I get out of this I'm going to do nothing that does not give me pleasure.

'Why don't you fucking well die!' he screamed eventually. And the man did. That was the awfulness of this fragment, that was what he could never forgive himself for.

He couldn't remember getting here in the same way as he had no recall of how he'd come to be in the crater with poor old half-head. He remembered the crater clearly, the mud, all soft and squelchy, not unpleasant, almost comforting, but at night so cold. And the rats. Oddly he'd found he did not mind the rats.

He could recall the lights at night. The Very lights, the phosphorous shells – probably because they were the last things he'd seen before the crump, the loud, earsplitting crump that should have sent him to Kingdom Come. Instead, he was in a bed somewhere in England.

'A visitor for you, Captain Boscar.'

'Hullo, old chap. I'm Richard Frobisher,' he felt his hand being taken in a firm handshake. 'I gather my father knows yours.'

He accepted the cigarette which Richard placed in his mouth and they settled down to exploring each other, noting a word here, an interest there, indicators that they might get on, might become friends.

'What's wrong with you?' Marshall asked.

'I got hit a couple of months back.'

'Where?'

'Delville Wood.'

'No, I meant where on you,' Marshall laughed, though he shouldn't have done so – for the sake of his eyes.

'Oh, chest. Unfortunately, I shan't be going back.'

'Unfortunately? Don't be such a bloody fool. Fortunately. Who but a lunatic would want to return to that hell?'

'Christ, what a relief, to hear you say that. I'm so tired of pretending. Everyone expects me to regret being invalided out.'

'To hell with what people expect. They weren't there, they don't understand.'

'When they told me I wasn't going back, I felt like dancing in the street. To be honest I don't know where I found the courage to stand up and get shot at in the first place,' he said, ironically. 'And you?'

'Me? I can't remember anything. Oh, I know who I am and everything about me until July 3rd and then – damn all. I don't know where I was, how I got here, I was in a crater, I know, but for how long . . .'

'You were in no man's land, for three days, one of the last to be found. It's a miracle you survived and an even bigger one that you're sane, that's what I've heard.'

'Sane?' Marshall laughed shortly, remembering the fragments and wishing he knew this man better and could confide in him. 'Who knows?'

'Your eyes? Are they . . . ?'

'Blind? I don't know. The bandages come off next month, then I'll know.'

'And the leg?'

'Hop and skip, I gather, but it's getting better.'

They chatted of this and that. Of whom they knew and where they'd been and where they planned to go. At the end of the hour they'd decided, both of them, that they probably would be friends.

*

'If you could just hold still, Captain.'

Hold still? He wanted to rip off the bandages himself. What was taking so long – sadistic bastards. He could feel the blood pumping in his ears as if his heart had shifted there. His palms were wet with sweat and he held his breath as the bandages were untwined.

'You can open your eyes now, the room is shaded. How many of my fingers am I holding up?' the doctor asked calmly.

Gingerly Marshall opened his eyes and quickly shut them again. Shaded the room might be, but the light felt as if it had pierced his eyeballs. Squinting this time, as if against the sun, he opened them again.

'Three, Doctor,' he mumbled having difficulty speaking as he squinted at the doctor's three stubby fingers splayed out in front of him. 'Three!' And in front of the doctors, the nurses, in front of them all, he wept with relief.

2

Marshall looked across the table at his new friend, Richard. He studied him closely for he knew only his voice, Richard had been discharged from the hospital before Marshall's eyes were unbandaged. Opposite sat a slim twenty-four-year-old man, of medium height, with a head of dark red hair which, despite a liberal dressing of pomade, was, much to its owner's annoyance, a mass of curls. His face was fine featured with delicate high cheek bones, a slim nose and fine pale grey eyes. He used his long slender hands expressively as he spoke.

A complete contrast to his companion. Marshall was well over six feet tall, and broadly built. At twenty-eight, and despite his time in hospital, he had the heavy muscular body of the sportsman. His square-shaped face with its firm chin and full mouth was normally a becoming shade of brown from hours spent in the open, but his months as an invalid had left him pale. Pale as he was, his blue eyes seemed larger and with his dark, almost black, hair made an immediate and dramatic impression. He had the bearing and the face of a man who was always noticed, and he knew it.

Both men were out of uniform, Richard because he had been invalided out and Marshall because, after his stay in hospital, his uniform was ill fitting.

'What shall we do? We should be celebrating the New Year, now that we've survived 1916 more or less intact.' Marshall patted the cane propped up against his chair.

'It's not easy to feel like celebrating, is it, when you think of the poor beggars still out there at the front?'

'We can drink to them. I'm sure they'd have drunk to us if our roles had been reversed,' Marshall said hurriedly, concerned that Richard might mean what he said. He himself had every intention of celebrating.

'I'm surprised they let you out of hospital on New Year's Eve of all days. Aren't they worried you'll get riproaring drunk?'

'I have every intention of getting drunk. But, they didn't discharge me, I discharged myself. Once you'd left I was bored to death. And, I'm sure they choose the ugliest nurses for the officers. That's what I want tonight, a woman – it's been a long time . . .' Marshall smiled a slow, lazy smile at the thought of female flesh.

'We'll go to the Empire, a friend of mine is in the show there. I'll ask her to bring a friend and we can go to the Eddington. I've taken a suite.'

'Daisy barred me.'

'When?'

'Back in 1914. For life, she said.' Marshall pulled a face.

'What on earth did you do?'

'I can't remember, I was so drunk . . . I think I might have pissed on her aspidistra.'

'Not *the* aspidistra?' Richard laughed.

'The very same.' Marshall held his head in mock shame.

'She'll have forgotten, and, in any case, dear old Daisy Lavender doesn't hold grudges.' Richard selected cigars for both of them from the ornate humidor held by a waiter.

'There's just one problem,' Marshall said once the cigars were satisfactorily alight. 'I'm afraid you'll have to go without me. I'm somewhat financially embarrassed at the moment – merely temporary you understand, and the Eddington is damned expensive.'

'My dear fellow, it was my suggestion, you're my guest. I wouldn't dream of letting you pay for anything.'

'Far too kind of you, old chap. When I'm back in funds you shall be my guest,' Marshall said with a marked degree of relief. He could not imagine when that day would dawn but by expressing the sentiment, Marshall felt free to accept the other man's hospitality.

'Excuse me.' They both looked up to find a pretty young woman in full evening dress standing at their table clutching a small embroidered evening bag.

'With pleasure,' they said in unison. Grinning at each other, they leapt to their feet, and both moved to pull the spare chair out for her.

'For cowards like you,' she said icily, clicking the clasp of her bag open and taking out two white feathers which she placed on the table.

'Oh, I say!' Richard exclaimed. 'This is damned unfair . . .'

Marshall said nothing but his expression said much as he lunged towards the young woman. She, fearing he was about to strike her, lifted her arm to shield her face. Instead Marshall snatched the bag from her grasp, snapped it open, and with a flourish shook the feathers high into the air. A draught from the window caught them and floated them in a wide arc about the dining room.

'So much for your feathers, Madame,' Marshall hissed at her with such vehemence that the woman backed away from him and into the arms of two burly waiters. Without more ado, they lifted her by the elbows and, ignoring her screeches and her flailing legs, carried her from the restaurant. Most of the other diners concentrated on their food in a mass display of embarrassment.

The head waiter, his face beetroot with consternation, hurried towards them. As he crossed the room, he bowed to right and left, muttering apologies to his clients in a mixture of Italian and English, his eyes darting about his beloved restaurant. With an agile leap he snatched a feather which had landed on a portion of filet mignon. Poised on a fork, midway between plate and mouth, it was about to disappear down a ducal throat. Without her realising, he caught two more feathers as they settled on a marchioness's tiara. With one fluid motion he swept the feathered glass of claret from in front of a baron, motioning to the wine waiter to hurry and replace it. He ignored a lowly esquire who found his mouth full of sole and plumage and, since he had not seen the incident, was unsure if he was eating fish or fowl. At last he slithered to a halt in front of Marshall and Richard.

'Captain Frobisher, I am mortified.' The head waiter's face was contorted with anguish. He began to wring his hands but was soon busily occupied plucking feathers from Richard's suit.

'It's all right, Luigi. It's not your fault. These bloody women pop up everywhere.' Richard tried to calm the man.

'It's far from all right,' Marshall blustered, brushing himself down. 'You should keep an eye open for trash like that.'

'Sir, my apologies . . . But, sir, you saw the young woman, she looked respectable,' Luigi said, his voice whining apologetically.

'It was our fault for not being in uniform. She was not to know,' Richard said, reasonably.

'I don't see why I can't go out to dinner dressed as I

choose. And it's not what you expect at the Ritz,' Marshall said indignantly. 'Come on, Richard, let's get out of here.' He picked up his cane, gave it a jaunty twirl, and with a limp that seemed dramatically worsened by the incident, hobbled towards the door. As one the other diners rose to their feet and applauded the two friends enthusiastically. Marshall acknowledged the applause with a wide grin and a theatrical salute as he left, followed by a deeply embarrassed Richard.

Out on the pavement Marshall roared with laughter.

'What's funny?'

'What good luck, that bitch turning up. It was worth it not to have to pay, wouldn't you say?'

'Good Lord, Marshall. I quite forgot,' and he turned to go back.

'Where are you going?'

'To pay, of course.'

'Don't be damned stupid.'

'Really, Marshall, we have to. It would be theft.'

Marshall stamped up and down in the freezing cold, hugging himself to keep warm as he waited for Richard.

'I hope you didn't pay for me,' he said as soon as Richard reappeared.

'They wouldn't let me pay for either of us, as it happens.'

'There you are then,' Marshall said with satisfaction.

'That's different. That's their choice. Taxi.' Richard held up his hand and they clambered in when the automobile drew to a halt. Richard gave instructions to the driver and then slumped back on the seat. The incident had upset him. It wasn't the woman's behaviour – that had been merely a silly misunderstanding – but Marshall's petty dishonesty which disturbed him. He hated meanness in any form and loathed dishonesty. He could not understand it in a fellow like Marshall. Moodily he looked out of the window of the taxi cab. But on the other hand he did not want to fall out with his new friend. He liked him.

And so many of his old friends were dead now, out there in the trenches, that he had few friends left. He rubbed the condensation off the window. Marshall could not help being out of funds. How could he be sure he would not behave similarly in Marshall's position? And in any case, in five minutes he'd be seeing her. This last thought completely cheered him and, as he offered Marshall a hip flask, he clapped him on the shoulder.

'Sorry I was boorish back there,' he said, sheepishly.

'Boorish? I didn't even notice, old chap, were you?' Marshall replied magnanimously as the taxi drew up at the theatre. Marshall fumbled in his pocket for change but Richard pushed him to one side, insisting on paying.

Richard ran nimbly up the stairs from the foyer while Marshall limped laboriously after him. Richard was waiting at the top with profuse apologies for his thoughtlessness.

'She must be something very special,' Marshall grinned as he finally reached the head of the staircase.

'She is, she is.'

The show was in full swing as they made their way to the dress circle bar and ordered two large brandies. The theatre was packed mainly with men in uniform chattering noisily amongst themselves and ignoring the comedian, in large plaid suiting, who was failing miserably to make them laugh. The two friends leant against the plush velvet top of the barrier which separated the bar area from the auditorium.

The heavy curtains came down and the comedian was rewarded with scattered applause. From behind the curtains could be heard the banging and cursing of the scene shifters. The audience moved restlessly in their seats, and the theatre was suddenly alive with anticipation.

The orchestra in the pit struck up with 'In a Monastery Garden'. The curtains parted to reveal a badly painted country scene. Clouds were painted on to an improbably blue sky, gaudy flowers nestled amongst unlikely trees and the whole back flap wobbled alarmingly. Incongruous in a country glade stood a rickety white staircase which disappeared into the wings.

To an ear-splitting roar of approval a row of chorus girls, dressed as milkmaids, danced on to the stage. They faltered in their steps as the wall of sound obliterated the music of the orchestra. Then, one girl taking the lead, they tottered into a ragged dance while the men clapped, stamped their booted feet, whistled and shouted.

Marshall yawned, bored by the amateurishness of the performance and wondered what on earth the creature who had lured Richard so far from the West End was like.

Fighting the racket of the men, the drummer, his arms flailing dementedly, crashed out a drum roll. The milkmaids divided into two rows, sank into uneven curtsies and pointed dramatically to the top of the staircase. There was a long pause. The men, as if instructed, quietened. The audience seemed to hold its collective breath.

First a foot shod in blue silk appeared, showing a neat ankle. Then with a swish of silk, at the top of the steps appeared a tall, slim woman, blonde hair peeping from beneath a large, ostrich-trimmed, picture hat which hid her face. Slowly she raised her head, paused for a second and smiled. The roar that greeted her smile should have lifted the roof of the theatre. Regally she acknowledged the applause and then gracefully, despite the full, spangled skirts of her crinoline dress, descended the staircase. So elegant was her bearing one forgot that the steps were an unstable, roughly painted stage prop – she could have been a princess descending a marble stair. Slowly she moved to centre stage and raised her hand imperiously to silence the cheers.

'We love you, girl,' a man from the gallery shouted.

She inclined her head and with her gloved hand blew a kiss in the direction of the gods. The audience erupted again. In the centre of the stage she stood, her head flung back, arms outstretched, and she allowed the adulation to flow over her. Then she nodded to the conductor and lifted her hand once more. To a man her admirers fell silent.

She sang them a medley of songs in a voice which was pretty enough but not exceptional. The magic was not her voice but the way she sang. And in the strength of her personality, which transcended the tawdry surroundings and bombarded the audience across the footlights. She manipulated them so that each man felt it was to him alone that she sang. It was as if, in some strange way, she were making love to them – each and every one.

'My God, she's good.' Marshall enthusiastically applauded the singer who was taking her bow.

'Isn't she?' Richard said, his eyes shining as he clapped even more energetically than everyone else around him.

'You mean . . . ? You lucky dog.' Marshall playfully pushed Richard who grinned back at him with all the pride of a small boy.

'Yes, she's my friend. And one day it'll be the West End for her. She'll be a star. I'm going to make sure of it. I've a friend I'm going to introduce her to, he'll help. That's her last song until the finale. Come on, we can go backstage now.'

Marshall was out of his seat with surprising speed given his stiff leg.

'Miss du Bois says as yer to go straight up, Captain Frobisher,' the stage doorman shouted from the warmth and comfort of his glass-encased office, his feet up on the desk and a large tankard of beer beside him as he studied the racing form in the evening paper.

'How are the feet, Fred?'

'Bearing up, sir. But I doubt as they'll ever be right. Mind you I'd rather be here than out there with them poor sods, if you know what I mean?'

Richard led the way along the corridor, its brickwork painted a dingy yellow, and dimly lit by sparsely placed

15

gas mantles, and up a metal staircase at the end. At the top of the stairs they were swamped by a tide of giggling chorus girls who twisted and flirted their way past them. Marshall stood stock still and inhaled their scent as they scuttled past.

'Ah God, I do love women so,' Marshall sighed to no one in particular, and stopped, turning to watch the gaggle of girls noisily clattering down the stairs to the stage. He swung round in time to see Richard slipping through a door further along the corridor. He arrived in the room as Richard disappeared into an expensive-smelling, lace fluttering, embrace.

'Darling, may I introduce my friend, Marshall Boscar. Marshall this is Miss Francine du Bois.'

'Mr Boscar . . .' a long slender hand was held out to him and Marshall found himself shaking hands with a woman who, despite heavy stage make-up, was the most beautiful he had ever set eyes on. Her long silver-blonde hair hung loose about shoulders which were creamy smooth and which Marshall longed to touch. Her full mouth seemed set in a permanent smile. But most extraordinary of all were her eyes – huge green eyes, true green not hazel flecked with gold. Round the rim of each iris was a line of darker green, and a double row of lashes guarded the beautiful eyes.

Richard watched his friend greeting the woman he loved with as much pride as if he had created her himself.

'We thought we'd go to Daisy's, see 1917 in there. What do you think, Francine?'

'What a lovely idea.' She spoke in a low husky voice, a voice so full of sexual promise that Marshall felt if she now ordered tea and toast, the spout of the teapot would stand as rampant as his own member threatened to do. 'And has Mr Boscar a friend with him or would he like me to bring one of mine?' She smiled at him, looking him straight in the eyes. The look told him she wanted him and the look said she would have him.

'He only got out of hospital today,' Richard explained.

'Oh, nothing serious, I hope, Mr Boscar.' She looked him up and down enquiringly, and he knew it was not his imagination that her glance lingered at the region of his crotch.

'No, nothing. Bit of a limp, that's all.' He patted his cane.

'Betty, go and ask Miss Flora Belle if she would care to join our party for supper,' she said briskly to a maid whom Marshall had not noticed standing in the shadows of the shabby room which was cluttered with discarded clothes and vases of flowers.

'Perhaps you'd like to help yourself to some champagne while you wait?' Francine indicated a silver tray with a magnum of champagne iced and ready in a silver bucket amongst the glorious paraphernalia of perfume bottles and powder puffs on her dressing table. 'I've just the finale and then I'll be free.' She blew them both a kiss as she slipped from the door and back to the stage.

3

'I thought I'd banned you.' Daisy Lavender stood statuesquely tall, her arms folded, barring the way into her hotel.

'You did, Daisy, you did,' Marshall said, giving her an exaggerated bow.

'You can stop showing off like that, I'm not impressed. And it's Mrs Lavender to you, mate.' Her cockney accent was at total variance with her elegant, almost regal bearing.

'I beg your pardon, Mrs Lavender.'

'He's most contrite, Mrs Lavender. Truly he is,' Richard attempted to sound serious.

Daisy eyed Marshall suspiciously.

'Boots,' she shouted with a raucous roar. 'Fevvers.'

Boots, the hallporter, shuffled towards them, so bent with age or lumbago that his face was rarely seen, and on feet which were obviously giving him great trouble. He offered Daisy a small basket into which she delved, selecting two long white feathers.

'Oh, not again,' Marshall sighed.

'I don't like cowards. Ripper!' she called and from the back of the hallway a small terrier of uncertain pedigree skidded across the floor, and with great enthusiasm began to snap and snarl at their feet for all the world as if he were ten times the size he was. 'Get 'em, Ripper,' she yelled excitedly.

'Mrs Lavender. It's me, Richard Frobisher, Basil's son. I'm staying here.' Richard sidestepped the snapping dog. 'Captain Boscar's a serving officer.'

'I don't like serving young men who aren't in uniform. What's wrong with your uniform? You ain't ashamed of it, are yer? Why ain't you in it?'

'Because I'm stuffing a pillow,' Marshall said laconically as his hand streaked out, grabbed the feathers and stuffed them into his breast pocket.

'Ha! I like him.' Daisy, hands on hips, threw back her head the easier to laugh. 'I see you limp . . .'

'He only got out of hospital today, Daisy.'

'Well, why didn't you say? That makes a difference. But, you . . .' and she pointed her finger sternly at Marshall. 'No repeat of last time or you'll be outside faster than you can say jerrybum.'

'Yes, Mrs Lavender,' Marshall half-saluted her, a mocking, self-deprecating smile on his face. Daisy looked at him shrewdly and decided she would need to keep an eye on him.

Proudly Richard led the way upstairs. It was the ambition of every Young Man About Town to stay at Daisy's. The address had kudos and there were never any questions asked of lady friends. The food was superb, the champagne flowed and if one were very lucky there was no bill to pay. But Daisy was most particular whom she allowed in. If one's father had been a favourite of hers back in the Nineties, when the Eddington had first opened its doors, then one was more or less assured of a place. Otherwise it could be impossible.

'Got to be one of the three As,' she was fond of saying. 'Won't let you in 'less you are.'

The three As were indicative of those whom Daisy admired the most in the world – Aristocrats, Americans and the Affluent. Little Lord Fauntleroy would have been Daisy's idea of perfection.

The workings of the Eddington were a mystery. If you took Daisy's fancy, your expenses were just as likely to be grafted on to the account of one of the Affluent. But staying there was a risky business for there was no telling when she might suddenly suspect you of Affluence and then everyone else's bill was added on to yours.

From the moment she awoke until she fell asleep in the small hours of the morning, Daisy drank champagne, steadily. Yet no one had ever seen her drunk, and no one could ever accuse her of not being aware of what was going on in her establishment. Nothing escaped her eagle eye.

Daisy's was the one place a young man could take a girl with no risk of embarrassment. As they sped up the stairs he would know it was with Daisy's blessing and, frequently, a magnum of champagne.

Though illicit passion seethed in the many rooms, Daisy also had a penchant for Bishops. Eddington's was high on the Church of England's recommended hotels. Many a gaitered cleric and his lady wife were fussed and fed by Daisy, blissfully unaware of what went on around them.

But just recently there had been a change in Daisy. The war seemed to be slowing her down, whereas previously she had seemed indestructible. The names of her young men, or sons of old favourites, appeared on the casualty lists with depressing regularity, and Daisy minded. She felt bereaved. Marshall need not have worried about whether or not he could afford the Eddington, for Daisy had decided not to cash the cheques of any of *her* young men while the war was on. Hence a drawer in her desk was rapidly filling with uncashed cheques. To those not in uniform she gave a feather and, having set the Ripper on them, she booted them out into the street without even bothering to stop and ask them why they were not serving. Consequently several who were not fit enough to fight, and some who had done so but returned wounded, found themselves on the wrong side of Daisy's door.

'I've no truck with cowards,' she would say, brushing her hands together as she rid herself of those she considered unworthy.

Richard, one of the fortunate ones, had been staying here since he left hospital. His father, Basil, in his youth, had been one of Daisy's most favoured customers, to the extent that his photograph hung on the wall in her parlour. Rumour had it that they had been more than friends; consequently Richard had one of the best suites overlooking the courtyard garden.

He held open the door to a large sitting room, where a table was set for four and the furniture and silver gleamed in the firelight. Off this room were two double bedrooms, again with fires burning, lamps discreetly shaded, and bed covers turned down. Each bedroom had its own bathroom – a novel concept but, then, innovation was Daisy's hallmark.

Richard and Marshall fussed about Francine and Flora. For Marshall it was a particular pleasure to be close again to warm, sweet-smelling female flesh. He had been too long surrounded by women in starched overalls who smelt of carbolic.

Flora was pretty, if a little on the short side, with dark eyes and a mass of dark curly hair. But beside Francine she paled into insignificance.

Assured of her beauty, and as if it gave her some special

right, Francine immediately took control of the evening. It was she who decided what they should eat, what they should drink. Since Marshall was not paying he let her do so, all the while wondering what Richard thought he was about. That woman needed a strong man, she was yearning for it.

As the meal progressed Marshall tried to concentrate on Flora but found it difficult. Francine flirted with Richard but he knew it was for him she meant the flirtation. She fed Richard tit bits, shared her glass with him, and all the time the great green eyes watched Marshall, telling him that this was what she wanted for him.

When Richard slipped his arm about Francine's waist and led her to the bedroom Marshall felt a bleak wave of anger engulf him. He wanted her. Frustrated, he turned to Flora.

'Well, little one, time for bed?' he said clumsily, aware that this was no way to seduce a woman. But it seemed he didn't care one way or the other.

'Just hang on a minute, ducks. There's things a girl's got to do,' Flora smiled archly at him as she made her unsteady way to the second bedroom door.

Marshall poured himself another glass of port and stared moodily at it. He had started the evening desperate for a woman, now one was in reach, just beyond that door, and he really felt almost too tired to bother. He got up, crossed the room, opened the door and slipped in.

In the dim light he could see Flora slumped across the bed, fully clothed, fast asleep and snoring. He chuckled as he looked down at her, pulled the coverlet over her and quietly let himself out. He stole along the carpeted corridor, down the stairs and was almost at the front door . . .

'Creeping out without paying, then?'

He swung round to see Daisy leaning, despite the late hour, on the doorway of her parlour.

'It's not like that. Captain Frobisher's paying. I was his guest.'

'Right one, aren't yer? Bet you never pay for nothing.'

'Something like that.' He smiled his charming, slightly crooked smile at her. Daisy looked him up and down, she had never been able to resist a handsome man and this one was one of the best. Tall, broad shouldered but slim of hip. Thick, straight dark hair. Large blue eyes and a full mouth – in her youth she had loved them like this.

'Fancy a glass of bubbly?' She gestured with her hand to the parlour, which doubled as her office. Marshall was aware that only the favoured were ever invited inside, it was indeed an honour she was bestowing on him.

'A brandy would be nice.'

'It's bubbly or nothing if you drink with me.'

'Bubbly will be fine,' he added quickly as she showed him into her cluttered inner sanctum. The room was so crowded with furniture that it was difficult for a large man like Marshall to move without sending something crashing to the ground. The large desk was littered with paperwork. The walls were covered with photographs and paintings of friends of Daisy's, all of whom were clients for she had no friends who weren't.

'Sit down then, rest yer plates of meat.' Expertly Daisy uncorked the bottle and held a champagne flute out to him. 'Here's to 1917, then, and all you want for yourself.'

'To 1917,' he repeated. He looked deeply into the glass and wondered what he wanted. This time last year he would have said money and women. This year? He still wanted women – that never changed. He needed money desperately and always did. But now . . . after the crater . . . after the man who called . . . He shook his head. 'To my son,' he heard himself say to his astonishment as he raised his glass to Daisy.

'How old?'

'He's not born yet.' He laughed at himself and his notion. 'In fact he's not even conceived. I'm not married.'

'Got a wife lined up?'

'No. I haven't.'

'Funny toast then.'

'Yes, I suppose it was.'

'That's the war for you. Makes you realise you aren't here for long, makes you long for continuity.' She refilled their glasses. 'Nice bloke that Richard. I've known his dad for years. It's nice when the sons come in their turn.'

'Continuity?' he smiled at her over the rim of his glass.

'Suppose it is.' She looked at him long and hard. 'What's he doing with that Francine? She's not for the likes of him. She's dangerous.'

'What do you mean, dangerous?'

'She takes what she wants, that one, and bugger anyone who gets in the way. I've seen her do it. Seen her destroy fellows . . .'

'Oh, I don't think Richard's likely to be that involved.'

'Don't you? I do. I think he's smitten. You're his friend, you try and wean him away from Francine *Blewett*.' She almost spat the name out.

'Blewett. Is that her real name?'

'Oh yes, calls herself du Bois or some such Frenchie name, don't she? I knew her mother. Now there was a woman. Straight as a die she was. No messing. You knew where you were with Ia. She ran the best whore-house in London. Tragic it was when she died, run over by one of them new-fangled motor cars. She was still young too. Gawd, how long ago was that, four, five years?' Marshall sat silent as she reminisced, he wanted to hear more. 'No one has ever been able to replace her. Blossom's has never been the same since.'

'I know Blossom's.' He sat up with interest.

'You should have known it in the old days, my boy. You've never seen women so beautiful – and their clothes! The best food, the best bubbly. I tell you, it was a palace. And what style Ia had. Why, when the old Queen died she had all her whores dress in deep mourning – black everything right down to the skin! What a sight. It doubled her week's takings, I can tell you. Then when she died it was sold, all the proceeds went to helping young girls. Ha! what a notion, most of them don't want helping, I can tell yer. Her girls bought it. She'd left them all provided for, you see, but it didn't work. Well, it wouldn't, would it? They was all at each other's throats and fighting amongst themselves. Tragic it was. Some foreigner's got it now – though what on earth she thinks she knows about the English aristocracy and their preferences I really can't say.' Daisy sniffed her disapproval of all things not British.

'And that was her mother?'

'Yes. She should be proud as punch of a woman like that instead of denying it. Mind you, she's not a patch on her mum.'

'How do you know all this?'

'Oh I knew Ia well, and she had a friend worked for her called Gwen. She works for me here now. Not that Ia didn't look after Gwen, 'cause she did, handsomely,' she said defensively. 'It's just that Gwen likes to work. That's how I know. Francine's often in here – I hope your mate don't think he's the only one?'

'Funnily enough that's where I was off to now.'

'Blossom's? No luck upstairs?'

'No. Mine drank too much. I'm not interested in necrophilia.' Daisy laughed loudly at his joke.

'Maybe you'd be interested in seeing me home then, Captain?'

They swung round to see Francine standing in the doorway. Swathed from head to foot in a white fur she looked like an ice maiden from a Nordic tale.

'But of course, Miss du Bois.'

'I'm very tired.'

Marshall was quickly at her side. 'Thank you for the champagne, Mrs Lavender.'

'You can call me Daisy,' she grinned. 'Perhaps that's a solution,' she said enigmatically as Marshall led Francine out into the freezing night.

24

Marshall lay back on the pillows, completely relaxed, and looked at the ceiling. He breathed deeply and contentedly, he loved the smell of a room after a night of love making such as they had just enjoyed. That strange musky smell of semen and sweat mingled with the scent of powder and perfume. A wonderful smell and one he had often tried to recall in the misery and stench of the trenches, in the lull between fighting. He liked women's rooms, the pinkness, the frillyness, the clutter of femininity.

'What are you thinking about?' she whispered. Absent-mindedly he stroked her hair. Without exception, women always asked that same question. Why did they think he thought anything? Why could he not be allowed, as now, just to lie and contemplate the ceiling? If you told them the truth, that you were thinking of nothing, they invariably became tearful and offended.

'I was wondering about Richard,' he said, to annoy.

'What about him?' Francine sat up, prettily covering her nakedness with a corner of the satin sheet.

'Why do you have satin sheets? I hate them, they slip,' he replied instead.

'I'll change them for you. I'll get linen ones,' she said quickly.

'I shouldn't bother for me. I shan't be back.' He swung his legs over the side of the bed.

'Marshall, why not? What have I done?'

She dropped the sheet and slid across the bed to him, putting her arms about him, pressing her breasts into his back. Just as he had known she would. He smiled to himself as he felt the wonderful sensation of her naked flesh against his. The soft, yielding, feel of them . . .

'He's my friend.' He turned abruptly to look at her.

'He's mine too.'

'Then we have behaved diabolically.'

'I know, I know. Oh, my darling, don't you realise the agony I'm in?' Francine said dramatically. Marshall smiled at her histrionics. 'But I can't help myself. When I saw you I wanted you so desperately. My darling, forgive me . . .' and she slipped from the bed and knelt before him. He allowed her to make love to him as he lay back and looked at the ceiling . . .

'Who's Rosemary?' she asked later, looking sideways at him as she poured the tea.

Marshall looked up sharply from the plate of bacon and eggs that Francine's maid had set before him. 'None of your business,' he snapped, feeling his stomach lurch at the sound of the name.

'I don't like other women being mentioned in my bed, even if you were asleep.' She pouted. He said nothing. 'Who is she?' He forced himself to eat. 'I said who is she? I don't like it. I won't have it.'

Marshall's knife and fork clattered on to his plate. 'Shut up, Francine, this minute, or I leave . . .'

Francine picked up her own cutlery but not before she had looked at him with her large eyes filled with tears – it was a useful trick she had learned years ago, to cry on demand. It always worked. But to her consternation, it didn't this time, as Marshall pushed his chair back, stood and announced he had to leave.

'I'll tell him if you like,' she said, desperate to keep him with her.

'Tell who, what?'

'I'll tell Richard about us. I'll say it was my fault.'

'You'll do no such thing.' He swung round and faced her angrily. For a second he studied her face and, certain she was playing games with him, he picked up his coat and slipped it on. 'Tell him what? There's nothing to tell,' he blustered.

'Marshall,' the great green eyes looked up anxiously at him, 'that was the most wonderful night of my life.'

'I'm glad you enjoyed it, madame, so did I, but I do not wish my friend to be told of our frolicking. Is that understood?'

'But Marshall, I can't stay with him when I feel like this about you. I've never felt like this before about any man. I want to spend every minute with you. My whole life!' She stood in a theatrical pose, swinging her long hair back over her shoulders and turning her head so that he found himself looking at her proud and beautiful profile.

Marshall laughed. 'I don't recommend it, Francine, my sweet. You're better off with Richard. He can afford you, I can't. I have £100 to my name. When that's gone . . .' he shrugged his shoulders, 'then, I don't know what I shall do.'

He was amused to note that Francine paused for a second, frozen like a statue, while she absorbed this information.

'I earn good money. I could keep both of us,' he was astonished to hear her reply.

'Don't be silly, my sweet. You like the good life too much for that.'

'No,' she shook her head, an intense expression on her lovely face. 'For you I'd give it up. I would, I truly would.' And she meant it. Francine had slept with many men but not one had given her the satisfaction he had, nor had made her feel so utterly female – she was not prepared to let him go.

He took hold of her shoulders. 'Listen, Francine. This talk is nonsense. We don't know each other, we have had only one night together, we shall never have another such night . . .' At this she let out a little cry of distress. 'I don't want Richard to know – he loves you, I don't. I promise you, if you tell him, you will never see me again.'

She stood silent watching him as if assessing him and then she laughed, a deep-throated chuckle of a laugh. 'I don't believe that, Marshall, my darling. You couldn't stay away from me now if you tried. Even if I do tell

Richard you'll still be back. I can promise you.' She looked boldly at him, on sure ground now. The tip of her tongue appeared and slowly licked her lips. As he watched her he knew she spoke the truth. He wanted them both, her to bed and Richard as his friend.

'If you say anything, I shall tell him who you really are – about your mother and the whore-house she ran so successfully.'

The green eyes flashed angrily. 'What are you talking about? My mother, what whore-house? There's nothing in my past that I'm ashamed of.'

'What about Blossom's?'

'That's a foul rumour,' she was almost shouting. 'It's been about for years, I don't know who started it but people spread it around because they're jealous of me. My father is an aristocrat – you only have to look at me to see that. My mother died in childbirth.'

'So who's your father?'

'I'm sworn to silence. When I went on the stage my father was furious. I promised him never to reveal my real name,' she lied with practised ease.

'What? Blewett?'

'My name is *not* Blewett!' She stamped her bare foot. 'My father is French, a duke, that's why I use a French stage name.' She tossed her long mane of blonde hair again proudly. 'It's that old harridan, Daisy Lavender, isn't it? She's always disliked me. Do you know why? Because I'm young and beautiful and she's old and past it . . . That's why, she's jealous.'

Marshall laughed, he liked her pride, he admired her spirited lying . . . 'Come here . . .' he ordered, and on the table, amongst the marmalade and toast, he took her again.

Marshall had only just climbed out of the bath at his club when Richard arrived.

'Oh my head,' he complained, slumping into a chair as

28

Marshall dressed. 'How much did we have to drink?'

'Too much.' Marshall laughed at his friend's woebe-gone face.

'You look fine.'

'A busy night made sure of that.'

'Flora?'

'No, she passed out. I saw Francine home and then I went to Blossom's,' he lied effortlessly.

'I was so ashamed when I woke to find Francine gone and I'd been sleeping like a pig. Thanks for looking after her for me.'

'You didn't mind my seeing her home?'

'Good God, no, if I can't trust you who can I trust?'

'That's true,' Marshall looked away as he adjusted his tie to his satisfaction.

'Marshall, I've come to ask you a favour. My parents are insisting I go home for a long weekend. Would you come? Help to relieve the unmitigated boredom?'

'It would be my pleasure.'

5

'Who'll be there?' Marshall asked as Richard's motor car shuddered its way through the January gloom.

'Not sure. My brother Charles is home on leave – hence the summons. You know mothers – she wants the whole family together.'

'Should I have come, then?' he asked, unsure, for he did not know about mothers and families. He was an only child, but in any case his own mother was not like others but was a law unto herself.

'Oh Lord, yes, there will be others there. Mother likes the house busy. She's keen for me to meet the daughter of a friend of hers, an American. She must be rich if Mother's that keen. Of course, what with the war, they don't entertain as lavishly as they used to.'

'Is she beautiful?'

'My mother?' The car swerved as Richard registered surprise at the question.

'No, no. Watch the road!' Marshall laughed. 'The American.'

'I doubt it, they rarely go together, do they? Money and beauty.'

'I wouldn't know. All my women have been ravishing and poor.'

The car passed the great mound on which stood Windsor Castle.

'Bet life was fun when the old King lived,' said Marshall as they spluttered up the main street.

'God, yes. But think of the money one would have needed to entertain. His son might be duller but he's cheaper.' Richard swung the car with more enthusiasm than skill around a bend as they left the town behind them, Marshall hanging on to the leather strap more for comfort than to steady himself. Ten miles and half an hour later they turned off the main road, and up a long twisting drive, eventually stopping in front of a large, crenellated Gothic-style building that loomed menacingly above them in the dark. The windows were shuttered so that no light escaped, for they were close to London and the threat of Zeppelin raids.

'So this is Mendbury. Good Lord,' Marshall said before he could stop himself. 'It's so . . . big,' he recovered himself quickly as Richard looked at him sharply. 'Like a palace.' He lowered his head as he got out of the car, so that Richard could not see the expression on his face. Marshall's own home was crenellated and battlemented, but appropriately in period. He was something of a purist where architecture was concerned and objected to the Victorians' refusal to allow a house to remain as it had been intended to be.

'My grandfather built it,' Richard said unnecessarily. 'It was a rather poky Elizabethan house before.' In the dark

Marshall winced. 'Mind you, I've often thought it was a shame to destroy the original, pity he didn't build around it really.' Richard swung the large door open and called out, his voice echoing in the cavernous hall. 'The gardens are lovely as you'll see in the morning. The Thames flows through the grounds and you can see it from almost every one of the main rooms,' he said almost defensively. Marshall felt that Richard had correctly interpreted his reaction to the house and was trying to put him at his ease.

The outside of the building might be grotesque, and the inside over-ornate, but the comfort was exemplary, Marshall decided as he dressed for dinner.

'And how's your father?' Lord Frobisher asked Marshall later in the drawing room, the moment introductions to the other male guests had been made, and the butler had served drinks.

'Very well, thank you, Lord Frobisher. I haven't seen him for over a year. Cornwall is so far away when you have only a short leave.'

'Still interested in insects?'

'Very much so. As a matter of fact he's had two papers published recently, both well received.'

'He should have been a scientist.'

'I think he rather regards himself as one, Lord Frobisher.' Marshall accompanied his reply with a gentle smile so that no reprimand could be detected.

'I mean a professional one . . .'

'Professional what, Basil?'

The men hurriedly jumped to their feet as through the door came Gertie Frobisher, Richard's mother. She was dressed approximately ten years out of date. Her husband did not approve of the fashionable shortened skirts which showed ankles, and Gertie, being uninterested in fashion, had allowed him this small victory which had confused her friends since she had, for years, been such a vociferous advocate of women's freedom. But this was no act of acquiescence. Gertie was merely relieved to be able to wear the clothes she had until they fell apart and no longer, each year, to have to waste precious time choosing a new wardrobe. She was a tall woman with a fine Edwardian figure which she carried with pride. Her face was intelligent more than beautiful but her smile, which was such a natural, spontaneous thing, could transform her face so that she appeared almost beautiful. Her best feature was her hair, a glorious titian red untinged with grey. It curled naturally and exuberantly and as she moved the curls bounced as though with a life on their own.

'Professional what . . . ?' she repeated.

'Marshall Boscar's father is a brilliant scientist but, cursed by birth, he remains an amateur.'

'So silly, Captain Boscar,' Gertie held out her hand in greeting, smiling brightly at him. 'So silly that our class is doomed to remain amateurs, don't you think?' Marshall bowed over her hand and did not have time to reply before Gertie was talking again. 'Let me introduce you to your fellow guests, Captain.'

Gertie had been followed into the room by three women. Two were middle aged, the wives of Basil's associates whom he had already met. He solemnly shook hands, his heart sinking at the dearth of pretty young women.

'And this is Miss Tregowan-Wakefield, the daughter of my dearest friend, Alice. Perhaps you know the Trego-wans of Gwenfer, Captain Boscar, since you come from the same part of the world?'

'Regrettably no, Lady Gertrude. I've heard of Gwenfer, of course, Miss Tregowan-Wakefield, but I have never had the pleasure . . .'

He shook hands with a pasty-faced young woman whose figure was too full to be wearing a frilled dress and whose blonde hair, tortured into an unbecoming frizz, did not suit her either. She seemed to be aware of her shortcomings for she stood hunched as if to make herself smaller. Once she had shaken hands she stepped back as if not wishing to inflict herself on anyone for longer than necessary.

'Dear Grace has been so brave, Captain Boscar. She came all the way from the safety of America, when she had no need to, to nurse the poor wounded soldiers. Didn't you, my dear?'

'Yes, Aunt Gertie.' Grace blushed an unbecoming magenta which, far from covering the whole of her face, merely formed unsightly blotches and accentuated its colour.

'Where have you been nursing, Miss Tregowan-Wakefield?' Marshall asked politely but with little interest.

'I was at Albert, and then at a base hospital. I became rather tired two months ago.' She blushed even more deeply, preferring to forget the ridiculous scenes she had made – constantly weeping, unable to stop. 'They sent me to Cliveden, it's lovely there,' she added hurriedly. She spoke in a beautiful voice, low and gentle. The merest hint of an accent only added to its charm. It should, Marshall thought, have accompanied a lovely face.

'So wonderful for me that she's so near, I can have dear Grace to stay as often as I like since she's now so close.' Gertie beamed at her protégée.

'Marshall escaped from hospital this week, didn't you old chap? He's searching for a nurse who took his fancy when he couldn't see. Aren't you, Marshall? Maybe it was Miss Tregowan-Wakefield.' Richard arched his brows as he teased Marshall.

Grace's mottled colour deepened to burgundy and she looked at Marshall with deep concern. 'Were you blinded? How dreadful for you. How fearful the dark must be, and not knowing whether you'll see again.'

'Yes, yes, it was like that,' Marshall looked at her, surprised at the intensity with which she spoke despite her obvious shyness. 'But I was lucky, I wasn't blind and all I have now is a limp.'

33

'And the memories . . .' she said softly.

'Yes, those too.' He frowned. 'You're American, aren't you? Where do you live when you're not in Cornwall?' he asked quickly for he had no desire to be reminded of the memories but wondered, fleetingly, what on earth she could know of them.

'In New York and we have a place in the country – and Gwenfer, of course.'

'A place in the country!' Gertie exclaimed. 'Dart House is one of the grandest, most luxurious houses I've ever stayed in. Warm as toast and enough hot water to launch a battleship.'

'The dear girl obviously doesn't like to boast, Gertie,' Basil intervened.

'Of course she doesn't, she's far too modest. That's why I'm doing it for her.' She laughed with the loud hooting noise that all her life had severely startled all those unfortunate enough to be in its vicinity.

The butler announced that dinner was ready and, led by Lord Frobisher, they filed into the great dining room. Because they were only ten, and given the massive size of the table, dinner was a far from intimate affair. The other guests were quite capable of shouting at each other to be heard but Grace found this virtually impossible. Frustrated, she sat silently isolated in her shyness and stole shy glances at the Captain when she hoped no one else was looking.

She thought he was the most handsome man she had ever seen. His figure, tall and broad shouldered, reminded her of her father's. She could imagine how safe she would feel in the Captain's arms – just as she did when her father held her tight. Good looking as he was, it was the humour and intelligence in his face which attracted her the most. She envied the ease with which he spoke with his neighbours and wished she had a little of his relaxed style. But she knew he suffered, for she saw it in his eyes. She would have liked to help him in some way to erase the dreadful memories she was certain were haunting him still. Not for the first time she wished she were beautiful instead of plain and overweight: then he might notice her, might want her to help him, she thought, as she morosely shovelled another potato into her mouth.

Basil visited his wife that night. He stood at the bottom of her bed in his long night shirt and endeavoured to look stern. It was an almost impossible task since Basil was a good-natured man with an amiable expression. So he did what he always did when he wanted to be taken seriously, he made a deep frown appear.

'Why are you looking so glum, Basil?' Gertie asked as she completed her nightly ritual by putting on soft cambric gloves over the cream she had carefully massaged into her hands.

'I don't think you should boast about Grace's wealth.'

'Why ever not?'

'Well, to begin with, it's vulgar.'

'Oh vulgar, rats.' She waved her hand as if vulgarity was of little importance.

'And, secondly it's not fair on the child.'

'Not fair? She won't ever push herself forward. Let's be honest, Basil – she's a sweet girl but while she looks as she does who is going to want to marry her? I'd fond hopes that Richard might take an interest but he didn't even seem to notice her. Did you see how quickly he took Captain Boscar off to play billiards? So rude, I must talk to him.'

'I should give up hoping, Gertie. I gather Richard has other interests.'

'Richard? Oh, Basil, how exciting, why have you not mentioned this before? Who? Do I know her?'

'Unlikely, old girl, she sings in a Music Hall.'

'Oh really, Basil. I thought you were being serious, that he had found someone. All young men have their little adventures with chorus girls before they settle down. How dreadfully disappointing.' She held her gloves up so that Basil could tie the bands around her wrists. 'What if Grace did some banting? Do you think Richard would notice her then? If she were thinner her face could be quite sweet.'

'Dear Gertie.' Basil smiled indulgently at his interfering wife, certain that if Gertie had decided the young girl should lose weight she undoubtedly would. It was a rare person who could resist his wife when she was set on an idea. 'But what about her background? Is she really what we want for Richard?'

'You mean being born illegitimate?' Gertie said, not shirking the unpleasant word for that was never her way.

'Well, yes . . .' Basil looked uncomfortable, not as much at home with bald truth as his wife.

'She's Alice's daughter, what more do you want? Lincoln adopted her. No one here would know the truth, only you and I ever knew and *I* have never told anyone.' She looked accusingly at her husband.

'Neither have I. How can you even suggest . . . ? No, but her real father . . . one never knows . . . blood and all that . . .' he fumbled for words to explain what he was trying to say.

'Chas Cordell was a charming, intelligent man. Not quite top drawer but Alice assured me that, apart from being married to someone else and forgetting to tell her, he was perfect. And Alice's background is impeccable, as you know.'

'I find it all rather worrying.'

'Oh piffle, Basil. With all that Wakefield money I'm sure no one is going to delve too far.'

'Money, there you go again, Gertie. Vulgar.'

'There's nothing vulgar about money, Basil, not with the estates you have to maintain. Stop being so bourgeois,' she said with the arrogance of long breeding.

Basil laughed good-humouredly. 'She is a charming girl.' He stroked his beard thoughtfully. Certainly the house in Sutherland would soon be needing a new roof, and the cottages here were in dire need of repair. He coughed, a loud rumbling cough. 'Until then, I think you should be more discreet about her, or you'll have the poor creature being taken up by fortune hunters. I was not too happy about the way young Boscar was eyeing her.'

'Marshall Boscar?' Gertie swung round, her face alight with sudden enthusiasm. 'Excellent. I should have thought of him. If Richard isn't interested, then he would be eminently suitable. Old family, breeding, why he's Cornish, too. He'd be ideal.'

'I agree he has breeding but he has no money and none to inherit. And, from what I hear, the family seat is falling down about their ears. He'd be most unsuitable.'

'Rubbish. You make them sound a perfect match – he so handsome and she so rich. Why, they'd be eternally grateful to each other.'

'Gertie, you're impossible.'

'I know, Basil dear, but matchmaking is such fun.'

'And why does she call us Uncle and Aunt? She's no relation.'

'Peculiar isn't it? Perhaps it's a quaint American custom.'

6

As they walked through the damp and dripping wood, Richard's dog bossily leading the way, Marshall felt sorry for Richard as he listened to him and his liturgy of praise for Francine. Not only had she completely taken over his life but it seemed she had also taken hold of his sanity. Such was his faith in her that his trust was absolute, which to Marshall seemed a very dangerous state of affairs. He knew, as he listened, that he should feel ashamed of himself for deceiving Richard but he didn't. He felt, in a way, that he was doing his friend a favour. The woman, it seemed to him, was incapable of fidelity, so it was better that she should be unfaithful with a friend who understood the situation. Without doubt, Richard was far too fine a fellow for the likes of her.

'Oh, blast! I've missed again,' Richard muttered as he reloaded. There, thought Marshall, the man was so besotted that it was even putting him off his shooting.

'Marshall, she's perfect. It's not just her beauty, she has such fine qualities. Do you realise that money means almost nothing to her? If I were a pauper she would still feel the same about me.'

'You're a lucky fellow, Richard,' he said, hoping that there was no hint of irony in his voice. Richard's dog put up a pheasant. Richard took the bird high and the shot echoed off the trunks of the great beech trees. Marshall jumped. At each shot he flinched. In fact, he found that he felt physically sick. The nausea had hit him the moment he picked up a gun in the gun room, and at each shot it worsened.

'Richard,' he said abruptly, 'do you mind if we go back to the house?'

'You all right?'

'It sounds damn stupid I know. But it's the guns, they make me feel . . . odd . . .'

'You poor chap.' Richard looked at him with concern, immediately broke his gun and removed the cartridges. 'It's not stupid. My cousin is exactly the same, he was on the Somme too. Even the sound of a door banging brings him out in a sweat. I realise now how lucky I've been. Don't worry, it'll pass.' Richard took him solicitously by the arm.

'I sometimes think it will never pass. I have such appalling dreams, Richard . . .' Then he stopped, he would have liked to tell Richard all about the nightmares but he could not, not even him.

'Marshall, my friend, we all have those.' There was the smallest hint of chiding in his voice.

'But I feel guilty, for God's sake . . .'

'We all do. You're not the only one. It's the knowledge that we've survived and have a future while our friends won't be coming back. And the responsibility for what we do with our lives now: it's terrifying, Marshall.'

They walked back towards the house. Marshall realised that, of all the men he knew, Richard was the only one to whom he could have confessed even this much of his weakness. With the rest he would have had to endure the guns rather than risk the shame of admitting fear. But Richard was different from his usual companions.

As they reached the house, and were climbing the steps, a figure cannoned into them. It was several moments before they realised that the bundle of cardigans, scarves, waterproofs, galoshes and old felt hat was Grace. A Grace who was being pulled along at speed by a robust setter, two labradors and four spaniels. Marshall steadied her, both men raised their hats and gave a half bow, and Grace blushed her magenta colour. In confusion she mumbled something which neither man caught before the excited uncontrollable dogs pulled her down the remaining steps and along the gravel path towards their favourite walk through the woods.

'Pity she's so plain. She's really rather sweet,' Marshall said, remembering, with a warm glow, her instinctive understanding of his suffering last night.

'Do you think she's plain? I don't think she is. She's a bit on the large side, that's all. Get rid of some of that puppy fat and she'd probably be quite attractive. Her mother, Alice, is a ravishing beauty even now and she must be well into her forties.' He held the large door open for Marshall to pass through. In the hall their clothes dripped rain on to the highly polished parquet as they passed them to an impassive footman.

'Fancy another breakfast?'

'Do you know, I think I could.'

'Grieves,' Richard called, as they entered the cavernous breakfast room.

'Do you really think she could be attractive?' Marshall asked once they were settled with their food and the staff had bowed their way out.

'Who?' Richard looked up from the fourth leader of *The Times* over which he was chuckling.

'Grace.'

'Ha! Do I detect an interest?'

'No, I was just curious.'

'Well, she's never going to look like my Francine who . . .'

Richard was away on his favourite subject and Marshall allowed his thoughts to ramble while appearing to listen, an art he had perfected. The insanity that certain women could inspire made him fear for his friend. Marshall had observed the same thing happen to other friends. The more physically besotted they were, the more ridiculous their behaviour became. He had never had the misfortune of falling in love and was glad of it. He was certain that, should such a fate befall him, he would run as fast as his limp would allow. He had a cool detachment where women and their Machiavellian ways were concerned. He liked women's bodies and enjoyed them, but he had no time for their scheming natures. He found them generally grasping, greedy for money and for what it could buy, greedy for his body. They were sexually insatiable, in his experience. The more one gave them, the more they seemed to crave.

And here was poor Richard waxing lyrical about a woman who had this week deceived him and would continue to do so. In many ways a man would be better off with a woman like Grace. Not being beautiful she would be less likely to stray and, no doubt, would be grateful to any man who took an interest in her. He wondered just how rich she was . . .

'What do you think? Should I?' he heard Richard ask him.

'Oh yes, I do agree,' he said instantly.

'I thought you would,' Richard looked satisfied and Marshall wondered, as he poured another cup of coffee, what he had advised him to do.

Grace walked for a long time with the dogs. She enjoyed walking, it was no trial, and she enjoyed the dogs. In fact she would much rather spend the whole weekend here in the woods with the dogs than face the agony of having to make polite conversation in the house.

She sat on a tree stump and let the dogs snuffle about in the undergrowth. Her greatest longing, once the war was over, and she was settled again, was to have a dozen dogs of her own. She and her father would have fun choosing which type to buy. Perhaps they could breed, perhaps she could build up kennels as famous as her father's stud farm. He would like that.

A smile transformed her face, as it always did when she thought of her father. She loved him so much that sometimes it hurt. And he loved her. To him she was beautiful. He never made her feel uncomfortable. How she missed him, how she longed for him. And although he was not her father, she never thought of him as her step-father: they loved each other as if they were of the same blood.

The last two years had been a terrible time for Grace. Until then she had lived in a privileged world. She had wanted for nothing. Because her father adored her it had never crossed her mind that she wasn't as he said she was – perfect. And everyone they knew had treated her in the same way. All her life, if she had wanted anything and her request was not promptly granted, she had found that a judicious sulk had invariably acquired it for her. And then war had been declared. At the age of nineteen, and against her father's wishes, she had sailed away, on her own, to England, full of a patriotism which verged on the devout. She felt a deep longing to help, and had enrolled as a nurse.

Then, she found that without the trappings of her father's enormous wealth, and with only herself to present to the world, she was frequently ignored. She was not perfect, she was dull. Apart from her background she had nothing to offer. She was her father's daughter, that was why she had been popular, that was why she had been courted by many young men, that was why people were nice to her.

This discovery had a devastating effect upon her. She began to think herself far uglier and duller than she really was. And in thinking, she was becoming. Her only consolations were dogs and food.

But last night she had met Marshall, and she had regretted the food. She wished they were in America, he would have noticed her there. She had never met anyone she had wanted so badly as she did this stranger. His presence had dominated the room. But she did not know how to go about getting him, not without her father to help her – he would have known what to do.

She swished her stick through the dead leaves at her feet, releasing the rich, damp musty smell of the earth beneath. Money. Money was the key to it. Everything and everyone had a price, her father was fond of saying. Marshall must be like everyone else, he must have a price too. Somehow, without appearing too obvious, she had to let him know that she was one of the richest heiresses in the Western world. She did not mind if it was her money that attracted him, it would be irrelevant – money was unimportant, she thought. Money was purely for getting what you wanted. Like so many people who have been heavily cosseted through their youth by wealth she was totally unaware of how important money was to her. She had often been heard to say that she would be quite happy to live without it.

She looked up through the tracery of branches on the leafless trees at the heavy clouds, pregnant with rain, above her. She did not notice the dullness of the day. To her the day was perfect, for Grace had found the only man she wanted to marry.

That night before she retired she confided her feelings to her diary.

'Marshall, I know it's a dreadful bore for you but if you could help me by taking Grace to dinner, I shall always be grateful.' Richard was pacing up and down Marshall's room.

'Of course it's not a bore, Richard,' Marshall lied. He had spent the past month, since they had returned from Richard's home, Mendbury, and between visits to Francine, breaking down the reserve of a chorus girl new to London, a virgin he was sure. He had planned tonight to take her to the Eddington and finally seduce her. But then, Richard had proved a good friend to him, he owed him something. Time without number Richard had come to the financial rescue.

'Of course I shall insist on paying,' he said as if reading Marshall's thoughts.

'My dear chap, I wouldn't hear of it,' Marshall replied contentedly, knowing full well that he would allow Richard to win this particular argument.

'No, I insist . . .' Back and forth the argument went and the five pounds travelled between them. With impeccable timing, Marshall gauged the exact moment to appear to give in graciously and accept the crisp white note. He congratulated himself on his expertise as he heard Richard thanking him expansively for accepting the money.

'What a relief, you're a true friend,' Richard sighed as he replaced his wallet in his pocket. 'I could hardly introduce Grace to Francine, could I? You see if Francine thought I were dining with another woman, even a woman like Grace, she would be mad with jealousy. She's like that about me,' he added, grinning with an inane pride.

Marshall, who, as it happened, had spent that afternoon in the arms of this selfsame delectable Francine, merely nodded sympathetically. 'You want me to collect Grace from her great aunt's house, take her to supper, and return her by midnight no doubt? Intact of course,' he said with a sardonic grin.

'That's right. She hates the aunt, apparently. My mother can't stand her either, of the old school, you know, fossilised in Queen Victoria's reign – so keep out of her way if possible. This is all my mother's idea. I've a sneaking suspicion that she's trying to match-make us.' He pulled a face. 'Grace has a few days' leave, it seems, and knows no one in London apart from her aunt, so Mother asked if I could arrange a party for her. I mean, how could one arrange a party for Grace? She's not the party type. I'll confess that I relied on your agreement and have told her that you would be joining me and a companion. If you wouldn't mind fibbing and saying I've been taken unwell? Francine and I are off to Bray for the night.'

'Will they mind Grace being unchaperoned?'

'It seems not. She's surprisingly independent. It must be being American.'

As he made his way to Wilton Terrace, walking to save the cab fare, Marshall wondered how cheaply he could arrange the evening so as to be able to pocket the maximum amount of change from Richard's five pound note. Expert sponger that he was, the £100 he had possessed at the beginning of January was, by mid-February, down to £50. He was being boringly careful with his expenditure. Life was unjust, he thought as he strode along, grateful that at least the weather was dry. He had been born with a good name and standing in society. He had all the interests of one of his class and none of the money necessary to support them. There were times when he despised his father who, despite his brilliant mind, was a child in business matters. If there was a bad investment to be had, then Halliday Boscar would find it. Mines in Australia, Brazil, Chile, Canada had all gobbled up money that Marshall had every right to expect to be his one day. Every inventor with an unsaleable notion made his way to his father's door so that the outhouses, the attics, at Boscar Manor were full of failed inventions which should have recouped their fortune. All Marshall had at twenty-eight were his looks, abundant charm, a smart brain and no desire whatsoever to work. What he really needed was a rich wife. He didn't want to marry, life was too pleasant without the chains of marriage, but it seemed the only solution. He stopped dead.

Perhaps Grace would be a solution. He began to stride along again. If the Frobishers wanted her for Richard she must be well provided for. If there was one thing to be relied upon, it was the British aristocracy's talent for marrying money. He wished now he had made more fuss of her during that stay at Mendbury. But newly out of hospital, intent on putting the war behind him, a woman like Grace had not interested him. Now, with his money depleted, his priorities were changing. He would have to ask Richard more about her. He quickened his pace. But what if she was really very rich – some of these American girls were – and what if Gertie Frobisher prevailed on her son to see sense? He might miss the boat. Maybe he should gamble and invest some of his £50 in Grace. After all he had, in the past, put as much as that on one horse: this was a similar situation really, a calculated bet. He had planned to take her to a cheap pie house, but perhaps he should take her to the Eddington. And luckily, tonight, he was in uniform. He smiled to himself. Everything would depend on the amount of money, but if there were enough, say a good £3,000 a year, then he would find it the easiest thing to overlook her appearance, you could ignore a lot for that amount. Should he make that the minimum or would he be able to get by on £2,000? He shook his massive shoulders. No, for £2,000 she would have had to be prettier. She seemed a pleasant girl. Depending on her income, he might decide to marry her.

Immeasurably cheered by these deliberations, Marshall strode along with a jaunty step, despite his limp, and a whistle.

'Where are Richard and his friend?' Grace asked, peering over his shoulder.

'He wasn't feeling too well. He asked me to offer you his sincerest apologies. I hope you won't mind being lumbered with me?' He smiled the lop-sided, slightly ironic smile that he knew, from experience, no woman could resist.

'No, not at all.' She could feel herself colouring and lowered her head to hide the blush as, taking her coat from the footman, he helped her into it. Once outside on the pavement he reluctantly hailed a cab; he could hardly expect her to walk as far as Piccadilly.

The cab drew up in front of the hotel.

'The Eddington?' Grace said, a mixture of interest and alarm in her voice as she looked up at its pretty Georgian exterior. 'I've heard about this place from my father.' She giggled nervously.

'We shall be dining in the public dining room – with bishops and country squires.' He laughed in return, such an open laugh that Grace was immediately reassured.

Daisy welcomed them personally and tapped him approvingly on the chest for being in uniform. When she saw the dog, Ripper, Grace quickly knelt on the floor allowing the dog to lick her in welcome, as she cooed over the creature. Daisy glanced enquiringly at Marshall and then at Grace, still crouched on the floor playing with the dog. She raised her eyebrows. Marshall rubbed his thumb and forefinger together in the time-honoured gesture. Knowingly, Daisy smiled and, suggesting to Grace that she leave the dog, showed them into the dining room. The long room was elegantly furnished in the French style, with panels painted dove grey, and a fine central chandelier. The vases, on grey and gold painted plinths, were full of out of season flowers. One wall was flanked with mirrors, making the room, which overlooked the courtyard garden, appear twice its normal size.

'The food is the best in London,' he said, once they were settled. He handed her the large parchment menu which, at six pages long, always took time to read.

Grace read the menu with the avid interest of a connoisseur. Her pale grey eyes darted about the pages, skimming over dishes that did not interest, lingering over those that took her fancy. There was so much she would like to try. Until now she had eaten only in the houses of friends and relatives in England and had been sorely disappointed in the food.

'There's no pheasant,' she said, a trifle put out: pheasant was her favourite food.

'One never eats pheasant after December, it's past its best,' Marshall said gently. 'I shall bring you here in the autumn and you can have ptarmigan pie, it's Daisy's speciality. The old King adored it.'

'Really?' she was blushing again. He had said he would bring her here again.

'Would you like me to order for both of us?'

'That would be very kind,' she said, hoping she did not sound as disappointed as she felt. To choose her food for her was to take away much of the pleasure of the meal. She sat silent, fearful that his choice would not be to her liking or, worse, that he would not order enough. She began to relax, however, as she heard him order the soup, the stuffed Dover sole, and the pie which had quite taken her fancy on the menu.

'Are you enjoying England?' he asked as they waited for their soup.

'I've seen so little of it. When I arrived I went straight to

47

France. And now we are so busy at Cliveden that I get little time to see anything.'

'The casualty figures don't get any better.'

'It's strange, isn't it, sitting here in this lovely room, waiting for delicious food, whilst across the Channel it's as if the end of the world has come.'

'I know. I wonder sometimes if we'll ever be able to enjoy ourselves again. An evening like this with a pretty young lady makes me feel almost guilty.'

Grace giggled at the compliment – only her father ever called her pretty. To her surprise she found Marshall easy to talk to and she found herself chattering about her experiences in France. She was touched by his interest in her parents and her home.

She enjoyed the soup and the freshly baked rolls. The sole was perfectly cooked. Best of all was the steak and oyster pie Marshall had ordered. As her knife broke through the delicate puff pastry case, the wonderful scent of the steam rose to her nostrils and she found herself salivating at the prospect ahead. Quickly she cut a portion of pastry, selected some meat and popped the forkful into her mouth. She thought she had never tasted such succulent pastry. The oysters were a joy to find nestling in the thin tender rolls of fillet steak. The roast potatoes were perfection with their crusty crisp skins. She would have liked to help herself to six. Instead, because she was with Marshall, she restricted herself to four. She knew she was drinking too much wine. But it helped her to relax so that she could talk to this man as if she had spent all her adult life laughing and joking with handsome, dangerous men.

Grace was in a daze. She could not believe her good fortune. She had thought of little else but Marshall for the past four weeks. With difficulty she had contrived this week's leave. Bravely she had asked her great aunt, Maude Loudon, if she might come to stay. It was a brave gesture because her aunt was an imperious old woman in her late seventies, whose temper was not improved by the arthritis that disabled her, and who had always filled Grace with terror. Her plan had been to see Richard and, perhaps, if she were very lucky, to meet Marshall again. Now here she was with him, tête-à-tête – something she had not even allowed herself to dream.

Marshall sat toying with his champagne, amused at the gusto with which Grace was attacking the large bombe glacé she had chosen. Curiously enough, he was enjoying himself. Maybe his plan was not such a bad idea after all. Grace was a good companion, she laughed at his jokes, she seemed to be delighted and content to listen to him, yet when she had something to say, he was surprised to find her interesting. It was relaxing, for a change, to be with a woman whose gaze did not wander about the room to see who was there, to check if they were being admired.

'Cheese? A savoury?'

'No, thank you. I think I've had far too much.' She patted her lips with her napkin. He poured more champagne.

'Oh dear. I shouldn't really,' she said with a giggle.

He didn't like the giggle but then, he reasoned, most young women of her age giggled. He studied her face across the table. Perhaps Richard was right: if she ate less and lost some weight she might be attractive. He didn't mind plump women but Grace, unfortunately, was fat, there was no other word for it. From judicious questions throughout the evening he had ascertained that there was a great deal of money there. She had spoken of her various homes, of a large number of horses. Her knowledge of wine, unusual in a woman, could come only from one who was used to a good cellar. She knew a great deal about art and jewellery. It looked as if he might be backing the right filly.

'I don't want this evening to end,' he said, suddenly, touching her hand so gently that she was unsure if she had imagined the touch.

'Oh, neither do I.' She looked at him, her eyes shining, all her longing for him to love her stamped on her face as if written in large letters.

'Darling Grace,' he said, noting her expression with satisfaction.

A week later they were engaged.

8

'Should you not wait until you get home to your parents, Grace dear?' Gertie said to the young girl sitting on a stool in her boudoir, and hoped the girl wasn't too heavy for it. It was French and rather valuable.

'No, I don't think so.'

'Perhaps you should ask your Aunt Maude to help you.'

'Never!' the young woman said. 'She doesn't like me. I don't think she has ever forgiven my mother for eloping with Chas Cordell.'

'She can hardly blame *you*,' said Gertie, aware that Maude Loudon, rigid in her principles, could easily do so. 'But I'm sure your mother has looked forward to planning your wedding.'

'I can't wait, Auntie Gertie. He might change his mind and then what would I do?' She turned to look at Gertie Frobisher, her large grey eyes devoid of expression. This dullness of mien tended to exasperate Gertie who spent her life careering from one acute reaction to another and who could never be accused of having a dull expression. At such times she felt they could have been discussing the most mundane subject in the world rather than Grace's future.

'If he is sincere, he won't change his mind. If he does, it means he does not love you enough.'

'He doesn't love me. I know that.'

'Grace, what are you saying?' Gertie looked at the

young girl with concern. They were sitting in her boudoir making plans since, in the absence of her mother, Grace had asked Gertie to help with the wedding arrangements. It was not a situation which pleased her. How could it be, when things were happening so quickly, too quickly? She felt an intense sense of responsibility towards Alice's daughter and, in going along with her plans, Gertie was concerned that she was neglecting her duty.

'Just that. He doesn't love me, how could he? Look at me. But we are good friends and maybe I can make him love me.'

'Then why has this handsome young man chosen you?' Gertie asked, knowing full well the answer but wanting to discover just how much Grace herself understood.

'My money,' Grace replied simply.

'That's a sad thing to say, my dear,' Gertie said as gently as she could.

'It's the truth.'

'You *told* him you were wealthy? Was that wise?'

'Yes. I feared if I didn't tell him, he wouldn't be interested in me and certainly would never marry me. And in any case he knew – others had already told him.' Grace looked slyly at Gertie.

'Grace, my precious child. Such a cool manner you have. And if you are right about his attitude, don't you mind?' Gertie swept on ignoring Grace's insinuation.

'No. I was only nine when my mother married my step-father, so for almost as long as I can remember, money has always given me whatever I want. This is the same thing really, isn't it?'

'But it – oh dear—' Gertie flapped her hands in the air, searching for words that would not come easily. It was not in Gertie's nature to talk so freely of emotions and feelings. But, never one to shirk her duty, she took a deep breath. 'To me it seems so – unromantic, so dreadfully cold.'

'Did you love Uncle Basil when you married? Mamma

has told me that she was expected to make a good marriage, that love was the last thing to be considered. She told me that her father disowned her because she fell in love with my real father who was poor.'

'Ah yes, but things were different then . . .' Gertie's discomfiture increased. To talk with this young girl about her husband and their feelings for each other seemed improper, to say the least.

'Were they?' Grace persisted. She really has a strong character, Gertie found herself thinking, with surprise.

'We did not have the freedom that you young girls have. We were so closely chaperoned that we hardly knew each other before we married. It is different now. This war has made a nonsense of how we were brought up. You young girls seem to skid about all over the place with not a thought for convention.' She paused and picked up the piece of petit point that she had been working on. She looked at it for a long time and Grace sat waiting politely for the older woman to continue. Gertie smiled and when she spoke it was as if her voice came from a long way off. 'But we dreamt of love. Oh, yes, we could dream. And we hoped for it.' And then, as if aware that she was telling too much, she coughed loudly, and bent her head over the needlework.

'But so do I, Aunt Gertie, don't you see? I love him. I dream that maybe one day he will love me. But I'm not going to wait. If permission does not come from my parents, then we shall have to elope.'

'And what if your step-father disowns you?'

'We shall be married before Marshall can find out. I shall have him, I shall be his wife. I could work to support us – I am a nurse, remember.'

Gertie shook her head, perplexed at the strength of determination Grace was showing. She had thought her such a quiet, weak little thing. It would seem she was her mother's daughter after all.

*

The telegrams that flew back and forth across the Atlantic, during the next month, were many and lengthy. As each argument against her marriage was presented to her, Grace countered it with one in favour. She had an answer to every objection, and each missile from her parents only seemed to make her determination more acute. In the end it was one of Gertie's telegrams which influenced her parents. In exasperation Gertie had sent – '*Regret Grace determined. Cannot take responsibility for consequences of your continued refusal.*' This finally decided Alice and Lincoln that they had no choice if they were not to lose their daughter.

The wedding took place in the neo-baroque chapel at Mendbury. It was as well the ceremony was held there, for the chapel was small and consequently the lack of guests was less noticeable.

Gertie had done her best, but as Grace appeared on Basil's arm, Gertie sighed. The girl should not wear silk – the colour did not suit her pasty complexion. The tucked, frilled, bowed and beribboned dress which she had insisted on made her appear even larger. She looked like a giant meringue as she moved awkwardly down the aisle. Thank goodness it was a short aisle, Gertie found herself thinking, as she watched Grace's ungainly progress towards her fiancé. Alice, her mother, had perfect deportment; it was strange that she had not insisted on a like bearing in her daughter. But then Alice had been perfect in everything – hair, face, figure . . .

Gertie stood with the rest of the congregation to sing the first hymn. She had insisted that they have only well-known ones since Mrs Wain, who obliged on the organ now that the regular organist was away at the war, was severely limited in her repertoire. As the notes of 'Praise my Soul the King of Heaven' lifted to the rafters, the cosy familiarity of the hymn allowed Gertie to sing the words perfectly while thinking her own thoughts. She decided she had been fair in the letter she had written to Alice after her telegram. She had been honest, as was her nature and as Alice would have expected. She had said that Marshall was without doubt, one of the most handsome, charming young men she had met in a long time. That he appeared fond of Grace but that, given his impecunious state, no doubt her prospects had been a great attraction to him. She liked the man but felt it was unlikely that he would be, as she put it, 'a trustworthy husband . . .' But then whose husband was? She knew for certain that Basil had been unfaithful on several occasions but he had always been discreet. She wondered how faithful Lincoln was? The unsuitability of such thoughts in the house of God stopped Gertie short and she changed tack rapidly. Provided Marshall was kind to Grace, did the rest matter? It was a pity he had no fortune; it was seldom a good idea for the woman to be the richer partner. It was not how things were meant to be and could make a woman intolerably overbearing and possessive – she had seen that often. A man would need immense character or a thick skin to weather the reactions of other men. Gertie sighed at the hopelessness of it all. The hymn ended, the ceremony began and Gertie concentrated her attention on the beauty of the words.

When at last the bride and groom turned from the altar and Gertie saw Grace's face so transformed by love and happiness that it verged on the beautiful she chided herself for being such an old pessimist.

Marshall and Grace had just finished dining in the small house in Belgravia that Grace said she had borrowed and which Marshall was certain, and hoped, she had purchased. He looked about him with satisfaction – the room was expensively furnished and decorated, as was the drawing room and his study. He had yet to see their bedroom but his dressing room had everything a man could want and an excellent valet already in residence. He took more wine. This was the moment, he thought. He drank the glass of wine quickly and refilled his glass. It would be best to have it out in the open, at the very beginning – now that the marriage knot was tied. He was delighted with the house to which Grace had insisted on bringing him straight after the ceremony. But it was clear that he could not afford its upkeep, or even the valet, on his Captain's pay.

'Grace. I've a confession.' He felt his body go rigid with tension.

'Yes, Marshall?' She smiled sweetly at him.

'I've no money, Grace.' He had been looking intently at the table. Now he forced himself to look up to see how she had reacted to this information.

'I know, Marshall.'

'How do you know?' He felt his muscles relax at the calmness of her response.

'Everyone was determined I *should* know,' she replied, smiling again, a placid smile that he found oddly attractive.

'And you don't mind?'

'No, why should I? I have more than enough money for both of us.' She spooned the last of her pudding into her mouth. 'I also know that you don't love me, Marshall. Even if you say you do. But there again, I have enough love for the two of us. You need not lie, Marshall, you need not say you love me. I understand.'

'Grace, you are an extraordinary woman.'

'Do you think so? Really?' She beamed with pleasure as if he had paid her the greatest compliment.

'Yes, I do. I shall look after you, I promise . . .'

'Yes, Marshall, I thought you would. Now, if you'll excuse me . . .' As she passed his chair she trailed her fingers gently across his hair. 'I think I'll go to bed now.'

Left alone Marshall poured himself a glass of port. What extraordinary luck: she was a remarkable girl. He would not have to maintain an act. He could be himself. He liked her, though, oh yes, he liked her more and more.

But now . . . ! Oh, Lord! He rolled his eyes to the ceiling, poured two glasses of port, and drank both in quick succession. Now he had to consummate the marriage. This had to be done if he were not to put himself at risk, legally.

Never had Marshall taken so long in preparing himself to go to bed with a woman. He smiled at himself in the mirror as he realised he must be behaving like the proverbial blushing bride, with his delaying tactics. He spent several minutes discussing with his valet which clothes he would wear on the following day. Twice he cleaned his teeth, four times he brushed his hair, and several times he washed his hands. Finally he could delay no longer.

Grace sat upright in bed reading, dressed in a voluminous nightdress trimmed with lace.

'At last. I thought you had run away,' she joked lamely.

'No, no, I was talking to Phillips.' He undid his dressing gown, aware all the time of the hungry eyes upon him.

He climbed into bed beside her and turned to put out the light.

'Oh, Marshall,' she sighed and put her arms up to be held. He took her in his arms and felt himself engulfed in flesh. She held him tight as if fearful that he might leap from the bed. He felt her large legs twining round him. He felt imprisoned by her body.

'Marshall,' she said softly.

Marshall closed his eyes.

9

'Married? What do you mean you're married?' Francine's slim body loomed over him in the subdued light.

'A couple of weeks ago. I didn't tell you because I didn't think you would be exactly pleased.'

'You bastard, Marshall.'

'No, Francine. I'm not. We have had no claims on one another. I've been a bastard to Richard, that I'll admit. But you and I? We knew it could not last.'

'What do you mean, couldn't last? Richard hasn't found out. Your wife needn't know either . . .'

'Francine!' Marshall sighed and looked with exaspera tion at the beautiful woman sitting astride him. 'We must stop seeing each other. That's what I'm trying to say.'

'Impossible. I won't let you go. I love you, Marshall. I love you.' Her voice rose histrionically on the last words.

'Don't try your dramatics on me, Francine. Be honest with yourself. We love each other's bodies, that's all it is.'

'No it's not "all it is" for me. I do love you. I knew it the moment you walked into my dressing room.' She began to move, swaying gently on his body.

'Francine. We must stop meeting each other . . .'

'Not yet, not now, my darling,' she said huskily.

Later he lay on the bed and listened to her singing as she went to fetch champagne. Nothing ever went to plan when he visited Francine. He had meant simply to come and tell her he was married, that their relationship was at an end. But, as always, he had ended up in her bed – she was difficult to resist.

She returned with the champagne, looking more beautiful than ever. He looked about the room. It was a small room and he admired the way she had attempted to make it pretty with draped silk on the walls and subdued, clever, lighting.

'What's that strange bowl?' He pointed to an azure-coloured bowl heavily decorated with roses in an alcove, a lighted candle beside it.

'Ghastly, isn't it?' she laughed.

'I don't know – it has a certain rustic charm about it.'

'A crazy woman left it to me. I don't know why I keep it, it's such an ugly thing,' she said offhandedly. In fact the bowl was her talisman and went everywhere with her. She touched it whenever she was about to go on stage – if she lost it she was certain she would never be able to perform again.

'Francine. We have to talk.'

'Why?' she smiled showing her perfect teeth. Everything about Francine was perfect.

'I didn't only come to tell you I was married. I came to tell you that I'm going to America.'

'Don't be silly, there is a war on. People aren't going to America.' She laughed shrilly.

'I'm being sent to Washington, to the embassy.'

'Is your wife going?' There was a hopeful tone in her voice.

'Yes, of course. She is an American.'

'Isn't it risky? What about the German submarines?'

'We'll get through.'

To his surprise Francine began to cry. 'Oh, Marshall,' she wiped the tears with the back of her hand just like a small child, 'I knew all this was too perfect to last. Of course you must do your duty,' she said, carefully judging the blend of admiration and reproach in her husky voice. 'I've had such a lonely life and you're the only person I've ever loved.'

Although he had not intended to, he found once again he was holding her and, inevitably, they were making love.

Six weeks later Francine sat in a tin bath in front of a banked-up fire in her small sitting room. Her face for once was not beautiful. Her expression was strained, the heat of the water had made her colour high, and sweat was pouring down it. The long blonde hair hung in damp hanks.

'More hot,' she gasped.

'Francie, I don't think you should. You're as red as a beetroot already.'

'Put more sodding hot in,' she snapped, glaring angrily at her friend Flora. 'And don't call me Francie, I don't like it.'

'It would do more good if you drank all of this gin. Don't sip it, knock it back in one go.' Tentatively she held the large glass of neat gin towards Francine who grimaced and shuddered.

'I hate gin, I've always loathed it – nasty common drink.'

'Common it might be but all the hot baths in the world won't work without the gin,' Flora said, practically. 'You'll loathe being pregnant a sight more.' Flora turned her head so that Francine could not see the smile that would insist on playing about her lips. She was supposed to be Francine's friend but she rarely felt herself to be on that footing. She knew that Francine merely exploited her good nature – she was a convenience, really, particularly on the maid's day off. Consequently Francine's present predicament pleased her. She was not normally vindictive, but she had heard Francine so many times sneering at girls who'd 'got themselves in a fix' – and now it was her turn.

'Pity you don't know who the father is, then you could get some money.'

'Of course I know who the father is. Don't be so bloody stupid. But he's married, isn't he?'

'I don't see how you can be so certain. You flitted from Richard to Marshall's bed like a little bee.'

'I know it's Marshall's. I know it in my bones. Do you imagine that I wouldn't know the father of my child? I knew the moment it was conceived.' She spoke in a dramatic style, flicking her damp hair which slapped against her shoulders. Of course she lied but she liked the idea that she had known the exact moment and immediately she had thought it, it became a fact. She bowed her head, tears formed in her eyes. 'Oh, Flora, what can I do? This isn't going to work, is it? And I'm terrified of an abortionist . . .'

'Have it,' Flora said matter-of-factly, pretending to study her nails.

'But how can I?'

'Tell each of them it's his and demand money from both. That should see you through.'

Abruptly Francine stood up, the water trickling down her bright red body. The heat and sudden movement made her dizzy and she swayed. Flora quickly moved to support her and help her out of the bath. Francine clicked her fingers.

'Towel,' she snapped.

Flora hurriedly picked up a towel, angry with herself for jumping so smartly to Francine's bidding.

'What are you doing? What have you decided?'

'I've decided it's too bloody hot in here. And, I've decided that Richard is to be a father. It's the only solution.'

Richard stood nervously waiting for his mother in the morning room. He suddenly felt like a small boy again, waiting with agitation for his mother to appear in order to reprimand him for some mischief.

He crossed the room and looked gloomily out of the window. The garden was a riot of colour, the lawns scattered with spring flowers, the branches on the trees bending with the weight of blossom. On the river two swans swam by shepherding their new family. A boat appeared full of young people noisily enjoying their outing in the glorious spring sunshine. But Richard saw none of this; he was so engrossed in his thoughts that nothing else registered.

When he had written to his mother telling her he was to marry and to whom, he had relied upon her somewhat radical views and unorthodox approach to help her come to terms with his decision. He had not been prepared for the curt telegraph which had summoned him here.

'Who is this young woman, Richard? Have we met her?' his mother was asking as she swept through the door, her husband in close attendance.

'No, Mama.'

'Well, do we know her family?'

'No, Mama.'

'When are we to meet them?'

'She doesn't have a family, Mama, she's an orphan.'

'Don't be ridiculous, Richard. Everyone has some family – aunts, cousins. Good Lord, look at us, we are awash with family.'

'Francine doesn't. She's alone in the world, poor thing.'

'What did you say her name was?'

'Francine du Bois.'

'Du Bois? A somewhat exotic name, isn't it?'

'Is she foreign?' Basil finally spoke.

'No, English, Papa.'

'Sounds foreign,' Basil said doubtfully.

'Her father was French,' he paused. 'A duke,' he added slyly, glancing at them to see their reaction.

'Bah! A French duke!' And Gertie dismissed a thousand years of French history with a flick of her fingers. 'I've never heard of a Duc du Bois.'

'She changed her name.'

'Why?'

'When . . .' he gulped, 'when she went on the stage.'

Gertie sat down suddenly and, had she been the sort of woman who was prone to the vapours, she would at this point have fainted or begun to fan herself with agitation. But Gertie was not like such women. 'The stage?' she asked in a grave voice with not a sign of emotion in it.

'She's an actress, Mama. A very good one.'

'And you intend to marry an actress?'

'Yes.'

'I don't think you have thought this through, my boy.' Basil stood, his back to the fire, his fingers looped in his waistcoat jacket, and frowned deeply.

'Richard, I don't think you understand the enormity of the step you are proposing. You know very well that no one of any standing would marry a writer or a painter let alone a stage artiste. You would be spurned by society.'

'I'm not interested in society, Mama.'

'You may think you're not but in fact we all need each other. You must cancel the arrangements immediately. I'm sure that we can make some sort of settlement on this . . . person.'

'Settlement? I beg your pardon, Mama. I don't understand.'

'I'm sure you understand fully what your mother is saying. No doubt we can come to some financial arrangement . . . I'm sure this young woman will understand even if you don't, probably better.'

'I love her, Papa. I wish to marry her. I don't give a fig what society says or does.'

'Oh, Richard. You're far too young. You're simply throwing your life away.'

'I'm not, Mama. I love her. I've told you she's from a good family. She has a talent and it's a talent she chooses to use.'

'Don't be so naïve, Richard. She's not of a good family – no French aristocrat I've met would countenance the thought of a daughter on the stage . . .'

'That's why she changed her name, Papa.'

'When we investigate this young woman I very much doubt if we shall find any connection with the French nobility. An actress is an unsuitable match for you, there is nothing more to be said.'

'All my life you've lectured me on the nobility of man! Who taught me that we are all equal, Mama?'

'That's theory. Family is a totally different kettle of fish,' Gertie said sharply.

'It's not for me. I don't care if she's noble or the daughter of a washer-woman. I'm marrying her and that's that. I'd like you to meet her but if you won't, so be it.'

'You cannot expect your mother to receive an actress, Richard. You simply can't.'

'Why not? What's she done? She's a sweet, adorable girl.'

'I think I should warn you that the consequences of such a match might be more serious than you realise.'

'Are you threatening me, Mother?'

'An ugly word but yes. I am.'

'Then threaten. I shall do as I wish.' Hurriedly he picked up his hat and cane. 'We marry next Thursday, St Giles at noon. You are most welcome.' And with dignity Richard left the room.

Richard was, however, totally unprepared for the letter that arrived three days later from the family solicitor. Basil Frobisher had acted quickly and a rapid investigation had confirmed to his parents that Richard's choice of bride was totally unsuitable. Gertie and Basil had sat long into the night before reaching the conclusion that the only way to bring the boy to his senses was to threaten him with disinheritance. Hence the letter informed him that should he continue with the marriage, then the great estate in Berkshire, the town house in London, the estate in Scotland would all be bequeathed to his younger brother. No doubt, had they been able to take from him his right to the title, they would have done so.

Richard was in a state of shock. The letter shook in his hands. He felt dizzy, and rushing to the lavatory he vomited and retched violently. He could not believe that his jolly, radical parents could behave in such a brutish manner.

'I'm sorry, darling,' Francine said, looking with wide-eyed horror as he told her the contents of the letter. 'It's all my fault. If you had never met me you would still have everything . . .'

'Nonsense, my sweet. You couldn't help being so irresistible that I fell in love with you. If I were King I'd give up my kingdom for you.'

'Oh, dearest Richard. You're much too kind to me.'

'You and my baby as well, now,' he kissed her gently.

'How shall we manage, Richard?' she asked as sweetly

as she could, guarding against any edge that might slip into her voice.

'Don't you worry, my darling. I shall get a job, of course. I've lots of friends. They won't desert me: one of them will help me find work.'

But Richard did worry.

10

Marshall, thinking that he had married a quiet, acquiescent woman, was taken by surprise when Grace refused to visit Cornwall. It was not just her refusal, but the vehemence of it which astonished him.

'But why don't you want to go?'

'It's too far away, the journey takes too long. I just don't want to go.'

'Don't you want to visit your family home?'

'No.'

'But it's where your roots are: you *should* go.'

'I "shouldn't" go anywhere. My roots are not there; my roots are in America where I was born.'

'But your mother is Cornish. Why, that almost makes you Cornish too.'

'What is it about you Cornish that makes you presume that everyone else wants to be Cornish? I have no desire to be Cornish. I'm American, born in New York, and proud of it. How can you be so arrogant about a place no one outside this country has heard of, and where nothing ever happens?' For once her face was expressive, bordering on angry.

Marshall laughed. 'Good gracious, that is the longest speech I've ever heard you make. Very well, my sweet Grace, I understand. But I shall be catching the morning train.'

'You'd go without me?'

'Yes.'

'Leave me alone in London? What would I do if there was another zeppelin raid?'

'My dear Grace, you would go to the cellar, as we did the other day. But I have to go. I have not seen my parents for over a year. I wanted you all to meet.'

'They don't seem too keen to meet me. They didn't come to our wedding.'

'My parents never go anywhere. You'd understand if you met them.'

'I don't want to be left alone.'

'Then come.'

Grace sulked for the rest of the afternoon. She had meant what she said. It had annoyed her as a child when her mother had talked constantly about her childhood home as if nowhere else in the world mattered. She found it insulting and ungrateful to her stepfather who had given both of them a luxurious life and beautiful homes. She had been to Gwenfer only once and had not been impressed. The house was cold, it had no electricity, and the local people, while adoring her mother, had not offered the same welcome to her and her step-father. Her mother always spoke of the place as if the sun always shone but Grace remembered the rain, mist and the endless booming of the foghorn on the Longships light-house. Moreover, the house unnerved her: she did not know why but she was convinced it was a house in which no one was destined to be happy.

She had no desire to go but was curious to meet Marshall's parents. He often spoke of them. And perhaps *his* home was a warm and welcoming one. In any case, she reasoned, if she were not with him he might meet someone else – on the train, at his parents', anywhere.

Marshall said nothing when, entering Grace's room later, he found her maid packing the suitcases.

The train finally ground to a stop at Bodmin Road station. Marshall was not surprised that there was no carriage waiting for them but he could not help the accustomed surge of irritation in the face of his family's vagueness. So it was that Grace arrived at Boscar Manor on the station baggage cart.

Because she had been told so often how poor Marshall was, she had not prepared herself for his home to be so large and grand-looking. It stood serenely in the middle of a great park. The centre of the house was Tudor, with spiralled chimneys that reminded Grace of a child's stick of twisted rock. The leaded windows winked at them in the weak rays of the dying winter sun. As they slowly approached across a park full of great oaks and beeches, lights began to appear at some of the windows. At the sound of the approaching cart the studded oak door swung open and a shaft of light pierced the gathering gloom.

Grace entered the great hall and was immediately struck by a chill draught. The house had appeared so warm and welcoming from the cart; now, inside, she could see that this had been an illusion. There was no fire in the great hearth. Cobwebs hung in grey gossamer swathes from the rafters of the hammer-beamed roof. The suits of armour, the weapons on the walls, did not glow in the light from the oil lamps but hung, dull, as if all aggression had been removed from them. The floor was dirty, what little furniture there was she could see was covered in dust, as were the two dogs which came to greet them, but to Grace's disappointment slunk off quickly, as if they were the wrong people.

'Cyril, there was no carriage at the station.'

'No, Mr Marshall.' The manservant held his lamp high and peered at Grace with what she regarded as far too familiar a stare.

'Why not, man?'

'The carriage has gone.'

'Gone?'

'The shaft broke, the horse died,' Cyril shrugged his

66

shoulders. 'I chopped up the wood, it went on the fire. We've still a little left.'

'We're very hungry, Cyril. Perhaps there would be enough kindling left to cook us some food?'

'I'll do my best. There bain't no cook, you'm realise.' He grinned at Grace who did not smile back. 'No wages see, Mr Marshall.'

'I see, the same old story. I'm sorry about all this, Grace, not much of a welcome for you. Where are my parents, Cyril? Did they not receive my telegram?'

'You father's in his workshop, your mother's gone out.'

'Ah. Well, if you could bring us some bread and cheese or something to the small parlour.'

Grace who was, as always, hungry felt despondent at the prospect of such a supper.

'Isn't there a hotel close by?' she asked hopefully.

'Not for miles, my darling. We can go to Bodmin tomorrow and get provisions in,' he replied, taking her arm and leading her across the hall. They were followed by a large dog, which had slipped in with Cyril and who, unlike his companions, seemed pleased to see Marshall.

If anything, the room which he showed her into was colder than the hall. He crossed to the hearth and knelt down, attempting to coax the remnants of a fire into life. Grace looked about her. She found herself standing in a room that time had passed by. There were no carpets on the stone-flagged floor, only a torn rug and what looked like grass strewn about. The panelled walls were bare of paintings, the mantelshelf devoid of ornaments. There were two high-backed and ornately carved chairs over which were thrown faded tapestries. At one side was an equally intricately carved chest on which stood a pewter tray and ewer. A dozen candles flickered, the smoke issuing from them indicative of their cheapness. Grace shuddered and pulled her coat closer to her.

'Is there no electricity or gas?'

'Don't be silly, darling, you don't get gas in the country.

In any case, my father would never permit either. Both my parents like to live in the past.'

'I can see that,' Grace said sharply. 'But I thought he was a scientist. Don't scientists like modern things?'

'Oh, yes, he has a generator for his laboratory but not for the house. Ah, thank you, Cyril, cheese.' He took the tray of food from the man who was looking slyly at Grace with a disconcerting grin on his face. She looked away.

Marshall poured two glasses of milk from a jug. 'At least the cow is still alive,' he grinned. He cut her a slice of bread from the half loaf and placed it with a slab of cheese on a plate which he offered her.

'Come close to the fire, Grace. You'll freeze over there.'

She shuffled over to the pathetic fire and sat huddled as she began to wolf her bread and cheese. The cheese had a strange taste. Looking carefully at it in the candlelight, she saw that it was covered in mould. Quickly she gave it to the dog who, in its haste, nearly bit her finger.

'This dog is starving,' she accused.

'Probably. If there's no food . . .' he shrugged his shoulders. 'My mother will feed them when she returns. She loves them, more than me I sometimes think.' He laughed but she did not respond. 'I did warn you I was poor.'

She managed a wan smile. 'Oh, I don't mind, Marshall, it's all a bit of an adventure, isn't it?' she said with a lack of conviction in her voice, and a rumbling from her stomach.

'When we've finished eating we'll go and find my father. I'm afraid I don't know when my mother will be back. When she goes on one of her trips she can be away for days. It is annoying, I wrote that we were coming, and my telegram confirmed it.'

'Is she visiting friends?'

'Oh, no, she's probably up on the moors – walking.'

'In this weather?'

'My mother never notices the weather. Finished? Come . . .' he held his hand out to her.

Nothing could have prepared her for the room into which he now led her. Brightly lit by electricity from a noisy generator it was full of gigantic models of insects. Grace jumped with shock at the sight of a beetle as large as a man which stood on the floor for all the world as if it was about to scuttle away. An equally large spider dangled from the rafters beside a swarm of giant locusts. The spider made her scream. A great bellow of laughter welcomed her cry.

'Marvellous, aren't they? See, frightened you, didn't they?' A large man, an older version of her husband, dressed in a long velvet gown that trailed on the filthy floor strode towards them, hand outstretched. 'So, you're Grace?' he said, beaming at her, and Grace smiled shyly back as she took his hand. 'You're a big girl, aren't you?' he barked and the smile slid rapidly from Grace's face.

'Pa, please . . .'

'It's true. What's wrong with that? I like them large, more to get hold of . . .' the raucous laugh rang out again. 'Sorry, my dear, I didn't wish to offend. Drink? We've still some port left in the cellar.' He re-crossed the room and rootled about on a paper-strewn desk until he found a shotgun. Instinctively Grace moved closer to Marshall. His father aimed at the ceiling and fired both barrels, the ear-splitting noise echoing around the cavernous room. Immediately Cyril appeared as if he had been listening at the door. 'Port, Cyril, the '39.' He replaced the gun on the desk, swung round and faced Grace. 'Do you like my models?'

'They're very interesting, Mr Boscar. Did you make them?'

'I did. Newspapers, that's what they're made of. Brilliant, aren't they?'

Grace nodded her head, unable to say anything since she could not understand their purpose.

'My father is cataloguing the insects of the world and the models are his hobby,' Marshall explained.

'So interesting,' Grace repeated inanely.

There was a large crash from the corner of the room. A lump of plaster, no doubt loosened by the gun shot, had crashed down from the ceiling above. Grace grabbed Marshall's sleeve. Mr Boscar merely roared with laughter and, as Cyril returned with the dust-encrusted bottle, he ordered him to clear up the debris.

As Mr Boscar carefully decanted the port he looked up, paused in what he was doing, and smiled at Grace. The smile unnerved her: it was identical to Marshall's most engaging smile. 'You see, my dear, my poor house is falling about my ears.'

'It would seem to be very dangerous to live here, Mr Boscar.'

'Perhaps I should send you some tin hats, Father?' Marshall said lightly.

'You're rich aren't you, young woman?' Mr Boscar finished decanting the wine and looked piercingly at her.

'Well . . .' Grace blushed. 'Quite.'

'Care to repair my house?' He smiled again.

'I don't think I'd have enough money,' she stammered. 'Maybe I could help a little. But I would have to ask my father . . .'

'Pa, she won't. I won't allow her to: it's not fair to ask her. This house is too far gone . . .'

'It's your ancestral home, Marshall, what do you mean? What is the point of bringing money into the family if we can't use it?'

'It could be beautiful, Marshall. And you told me your family has lived here for centuries.'

'It's my responsibility, Grace. I shall raise the money myself. I want none of yours,' he said emphatically. Grace looked at Marshall adoringly. Mr Boscar snorted with derision as he handed round the glasses.

An hour later, much warmed from the port, Marshall

was escorting her to bed when the great hall door swung open and in strode a tall woman. Her face, though ravaged by age, was still beautiful, her luxuriant hair flowed loose; she was dressed in an assortment of furs which swept the floor and beside her padded two deerhounds who sprang at Marshall with pleasure. From the back of the hall the other two dogs leapt at their mistress, hysterical with joy at her return. It was she, obviously, for whom they had been waiting.

'Mother!' Marshall smiled broadly.

'Such a lovely day . . .' the woman waved her hand vaguely. 'You didn't get killed then. I'm so pleased.'

'Yes, Mother, I managed to say alive. May I introduce my wife Grace.'

The woman seemed to glide across the great hall towards them. She peered myopically at Grace. 'You're rather ugly, aren't you? And far too fat. Join me in my room, Marshall, put your wife to bed.' And with the same strange gliding motion she disappeared into the gloom and a door shut.

Grace felt tears begin to prick behind her eyes. 'I would like to go to bed, Marshall, if you don't mind. It's been a long day. And could you check that those poor dogs are fed?'

'Take no notice of Mama. She's eccentric.'

'Really? I should have thought *rude* a more fitting adjective.'

Shivering in the narrow damp bed and longing for her husband to come, Grace decided she hated this house and loathed his family. Even Gwenfer would be better than this. Longing for sleep, she was too afraid of the flickering shadows and creaking sounds to get up to blow out the candle. As she turned in the bed and her foot slid over the side, she realised suddenly that there was no room for her husband here. Had his mother put her in this room with the small bed or was it Marshall's choice? They had been married for nearly two months and he had made love to her only once. Although the experience had been deeply disappointing to her – it was all over so quickly – and although she was ignorant of how husbands and wives behaved, she felt it should have happened again.

Alone in her room she missed the monumental row that ensued between Marshall and his parents. His careful plans to prise money out of Grace to repair the house were now, thanks to his parents' rudeness, no doubt scuppered. Mr Boscar was disgruntled, and Mrs Boscar unrepentant. 'I don't like ugly things, you know I don't,' she said sulkily.

The next morning Grace awoke alone. When her husband finally came to her room, she announced that she wished to visit her own ancestral home – Gwenfer. Marshall raised no objections.

That night at Gwenfer, in the four-poster bed, with a gale of terrifying proportions whipping in from the Atlantic, Marshall's nightmare returned. Once again he was back in the shell hole, the young man with his head half blown away, howling in agony.

'*Rosemary*,' Marshall screamed as he sat up in bed, covered in sweat.

'My poor love,' Grace said, taking him into her arms and cradling him against her soft breasts.

Marshall sighed, still half asleep, enjoying the once-familiar soft, yielding feel of her breasts. He remembered . . . As she comforted him, so she aroused him. A short time later, in the land of granite on the great Tregowan bed, a child was conceived.

11

Richard Frobisher stood at the foot of the nursing home bed and gazed at his wife with naked adoration. Every morning for the past seven months, he had awoken amazed that Francine was his wife – that of all the men in her life she had condescended to marry him. For Richard the baby had been a godsend: he did not like to dwell on the thought that, but for the baby, she might not have married him.

Francine sighed. Richard glanced anxiously at his wife. Petulantly she thumped her pillow and flung herself back upon it.

'God, I'm going to get so bored in this flaming hole. How many days did the quack say?'

'Fourteen, my precious.'

'I can't stand it here for one week let alone two. You'll have to get me out, Richard. I insist on being home for Christmas. Get a nurse in. Anything!' she complained in her deep, husky voice.

How Richard loved her voice. He put out his hand to stroke her beautiful long, blonde, hair.

'Oh, Richard, don't! You know I hate the way you stroke me – like a flaming dog.' Francine shook her head away from his touch, her green eyes flashing menacingly. Incredible eyes, thought Richard, eyes that gave her face such an air of innocence – fascinatingly at odds with that low, vibrant voice and its matching chuckle. Everything about Francine was at odds – he knew that's what fascinated him about her. Life with Francine was heaven and hell. Life with Francine was dangerous. It was a danger that attracted and frightened him. But she made Richard feel alive as no other woman had ever done.

'What shall we call her?' he asked, removing his hand and gently stroking the fine down on the baby's head instead. 'She's so beautiful,' the new father's voice shook with emotion as he looked at the other female with whom he was in love. 'What about Francine?' he looked up smiling.

'Don't be silly, Richard. I'm Francine Frobisher – I don't want another – it would be too confusing for words.' She studied her nails intently, already bored with the subject of her daughter's name. The whole business was tedious: she could not think why she had been so stupid as to get pregnant in the first place. Then a secret smile hovered about her mouth. She remembered only too well how – making love to Marshall, floating along on a sea of passion – it had been so easy to make the slip. Why did something so glorious carry the risk of a consequence so unutterably drab as pregnancy and the ghastly business of childbirth?

'What about Elizabeth or Ella?' Richard continued, helpfully. 'May or Margaret?'

'Unoriginal.'

'Penelope? Pamela?'

'Polly. That'll do.' The beautiful young woman began to flick through a magazine; her decision made, the subject was closed.

'It's not a very pretty name.' Richard sounded disappointed.

'She doesn't look as if she's going to be a pretty child, just look at her nose – enormous. It's best to play safe – if she's going to be plain she had better have a plain name.' The green eyes flashed warningly; Francine did not like to be crossed. Richard frowned – the frown of a man who knows that once again he has been beaten.

Francine shook her long hair and chuckled, the expression in her huge eyes changing immediately to a soft, limpid mood – no wonder she was famous for her eyes. 'See, Richard, I always know best. Don't I?' She pouted prettily at him. He adored her when she did that, for Francine's pout meant she was in a good mood again and was playing games with him.

'Polly it is then. Pretty Polly – she might be after all – it's early days,' he said, peering at the sleeping child. He wondered why his wife should think her plain when to him she was the most wondrously beautiful child he had ever seen.

A nurse bustled in, her face virtually obscured by the

bouquets she carried. Francine sat up immediately, her long-fingered hands stretched out towards them, her face aglow with interest. She dived her hands into the flowers, ripping apart the florist's creations in her search for the cards. Impatiently she tore at the envelopes. Richard watched her with an indulgent smile – how like a child she could sometimes be.

'Richard, listen, from Phillip Treacher. "Darling, hope this production has only one act – Hurry back to us." Do you think that means he wants me in his new production?' She clasped her hands together and looked up at her husband, her eyes shining, reminding Richard of a madonna. 'Oh, Richard, imagine, little me in the West End. Think, I'll never have to appear in that dreadful music hall ever again.' She picked up a mirror and studied her face. 'God, I must get myself back to normal fast.'

'You look perfect to me,' he said adoringly. She glanced at him, irritated. 'But yes, it looks as if Phillip is interested in you.' Richard tried to keep the disappointment from his voice. He had been so proud to be able to introduce his wife to Phillip in the hope of helping her career. He hadn't thought through the consequences of his actions. He had hoped that when she had a new baby to care for he would have had his winsome wife to himself for at least a year. He looked at his watch.

'Darling, I have an appointment. I'll be back this afternoon to see you both. Anything you need?'

'No, nothing. Not now you've got the telephone organised for me.' She patted the instrument beside the bed. 'So clever of you, my darling.'

'Not at all,' he said indulgently, smiling at the memories of the fight he had had with the Matron to have his wife moved to a room with an instrument installed. The Matron had not understood Francine's addiction to the telephone and had serious doubts whether her patient would rest sufficiently if she had access to one. But somehow Richard had finally persuaded the formidable woman to give way.

'See you later then.' He turned to the door.

'Darling, not this afternoon – I'm very tired and quite honestly, my sweet, I'd like an early night. I'll see you tomorrow, I'm completely exhausted. Having your baby was very hard work.' She lay back against the pillows looking so small and wan that Richard regretted that he himself had not suggested she rest.

'I'm a thoughtless oaf. Of course you must rest. Until tomorrow.' He kissed his fingers, blew her a kiss across the room, and gently closed the door behind him.

'Nurse,' said Francine, sitting up straight and alert as she addressed the woman busily arranging the flowers. 'Take the brat out and shove her in the nursery or somewhere, there's a pet.'

'Oh! Mrs Frobisher, you are a one!' the thick-ankled nurse giggled, gazing adoringly at her glamorous patient, as she picked the sleeping baby up.

Alone in the room, at last, Francine grabbed the phone and dialled a number.

'Buttons, thank you for the adorable flowers, my favourites,' she said vaguely, unsure of which of the many bouquets was Buttons's. 'Buttons, be an absolute darling. It's like a morgue in here. Come and see me this afternoon – bring whoever you can find. I'm so bloody bored.' Smiling, she listened to his voice. 'Divine! Bring some fizz too, I'm gasping.'

The phone call disconnected, she dialled again.

'Flippy? Flippy darling . . . God it's wonderful to hear your voice . . . thank you for the heavenly flowers . . . No, I didn't read the card out – too naughty. Did you mean it?' She smiled coquettishly at the mouthpiece. 'A girl.' She shrugged. 'Darling, I don't know. You know me and sums, I think they said 6lb something.' There was another pause. 'Polly . . . I think it's chic . . . No, it was my choice. I couldn't leave something as important as her name to Richard . . . No, he's not coming in, he's got some boring business dinner to attend . . . Come early . . . Oh, Flippy, I love you too, and now my body's my own again . . . !' She chuckled.

Francine replaced the receiver gently, resting her hand on it awhile as if loath to lose contact with the other party. For a second she lay back on the pillows, a dreamy smile playing about her mouth.

Suddenly, she sat up, and rang the bell for the nurse. Francine was hungry.

Richard sat in the empty flat off Park Lane, a drink in one hand and stared at the telephone. The flat seemed emptier than empty without Francine. When she was there, her personality filled rooms she was not even in.

He looked about the starkly modern room, still unsure if he liked it. Beautiful it might be but comfortable it was not. And so white – blindingly white – but for how long? No doubt it would soon be changed. It could become anything – an Arab tent, a Chinese salon, a Regency dining room. Who could tell with Francine? No sooner had he got used to the decor in their bedroom than Francine had changed it – twice. It looked as if the only time the flat would be safe was if she was in a play, then her restless spirit would be otherwise occupied.

He put his head back only to find that this modern chair had no backrest, and sat bolt upright again. God, he was tired. It took hard work in the firm of stockbrokers for Richard to earn enough to keep Francine in clothes and decorators.

She wanted him to sell Hurstwood. In fact she nagged him constantly – Hurstwood and the country were anathema to Francine. But it was the one thing on which he would not give way. He was sad when his Great Aunt Agnes had died but overjoyed that she had left him the small estate in Devon. Now his dream, and the one thing that helped keep him sane at the office, was the thought of making enough money to retire to Hurstwood with

Francine, and now Polly, to lead the life of a country gentleman. He sighed. The dream seemed a long way off even if he took into account the money Francine could make once she was back on the stage. These days every penny seemed to disappear so fast.

Intently he studied the phone again. Should he call? Hear her voice? Perhaps he had better not, for one thing it might wake her, but secondly, if he heard that irresistible voice it would take all his self-control not to go crashing round there.

But there was one phone call he had to make. First he lit a cigarette and puffed nervously at it. He dialled the operator and asked for a number in Berkshire and waited, twisting the cigarette between his fingers as the connection was made.

'Lady Gertrude, please.'

'Who shall I say is calling, sir?' an unfamiliar voice replied in measured tones.

'Her son,' he answered shortly, embarrassed at having to identify himself to the stranger. John English, the old butler, must have been retired. He sat drumming a tattoo on the white marble table beside him. A discreet cough from the receiver attracted his attention.

'Mr Frobisher. I regret her Ladyship is not at home to calls.'

'Thank you,' Richard said, his natural politeness disguising the crushing disappointment he felt.

What had he expected? But, for him to telephone after all these months should have told his mother that he had something important to say. He felt bitter, and miserable: if only they would give Francine a chance. Still, his mother would read the announcement in *The Times* tomorrow – perhaps she would contact him then. He so wanted his mother to meet Polly.

In the depths of Berkshire the logs crackled in the great stone fireplace, the beech trees rustled in the park. The black labrador, Duxford, lifted his head as his master coughed, and then slumped back on the Persian rug – no action at the moment – the dog returned immediately to sleep.

Basil coughed again. He was coughing because he knew he should say something but was uncertain what would be appropriate. It was not a cough caused by illness or irritants.

'You can cough all you want, Basil. I don't see the point in speaking to him,' his wife said sharply.

'But hasn't it gone on long enough, old girl? He telephoned, he must want to bury the hatchet. Perhaps the baby has been born.'

'Then do your sums, Basil. How long have they been married? It's obvious now that the boy was tricked into marriage,' Gertie said crisply while still concentrating on her petit point. Only the jerking of her needle as she stabbed at the canvas indicated the strain she was under. It would have been so easy and yet so difficult to talk to him. She wanted to – there were days when she ached with longing for Richard, the son whom her younger son and daughter could never replace. But principles were at stake here, and Gertie was not one to shirk a principle.

Basil, on the other side of the enormous fireplace, settled his bulk into his favourite wing chair. His hand stretched out for his glass of brandy – always in the same position so that he need never look – and it made contact like a homing pigeon. Inwardly he sighed and his highly coloured face with its large walrus moustache settled into an even more lugubrious expression than normal. He admired Gertie. If pressed, though he never was, he would admit to loving her. But she was stubborn, certainly. He had given up arguing with her, when a principle was at stake, years ago. He simply wished that the whole sorry mess could be resolved.

When news had first reached him of Richard's infatuation with Francine, he had thought little of it. When the

79

fixation had persisted, goaded by Gertie's increasing concern, he had gone himself to the theatre to see the girl who was causing such disruption to his domestic tranquillity.

As soon as he set eyes on Francine he understood his son. The boy had been wounded in the trenches, had seen his friends dying, and God knows what other horrors. Invalided out, was it any wonder, after living through that hell, that he should have fallen for this young woman?

What a beauty she was. Luxuriant golden hair, the most improbably innocent, green eyes and certainly the longest legs in the business. Good God, he could probably have raised a gallop for the girl himself.

In his youth he had had many a young actress. But he would never have married one. Basil grunted at the very idea – his wife's needle paused for a second, the labrador lifted his head. The brandy glass made the return journey to the table.

The difference between him and his son was that Basil knew his place, knew his position in the scheme of things. He had sown his wild oats, had married Gertie, had continued to manage the occasional discreet adventure. Why could Richard not do the same?

He thought that Gertie's insistence on cutting him off without a penny was extreme but felt he could not do otherwise – one had to stick by one's wife even if the principles were a bit rigid for comfort.

He had been glad, when his aunt had died, to hear she had left his son Hurstwood – a nice, useful little estate that. Nothing to compare with this one, however, the one that should rightly be his. Not that he thought Richard would hold it against Charles, his younger brother, for Richard had a good heart and a character for forgiveness.

Basil grunted again – tonight he might be a grandfather and not even know what sex the baby was. Bloody women!

*

At the hospital Francine's door displayed a 'Do Not Disturb' notice. She had artfully draped silk scarves over the glaring hospital shades. In the softened gloom of the room two heads were close together, hands were firmly held. Early in her pregnancy Francine had met this young man and had decided he was a worthy replacement for Marshall. The air was full of the sighs and promises of undying love that Francine and the Honourable Frederick, otherwise Flippy, Sigford were making to each other.

Chapter Two

1

Alice Tregowan-Wakefield looked about the bedroom to see if she had forgotten anything. This was unnecessary since Alice was a perfectionist in matters of entertaining and she had never been known to overlook anything.

Nevertheless she always checked each room before a guest arrived, though this time it wasn't a guest but her own daughter and her daughter's new husband. How strange that will be, she thought, as she shook the cushions on the chaise. She straightened the curtains and looked out of the window at the New York traffic streaming by. It was only Tuesday; she would have to wait until Friday morning before she could escape to Dart Island where she was happiest. If only Lincoln would retire, she thought, not for the first time, if only they could spend more time in the country.

Lincoln was always promising to do less, to spend more time there – he never did. She had learnt over the years that his promises were not to be relied upon. Long ago she had believed him when he said they would spend six months of each year in England, at Gwenfer, her family home. But they had only been there twice. Of course Lincoln could not help the intervention of the war – all visits were impossible now until that horror was over. But when peace came she doubted if she would often see her home. He had gone to such trouble to buy it for her too, tracking down the new owner after her father died and they discovered that he had sold it. It was typical of Lincoln to make such a grand gesture to please her, but now it was almost as if he had forgotten about the place.

She paused in her tidying. It was odd that after all these years she still thought of Gwenfer as home. It was silly really, here she was, a woman of nearly forty-two, who had spent more of her life in America than in her own country. In her heart, though, she still clung to those roots, snaking down deep into the granite of her native land, the land that would never, it seemed, release her.

She checked the bowl of fruit. She wondered if the war and the suffering she had seen had changed Grace? Would she be more mature, more considerate? She hoped so, for there had been much need of improvement in the spoilt and petulant young woman her daughter had become. She could honestly say that Grace's faults could be laid at Lincoln's door. He had adored the child to the point of ruination, and her own attempts at discipline had been ignored by both husband and daughter. She had been surprised when Grace announced she was going to Europe on the outbreak of war. Knowing how lazy she was Alice had pointed out that the work would be hard. On the one hand, she had been concerned for the girl's safety, but on the other she had secretly thought it might be the making of her. She was proud of Grace and the stand she had made against Lincoln's objections. There was no need for her to go: she was an American citizen and America was not even involved then. The gesture was brave and totally out of character – Grace was the last person one could imagine toiling in the wards of a hospital for wounded soldiers. Alice was excited at the prospect of seeing her again but, more than that, she found she was curious to know what Grace had become.

Lincoln had been impossible since the telegram arrived announcing Grace's impending marriage. Frustrated by the difficulties of trans-Atlantic communications in wartime, it had taken too long, for one of his impatience, to find out about Marshall. It was Lincoln who, pulling strings and bribing officials, had arranged for Marshall's transfer to the British Embassy in Washington as military attaché. There he could keep a better eye on Marshall, he reasoned. He had then used strategic blackmail on Marshall's commanding officer – whose business affairs Lincoln knew too much about for that gentleman's comfort – to have his son-in-law discharged from the army. Hence their arrival in New York where, Alice presumed, Lincoln hoped to have more control over Marshall. Alice was concerned that Marshall might have learnt what interference her husband was capable of – she hoped not, it would not bode well for the future. Since they had first heard of him, Lincoln had lathered himself into a rage, claiming that Grace's husband was obviously not good enough for her – but then who would have been?

Alice doubted if Lincoln could have loved Grace more if she had been his own flesh and blood. After each miscarriage Alice had suffered – his love for his step-daughter simply increased. He must have been disappointed at Alice's inability to bear him a son and heir, but if he was, Alice was never aware of it. After four miscarriages Lincoln had taken it upon himself to ensure that Alice never became pregnant again. He loved her too much to risk losing her, he said. So, all his hopes and ambitions had become centred upon Grace. There were times when Alice felt sorry for the girl, deluged with love but hemmed in by expectations as she was.

Lincoln was an enigma. Even after fourteen years of marriage Alice recognised that she did not really know him. His character seemed to have so many facets but she was allowed to know only some of them. There was the kind and loving family man, intensely loyal, generous to a fault. But there was also the man who could fly into a screaming rage if she was two minutes late, or dinner was not perfect, or he imagined she had smiled at another man. Such opposites in one man. A friend had explained that it was because he was born under the sign of Gemini – always torn between the two characters within him. Alice had no time for such fancies but, whatever the cause, this lack of consistency exasperated her. Alice preferred people to be more equable in their approach to life, as she was herself.

And then there was the Lincoln she was not supposed to know but of whom she had caught glimpses over the years. He was totally ruthless in business and feared by many of his associates. And, she had realised reluctantly, this was a state of affairs that Lincoln enjoyed – he wanted to be feared and was undoubtedly proud of his reputation.

Alice felt cheated by this aspect of him. When they had first met he had taken her to the factory he had built in the town of which he was the chief benefactor. She had been impressed by his benign paternalism. His employees seemed genuinely to care for him and he for them. But this factory, this town, had a position rather like Alice's in his life – they were like family, they were protected and loved. Business enterprises he had subsequently founded did not enjoy this protection, and she pitied those others he employed and with whom he had dealings.

He strode through life with a mission and with enormous confidence and yet, paradoxically, he suffered from a degree of insecurity. He wanted, needed, to be accepted, and there lay a problem. For in many cases he wasn't. He was rich and he wanted to stand in society with the Astors and the Vanderbilts but they had turned their backs upon him and refused to accept or invite him. Alice had soon learnt why – he had done too many deals that bordered on the criminal or had been too ruthless for their newly developed sensibilities, for they had long ago lost the swashbuckling courage of the founders of their own fortunes, and swathed themselves in discreet respectability. This rankled in the darkest recesses of Lincoln's complicated mind. When Alice had met him, he had seemed to care nothing for society. But once they were married acceptance was what he wanted, almost demanded – for the sake of Grace and Alice. He felt ashamed that, because of him, they were not invited into the grandest homes, to the biggest balls, to the great dinners, to the Norfolk Island estates. Alice told him frequently that this rejection mattered not a jot. But Lincoln could not be reassured. To compensate, the house on Dart Island grew grander by the year and at this very moment a vast house overlooking Central Park was being built for her, which she did not want and knew she would hate.

Like many women Alice realised she had not known her husband when she married him. Did she love him? She still did not know. She cared for him, for everything he had done for her and her daughter. But persistently in Alice's head remained the memory of so long ago when at the age of eighteen she had fallen in love with Chas Cordell and had eloped with him to America. So great was the excitement he had sparked in her that she had lost country, friends and family with barely a backward glance. Over the years the memory of the happiness with him had remained, completely obliterating the pain she had felt when he deserted her; the anger when she discovered he was already married; the fear when she learnt she was to bear his child. The luxury in which she now lived had helped soften the memory of the poverty she and Grace had been forced to endure in the rat-infested tenement. Now she could barely remember the long hours she had worked in her bakery to survive, and the mind-numbing fatigue. Lincoln had rescued her from all that, and for that her gratitude was boundless.

Alice was aware that these memories of Chas were dangerous. It was those memories, she was certain, which prevented her from loving Lincoln as she should.

She took one last look at her daughter's room. Glancing at her watch she realised she had only one hour to bathe, and to prepare herself with the degree of perfection that Lincoln demanded of her, especially tonight, Christmas Eve.

*

'But I had rather hoped, despite my leg, to stay in the army, sir.'

'What on earth for? You can't support my daughter on an army captain's pay, can you?' Lincoln smiled at his new son-in-law, and Alice found herself playing agitatedly with the pearls at her neck. It was not one of Lincoln's genuine smiles. She found she was willing Marshall to agree.

'No, sir, but I had every reason to hope for promotion.'

'There's no point in hoping, young man. You can't eat hope.'

'Of course not, sir. Then I shall look for employment.'

'Now you're talking. And where are you planning to live?' Again the smile. Lincoln was enjoying this, this cat and mouse game was one of his least appealing traits, Alice thought. She knew that, only the month before, Lincoln had learnt from friends in England exactly what Marshall's financial position was. He had found out that there was no question of Marshall being able to afford a house, not in New York where property was prohibitively expensive, and certainly nothing that Lincoln would consider suitable for Grace to live in.

'Papa, you are being a mean old bear,' Grace cajoled him. 'Stop it, you'll frighten Marshall away, then what should I do?'

'Papas have to find such matters out, Grace, my princess.'

Marshall saw the warm, genuine smile which Lincoln offered to Grace, in total contrast to the cold grimace Lincoln had bestowed on him, and judged that he was dealing with a sadistic bastard who would need handling with kid gloves, if he were to get the life-style he wanted. He looked across the drawing room at his mother-in-law and knew, without doubt, that she would be his ally.

'I've worked it all out, Papa. If you and Mama are moving to your new house soon, then Marshall and I can have this house, I like this house, you know I do, Papa.'

'Husbands house their own wives.'

'Oh, Papa, please, don't be such a fuddy duddy. And surely, if you want Marshall to work, though I don't see why he should – you give me plenty of money . . . But if you insist, couldn't Marshall work for you? He's wonderfully clever.'

Lincoln's expression softened, it always did where Grace was concerned, but he had hoped to play this game a bit longer. He did not like this young man: he had decided that the moment Marshall had strutted into the house. He was an opportunist: Lincoln knew the type too well. He had noted, too, that Alice seemed to be taken by him; women were always stupid where this sort of man was concerned. But he didn't want to worry Grace, especially so close to the birth of her child. Not that he liked to dwell on how she had become pregnant – his little girl in this mountebank's arms! He shook his leonine head.

'All right, my darling, you can have this house. Maybe I can find work for your husband.'

'There, Marshall, I told you what a dear man my father was. I knew he would help us.'

'Thank you, sir.'

The two men looked across the room at each other with mutual loathing.

2

Standing in the ornate, over-scented, over-heated bedroom, Marshall looked across the bed at his wife and marvelled that he had ever found the courage to impregnate her.

'I'm sorry, darling,' Grace said in her beautiful, low voice, a voice which deserved an equally lovely body instead of one bloated with fat. She flopped back against the silk, cream-coloured pillow. 'So dreadfully sorry,' she repeated, apologising, as always, in fear of losing him.

Marshall's jaw tightened a fraction. There were things about his wife he could admit to admiring but her increasingly apologetic and cringing manner irritated him beyond endurance.

'Why are you sorry, my love?' he said, smiling at her. It was a practised, professional smile, one he had perfected in front of his looking glass. Perfect white teeth flashed in an evenly tanned face but the eyes were devoid of expression.

'That it's not a boy, Marshall.'

'My sweet, why should I mind? We have all the time in the world, you and I. Next time it will be a boy.' Again the slick smile streaked towards her across the wild silk coverlet. 'Next time, be damned!' he thought to himself. He had done his duty. He was not going to sleep with her again – ever. He couldn't. The old man had an heir. He would stay with her – he could not afford to leave, not if he didn't want to work – but from now on he would insist on separate rooms. He'd start right now, using the baby and his wife's fatigue as an excuse for sleeping in his dressing room. Then, after a month or two, he'd arrange for a suite of rooms of his own. It wasn't as if he were depriving her of anything. The few times they had made love she had not known what to do and had obviously not enjoyed it for one moment. Yes, that was it, he would be doing her a favour, really – that's how he would handle it. He snorted with amusement at his own cleverness. Grace looked at him questioningly.

To avoid her stare, Marshall bent over the ornate bassinet. His large, strong hands gently held back the delicate lace canopy woven fine as gossamer. He looked at the sleeping child. The down on her head was glinting golden. One tiny fist was held clenched against the perfect, smooth cheek. Tentatively he touched her other hand with his forefinger; her miniature fingers clenched tightly around it. The baby snuffled gently. Marshall stared at her with a dazed expression – for the first time in his life he had fallen in love.

'Grace, she's *perfect*.' He looked up. This time as he smiled at his wife he glowed with pride, and his smile was full of genuine pleasure. Grace leant forward eagerly, stretching out her hand to her husband, as if trying to catch the smile, responding to this unaccustomed warmth.

'Look at her hands. They're so delicate. She's going to be blonde, I like fair-haired women. She's got my mouth . . . Yes, she looks like me, she really does . . .' The words tumbled from him as, with a sense of astonishment, Marshall adjusted to this strange, unfamiliar emotion. Even as he spoke, even as he came to terms with it, he realised that he could never leave Grace now, even if he wanted to. He was trapped: his daughter would keep him here as nothing else could have done.

'What shall we call her? Perhaps Alice, after my mother. That would please Papa so much.'

'No,' Marshall replied abruptly.

'Of course, darling,' Grace said hurriedly. 'Of course you'd prefer Mathilda, after yours?' She said it as graciously as she could. She had wanted a pretty name for her baby. She waited as her husband stared a long time at the sleeping baby.

'Juniper. That's what we'll call her.'

'Juniper?' Grace sounded seriously unsure.

'Yes, Juniper. An unusual name for someone who is going to be an unusual lady.'

The christening of Juniper Wakefield Boscar was the highlight of the Dart Island summer season.

The large, glittering white mansion – a sprawling mixture of American colonial, English Regency and neo-classical pillared grandeur – was thronged with people. They eddied about the great house, peering into the ornate salons. They moved with care amongst the crowded, expensively furnished rooms, wove as if in a minuet between the many tables heavily weighted with silver-framed photographs and cluttered with enamel boxes, and slid through the jungles of aspidistra. Groups made tableaux on the immaculately mown lawns. They dallied by the great Italianate fountain and everyone endeavoured not to look impressed.

A string quartet played Mozart. Five hundred bottles of champagne were drunk. Lobsters, salmon and oysters beyond number died for Juniper's baptism.

In the ballroom Juniper's presents were displayed. Baby rattles in every material and precious metal known to man, solid silver mugs, in quantities sufficient for an orphanage, glinted in the sun. Fine cases of silver cutlery, silver candlesticks, a silver punch bowl. Jewelled trinkets and, the *pièce de résistance*, from Juniper's grandfather – a tiara studded with diamonds. It was as if Juniper were a bride instead of a baby.

This first grandchild of Lincoln Wakefield was being launched into society in a manner befitting a Princess of the New World.

Lincoln watched the colourful scene on his lawn. Despite being nearly sixty he had the upright carriage of a much younger man; his large impressive head was in proportion to his wide-shouldered body. He had the far-seeing look of a sea captain in his pale blue eyes, strange in a man who loathed the sea. His face was lined with deep furrows chiselled by the scepticism and suspicion that were his keenest tools of trade. It was a hard face and one that sent tremors of fear through his competitors, and through those of his employees who were incompetent. But those he cared for, and those who worked hard, had no need to fear him.

He watched the milling crowd with a mixture of pride and cynicism, the mixture with which he surveyed most aspects of life. His pride today was overwhelming. Lincoln never thought of himself as Grace's step-father.

She was his little princess whom he loved more than life itself. Thus her child would be as precious to him as if his blood flowed in her veins. Until the baby was born he had not realised how great was his longing for this child, this member of the next generation. The fact that she was a girl was irrelevant. If no other children were born, if no grandson appeared, so be it. Lincoln would make certain that this child would be a fitting heiress to the Wakefield millions.

He smiled to himself as he habitually did when he thought of his money. He had done well, this occasion was proof of it. If Lincoln sneezed Wall Street trembled.

In under forty years he had risen from the poverty of a small farming family, scratching a living from soil that was heartless, to become a multimillionaire with a mansion in New York as well as this island. A millionaire who had built his own town, who owned his own train, with more money than he could ever spend, an estate in England, an employer of thirty thousand. From a secret family recipe he had become the largest manufacturer of pickles and sauces in the whole of the United States. From that foundation he had invested shrewdly and well. Lincoln was the embodiment of the American Dream.

Lincoln worked harder than any man he had met. If a deal was in the offing Lincoln would not rest until it was completed. And as soon as one deal was completed, he would be off in search of another. He toiled, saved, wheeled and dealt assiduously for the sake of his family – Alice, Grace and now Juniper.

A frown replaced the self-satisfied smile. He often frowned these days when he thought of his daughter. She had been a dear, sweet child, occasionally wilful but then which woman wasn't? Dutiful she *had* been, until she became besotted with that dolt of a husband. Marshall's interests seemed to extend no further than polo, champagne and that over-large lump of meat which dangled between his legs.

Lincoln encouraged the polo. In the half year since Marshall's arrival, Lincoln had lavished a small fortune on his son-in-law's stables – all in the hope that one day he would fall from a horse and break his limey neck.

The frown deepened to a scowl of anger. Lincoln shook his head – this would not do. He should not allow thoughts of that bastard to spoil this perfect day.

Grace sat in the shade of the large copper beech tree. She always tried to sit in the shade for the sun was unkind to Grace and within an hour could spitefully turn her pale skin to an unbecoming red, followed irrevocably by unsightly peeling. She sat because, in sitting, she hoped her size would be less evident. Juniper was six months old but Grace was larger now than she had been when the child was born.

Beneath her brimmed hat heavy with satin and mauve roses which matched the finely pleated lawn dress that did nothing for her colour or shape, Grace watched through slanted eyes the slim women, skittling about the lawn in daringly short dresses which exposed elegant ankles. Grace adjusted her long skirt in a vain attempt to hide her own puffy ankles above swollen feet which were in agony from the fashionable, tight barred shoes which cut into her flesh.

Her glance swept across the lawn to the terrace where her husband, looking handsome and cool in his perfectly cut suit, leant elegantly against the balustrade. He was surrounded by a bevy of beautiful women who fluttered about him like exotic moths. She watched him lean over and whisper in one beauty's ear, watched his hand slide over another's perfectly proportioned rump – and felt the familiar pain worm its way deeper inside her.

The pain was a physical manifestation of Grace's mental torment. But as the pain increased until her hands became damp with sweat – Grace still smiled. For Grace's agony of jealousy was a private matter to be hidden from the world. She had taught herself, whatever the provocation, no matter how strong the pain – to smile, to smile – while she slowly disintegrated within. She could no longer afford the luxury of the spoiled child or the beautiful woman – a tantrum – for she knew she could not bear to risk losing Marshall.

After nearly eighteen months, it was still a miracle to Grace that Marshall had married her. She knew she would never be able to keep him faithful. She had prepared herself for that. She had had warning enough – as soon as the baby was born, he had insisted on his own rooms, and not once since Juniper's birth had he visited her at night. He must be getting comfort somewhere else, she reasoned. Prepared she might have been, but not for the deep pain she felt when Marshall was late home, or the nights when he did not return at all. He lied of course, brilliantly, but she knew . . . Her one hope had been that when she lost weight he would return to her bed and the philandering would stop. But it had not, and she had turned for consolation to her old love – food.

Perhaps when Papa died it would be better. Grace brushed her face as if trying to erase such a thought, but it kept creeping disloyally back. But, all the same, when he died and when all the money was hers she would be able to give Marshall whatever he wanted. Why, she would even give him all the money if he asked for it. Then surely he would begin to love her and stay faithful to her.

Marshall stood amongst the group of admiring women and was bored. The ease with which he made his conquests frequently bored him these days. Women were such fools, he thought. He despised women and the lengths to which they would go to entice him to make love to them.

Over the heads of the clacking females he saw his wife watching him. For a minute he stopped flirting: perhaps his behaviour was too blatant? But she never seemed to mind. By the same stroke of luck or genius, he had landed himself with a rich, tolerant wife. He was even quite fond of her but, if he were honest with himself – which was rare – he had to admit that it was a fondness similar to that he felt for his dog and his horses. He couldn't understand how despite all her money she contrived to look so frumpish. He gave her a half wave, a wave more like a small salute, and turned back to the other women as he felt a silk-clad thigh press suggestively against his own. He looked down into the pert face of a redhead he had not met before. A rather vacuous face, he thought, but the lips parted and a little pink tongue ran gently back and forth across her upper lip. After all, thought Marshall, it was not her brain he was interested in. From her hand he took the neatly folded card, slipped it into his pocket, and effortlessly carried on the social banter. 'What else was a man to do?' he thought. No one could blame him. One thing was for sure, his Juniper would not be like these women, hanging about him like bitches on heat. He would see to that.

3

The guests had left. An army of servants had moved with well-organised precision through the mansion, about the grounds. All evidence of the party had been removed so that by dinner time it was as if there had been no great reception.

Lincoln sat at the head of the highly polished mahogany table. His wife Alice was a long way away at the other end. His daughter sat slumped half-way down, opposite the army place-setting of her husband. The candles glinted on the silver. The butler and footman retreated with discreet shuffles. An uncomfortable silence reigned, broken only by the rattle of the cutlery, the occasional clink of a wine glass being replaced on the table.

Lincoln surveyed his food morosely – a delicate stuffed

chicken breast with a suspicious looking sauce of a strange Chartreuse colour. He prodded it tentatively – from inside the breast a cascade of finely chopped mushrooms settled into the sauce like miniature rocks in a green sea. He sighed. He loved his wife, admired her elegance, her sophistication, her taste. But there were times when he wished she were not so bloody European.

'Why can't we have a good honest steak once in a while? Or meat loaf? I like meat loaf,' his voice boomed, causing Grace nervously to drop her fork. God, the girl was a bunch of nerves these days, he thought.

'Of course, Lincoln. Would you like me to ring for Septimus to bring you a steak?' his wife said, smiling reasonably at him.

'No, no, not now. I don't want to waste good food. Food costs money.' He scowled at them, wishing not for the first time that his wife was not always so reasonable about everything. 'But, tomorrow – tomorrow I want steak.'

'And so you shall have.'

Lincoln sulked and gingerly placed the perfectly prepared chicken in his mouth. It tasted good, it always did, so he did not really know why he complained. It was just that sometimes, even after all these years, he longed for some good, plain American fare such as his mother had served.

The silence descended again. He knew why he had spoken out about the food – to stop himself saying what he really wanted to say. He chewed slowly, sipped his wine, sipped his water, ate more chicken and could contain himself no longer.

'Where's Marshall?' he demanded.

Grace flushed and looked quickly from mother to father as if her husband's absence were all her fault.

'He had a call. Business, Papa.'

'Business?' Lincoln snorted the word. 'Business on Sunday?'

'You do business at weekends, too,' she said with some spirit in her voice.

'I do, but then I'm a *businessman*!' he replied in the ironic voice he used for underlings. 'I wasn't aware that the illustrious Marshall was one.' He regretted his tone as soon as he saw the blush on his daughter's face deepen, the tears form in her pale grey eyes. 'What business, Gracy?' he asked more kindly, reverting to her childhood name.

'Something to do with ice-cream parlours, Papa.'

'It was boat-building last week,' he grunted. Try as he might he could not keep the irritation out of his voice.

'He didn't like the man, Papa.'

'Like? What's liking got to do with making deals? Why, some of my best deals have been done with my worst enemies. I don't understand the boy.'

'Evidently,' his wife said briskly, her accent still, after so many years, untouched by the Americans she lived amongst.

Grace shuffled her bulk uncomfortably in the chair and piled far too much food on her fork. With lightning speed she put it in her mouth and swallowed it with a minimum of mastication.

'Ah well, I suppose the boy will eventually find what it is he wants to do,' he said more kindly.

Boy! he fumed to himself. A thirty-year-old layabout content to live off his wife's allowance. A kept man. What sort of man was that? Every position he offered the skunk, Marshall found some excuse not to take up. A parasite was what he was. Alice had often explained to him, and at great length, how Englishmen of a certain class did not work: their land was occupation enough. If that was the case, the idle good-for-nothing should have stayed in England. This was America where men worked – worked to make money, to build for their families, to lay down for the future. Their sons in turn worked that lode of wealth, and mined for more.

Business, the lying bastard! More likely humping some dirty whore at this moment, while Grace fretted and Lincoln grew more frustrated at his inability to ease her pain.

Gloomily he stared into space. He should never have allowed the wedding in the first place. But Grace had taken them unawares. Overnight his dutiful daughter had become a determined, stubborn advocate for her own future. And what had happened? He had given in. Given in rather than have her elope, and risk losing her for ever.

He looked at his despondent daughter morosely pushing the last piece of chicken about her plate the better to mop up the final drop of sauce. She always looked defeated these days but, give her her due, she maintained a serene façade in public.

He should have had the bastard killed. It would have been easy enough to arrange: he had done as much before. For the one and only time in his life he had wavered and now he was having to face the consequences.

Viciously Lincoln tore at the remains of his bread roll. How could she ever find happiness with a waster like that? Charm, ah, he had charm in abundance, but, that apart, his only claims to fame were the noble families to whom, he incessantly told them, he was related; and that huge organ between his legs . . . hung like a donkey, he had heard at the club. And women queuing to find out the truth of the rumour.

As Lincoln's anger rose, the room began to blur. He fought to calm himself, to lower his dangerously high blood pressure. He was not about to give his son-in-law the satisfaction of seeing him die.

'If you'll excuse me, Mother, I think I'll go to bed. I'm very tired. Thank you both for such a perfect day.' Grace smiled as she waddled awkwardly from the room.

'I bet that bastard's out fornicating.'

'Most probably,' Alice replied, calmly.

'How can you sound so matter-of-fact about it?'

'There's not a lot we can do about it, Lincoln, is there? She chose him, though we both warned her. We did our best.'

'In fact there's one hell of a lot we can do about it.' Lincoln stood, abruptly pushing the heavy carver back as he did so. 'Get Septimus to bring my brandy to the study. I've work to do.'

Three hours later Alice sat in the giant bed with its ornate hangings. Across the room she could see herself reflected in the heavily embossed mirror on the mahogany dressing table. A book was open before her but Alice was not reading it. She was thinking. Deep in thought, she laid her head against the pillows. She was a beautiful woman, one whom time had treated favourably.

Alice felt sorry for her daughter but it was a sorrow tinged with irritation. Grace had left them a petulant and wilful young woman intent on getting her own way – a young woman difficult to like. She had returned miserable, whining and apologetic – like a young horse whose spirit has been broken, a young woman still difficult to like. It seemed that Grace's behaviour was always on the edge of extremes. There had been a time, all those years ago when they suffered together in the tenements, when she had lived for her daughter, when her love for her consumed her to the point where she had fought to survive not for herself but for Grace. Yet now, this woman was like a stranger to her. There were times when Alice knew without doubt that her daughter felt nothing for her, and on these occasions she admitted to herself that she found it difficult to feel for Grace the unconditional love she had felt so long ago. It was a situation which saddened her but to which there appeared to be no solution.

But why was Grace so changed? When they had first arrived, Marshall had been kind and considerate: Alice had seen it with her own eyes. Now she could hardly blame him for spending less time with Grace, who seemed incapable of amusing him, or of being light-hearted. And, even Alice had to confess, her daughter was beginning to look a sorry mess. She stuffed food into her mouth like a navvy; she did not care about her complexion or her hair. Grace's pitiful devotion to Marshall was plain to see, and for the sake of her daughter's sanity Alice had tried – though it went against the grain – to make Grace see sense. If she wanted Marshall's approval, she must eat less, must take more interest in her appearance and try to be more lively. But each time she raised the subject, she seemed to goad the young woman into eating more, and behaving still more morosely. Recently Alice had taken to biting back *any* comment that could be construed as criticism. Alice was sadly aware that she had lost the key to understanding her daughter's complex character.

Most of all Alice felt sorry for her husband, knowing the terrible impotence he must feel as he watched his adored daughter slide into despair.

She had liked Marshall on sight but had recognised at once how impossible he would be as a husband. She had felt it her duty to warn her daughter of what the future with Marshall might hold. Blushing deeply she had even mentioned to Grace, during one of Marshall's increasingly frequent absences, that she must take care, that with such a husband there was risk of infection. Grace had been furious with her, had told her to mind her own business and to stop interfering. Alice, frustrated in every attempt to help her daughter, had answered with aggrieved anger and the ensuing quarrel had widened the rift between them.

Alice knew that she should dislike Marshall, as her husband did, for what he was doing to her daughter. But she found she could not, she acknowledged that she herself was susceptible to his charm. She forgave him when he was late, frequently found herself defending him.

She suspected that he was an easy-going, generous man, out of his depth, that his behaviour was more amoral than immoral. Perhaps she should speak to Marshall himself. He was at risk, of that she was certain. She might not understand her husband entirely but she knew what he was capable of. But Alice came from another world, another generation. The sensibilities, so deeply ingrained within her, would never allow her to speak of such matters to her son-in-law.

Suddenly she thought of her old friend Gertie. She wished she were here to talk to, to give her some sound, down-to-earth, advice. But Gertie wasn't here and she hadn't seen her since this wretched war had prevented travel. Apart from her one childhood friend, Gertie had been the only real friend in the whole of her life. The sort of friend to whom she could always turn in trouble, the kind who sometimes, it seemed, knew she was upset without needing to be told. Gertie was the only person to whom she had ever been able to confide her deepest thoughts. She owed her much. When society had ostracised her, only Gertie had welcomed Alice and Lincoln into her home when they had visited England. With her steely determination she had worked at the task of filtering them into the society which had so abruptly rejected her when she had eloped with Chas. To Gertie, acceptance by that élite was essential – to Alice it no longer mattered. But rather than hurt her old friend she had smiled her way back into favour and had benevolently enjoyed Gertie's sense of triumph, as barrier after barrier had fallen.

Why were children such a worry? Had her own father worried about her like this when she had run away to America? She smiled, knowing the answer – he had not given her one thought. Her father had been angry because he felt his name had been damaged by her behaviour. She had always resented this; now she envied him his lack of concern. If you didn't care for your child, you were spared the worry and the sense of inevitable frustration as you watched that child, now an adult, wreck its life.

Her thoughts were interrupted by her husband entering the room from his dressing room, dressed in his habitual long night-shirt.

'I've seen to it,' he said, climbing into bed beside the beautiful woman who still excited him and who, in all their years together, he had never once betrayed. 'I've seen to that useless parasite.' And in detail he explained to his wife what he had done.

Grace Boscar's pillow was soaking. She had cried so much that she now felt sick.

She tossed and turned, on the rumpled silk sheets, discarding the damp pillows, one by one, on the floor. Which of those slim elegant bitches was he with? Which firm pair of breasts were his hands upon, his lips sucking? Grace's huge form thrashed about the bed in torment.

She was driving herself mad with these thoughts but could not stop, could not remove from her mind's eye the image of her husband giving pleasure that should be hers, to another woman. Agitatedly she tore at her handkerchief – a scrap of lace which was totally inadequate for the torrent pouring from her eyes.

Grace heaved herself from the bed and padded into her bathroom. With disgust she surveyed her reflection in the mirror.

'Look at you,' she said aloud between shuddering sobs. 'You're a fat, ugly, *pig*!' she yelled.

Angrily she stripped, and stepped into the shower, purposely allowing only cold water to cascade over her body. Somewhere she'd read that cold water would firm her breasts. She stood beneath the torrent of chill water until her skin was blue and her body ached. By punishing her obese flesh Grace made herself feel a little better.

In front of the floor-length mirror of her closet she critically studied her large melon-like breasts with brown aureoles the size of coffee saucers. She patted her swollen belly and watched with disgust as her flesh vibrated. And she stood and hated herself. Everything was her own fault. How could she blame Marshall if he preferred prettier women? What man could possibly find beauty in her bloated body?

She covered the offending flesh with a fresh silk peignoir. She brushed her hair. She perfumed herself and tried, in vain, to make her face look prettier. She returned to bed and sat and waited for her husband.

But that night Marshall did not return.

He slipped into the house at seven the next morning, cursing himself for being late – the servants were already about. He had not meant to be out all night but that redhead – God, what a night it had been. The woman had been insatiable and now Marshall was exhausted.

If only he had his own separate suite of rooms, as in New York, instead of having to share a suite with his huge mare of a wife, he thought, as he quietly opened the door.

The room was empty.

The bed was in chaos – the bed clothes flung back trailing the floor, the pillows scattered about the room. He peeped into the bathroom. It too was empty. In her dressing room, he saw with a jolt that the cupboards were open and clothes had been removed.

'Damn,' he said out loud. Had he overplayed his hand? Ah well, it would have to wait – he had to sleep. He crossed to his own dressing room. Propped against the mirror was a note, beside it a shredded, damp lace handkerchief.

'*Marshall. I shall be back – Grace.*' That was all. Excellent, he thought sleepily, he could spend another night with whatever she was called – Marshall was not very good at names.

For six months there had been no word from Grace. Lincoln Wakefield had private investigators scouring the country for her but Grace had covered her tracks well. She had disappeared.

The one fact they had discovered was that she had taken $15,000 in cash from the bank. With such a large sum of money in her possession, finding her had proved an impossible task – the money had enabled her to go to ground. Lincoln had concentrated on searching in North and South America, reasoning that, with the war in Europe, she could not have gone there. Travelling would be too difficult. No one liked to point out to him that, since she had been a nurse, it would be the easiest thing for her to travel on a troop ship to England or France.

Marshall almost felt sorry for his father-in-law – it was to be the first and last time he did so. Lincoln began to lose weight, his bluster diminished and he seemed to shrink both mentally and physically.

Alice alone appeared calm amidst the drama. She was angry at her daughter's lack of consideration for Lincoln's feelings; she could at least have let him know that she was safe and well. She had no idea what Grace was about but felt certain that, whatever it was, it had to do with Marshall. She was convinced that Grace would return when she was ready. She did not worry, as Lincoln did, for her daughter's safety. As she had pointed out, no one would take so large an amount of money to go off and kill themselves. Also, she was certain that a young woman who had seen and survived war at close quarters could manage in any circumstances.

Despite several dreadful scenes during which Marshall stood firm while Lincoln abusively accused him of bringing this trouble to the family, Marshall, to everyone's surprise, behaved like a dutiful son-in-law. Lincoln and

Alice had moved into the new mansion overlooking Central Park. It was Marshall himself who suggested that Juniper should move to her grandfather's until her mother returned. His intentions were largely compassionate – Lincoln was in a bad way, behaving as if Grace were dead, slipping daily into a deeper depression. He hoped that Juniper's presence might help lift the old man's spirit and therefore Alice's too. So, the child with her entourage of two nannies and four nursemaids decamped to the enormous hundred-room mansion, to the luxurious suite of nurseries which had been prepared for her.

On the other hand, Marshall was the first to admit that without Juniper in the house he had much more leeway to entertain at home just as he wanted. Consequently a procession of mistresses climbed the steps of the brownstone and were well and truly bedded in Grace's opulent and vast bed – a bed made for sexual adventures of the type Marshall was now enjoying.

When Grace had first disappeared Marshall had a couple of weeks of anxiety that he might now have to look for work. But when his allowance from Grace continued to arrive in his bank account, he ceased worrying. Now there were no mournful, reproachful eyes to face as he set about copulating with a large section of New York's female population.

The atmosphere eased dramatically on Christmas Day when a hand-delivered note dropped through Lincoln's letter box. No stamp, no postmark and, although footmen were immediately dispatched through the snow-covered streets, no delivery boy was found. The note was to Lincoln and was short and to the point. She was well. She was not to be looked for. She would be back and she loved him.

Lincoln slowly replaced the lost weight, his bluster returned, his loathing for his son-in-law intensified and Marshall no longer felt any pity for him. He would have stopped visiting the house altogether but for Juniper. But

Marshall could not let a day go by without seeing his child and would take nursery tea with her each afternoon. Even Lincoln grudgingly had to admit that, though Marshall was a lousy husband, he was a good, caring father.

During the following year there were two cards from Grace. Both were postmarked New York, but since Lincoln had every policeman and a dozen private detectives looking for her in the city, it seemed unlikely that she had posted them herself. So, although they did not know where she was, at least they knew she was alive.

A degree of normality returned to the mansion. Grace was rarely mentioned, her name being spoken tended to bring Lincoln's depression back. So Alice instructed the staff, and asked friends, not to mention Grace in front of Lincoln. After nearly eighteen months Marshall found that he had almost forgotten what it was like to be a married man.

It was Christmas Eve – the second Christmas without Grace. Marshall had stepped out of the house to pick up the new dress suit he had had made and wanted to wear to the large dinner Alice was giving tomorrow on Dart Island. His Christmas present for Juniper, a fine rocking horse, was already stowed in the Wakefield private carriage on the train. The Wakefield coach would be hitched to the Dart County Express which left Grand Central at one. Marshall had no other plans but to change, take the train, and to spend the next two weeks in the country with his daughter.

The butler let him back into the house. He crossed the hall to the stairs.

'Marshall?'

He stopped dead. One foot, lifted above the stair tread, remained poised in the air as the familiar beautiful voice called from the drawing room. Quickly he swung round and entered the room.

A slim, beautifully dressed woman, her hair expertly

coiffed, her make-up discreet, stepped forward to greet him. It was several seconds before Marshall could believe that this transformed creature was Grace.

'Well?' She smiled at him, her smile making her almost beautiful – almost, not quite.

'Grace,' was all he could think to say, standing there, knowing his mouth was hanging open with astonishment.

'Surprised?'

'Stunned. You look wonderful,' he said with genuine pleasure.

'I'm glad.' She moved gracefully across the room towards him and slowly and lovingly touched his face as if assuring herself he was there. He put his own hand up to take hold of hers but, before he could do so, she had slipped away from him and sat down in one fluid, elegant movement. She crossed her legs – legs which he observed were now shapely with trim ankles. She smoothed her skirt with long languorous movements of her hands so that he found himself being made aware of the shape of her thighs. She was a woman, an attractive woman and one whom he found he wanted to possess – now. He coughed abruptly, astonished at the turn of his thoughts and feeling somewhat embarrassed that he should be regarding his wife, of all people, in this way.

'So?' she looked up at him with a strange sideways motion of her head that reminded him of a cat. 'So?' she repeated opening her eyes wide. Her eyes, he remembered, had once been a dull watery grey but now her pupils were huge and their black centres, verging on purple, looked like the soft petals of a pansy, rimmed with a thin line of grey. She opened her mouth just slightly and licked her upper lip, a gesture which, when made by a pretty woman, always excited Marshall. He could not contain himself but quickly crossed the room, pulled her up into his arms and began to kiss her with a longing which would have taken him by surprise if he had not been so sexually aroused.

Beneath the ornate chandelier, against the overstuffed sofa, beside the tall aspidistra on the antique Persian rug he took her violently, and Grace screamed with a passion he had never heard from her before. Through the haze of his own pleasure he heard her using language that he had never dreamt he would hear from her.

Together they sat opposite each other in Lincoln's plush, private, railway car. Marshall was staring with stunned amazement at his changed wife.

'I don't understand,' he had said.

'There's nothing to understand, my darling. I wanted to change my appearance for you so that you would want me more. I'm sorry it took so long.'

'I don't mean how you look, though of course that is charming. You're different . . . I mean back at the house . . .' Marshall found that he was embarrassed. He had never had any problem talking with his mistresses about matters of sex, and what he wanted of them. He had even enjoyed their occasional use of foul language. But his wife . . . ?

'Don't worry, darling. I know what you're trying to say. I wanted to be as . . .' she stopped, not yet able to speak of the women in his past. She had wanted to be like them, for him to want her, take her as he did those others. She wanted to be his mistress not just his wife. It seemed she had succeeded. She smiled at him. 'You can talk to me about it.'

'I'd prefer not to, if you don't mind.' He grinned bashfully.

'Then you would prefer me not to use explicit language?' she asked in a strangely businesslike voice.

'Well, yes.'

'But you like me to *act* explicitly?'

'Well, yes.'

'Very well, my darling.'

Marshall had taken the precaution of telephoning Alice

before they left New York. He was concerned that if the new Grace turned up out of the blue, Lincoln might have a heart attack. He had better be prepared. He ridiculed himself afterwards. Now that Grace was back in his life, for the old bastard to die and leave her everything would have been the best thing that could happen to him. He was too kind for his own good, he thought. However, the reunion between father and daughter brought a lump even to Marshall's throat as Lincoln hugged Grace to him, tears pouring down his crusty face, and Grace clung to him as if she would never let go.

'Grace, my darling, I've been so worried. Where have you been? Why did you go?'

'I'm sorry, Papa. I had to do it this way. I knew that if people knew where I was, they would visit me and I'd only get all confused again . . .'

'Was it because of Marshall that you went?' he asked, glowering across the room at his son-in-law.

'No, Papa. It was no one's fault but my own,' she lied loyally.

'You look wonderful, my darling. As pretty as a princess.'

'Do you like the new me?' She twirled around. 'I'm determined to stay this way. I want to be pretty for Marshall. Don't I, darling?' she smiled coyly at her husband.

'I hope so, darling,' Marshall replied, the memory of their lovemaking causing his member to stir so that he had to sit down hurriedly. Grace laughed merrily at him as if she knew what he was feeling, certain that she had power over him now.

The doting parents and grandparents visited Juniper's nursery. Juniper refused to go to Grace but held her arms up eagerly to Marshall. Grace burst into tears.

'What did you expect?' Alice found herself saying with irritation. There was much for Grace to explain as far as she was concerned.

'Don't be cross with me, Mama, please.' And Alice saw a strange expression in her daughter's eyes – she had the look of a sleepwalker.

Later, Marshall and Grace were in the suite of rooms always kept ready for them. And tonight Marshall made no move to go to his own bedroom next door.

He waited in bed for his 'new' wife. He smiled with genuine pleasure as she entered from her dressing room. She was dressed in a soft grey negligée, her hair, which had once been lank, shone like a gleaming cap. But it was the way she moved that pleased him most. She seemed to float rather than walk to the bed, a strange, sinuous movement making the soft chiffon of her gown ripple across her body, one moment revealing and the next hiding the contours beneath. He put his arms up to her, she touched him gently, and then moved away across the room – he could not take his eyes off her. She returned to caress his naked body, her fingers running swiftly and softly over him, and then she slid from the bed smiling provocatively at him until he found himself calling out, almost pleading, 'Grace, come here to me . . .' He leapt from the bed, lunging at her. She laughed, huskily, as he tore at her clothes and lifted the now light form, and carried her to bed. Twice in one day – he could not remember this ever happening in their relationship.

'I've something to show you,' she said as later they lay in each other's arms. Nimbly she slipped from the bed and returned with a large book of photographs. 'But I wonder if I should show you them,' she said like a naughty little girl, fuelling his curiosity.

'What *is* this?' he asked, sitting up and puffing out the pillows behind him. As he turned the page he looked with disbelief at his wife, who sat crosslegged before him, her eyes, with their enormous pupils, shining with excitement.

'Aren't they exciting?' she said, almost ingenuously.

'They are the best I've ever seen,' he admitted as he

studied one pornographic photograph after another. 'And when and why did my naughty wife get these?'

'I thought they might amuse you.' She looked enquiringly at him as her hand trailed sensuously up his leg. Marshall slammed the book shut.

'No, Grace, they're obscene. You shouldn't have anything to do with pictures like this. How could you?'

'Whatever you say, Marshall . . . Whatever you want . . . I only wanted to please you.' She slipped from the bed and, taking the book, dropped it into the wastepaper basket. She rubbed her hands together as if drying them. 'There, all gone.' And she jumped back into bed and twined her legs about him.

As he began to make love to her *again* he made a mental note to rescue the album of photographs. It would be most unsuitable for the servants to see. And in any case he knew just the woman whom the photographs would arouse to fever pitch.

5

Marshall had packed for a two-week stay. He had several new polo ponies he wanted to work on and had looked forward to the time with Juniper. To his surprise, and a degree of annoyance, Grace insisted they return to the city the moment the Christmas holiday was over. He was on the point of refusing when Grace totally disarmed him by telling him she wanted to be alone with him, she did not wish to share him with anyone. He was so charmed and fascinated by her metamorphosis that he found himself agreeing. They returned to their brownstone leaving Juniper with her grandparents.

What happened next was an insidious series of events which even later Marshall could not explain. He was sure he had not suggested their first visit; he would never have insulted his wife by doing so. But by the time they arrived at a strip show, in the village, he had almost persuaded himself it was his idea.

Marshall had taken his mistresses to such shows in the past without a second thought. He found they were a good way of arousing a woman who was being slow about tumbling into his bed. But his wife? That was a different matter. What on earth were they doing here? he asked himself. But, as he sat opposite her in the darkened night club, he saw a blush, not of embarrassment but of excitement suffuse her face. With a mounting excitement of his own he watched the glint of sexuality in her eyes.

From this small start they unleashed themselves on a sea of sexual adventures. Marshall, who had frequently found himself bored with a woman after one night, now found he could never have enough of his wanton wife. From day to day, from hour to hour, he had no idea what mood he would find her in. She might be like a wild, sensuous animal excitedly leaping upon him, almost devouring him with passion. Or she could be docile, somnolent, acquiescent to his every need. In their bed, she was so expert, that she could awaken him time and time again. His pleasure was her only concern. If he wanted her to take the initiative she did so. If he wanted to whip her, she complied, screaming so prettily that it drove him to greater frenzy. And, from somewhere, she had acquired an extraordinary collection of clothes to excite him. Whatever sort of woman he wished to bed, Grace, with the aid of make-up and her costumes, was able to become. So he had bedded her as a whore, as Cleopatra, as a nun, as a society lady complete with tiara, as a nursemaid – the possibilities seemed endless.

They were frequent attenders of the strip-tease clubs. And then one night they found themselves at a live sex show. He couldn't remember suggesting it, and he felt uneasy. Even he had never been to such a show before and the new elegant Grace looked utterly out of place in the seedy audience. But she seemed happy with the arrangement, so after that they went to other such clubs. It seemed a natural progression that he should move on to escorting his wife to brothels. They lay on a couch behind a two-way mirror and watched as the whores performed. The natural, anonymous bodies flailing about on the beds excited them both.

Of one thing he was sure – the idea of going to an orgy had nothing to do with him. Such gatherings gave him no pleasure. He had never understood how some men could enjoy watching their partners being handled by others. So this suggestion must have come from her. Not only was she subtle in bed but, he had to conclude, she was subtle in manipulating him to do what she wanted. The change in Grace was mental as well as physical – it was as if he were married to a different woman. In an attempt to retain some dignity, he rented an apartment a long way from their home. Marshall felt safer pursuing the adventures in private.

Marshall was in an unenviable quandary. He did not understand what was happening to them. His feelings for Grace had changed too. Was it love? He was not sure, since these feelings were nothing like those he had for Juniper whom he knew he loved. But certainly he felt a much greater affection for Grace than he had ever believed possible. There was a vulnerability about her, almost as if she was not completely in control of her own life any more. Something extraordinary had happened in the time she was away from him, but this was a subject she refused to discuss, no matter how often he asked. He found himself wanting to protect her. These new emotions he thought might be bordering on love, or at least the degree of love that Marshall would ever be able to feel for a woman. He had always liked Grace, but now he did not want to be without her. This new Grace, however, was sexually insatiable, and he feared that if he did not comply with her demands, she might leave him for another man who would share her tastes more enthusiastically. Her money was no longer of paramount importance – though admittedly it mattered. No, he simply did not want to live without her. He found himself, for the first time, afraid of losing her.

But he could not bring himself to kiss her. Not since the night, soon after her return, when he discovered the reason why she remained so thin. Unexpectedly tired he had gone to their room early, only to find Grace, her head over the lavatory basin, her fingers down her throat, vomiting her expensive dinner away.

What was happening was perverse, he knew it was, but he seemed to have become trapped in a web of sexuality. He had, time without number, tried to explain his confusion to her. He tried to explain that he was happy with her now, that he had no need for other women. He suggested that they revert to a more normal married life. He told himself that he should insist, but he found he was not prepared to take the risk of losing her.

Grace would listen to her husband's explanations and, though she was touched, she could not believe he spoke the truth. She had to refuse. For, although Grace hated their lifestyle, although she frequently loathed herself, and night after night had to steel herself for the adventures ahead, she could not stop. She was certain that this was the price she had to pay to keep her husband amused. In the time she had been away, Grace had learnt much about men, or rather a certain kind of man. Now she believed she knew about all men and their fantasies and no one could have persuaded her otherwise.

She had not told Marshall where she had been for the thought of it still filled her with shame, a shame she could only confide to her diary. She had gone straight to Boston and re-enrolled as a nurse. It was evident that the war could not go on much longer but travelling by troop ship was still the easiest way to get to Europe. It was not, however, until the Christmas of 1918, by which time the war was over, that she reached France. It took her over a month to travel across the war-torn country to Switzerland, where, she had heard, there was a doctor who would transform her. In his clinic she had been drugged for three months – sufficient to keep her in a twilight world, and had been fed a controlled amount intravenously. When the course was over she was weak, she was slim, and she was changed for all time. Daily the doctor had given her increasing doses of his 'tonic', the contents known only to him, mixed only by him. If she stopped taking it, she became listless, irritable and so discomfited that only another dose of the elixir could help her. She never asked what it contained but, having total faith in her doctor, happily took the prescribed amount, which made her feel confident, brimful with energy, as if she could conquer the world.

Six months later, with a good supply of 'tonic' in her bags, she had travelled to Paris. In 1919 it was a city of relentless gaiety, its inhabitants intent only on celebrating their survival. There she had her hair restyled; she bought a complete wardrobe of chic and expensive clothes for her new slim figure; then she searched out experts who would teach her how to use make-up discreetly, and to her advantage, and others who taught her how to walk and sit so that she would always look alluring.

Eventually, gathering all her courage, she visited a famous brothel. The Madame was only too pleased to accept the large sum of money she offered to be taught the intricacies of making love. It was not the unusual request that Grace supposed – before the war Madame had run a most profitable sideline in teaching society women, wives of eminent men, the secrets of the brothel. There Grace had been initiated night after night. And it was there she had learnt what men desire.

Of course she could not believe her husband when he claimed he wanted a normal life. How could she? For Grace was certain she knew what men wanted.

*

Lincoln was no longer so offensive to Marshall. Once or twice his behaviour to his son-in-law even verged on the polite. Marshall was fully aware that this was not because of any new fondness on the part of his father-in-law, but rather that Lincoln feared his former attitude might make Grace take off again. Marshall rather enjoyed this new-found power.

Juniper stayed with her grandparents. The arrangement had been Grace's idea. Marshall would much have preferred to have Juniper at their own home, but Grace was adamant – it was better this way. It was not that she did not love the child, rather that she seemed to want to devote every one of her waking moments to her husband, and to making herself attractive for him. Everything else was of no consequence. Juniper must be elsewhere. She dropped her few friends, her few interests; even her plan to breed dogs was forgotten. Nothing must come between her and Marshall.

But together they always went to tea with Juniper when she was in New York with her grandparents.

It was on one of these visits that Alice came into the nursery.

'Grace, Marshall, we are all invited to England for Christmas, by Gertie Frobisher. What do you think? Wouldn't that be fun?'

'It was Aunt Gertie's son Richard who brought us together, Mama.' Grace put out her hand to touch Marshall as if making sure it was true.

'Really? Gertie and Basil don't speak to him, you know. So I doubt if he will be there.'

'You can hardly blame them can you, Mrs Wakefield? The young fool married an actress, Francine du Bois she called herself. I'd heard her name was really Bloggs or something,' Marshall said dismissively.

'I think I'd call myself something different too if Bloggs were my name. Perhaps not quite as grand as du Bois.' Grace smiled.

'She's a very beautiful woman, mind you. She's done quite well on the stage since, I gather.'

'You know her?' Grace asked sharply.

'Not really,' he lied. 'I met her once with Richard and I saw her perform several years ago,' he smiled at the thought of the various 'performances' he and Francine had enjoyed. 'Someone at the club was saying the other day that she's really quite a big name in the West End these days.'

'She's not "du Bois" any more. She's trading on the Frobisher name, according to Gertie. Anyhow, enough gossip,' Alice said briskly. 'We're invited for a month. Lincoln says he is happy to be away for two months, so I shall be able to visit Gwenfer – I do hope you will come. If we're going we must book at once – the staterooms are filling up fast. Everyone's off to Europe, it seems, now the war is over.'

'I'd love to go,' Marshall replied enthusiastically. He had not been home for three years. He'd like to see his old friends again – and Francine.

'Perhaps we could pop over to Paris, you and I?' Grace suggested, her deep voice rich and caressing. 'I gather one can have such fun in Paris.'

6

'You can't possibly imagine how ghastly the whole experience has been. I feel I've aged years.'

'You don't look as if you've aged a day, my dear Gertie.' Alice laughed at her friend. It was true she did not look a day older than the last time they had met, back in 1912. That date might just as well have been in a different century for everything else, it seemed, had changed even if Gertie hadn't. London was so crowded, full of motor cars and bad-tempered people. The streets were dirty in a way they had never been before. Young women walked about unchaperoned and no one thought the less of them. They wore make-up, smoked, drank, and had a pride in themselves that only their usefulness in the war could have given them – they were no longer merely decorative items in men's lives. And, walking in Hyde Park upon her arrival in England, Alice had noticed a dearth of young men, and had been saddened.

'You couldn't possibly know how awful it has been. We had to close up three quarters of this house. It would not have been patriotic to keep it open and employ staff.'

'If you could have found any staff,' Alice said quietly.

'Well, quite. All the footmen were eventually conscripted, you know. And the chauffeur – I think that was even worse. Basil had resisted having a motor car for so long and then the only man on the estate who knew how the infernal monster worked went away to war. Of course we had sent all the horses to the army. So Basil had to learn to drive. I can tell you, Alice, his ability is minimal – I suffered in the war!' She hooted with laughter at the memory of Basil's erratic progress in the motor. 'And the house in Scotland was taken over by the Navy – you should see the mess they left. Of course, Basil has taken it up with the authorities – one doesn't mind making sacrifices for one's country but the state of the plasterwork was appalling.'

Alice tutted in sympathy as she accepted a cup of tea from Gertie. The friends sat on either side of the fireplace in Gertie's boudoir in the sprawling mansion in Berkshire. Outside, the chill winter day was drawing to a close. The trees in the park stretched skeletally against a yellowing sky, which everyone hoped meant snow and a white Christmas. The menfolk were out shooting, the women resting, but these two had fallen into the habit of taking tea together at this time of the day. Thus, they could talk of old times without interruptions from the large house party that was gathering for Christmas.

'Thank God your sons survived.'

'I still go down on my knees and thank God daily. Those dreadful lists, you can't imagine the pain each day of reading them, Alice, seeing the names of young men one knew, and then, as the war progressed, and more men were needed, the names of our friends. Oh, yes, Basil and I were lucky, but others weren't.'

'My cousin, Alfred Loudon, was killed I heard.'

'Yes, and it finished poor old Maude. She just wasted away after that – too sad. And did you hear of poor Alexandra Popplewhite? She lost both her sons – and on the same day.'

'It was the one time I was glad I had no sons and that my cousins were not close to me.'

'But your Grace was so brave, I've always admired her for that. I cannot imagine the dreadful scenes that sweet child must have witnessed.'

They sat silent for a moment thinking of their good fortune, feeling sadness for their friends. But Gertie was never completely happy with silence.

'And of course the greenhouses had to be closed – the heating you see, too wasteful. And the gardens were wrecked, no gardeners. It will take years to get them back to how they used to be.'

'Nature is very resilient. We had shortages, too, and young Americans also died,' Alice said with a hint of irritation, for she felt as if Gertie regarded this war as her own.

'Ah yes, but you didn't have the zeppelins and then those frightful aeroplanes. We had to blunder around in the dark – so dangerous. And of course our struggle was longer than yours.' She sat back and folded her arms, her whole body indicating that she felt she had won this particular argument.

'Just listen to us, Gertie.' Alice laughed softly. 'We suffered more than you suffered – we sound like fractious children.'

'Oh dear, I suppose we do. But all that time it seemed

one measured one's discomfort against others' suffering. How silly. And we should forget, we should be looking forward.'

'Yes, most definitely. And speaking of the future, when are you going to see Richard?'

'Ah well, I blame the war for that, too. The whole world has turned topsy-turvy. Standards don't seem to matter any more.'

'Quite honestly, Gertie, I think you're being extremely pigheaded about the boy.'

'But Alice . . . how could he behave in such a way, to us?'

'Well he did, and it's done, and all you are doing is cutting off your nose to spite your face. It's ridiculous. You have a son you love whom you never see, and a granddaughter you've never even met.'

'But it's the principle, Alice. How can he expect me to receive a creature like that?'

'Gertie, you've never met the girl. She might be quite charming.'

'She smokes.'

'Many young girls do these days. If we were younger no doubt we would.'

'And drinks.'

'And who's partial to her sherry?' Alice laughed at her old friend.

'I would like to see the child, though,' Gertie said wistfully.

'Of course you would. Oh Gertie, principles are such a burden. Look at my family. My father didn't even know Grace existed. Look what you did for me and Chas when we eloped. You understood about love then. And you haven't let society dictate your attitude to me and Lincoln. I know we would never have been accepted over here had it not been for your intervention.'

'That's different.'

'Family is different too. Why not invite them for

Christmas? Juniper's here to play with Polly. You'd have your whole family about you . . . Gertie, it's an ideal time to forgive and forget.'

'Do you think so, Alice? Do you think I could manage such a difficult situation?'

'You, Gertie? Gracious, you could manage any social situation.'

'One shouldn't have favourites, I know, but I'll admit to you – of my three I love Richard most.'

'That's why you took it so hard when he went against your wishes. I'm sure if Emmeline falls in love with someone unsuitable you'll forgive her.'

'Not my Emmeline, she wouldn't do such a thing. I've high hopes, that she might make a match with Peter Merchant.'

'Who's Peter Merchant?'

'You know – Augusta Portley's son. She married Alfred Merchant the season before ours. A nice boy and I've seen the odd little spark there between them.'

'How eminently suitable. So Gertie, your Charles is marrying Fiona Duckforth – who couldn't have a better pedigree. Maybe Emmeline will marry Peter, with an equally good standing. So, can't you in your heart allow Richard to be the odd one out?' She smiled slyly at her friend.

For what seemed an age Gertie looked out of the window, a faraway look in her eyes. Suddenly she shook her shoulders and sat even more upright. 'Alice, you're always right. It's been too long. I'll write a note and send it up on the evening train.' She forsook the tea and poured them both a sherry. 'You mentioned Chas . . . do you often think of him?' she asked in her forthright manner.

Alice looked at her friend a full minute as if deciding what to answer. Gertie, with her expertise in dealing with people, realised a confidence was about to be imparted and remained patiently silent.

'I've never told a living soul this, Gertie. But . . .'

Gertie waited.

'Yes, I do think of him – I fear, too often. I love Lincoln – don't misunderstand me – he's been good to me and Grace. But there's never been the same delirious excitement I felt with Chas . . . that feeling of being totally alive.' She did not sigh but her voice sounded as if she did. She looked wistfully into the fire and was silent.

'I wonder sometimes if I married Lincoln mainly for security. It makes me feel guilty.'

'Oh rats, Alice, the man adores you. There's always one who loves more in a relationship – it can't be helped.'

'You really think so?'

'Absolutely. Another sherry?'

Three more days, thought Richard, and Francine's play would have finished its run – thank God. During the pantomime season she would be at home for a good month before she had to go into rehearsal for Teddy Triumph's new play.

He was relieved for the simple reason that when Francine was working they hardly saw each other. She was never home before midnight and frequently later. Her excuse, one that he tried to understand, was that she needed to relax after her performance. The only way she could do so, she insisted, was by taking late-night dinners and visiting the new 'night clubs' that were taking over from the cosy supper clubs.

At first Richard had gone with her. He would wait each night in her dressing room to escort her wherever the mood, or her noisy gang of friends, decided the evening was to be spent. But with the office to attend in the mornings, he could not keep up the pace.

As Francine did not rise before noon he never saw her in the mornings: because of the late hours she kept she had suggested separate rooms so that she would not awaken him. The only time they seemed to meet was for an hour after he returned from the office and before she rushed off to the theatre. If Francine was invited to a cocktail party, as she often was, they did not see each other at all. And she always seemed to be exhausted: too often recently he had visited Francine in her room at night only to be sent away and made to feel a cad for wanting her so desperately when she was so tired. These days there seemed less and less chance of a brother or sister for Polly.

If it had not been for Polly, Richard's life would have been dismally empty. But the whole of the Christmas period stretched before them and he had arranged to take two weeks' leave from the office to be with his wife and daughter.

Richard was reading in his study – he managed to read a lot these days. Quietly the maid entered the room with a letter on a silver salver, which she presented to him with a bob. Richard's heart faltered as he recognised his mother's handwriting, his first thought was for his father.

With shaking fingers he tore open the envelope. He couldn't believe what he read. An invitation from his mother for Christmas. He jumped from the chair with a whoop and hugged the startled maid.

'Is the messenger still here, Molly?'

'Yes, sir. He said as he was to wait for a reply.'

Quickly Richard scribbled an acceptance, ending the note 'with love'. He raced from the room to hand the note to the messenger – a footman dressed in the Frobisher livery. He grabbed his hat and coat and raced into the street. He had to tell Francine.

The cab seemed to take an age to reach the theatre. Richard turned the corner in time to see his wife emerge from the stage door. He smiled with pride as he watched her graciously sign the autographs of the faithful. He stepped forward to call her name, but as he did so, another man appeared from the shadows. He put his arm about Francine in a possessive way and ushered her into a large gleaming Rolls-Royce. As the car slipped past him Richard saw his wife in another man's arms.

Richard waited up for her that night. It was three o'clock before he heard Francine's key turn in the lock.

'Richard, what on earth are you doing up so late? Is it an emergency?' Her laugh, he realised for the first time, was brittle.

'I went to the theatre tonight to collect you.'

'Oh, you silly boy. You should have telephoned and let me know you were coming – I was off and away as quickly as possible.'

'I know. I saw you,' Richard said bleakly.

'Saw me?'

'In a car. In some bastard's arms.'

'Darling, don't be silly. That was Rudolf Hensel. He wants me to do a tour with him next year.'

'Will you have to kiss him, too?'

'Oh poor darling, Richard! You've been jumping to conclusions, haven't you? You know us theatre types – we're always falling into each other's arms – I do believe you're a teeny bit jealous – too divine!'

'Is that all it was, Francine?' Richard asked urgently.

'Of course, my sweety. What on earth makes you think your lady would ever do anything to hurt you?' She smiled beguilingly at him as she resolved to be more careful in future.

He looked pleadingly at her, and was about to speak again. Quickly she went on, 'Why were you at the theatre? You never come these days,' and she turned away so as not to see the look in his eyes – the look that always annoyed her.

'I had a letter from my mother. She wants us to go to Berkshire for Christmas.'

Francine sat down quickly. 'I don't believe you. Let me see.' She grabbed the letter from him and read it quickly. 'Why? Suddenly?'

'I don't know and I don't care. It's the best Christmas present I could ever hope for.'

'I'll need new clothes, masses of them. I've nothing to

wear to the country. Dicky, I've spent every penny I've got . . .'

'Buy what you want, my darling. Whatever you need,' he said excitedly, all money worries forgotten for the moment.

7

Mendbury was one of those houses that looked forward to Christmas. Its Gothic, marbled coldness welcomed the softening effect of the holly and mistletoe draped in profusion about it. Its large echoing rooms needed the bustle of people. It seemed almost as if for eleven months the house slept, coming truly alive only at Christmas.

Gertie Frobisher looked forward to Christmas, too, for she was of that breed of woman who enjoy organising on a grand scale and Christmases at Mendbury were grand. She sat in her morning room making innumerable lists – lists of guests, train times, food, menus, presents, and a second set of lists for the estate workers' festivities. Years ago she had the estate carpenter make her a large chart, which each Christmas was hung on her wall. On this, using different coloured markers, she plotted which rooms to allocate to whom and as some guests left and others arrived the names were changed so that she always knew where people should be sleeping – should be, for Gertie was a woman of the world and was fully aware that the corridors of the house witnessed many a night-clothed, surreptitious, tiptoeing change of room.

In addition she had a comprehensive filing system that would not have shamed a large professional office. Everything was cross-referenced. Each meal she had ever served to every guest she had ever entertained was listed. The rooms they had slept in, the china used, the flower decorations, their likes and dislikes, any gifts she had given or had received. What their interests were, even what illnesses they had suffered. The names and ages of their children and grandchildren were kept. Even the breed and names of their dogs were important enough for Gertie to file. She was famed in society for her prodigious memory: few knew of her secret system.

Like a general Gertie moved about the house checking the linen, the cutlery, choosing which of the priceless sets of china would be used. The housekeeper annually retired to her room in a sulk at having her domain invaded. The cook reluctantly and with an audible sniff agreed to alterations to menus over which she had spent hours but which Gertie could never resist changing.

Gertie was born before her time – she would have made an excellent corporate woman.

In the week before Christmas the guests began to arrive. The first were Charles and his future wife, Fiona, with her parents and their younger children plus two maids, two valets and a nanny. Juniper was beside herself with excitement as the new nursery occupants joined her. Emmeline Frobisher's best friend, Caroline Bathurst, arrived with her parents and two maids and a valet. Three army friends of Charles with their wives arrived in a flurry of squealing tyres and scattered pebbles. Their entourage of three maids and three valets were to arrive later by train.

The arrival of Victoria and Beatrix Frobisher, Basil's spinster sisters, in their large black Daimler was more sedate. They had only one maid between them but six King Charles spaniels who had never been house trained and who slept with the sisters and hated Basil's labrador, Duxford, a hatred of long-standing.

Eighteen guest bedrooms were filled and the twenty visiting servants settled below stairs. All the servants rated Christmas at Mendbury high on their list of 'good stays' – the food was excellent, the beer was plentiful and the resident staff obliging.

*

The house party was complete and waited agog for the return of the Prodigal Son.

'Dear God, he's aged so much,' thought Gertie as she watched her son alight from the family Rolls-Royce she had sent to the station. She wanted to rush straight up to him and kiss him, hold him. Instead she waited, tall, matronly, in her long unfashionable skirt at the top of the stairs with Basil beside her. The other guests had unanimously decided to disappear discreetly, which did not stop any of them watching from the windows.

'Mother,' he paused, uncertain what to do. Gertie proffered her cheek and he kissed her quickly, shook hands with his father, and introduced them to Francine.

'Lady Gertrude, too kind of you to invite us,' said the husky voice bubbling, it seemed, with laughter.

'How do you do,' Gertie replied stiffly, looking straight at the innocent green eyes. 'And this is Polly?' She looked intently at the curly haired toddler, held in her nanny's arms, whose large brown eyes, the colour of Gertie's own, solemnly returned the gaze. To her disappointment, Gertie could see no other sign of Frobisher in the child. On the other hand there did not seem to be anything of Francine either. The child was as dark as her mother was fair.

'You must be wanting tea.' She led the way through the great hall and into the drawing room where the other guests had quietly assembled.

She was beautiful, Gertie thought grudgingly, as she watched her daughter-in-law across the room. She found herself admiring her long-legged slimness, the beautiful fine-boned face, the silver-coloured hair, the magnificent eyes and the elegant turn of her head as, smiling, Francine turned from one guest to another in greeting.

But Gertie's sharp eyes missed nothing. She noted how quickly dismissive Francine was when she greeted the women guests, passing on swiftly to the men over whom she lingered like a bee looking for pollen. Gertie noticed the boldness of her daughter-in-law's gaze as her eyes fluttered over the men to whom she was introduced, how long it took her to relinquish their hands, how artfully she stood, one hip jutting forward provocatively. 'Trollop,' thought Gertie and almost missed the cup into which she was pouring tea.

Grace watched this beautiful creature flitting about the room and dreaded the moment when she would approach her and Marshall, for Grace thought that Francine was the most beautiful woman she had ever set eyes on.

She had arrived in front of them. Grace felt a limp hand in hers and found herself looking into eyes that held no warmth. The vision moved on to take Marshall's hand. He was aware that, as he had watched her wend her way round the company, he had found the old excitement she had once stirred in him returning. She looked boldly at him, her hand giving his a slight pressure.

'Mr Boscar, we meet again.'

'You know each other,' Grace said, feeling a sinking dismay.

'Only fleetingly, Mrs Boscar. A long time ago, when he was a bachelor. Your husband was not interested in me, were you? If memory serves me right it was a Flora Belle who took your fancy,' she chuckled.

'A sad omission . . .' he bowed sardonically.

'Dear Flora. She's dead you know,' she said, quite coldly, and those women who heard her decided unequivocally that they did not like her.

Alice was the last to enter the room. She stood in the doorway, her face drained of colour, staring at Francine. Bossily Gertie ushered her friend forward to make the introductions.

'I must apologise for staring, Mrs Frobisher,' Alice stammered, 'but you're uncannily like a childhood friend of mine, or rather how I imagine she would have looked as an adult.'

'Really?' Francine replied in the hard voice she reserved for women, especially beautiful ones like Alice. 'What was her name?'

'Ia Blewett.'

The name fell like a stone. Lincoln moved swiftly across the room to take his wife's arm, and Marshall, with an amused smile, watched Francine closely for her reaction. Francine did not falter. 'I'm afraid, Mrs Wakefield, the name means nothing to me,' she said tossing her hair over one shoulder.

'Who is Ia Blewett?' Marshall asked mischievously, looking straight at Francine.

'She lived on my father's estate in Cornwall. We became best friends for a few years . . . and then, oh, it's a long, sad story . . .' Alice stopped speaking.

'No, Mama, tell them, it's a lovely story,' Grace insisted, pleased that for the moment the attention was on her mother and not on Francine.

'She was very ill. And my nursemaid, Queenie, well she had never approved of our close friendship – because Ia's family was poor – and she told me that Ia had died. It wasn't till years later that I found out that Queenie had lied but by then I had lost touch with Ia . . .'

'Did you meet again?' Francine surprised everyone by asking, almost urgently.

'No, never. But the strange thing was that on our last visit to Gwenfer, just before the war began, I had instructions to go to a lawyer about a bequest from an Ia St Just. Ia is not a common name – I felt it must be the same person. Why would someone I'd never met want to leave me a small fortune in jewels?'

'A fortune in what?' Francine snapped.

Gertie looked at her daughter-in-law closely.

'My family jewellery. My father sold it when we were estranged. I thought never to see it again. But there were all the familiar pieces in the lawyer's office, no note, anything. Only a lawyer's instruction that a Mrs St Just, who had died the year before in a street accident, had left them to me.'

'But didn't you find out more, Mama?'

'Lincoln tried, didn't you?'

'I came to a dead end. She was a wealthy young woman who left the rest of her fortune to a home for young women on their own in London,' Lincoln said, not looking at his wife.

'So typical of Ia. She was always so caring,' Alice said sadly.

'But how did she come to have your jewellery?' There was a distinct edge to Francine's voice as she asked the question.

'We don't know, Lincoln, do we?'

Lincoln looked uncomfortable as he muttered that indeed they didn't. Marshall watched the proceedings with great interest.

'I'm just glad you got your family jewellery back, Alice. Such injustices you suffered,' Gertie fretted.

Alice took her hand. 'Dear Gertie, always my champion,' she said lightly, but there was a guarded expression in her eyes which belied her tone as she looked closely at Francine before she moved away.

8

Despite Gertie's fears, the dinner that evening went well. She noted with surprised approval that her daughter-in-law certainly knew how to behave. To avoid trouble from the outset, she had purposely placed the young woman between two much older men and she saw that Francine was charming and attentive to both of them. After dinner, when the ladies retired from the dining room, Gertie suppressed her irritation as she saw Francine light a cigarette. She even instructed the butler to bring brandy when Francine refused the lemon barley water which it was customary for the women to drink. And Gertie frowned only fleetingly when Francine refused to join the rest of the party as they gathered in their coats and wraps to attend Midnight Mass in the chapel. All in all, it had not been a bad evening, she conceded, and dear Alice had been at pains to point out how charming Francine was. Perhaps she had been too hasty in her judgement.

Grace felt far from pleased as she wrapped herself in her sable coat and hurried off after her mother and father. What others saw as charm, Grace interpreted as a predatory seductiveness. There was something about Francine which made her feel very uneasy.

The party walked across the newly fallen snow which blanketed the knot garden, towards the candlelit church. Light streamed through the stained-glass windows of the chapel where the rector and the estate workers awaited the arrival of their master and his guests.

Grace knelt on the hassock and prayed very hard. She prayed that she might only have imagined the flame of interest in her husband's eye when he met Francine. She prayed very hard that Francine should not find out that Marshall had also cried off Midnight Mass and was, at this moment, playing billiards with Charles Bathurst, a confirmed atheist, who had refused to join them. They were the only prayers Grace offered up that night.

Left alone in the drawing room Francine kicked off her shoes. She roamed the room, studying its contents. Surely this summons meant only one thing? That Richard was to be reinstated within his family, which meant that all this would be his one day. So she amused herself planning how she would rearrange and decorate the room when this house was hers. She wrinkled her nose with distaste at what she saw – there would have to be a lot of changes. If there was one thing Francine could not stand it was anything old. If she could persuade Richard she would much prefer to have the whole house knocked down and a spanking modern one with large windows, shaped like a liner she envisaged it, put in its place.

She poured herself an enormous brandy, lit a cigarette and curled up on the sofa. She liked her father-in-law. She smiled as she remembered the glint in the old boy's eyes as she had decorously kissed his cheek in welcome. To her surprise, the old trout, Lady Gertrude, was not as bad as she had imagined, a bit stuffy but then one expected that from her generation.

She stretched. Should she go to the billiard room and seduce Marshall now, or go to bed? . . . She drained the brandy and chuckled to herself, remembering the many nights they had enjoyed in the past. There was no doubt that he was the most proficient lover she had ever enjoyed and certainly the best endowed. It amused her to think that his daughter, Polly, unknown to him, was asleep upstairs. Should she tell him? she wondered. Thoughtfully she weighed the pros and cons. Perhaps it would be wiser to keep the secret for the time being. The knowledge might prove more useful in the future – one never knew when information as stupendous as that might come in handy. What a dreadful wife he had: no amount of money would ever make her really beautiful – she was no competition at all. Finally she decided she would wait for another opportunity to get him back into her bed. Later, in London perhaps. It would be a little risky to do anything here when so much was at stake. The most important thing, for the moment, was to get Richard back in favour with his parents. Francine picked up her shoes and quietly made her way up to bed.

Christmas Day passed happily. In the morning Francine surprised everyone, including Richard, by presenting herself in the hall, swathed in white fox fur and announcing she could not possibly miss matins on Christmas Day of all days.

Francine entered the church as she entered anywhere –

with panache. She didn't seem to walk but rather to swirl, in clouds of Patou's Joy, down the aisle. With an elegant twist to her body she slipped into the family pew, and with one fluid motion sank to her knees on the hassock, raised her head to the beauty of the stained-glass window, and wondered if the lighting was doing her justice and if Marshall was looking at her. The estate workers sat with mouths agape at such beauty in their midst and talked of nothing else for weeks to come.

The day unrolled in the relentless pursuit of excess typical of any Christmas. The guests' luncheon did not finish until four and since Gertie had moved dinner forward an hour to eight o'clock, the staff had only four hours to clear away, reset and cook the gargantuan dinner which was to follow the gross luncheon.

After dinner the house guests played games and – since most of these were theatrical – Francine shone. She really could not remember a Christmas she had enjoyed more.

The unusual amounts of alcohol she had taken relaxed Gertie. She watched with pleasure as her glittering daughter-in-law swooped about the drawing room, managing to cajole even the spinster sisters into a game of charades. Today Francine was as charming to the women as she always was to the men. The house party retired in a euphoric state of happiness.

On Boxing Day morning the male members of the party went shooting. Francine stayed in bed – she had a hangover, a monumental one. It would take at least until after luncheon before her face was presentable enough for her to re-emerge from her bedroom.

By the evening, tensions began to surface. Gertie was not the only one who had seen Francine kick one of the elderly sisters' King Charles spaniels out of her path. This had reduced Beatrix, the younger of the sisters, to paroxysms of weeping so fierce she had to be led away to bed.

The moratorium of Christmas Day seemed to have

come to an end and Francine began to flirt again. Unknown to her mother-in-law, Francine was becoming bored – a dangerous state of affairs. The women in the party became restless and fretful as, with sly eyes and murder in their hearts, they watched Francine enslave the men one by one. By bedtime the room was divided into two – the women at one end trying desperately to talk, and look, as though they did not care, and the men at the other with Francine in their midst.

'Stupid old goat,' thought Gertie as she watched Basil gamely pulling in his paunch and smiling benevolently at his daughter-in-law.

'He won't resist that one, there's nothing I can do to divert him from her . . .' Grace sat, pretending to read, while her mind was verging on panic.

'Trollop,' and less ladylike words, thought the other women.

'She's very beautiful,' said Victoria, the elder, and vaguer of Basil's sisters, but she was quickly silenced by the unanimous glare of the assembled women.

Gertie could stand it no longer.

'Ladies, I suggest we retire,' she said looking pointedly at Francine.

Like a fluttering covey of doves the ladies of the house party rose as one, gathering their bags, their petit point, their pince-nez, their novels.

'I think I'll play billiards,' Francine announced gaily. 'Far too dreary to go to bed all on my lonesome.'

There was an almost perceptible groan from the assembled men. There were gasps of astonishment from the ladies. Gertie ran a correct house party, not for her the strange behaviour she had heard of in some houses. She was aware that at night bed partners could and did change but, in public, rules were observed. And one of these rules was that the women retired en masse and left the men to their billiards and brandy.

'I do not think that is a good idea, Francine.'

'Don't you, Lady Gertrude? I do,' Francine said, staring hard-eyed at her mother-in-law.

Gertie was unused to being crossed, especially in her own home. She floundered, unsure what to do.

'Francine enjoys billiards, Mother. Just one game,' Richard said gently. Gertie looked at the son she adored and heard the note of appeal in his voice. With a shock she realised that her son was nervous. Was he frightened of his wife? Frightened she might make a scene?

'Very well. But I find it extraordinary behaviour,' she said stiffly, as she led her ladies from the drawing room.

Alice went straight to sleep. The Frobisher sisters, surrounded by their dogs, were soon snoring nearly as loudly as the spaniels. Gertie lay in the dark worrying. In all the other rooms the young women tossed about their beds fearful that Francine might be thrashing about in bed with their husbands.

Gertie had a dreadful night. At six she gave up the idea of further sleep, and got up. It was far too early to disturb her personal maid so she dressed herself in comfortable tweeds and decided to go and look at the horses – they would be awake. When Gertie was worried she liked to go to the stables where the ordered routine, the warmth, usually returned her to good humour.

Slipping quietly from her room she walked almost silently along the corridor. She stopped dead in her tracks as one of the doors opened and from her daughter-in-law's room emerged one of her footmen, shoes in hand, his shirt hanging out of his trousers, jacket over his arm, his hair dishevelled. He began to tiptoe down the corridor away from her.

'Harris!' Gertie's voice thundered along the corridor. The young man stopped dead in his tracks, still on tiptoe, his shoes dropping with a clatter on to the floor. 'What are you doing on this floor, Harris?' Gertie continued as she bore down upon him. 'Turn round, young man,' she ordered. 'Turn round when I'm speaking to you.'

As if hypnotised the young footman turned slowly to see his employer, her face quivering with indignation.

'Answer me. You know footmen are never allowed on the upper floors.'

'Mrs Frobisher . . .' he gulped. 'Mrs Frobisher, she rang, M'Lady.'

'And why did you not summon a maid?'

'I . . . I . . . I . . .' In his terror speech deserted the footman.

'It's all right, Peter. I'll handle this.' Francine appeared at the doorway dressed in a green silk peignoir, which matched exactly the colour of her eyes, her golden hair cascading about her shoulders. She looked at her mother-in-law brazenly. 'Is there a problem, Lady Gertrude?'

'There certainly is, young woman. No footman is allowed above stairs. What is Harris doing here?'

Francine smiled a sly smile. 'I wanted some tea.'

'You hussy, you unspeakable hussy. How dare you,' Gertie's deep voice boomed, her mounting fury making her oblivious of other bedroom doors opening, of faces peering out inquisitively. For a fleeting seconds she was aware that she should be conducting this interview behind closed doors, but anger swamped propriety and a dreadful blinding rage swept over her.

'How dare I what?' Francine said in a dangerously quiet voice.

'You have abused my hospitality. With my son under the same roof . . .'

'Perhaps you are jumping to rather unfortunate conclusions, Lady Gertrude.'

'No, I don't think so. Harris, did you fornicate with Mrs Frobisher?'

The footman looked from one to the other woman with naked fear in his eyes. He gulped, looked wildly at his employer and, turning quickly, ran in panic along the long corridor.

'You are dismissed. Pack and leave. You'll get no reference from me!' Gertie bellowed after him.

Several heads disappeared discreetly, doors were firmly shut, each guest obliged to follow the proceedings with an ear pressed closely against the woodwork.

'You rotten old cow,' Francine shrieked, her carefully modulated voice and accent reverting to the tone and accent of her youth.

'I beg your pardon! How dare you speak to me in that way! He has misbehaved: he must take the consequences.'

'And what are you going to do with me? Dismiss me too?' Francine laughed a loud, screeching laugh. 'You miserable bitch . . . You shrivelled-up old crone.'

Gertie stood, her back rigid with indignation. 'Francine, such language does not impress me one little bit. You are behaving exactly as I would expect someone from the gutters to behave,' she said coldly, her dignity fast returning.

'And you are behaving just as I would expect a bigoted hypocrite like you to behave. You're just lucky it wasn't your precious Basil creeping out – it could have been, you know. I just preferred something younger – for tonight.' It would have taken a fool not to notice the implied threat.

'Get out of my house.'

'With pleasure. With the utmost pleasure. I've never been so bored in my life . . . If this is what life with your lot is like I'd rather go back to my own life, ta very much.'

'To your stews, you mean,' Gertie thundered.

'*Stews!* Christ, you're like a dinosaur. Stews . . .' And she began to laugh hysterically, a shrill ear-piercing shriek that grew ever louder as she clung to the door for support.

'Mother, Francine, what's going on?' Richard rushed along the corridor towards them, summoned in haste by his brother.

'I regret to have to tell you this, Richard, but . . .'

'Then don't, you malicious bitch.'

'Francine!' Richard looked anxiously from his wife to his mother.

'I found one of the under-footmen sneaking out of your wife's bedroom.' Gertie was speaking calmly now, but her breast still heaved with righteous anger. 'I have, of course, dismissed him and I've requested your wife to leave. You and Polly are welcome to stay.'

'The brat goes with me,' Francine spat out.

'Francine,' Richard looked imploringly at his wife.

'Your mother has a filthy mind, Richard. I rang for some tea, that's all. The old bitch is jumping to horrible conclusions just because she doesn't like me.' Tears began to well up in the famous green eyes.

'Mother, really! How could you?'

Gertie's mouth opened in dismay. 'Richard, don't be so naïve,' she blustered.

'Did the footman confess?'

'He didn't have to, Richard. He fled in guilt.'

'Maybe you *are* jumping to conclusions, Mother.'

'Richard! Really. You know how this house is run . . .' she began and then saw there was no point, her son was lost to her again.

'Ring for your maid, Francine, and pack. We're both leaving.'

Richard turned and marched back along the corridor.

As the shouting had subsided the bedroom doors once more opened a little, curious eyes peering out in time to see Francine poke out her tongue at the noble form of Gertie Frobisher and to hear her say, 'See, he loves me, you dried-up old stick – but you wouldn't be able to understand that. As to this stately pile,' Francine waved her hand to encompass the corridor and its priceless paintings, tapestries, porcelain and Persian carpeting. 'Well, Gertie, old girl, you can stick it up your flaming arse for all I care . . .' and with a flourish, and an imperious toss of the head, Francine disappeared into her room.

The curious eyes were astonished to see tears begin to tumble down the redoubtable Gertie's weatherbeaten cheeks.

9

In the first-class carriage on the train back to London the atmosphere was strained. There was much that Richard wanted to say to his wife but the presence of Polly and her nanny prevented him. Instead he sat morosely gazing out across the landscape, doubt and fear festering in his mind.

He had set such store by this holiday. He had allowed his hopes to soar too high. The elation of the past two weeks at the prospect of seeing his parents, returning to his home, of being a full member of his family once again, now lay in tatters. He realised this had been his one chance of reconciliation. He doubted if his proud mother would ever relent now.

He looked across the carriage at his wife. She too stared moodily out of the window, toying with the walnut acorn of the blind. All morning he had been trying to believe her version of events. All morning his inner voice had been arguing against it. It was perfectly reasonable that she could have rung for tea but then why did a footman and not a maid answer? Perhaps a maid wasn't available. His mother was of a different generation who could easily, with her own high standards, have jumped to the wrong conclusion. After all she was not predisposed to like or trust Francine. A footman! But what did he really know about his wife or her background even after these past years together? He had long doubted her story of having a French aristocrat as a father. For one thing her French was limited and poor and, secondly, she resisted every sugges-tion he made that they should travel to that country and hopefully mend the feud with her family. Nor had she ever had a single visitor from France. Surely one of her family would have searched her out? His own brother visited him, secretly and regularly. Even his young sister had given her chaperone the slip one afternoon and found him in his office. What, then, was the truth? Where did she come from? He would have to have been deaf and stupid not to notice that when she was angry her voice changed dramatically to Cockney. Not that any of this mattered to him. Long ago, he'd realised that nothing could alter his love for her. But if he knew more, perhaps it would explain her to him, make it easier to understand and to deal with her many moods.

Would she, could she, deceive him? For his own sake perhaps he should begin to contemplate this possibility.

Abruptly he stood and went out into the corridor. He needed to walk up and down, he needed to think, needed a cigarette.

Francine watched him leave the carriage. The slope of his shoulders made him look so dejected that even she could begin to feel sorry for him. She had been rash, but then she had been bored and the young footman was certainly a fine specimen and really quite skilled in the bedroom arts – for a servant. After all, it wasn't her fault but Richard's that she was bored. He knew how much she needed to be entertained . . . If he were more interesting, if he was not so relentlessly dull, if he was better in bed . . . !

She snapped open her bag and took a cigarette from the heavy gold case and lit it with her matching lighter. She was aware of the look of disapproval on the nanny's face so she deliberately blew smoke in the woman's direction. Supercilious cow, she would have to go . . . She was quite relieved she need not go to Mendbury again. It was a grim place, too old fashioned and fussy, and with no modern style. Life was too short to waste time with Richard's dull family – not only dull but rigid and pompous. She chuckled softly, how those old sisters had smelt of moth-balls as if they were trying to preserve themselves as well as their old-fashioned clothes. Really, it astonished her how ghastly people who considered themselves 'quality' so often were. Not one of them had the finish, the style, the chic that she had, and she the daughter of a . . . She shook her head quite violently, that was a thought she never allowed herself.

She settled back against the seat and at last allowed herself the pleasure of thinking about Marshall. Just being in the same room had brought all the memories flooding back. It was as though it was only yesterday that he had been caressing her body, just a day ago when she had felt his heavy weight upon her. She moved restlessly in the seat, finding that just thinking about Marshall excited her. What a man he was, a real man, not like her gentle, sweet, but boring husband. She wondered how long it would be before he got in touch. She did not doubt that he would. She had seen the look in his eyes. She was not the only one who remembered those illicit hours they had spent together.

The snow was turning to rain. She watched without interest as several spots of rain slid down the outside of the window, the light reflecting on them, making them look like round, even diamonds . . . The jewels! She sat upright, Marshall banished from her mind. What had that woman meant? What jewels had Ia left, what was their worth? How much had she been cheated of this time? God, she hated her mother. She could still remember the pleasure and elation she had felt when, over seven years ago, after the late performance in the rowdy pub where she had to compete with drunken brawls, she had idly glanced at the evening paper to see that her mother had been killed in a traffic accident. The death of a celebrated whore-house keeper had made large headlines. That night had been a sleepless one as Francine had tossed and turned, calculating the worth of the property off

Piccadilly and wondering how much money Ia had in her bank accounts and hidden away in the safe. Francine knew where the safe was, and its combination: she had made sure of that during the short time she had lived with her mother. For a while she toyed with the idea of keeping the business going – after all it had made her mother rich beyond most people's dreams. But, at about four o'clock in the morning, she had rejected the idea: if word ever got out that she owned a brothel it would damage her stage prospects. The desire to be a star was the driving force in Francine's life, more important even than money. No, she would sell the lot, buy a decent house, new clothes, a few jewels, and invest the rest. With the right clothes and a good address she could get herself noticed: sing in a real music hall; become a success.

The following morning she had rushed round to the brothel, snapped at the weeping whores, booted her mother's favourite, Gwen, out of the study and rushed to the safe. The money she found there was disappointing, a mere seven hundred pounds which she stuffed into her handbag. She was irritated to find a large locked wooden box. She thought of searching for a key but when she saw a label announcing it to be the property of an Alice Tregowan, she thought better of it. Best not to be accused of stealing. She delved further into the safe and quickly riffled through a pile of papers until she found what she was searching for – the will.

She crossed to her mother's desk to read it. She did not like what she found. Her mother had left instructions that everything was to be sold, a home for young women alone in London was to be set up. She was furious at the bequests to each of her mother's whores. But worse was to come. She was virtually blinded with anger when she read the last line. *'To my daughter, Francine Blewett, I bequeath my azure bowl. It was all I had at the start of my life in London. Let us see how well she does with it.'*

'Old cow,' she muttered out loud at the memory. Polly's nanny pursed her lips in disapproval. Francine continued to stare out of the window. How smart she had thought herself when she burnt the will in the grate. It was a shock to discover two hours later, after she had sacked Gwen, that it was only a copy. Her mother's lawyer arrived with the original. Francine had nothing.

She took legal advice. But to contest the will, especially of someone as notorious as her mother, would have led to unfortunate publicity. Her ambition to be a star triumphed over anger.

Now she was a star. A famous star. And one day, when Basil died, she would be a baroness – that was something her mother had not achieved. So much for her mother and her azure bowl. But for the time being she was not rich enough, and it did not seem as if Richard would ever earn sufficient for her needs. For Francine wanted to be enormously rich, after all, someone as beautiful as she deserved the best, she thought. Now it appeared that she had been cheated of a small fortune in jewels. What annoyed Francine even more was that they must have been in the wooden box in her mother's safe. To think that she had handled them and put them back!

She would never understand why her mother had hated her so. Why, the woman hardly knew her. She had not even met her till she was thirteen and had run away from her foster home; by fifteen Francine had run away again – this time from her mother, who kept insisting that Francine's father was a footman, whereas anyone could see from her aristocratic beauty that he must have been a Lord. *Admittedly* she had stolen from her mother, but only a little, and only because she was so mean to her. *Admittedly* she had killed her dog, a nasty creature . . . but she had hated it. What was its stupid name? – Dog, that was it, a silly name for a horrid animal. But who would disown a daughter just because of a dog? After all, she'd done it in a temper to punish her mother for not loving her enough to give her the money she needed, so it was Ia's fault really.

Now all she had was the bowl. She hated that bowl as she had hated her mother. At first she had wanted to smash the bowl, but oddly enough whenever she tried she found she could not bring herself to do so – and now it had become her reluctant talisman. Silly really, she thought, as the train entered a tunnel and Francine admired her reflection in the darkened window . . .

Alice had to delay her departure from Mendbury for Gertie needed her. Sadly her visit to Cornwall would have to be postponed while she was required here. Uncharacteristically, Gertie had taken to her bed prostrate with dismay over the dreadful incident with her daughter-in-law. Like her son, Gertie had set great store by their meeting.

Most of all she was angry with herself: her violent reaction made any reconciliation impossible. What had she expected? That her unsuitable daughter-in-law was a quiet, docile wife to her son? No, she had always known the woman was a trollop. Nothing had changed except that she now knew for certain the kind of wife her son had acquired. She should have said nothing, done nothing. Francine's behaviour would have led eventually to her son's disillusionment. But she, with her temper, had put Richard in an impossible situation – he had had to leave with his wife, he had had no choice.

Gertie's only hope now was that Francine would continue to dig her own adulterous grave. And, shameful as divorce was, it would be a price worth paying for Richard to be rid of the woman. Then she would be able to welcome her son back again.

Her conviction that it was only a matter of time cheered Gertie so that she rose from her bed, descended the stairs and, with dignity, carried on as if nothing had happened.

Grace and Marshall had gone to France. Lincoln had a

business meeting in London, so Alice ordered a taxi as soon as they arrived there and went to the theatre. Alice had never been to the theatre on her own before and she was glad when the lights went down for she had not enjoyed the curious stares focused on her alone in her box.

Watching Francine, it was not easy at first to understand why she was a success. Her acting was mediocre, her voice was sweet but not strong, her dancing was better. But, as the musical comedy progressed, Alice realised that, in a way she could not comprehend, Francine was dominating the stage and overwhelming the other actors with her personality. She played exclusively to the audience and they loved it; she flirted with them, toyed with them and they adored her for it. On stage she had a presence which was magical. It was that and her extraordinary beauty which made her a star.

At the end of the performance, while Francine was taking one of a dozen curtain calls, Alice sent her card backstage. Ten minutes later she was summoned. As she made her way along the corridor, past the dressing rooms, around the props, she still wasn't certain why she was here. She felt sure that Francine was, in some way, related to her old friend Ia but she was equally sure that Francine would continue to deny it.

In her dressing room Francine lay exhausted on a chaise surrounded by a bevy of admirers all clamouring to speak to her, all wanting to give her presents, invite her for supper, to pour her champagne. If Alice had thought they would be able to have a quiet talk, such an idea was quickly cast aside. And then Alice saw it – the bowl, an azure bowl.

It was a large bowl gaudily decorated with red roses – a fairing from a past age. It stood on Francine's dressing table full of odds and ends – combs, clips, small change, a powder puff. Alice touched the bowl lovingly, for in doing so she was touching her own past.

The last time she had seen this bowl was in Ia's home the day she had found Ia and her family stricken with typhoid fever. It had been the only pretty thing in the whole cottage. It had attracted her attention then as it did now. She had never seen another like it. There was no question in her mind: this must be Ia's bowl, and she would have left it only to someone close to her.

Alice did not bother to fight her way through the crush to Francine. There was no need. She was certain now that she had found Ia's daughter – Francine.

She made her way out of the theatre. She wished she could feel pleased; instead a sense of desolation swept over her. She had found all that was left of Ia but, from what she had seen this past week, Francine was not a person she wished to know.

Had Ia herself liked her? Alice could not imagine it so, for the Ia she had known had been straight and honest. She might have been proud of her daughter's success but of the woman she'd become – never!

10

Alice was met at Penzance station by a chauffeur with a brand-new Rolls-Royce. It was typical of Lincoln to have thought of her comfort but, in a silly way, she was disappointed that it was not the cumbersome Tregowan coach awaiting her. That old coach had been so much part of her childhood that each time she had been away the sight of the coach on her return made her feel securely home. Now she regretted promising Juniper a ride in the old coach. She saw the disappointed expression on the child's face as she climbed into the shiny motor car. The coach would have been an adventure for Juniper who had never ridden in a horse-drawn carriage in her life. Lincoln had a garage full of motor cars, and Marshall had three. She leant her head back on the plush cushion as the chauffeur drove smoothly along the promenade. What a difference from the rocking coach, which always reminded her of being on a boat, but a boat with the comfortable smell of horses about it. Despite the car she was excited. It was now six years since she had seen her old family home. Her love for it had never left her and her longing to see it again was a deep physical ache, one that was about to be relieved.

She was sad that, on this visit, there was just herself and Juniper. On the trip across the Atlantic she had planned this home-coming to Cornwall with her family meticulously. She had planned to give a party for the local gentry and an even larger one for the villagers and estate workers. She had wanted Lincoln to investigate the feasibility of re-opening the tin mines to bring prosperity back to the area. Most of all she had hoped to interest Marshall and Grace in coming here to live, to manage the farm, so that the house did not stand empty and lonely for years at a time. But because of their delay at Mendbury, Lincoln could not afford to take more time from pressing business engagements. She had known that it would be pointless to ask him to change his plans: with Lincoln business always came first. To her intense annoyance, Grace and Marshall had returned to France almost as soon as Christmas was over. So much for her fond plans there. She had never been able to instil in Grace her own love for the county and Gwenfer. With Marshall, a Cornishman, at her side, she had thought it reasonable to hope that Grace might see things differently. But they had not even set aside time to visit Marshall's parents near Bodmin. Alice supposed she would have to visit them now, in order to introduce Juniper.

For Alice, Gwenfer was everything she desired in the world. She would quite happily never set eyes again on the mansion in New York, the great sprawling house on Dart Island. For all her years in America, Cornwall had kept an enduring hold on her; she still had frequent dreams of

Gwenfer. She smiled to herself as she remembered how adamant she had been as a young girl that she would *never* leave there.

But she had left. Though she had never wanted to go to London as a debutante, her governess had persuaded her she must. How different her life would have been if she had ignored the advice. She would never have met Chas Cordell, that handsome, charming American who was the author of her downfall. By eloping with him she had heaped disgrace on her head and caused her father to disinherit her. In turn, Chas had deserted her, left her alone and almost penniless in New York. But she had never forgotten him – unlikely that she should with Grace as her legacy from him, she told herself, sharply. Had she stayed at Gwenfer, there would have been no Grace, no Juniper and no Lincoln in her life.

Would she have married someone else? Would she have loved someone as she had loved Chas? She doubted it. The house was too isolated in the far West of England for her to have met a suitable young man to love and marry. Would she have been happy? At this thought a sudden chill feeling went to the very depth of her body. She loved her family dearly, but with an extraordinary clarity she knew she would have been happier had she stayed.

The car sped across the scrubland and into view came the tall chimneys of the tin-mine pump houses. In her early childhood the relentless clamour of the sea and the reverberating boom of the pump houses had always been there, a noisy part of her life. When her father had closed the mines, bringing untold misery to the community, those same pump houses had stood in stark, silent reproach to her for her family's cupidity. Once tall and proud, she saw to her dismay that the stone work had begun to crumble. They stood as half-ruined reminders of her forebears' rape of this land, and of the countless men whose spirits and health had been broken to supply her family with luxury and the wherewithal for her father's final downfall – gambling.

The car turned off the cliff road and through the gate-posts topped with the great stone falcons which were part of her family crest and had stood there for centuries. The chauffeur slowed appreciably to negotiate the steep drive-way, cut from the cliff. She looked about her, the driveway had never looked so well cared for when she lived here. The grass verges were neatly trimmed, the shrubs were contained. In front of the house, the wild garden she had loved had been tamed. When spring and summer came the roses would no longer snake wildly over the walls and down the steps. No longer would the clematis and honeysuckle twine with abandon on any object that took their fancy. Now they grew where they were ordered to grow, controlled by twine. The grass was lush and smooth as velvet; there would be no daisies, no buttercups. In the flower beds, smiled on by the balmy Cornish climate, plants were already thrusting their way through the sifted, stoneless, weedless soil. Plants that would flower in ordered rows. Alice looked at it all and hated it. This cultivated excellence was alien in such a wild place as Gwenfer.

She stepped from the motor car and looked up at the beautiful, granite house that had housed her father's Tregowan ancestors for centuries. She loved the building as if it were a breathing human being. As she looked at it she felt the house was studying her, was remembering her, and its welcome to her was a tangible thing.

The large oak studded door began to swing open. Alice held her breath for she felt at any moment that Queenie, her old nursemaid, would bustle out to welcome her, with Ia, her childhood friend, not far behind. Instead, it was the rather stooped form of Mrs Malandine, the housekeeper, who approached her, arms outstretched in welcome. How old she was, Alice thought. She should not still be working, Alice worried. She must make arrangements for the woman's retirement before she left.

'Mrs Malandine, how wonderful to see you.' She grasped the hand warmly.

'Mrs Wakefield, oh, welcome home.'

'Yes, it is home, isn't it? My home.'

'I've laid tea in the parlour, Mrs Wakefield.' She bent down. 'And this is Juniper. My, what a pretty girl, almost as pretty as your grandmother was at the same age,' the housekeeper fussed over the little girl. And Juniper, a child well used to fussing and attention, complacently accepted the homage.

'And how old are you, Juniper?'

'Three this month.'

'What a big girl you are!'

Juniper smiled patiently.

Regretfully, Alice entered the house. She had not wanted to go inside immediately. She had planned to do what she had always done as a child when arriving at Gwenfer. She wanted to kick off her shoes and run through the garden, down the valley where the small river ran to the sea, and race to her favourite rock and sit and allow the magic of the sea to enter her soul.

Instead, she ushered her granddaughter across the great hall where the standards of her ancestors hung above the shields and armour that had once covered their bodies. In the small parlour she paused as she saw the unfamiliar sight of an electric light glowing in the corner of the oak panelled room.

'Electric light?'

'Yes, Mr Wakefield wrote with instructions to have it installed. We've a fine generator which Mr George's son cares for. Do you remember Mr George, the coachman? He died, poor soul, only three years ago, ninety-four, a great age . . .'

'Is the electricity everywhere?'

'Oh, yes, Mrs Wakefield. Even in the servants' quarters. What a difference it's made to our lives, wonderful it is. We've even a refrigerator. Mr Wakefield has been so thoughtful. And the bathrooms, oh, Mrs Wakefield, the luxury . . .'

'Bathrooms!' Alice exclaimed.

'Yellow cake,' Juniper lisped.

'That's our famous saffron cake, my dear, you'll enjoy that.' Mrs Malandine was busily removing Juniper's coat.

'Please see to Juniper's tea, Mrs Malandine, I'm going for a walk.' Abruptly Alice left the room, walked out of the front door and down the garden steps towards her rock. How dare he, how dare he change a thing here, she thought angrily as she hurried along. This was her house, her place, her land, she would decide how it was to be. He had given it to her, the house was in her name, how could he presume to interfere – he knew how much the place meant to her. The garden was bad enough, but not the house also. She wanted it to stay exactly the same as it had always been, he was spoiling everything . . .

Sinking angrily on her rock, she looked out across the restless sea towards the great dark rocks of the Brisons. As she listened to the rhythmic music of the ocean she felt her anger fade. She felt the peace she had known she would find here, a peace that she found nowhere else in the world.

'I knew I'd find you here . . .'

Alice swung round to see a small woman standing on the path, smiling at her. Alice knew it was a smile because she knew the woman, but a stranger might have been forgiven for thinking it a grimace, for it came from a face unique in its ugliness. Through the gold pince-nez perched on the large, Roman nose, one blue eye and one brown eye looked at her with the sharp intelligence of a small bird. Tiny hands were held out in welcome.

'Miss Gilbey!' Alice jumped up and raced towards her former governess and flung her arms about her in welcome, no longer the elegant middle-aged New Yorker but an excited child again.

Alice loved Philomel Gilbey for she owed her much. It

was Philomel who had kept her sane when she thought her friend Ia had died, and after the deaths of her mother and her beloved Queenie. It was Philomel who had consolidated her random knowledge: until the governess's arrival, Alice had been self-taught. When her brother Oswald had drowned and her parents had all but deserted her, left her alone here with the servants, she had taught herself as best she could from the books in her father's library. Philomel had efficiently uncovered what Alice knew and what was lacking. Within two years she had brought all the threads of knowledge together so that when Alice had entered society she did so better educated than any of the other debutantes, except Gertie.

They cried in welcome as they held each other. Then side by side they sat on the great slab of rock. There they caught up with the happenings in their lives. Alice talked of New York and Juniper and apologised for forgetting once again that Philomel was married and was Mrs Trenwith now. Philomel laughed for she understood. Given her ugliness and ungainliness it was still, after all these years, something akin to a miracle that Ralph, now the local vicar, had proposed.

Philomel reported on the dairy, and the souvenir factory – both enterprises started by Alice to give employment when her father had closed the tin mines. Her face glowed with pride as she reported on the school which was her responsibility and her joy. Her small frame puffed up with pride as she told how one village boy she had tutored was to enter Cambridge University this coming autumn on a scholarship. His success was the absolute pinnacle of Philomel's career.

'It will be a hard society for him to enter, amongst young men who lack nothing. He will need things if he is not to feel a complete outsider. You must let me know what clothes he will need, what books. I'll supply it all and an allowance.'

'Dear Alice, always so sensitive and so generous.'

'It's nothing, Philomel, I have so much.'

'You may be rich, but you're not happy, Alice.'

'I wouldn't say that.' Alice turned her face to avoid the penetrating scrutiny of her old governess.

'I do. I know you too well, my dear. Just now you spoke of your life but there was no spark in the telling. And you speak of a city and your granddaughter but not of Grace, nor your husband.'

'Grace is married now. We are not as close as we were, I don't expect to be. I see more of Juniper than I do of her, so, of course, I have more to say about the child,' she said a shade defensively.

'And your husband?'

'I apologise. An oversight. He is well and he continues prosperous,' she laughed gently.

'No, Alice, I sense something. I fear you are being a dutiful wife and not a fulfilled one. Forgive me for speaking so, but I think I can presume on our years of friendship.'

'Please don't worry, Philomel, I'm not unhappy, that would be wicked of me, I really am so fortunate. But you see . . . Oh, I can tell you, Philomel . . . I do seem to spend a lot of my time wondering what might have been . . . so silly . . .' She shook her head as if to shake the notion away.

'If you were truly happy you would never even consider any alternative. Believe me, Alice, I know for I am the happiest woman on earth.'

'Dear Philomel, then your happiness makes me happy. To be honest, I think I know what the problem is. I'm beginning to realise that I can never be truly happy away from Gwenfer. It has an uncanny hold upon me. Sometimes I think . . .'

'Will Lincoln retire one day? Will it be possible for you to live here then?'

'Lincoln retire? Hell will freeze first. No, it is something I have learned to live with. It is probably being here that is making me seem more melancholy than usual. I really am most happy,' she said firmly and seeing the unconvinced expression on her governess's face, changed the subject. 'Tell me, have you ever seen the green flash when the sun slips into the sea? Ia and I used to spend hours searching for it.'

'No, I've heard of it, of course, but I've never seen it.'

'I think if I was ever fortunate enough to see it then I would be certain that my life was truly content.'

For two weeks Alice could honestly say she felt more, if not wholly, content. She changed many things around the house. She had the oil lamps brought out and cleaned and the wicks trimmed. She ordered them to be placed in the rooms, but she would not go so far as to deprive the staff of the convenience of the electricity. In the evenings she would sit and read to Juniper, enjoying the hiss of the lamps about her, their familiar smell. As Juniper sat at her feet and she stroked her fine blonde hair, she could imagine herself back in time, stroking Ia's hair and reading to her. She had taught Ia as she was now beginning to teach her granddaughter.

She ordered the hip bath to be placed in front of Juniper's bedroom fire. And she laughed with the child as the maid poured the water over her in a cascade from a jug. And she remembered the comfort of her own bath times, warmed by the log fire, the flames turning the water into pretty jewels. Such thoughts made her long for Queenie to be here to play with them. Queenie, the nursemaid she had loved more than she had loved her mother.

Alone, she climbed the stairs to the old schoolroom. From her pocket she took the key with which she had locked the door when she was last here and which she had taken back to America. She entered, her oil lamp held high, and she sat at her desk and for a long time thought of Ia, whom she had loved as a sister.

In the daytime she visited the villagers, inspected her dairy and the factory that made Cornish pixies. She presented prizes at the school. She frequently visited and tended Queenie's grave, and once she visited the mausoleum of her parents.

Two weeks she was there but in that two weeks she felt as if she had never been away. She longed to stay and she wept when she had to leave. Her last instruction to Mrs Malandine, as she said goodbye, was to tell the gardener that the garden was to be allowed to run wild again.

Chapter Three

1

Lincoln Wakefield sat impatiently behind the large, ornate desk at which Napoleon also had sat. He looked gloomily about the study of his house on Dart Island: he looked but did not see the paintings in their heavy gilt frames, the deeply embossed and gilded ceiling, the rows of books he had never bothered to read. All these objects normally gave him pleasure but this evening he was unaware of them. His fingers beat an impatient tattoo on the desk. Where the hell had the child got to?

He jerked the tapestried bell pull.

'Where's Miss Juniper?' he demanded of the butler the moment the man appeared.

'She has gone sailing, sir.'

'Sailing?' Lincoln exploded, half rising in his chair. 'Who said she could go sailing? I didn't say she could go. The boat is dangerous.'

'Her governess and the boatman are with her, sir,' the butler replied in his expressionless voice.

Lincoln relaxed in his chair which, it was alleged, had also belonged to Napoleon but which lacked the impeccable provenance of the desk. 'Ah, yes. I'd forgotten about the boatman.' He felt better now he knew the large capable seaman was with her. Juniper would be safe with him. 'Whisky and soda, Septimus.'

'But, sir. Mrs Wakefield . . .'

'Whisky and soda,' Lincoln said in a dangerously controlled voice.

'But, sir . . .' the butler gently touched his pocket watch. He did not need to look at it: the action was sufficient.

'God damn the time,' Lincoln barked.

'But the doctors, sir.'

'To hell with the doctors. What are you, Septimus, my butler or my bloody keeper?'

'Yes, sir. I'm sorry, sir,' and the man expertly negotiated his way between the many cluttered tables that filled the room.

'Goddamn cheek,' Lincoln growled to himself. What the hell was the world coming to when his own butler argued with him? One whisky a day and no cigars, the doctor had ordered. It was hardly worth the effort of living, he continued to mutter. He fumbled in the humidor for one of his forbidden Havanas. He cut it, lit it and puffed with immense satisfaction.

So, Juniper had gone sailing? He should not complain. It was his fault she had a boat. Trouble was, when Juniper wanted something he could not resist the enormous pleasure it gave him to indulge her – whatever it was. The child was always so appreciative and grateful. If it was anybody's fault, it was that of his flaming neighbour on the mainland – Skintle or some such name – who'd bought one for his boys. As soon as Juniper had seen the little boat, she had to have one of her own.

What Lincoln liked most about Juniper was her forthrightness. If she wanted something, she asked for it outright. No deviousness, no wheedling – he found it totally disarming. He'd never refused her anything but he knew that if he did, she would accept his decision without question.

But in giving her the boat he had only added to his great burden of worry. For ever since the child was born Lincoln's days had been filled with fear and worry about all manner of dreaded catastrophes that could befall her.

If only Juniper had been a quiet, docile child like her mother – content with dolls and things like that. But no – Juniper wanted action. Within Juniper's female form burned all the fire of the male Wakefields. This was

Lincoln's frequent thought, conveniently forgetting, as always, that she had not one drop of his blood in her.

How long had the Shetland pony lasted before the cry went up for 'a proper pony, Grandpa, darling?' The man smiled at the memory. Of course the child was a natural horsewoman and the leading rein was soon dispensed with. The walking gave way to the trot and the trot to the canter and the canter to the gallop. Hunting was the latest craze – something else for Lincoln to worry about.

He wished Dart Island were a deserted island where Juniper would be safe, where there would be no other people to influence her and make her want to pursue these dangerous hobbies. Just him and Juniper, miles from anywhere and anyone, what a delightful thought.

He glanced at his watch. An hour late. An hour out of his favourite time of the day when, for two hours between tea and dressing for dinner, Juniper and her grandfather talked, played games, or just sat quietly reading together. He did not like it that she was so late. But more to the point he did not like the idea that she might be enjoying herself more elsewhere.

He looked down at the sheaf of papers his lawyer had left him with the cryptic note that he thought Lincoln might like to study them more fully. 'What's this?' he thought, pulling them towards him.

The butler reappeared with the silver tray and heavy glass decanter.

'Took your time.'

The butler silently inclined his head and poured a glass of whisky. He placed the glass beside his master. He stoppered the decanter and picking up the tray began to leave the room.

'Leave the decanter,' Lincoln ordered.

Uncertainly the butler replaced the decanter beside Lincoln. 'Congratulations, Septimus, you managed that without a *"But"*.' He grinned mischievously up at Septimus who, imperturbably, bowed his head and again withdrew.

Ensconced with his cigar and glass, Lincoln returned to the pile of papers. A photograph caught his eye.

'What's this?' he muttered. It looked like a castle. 'What the bloody hell do they want a castle for?' he asked aloud of the empty room. He frowned. Bloody expensive things to maintain – castles. Without reading further, he knew it was to do with Grace.

Sometimes Grace's extravagance annoyed him. But on the other hand, what was money for except to be able to give to those you loved? The only thing he had refused her was the steam yacht – too ostentatious by far and, in any case, Lincoln hated the water. It was bad enough crossing the Atlantic in a liner, let alone having to imagine his loved ones on a bloody steam yacht a fraction of the size.

A castle . . . pretty place, he studied the photo again. He'd been mistaken, it was a house with battlements and tower which looked very like a castle. But why did Grace want another house?

Ten thousand acres – not bad, even if it was a drop in the ocean compared with his land holdings in America. Cheap at the price, too, compared with prices here.

He took up his pen to sign . . . The pen remained poised in mid-air . . . *Boscar Manor, Cornwall, England*, he read. And as he read he felt the blood within him rising, felt the now familiar pounding in his head. What game was this?

Rapidly he dialled his lawyer's number.

'Charlie, this house, is it owned by a Boscar?'

'That's right, Mr Wakefield.'

'Which Boscar?'

'I gather it's your son-in-law's father, sir.'

'Is it, by God?' Lincoln replaced the receiver not bothering with any of the niceties of social chit-chat.

He frowned deeply. No doubt Marshall had hoped he would sign without reading the papers. It was well known that these days he often took Charlie's advice on smaller matters and signed a pile of papers without checking them. He trusted Charlie implicitly to pull out the ones that needed his personal attention. Perhaps Marshall had tried to bribe Charlie to push this one through. There had to be something fishy here, or else Grace would have approached him directly about it.

They had the gall to expect him, unquestioningly, to buy something that would be Marshall's one day anyway.

'Grandpa!' The door flew open and Juniper burst into the room. With arms outstretched she skipped across the room towards him, her blonde hair flying from beneath the jaunty sailor's cap she wore. Her eyes glowed with health and excitement.

'Grandpa, such a day I've had!' She flung herself into his arms and with a deft twist of her body elegantly manoeuvred herself on to his lap. 'Grandpa, you smell lovely,' she announced.

'And you smell of the sea and . . .' he kissed her on the cheek, 'and I can taste the salt on you.'

She sniffed again. 'That's a cigar smell,' she said accusingly, at the same time spying the rest of the cigar smouldering in the ashtray. 'And what else do I smell?' she sniffed the air like an inquisitive puppy. 'Whisky, too, Grandpa that's bad.'

'Just a little one. Don't tell your grandmother. Keep it a secret, eh?'

'You won't die, will you?'

'What on earth gave you that idea?'

'I overheard Daddy talking to Mummy.'

'And what did you hear?'

'Daddy said,' the child put her head on one side with great concentration, as if searching her mind for the exact words. 'He said . . . "if he keeps on the cigars and whisky he'll be dead within the year . . ." It's not true, Grandpa, is it?'

'What nonsense. Of course it's not true. A little whisky never hurt . . .' He looked at the anxious face, the hazel eyes, flecked with gold, studying him intently. 'The truth is, Juniper, Grandpa is getting on and the doctors said I was to cut down a little, that's all. I intend to live for ever or at least until I see you happily married to a wonderful man who will always love you as much as I do.'

The child nuzzled into his cashmere jacket. 'I'm so glad, Grandpa. I couldn't bear it if you died. I really couldn't. No one loves me like you do. Oh, what's that . . . ?' her small hand snaked out across the desk and picked up the picture of the house. 'What a pretty place. Where is it?'

'Would you like to live there, Juniper?'

'With you? Only if you and Grandma live there, too.'

'Perhaps.'

'Oh, please.'

'We'll see.' He pushed the papers from him. 'You shouldn't have gone sailing, Juniper, it's too cold.'

'Oh, Grandpa, I was well wrapped up.' Lincoln grunted. 'You should have come with us, it was lovely. Miss Launceton was so funny. She didn't want to go, of course. She never wants to do anything exciting. But I insisted. Grandpa, it was so funny. First she went white, then grey, then sort of yellow and last, oh last was best of all – she went green. Then she was sick.' The girl clapped her hands at the memory. 'But Grandpa, you see she'd never been on a small boat before and she was sick *into* the wind.' The child shrieked with laughter.

'Juniper!' Lincoln admonished. 'That's not kind. Poor Miss Launceton.'

'I know it's not kind, but I can't help myself. She's always telling me off for being untidy and there she was covered all over in sick. She looked so cross with herself. I didn't laugh in front of her,' Juniper added, suddenly serious. 'I waited until after.'

'That was better of you, Juniper. I suppose she'll be handing in her notice now,' he sighed.

'Oh, I do hope so, Grandpa. She is dreadfully boring, you know, and never wants to do anything that's fun.'

'But how many governesses have you had this year, Juniper?'

'Only two.'

'But it's only February, my darling.'

'I'll try to be better, Grandpa, honestly I will. If perhaps you could find me a young one who likes boats and horses . . .' She smiled up into his face, which when he looked at her always had a benevolent expression.

'We'll have to see. There now, there's the dressing gong. See what your beastly sailing has done to our time together.'

'I didn't think, Grandpa. I promise I'll never go sailing at this time again.' She slipped from his knee. 'See you in the drawing room.' The child raced from the room.

Lincoln puffed on the remains of his cigar. It had been a good idea of his to insist that the child came down for dinner. This had meant moving the meal forward an hour to fit in with her bed time and Alice had made a bit of a fuss. But they had got their way in the end.

His hand went out to the whisky decanter. He paused. Then he pushed it away and stubbed out the cigar. He opened the humidor and emptied the contents into his wastepaper basket. He would listen to his doctors. He had no intention of giving Marshall the satisfaction of seeing him dead – not yet. And he could not break Juniper's heart – he owed it to her to go on living a good while longer.

He pulled the papers towards him. Wherever Grace Boscar's name appeared on the document as purchaser of Boscar House, he crossed it out and in his distinctive handwriting wrote *Juniper Wakefield Boscar* instead.

That night Juniper lay in her white-frilled colonial bed and watched the shadows flit across the ceiling of the pretty room. The curtains at the open windows lifted in the sharp winter's wind. Juniper loved being here on Dart Island better than anywhere else in the world. If she listened carefully she could hear the sea slapping on to the beach away across the wide lawns and past the magnolia tree. She could imagine her little white boat, *Firefly*, bobbing briskly on the water.

If she strained her ears even harder, far away from the house she could hear the horses snuffling and pawing in their stables. All her father's polo ponies were there and among them Sparkle, her own pony. He was called Hannibal really but Juniper had thought that such a heavy name for so sprightly a creature that she had named the jet black colt 'Sparkle' instead.

She loved the boat, and Mark the boatman. Sparkle she loved even more, though.

In truth Juniper loved everyone as much as they loved her. That was not quite true. She did not love Miss Launceton, in fact she had never managed to love one of her governesses – perhaps no one ever did, she thought, they always seemed such unlovable women.

Most of all in the world she loved Grandpa Wakefield. She loved him with an ache that hurt sometimes and a fear that one day he might leave her. She had been frightened when she had seen the cigar and whisky. She had heard far more than she had told him. She knew his heart was not strong, she knew if he was to live he must stop smoking and drinking – she had eavesdropped when the doctor called. He must be stopped from hurting himself.

She was certain she had been right to tell him of the conversation she had overheard. She knew it would have hurt her grandfather even more to know her father's exact words: 'At *last* he'll be dead . . .' Nor had she mentioned the funny little laugh her father had given – unaware that she was outside the door.

She had been told often she should not listen at doors. But it could be such fun, for grown-ups had much more interesting conversations than children and it was not her fault if they talked so loudly.

It was a continuing puzzle to Juniper why the two men she loved most in the world did not seem to love each other. For in Juniper's heart, just a fraction below what she felt for her grandfather was her love for her father.

If her grandfather represented love and security, her

father was love and excitement. Juniper was so proud of her handsome, glowing father that she knew she would have to search the world to find a husband as brave and gallant as he and – more importantly – as much fun.

In New York Juniper saw her father every day and she missed him when she came to Dart Island. She always came here for three weeks at the time of her birthday and then from late spring to autumn Juniper stayed here with her grandparents when her parents travelled to Europe. She was disappointed that they never suggested she go with them, but if they had taken her she would not have the long idyllic summers with her grandfather.

Why they had to live in separate houses in New York was a mystery too. Grandfather's house was ten times larger and a hundred times grander than the brownstone where her parents lived, and it overlooked the Park. Both Juniper and her grandfather would have liked them all to live together all year but Daddy would not hear of it.

She loved her mother too. But, to be honest, she sometimes found her rather dull – not nearly so boring as Miss Launceton, but she only seemed interested in clothes and make-up and gossip. And when they went out shopping together she never allowed Juniper to have milkshakes or cream cakes as Grandma Wakefield did.

Juniper stretched and yawned. Still, next week she would be six and everyone would be here and would not that be lovely?

2

The following week Marshall stepped along Park Avenue, in the surprisingly warm February sunshine, with the stride of a man well pleased with himself. He had had an exceptionally good day. He had lunched at Domingo's with an old army friend, newly arrived from England, and had caught up with the latest news and gossip from home.

The talk over luncheon had made him sufficiently home-sick to go straight from the restaurant to Cooks where he booked a passage for himself and Grace for their annual trip to Europe – a month earlier than usual.

Marshall still regarded England as home. He would never really belong here, he had long ago decided. It was not that he was unhappy but there were times he felt most misunderstood by the Americans, who did not seem to share his dedication to doing as little as possible as profitably as possible. Nor did they understand his total absorbtion in looking good – a well-cut suit gave Marshall more pleasure than a good lay if the truth were told. He twirled his cane in the air . . . it should not be long now and once again England would be his home. Grace had told him the doctor's latest reports on her father. It seemed the old bastard had not long to go, if he carried on as he was doing – in fact he could keel over any time.

From an excellent lunch to a good afternoon, too. A fine, energetic afternoon with that young actress . . . Good Lord, he paused in his step, he'd already forgotten her name – Doreen . . . Doris, yes that was it, Doris some-thing or other fresh over from England, keen to make her fortune on the Broadway stage.

Doris was one of several young women on whom Marshall had bestowed his interest in the past eighteen months. He really had intended to stay faithful to Grace, but, well . . . he had persuaded himself, a man needed normality in his life. It amused him that he was different from other men: whereas most men were unfaithful because their wives were frigid and their home life lacked excitement, he was unfaithful because he needed occa-sionally to have some relief from his wife's sexual demands. These affairs were never serious, oh, no, Marshall saw to that. As soon as one of the girls looked as if she was falling in love with him she was summarily dismissed – he wanted no emotional confusion, no further complications in his life.

As he strode along a broad grin etched itself on his handsome features at the thought of the house. That was the best news of all. He had phoned Grace from his club to be told the old bugger had signed the deeds. He twirled his silver-topped cane again, raised his hat to a pretty woman, and continued purposefully – much to her disappointment.

Not only was the house now his – whatever belonged to Grace was his, the sweet woman was always at pains to tell him – but his father, in return for being allowed to stay on at Boscar, had agreed to give Marshall fifty per cent of the proceeds.

He leapt up the steps of the brownstone; the door was opened by a footman as he approached. He loathed this overstuffed house with its ornate furniture – it was a house for old people not for a young married couple. He would have preferred one of those shiny new apartments overlooking the Park – far more modern.

Once the old man was dead they could knock down Lincoln's mansion which he alone liked, and build a soaring skyscraper. At the top would be a penthouse – where he and Grace and Juniper would live. That was his New York plan. Marshall's mind frequently reeled at the figures involved in his many plans – all unattainable until Lincoln turned up his toes.

In the drawing room he poured himself a drink just as the door opened and his heiress whore of a wife slipped into the room.

'Darling,' he kissed her cheek. 'Drink?'

'Please. God, I'm so tired. I had to go to my Aunt Sophie's – so dreary. She had a present for Juniper.'

'What time do we leave for Dart Island?' he asked, pouring a small bourbon for Grace and a larger one for himself.

'I promised Papa we would be there for luncheon. Juniper's party starts at three. I've bought her a fur coat,' she said casually.

'A fur coat for a six-year-old? You Americans never fail to amaze me.'

'It gets cold in New York and she's such a little thing,' she replied defensively. 'And you?'

'I've got her a new horse blanket for Sparkle with my crest on it.'

'She'll love that, probably more than my coat.'

'Darling Grace, I doubt it – what little girl could resist a fur coat?' But secretly Marshall thought she was right. Juniper would much prefer the horse blanket. 'And what about Boscar Manor? Isn't that the most marvellous news?'

'I'm not so sure I want to go to Cornwall, I've never liked the place. All my mother ever talks about is dreary Gwenfer, I even hate the sound of its name.'

'We shan't live there, my sweet. I've no intention of burying myself in the back of beyond either. I wanted security for my parents and some money to call my own, at last.'

'But you *know* you can have all the money you want.'

He kissed her on the tip of her nose. 'But don't you see, this will be Boscar money and I've such plans . . .'

'I think it's silly, Marshall. You call it Boscar money but where has it come from? My father. We need only have asked him to help us.'

This conversation was getting them nowhere. Grace would never understand how he longed for some independence. In fact it was probably better she did not know . . . He decided to change the subject. He poured them fresh drinks.

'Do you know what happened today? I suddenly had this overwhelming longing to be back in England. So, I've got our tickets. We sail at the end of this month.'

'I'm worried about the house, Marshall,' she persisted, making no comment on their travel plans. 'I do think we should have asked Papa outright. I don't like to do things behind his back. He would be so angry if he found out.'

'You do lots of things behind his back that he wouldn't

'approve of,' he reminded her, playfully slapping her rump.

'Oh, Marshall – that's different,' Grace said softly, running her hand down his thigh.

'You know he wouldn't have bought it, if he had known it was for me. I think it was damn nice of Charlie Macpherson to go along with us on this.'

'We paid him enough,' she said sharply, moving away from him. 'You don't understand about Papa. He just wishes you would get a job, that's all. He doesn't realise I keep you so busy.' She smiled and suggested they changed for dinner. At least it was to be a respectable dinner at the British Consulate, Marshall thought with relief.

Though his life style suited him, indeed was what he had dreamt of, there were times when he felt trapped in a gilded cage. There were times when he feared the future, wondered how long he could exist this way. But then he sometimes shuddered with terror at what would happen if he woke up one morning impotent. Marshall tried not to dwell on such misgivings and found it best not to think too long or hard about his future.

Juniper had been in a whirl of excitement all morning. The night before she prayed as hard as she could for good weather and had woken up to sunshine and an unseasonal warmth. Immediately after breakfast she had taken Sparkle for a ride. She had helped the boatman make *Firefly* shipshape. She had watched the workmen putting up the funfair and had pestered her grandfather for her present. But he had refused to give it to her. Luncheon, when her parents were there, that was to be present time, he had said firmly, but his eyes twinkled at her.

Juniper was excited about the funfair. She had been disappointed last year when Grandpa had organised a circus. There had been such a fuss when she stopped it – but she had to, there was nothing for it. She could not stand seeing animals perform: it was cruel. No, the roundabouts and the water-chute, the dodgems and the candyfloss were a much better surprise. Each year her grandfather thought up more and more wonderful surprises, and each year Juniper's friends turned green with envy.

Juniper lurked in the hall whiling away the time by playing hopscotch on the black-and-white marble floor. She heard the swish of tyres on the gravel and ran pellmell out of the open door, down the broad flight of steps and into her father's arms.

'Daddy, my darling Daddy,' she hugged him somewhere about his legs. He swung her up in his arms and studied her.

'Good gracious, Juniper. I haven't seen you for one week and in that time you've grown even more beautiful.'

'You're a dreadful flirt, Daddy.' She kissed him full on his mouth and he licked his lips where her kiss had been.

'My, you taste good,' he said.

'Don't I get a welcome?' Grace asked, trying to make her voice sound natural even though, as usual, she felt left out when Marshall and Juniper were together.

While the luggage was unloaded by the footmen from the back of the car, Juniper, still clinging to Marshall, was already making plans with him for this short holiday.

'The suitcases to our rooms. These boxes to Miss Juniper's room. These to the grand salon,' Grace ordered the footman. 'Is it presents in the grand salon . . . ? Juniper . . . I just asked you a question,' she said with irritation.

'Sorry, Mummy,' Juniper slid to the ground and dutifully concentrated her attention on her mother. 'Yes, there's piles there already. What are these?' she pointed to the boxes destined for her bedroom.

'Why, your party dress of course and new shoes and the most divine petticoat that Bloomingdales had. And I found a sweet nightdress and négligé just like I wear.'

'Thank you, Mummy, you're so kind to me,' the child said ingenuously.

They trooped up the steps leaving a chauffeur to park the gleaming Bugatti in one of the garages. In the hall Alice awaited them. She looked intently at her daughter. The girl went from one extreme to the other – she was far too thin now and there was a brittleness about her, a guarded look to her eyes, which worried Alice. Lincoln had assured her that their problems were over, that Marshall was behaving himself. But at what cost to their daughter, Alice was not sure.

After she had kissed the new arrivals welcome Alice instructed the butler to call Mr Wakefield and they entered the grand salon for champagne and the ritual opening of Juniper's presents.

Juniper's presents were another thing which worried Alice. They were a tangible sign of the constant battle waged between the parents and grandfather for Juniper's affections. Alice felt there was something distressingly undignified in these adults vying with each other for a child's love. Alice never stopped marvelling at how normal, sweet and generous Juniper seemed to be, despite the grown-ups in her life. But no one would listen to Alice, least of all Lincoln. And to be fair to the child, so far, she seemed touchingly grateful for what was given her.

Lincoln entered the room, kissed his daughter, grunted at his son-in-law and bestowed on his granddaughter such a look of unadulterated love that Alice had to smile.

The ritual of the present opening was always the same. First the champagne toast when even Juniper was allowed a small glass of watered-down champagne. Then the presents. Those from cousins and aunts, from business associates of Lincoln who needed to ingratiate themselves with him, all these were quickly dispatched. Next came Alice's present.

Juniper looked at the basket-weave needlework box lined in pink satin, the cottons glowing untouched in special pockets, and she clasped her hands with genuine joy.

'Oh, Grandmother, how did you know? I've always

wanted a real work box just like yours.' The child ran across the room to plant a kiss on Alice's cheek. 'Gracious, *two* from Mummy and Daddy. Which one do I open first?'

'Ladies first wouldn't you say, Juniper?' Her father smiled at her.

The child squealed with joy as the pale-beige miniature fur coat cascaded from its wrappings, and she slipped it on immediately. She paraded around the room as she had seen the models do when her mother had taken her to the couture houses. The pale colour of the fur accentuated her own blondeness and those present could see the beautiful woman she undoubtedly would become. Marshall glowed with pride, Lincoln beamed with satisfaction, but Alice felt suddenly chill, fearing for someone with so much beauty.

'Oh, why is it so warm today? I shan't be able to wear it, not until the cold weather returns. Oh, Mummy it's lovely.'

Picking up Marshall's large box, gaily wrapped and with a bouquet of silk red roses on the top, she smiled shyly at him. 'What have we here, Daddy? It's so big!'

When she saw the rug with her initials and her father's crest upon it, she burst into tears.

'Sparkle will be so very happy. He really will.'

Marshall smiled, well pleased with her reaction. From the corner of his eye he glanced at Lincoln and thought, 'Got you, you old bastard, beat that.'

Lincoln's gift, always the last to be opened, was a large wooden box with no fancy wrappings. Gingerly the child opened it. On top was a small oil painting. Beneath it a stack of papers, heavy with wax seals.

'Grandpa, what's this?' She smiled mischievously at him and taking the painting studied it carefully, a puzzled look on her pretty young face. She looked up at her grandfather. 'It's a lovely picture, I'll treasure it always, just like the pictures in my fairy books. You are so kind to me,' and she kissed him soundly and gave him one of her special hugs.

'You don't understand, Juniper. It's yours.'

'I understand, Grandpa, I'll hang it by my bed.'

'No, my darling, I mean it's really yours. Remember how you said you'd like to live there?'

Juniper squealed with delight. 'Oh, I don't believe it. Look, everyone, Grandpa's given me my own fairy castle.' And into Marshall's hands she thrust the oil painting of Boscar Manor, Cornwall.

'Oh Papa!' Grace exclaimed, looking nervously at her husband. He was so good-tempered these days, but this . . .

'Lincoln, you are quite ridiculous,' Alice tutted anxiously.

Marshall said nothing but his face was a mask of badly controlled anger. His hands shook as he handed the painting back to Juniper.

'It's lovely, my darling. I'm glad it's yours.'

Grace looked admiringly at her husband, knowing better than most the great self-control he was exerting. She saw the smug smile on her father's face and was angry, bitterly angry.

'Papa, how could you do this?'

'Do what, Grace?'

'You knew that was Marshall's family home. You must have realised how much he wanted us to have it. What you have done is despicable.'

'Your daughter owns it, what difference does it make?'

'All the difference in the world, Papa.'

'Then you should have asked me outright. I like people who are open with me.'

'If I'd asked you outright, you would have said no.'

'Do you know that for certain, Grace?'

'Yes I do. You've always hated Marshall, ever since the day you met him. Why can't you be kind to him, why can't you . . .'

'Kind?' Lincoln's voice exploded out of him. '*Kind?* I think I'm remarkably kind to your wastrel of a husband. Do you know how much he costs me a year? There are the ponies. There's your inflated allowance. There's the brownstone, who pays the bills on that may I ask? Your travelling expenses when did you last pay for a ticket from the very generous allowance I give you? How many times have I paid off his gambling debts, answer me that?' Lincoln bellowed, his voice echoing about the large cavernous room. Grace was shaking; she had never seen her father so angry before.

'Everyone, please, the child,' Alice pleaded.

Juniper stood in the middle of the room, tears tumbling down her cheeks as she looked with horror from one parent to the other, and to her grandfather.

'Please, Daddy, please. You have the house, if that's what you want, then you'll all love each other again, won't you? Please take it . . .' and she thrust the painting towards her father.

'You can't give presents away, Juniper. It's ill mannered.' Unbelievably her grandfather was growling at her. He had never done that before, never.

'But I don't want people to be angry, Grandpa!' she sobbed.

'If you give your father that house I shall be very angry with you, very angry.'

'Then what am I to do, Grandma? Help me, please. I don't want the horrid house any more.' The girl appealed to Alice in despair.

'You ought to be ashamed of yourselves, all of you. Spoiling the child's birthday like this. You go too far, Lincoln. Come, Juniper. Let's go to your room, wash those tears away and change into your new dress. Your guests will be here soon. Don't worry, my precious, we'll sort something out about the silly old house.'

Alice marched the child briskly from the room. Once in her bedroom Juniper was immediately sick. Alice fretted about her but the child would not stop crying. There was nothing for it, the party would have to be cancelled.

In the salon the three remaining adults glowered at each other across the room.

'Does it matter who owns it?' Lincoln finally barked out, beginning to feel that this time he might have gone too far.

'Yes, Papa, it does matter. Giving it to Juniper has humiliated Marshall – just as you planned, no doubt.'

'Huh!' Lincoln downed a glass of champagne in one.

'I thought, sir, that you loved Grace and wanted her to be happy. I had also always assumed that you *enjoyed* being generous. I was unaware that I was supposed to be humiliated by it. I'm sorry to disappoint you, sir,' Marshall said quietly.

'Happy? Do you really think my daughter is happy with you? . . . sir,' Lincoln added as a sarcastic afterthought.

'I do my best.'

'Best? You're an evil bastard, Boscar. You have brought nothing but dissent and unhappiness to this family. Look at her eyes – you think that's happiness there, *sir*? The only good to come out of this marriage is Juniper. And what sort of father do you think you are? What sort of example do you set? Why, she spends more time with me than with her parents.'

'We must put that right at once, sir.'

'And what does that mean?'

'It means, Mr Wakefield, I'm taking her with me – now. Grace, go and tell her maid to pack.' Marshall spoke quickly but still quietly.

'Grace, sit down,' her father shouted as Grace began to cross the room. 'The child stays here.'

'She's our child, we take her with us if we so wish,' Marshall's voice rose in anger.

'And what will you live on?'

'We'll manage. I can find employment, though I know you think I couldn't.'

'I've money of my own, Father, you forget,' Grace interjected.

'Really? You think you've enough? Your allowance stops as from today. The interest on that small amount I settled on you won't keep your parasitic husband in brandy and tailors, believe me. Grace, you're a fool if you think otherwise – you make me laugh.'

'How dare you speak to Grace in that manner. You've gone too far! Get the child, Grace . . .' Marshall was shouting loudly now, his face was white with anger, a pulse throbbing rhythmically in his temple.

'No. You will not remove that child from under my roof,' Lincoln said in a voice so dangerously quiet that it frightened Grace.

'Will you keep her here by force?'

'If necessary, I've guards enough. I shall enjoy seeing you thrown out, Marshall.'

'Then we shall go to court and sue you for her return.'

'I wouldn't do that if I were you, Marshall. It could be a very unwise move.'

'No court would let you keep her from her natural parents.'

'Really? You certain of that?' With mounting horror Grace realised that her father looked completely relaxed now and was smiling a knowing sort of smile.

'Marshall, don't, he knows,' she faltered.

'Knows what?'

'About us. Don't you, Papa?'

'Yes, Grace. I know everything. And I cannot tell you how painful it was to find out.'

'What on earth do you mean?' Marshal was blustering now, unsure of his ground.

'The drugs for a start.'

'What drugs?' Marshall laughed dismissively, more sure of himself.

'Don't lie to me, you son of a bitch. The drugs you force on my daughter to make her . . .'

'I don't understand a word you're saying. Me? Drugs? You're mad.'

'The drugs, the apartment, the brothels, whom you entertained last night, I know everything. I have a good intelligence network – I use it to check on clients or *employees* – such as you,' he sneered. 'So you see, Boscar, I don't think any court will allow you your daughter – I'd get custody. But we don't want it to come to that, do we? We should have a really messy scandal on our hands – imagine with what relish the newspapers would take it up.'

'Oh God!' Grace moaned and covered her face with her hands. 'Does Mummy know?'

'No, Grace, she doesn't! Nor shall she. I assure her you're happy. Mind you, it doesn't stop her worrying – she's not blind.'

'Papa . . . I'm sorry . . .'

'I'm sure you are, Grace. I don't understand what you do, but it can't stop me loving you.'

Grace shuddered convulsively. Tears began to run down her face. Her husband put a protective arm about her. 'I think we should go home, Grace.' He pulled her to her feet. 'Come on, old girl, you mustn't cry and spoil that pretty face. I'll get the car.' He moved quickly from the room. Grace picked up her handbag and slowly followed him.

'Grace,' her father called. She turned, looked expectantly at him. 'Why, Grace? Why?'

'I can't help myself. It's the only way I know to keep him, Papa,' she replied through her tears.

Alone in the room Lincoln Wakefield's shoulders began to shake. Tears that he had not shed since he was a boy tumbled down his cheeks. He was afraid he had lost Grace, his little girl . . . but he had no choice. Juniper had to be protected at all costs, even if that meant he never saw his daughter again.

Chapter Four

1

For nearly two years Marshall and Grace had been living with his parents at Boscar Manor in Cornwall. It was an arrangement that suited nobody.

Grace found she could not forget or forgive Marshall's mother for her rudeness on that first visit years before. She refused to speak to her.

Mrs Boscar was confused. The whole of her life was scattered with such puzzling incidents: she never understood how she had offended. But she was not the only one to be confused; those she had upset were usually equally muddled. For Mathilda Boscar was a beautiful, fey creature, who looked incapable of cruelty. Tall and willowy, she dressed in unique, jewel-coloured clothes, which she designed herself. Her long, free-flowing, black hair framed her face with exuberant curls, and her large blue eyes had a soft, dreamy quality. She lived in a world of her own creation, a fantasy world inhabited by fairy folk, goblins, moorland giants, and water spirits who lived in bottomless pools. It was a world of poetry and music. She looked so romantically whimsical and harmless that everyone was doubly shocked when she made an apparently waspish or offensive remark. But to offend was not what Mathilda intended. She had told Grace she found her ugly because she *was* ugly – it was simply the truth. A fact, not an insult. She was far better at communing with nature than with her fellow human beings.

Marshall had tried to bring his wife and mother together. Patiently he explained to Grace that his mother was not like other people, that she spoke before she thought. Grudgingly, Grace agreed to talk. In the small parlour, over tea, Marshall explained to his mother, with equal patience, how sensitive Grace was and how unkind her remark had been.

Mathilda was incensed. This was so unfair, she protested. Everyone knew how kind she was. She had never been cruel to a living creature in her whole life – especially dumb and stupid ones.

At this added injury to her sensibilities, tears leapt into Grace's eyes and she stumbled from the room. The rift between her and Mathilda was irrevocably widened.

Halliday Boscar did not help either. He was quite fond of his daughter-in-law, though rather disappointed that there was so much less of her these days. His problem was that whereas with insects his memory was prodigious, it failed him miserably and without warning where fellow humans were concerned. He might spend a pleasant evening chatting to Grace of his beloved creatures or his wild inventions, and yet, the following morning, upon meeting her in a corridor, he was quite likely to find his step faltering. He would stare at her vaguely, with the expression of a man who felt that he should know her but for the life of him could not remember where they had met. He would shake his head in frustration and shamble on. His attitude only added to Grace's highly developed feelings of inadequacy and inferiority, and she retreated further into herself.

But hardest of all, six months after their arrival the last of her precious store of drugs from the Swiss doctor was used up. With little money she could not afford to send to Switzerland for more or go to London to try and find a sympathetic doctor. She suffered, she suffered greatly as the fog of drugs which had made her life possible lifted and she had to cope without this crutch. She sweated, she shook, she was nauseous and short tempered but finally she came through.

Freed from the drugs Grace became fully aware of her surroundings. Partly to give herself an aim and a focus she tried to organise the large, mouldering mansion. Though she had been a nurse her domestic skills were negligible. It took her over a week to arrange a small sitting room for herself and Marshall. Her sewing was not neat and when she patched a sheet the result was an uncomfortable ridge that would cause many a sleepless night. Since much of the linen just fell apart in her hands she eventually gave up. With no washerwoman it was only a matter of weeks before she had ruined most of her own clothes and virtually all of Marshall's shirts.

Cyril, the one servant, was no help at all and resented her efforts. He sat by the large kitchen range and sulked as Grace turned out drawers and cupboards. He watched with an unpleasant smirk as, seething with anger, she scrubbed the tables and floor. There was nothing she could say to him. He had not been paid for months. If he left she would have to chop the kindling, tend the fires and light the monstrous kitchen range, which seemed to have a mind of its own, understood only by Cyril.

The work was hard but, to her surprise, Grace found it satisfying. She was proud of the great hall she swept daily, the furniture beginning to shine from her efforts. But her mother-in-law would return from one of her long, solitary walks on the moor, carrying large bunches of wild flowers, the heads and seeds of which she cast about the floor with a seemingly spiteful abandon. Mrs Boscar did nothing but lavish love on her dogs, take her walks and play the piano. She played beautifully but it was a sound which, tired as she was, began to irritate Grace out of all proportion. Since no one seemed to notice the improvements, let alone appreciate them, she lost heart. Once again the dust settled on the contents and inhabitants of Boscar.

Food meant nothing to the senior Boscars. Both of them were content to live for weeks at a time on lumps of cheese and bread and Cyril's rabbit stew. Grace spent much time trying to cajole him into attempting something else. He would grunt, promise to try, and she would think she had won, only to find, that evening, another stew being served by Cyril who grinned slyly and looked half-wittedly at her. Her own attempts at cooking had resulted merely in burnt pans and many tears.

Grace could not understand why they should live like this. Her father had paid a handsome sum to acquire the house and Marshall had received half of it. Whenever she tackled Marshall on the subject of money he became infuriatingly vague.

By dint of wheedling and cajoling she finally discovered the truth. Marshall's father, it appeared, overjoyed at having money in his hands, had embarked on a massive spending spree. Marshall listed for Grace the various expenditure. His old laboratory had been gutted and a spanking new one built with brand new microscopes, an incubator for his insects and several large herbariums with complicated heating systems were installed. More money had been spent tracking down further rare insects which were sent to him from all corners of the globe. His large papier mâché models had been thrown away and a professional model maker employed to build new vastly improved ones with clockwork motors. Now giant locusts with flapping wings whirred about the ceiling of his laboratory and enormous spiders, cockroaches and ants scuttled about the floor.

Numerous patents had been taken out. One was for a mechanical cure for snoring, which unfortunately damaged the nose; next an artificial limb which the inventor, who lived with them for six months, claimed would work from the body's electrical impulses – it did not. A large shed was built for a machine which would revolutionise farming – an automatic cow milker – but sadly it exploded and electrocuted the cow. Flight then took his fancy and the wrecked cow machine and its inventor were summarily removed, to be replaced by a flying ace from the Great

War who had designed a machine with one blade which would take off vertically and land anywhere. It crashed in the lower meadow and the pilot joined the cow.

That, Marshall explained, was how Halliday had happily dissipated his money.

'But what about your share, Marshall?' she ventured to ask.

'Ah, well,' he said, not caring to look at her. 'I lent it to my father, I'm afraid.' He shrugged his shoulders as he lied. In fact most of his money was safely invested in gilt-edged securities. He was saving his money in case the day ever arrived when she, rich in her own right, would tire of him and he would have nothing.

Things improved slightly when money from Alice began to arrive on a more or less regular basis. But the amounts were limited and there was no question that they could return to their previous way of life. At least Grace could now employ someone to wash and iron their clothes, the food improved and a woman came in twice a week to help her with the heavy cleaning. Lincoln had been right about her own, limited allowance: it covered Marshall's consumption of claret, port and brandy and the restocking of his wardrobe. Marshall would have given up the port and brandy rather than allow his appearance to fall below his exacting standards.

Her strange sexual appetites had calmed down – much to Marshall's relief. He presumed this was because she was older and more content. What he had not realised was that since they never saw anyone of note, Grace felt she could relax where her errant husband was concerned – there was no one here for him to be unfaithful with.

She was frequently listless and bored. Once she would happily have walked in the parkland, the woods and the moors which surrounded the house, but these days she did not seem to have the energy and they held no attraction for her. She never accompanied her husband on his rides over the estate; and Mathilda's dogs had eyes only for their mistress so were no company for Grace. Deprived of shopping, visits to the beauty parlour and luncheon with her friends, time hung heavy on her hands and she began to become seriously depressed.

There was no question of Grace having to concern herself with diet to control her weight – hard work and lack of rich food saw that she remained slender. But her face suffered. She began to age rapidly as anxiety and discontent took their toll. Like so many wealthy people, Grace had always imagined that she did not need money, she had often thought that those who were poor were happier than she. She knew better now. She longed for money, she thought about it constantly, she even dreamt about it.

Marshall, however, had not felt so happy for a long time. He was fond of his parents and passionately loved Boscar Manor. He had always thought that a quiet life in the country was not for him. Instead he found that, with the help of Alice's money, he enjoyed being lord of the manor, took pleasure in the trips to the market, chatting with the farmers, drinking cider with them, selecting a pig, some chickens, and a new cow to replace the electrocuted one. He loved riding and checking the land, giving a hand with the fencing, helping when the new cow calved. Occasionally he would take a trip to the ale house in Bodmin, to see old friends who were now the town worthies. He enjoyed the way they looked up to him with his smart clothes and his talk of America. He was fitter than he had been for years and imagined that his wife was as happy as himself.

But, eventually, even Marshall became aware of Grace's misery. And being unable to ignore it, he decided he would have to avoid her.

'I'm going to London,' he announced one morning at breakfast.

'What for?'

'I need a new suit, shoes, hats. My shirtmaker calls. I

want to go to Purdeys, have my guns checked.' He noted her frown. 'I shall choose a gift for you for Christmas.' He beamed at her, satisfied with his own stratagem.

'You've dozens of suits and shirts.'

'But they're passé, my sweet.'

'I shall come too.'

'Why?'

'Maybe I'd like to buy some new clothes too.'

'What for? We never go anywhere nor do we do anything.'

'Then why do you need new suits?'

All the same, Marshall went to London – and on his own.

Within two hours of arriving in the city he was glad he had come, and without his wife, for who should he contrive to bump into but the delectable Francine Frobisher?

2

Richard Frobisher sat at the dinner table set for three, with Polly beside him; Richard looked despondent.

'It doesn't matter, Daddy. I really don't mind Mother not being here. After all she hardly ever is, is she?' She smiled at her father, her brown eyes full of concern. He put his hand out and touched her small one.

'But on your birthday . . .'

'Really, Daddy. I have you. And we always have such fun together, don't we?'

Richard smiled. It was true. When he was with Polly, he needed no one else. That a child could be such engaging company had surprised him at first. Now, truthfully he preferred an evening alone with Polly to one with anyone else.

He signalled to the maid and dinner was served.

Later, once Polly was in bed, Richard worked in his

study on the farm accounts. Despite the pleasant evening he was angry. It took a great deal to make him so – but Francine had tried his patience too far tonight.

From the start, when Polly was four, Francine had resented the move to Hurstwood. At the time another of Richard's great aunts had died, leaving him a good sum of money – enough for him to be able to give up his work in the city and do what he had always dreamt of – work his land at Hurstwood, ride his horses to hounds, and give Polly a healthy country life.

He had agreed to Francine keeping on the flat in London even though, as he had pointed out, it was rather large for one person. But he had expected that, with no theatre on Sunday, she would make the effort to come for the odd weekend. And he had thought it reasonable to assume that, when she was between plays, she would come to Hurstwood. Francine thought otherwise. From the start her visits were intermittent and, as the years slipped by, had virtually ceased. To ensure that Polly saw her mother, the onus had been put on Richard to travel up to London with the child. He sat working out dates, it must be nearly six months since she had last been here.

He had been patient with her, realising that she was a child of the city and that the countryside bored her. He knew also that it was necessary for an actress to be near the theatres, the agents and producers. But just this once he had insisted she come. It was Polly's ninth birthday, she must come – it was a Sunday, after all, with no theatre performance. His present for Polly was a new pony; they could hardly bring it to London and the child would be desperate to try it out.

And the bitch had let him down.

Bitch she was. There was no other word. It was humiliating that his mother had been right all along. The sacrifices he had made for Francine did not sadden him now but rather angered him. He had lost his family, his inheritance, and for what?

Years ago he had come to the reluctant conclusion that she was unfaithful. He could not be certain, for Richard was too kind and popular a man to be given such information by friends and he had no enemies. Nor would his sense of dignity allow him to employ a detective. But he knew instinctively. He himself had often been tempted. There were many women in the local hunt who would have been only too happy to relieve his tensions. But Richard never succumbed; he had Polly to think of. If he went to London, Polly was always with him, so the opportunity for him to be unfaithful never occurred there.

Nowadays he could think about Francine's infidelity quite calmly but this had not always been so. At first he had minded – minded desperately. But in the last few years what his wife did mattered to him less and less.

Very occasionally, in the past, when she came they made love and for a short time he would allow himself to hope that the old magic had returned. But it never lasted, then she was away again and with each visit seemed further from him.

They might as well not be married, he thought, as he shifted the lamp closer and poured himself another whisky. But Richard was of the old school and did not believe in divorce. He had always thought that, provided Francine was discreet in her behaviour and Polly was not hurt in any way, he would be content to let things ride. She still seemed to enjoy using his name – the name of one of the oldest families in the land. No doubt that was why she herself had never mentioned divorce. Of one thing he was certain, his wife was a snob.

But now? What had his tolerance brought him – only sadness. Polly needed a mother. There would come a time, soon now, when he would be inadequate, when Polly would need a woman to turn to. He downed his whisky. Francine had finally gone too far: tonight she had shown how little she cared for both of them. It was time for an ultimatum.

It was two in the morning, the stable clock was chiming as he heard the wheels of the car enter the driveway and screech to a halt outside the front door.

He poured himself a stiffening drink and listened as her shoes clattered across the flag-stoned floor.

'Richard, darling. I'm sorry. Where's Polly? Is she cross with me too?' His wife stood in the doorway, one foot in front of the other, one hand on hip, elegant as always. 'I can't tell you the drama I've had.'

She swept into the room followed by a wake of expensive perfume, her sable coat trailing dramatically on the floor behind her.

'Where were you?'

'Oh, Richard, you do sound cross. That's your angry-with-Francine voice . . .' she pouted at him but the pout did not work as it used to do. 'I got stuck with a dreary producer in London. I set off late and had a puncture. There, you see it wasn't totally Francine's fault. Any fizz about?'

'Why didn't you telephone?'

'I thought I could make it in time.'

'When you broke down?'

'Oh Richard, don't be silly, I was miles from anywhere. I had to walk for ages to get help.'

Richard glanced quickly at the immaculate, high-heeled evening slippers. No mud or scuffs marred them.

'Who were you with?'

'I told you, an awful producer who wants me in his next play. But if it's as boring as he was, the answer is most definitely *no*. Darling, I asked you, any fizz?'

'I didn't order champagne to be brought up tonight. I want to know who you were with.'

'Then ring for some.'

'The servants are in bed,' he said coldly. 'Stop this charade, Francine. Tell me who you've been with. You don't come home for months and then you miss our only child's birthday.'

Francine laughed her husky laugh. 'Richard, don't be

186

silly, you and Polly hardly need me – a dear little twosome you make.'

'I want you here more of the time, Francine. If you can't manage it, then I shall insist you give up the stage. Polly needs a mother.'

'Oh don't be stupid, Richard. Polly doesn't need me. I don't think the child even likes me,' as she spoke she was picking up the bottles from the drinks tray, looking for one that took her fancy. 'The least you could do would be to have some decent liqueurs,' she complained.

Richard crossed the room and grabbed her wrist.

'I want to know, Francine, once and for all. Who were you with? Who is it?'

'Good heavens, Richard, are you jealous at last? I thought such emotions were beneath you.' She laughed. It was probably the laugh that was Richard's downfall; his hand swung almost involuntarily through the air and he struck her across the face.

She looked at him, stunned. 'Don't you dare hit me, you bastard,' she shrieked.

'Then tell me,' he shouted back.

'I went to a party and then on to dinner. I didn't want to come here, if you must know, for a dreary evening with you and that simpering miss.'

'You bitch,' he hit her again.

'I told you, you bleeding bastard, don't you touch me. I'll have the police on to you if you don't watch out.'

Richard laughed, an empty, hollow laugh. 'My, my, Francine. How your accent slips when you're angry.'

'Sod you, Richard. Sod you . . .' she screeched, stamping her feet with rage, knowing only too well he spoke the truth.

'For the last time, I want to know where you've been,' Richard said quite calmly.

'With Johnnie Bates, if you must know,' she lied. Her instincts of self-preservation told her not to mention the name of his old friend, Marshall.

'Good God, Francine, he's a drunkard, a liar, a lecher . . .'

'And he knows how to please a woman, knows what to do with it . . . not like some I could mention.'

'God, how vulgar you are.'

'Yes, and that's what you used to like about me. Or can't you remember?' Noisily and with shaking hand Francine poured herself a brandy.

'If you don't stop seeing Bates and others like him, I shall divorce you,' he heard himself saying with surprise. Francine swung round and looked at him with equal astonishment.

She laughed a short, dismissive laugh. 'You wouldn't. There's never been a divorce in your family. What would your sainted mother have to say about that?'

'She'd be pleased for once that I'd done something sensible, something I should have done years ago. I mean it, Francine. Bates or me.'

'Ha! You try. You divorce me and I'll make sure you never see your precious Polly again.'

'You've no time for the child, why bring her into this now?'

'That wouldn't stop me. I promise you, Richard, you try anything and it's the last you'll see of her.'

'I'll fight for custody. The court would find you an unfit mother.'

'Don't try it, Richard,' the green eyes flashed menacingly.

'I will, Francine. I'm finished.'

'Then I think it's time we had a talk, Richard. You divorce me – I'll take the child. No court will give her to you for the simple reason, Richard my pet, that she isn't yours.' Francine's shrill laugh rang out. The agonised surprise on Richard's face seemed to whip her into even greater paroxysms of mirth.

'That's not true.'

'Oh, isn't it? Who should know better than me?'

'You bitch.'

'Yes, I suppose I am.' She looked closely at her long nails as if only partially interested in this conversation. 'So, who's going to tell Polly you're not her daddy then? Um? Shall I? . . . I can just imagine how I'll play the scene.'

Richard wanted this obscene conversation to stop and knew that it would not; knew with a strange clarity that he was trapped in this marriage for ever; knew that if he hit her again he might just end up killing her.

'I'd close your mouth if I were you, Richard. It makes you look like a dying fish. God, you bore me.'

'Why stay with me then, Francine?' He tried to stay calm.

'It suits me. I want to be Lady Frobisher when your old man pegs it. Oh yes, being married to you has done wonders for my career . . . being a lady will help even more and I don't intend to give that up lightly.'

He turned from her and looked into the fire, his shoulders slumped with defeat. 'All right Francine. You've played your cards brilliantly. You knew I would never do anything to hurt Polly. I've only your word I'm not her father and it's irrelevant. I love her, that's all that matters to me. So, you win, no divorce – but for your daughter's sake be discreet. And for God's sake, Francine, try to come and see the child more frequently.'

'I don't promise anything, Richard. All I can promise you is that I'll die your wife . . .'

'Who is her father?'

'Ha! Wouldn't you like to know? I'm not telling you. You can just spend the rest of your life wondering who, of all the men I've known, succeeded where you failed.' Her harsh laugh rang out obscenely, cutting through the tension in the room. 'Now I'm tired – it's been a long day. I've a hair appointment tomorrow in London. I'm off to bed. And do me a favour, Richard – don't creep in – your attempts at lovemaking are so unutterably tedious.'

She picked up her fur and with effortless style walked from the room, her fragile beauty seeming to belie the recent scene.

Richard poured himself another large whisky, he was shaking. For the first time in his life he wished somebody dead.

He remembered the young man he had been – so in love, so smitten . . . but Francine had not changed. Francine had always been the same . . . he had been blinded by love and her beauty and now he had to try to live the rest of his life with the consequences.

He downed the drink in one gulp, switched off the lights and climbed the stairs. Quietly he let himself into Polly's room. From the glow of the landing light he looked down on the sleeping child, her dark curls on the pillow, the features already beginning to suggest the strong-faced woman she would one day become. He touched her face gently with his finger. Her eyes opened, she looked at him dazed with sleep.

'Hello Daddy, what's the time?'

'Sorry I woke you, Polly. I just wanted to see you and tell you I love you.'

'That's nice. I love you too.' Polly turned over and went back to sleep immediately.

3

Lincoln had said nothing for the past five minutes. The atmosphere in the room was tense. They were in the study of his New York house, which he often used as an office instead of his official one in the Wakefield building, down town. He sat in the large, ornate, gilt chair which had come from Italy and which, he had been assured, had once belonged to a pope. Across the wide desk – a desk he had had made with the specific instructions that it should be twice as wide as any normal desk – the two men were beginning to sweat; the younger of the two, who had been doing most of the talking, had finally lapsed into silence. The clock on the mantel shelf ticked the silence away. Outside on Fifth Avenue the traffic rumbled by, its sound muted by the thick glass of the windows and the heavy velvet drapes.

Lincoln made a steeple of his fingers, nodded his leonine head, studied the two men through eyes so heavily lidded that they could not be certain he was looking directly at them – and still he said nothing.

This was the moment that Lincoln liked best in a negotiation – the testing of nerves. To an inexperienced businessman, it might have seemed that the two men opposite had offered all the goodies they had – the percentages, the halves of a quarter, the quarters of a quarter, the expenses, the profit forecasts, the interest rates. He was fully aware that they had laboured over these calculations for weeks, maybe months, before approaching him for what he had and they had not – money. But Lincoln was skilled in negotiations and knew full well that still lurking in their briefcases, noted on a slip of paper to be used only as a last resort, or wedged in their brains, were further irresistible slivers of percentages that, if he won the battle of wills in which he was now engaged, would be his.

He knew that whoever broke the silence would be the loser. And he was pretty certain that these two hicks were unaware of that fact. The sweat on their faces was more visible now – not much longer.

A car braked outside on the avenue, its tyres squealed, followed by the angry hooting of a dozen horns. The men from California swung round in their chairs and stared at the window. Lincoln did not even blink, his fingers remained in their steeple shape, his large body was immobile and almost threatening in its stillness.

'Well, perhaps we could come to a better arrangement over distribution, Mr Wakefield,' the older of the two men said suddenly, finally unnerved by the silence. Lincoln raised one eyebrow questioningly.

'Say . . . forty per cent.'

Lincoln watched the trickle of sweat roll down the over-indulged face of Bob Zimmerman. He had them – the jump in percentage was too big, they were panicking. He waited another twenty seconds before collapsing the steeple of his hands. It was as if the other two had stopped breathing. He spread his hands on the desk and appeared to study them.

'I don't think so, Mr Zimmerman. I see rather ten per cent interest on the loan and fifty-five per cent overall.'

'I like the ten per cent but the fifty-five . . . ?'

Lincoln shrugged his shoulders. 'The alternative is twenty-five per cent interest and your forty per cent.'

'But Mr Wakefield,' they said in unison.

'That's too high,' Zimmerman blustered.

'It's hardly fair,' said the other.

The steeple was reformed. The clock ticked. They were once again surveyed from beneath the hooded lids. He knew they had no choice, they had had no choice the moment they had walked through his door. Lincoln knew everything that happened in this city. He knew which banks these two had approached, which financiers had turned them down. He was fully aware that because of his hard reputation, he was their last resort. There was no one left with the sort of money these two needed.

It was all a game to Lincoln. He had his fortune in four distinct categories. There was his great food empire which now spread all over America – there wasn't an American table that did not have his sauces and pickles on it. Then there was his real estate which also reached right across this great country and was so diversified that his family would never want for anything. And then there was the fortune he played with. The stock market to Lincoln was a playground. Others had their entire fortunes invested in stocks and bonds but Lincoln saw that as a fool's way.

Buoyant as the market was and easy as it was to make money there, Lincoln did not trust it. He saw himself as a wild courageous knight making sudden forays into the market where his actions caused jubilation or despondency. And finally there was what he called his indulgence money – little ventures on which he embarked just for the fun of it. Where other men would have a flutter on horses or at the cardtable, Lincoln gambled on businesses. Over the years, with his unerring instinct, not one of his gambles had let him down. He had already decided before Zimmerman and his sidekick appeared in his life, that this year his play would be the motion picture business – there were fortunes to be made and to be lost in this industry. He liked the smell, the uncertainty of it.

The making of films did not interest him, only the business of making money from them. He never went to the theatre let alone to the moving picture theatres. The sight of grown men and women leaping about a stage pretending to be someone else had always struck him as ridiculous in the extreme. And for them to do the same as flickering shadows on a stretched, white sheet took the whole thing to incredible lengths.

However he had made a point of walking past the many motion picture houses that had sprung up and had noted the queues snaking along the sidewalk for several blocks, impatient to be admitted. He had seen society women, businessmen, shop assistants and servants all standing in line. He could not understand why they should choose to stand in the cold, dirty air but could smell a profit lurking there when they did.

'You've got us over a barrel, Mr Wakefield.'

Lincoln allowed them a warm smile across the expanse of the desk. Now he had almost won he could afford to be pleasant.

'I tell you what, fellows. It's a big decision for you and you won't want to be rushing into anything. Today's Wednesday, my wife and myself would be honoured if you would join us at my Dart Island estate on Friday for the weekend. Then, if you've made your minds up, we can work the details out. And if you decide against me,' he spread his hands wide, an innocent expression on his face. 'Why, we can just have a pleasant weekend – no point in business interfering with pleasure, wouldn't you say?'

With satisfaction he saw the men relax and beam at him. He'd won.

Alice was quite resigned to the weekend being an extension of Lincoln's working week. It was rare for them not to entertain at weekends – always business associates of Lincoln's. She did not resent them; what she did resent was having to entertain the frequently boring wives who were her responsibility.

They were never alone these days. In fact she could go for days without seeing Lincoln, except in bed. During the day she led her own life, supervising their homes, visiting museums, art galleries, reading. She still had her consultant's role in the catering business which she had created all those years ago when she had found herself alone and disinherited in New York. But these days she was called upon less and less often. During the week Lincoln rarely required her assistance to help entertain in the city so she frequently dined alone. She would have liked to go to the opera or theatre on these solitary evenings but she knew that Lincoln would never have sanctioned it. So she would wait for him, and if she were lucky he might tell her, before they fell asleep, what he had been doing. Twice a week, as regular as a clock, he possessed her but the joy had long gone out of it for her. She responded to him out of a sense of duty.

This weekend she was pleased to find there were only two guests who, since they were from California, had left their womenfolk back in the West. She would have time to herself to walk by the sea, maybe paint a little.

'Grandma, is it true?' Juniper was racing along the wide

corridor towards her. She was nine now, small for her age, but more beautiful than ever.

'What, my darling?'

'That Grandpa is going to make moving pictures?'

'Darling, I don't know.'

'One of the maids told me.'

'Ah well, if one of the maids told you, it is undoubtedly true,' Alice said with a gentle smile.

'Maybe we'll be going to California, that's where they make them now. Gosh, it's so exciting. Maybe we'll meet Mary Pickford, maybe she'll invite us to luncheon.'

'Calm down, darling. You don't know for sure . . . And don't say "gosh!"'

'I'm going to ask him the minute he arrives.'

'You do that, Juniper, then perhaps you'll let me know.' She smiled indulgently as the child raced back along the corridor.

Alice let herself into her own suite of rooms to bathe and dress, for the guests were due in two hours. She felt suddenly despondent. If the child was right and they were going to visit California then once again she would have to give up all idea of a trip to England this year. It would be six years since she had last been home to Gwenfer. Her feelings of homesickness for the place never left her. Once she had suggested that she go alone. Lincoln's temper had been so great that it was not a suggestion she ever dared make again.

Alice knew that it was not only business which kept Lincoln in America. So great was Lincoln's hatred for Marshall that he refused to be on the same continent as the man, let alone in the same country.

Alice still did not know exactly what the argument had been about, nor why Juniper now lived permanently with them. She had asked, even demanded, to be told, but all Lincoln would admit was that Marshall had done something so unspeakable that he could not tell her what it was. Nor was Grace any more forthcoming in her letters.

Alice hated to be patronised in such a way. she had experienced much in her life; she doubted if she could be as shocked as her husband supposed.

Alice was left with a deep anger towards her husband, an anger that had marred their relationship in the past three years. Without consulting her, he had deprived her of half her family. She was angry that Lincoln had created for Juniper the same unhappy situation that she had suffered – a childhood without parents. The conclusion she had tried hard not to reach was that this was exactly what Lincoln had wanted all along – to have Juniper for himself. Sometimes she feared that his infatuation with the child was dangerous and harmful to them all.

Secretly, Alice wrote to Grace and enclosed letters from Juniper. She could not risk their replies being delivered to the house so she had Grace write to her poste restante. She found it ironic that Grace, who had so hated Cornwall, should now be living there – and how she envied her.

Persuading Lincoln to allow them to live at Boscar Manor had been her only triumph in the whole sorry mess. Lincoln would have preferred Marshall to be homeless, to have him and his parents evicted, but Alice had prevailed upon him at least to allow her daughter a roof over her head.

Alice still had some income from her catering firm and now that Grace's large income from her father had stopped Alice sent what money she could afford. Even then she had to be careful, she could not send as much as she wanted. Lincoln, suspicious that this was exactly what she would do, had taken to checking her accounts and bank statements. It enraged Alice that she had no privacy in her affairs but he had the right to do so and there was nothing, no argument, no pleading which would dissuade him.

In the face of Lincoln's attitude, Alice had become dishonest. She had discovered a dressmaker who could copy clothes for a quarter of the couture price. Alice had cut the couturier labels out of her old clothes and in case Lincoln took to snooping in her wardrobe had sewn them into the new; the money she saved she sent to Grace. She resented being made to behave dishonestly. She resented being spied upon. And she was angry with herself for allowing this disintegration of her family to occur.

Juniper, after an immediate period of grief, had adjusted well to her parents' absence. Perhaps the pain was less because she was used to spending so much time with her grandparents. But Alice knew the whole situation was wrong. Whatever Marshall had done no one had the right to deprive the child of contact with her mother and father.

It was not surprising that, these days, Alice frequently found herself wondering what had happened to the Lincoln she had married twenty-four years ago.

An hour later she entered the long salon whose floor-length windows opened on to the wide lawns that swept down to the sea.

'Gentlemen, I hope you're comfortable in your rooms?' she said politely. The two men turned from the window where they had been studying the view and advanced, smiling, towards her. Alice felt the room close in on her until she seemed to be looking down a long tunnel – approaching her was Chas Cordell, the father of her child.

4

Chas Cordell advanced across the room with hand outstretched and with a broad smile on his face. He was half-way across when his step wavered. In front of him stood a tall woman. Her hair, which once must have been very blonde, was still fair and styled in a heavy chignon in which small diamonds glistened. Chas approved: he liked long hair and did not favour the new cropped hair styles which, in his opinion did nothing for women but make them look like men. She wore a soft grey, chiffon dress, low waisted as fashion dictated and from which tiers of fabric fell to the floor. When she moved Chas was reminded of waves rippling. The grey of the material complemented the colour of her eyes, the finest feature in a face whose delicate bones cast exquisite shadows on skin devoid of make-up. Chas admired what he saw. For him there was nothing more pleasing than the beauty of a mature woman: not for him the obsession of his friends with young starlets who were more like children than women. Around her neck she had twisted a long string of pearls; suddenly her hand shot up to them and nervously she began to play with them. With this gesture Chas experienced a strong feeling of déjà vu – of being in a ballroom in England many years ago and seeing a beautiful debutante, her hand at the pearls on her neck . . .

Chas stopped dead in his tracks. Good God, he thought, she must be at least fifty and yet, if anything, she was more beautiful than he remembered her. His mouth began to form the word *Alice*.

'Mrs Wakefield?' his companion, Bob, said, advancing with hand outstretched. 'Might I introduce myself. I'm Bob Zimmerman and this is my associate, Chas Cordell.'

'Mr Zimmerman, Mr Cordell, welcome . . .' she said with only the trace of a tremor in her voice as she shook their hands in turn. Chas felt the years slip away; he suddenly felt young again.

'I expect you would like a drink,' she said, grateful for the social niceties behind which she could hide her confusion. But, as she reached for the bell pull to summon the butler, her hand fumbled with the cord. She was frightened by the way her heart had lurched at sight of this man from her past, a man she should despise and hate. Instead, she found her heart betraying her, and felt an intense excitement within her – a sensation once so familiar but which she had not experienced for many years.

Unnecessarily she pulled the bell again – it was something to do. She was afraid of such feelings. She would have liked to run from the room, from the house, across the lawns to the safety of the shore. But she forced herself to turn and face them. Somehow, she never knew how, she began to make polite conversation. They discussed the weather. She answered their questions on England. She accepted their admiration of the gardens, the views . . . when all the time she longed to ask if he were married, how many children he had, was he happy . . . ?

She feared Lincoln's arrival lest, in some way, she betray herself. Regularly, over the years, he had tried to find out the name of the man who had deserted her; always she had refused to tell, fearing what Lincoln was capable of towards someone he regarded as a mortal enemy. And yet, when the door opened and he entered the room, she felt nothing but relief as her husband, as always, took control of the social situation.

She excused herself and hurried from the room in search of Juniper. She had to find her and prevent her, somehow, from joining them. Sometimes, bursting with pride, Lincoln liked to show off his granddaughter to guests even though Juniper often complained that it was 'boring'. Chas must never meet Juniper, she thought, just in case somewhere in her face, unbeknown to Alice, was a likeness to his own family. It was imperative he never knew of Juniper's existence.

As she raced up the stairs she was full of real fear. Whatever business Chas was trying to arrange would cease if Lincoln found out the truth. Not only would her husband's past anger towards Chas flare up again, but Alice knew that Lincoln could not allow Juniper's true grandfather into her life – his jealousy would be awesome and a dangerous thing.

When she found Juniper it was to discover that the child was running a slight fever. Alice felt ashamed of her relief as she packed her off to bed with a light supper and turned on her heel to return to the ordeal ahead.

The dinner was the longest of her life. Each time Chas

looked at her, Alice had quickly to look away. Once, she allowed her own eyes to linger and she had found herself blushing. She was so nervous that during the meal she knocked over a glass of wine, dropped her spoon, lost her napkin, and twice forgot to ring for Septimus. As the meal progressed, she convinced herself that Lincoln was watching her carefully, which only made her more edgy.

At last the meal was over and she could leave the men to their port and brandy. She stood up and in her haste knocked her chair backward. Muttering her apologies she hurried from the room. She was half-way across the hall when she heard Lincoln call her. She turned slowly to face him, her heart thudding.

'Alice, what is the matter with you? Are you unwell?'

'I'm very tired, Lincoln.'

'I trust you've not caught Juniper's fever?'

Yes, she thought, she could use that as an excuse. She put her hand to her forehead, it was ice cold. She could not lie. What if he insisted on feeling her brow to see how hot it was? 'No, no, Lincoln, I've no temperature, I'm just very tired.'

'Then go to bed, my dear. My guests and I will only be talking business.' He kissed her on the cheek and Alice, longing to run up the stairs but conscious he was watching her, walked sedately up the long staircase. But she was filled with such guilt at her deception that it was as if, already, she had been unfaithful to him. At such a thought her hand shot up to her pearls, she stumbled and had to hold the banister for support. What on earth had made her think such a thing? How stupidly she was behaving; she must pull herself together.

'Goodnight, Lincoln,' she forced herself to call down to him, where he still stood watching her progress up the stairs.

She did not sleep well that night and at one point slipped quietly from their bed. She wrapped herself in a fur stole and sat a long time in a chair by the window waiting for the winter dawn to break. She wanted to collect her thoughts, retrieve some sanity. Instead, she found herself remembering the past, the weekend at Bear Mountain when she had willingly given Chas her virginity and Grace had been conceived. Of course, everyone thought she had been seduced, but that was not the case: innocent as she was, she had welcomed what happened to her. She could not forget the happiness of that period in her life and found she did not wish to. Not for the first time she wondered how different her life might have been. She should have been thinking of her husband but as the dawn broke, she had hardly given him a thought.

In the morning she was genuinely tired and it was the easiest thing to get Lincoln to insist that she stay in bed and rest. She could not remember the last time she had had a whole day in bed. It should have been a treat, but instead she spent the day in fretful guilt worrying about her reaction to Chas.

On Sunday, she forced herself to come downstairs; it would have been too rude not to be on hand to say farewell to the guests. Over lunch they made polite conversation again. Alice found she was less nervous. Lincoln was behaving normally: she must have over-reacted the other night. Chas was being very discreet and had obviously given nothing away. She could ask now how the business meeting had gone. She could smile and congratulate Chas and his partner when they told her, with beaming pride, that Lincoln had agreed to finance their new film studios. Since everything Lincoln touched turned to gold, it was only a matter of time before Chas was what he had always longed to be, a rich man – the thought made her strangely happy.

She joined in enthusiastically as plans were made for their trip to California in two months' time. She smiled indulgently at Lincoln when they told her the name of their new company – *Juniper Productions*, JP for short.

Alice was relaxed, was her normal self again.

Finally they stood in the hallway saying their goodbyes. In a few moments he would be gone from her life again, she would feel safe once more.

'It's been such a pleasure meeting you, Mr Cordell,' she said with her hostess's smile.

'It's been an honour, Mrs Wakefield.' He made a half bow over her extended hand, his own hand took hers to shake it. With a start Alice felt a small, crisp, folded note pressed in to her palm.

5

'I really should not be here, Chas,' Alice said, looking anxiously around the entrance hall of the fashionable hotel, worried that she might see someone she knew amongst the crowds.

'Thank you for coming, Alice. I realise the risk to you. The last thing I want is to compromise you in any way, but I had to see you before I left.' He took hold of her elbow and the pleasurable feeling she felt at his touch alarmed her, as he steered her towards the elevator.

She walked as if mesmerised. When she had read the note which he had pressed into her hand she had felt fear, elation and anger. Fear that Lincoln would find out; elation that Chas wanted to see her privately; and anger that he should presume she would even deign to see him after the way he had behaved. To her shame, elation had won the battle in her mind.

'Where are we going?' she whispered in the elevator so that the operator would not hear.

'I've a suite.'

'Oh, Chas. I don't think . . .'

The machine stopped. Taking her arm again he propelled her rapidly along the corridor. She walked with head down, frightened of the prying eyes of other guests. He opened the door of his suite and ushered her in.

In the doorway she paused. 'Chas, I still think . . .' she began before it was too late and the door was closed.

'Alice, where else can we talk?' The public rooms are too dangerous for you, undoubtedly you would be seen. I'm not known in this city, but you must be. I thought it best here, in my rooms, I don't want to make trouble for you with your husband.'

'He would ruin you.'

'I realise that.'

'If he knew I was here he would . . .'

Gently he placed a finger on her lips to stop her. 'Darling, don't even think about it. He won't know, don't worry.'

She looked at him, her large grey eyes full of fear, but her senses reeling at his use of the endearment. She stepped forward. The door closed.

'I wrote, Alice, to the hotel we stayed in but my letters were sent back to me.' She looked at him, studying his face intently, the face she had so often conjured up from her memories, studying it for a sign that he spoke the truth. 'And I returned. A year later. I searched for you.'

'Did you? she said uncertainly, allowing him to lead her to the couch.

'No one knew where you had gone, I tried all our friends, all our old haunts. Most thought you must have returned to England. All the same, I put adverts in all the papers that I thought you might read.'

She laughed a short, mirthless laugh. 'I did not have money for newspapers.'

'What happened? I have to know. The thought of you alone in this city haunted me for years.'

She looked at him steadily. Yes, she would tell him, he should know how she had suffered, the poverty, the degradation. So at length she told him of the tenement, of the rats, of her hunger, of her terror alone at nights listening to the sounds of violence in the streets below. As her tale progressed his expression changed from guilt to anguish – she was glad he suffered. And then she paused, shocked at herself for feeling such bitterness. So, she began to tell him of her cooking, of the business she had created, how well she had done. And she found she was pleased to see him smile with relief. But she did not tell him of Grace nor of Juniper. Of them, she knew she must never speak.

Then it was his turn; she too needed to know.

'Why, Chas? Why did you disappear that night so abruptly, so cruelly? How could you leave me?'

'Fear, Alice, I'm ashamed to admit. Fear and panic. You remember the legacy from my aunt?' She nodded. 'Every cent had gone. I was fearful of being sent to jail and I was too ashamed to tell you the truth. You had left your country, your father disowned you, all because I promised you a good life with me, and I had let you down disastrously. I just hoped and prayed that you would have enough money to pay the hotel bill.'

'And it didn't matter if I went to prison?'

'I knew you wouldn't go to prison – you were too well-connected. But my God, Alice, please try to imagine the guilt I've felt over the years, for putting you at risk. I hated myself for what I had done.'

'If you had no money, then how did you get the ticket to go to California?' she asked suspiciously.

'That evening, when I left you, I went downstairs for a stiff drink. God, I needed that drink – I still remember it. In the bar I met an old friend who had a train ticket he did not want. He let me have it on the promise that I would pay him back as soon as I could. Somehow it seemed that fate had taken over, that I was meant to go, that I was no longer in control of what was happening. It all seemed so simple, too. I would go West, make money and send for you as soon as possible. And I did write all this to you, but you had left.'

'And what about the wife whom you forgot to tell me

about?' Alice managed to say but the words emerged stiltedly and her face felt stiff as wood as she asked.

'I should have told you.'

'Yes, Chas, you should have done.'

'I worked in San Francisco doing . . .'

'I was asking about your wife.'

'I did not tell you because, as you found out, I was hoping for a divorce. It had never been a proper marriage, we'd never lived together. It was the result of a stupid, drunken, student prank when I was at Yale.'

'Your friend Delaware . . .' she interrupted, but he held his hand up to silence her.

'Please, Alice, let me finish. I admit I had hoped to keep the divorce a secret, sort it out somehow. But when I saw him a year later Delaware confessed he had let the cat out of the bag. Six months after I left you, my wife was killed in a fire . . .'

'Oh, Chas, no,' Alice's voice sounded like a sad wail.

'Funny isn't it? No doubt you would never have married me as a divorced man and there I was a respectable widower but I couldn't find you. Well, anyway, for a year I worked my butt off, doing anything I could find. I saved every cent I could and by the end of the first year I had enough for a deposit on a house. It was very small but I didn't think you would mind that, you'd always said you would like a simple life . . .' He smiled at the memory. 'So, as I said, I came back to New York and it was as if you had disappeared off the planet. I was beside myself with worry, I searched this city like a madman. I returned to California. I drifted a bit after that, there didn't seem much point in anything for a long while. But then I pulled myself together. I got a job in real estate and now, as you know, for the past five years I've been learning the movie-making business. Life is good now, I've money, a nice home.'

'I'm glad,' she said with genuine pleasure. 'And are you married?'

'I'm afraid so, for the past fourteen years.' He looked down as if ashamed, as if in marrying he had betrayed her again.

'And children?'

'Four sons, but sadly no daughter.'

That was the worst moment for Alice, when she had to fight with herself not to tell him he most certainly did have a daughter, and a granddaughter. 'Don't look so ashamed. Why should you not be married? I am,' she said instead.

'Are you safe with him, Alice?'

'Safe? What an extraordinary thing to say. Of course I'm safe with him, he's been very good to me . . .'

'But he's ruthless.'

She laughed. 'I'm not one of his businesses, I'm his wife. There is a difference.'

'But I heard he had packed his daughter off to Europe and cut her off without a penny . . . and that you don't see her any more.'

'That's none of your business, Chas. Lincoln had his reasons.'

'Oh, Alice, it *is* my business. You don't understand. When I saw you at Dart Island and realised you were his wife, I felt so afraid for you. I wanted to take you away from him so badly.'

'Chas!' Her eyes widened with alarm.

'I never stopped loving you, Alice, not for one minute of one day.' He took her hand and gently lifted it to his mouth and kissed it. She snatched it away and moved further along the couch.

'Chas, please . . .'

'Those months we had together and that last weekend when you finally gave yourself to me. All those memories have haunted me over the years.' He slid along the couch towards her. 'What have we lost, my darling, what have we lost?'

'But your wife . . . ?' she said breathlessly, afraid of the happiness his words were giving her and clinging desperately to the fact that he was married, as if that state of affairs could preserve her sanity.

'I love my wife, she's a good woman. But never as I loved you, Alice. It's never been as it was with you. I want you, Alice, I need you.'

'Oh, Chas,' she sighed as his arms wound about her and she felt his lips on hers and found her own lips parting of their own accord. Yes, this was how it should be, she thought, as she felt her body moulding to his.

'Come,' he said softly and taking her hand helped her to her feet and led her to a door. He opened it, revealing the bedroom beyond. She stopped dead, her eyes seeing only the large bed, and a look of horror spread over her face at the step she was contemplating.

'Chas, we can't, it would be wrong.'

'How could it be wrong when we have loved each other all these years? We are meant for each other . . .'

'No! It cannot be. We're married to other people,' she cried out. 'How could you even imagine that I would . . .' She turned on her heel and raced from the room, and from Chas. She did not wait for the elevator but ran down the endless flights of stairs. Rapidly she wove her way across the busy foyer and hurtled down the steps of the hotel still propelled by a sense of panic at what she could so easily have done.

So quickly did she move, so engrossed was she in her own thoughts that she did not see her husband alighting from his motor car outside the hotel.

Two days later Chas Cordell was dead.

6

Alice began to shake uncontrollably as she read the morning newspaper report. Nausea and dizziness followed quickly. She stumbled to the window, threw it open, and leaning against the sill she took deep breaths, determined not to faint. Below her the rush-hour traffic of Fifth Avenue inched and lurched its tortuous way. Each day, at this time, exhaust fumes fouled the air. The unpleasant smell usually made her long to be on Dart Island in the clear, clean air, but this morning she did not even notice.

Dazed, she moved back into the room and, because of the tremor in her hands, had difficulty pouring herself a cup of black coffee. The liquid spurted over the clean, monogrammed tray cloth. Careful housewife that she normally was, she failed to observe the spreading stain.

She slumped into a chair and reread the report in case she had made some dreadful, inexplicable mistake. She had not. The headlines stated baldly that Chas was dead, found the night before at his hotel, drowned in his bath.

But why hadn't Lincoln told her? Why had he not come when her maid woke me to break the news to her himself? Always up and about by six, he would already have been up for a couple of hours and would, as usual, have read the papers while he took the solitary breakfast which he preferred.

She sat looking into space . . . unless, of course, he wanted her to find out this way, wanted her to be shocked. And if he did, there could only be one reason – that he had found out about her relationship with Chas all that time ago.

This idea angered her. Such cruelty enraged her. She must find out. Quickly she put on her robe and, still shocked, felt almost as if she were floating as she made her way down the stairs to Lincoln's study.

She found him sitting at his large desk, beside him a pile of newspapers, roughly folded as if recently read. He was studying a document, pen in hand, and making alterations to it.

'Have you seen this?' she found herself asking, unnecessarily given the newspapers beside him.

'Terrible, isn't it? Why, imagine, I had lunch with him only a couple of days ago. He was right as rain then. At least we should be grateful he had signed the agreements on Juniper Productions . . .'

'Lincoln, how could you think of business at a time like this?' Her distress was patent in her voice.

'Easily, it's what makes me a success,' he said. 'But at a time like what Alice?'

'He was a friend of yours.'

'I would not care to call him my friend. A business acquaintance merely. You can hardly expect to find me grieving.' He laughed, at least his mouth opened and a noise which sounded like a laugh emerged but there was no mirth to it, no jollity. It was a chilling sound.

'But, I don't understand. It seems very strange to me,' and she stabbed the paper with a shaking finger. She was finding difficulty in speaking as if a tight band was compressing her chest.

'Death frequently is strange, especially when it's least expected. You seem to be mighty upset?'

'Of course I'm upset. I knew him, he was a friend.' The paper rustled in her hands like dried leaves and she felt tears begin to form in her eyes.

'Well, hardly, my dear. A friend? After one dinner and one luncheon? I did not know that you cared to make friends that easily. I had always thought you were far more discriminating. Why, you can hardly say you knew him.' He smiled up at her, but it was not a loving or pleasant smile, rather a quizzical one with no warmth to it, empty as his laugh had been. The dizziness returned and she sat down hard on the chair opposite him.

'He seemed a very pleasant man,' she said faintly.

'Oh, I agree, extremely pleasant. And handsome too, I suppose – to women.' She was aware of him looking at her. She did not return the gaze but looked down at her hands which, she found to her alarm, were still shaking. 'I should imagine he was very handsome as a young man.

The all-American guy, wouldn't you say? Beefy, blond and blue eyed. The kind of man whom silly women would fall head over heels in love with. Don't you agree?'

Only a fool would have not realised that Lincoln was playing a game with her. A cruel and frightening game. Alarmed, she felt a tear begin to roll down her cheek, and surreptitiously she tried to wipe it away, knowing her tears would confirm his suspicions. She heard his chair scrape as he stood up and walked around the desk to her side.

'Tears? Tut tut, Alice. I fear your reaction is somewhat extreme,' and from his pocket he handed her a large white handkerchief with which she wiped her eyes. 'But then, perhaps your tears are because you really did know him.'

At first she could not look at him but was aware that he was sitting on his desk, his long legs stretched out in front of him, brushing her robe. He said nothing. Finally she slowly raised her head to see him, arms folded across his chest. With relief she saw that her fear had been unnecessary for on his face was a kindly expression. The look lulled her, common sense took over. Why should he be angry, there was nothing to be angry about. She had over-reacted, no doubt from shock. There seemed little point in his not knowing now. He could no longer harm Chas.

'Yes, Lincoln, I knew him. He was Grace's father, but you knew that didn't you?'

'I did.'

'How long have you known?'

'My dear, I'm a clever man but not psychic. Only this past weekend when you behaved so strangely. Then I began to suspect.'

'Because I was tired?' she said with disbelief.

'Not tired my dear, shall we say avoiding someone? And then I thought, why? They were both pleasant enough and well mannered so it could not be their personalities. I came to the conclusion it was because they were from California. Now why, I thought, what is it about Californians upsets my dear wife so? And of course I remembered, that's where the bastard who deserted you had scuttled, lacking the guts to face you. It could not have been Zimmerman, I knew the man in your life was an Episcopalian not a Jew – it was simple.' He said almost proudly, 'Of course I checked, and I was right.'

'I behaved stupidly. I feared your anger.'

'You were wise to do so.'

'But he did not matter any more.'

'It mattered very much to me, Alice.'

'But it was all so long ago.'

'Your visit to him on Monday was not so long ago.'

She knew she looked at him with horror etched on her face. She realised that her very reaction to his words made denial impossible. 'You knew?'

'You're not very good at committing adultery, Alice, one has to be far more discreet than you were.'

'Oh, Lincoln, my poor darling. You didn't think that, did you? What torment you must have been in.' She put out her hand to touch him, to reassure him, but he moved his arm away from contact with her. 'Lincoln, nothing happened, you have to believe me. I was there less than an hour.'

'A lot can happen in an hour.' The expression in his eyes was so cold that for the first time Alice felt real fear.

'It was foolish of me to go there, I realise, but I wanted to talk to him.'

'What about? What, after all this time, could you possibly want to talk over with him? Did you want to tell him how much you had missed him, how much you still loved him, eh? Was that it?'

She wished he would shout, she found the calm, almost conversational, tone of his voice alarming.

'We did not speak of such things,' she said, her voice shaky with emotion. She looked away quickly to avoid his gaze. Never one to lie, she found it the hardest thing to do.

'Oh, Alice,' he laughed a mirthless laugh which fuelled her fear like kindling. 'After what happened in the past am I expected to believe that you spoke of the weather, the latest play? I'd prefer you didn't insult my intelligence quite so blatantly. I wish to know what you spoke of.'

Alice remained silent. Hers was not a wilful silence: she simply had no idea what to say. Her mind was in a turmoil of panic. Suddenly he grabbed her wrist and twisted it. There was a burning sensation and a sharp pain shot up her arm. She grimaced but no words would form: it was as if her mouth was paralysed. He twisted her wrist again and bent her arm back. At last she cried out.

'What did you talk about?' he said very slowly between clenched teeth.

'He told me where he had been . . . his jobs . . . his wife . . . his children . . .' Tears of pain were pouring down her face.

'And?' Further back he wrenched her arm.

'I told him about the bakery . . .' she sobbed. 'About meeting you . . .' He bent her arm back further so that now her body was contorted forward as she tried to relieve the pain. 'All right,' she gasped. The pain eased a little. 'I asked him why he had deserted me. Please, Lincoln, you will break my arm.'

'What about Grace? Did you mention her or Juniper?'

'I didn't tell him. I thought it was better he should not know,' she managed to shout this time, pain giving her voice substance.

He dropped her arm. 'That was very sensible of you, Alice. The only sensible thing.' He let go of her and resumed his seat on his desk.

'It wouldn't have mattered if I had, would it? He's dead now, he can do nothing.'

'Exactly.'

She did not know what made her realise the truth. Whether it was the smug way he said, 'Exactly', or whether it was the equally self-satisfied smile. But suddenly she knew – Lincoln had killed him. And she also knew he wanted her to know, as if he were proud of himself.

'You?' She did not say the word but rather exhaled it and clutched at her throat, but this morning there were no pearls there to comfort her. 'You!' she repeated with mounting horror.

He bowed sardonically. 'Me.'

'But why?' her voice came in a barely audible whisper.

'I did not like him.'

'But that's no reason to kill a man.'

'Don't be melodramatic, Alice. I did not kill him.'

She felt herself slump back in the seat with relief. 'Oh, thank God for that.'

'I had him killed. There is a difference.'

With the speed of an express train the horror returned. The walls of the room appeared to be flexing, as if made of rubber, or like distorting mirrors at a fairground. His voice came as if from a long way down a tunnel. He was speaking to her but she could not take in what he said for her brain seemed incapable of interpreting the sounds.

'Please tell me this is all a nightmare,' she interrupted him, only to hear him laugh. With horrified and rapid comprehension she realised that because of her a man had died. Because of her a woman was widowed, her children fatherless. That she should be the cause of such sorrow, such injustice appalled her. She had already felt anger, fear, horror. Now anger returned, great waves of fierce rage at his arrogance, at his inhumanity. She stood up abruptly and faced him, her eyes not lowered now but meeting his stare, unwavering. Her large eyes which had been diminished by fear now sparkled with fury. 'But, he was innocent, we did nothing. How could you do it?'

'My dear, Alice, I have only your word. And I have to ask myself what sort of a woman would visit a man in his hotel room?'

'Because we did not want to be seen. He was afraid I could be compromised.'

'Precisely. Now, why would you not wish to be seen by our friends and acquaintances? I'm afraid the conclusion is very obvious to me.'

She shuddered. If he had killed Chas from jealous fury then why was she still alive, why was she not lying cold in a coffin? Unless he had not finished with her yet? Again her hand went to her neck, her fingers flexing, as if her habitual pearls were there.

'I swear to you on everything sacred to me, I did not commit adultery.'

'I did not kill him because of you. Oh no. He might have found out about Juniper, and that would never have done.'

Alice's shoulders slumped. She looked at her husband and saw a cruel ruthless man, perhaps known to others, but whom she was seeing for the first time. He was mad. In that moment she knew she had to leave, that she would never again be safe, that neither of them would be able to trust the other ever again. There would never be a moment's happiness with him if she stayed.

The decision made her mind clear. He must not know she was going, he would force her to stay. She must get out of this room, pack her cases and somehow slip out with Juniper without his knowing.

She looked him straight in the eyes. 'I don't believe you, Lincoln, I think you are being melodramatic,' she said in her best, haughty English manner. She turned and with heart thumping and terror stalking her she walked from the room.

In her bedroom, she locked the door and then, with difficulty, manhandled a heavy chest in front of it. As she packed, she planned.

She would go to England, to Gwenfer. She would be safest there: any strangers, any assassins would be quickly noticeable in such a sparsely populated place. Her own people would guard her. She paused in her packing horrified at the way her mind was working – assassins, such dramatics! Surely he would not . . . she was panicking, over-reacting. But she did not know, she could never be certain – ever again.

She threw open the large closets, looked at the furs, the long line of evening wear and decided that she would not need them where she was going. She could carry one case; she would have to pack only sensible clothes. From her jewel case she took only her engagement ring and reluctantly replaced the pearls which were almost her trademark. She wanted none of his gifts.

She dialled a number and spoke to an attorney she knew – one who was unconnected with Lincoln's affairs – and instructed him to sell her bakery and catering business for her. She called Cooks and had her first stroke of luck: there was a sailing that night with berths available. She booked a stateroom for herself and Juniper.

Then she stationed herself at the window concealed by the curtains, and watched the steps, waiting for the moment when Lincoln left for a business appointment – which undoubtedly he would. It was an hour before her patience was rewarded and Lincoln appeared and entered his waiting car.

Immediately she removed the barricade from the door and rushed to Lincoln's study. She swung back the large painting that concealed the safe and with surprising dexterity, given the circumstances, twirled the combination lock. She removed her own and Juniper's passports and enough cash for the journey.

Juniper was intrigued by all the haste and excited by the news that they were to travel to England that night. Having dismissed the nursemaid Alice hurriedly packed a small case with clothes for the child and told her to select only those favourite toys which would fit into the bag she gave her.

Wrapped up against the winter chill and the winds

which funnelled through the canyons of skyscrapers, Alice bundled the girl down the stairs. They were opening the door when Lincoln appeared.

'And where do you think you are going?' He glared at Alice. Terrified, she stood speechless.

'We're going to England, Grandpa. Isn't it exciting?'

'You're not going anywhere, Juniper. Go up to your room.'

'No. I don't want to.'

'Go, this minute,' he shouted angrily at her and, shocked by the expression on his face, she ran towards the stairs.

'You bitch!' he swung round to confront Alice. 'You think you can sneak out of here and take my grand-daughter with you.'

'She isn't your granddaughter, Lincoln, she's mine. It's my blood in her veins and she's not staying here with you.'

'Oh, yes she is. I'll kill you rather than lose her. And I mean that, Alice. These are not mere words.'

Alice felt herself swaying and leant against the wall. What choice had she? She could not stay, not now. But Juniper was safe, he would never hurt her. She would have to go and somehow, with the help of her lawyers, she would get the child back later. She turned to the door, her hand on the heavy door knob. She felt her whole body slump. She could not leave the child. How could she even think of such a thing? She turned to face him.

Juniper, her courage returned, had come back down the stairs. She was standing at the foot, watching her grand-parents, a bemused expression on her face.

'Juniper, come with me, now,' Alice called, quickly opening the door and feeling the cold blast of the wind.

'Stay, Juniper,' Lincoln ordered.

The child looked with bewilderment from one adult to the other.

'I beg you, Juniper, don't ask questions, come with me, there's a good girl.'

'I can't leave Grandpa if he doesn't want me to go. I love him, Grandma, more than anyone in the world.'

'See,' Lincoln smiled with the triumph of a man who knows he has won. Courteously he held the door wide open for Alice and gave her a courtly bow.

'I'll fight for her, Lincoln.'

'I shouldn't waste your money, if I were you.'

Alice slipped out of the door, without looking back at the child. The great door slammed shut. Lincoln leant against it, his head bowed for a moment on his arms. Quietly Juniper approached him.

'Grandpa, why has Grandma gone? Why are you angry with her?'

He turned to face the child. 'She doesn't love us any more, Juniper.'

'Oh, Grandpa, I'm sorry.'

'There's just you and me now, Princess.' And he slid to the floor, his large body shook but he made no sound.

Juniper knelt beside him and put her small arms about him. 'Don't be upset, Grandpa. I love you. I'll never leave you, never, never . . .'

Chapter Five

1

The moment Alice walked over the threshold of Gwenfer she felt finally safe and at peace. It was as if the walls of the old building were closing protectively about her. She knew, with certainty, that nothing evil could befall her here.

Her business in New York had been sold quickly and profitably. Knowing that, if she were to survive, she must be careful with her money, she invested it cautiously in safe bonds and shares. Having once known great poverty, she was not frightened by the future. This time she had some money; whereas in the past she had had nothing. Now she was more than fortunate: she had her Gwenfer, a grand roof over her head. She had, however, decided to close a large part of the house. She would use the small parlour at the front and, otherwise, would live at the back in the servants' quarters, just as she had as a child. Mrs Malandine had retired. She kept one maid to help her – Flo, who had worked at the house since she was a child and whom she did not have the heart to sack. She needed little for herself: she had to husband her money for Grace and Gwenfer.

She had hardly been in the house five minutes when Philomel hobbled in, an old woman now, bent from severe arthritis but with a mind as razor sharp as ever. Alice thought it best to tell her old friend her new circumstances right from the start. Philomel was sympathetic and practical. Alice must share her gardener to grow her own vegetables, she must get books on farming to enable her to revitalise the home farm which had been allowed to moulder and die.

Discreetly she let key people in the village know of Alice's newly straitened circumstances. In the following days Alice had a string of visitors bearing gifts – eggs, bread, jam, a duck, chickens, an apple pie. Alice was overwhelmed with their kindness but the village was pleased and proud to be able to pay her back for her kindness to them all those years ago. Eventually she had to call a halt, times were no longer as bad in the village as they had once been, but Alice knew well enough that they did not have sufficient to give away so much. She invited to tea all those who had given her presents and explained as graciously as she could that though she appreciated their generosity, she had sufficient money to eat, but what she needed was help in cleaning up the house, for a man to replace the odd tile on the roof and anyone willing to dig over the kitchen garden, which was a wilderness – the gardener had taken her at her word and had let everything run wild. She was swamped with volunteers.

The evenings were the worst. During the day she was too busy to fret but by nightfall the villagers who were helping had gone and, alone in the small parlour, Alice would go over and over in her mind what she had done. Should she have? And had she over-reacted?

In many ways she regretted that the berth on the liner had been available. Perhaps it would have been better if she could have stayed in a hotel for a week or two while waiting for a sailing instead of leaving on the selfsame day. Then she could have written to Lincoln, telephoned him, tried to reason with him. Maybe she could have contrived to see Juniper, persuaded her to come with her.

Then reason would tell her that Lincoln would have prevented her from seeing the child. She feared that Lincoln must hate her now for what he imagined she had done. He was too proud a man ever to change his attitude to her now.

She grieved for Chas whom, she now acknowledged,

she had never stopped loving, and she grieved for the past with Lincoln.

The lawyers gave her no hope of getting Juniper. For a start she could not compete with Lincoln in the courts – she did not have the money. And it would be money wasted for, although Juniper was her granddaughter, it was Lincoln who had been awarded custody of her. She could only hope that he would not poison the child's mind against her.

After two weeks she travelled to Boscar in the Rolls-Royce that, despite standing unused in the garage for all these years, started at the first attempt. Beautiful car though it was, it would have to be sold, she reluctantly decided.

Her welcome at Boscar Manor was not quite what she expected. Mathilda Boscar graciously shook her hand and without explanation seemed almost to float from the room. Halliday Boscar, having shown her his model insects, seemed to forget she was there. She did not mind this vagueness; she had come here to see Marshall and Grace.

'What do you mean, you've left my papa? How could you do such a thing?' Grace faced her angrily. They were in the small sitting room that Grace had furnished for herself and Marshall. Alice was distressed at the poor furnishings, her daughter's pathetic attempts at making the room pretty.

'He has Juniper.'

'And that's another thing. How dare you leave our daughter as well? She needs you now that she hasn't got us.'

'It was hard for me to leave her, you can't imagine how I fought with myself. But I had to, Grace. She is safe with him, you know how much he adores her. But I had to go, I feared he would harm me if I stayed.'

'The bastard!' Marshall spoke for the first time.

'Don't you call my papa that.'

'He's hardly treated you well, has he?' Marshall snapped back. 'I should think you would hate him.'

'Well, I don't. We know why he did what he did, don't we, Marshall? He was right. I still love him, I'll always love him. But you, Mother, I can't forgive.'

'Grace, listen to me. Your father isn't as you think. He is capable of great wickedness . . .'

'What wickedness?'

Alice looked despairingly at her daughter. How could she tell her that the stepfather she adored had killed the real father she had never known? 'You must take my word for it, Grace.'

'Lies, lies! It's all lies!' Grace was shouting hysterically.

'I've never lied to you, Grace. Never.' Alice felt shocked at the vehemence of Grace's reaction. She looked at the bitter expression on her daughter's face. She felt sorry for her. Since the age of nine Grace had known only luxury, whatever she had wanted she had had. Now Alice was looking at a deeply embittered woman. But, for all her sympathy, Grace's reaction would make what she had to say easier.

'I haven't come here to argue, Grace. I'm sorry you're upset but I assure you I had no choice. Arguing will help neither of us. I need to discuss money with you.'

'God damn it, how can you talk of money at a time like this?'

'I've supported you as much as I could and I shall continue to do what I can. But, unfortunately, I cannot give you both as much as before.'

'Why not?' Grace demanded, very much as she had as a small child when not allowed something on which she had set her heart.

'Because I don't have it. It's as simple as that.'

'You sold your business, you told us so,' Grace said petulantly.

'Yes, but it has to be invested safely. The income has to be stretched very thinly – Gwenfer is an expensive house to maintain. It's the sea air and the winds, they are so destructive . . .' she said to no one in particular but with a desperate need to explain herself: Grace was making her feel guilty. Marshall was listening carefully to every word.

'Gwenfer! It's always been that bitch of a house with you, Mother, hasn't it? There are times when I think you love that place more than me.' Grace sulked.

'Grace, don't be so silly. I . . .'

'Then sell it.'

Alice swung round in the chair, shock and surprise registering on her face. 'I couldn't do that! I couldn't let it go. I think I'd rather die . . .'

'See. See what I mean, Marshall? She's crazy about that house, she'd see us starve rather than get rid of it. Mother, I think you are being totally selfish.' At which she stood up, turned abruptly and stormed from the room, slamming the door violently and leaving a stunned silence behind her. As if hypnotised, Alice and Marshall watched the lintel of the door shiver, slip and in a slow motion fall to the floor with a crash. Marshall crossed the room, picked up the lintel, studied it intently, tried to replace it and caught the piece of wood as it wobbled down again. Sighing, as if to say that such complicated work was beyond his capabilities, he placed it on the table.

'Some days I think it's a miracle we've still got a roof on.' He grinned sheepishly at his mother-in-law.

'These large houses are a curse on us, Marshall.'

'I'm afraid so. If I had my time over again I'd make certain I never loved a building. Houses are far more rapacious and ungrateful than any woman . . .' and then, aware of how tactless he was being, he turned away, and looked moodily out of the window, a worried frown on his face. The silence returned.

'I'm sorry,' they both began in unison and laughed with embarrassment. He bowed to Alice.

'I was going to say I'm sorry I've upset my daughter.'

He laughed. 'Touché. I was about to apologise for my wife.'

Again they laughed awkwardly. Marshall continued to look out of the window across the land he had grown to love.

'Look, Mrs Wakefield, perhaps it would be better . . .' he began as she said, 'Marshall, I wonder . . .' They both stopped and having reached this conversational impasse both stared at each other.

'You first, Mrs Wakefield.'

'Grace is probably right. It's madness for me to try to keep Gwenfer.'

'No, no, she's totally wrong. I do understand how you feel. You're not being selfish. Why, you could sell up, get a smaller house, perhaps somewhere near to Lady Gertie and lead a very comfortable life. But I know why you want to keep it. Grace doesn't understand. It's not for you, it's for future generations, isn't it? You feel you don't have the right to sell.'

'Exactly, Marshall,' she said, somewhat surprised at this indication of sensitivity. 'I'm so glad you understand. But what on earth am I to do . . . ?'

'I think I've the solution, Mrs Wakefield. It's not ideal but it might help . . . We could all move in together at Gwenfer.'

'Gwenfer?' She did not know what she had expected him to say but it was not this.

'Mrs Wakefield . . .'

She held up her hand to him. 'Please call me Alice.' She was not just being friendly to him; she found she did not like the sound of that name. She would see what she could do about divesting herself of it.

'I'm honoured, Alice . . .' he gave a small bow. 'You see, we have two houses. Two houses we are both desperate to save. You have a little money and Grace has her minuscule amount. And I have none – the poor relation.' He laughed woodenly but found he could not look at her as he said it, certain she would read on his face that he deceived her about his own money.

'Marshall, I've never minded helping you.' She smiled at him.

It was her gentle smile that finally pricked Marshall's conscience. 'Well, that's not strictly true. I do have a small amount of savings, I can help a little, but not enough to keep this house going,' he finally confessed. 'So, we pool what money we have and live in one house. I can help, I'm not quite the waster I used to be. I've learnt a lot about farming. We could get your farm going again. Of course my parents can't help in any way . . .' he shrugged helplessly.

'But you love, Boscar.'

'I do and I want Juniper to love it too, *when* I'm allowed her back again,' he said with bitterness in his voice. 'But don't you see, Alice? This house is Juniper's. There's nothing he can do about that. We inform the lawyers that we've moved out; Lincoln won't allow a material possession to fall into disrepair. He'll keep it repaired and water-tight. It can't be sold until Juniper is twenty-one. By then surely the old devil will be dead and Grace can buy it from Juniper?' He sat down and faced her, his face eager with the plan he outlined.

Alice shivered; a lot had happened. Lincoln had behaved atrociously, she feared him but . . . she shivered again . . . she found it wasn't in her to wish him dead. However, what Marshall said made sense. She held out her hand and took his. 'You've made me very happy, Marshall. I shall always be grateful to you.'

'Can you tell me what it was, why you ran away?'

Alice looked at him closely. She had vowed never to tell anyone, but how she longed to confide in someone. Could she trust Marshall? Perhaps because of his loathing for Lincoln he was one of the few people whom she could tell. 'Only if you promise never to tell Grace?'

'I promise.'

'Grace's real father, Chas Cordell, turned up out of the blue. Lincoln had him murdered.'

A long drawn-out whistle escaped from Marshall. He had realised it must be bad for Alice to have run, but this . . . ? His mind whirled trying to find in it an advantage to himself. He slapped his thigh. 'We can get Juniper back! He's gone too far. Oh Alice, I miss her so.'

'I don't think so, Marshall. He will have made certain that the murder can never be traced back to him. We would be pouring away money we can ill afford on lawyers. She is happy with him, and he will never hurt her. We shall just have to be patient, Marshall, and I know how hard that is for you. I miss her desperately already.'

From the elation of a moment ago, Marshall slumped in the chair, his head in his hands. Alice said nothing but allowed him to assimilate what she had said. She wanted to find out from him what it was that had enabled Lincoln to get custody of Juniper. And then, to her horror, she realised that his wide shoulders were heaving: he was weeping, silently. She could not ask him now; maybe she would never ask.

'Dear Marshall. I'm so sorry for you. But she still loves you, I know that . . .'

He looked up at her with a tear-stained face. 'Alice, each day, each week, each terrible year away from that child, I feel only half alive. This place saved me, kept me sane. I work the land here for Juniper, I dream of taking her round, showing her what I've done . . .'

This was a side of Marshall which Alice had suspected, but never seen. The years away from New York had worked a change in him. She was moved but could say only, 'Maybe we shall have her with us again – we must not give up hope.'

Grace was furious that she had not been consulted about the move. Halliday, once he had been assured that his laboratory could be moved and set up again in the old stables at Gwenfer, did not mind nearly as much as Marshall had feared. Mathilda ranted uncontrollably for days. And Cyril said he wasn't going anywhere.

Within a month Mathilda had discovered the sea and the cliffs and was content. Grace was not speaking to anyone. Halliday was happily setting up his laboratory. And Cyril had fallen in love for the first time in his life – with Flo.

2

Once Halliday had been persuaded not to fire his shotgun at the ceiling to call Cyril, Alice felt that in the circumstances everyone had settled reasonably well. Primarily, this state of affairs was thanks to Alice herself. At first she was a frequent arbiter in the spates of temper and irritation which erupted all round her. But finally the situation became too much even for a woman of Alice's patience and she lost her temper with all of them. The sight of the normally calm Alice stamping her foot, and furious, had a salutary effect on everyone and a truce, if a sometimes tenuous one, reigned at Gwenfer.

Alice could not say that she liked the Boscar parents. Rather she found them peculiar people and she regarded their eccentricity with a good measure of scepticism. She felt it was too purposeful, too self-conscious. She dealt with them rather as she would have dealt with children who behaved outrageously to get what they wanted.

Of the two she preferred Halliday, who attempted to communicate with the others – if vaguely – and who tried to fit into the routine of the household. The same could not be said of Mathilda who never kept to mealtimes, demanded food at all hours, and could never be found when she was needed. But Alice found she could forgive her much when, of an evening, the logs crackling in the fire, the oil lamps hissing comfortingly, Mathilda would sit at the piano and play so beautifully that all of them could for a few precious moments forget the anxieties that beset them.

Alice had a new respect for Marshall. Frequently, when she came down to the kitchen at seven he was up and away into the fields, with Cyril in attendance, trotting along behind like a faithful cur. Cyril's keenness to work surprised everyone, including Cyril, but Alice was certain it was to impress Flo and prove to her what a good husband he would make.

Marshall's efforts, helped by Mr George's grandson Zack, quickly began to show results. The farm machinery was mended, the land was ploughed, seeds were sown, soil hoed, the cow was calved, sheep were brought to join the pigs, and soon their own vegetables began to appear on the table.

Marshall worked from dawn to dusk. He worked himself into exhaustion for he was working to forget . . . No one would ever know the agony of spirit that Marshall suffered at not seeing his daughter. Regularly, in the depths of the night, he would slip from his bed and sit alone in the parlour, longing for her, and rereading the letters he had received from her. But since Alice's departure from New York, the child's letters had ceased.

When he had first arrived in England he had consulted solicitors and barristers. He had been circumscribed by the fact that he could consult only those lawyers he did not know socially. For he had to be honest with them and the tale he had to tell of Lincoln's investigations, and of his and his wife's lifestyle, was not a pretty one. All of them had agreed – he did not stand a chance of getting custody of Juniper, not with the evidence that Wakefield had stacked up against them.

In a way he knew the old bastard was right. The way he and Grace had been living was not the right atmosphere in which to bring up a child. From Gwenfer it all seemed like a strange, wild dream. His hope now was that, since they no longer lived such a life, he might get his daughter back, given time. This was the one good thing to have come out of their new circumstances. But, ironically, now they did not have enough money to employ the lawyers to argue their case.

He went to London on a regular basis now, every six weeks, but always on his own. He told Alice he was going to ensure his investments were safe, to consult lawyers. He informed Grace that he went because he had to get away occasionally to see old friends, to sit in his club, to pretend for a short time that his life was normal again. He used their shortage of money as an excuse not to take Grace with him – but he always brought her back a present. Grace, forever fearful of losing him, controlled her temper and forced herself not to protest. Instead, she would drive him to Penzance, kiss him dutifully goodbye and tell him to have a nice time. Then she would return to Gwenfer full of fear and terror, certain in the knowledge that he was going to be unfaithful. She began to eat large amounts of food to console herself, but this time she could not bring herself to follow her bouts of eating with bouts of hideous vomiting and insidiously her weight increased again. She was unable to sleep until Marshall returned from his trips, for she lay in the dark, torturing herself by imagining him in bed, making love to a beautiful woman.

She was right to suffer. Always his first call, upon arriving in the capital, was on Francine Frobisher.

It was difficult for Alice to understand how she felt about Grace. She loved her but that did not stop her finding the young woman irritating beyond measure. Grace was always depressed, always to be found sitting vacantly staring into space, invariably pushing food into her mouth. Nothing seemed to interest her – no household duties, no books, no animals. Whereas Alice could not be idle. In the afternoons, the minute her duties in the house were finished, she quickly donned her hat and coat and, whatever the weather, would go out for a walk, sometimes to her rock, sometimes to the cliff. In the evenings, if she was not reading she was either sewing or painting.

Frequently Alice wished she were alone at Gwenfer. She felt ashamed of her selfishness, but she could not help herself. Often she would allow herself to plan how it would be when all the Boscars left her. For the one constant in Alice's life was the peace which Gwenfer gave her and the great love she felt for the place.

But she did have Philomel. At least twice a week she visited Philomel for tea. A bad fall, a few weeks after Alice's arrival, had left her bedridden. Ralph, her husband, tended her with such loving gentleness that Alice was moved when she saw the two of them together. For all her adventures, all the wealth she had enjoyed, she had never experienced the solicitous, strong devotion that these two shared in their tiny, modest cottage – for they had never moved into the vicarage, preferring the simplicity of life in their first home together.

'Promise one thing, Alice.'

'If I can.'

'Never leave Gwenfer. This is where you belong, this place gives you peace even if you do feel you are alone and disappointed. Your disillusionment would be worse if you weren't here.'

'I know that, Philomel, I've always felt it. I shouldn't have listened to you all those years ago when you insisted I went to London for "the season".' She forced a laugh, fearful Philomel might be offended.

'It was not good advice, was it? I regret it now.' She sat up and reached for Alice's hand, but the effort made her cough. Alice helped her drink some water and then knelt and put more logs on the fire for the day was chilly and the winter winds were howling outside. They lapsed into a companionable silence, the only sound in the little room the ticking of the clock on the mantel, the crackling of the logs in the grate.

'You know I'm dying, don't you, Alice?'

'Philomel, don't say such a thing!'

'It's the truth.'

'Nonsense, you'll be yourself again when the spring comes and the weather is kinder.'

'No, Alice. I know, it's as if God were warning me, preparing me. There are nights when, as I fall asleep, I think I won't see the morning. It's always such a delightful surprise when I do.'

'Philomel, my dear, I'm sorry.'

'I'm not frightened. I've had a wonderful life. Ralph has given me happiness that I did not imagine could exist. Through him I have found God again. No, I have no fear, just a deep sadness that I shall be leaving my husband.' A tear appeared first in the blue eye and then in the brown. Alice held the little woman close to her, the woman who had saved her own sanity so long ago, and stroked her hair gently.

And then one morning, a year after Alice had returned, when the air was full of the promise of spring, the sun turning the sea back to azure, proclaiming the summer to come, a morning when the wild daffodils on the cliff top were a moving golden cloud – Philomel did not wake up.

Alice wept for the loss of her friend, the last link with her childhood.

From the moment she had arrived in England from New York Alice sent letters regularly to Juniper. She wrote direct to her, she wrote care of Lincoln, she wrote care of the housekeeper, the cook, the chauffeur, the boat man – there was never a reply. Reluctantly she had come to the conclusion that her letters were being intercepted by Lincoln, or worse, and a thought she did not care to dwell upon, that Juniper's mind had been poisoned against them all to such a degree that she did not want to hear from them, perhaps even hated them.

Therefore, when, after nearly eighteen months a letter arrived for Alice from Juniper, Gwenfer took on a carnival mood. It was addressed in childish handwriting to Gwenfer, England and had found her. The letter told them of her boat, her pony but most importantly it told them she loved and missed them. Alice and Marshall replied immediately with long, loving letters and even Grace was moved from her lethargy to write a note. It was then that Alice remembered how she had kept contact with Grace by using the poste restante system. That was where they addressed the envelope, hoping that Juniper would remember the trips with her grandmother to the post office. The effect on Marshall was electric. He worked harder than ever: he wanted Juniper to be proud of him when she came.

They had been at Gwenfer for two years when the invitation from Gertie arrived. There had been several invitations from Gertie since her return, but Alice had felt she could not leave the others alone at Gwenfer nor could she afford to repay any hospitality. So it was now some years since she had seen her friend. Now it was May and Gertie was inviting them to join her at her London house for the season.

At first Alice was in two minds whether to go. There was the expense. Even modest clothes for Grace and herself would take money they could ill afford. And never having enjoyed the social whirl, she was certain that she would miss Gwenfer intolerably the moment she arrived in London. But then she thought of her old friend. What bliss it would be to sit with Gertie and unburden herself to the one person in the world she trusted implicitly, who understood her well and who always told her the truth. And, certainly, she was tired and the thought of a month of being waited on hand and foot attracted her. It was a combination of all these thoughts that finally persuaded her to go.

Marshall felt it was time he too had a holiday and that Cyril and Zack could manage well enough without him for a month. His regular trips to London lasted only a couple of days, three at the most: it would be pleasant to have a whole month to look up old friends.

Grace did not want to go. The thought of a London full of beautiful women up for the season and all lusting after her husband was her idea of purgatory. But once Marshall had decided to go she had no choice but to pack her bags and join them – she could not trust him away from her for so long.

The moment they arrived Grace excused herself and went to Harley Street and returned bright eyed, excited, and with a small package in her handbag. To Marshall's horror she began to seduce him again and he knew what that boded. He had enjoyed the normality of the past years – rather, his idea of normality, which meant not sharing a bed with Grace, but finding a cosy wench to bed and comfort him on his trips to London. This time he argued forcefully against any 'adventures'. He pointed out to her that if they lived a life of spotless domesticity they stood a better chance of having their daughter returned to them. Grace had immediately collapsed in wailing hysterics, shrilly accusing him of having found someone else. Aware that her shrieking could be heard all over Gertie's house and no doubt out in the street as well, for the sake of peace he gave in. That evening, late, he allowed himself to be led down dark alleyways in Soho, to dimly lit rooms whose doors were bolted behind them. But this time he was adamant; they could never go back to their previous life of debauchery. Grace must regard this as a holiday diversion, nothing more.

Marshall threw himself with enthusiasm into the social whirl and Grace, always shy, was now even shyer – convinced that wherever she went people were whispering about how fat and how ugly she was. She was neither. Certainly she was beginning to put on weight but her face was still pleasant and her body for the time being was more voluptuous than fat. Painful as society was to her, she dared not risk allowing Marshall to go alone to the balls and glittering soirées. So she forced herself to accompany him, ever watchful for predatory women.

3

At twelve Juniper was still small for her age, but she was beautiful. Her summers in the sun had bleached her hair to an almost silver white. Her face, with its fine chiselled features, was dominated by the large, gold-flecked hazel eyes. Despite the attempts of a succession of governesses to persuade her to wear a hat and to cover her skin, lest she look like a gypsy, Juniper was tanned a becoming peachy brown.

The routine of Juniper's life never varied. Winter in New York, Dart Island for the summer. She and her grandfather moved from one to the other in an organised ritual. Dart Island remained her favourite, not for the enormous, luxuriously appointed mansion, but for the freedom she had here, and the fact that, best of all, she had the sea.

Sparkle, the pony, had long been replaced by other horses but he was still with her, still loved, lording it in the stables now that her father's polo ponies had gone. Fat and lazy, the pony was enjoying his retirement.

Juniper had her horses, her boat, and a large group of friends from the many mansions that now dotted the main foreshore. Lincoln had been the first to come but he had been swiftly followed by the new rich, who, unwelcome at the resorts colonised by old money, had built their own, secure estates away from the teeming city.

It was a rare day in summer when there wasn't a party, a clam bake or a dance at one of the houses. As one of the most popular of the young, Juniper was always invited. Not that she always went; she made a point of rationing her absences from the house and her grandfather, for she knew he needed her.

Much had happened in the three years since her grandmother had left so dramatically – she had been replaced.

First there had been Lola Banks, a fluffy blonde who dreamt of becoming a movie star and whom Lincoln had met at the studios in California, a mere month after Alice left. At first Juniper, still desperate for her grandmother's return, had resented her presence, but there was nothing about the woman to dislike. She was a soft cuddly kitten of a person, who was never cross, who laughed at everything and whose interests were limited to clothes, her face and the trinkets which Lincoln showered on her, and which she accepted with the pleasure of a child. She did not offend for she talked of nothing of any consequence and she slept half the day. She obviously made Lincoln happy for it was she who had made him smile again for the first time since Alice left. Not that Juniper was supposed to know how close was Lola's relationship with Lincoln. They had separate rooms, they never touched in public; but Juniper knew. She had learnt to watch for glances across rooms, snatched and whispered conversations, the sudden silences when she entered a room. When Lola left, as suddenly and as quickly as her grandmother had done, Juniper found she missed her.

Within two days she was replaced by Doreena Laski. Juniper presumed that she had been waiting in the wings, like the actress she was, to take Lola's place. Doreena was a dark-haired, dark-eyed beauty of Yugoslavian blood. She dressed only in black and she was so chic, so sophisticated that Juniper found her intimidating. She smoked, using a long black, diamond-studded holder, held between fingers whose long nails were painted blood red. These fascinated Juniper who had never seen such painted nails before. She drank cocktails with strange exotic-sounding names, at all manner of times of the day; Juniper was convinced she had them for break-fast. But she steadfastly chose to ignore Juniper.

Juniper watched the relationship and noted that her grandfather did not laugh as much as he had with Lola. She saw that the trinkets were larger and sparkled more, she assumed they had cost more than Lola's gifts. Juniper had never seen Lola drink but Doreena did so all the time and, worse, she insisted that Lincoln join her, calling him a boring old bear if he did not. Juniper monitored the situation for two months and finally decided it was not good enough. Doreena would have to go. This was quite simple to arrange: she merely told her grandfather that she did not like the woman. In less than twenty-four hours not one shred of Doreena's brief reign remained. The woman sat in the train back to California completely perplexed and confused as to why she had been so humiliatingly dismissed, how all her plans to become the next Mrs Wakefield had gone astray.

After that there was a long string of young women who came in all shapes and sizes and hues. So many that Juniper rapidly forgot their names. That was until, after eighteen months, Thomasine Randolph arrived.

Thomasine, quickly known by everyone as Tommy, was completely different from all the others. Her father had lost his fortune in the great Wall Street crash of the year before, a crash that Lincoln had foreseen and in which he had not lost a cent – rather, he had made another fortune from the catastrophic debris. Tommy, who all her life had known great wealth, woke up one morning to find herself poor. She had immediately learnt to type and had set out to find work. Her first interview had been with Lincoln who needed another secretary. She never com-plained and was completely philosophical about what had happened to her, managing to send three quarters of her wages back to her parents who were not coping as well as she.

She was a tall, willowy redhead, with dark brown eyes.

She could have been beautiful but it was as if she did not wish to be. She dressed rather sedately and she wore her glorious red hair firmly clipped into place. The fine dark eyes looked at the world from behind large tortoiseshell spectacles and, if asked, she would have chosen a book as a present rather than any bauble. She might dress plainly but she could not disguise the lissom body, nor the fluid elegant way she walked, which made men look instantly at her. She was calm and practical, clever and funny. She reminded Juniper of her grandmother and she watched impatiently for her grandfather to see the likeness. She did not have long to wait. Within a month Tommy was in Lincoln's bed and out of his office; the procession of young women ceased. Lincoln laughed again, and Juniper approved.

Her love for her grandfather was as strong as ever and his for her was, if anything, greater now that Grace and Alice had gone. The only person they never discussed was Alice. In the beginning Lincoln had never let an opportunity go by to speak harshly of Alice to the child. Frequently she was told what a bad woman her grandmother was, how little she had loved her. Time without number he pointed out how Alice had deserted Juniper just as her parents had done. He carefully underlined such statements by emphasising his great love for her and the fact that he would never leave her.

During the first year after Alice's departure Juniper had been puzzled and deeply hurt. It was true what her grandfather told her: everyone she loved – except him – left her. And then one day, during Doreena's reign, it was raining, her governess had a cold and Juniper was sitting in the great salon idly leafing through an old photograph album. She studied each photograph of Alice carefully, she even went into Lincoln's study and from his desk took the giant magnifying glass. How could such a sweet-faced woman be all the things her grandfather said? She sat alone, dreamily looking out of the long sash windows across the rain-swept lawns towards the sea and remembered the happy times . . . the picnics her grandmother had arranged, the painting lessons she had given her, the woman's kind patience. She remembered the small, always practical and, frequently, favourite presents that Alice had given her. She thought of the many kindnesses she had seen her grandmother perform, for people who were ill, or lacked food and money. She recalled what fun Alice had been. She could call clearly to mind the calm influence Alice had been in her life when so often Juniper, torn between Lincoln and her parents, had felt herself trapped in the vortex of emotions swirling about her. Suddenly she felt certain that her grandfather lied.

The next time Lincoln blackened Alice's name, he was taken unawares by Juniper's reaction.

'I'd prefer it, Grandpa, if you did not speak about my grandmother in that way, I love her.'

'After she left you? After she just walked out of both our lives?'

'I'm sorry that she hurt you, Grandpa, but she must have had her reasons for going the way she did. My grandmother would not hurt a living soul if she could help it.'

'She's selfish and wicked . . .'

'I warn you, Grandpa, I will not listen to you. I never want to hear such talk ever again . . . and I want to write to her.'

'You'll do no such thing. I will not have you contacting her, do you hear me?'

Juniper glared defiantly at Lincoln, whose colour was rising dangerously, and said nothing.

'I asked you if you heard what I said?'

'I heard you. I could not help it, you are talking so loudly.'

For the first time ever Lincoln found, to his horror, that he wanted to hit the child. He turned from her, clenching his fists in his anger. He had seen the defiance in her face, the determined set of her chin; without doubt she meant what she said. He would have to watch himself if he was not to alienate her for ever. If that happened, his life would not be worth living. 'I forbid you to contact that woman,' was his parting shot as he stormed from the room.

If she were right and her grandfather had lied, then the most perplexing question was why her grandmother had not written to her. She was not to know that every letter Alice had sent her, and all those she had sent care of the servants, was destroyed by Lincoln. It was difficult for the servants, who had loved Alice and adored Juniper: they wanted her to have the letters. But jobs were difficult to come by these days.

After the scene with Lincoln she had gone straight to her room and had written to Alice. Not knowing where she was, she had written Gwenfer on the envelope for she felt that if she herself ever ran away that was where she would go.

When no letter came in reply she began to suspect that her grandfather must have intercepted the mail but was too proud to ask him. Then, back in New York for the winter, she passed the post office one day and remembered how in the past she had gone there many times with Alice to collect letters from her mother. Entering she asked if there was any mail poste restante for her. She was overwhelmed with happiness at the pile of letters waiting for her and locked herself in her room to read them. She kept them carefully hidden for she would not have put it past her grandfather to have her room searched. She loved him but she did not trust him.

For the first two years governesses had come and gone until Tommy, concerned that the girl was learning nothing, finally took her education into her own hands. Tommy was fluent in French and German. In history lessons she could take Juniper's mind racing back across the centuries. In geography she could transport her across the world, and in literature, could awaken the imaginative sensitivity which was at the core of Juniper. Tommy even brought maths alive for Juniper. She was a fund of funny stories and found she enjoyed teaching; Juniper found she could enjoy learning. It was as if a sigh escaped the lips of all those who inhabited the Wakefield mansions when at last Juniper had a teacher whom she liked.

Alice had always countered her husband's spoiling of the child. She had balanced his generosity with common sense and practical advice. She had taught Juniper to sew a seam, to turn a collar, to cook, to preserve – the rudiments of housekeeping. Her own life had taught her the advantage of a young woman, no matter how rich, having a skill to fall back upon.

Her own experiences had brought Tommy to the same conclusions and she continued the regime. No one knew what the future would bring Juniper, she thought. Who could tell if a time would not come when she would displease Lincoln? Tommy understood her protector well enough by now to realise that he was quite capable of cutting Juniper out of his life, just as he had his step-daughter and wife.

Juniper had stolidly accepted these domestic tasks because she loved Alice, and now complied because she was fond of Tommy and wanted to please her. But she found them increasingly boring. In the girl's logical mind there seemed little point in learning such mundane crafts with so many servants to perform them for her, and she was not likely ever to need such skills. No, Juniper preferred the world outside the stillroom and sewing room.

Without Alice to control him, Lincoln's generosity to the girl knew no bounds. It was as if Juniper had only to *think* she wanted something for it to appear. Despite his attitude to Alice, Lincoln was central to Juniper's life; she loved him. Arguing, she decided, was silly, it brought only pain and confusion.

Lincoln stood on the quay, his hand in Juniper's.

'Well my darling. What do you think?'

Juniper looked at the gleaming new boat tied to the jetty.

'Mine?' she said, smiling up at her grandfather beguilingly.

'Who else am I likely to buy a boat for?' he said in the deliberately gruff way he used to her – and which fooled nobody.

'Oh, Grandpa – it's wonderful. Much better than my little dinghy. You wait until those boys over at Greenacres see this, they will go pea green with envy.' She was jumping from one foot to the other with excitement.

'Not too big for you, my sweet?'

'Don't be silly Grandpa – I can manage it, it'll be easy. Come on,' she jumped nimbly into the boat holding her hand out to her grandfather. 'Come on, Grandpa.'

'No, Juniper, you know I don't like the sea. And you get back here also. You know the rules, you're not allowed on the boat on your own. Wait for Mark to come.'

'I'm not alone, you're with me.' She smiled up at him slyly. 'Oh, come on Grandpa, do!' she sighed with impatience.

'I hate the sea, don't know why I buy you the beastly boats.'

' 'Cause you love me,' she sang at him. 'Just sit in it, Grandpa, there's an angel. We're not at sea, look we're safely tied up,' and she pointed to the painter.

'Very well then, just for a minute.' And tetchily the old man lowered himself carefully into the boat, still pleased at the pleasure this new present was giving her.

'Let's try her out.'

'No darling. Not until Mark gets here. Drat the man,

where is he? I said to be here at two.' He looked with irritation at his pocket watch.

'Oh please, Grandpa. I can sail her. I always sail *Firefly*, Mark just sits there, says it's the best job he ever had,' she pleaded, looking up at him, her even white teeth shining even whiter in the tanned face.

'I promised to take Tommy for a drive.'

'She's gone to the library, she told me. Oh, come on, just a tiny weeny trip, we'll be back by the time she returns.'

He looked at her eager face, and smiled at her – he never could refuse the child a damn thing . . . 'Just out a little way then,' he replied, looking at the calm sea and noting there was not one cloud in the sky.

Juniper shouted to a boy to cast them off, expertly raised the sail and then a puff of wind stretched the canvas and the little boat slid smoothly away from the jetty. They gathered speed across the small natural harbour, Juniper tacking the boat and smoothly catching each small pocket of available wind.

'That's far enough, Juniper,' Lincoln said as the land began to look too far away for comfort.

'Oh, Grandpa, don't be so boring. It's such a perfect day for a little sail,' Juniper replied, heading the craft out to sea.

Lincoln watched Juniper with pleasure, admiring her expertise. He'd always admired people who were expert in what they were doing and she was no exception. What a beauty she was. These next few years would be the most precious, watching her turn into a beautiful woman before the beaux started sniffing around. Lincoln shuddered at the very idea. It would have to be a fine, upstanding young fellow who would ever receive his permission to court someone so precious. He slumped back on the cushions, to his surprise finding that he was enjoying the motion of the little boat, the slap of the sea against the wooden hull. At moments like this he found he could forget everything, Grace, Alice, all the bad things in his life. This child could erase all such memories. He sighed contentedly.

Far away on the horizon, unseen by either of them, a small black dot appeared. Inexorably the dot grew larger as it sped rapidly towards them.

Lincoln moved his shoulders, altering his position on the cushions to ease the sudden discomfort of an attack of indigestion. He rubbed his chest. On the horizon, growing larger by the second, the dark squall approached.

'You all right, Grandpa, you look worried?'

'Fine, Juniper. Touch of indigestion.'

'You shouldn't have had so much pudding,' she said gaily.

The pain increased, the cloud scudded nearer. He fumbled in his pocket for the pills the doctor had insisted he carry but which he'd never needed. He was panicking unnecessarily, of course it wasn't his heart, it was his lunch. Still, all the same, a pill wouldn't go amiss. He began to unscrew the bottle. As if a switch had been thrown the sunshine disappeared. That was when he felt as if he were being punched in the chest and a pain of such excruciating intensity swelled up that he felt he was about to burst. He dropped the bottle and clumsily began to get to his feet . . .

'Grandpa, careful, sit down, you'll capsize the boat,' Juniper ordered sharply.

Clutching at his chest Lincoln lunged towards her, his mouth distorted, his face a strange blue.

'Grandpa!' Juniper called with alarm as he stumbled, grabbing for the mast and making the small boat rock. Hanging on to the tiller for dear life Juniper screamed at her grandfather. 'Sit down, you'll have us over . . .' But the words were barely out of her mouth when, before her horrified stare, her grandfather swung round, looked at her for a long beseeching moment, lost his footing and hurtled overboard.

Within seconds Juniper had the boat under control, the sea anchor out, the sail down. She grabbed the lifebelt, scanned the water, and taking careful aim, threw it to her grandfather. She leant over the side as with beating heart she saw he made no effort to swim towards it.

'Please, Grandpa, try . . .' she screamed, panic making her voice ugly and shrill. Why didn't he try? Quickly she assessed the situation. It would take her longer to raise the sails and steer towards him than it would to swim to him. She kicked off her shoes, dived into the water, and with a few swift strokes was beside the lifebelt and her grandfather. 'Hold on to this, Grandpa, please, then I'll get the boat, please . . .' she was sobbing now. The wind was freshening, the water beginning to churn, as she trod water, and each time she spoke she swallowed great mouthfuls of salty sea. 'You must hold on.' Clumsily, the chill making her fingers feel dead, she fumbled for his hands and, finding them, placed them on the lifebelt. His eyes opened, they rolled in his head, and a groan escaped. 'Thank God, Grandpa, I thought you had drowned. Please help me, look. You must hold on, I'll get the boat . . .'

A wave larger than any of the others knocked her away from him. She recovered, turned round and all there was to see was the lifebelt bobbing on the water.

'Grandpa!'

She kicked her legs up and dived down. Deeply she swam until, her lungs bursting, she shot to the surface gulping the clean air into her. Back down she went, her young legs propelling her deeper into the sea. Back. Breath. Down. She repeated the procedure again and again.

At the twelfth dive Juniper knew she was exhausted. Knew she could not dive again. Wondered if she had left herself with sufficient energy to get back on board. Weakly she began to swim to the boat.

Suddenly the waves subsided, the wind abated, the sun reappeared, and the sea looked blue again.

Marshall was dining at his club. Tonight there was no ball or dinner of significance and, despite Grace's mistrust, he had taken himself to the club. Meeting his old friends there made him realise just how much he missed being a man about town. Gertie's hospitality was legendary but his movements were too restricted – why, he had only managed to see Francine for one afternoon. This evening had shown him that he had to get his finances better organised to give himself more freedom, and he wasn't going to be able to do that buried at Gwenfer.

The talk tonight was of particular interest. Billy Swiverton and Flippy Sigford were looking for investors to join them in buying a mansion near Windsor which they intended turning into a health spa. Banting was all the rage and women were prepared to spend fortunes by going twice a year to Baden Baden and other spas, to torture themselves into the required shape for the new slim-line fashions. Flippy had hit on the idea of starting an exclusive clinic in England. It was a brilliant idea and one, given their contacts in society, which was bound to succeed.

He loaded his fork with the last morsel of treacle tart and clotted cream and thanked the good Lord for making him a man so that the vagaries of the fashion designers did not throw him into a panic if an extra inch appeared. Even so, Marshall would never allow himself to get fat – that same good Lord had given him the sort of body that enabled him to eat and drink whatever he wanted without any damage to his slim, still muscular frame.

The group ordered coffees and large Napoleon brandies and made their way from the dining room to the library and the large, comfortable leather chairs, spaced judiciously about the room and ideal for confidences. They were soon engrossed in a whispered conversation while

Flippy excitedly did projections and calculations on a piece of paper.

Marshall was excited by what he heard. Times were difficult. Since the Wall Street crash, money was much harder to make but from what Flippy said, with this project they could just sit back and count the profits.

They all looked up when a commotion erupted at the door. Marshall was annoyed to see one of Gertie's footmen arguing with the doorman, insisting loudly that he be allowed to see Mr Boscar. The man knew better than to interrupt him here, Marshall thought, noting the frowns on other members' faces, the irritated rustling of several *Times* newspapers. The footman, seeing him, pushed the doorman to one side and scurried across the room towards him.

'What on earth do you mean by coming here?'

'Mr Boscar, sir. I'm sorry. The butler said as I was to tell you confidential like,' he looked about anxiously and lowered his voice. 'It's Mrs Boscar, she's in a terrible state, sir.'

'Mrs Boscar?'

'Yes, Mr Post said as I was to tell you to come quick as he can't take the responsibility himself. Lady Gertrude and Mrs Wakefield are both out but they've been sent for.'

Exasperated, Marshall excused himself to his friends, promising to be in touch in the morning. The footman turned to follow, knocking into the old waiter who was bearing a tray loaded with brandy for Marshall's party.

'Sorry, mate. Can't stop,' the footman yelled as he raced after Marshall. Tray, glasses and waiter crashed to the floor. The clubmen were not so much concerned with the waiter as with the loss of good brandy and the noisy interruption in their sacred sanctum. Young Boscar had learnt some strange habits over in America, they agreed.

'What's happened?' he asked in the relatively empty hall as he was helped into his coat.

'It's her father, sir. A boating accident . . .'

'Juniper. My daughter. Is she all right?' Marshall felt as if the blood had frozen in his veins.

'I'm afraid I don't know, sir. Mr Post just told me to come and get you . . .'

The man's voice tailed off as Marshall strode rapidly away from him and through the glass doors hurriedly opened for him by the doorman. On the street a taxi had already been summoned and as the footman emerged it was to see Marshall disappearing into it. The taxi roared away from the kerb leaving a disgruntled footman to walk home.

In the taxi Marshall felt fear in a way he had never known it in his life. The boat . . . The old man never went in the boat . . . it was Juniper's boat . . . God. Dear God. For the first time in decades Marshall prayed to his long neglected Lord. He bargained with him, promised everything he owned, promised to mend his ways, so long as Juniper was alive.

As he paid off the taxi he could hear Grace's screams coming from an upstairs room. Curtains twitched in the elegant Mayfair house, servants' heads popped up, peering through the railings of the area steps.

In the hall Marshall found the Frobishers' servants clustered, maids wide-eyed with horror at the terrible wailing from the room above. The butler, normally impassive, approached, wringing his hands with worry.

'I've sent for the doctor, sir.'

'My daughter, Post. Have you news of my daughter?'

'No, sir. None, sir. Mrs Boscar opened the telegram. All the maid could gather was there had been an accident with a boat and then this . . .' he nodded towards the raucous, animal noises emanating from the first floor. Taking the stairs two at a time Marshall raced towards the noise.

'Marshall . . . !' Grace rushed towards him, her face blotched, tears pouring down the mottled cheeks. 'Marshall, my papa,' she sobbed.

'Juniper. Is Juniper all right?'

'He died despising me,' his wife began to wail again.

'Grace.' He grabbed her shoulders and forced her to look at him. 'Try and pull yourself together. What news of Juniper?'

'Juniper?' Grace looked at him, dazed, as if she did not understand the question.

Marshall let go of his wife with irritation. 'Where's the telegram?'

'Here.' Crumpled in Grace's fist was the buff sheet of paper. Instead of giving it to him she closed her fist tighter around it. Marshall prised it from her.

'REGRET LINCOLN WAKEFIELD DROWNED THIS AFTERNOON. BOATING ACCIDENT.' Shaking, Marshall read the paper in his hand. There was no mention of Juniper. She must be safe. She had to be safe.

He crossed to Grace's desk and rapidly penned a reply. 'ARRIVING FIRST BOAT. HOW IS JUNIPER.' And he signed it 'GRACE' and then shook his head and crossed her name out and signed it with his own. Stupid of him, Lincoln was not going to read it and be enraged at sight of his name. He gave a short laugh, it was the only amusing thing that had happened this evening.

He rang for the butler to send the cable and then turned to his wife whose screaming had subsided but who now was lying in a huddled heap on the floor, her body racked with dry sobs as if there were no more tears in her.

'My papa, my papa,' she was repeating to herself over and over again.

'There, there, sweetheart. Be a brave girl. Come on, old girl, you can do better than this.'

'He despised me,' the watery grey eyes looked up at him with naked despair. 'Oh my God. What have I done?'

'I'm sure he still loved you.'

'No, not my papa, he hated me. You don't know what you're talking about.' Suddenly her eyes flashed with anger and she was looking at him with loathing, a

247

loathing that made him back away from her. 'It's all your fault – all your fault.'

'My darling. How could it be my fault? I was here, you know I was. Don't be silly.'

'You made me what I am. You made him hate me,' she shouted.

And from somewhere within her more tears were found to gush out of the pale grey eyes, to puff up her discoloured cheeks further. With relief Marshall welcomed the doctor. Duly injected with a sleeping draught, Grace was led away to bed. Marshall instructed the maid to pack.

Feeling very shaky he let himself out of Grace's room and ran down the stairs to the library. There he sent for a decanter of brandy and gave Post instructions to arrange for a stateroom on the first available ship. As an after-thought he called the man back. He had forgotten Alice, she might want to come too. He told Post to book two staterooms.

The minute the brandy arrived he poured himself a stiff drink and sat down to think. He puffed nervously on his cigar. He would not really relax until he received a cable with news of Juniper but still . . . a smile hovered about his mouth. At last the old bugger had gone. All that money virtually his. He lifted the glass to his lips but then paused, frowning as he recalled Grace's accusations as she mourned her father. What if he'd put up with all that nonsense for all those years only to find she had turned against him, now that she was rich? Christ, he gulped at the brandy, it didn't bear thinking about. He poured another brandy. Well, all that business would have to stop now. Not only had he just made a bargain with God back there in the taxi, but soon Juniper would be theirs again, and he would have no funny business with his daughter about.

The door swung open and Alice and Gertie burst into the room in a flurry of agitation.

'Post says that . . .' Alice stopped in mid-sentence as if she couldn't say the actual words.

Marshall crossed the room and took both her hands in his. 'Alice, I'm sorry, but I'm afraid it's true. Lincoln . . . a boating accident,' and to his surprise found he could not say it either.

'Juniper?'

'I don't know.'

'It would have said so, Marshall.'

'Do you think so? That's what I'm hoping.'

'I'm certain. Don't you think so, Gertie? If it had been both of them . . . it would have said . . . it would have said,' she repeated as if by repetition she could make it so. She felt cold fear for Juniper and a sudden terrible sadness for Lincoln. It seemed impossible that she would never see him again.

'Undoubtedly, Alice. Have you cabled, have you booked berths? Where's Grace?' Gertie asked briskly.

'She's asleep. I'm waiting for Post, I sent him to book two staterooms.'

'Two?' Alice asked.

'For you, Alice.'

'Oh, I don't know, Marshall. I don't know if I could go,' her hand shot up to her neck in the gesture she had always made when greatly upset. 'So much has happened . . .' and her voice trailed off.

'Don't be ridiculous, Alice. Of course you must go, the child will need all of you with her,' Gertie said in the tone of voice with which no one ever argued. 'Now what about money?' she asked practically, snapping open her purse and taking out her cheque book. Gertie was in control.

6

For several days the staff in the large mansion on Dart Island despaired of Juniper's sanity. Since Mark the boatman had found her and brought the boat back to shore, the young girl had not spoken a word but had sat staring blankly into space. She had not cried, she barely slept, she would not eat.

The police had come and had tried unsuccessfully to learn exactly what had happened. But Juniper would not speak to them. Even Tommy had failed. Patiently she had explained to Juniper that her grandfather had not been found and that the police had to know what accident had befallen them, but the girl just stared vacantly at her. After four days the doctor was at his wits' end. It was as if the child had lost all will to live, almost, he confided to Tommy, as if she were willing herself to die.

At first no one could believe that a man so vital as Lincoln could possibly be dead. The staff sank into paroxysms of grief, his office staff ground to a virtual halt. It was Tommy who forced everyone to pull themselves together. It was she who made certain that the house and estate cranked back to normal. She began to issue instructions like a general. She made meticulous plans for the funeral so that when Lincoln's family arrived from England there would be little for them to see to in their grief, and she dealt firmly with the Press. This last was essential since already rumours were beginning to filter into the newspapers that Juniper was in some way to blame. All such reports found their way into the furnace and were followed up by a sharp letter from Tommy to the editor threatening legal action unless such innuendo ceased. The gossip receded, but Juniper stayed alone in her rooms.

'Daddy,' Juniper held up her arms, now as thin as sticks, to her father. For the first time since the accident, she spoke.

'My Juniper. My dearest one. How I've missed you! I love you,' Marshall said in a quick torrent, holding this most precious person close to him.

'My Grandpa's dead, Daddy.'

'I know, my sweet. I'm sorry.'

'I tried to save him, Daddy, I really did. I just wasn't strong enough.' She looked at her small hands which still felt cold and which she was certain would never be warm again. 'I dived and dived. I looked and looked, Daddy.' The hazel eyes at last filled with tears. 'But he had gone. I know what people are thinking . . .'

'What does it matter what people think? You did everything you could, Juniper.'

'Have they found him, Daddy? I can't bear to think of him alone out there in the cold water. He hated the sea, it's all my fault . . .'

'I understand, my darling. Of course it's not your fault, accidents happen . . .'

'But have they found him?'

'They will, they will. If not, I'll find him myself.' He held the child close as at last, between her sobs, she related the full story to him. For the first time since Lincoln's death, the child slept fitfully.

Even as Marshall settled his daughter the boats were out in the bay trawling back and forth in the search for Lincoln's body. Once he was certain that Juniper would not wake for some time, Marshall made his way to the shoreline to watch the operations. He was just in time to hear the yell from one of the boats and to see a large object huddled under a tarpaulin. He waited, deep in thought, as the boat was rowed to shore. It seemed to take an age, it seemed to take even longer for the body to be manhandled on to the beach.

Marshall was fearful to look, expecting to see Lincoln bloated and nibbled by fish, or even worse that an eye would snap open and look accusingly at him. He lit a cigarette, inhaled deeply, and forced himself to look . . . He was surprised. The old man looked almost pathetic with a wig of seaweed askew on his head. There were a few bruises and he was a strange colour, but apparently no fish had fancied him. He looked much as Marshall remembered him. No eye opened, no abuse issued from the half-open mouth that looked as if he had died smiling. He really was dead. He'd gone. They were free. Marshall felt like dancing a jig there and then on the sand in front of the boatmen who stood with heads respectfully bowed. He felt he should say something.

'I didn't expect him to look . . .' he paused, not knowing quite how to say it. 'To look so well,' he finished.

'We found him wedged in the rocks off Crab Point, sir,' one of the men explained.

'It wasn't the water that killed him. Heart more like.'

They carried the heavy body on a makeshift stretcher up to the house. The morticians descended upon him and stripped and bathed him, dressed him in clean shirt with a neat tie and a smart suit. His cheeks and lips were rouged, his hair was trimmed. They lowered him into his coffin, summoned his family and stood back, proud of their handiwork.

Alice stood in front of the coffin, which rested on a table, swathed in black velvet, in the centre of the large salon which had always been used for formal occasions. She looked down at the man with whom she had shared so many years of her life. She felt a deep sadness but it was for the Lincoln she had known long ago. She remembered with affection the man who had built this home for her, had given her Gwenfer back again. But she found she could not grieve for the Lincoln Wakefield who had shown himself so ruthless, whom she could never forgive for Chas's death. Part of her mind felt only relief that she need no longer fear him.

The door opened quietly and she looked up, peering through the shadows, for the drapes were pulled and the only light was from the four great wax candles that stood at each corner of Lincoln's bier.

'I'm sorry, Mrs Wakefield. I did not realise anyone was here.'

'Please, Miss Randolph. Come . . .' She held her hand out in welcome to Lincoln's secretary for that was how she had been introduced to her. Alice looked at her with concern, for she was extremely pale and seemed to sway in the candlelight. The young woman approached the coffin with her eyes cast down and stood for some time before she looked into the casket.

'Oh, no . . .' she whispered and immediately her hand shot to her mouth as if to stop herself saying anything more. Her shoulders slumped, she swayed visibly and her face was contorted as if she were fighting back tears. In that moment Alice understood who Tommy was and felt nothing but pity for her. She put her arms around her.

'There, Miss Randolph, let the tears come, it will help you . . .'

Tommy looked at Alice, her eyes full of anguish behind the glittering tears. 'If only I hadn't gone to the library. I didn't have to go, I just wanted time alone . . . If only I'd been here, I'd have been with them . . . I might . . .' and she began to sob.

'Don't torture yourself, my dear. The doctors have assured us it was his heart. It was very quick, there was nothing anyone could have done.'

A cry escaped from Tommy and Alice gathered her into her arms and held her tight as the tears cascaded down her cheeks and she shuddered with grief. As she held her Alice found she was crying too, crying for the man she had known a long time ago . . .

Grace was still sedated. During most of the journey across the Atlantic she had slept. Now, in the large mansion beside the sea, she seemed to move like a ghost through the ornate rooms, conjuring up memories of happiness from the past. And she began to eat in earnest.

On the day of Lincoln's funeral, Grace began to wail again. Marshall did everything in his power to stop her but she was past hearing him. Juniper looked first with horror at her mother, and then with a look of disbelief she left the room. Marshall slapped his wife's face and recalled the doctor. Once again Grace was drugged to sleep.

Marshall stood beside the open coffin wishing the men would hurry up and screw down the lid. Lincoln lay almost as if he were sleeping. Gingerly Marshall prodded him, still finding it difficult to believe he was dead. The skin was reassuringly cold. He looked at the crusty face, benign in death, and lifting his hand to his forehead gave a small salute.

'One thing you couldn't control, Lincoln. Your own death,' he whispered to the corpse.

It was decided that Juniper had been through enough and should not attend the funeral. Grace was too sedated, so Alice and Marshall were the chief mourners before the large mausoleum. It had been Lincoln's intention that they should all be buried there in time, but Alice knew her bones were destined to lie at Gwenfer and Marshall was determined that even in death he had no intention of sharing space with the old bastard.

The wake was long and expensive, one that Lincoln would have approved of. Every business associate with whom he had ever had dealings made the long journey to Dart Island to pay their last respects. But Marshall wished it would end; he wanted the Will to be read, he could not wait to learn at last the full extent of his wife's wealth. He wanted to start planning how to spend it.

At last the guests had left and the family and staff were gathered in the drawing room for the reading. Marshall fussed over Grace who lay, still drugged and looking wan, on a chaise-longue. He had argued with Charlie Mac-pherson, Lincoln's lawyer, that it was not necessary for Grace to be present but Charlie had insisted. Alice sat at the front beside Marshall. Behind them – the seniors sitting, the junior members standing – were the staff and retainers from both houses. At the far side, as far away from everyone as she could get, was Tommy. Marshall frowned as he saw Charlie snap open his briefcase. Marshall was not a vindictive man but he would never forgive Charlie for shopping him to the old man over Boscar House. No doubt about it, he thought with satisfaction, Charlie would be the first to go.

Marshall fidgeted restlessly while Charlie itemised the list of bequests to family and retainers. He heard with surprise the size of Alice's bequest – sufficient income to keep her in comfort for life whether or not she remarried. That was an optimistic sign. At least the old man appeared to have forgiven her, and had not been prepared to take his vindictiveness to the grave. He smiled with satisfaction as he heard Charlie say, 'And finally . . .' Marshall sat bolt upright, immediately alert, and nodded with satisfaction at the long list of companies, interests, properties listed by the lawyer, 'I bequeath to my grand-daughter Juniper Wakefield Boscar. I appoint as trustees my dear friends Charlie Macpherson and Thomasine Randolph to act for her until she reaches her majority or marries.'

'I beg your pardon . . .' Marshall blurted out and from behind him there was a burst of exclamations and the buzz of conversation.

'I further request that Miss Randolph has care and custody of my granddaughter until she marries, for which a sum of $20,000 per annum is to be paid for life.'

Marshall was on his feet. 'Would you repeat that?'

'It's all Juniper's,' Charlie answered simply. The muttering from the staff swelled. 'Surely you don't want me to read all this again?' he said, waving the large document at Marshall.

Marshall swung round to the assembled staff. 'Get out, all of you, you've heard enough.' He was shouting. Reluctantly the staff began to shuffle from the room. 'Get a move on,' Marshall roared. 'Not you, Miss Randolph. I want a word with you.' Looking nervous, Tommy turned back into the room.

'When was the will made?' Marshall demanded.

'1918. I can, in fact, tell you the very day we started working on it – it was June 11th – Juniper's christening. Of course it's been amended over the years as businesses have been bought and sold. Lincoln was very meticulous, he wanted everything listed so that there could be no mistakes.'

'Juniper's christening!' Marshall repeated, aware he sounded half-witted. 'But he didn't know this woman then,' he pointed at Tommy with a dismissive gesture, the time-honoured gesture of any family member who sees money he thinks is rightfully his disappearing from his grasp.

'No, Miss Randolph was added as a trustee earlier this year. Prior to that it was Mrs Wakefield,' he bowed to Alice. Suddenly into Alice's mind flashed the picture of Lincoln sitting on the end of her bed, telling how he planned to stop Marshall from touching his money. She had never thought he would go so far, not when he was so fond of Grace . . . but then so much had happened. Never interested in money herself, she had quite forgotten the incident till now.

'Mr Boscar, I assure you I did not know anything about this,' Tommy said anxiously.

'Huh!' was Marshall's cynical reply.

'She did not know. For obvious reasons, Lincoln was determined she should not know,' Charlie said in his most reasonable voice.

'But this isn't fair to Grace. She had a right to expect . . . And you did nothing to stop him.'

'No one could stop Lincoln from doing what he wanted,' the lawyer pointed out.

'And how is my wife supposed to live? Answer me that.'

'Marshall, don't distress yourself. I realise how bitterly disappointed you are, but don't you see? Lincoln has been most generous to me. I'll be able to help more now,' Alice said gently.

'Vindictive old bastard!' Marshall muttered as he slumped back in his chair, his mind whirling as he tried to find a way out of this.

'Might I say something?' Tommy stepped forward. 'I've known Juniper for almost three years. The one thing that has been consistent is her loyalty to her grandmother and parents – she would never hear a word against any of you.' She smiled nervously at Marshall. 'In my opinion, Mr MacPherson, she should live with them. She loves and needs them . . .'

'I see. You're quick to opt out of your responsibilities. I suppose you're going to take the money and run . . .'

'Marshall!' Alice interrupted. 'Don't be stupid, listen to what Miss Randolph has to say.'

'No, Mr Boscar, I have no intention of running. I regard this as a sacred trust from Mr Wakefield. You see, I happen to love Juniper as well.' Marshall had the grace to lower his head. 'My suggestion is that we should live with the family, or if not with, at least close enough so that she can see you every day.

Alice and Marshall looked with eager expectancy at Charlie. He shuffled his papers, enjoying these moments of power over Boscar whom he had always despised. 'Well, he makes no stipulation that she should have no contact, nor does he state where the child should live. Should there be any objection, though I can't see from whom, then, given that the original custody order to Mr Wakefield was a purely amicable one,' he paused, looking pointedly at Marshall, as he recalled how hostile had been Marshall's signing of the documents, 'I should think there would be no trouble.'

Marshall pondered these suggestions. 'What if we contest the will?'

'It wouldn't be wise, Marshall. He left instructions that, in such an eventuality, I was to present all relevant documents to the courts.' Alice looked perplexed at Charlie's words but Marshall glanced away; he knew when he was beaten. If they all lived together, Juniper's estate would pay the bills. He looked across at Tommy. She looked a reasonable woman, if she let her hair down and threw those spectacles away she could be very attractive . . . that was another possibility . . .

'I suppose there's not a lot I can do then,' he said eventually.

'Not really, Marshall.' The lawyer smirked unpleasantly as he packed his papers away.

Chapter Six

1

Adjustments were made. But the wealthy, although grieving in the same way as the poor, are spared the necessity to adjust to straitened financial circumstances. This family's adjustments were limited to consideration of which house to sell, and which to buy – where Juniper was to live.

No one but Lincoln had ever liked the cumbersome mansion on Fifth Avenue. Thus the decision was simple: either it should be sold to a developer, or it could be knocked down for Wakefield Enterprises to redevelop themselves. They settled on the latter and in the new plans a penthouse was to be reserved for Juniper's use when she was in New York. Marshall's dream of an uptown modern apartment was to be realised. And everyone involved was agreed that, given the unhappy circumstances surrounding the Dart Island estate, it was to be sold – lock, stock and barrel.

Unfortunately for everyone, no one had thought to include Juniper in the discussions. Hence, one day, three months after Lincoln's death, when driving up Fifth Avenue in the family limousine, she glanced out of the window to see a large ball and chain hurtling at her grandfather's house. Sharply she tapped the chauffeur on the shoulder and ordered him to drive immediately to her grandfather's office.

She had never been to these offices. In the latter years of his life Lincoln had rarely gone there himself, preferring to work from home. Consequently the doorman did not want to let her in, refusing to believe that this small slim girl could possibly be his employer.

It was the way she said, 'I think, for your own sake, you'd better take my word for it,' and the steadfast way she looked at him that made him hand her over to the receptionist.

The receptionist, more interested in her nails than this slip of a girl, merely laughed. Juniper looked quickly at the board to see on which floor Charlie Macpherson's office was situated and quickly slipped into the lift the next time the doors opened. As the doors closed she glimpsed the receptionist squawking impotently and waving her hands at the guard. On the twentieth floor Juniper did not even bother to ask the many secretaries to announce her but, before their astonished eyes, swept up to the largest door and strode in without knocking.

'Mr Macpherson, how dare you!' she said without preamble as she marched into his large office, which was furnished to resemble the noblest Englishman's library. 'They're knocking down my grandfather's house.'

'Why, yes, Juniper, we decided . . .'

'Who's we?'

'Why myself, the board, and . . . your father.'

'My father isn't one of my trustees.'

'No, but I thought it courteous to ask him.'

'Did you discuss this with Tommy?'

'Well,' he began to look discomfited as Juniper stood with anger in her eyes and defiance in her posture. 'Um, we felt . . . we felt that she was more involved with your day-to-day care . . .'

'She's my trustee, with you. She should have been consulted, I don't know what she will have to say about this. At least she would have had the courtesy to ask me what *I* wanted.'

'I apologise,' he thought it expedient to say.

'I accept your apology,' she replied with serious graciousness. 'From the mess I saw it is evident that it is too late to save the house now.'

'I'm afraid so. The new building work starts in ten days . . . it doesn't take as long to knock a house down as it does to build . . .' he laughed feebly, but stopped when he saw that Juniper did not even smile. 'We've a sparkling new building going up, you'll love it. We've reserved a lovely apartment for you at the top. Why, you'll be like an eagle in its nest with the whole of New York at your feet. And a wonderful swimming pool in the basement for you to play in . . .'

Juniper looked at him with disdain. She was not used to being spoken to as a child. 'Dart Island. What have you all decided to do with that?'

'Ah well, because of the sad circumstances . . .' he coughed discreetly, and straightened up in the large black leather chair, certain he was on surer ground here. Surely she would never wish to return there. 'We have several purchasers interested.'

'Then you can tell them it's no longer for sale.'

Through Charlie's mind flashed the large sum he had arranged as backhanded commission on the sale. Equally quickly he calculated his large salary over the years until this difficult young woman married – possibly only four or five years left – before she had total control over whom she employed. He did not want to lose this job. And he had plans, vague as yet, but ones that would net him a sound future. Young as she was, he could not afford to cross her: she looked the type who would never forget, let alone forgive.

'Of course, Juniper,' he said smoothly, congratulating himself on the nonchalant way he was kissing that commission goodbye. 'Have you plans to live there?'

'No, not for the time being. I still need to forget some things . . .' Then she stopped, why should she explain herself to this employee? 'I don't wish it to be touched. I suggest you leave it, just as it stands. My grandfather loved that place, he built it for my grandmother. He lies there . . . you will not alter a thing.'

'Yes, of course, Juniper. Would you care for some tea, or perhaps some lemonade?'

'No thank you, Mr Macpherson, I'm late for my dancing lesson.'

What had surprised Marshall most of all was how helpful and quiescent Charlie was being. Marshall had expected trouble with the man, instead he found himself consulted – a pleasant surprise. Things were turning out far easier than he had dared to hope. Since it had been decided that Juniper and Tommy were to live with them, it was the easiest thing to prise from the trustees a large allowance for Juniper's needs since the child must be kept in the manner to which she was accustomed. So, while not rich himself, he had access to wealth and in appearance was a rich man.

Alice had returned to England immediately after the funeral. At the time it had upset Marshall: he felt she should have stayed longer for Juniper's sake. But, as it turned out, her going was a good idea. Had she been here, Charlie might have consulted her, too, and then some of his plans might have been scotched. As it was, it was easy to claim from Charlie a large sum of money for the repair of Boscar Manor – it was Juniper's after all. He had made the estimates on American prices, intending to pocket the excess; Alice might have pointed out the discrepancy. Undoubtedly it was better she had gone.

Confident that he was now financially secure, he wrote to Flippy Sigford telling him to regard him as a partner in the Health Clinic – he could confidently risk his own money now. Most of the time he was busy planning the penthouse, consulting with the architects and designers, scouring the shops for suitable furnishings. He did not want one item of Wakefield's to remain. He'd show these damn Yankees what good taste was.

Slowly it dawned on him that nothing had changed for him here. He was still not treated with the respect he craved, and which was his by right of birth in England. Everyone here knew it was his daughter's money he was spending, everyone knew that Grace had been cut out of the will. He noticed the whispering as he passed by, the snide grins . . . he began to know how a gigolo felt. He began to long to return home where no one would know the circumstances, but could not see how he was to persuade Juniper.

At first Juniper had been overjoyed by the presence of both of her parents but as the months slipped by she felt an exasperation towards her mother that had not been there before. Daily Grace grew fatter and vaguer. She lay in bed all morning and half the afternoon. The shopping expeditions became shorter and it was as if the woman had no interest in anything at all apart from her adoration of Marshall, which shone out of vacant eyes. In fact, the only time Juniper saw any animation in her mother's face was when Marshall entered the room. Juniper began to feel that she could disappear from her mother's life and Grace would barely remark her absence.

Eventually even Marshall was forced to notice the deep depression from which Grace seemed incapable of recovery. Her grief for Lincoln made even Marshall feel sorry for her.

'Daddy, I don't think Mummy is ever going to get better the whole time we are here.'

'What do you suggest, my sweet?'

'I think we should go to England. There won't be memories of Grandpa there, it might help her.'

'If that's what you want, my darling, then we shall go.'

'It's not what I want, I'm happy here. I think it's best for Mummy,' she said in a voice of such sharpness that Marshall looked at her with surprise.

'Of course, of course. Your mother's happiness is all that concerns me,' he said seriously while his heart sang at the thought of returning home.

The voyage across the Atlantic was difficult for Juniper. She who had loved the sea now found she was terrified by it. As soon as she boarded the liner she began to shake uncontrollably. She went straight to her stateroom and to bed and lay under the covers shivering miserably. The ship's doctor was called but declared her fit as a fiddle and when he suggested she take a walk on the deck, she looked at him with disbelief. Marshall came and chivvied her but Tommy was the only one who understood. She sat patiently and talked gently to Juniper, explaining how her fear was a natural reaction that, given time, would pass. It was she who insisted that the girl be left alone and it was she who held her close when the fear became almost too much to bear. Juniper had always been fond of Tommy but on the crossing a bond of deep friendship was forged between them.

The crossing was not a happy one for Grace either. Marshall had talked at length with her. There, in the ornately furnished stateroom, he told Grace that they could no longer continue in their old perverted ways.

'You've found someone else?'

'No, Grace. I have not. There's only you, as there has only ever been you,' Marshall lied. 'We have to think of Juniper now, she'll be under our roof, I want nothing to damage her.'

'But, Marshall, you've always needed excitement and . . .' – desperately she searched for words, '– I know you'll tire of me,' she whimpered.

'No Grace, I won't tire of you. I will always stay with you.'

'Stay with the money, you mean,' she retorted with more spirit.

'Darling, that's unfair and you know it. The Wakefield money has never meant anything to me,' he lied again with practised ease. 'And Grace,' he went on, determined to grasp the nettle, 'those drugs are destroying you. Can't you see what they're doing to you? If only I'd known about them at the beginning, I would have insisted you stop years ago.

Grace was silent for a moment. 'I can't, Marshall. It's too late,' she said simply.

'No it isn't. I'll be with you, I'll help you, I promise.'

2

Alice had not expected to be as affected by Lincoln's death as she was. She had thought that fear had killed any love or affection she had for him. She was wrong. She grieved.

It was this grief which had decided her to return home as quickly as possible. When she had explained to Juniper why she was going, the child had understood immediately with the instinctive sensitivity of the young. She had no worries for Juniper: she had watched the affection between her and Tommy and was fully aware of Marshall's great love for the girl. For herself she had to get back to Gwenfer, knowing that only there would she be at peace, that there the grief and the sad memories would fade.

Marshall had written to his parents requesting that they return to Boscar Manor to supervise the repairs he had arranged. Alice was therefore more than a little put out to find, upon her return, that the Boscars were still firmly in residence at Gwenfer. They informed her bluntly that they had no intention of leaving Gwenfer for the discomfort of Boscar.

'We shall return when the men have finished,' Mathilda announced grandly, oblivious to Alice's displeasure. 'Noise makes my head throb.'

'But someone should be there to supervise the builders.'

'Cyril's there. He went yesterday.'

'Ah, I see. Poor Flo, she will miss him.'

'She's gone too. They refused to be separated,' Mathilda said serenely. 'So of course we had to let her go.'

'But Flo is the only help I have.'

'We know. Last night was most inconvenient. We

insisted they should not go until your return. But now you're back . . .'

Alice looked with irritation at the selfish, idle couple before her. She needed time to think, not to spend her time waiting hand and foot on this demanding pair. 'I'm sorry to disappoint you, I'm not back. I'm leaving immediately. You can fend for yourselves.' And she swept from the house, into the car and returned to Penzance. She booked into the Queen's Hotel, telegraphed Gertie, had a good dinner, slept like a top and caught the first train in the morning for London.

She spent a busy few days staying in Brown's Hotel. Thanks to Lincoln, she could now afford the luxury of a good hotel and she felt as excited as a child. She looked for a house for herself. And she took pleasure in shopping for gifts for Gertie, something she had not been able to do for a long time. With the same sense of excitement she took the train to Berkshire.

Staying with Gertie, Alice always felt that time had stood still. She was sure that Gertie's unfashionable clothes helped create this atmosphere, but the house added to the impression, for nothing had altered, everything was just as it had been before the war had changed everything and everyone else for ever – everyone, that is, except Gertie.

'But why on earth don't you buy a house close to us? The Thames Valley is teeming with beautiful houses and it's so convenient for London,' Gertie said bossily, as she poured tea for them both in her boudoir.

'What would be the point of having two country homes? No, I want a small pied-à-terre, that's all, nothing grand. I'm beginning to wish I hadn't even mentioned it to you.'

'It wouldn't have made any difference. Agnes Cobble-stone told me. She said she had seen you coming out of the pokiest little house, close by her dressmaker's!' The latter was said with an arched eyebrow.

'Good gracious, can one do nothing in this country without your knowing?' She smiled tolerantly at her friend who seemed to make it her duty to know exactly what Alice was doing. 'It's a dear little house, with a sweet garden quite big enough for me.'

'But *Chelsea*, Alice! A haunt of bohemians and goodness knows what riff-raff. I know no one who lives outside Mayfair and Belgravia.'

'You do now,' Alice said firmly.

'But what about Juniper?'

'When they come, I'm sure they will either lease or buy a large house somewhere you'll find quite suitable. When Juniper is older she will be very welcome to come and stay in my tiny house, but as it is there would not be room for everyone, which is exactly what I want.'

'The Boscars have been difficult, I presume.'

'Yes, demanding would be the precise word. I seem to have spent my life doing what other people want me to do. I've decided to become utterly selfish and live as I want and do what I want.'

'You couldn't be selfish, no matter how hard you tried.'

'Yes, I can. If you will have me, I intend to stay here until the house is mine, or until those dreadful people leave Gwenfer and I can return home.'

'My dear Alice, you are welcome to stay here for ever.' She leant across and patted Alice's hand. 'And how is Juniper?'

'She's a dear. Remarkably unspoilt given the circumstances. She's strong, I feel she will be able to cope with life and the dreadful responsibility of her riches.'

'Is she beautiful?'

'Too beautiful for her own good, I'm afraid. I've some photographs here.' She opened her handbag and handed them to Gertie. 'And Polly?' she said quietly. Gertie's back, ramrod straight at the best of times, became even straighter. 'You never see her, do you?' Alice asked in an almost accusing tone.

'Never,' Gertie replied, tight lipped.

'It's hardly fair to continue to punish the child, is it? It's not her fault . . .'

'I hear rumours.'

'What rumours?'

Gertie looked about the room so suspiciously that Alice thought she was about to leap up to check for eavesdroppers at the door.

'That she's not Richard's child,' she eventually whispered.

'Oh, Gertie, how dreadful. It's not like you to listen to appalling gossip like that.'

'I can't help what people are saying,' Gertie said a shade too defensively.

'Are you sure you are not listening to such rubbish because deep down you want it to be true?'

'You always were too modern for your own good, Alice – that comment sounds positively illogical – psychoanalysis and such rot.' Gertie sniffed dismissively.

'You can sniff, Gertie, but there's a lot of wisdom in it.'

'You'll be wanting to analyse my dreams next,' Gertie snorted in derision.

'And maybe that wouldn't be such a bad idea,' Alice retorted, taking another of the wafer-thin cucumber sandwiches, always her undoing when she stayed at Mendbury.

'And what does Richard say? I presume he's heard these rumours too?'

'I should think so. The whole of London was full of it a few years back. He dotes on the child as far as I can make out – absolutely dotes.'

'If he can accept the situation, why can't you?'

'You know why not, there's no point in going over that.'

'I'd like Juniper and Polly to do their season together. If Juniper hates it as much as we did it will be more fun for them to be together.'

'I shouldn't think she would be much of a companion for Juniper unless she too is mad on horses and farms.'

'And how would you know that?' Alice smiled slyly at her friend.

Gertie seemed discomfited for a moment then looked at her friend and laughed. 'Maggie Blunt, her nanny, was Richard's too. She's semi-retired now but she lives with them at Hurstwood.'

'So you're interested enough to keep a check on them?'

'Well . . . It's only natural, isn't it?'

'Oh quite, Gertie, quite . . .' Alice said non-committally.

3

The move to England had been the best possible thing for Juniper. Freed from the memories of her grandfather, which were at every corner in New York, she began to recover her old sparkle. She would never forget him but now she found she could think about him without wanting to burst into tears.

Her father had leased a large house in Belgravia for them and had arranged for her to use the local livery stables and to ride daily in Rotten Row. And there was the excitement of trips to the theatre, opera and ballet.

On Tommy's insistence she had been enrolled at Miss Lambert's school for young ladies recommended by a friend of Tommy's. At Miss Lambert's she learnt with a speed that surprised and delighted her. It was the school-room atmosphere she had needed, the competition of girls of her own age. Quickly she climbed from bottom of the class to near the top.

England had not had the same effect on Grace. She spent more time than ever in bed and Juniper watched with alarm as her mother began to swell like a slowly inflating balloon until Juniper felt ashamed to be seen with the waddling figure. When she was not in bed Grace wrapped herself in layers of jumpers and mismatched shawls and huddled shapelessly over fires which, given the warmth of the spring, no one else needed.

Of course everyone was sympathetic since they were sure that Grace was still in deep mourning for her step-father. She was, but Marshall was the main cause of her depression. She could no longer remember the last time he had shared her bed and, as her misery and insecurity increased, she consoled herself with chocolates and cakes, knowing all the while that the fatter she became the more she repulsed him. Once again she tortured herself with the agony of speculating about his infidelity.

She ached inside, ached with the old familiar pain of years ago and recognised that she had lost the strength of will to regain her sexual hold on him. She consoled herself that most men of her acquaintance kept mistresses – suitable mistresses, showgirls and shopgirls – hardly a threat to her married status. But there was a new and insidious misery for which there was no consolation, misery born of the growing realisation that since Juniper's inheritance Grace herself no longer had even a financial hold on Marshall. When food was no longer a solace she sought out doctors in Harley Street who asked no questions when it came to prescribing for rich, bored society women. Then she hired a private detective to watch Marshall.

Within three months of their arrival in England Marshall had installed a pretty chorus girl in a small house he had leased in St John's Wood. He settled into a safe routine of visiting her of an afternoon when he would normally be at his club and Grace would be resting.

He avoided Francine. It had been a hard decision to make but her flat was too public – there was too much risk of being recognised by other visitors – and London was a hotbed of gossip. Juniper might hear of it, and though Grace might forgive him a little chorus girl she would not countenance someone of Francine's standing – the most famous musical comedy star of the West End and a baroness-to-be. And, if he thought deeply about it, there was another reason: he did not want Richard to know he had deceived him over the years. It was something of which he had never been proud.

It was summer and school had closed. Accompanied by Marshall and Tommy, Juniper travelled to Cornwall to visit Boscar Manor. Grace had intended coming with them but, given the news that her in-laws had returned to the house, she changed her mind. As the train travelled west Juniper felt hope that in Grandfather Boscar she might find another Lincoln. She was to be sadly disappointed.

Juniper was perplexed, she had never been ignored in her life before. She was polite, she smiled at them, she tried to make conversation, she used all the charm of which she was capable. She might just as well have tried to befriend two statues. They looked at her so vaguely that she became convinced they did not know who she was. Frequently flickers of irritation crossed their faces. They had no time for her: her grandfather wanted only his insects and her grandmother needed only her piano and her solitary walks.

But worse was to come. Even Marshall was too busy for her. The realisation of this came as a great shock. Now her grandfather was dead, her father had all her love and devotion, and she expected as much in return. From the moment of her birth Juniper had been the centre of someone's attention. In New York her father had lavished time on her, had searched her out to take her for treats – a different one every day. In London it had been he who insisted on showing her all the sights. But here at Boscar Manor it was a different matter. He had other things to do, occupations which amused him more than she did. It was a new experience for her to hear her father say – 'In a minute, Juniper', or 'Not now, my Princess'. She did not know how to deal with this state of affairs. She would put on a new dress in the hope of catching his attention, or she would restyle her hair to distract him, but he failed to notice. The problem of the roof or the intricacies of the plumbing interested him more. From being puzzled she became hurt and from being hurt she finally became angry.

'Tommy, I want to visit my Grandmother Wakefield,' she announced one day, having decided that she hated Boscar Manor and did not wish to stay where she was not wanted.

Juniper had no memories of Gwenfer, she had been far too young the last time she was there. But, as Tommy swung the car between the gateposts with their large stone falcons and slowly inched the vehicle way down the steep driveway which clung to the side of the cliff, she looked about her with a strange sense of excitement. The rhododendrons had been allowed to grow wild and in places arched over the driveway making a dark cool green tunnel. The car emerged at the bottom and came to a halt in front of a long, mellowed granite house. The ranks of mullioned windows glistened in the sun. Juniper leapt out of the car, looked up at the house and felt as if it was welcoming her. From the terrace she looked down at the garden through which a stream cascaded and where plants grew in wild, colourful profusion. Standing on tiptoe, she could see the sea far down the valley, white waves cascading on the rocks, spray leaping into the air as if the sea itself was greeting her too. She stood entranced and, as she stood there, she fell in love – with Gwenfer.

'Grandmother, it's the most beautiful place I've ever seen in my life,' she said as she hugged Alice who had hurried from the house.

'Oh, Juniper, you don't know how happy your words make me.'

'It's most odd, I feel I belong here. Does that sound silly?'

'No, my darling, not at all. This *is* where you belong, these are your roots, this is your true home,' Alice said with feeling, and found she could have cried with joy, as they looked at the valley that throughout her life, even when thousands of miles away, had always sustained her.

4

Neither Alice nor Juniper would ever forget that summer together. They had always loved each other but now, despite Alice's fifty-eight years, and Juniper's fifteen, they became friends.

Frequently, as they sat on Alice's favourite rock at the mouth of the cove, and chatted of everything under the sun, and she tried to answer Juniper's many questions, Alice was reminded of Ia. It was not only the circumstances – sitting on the rock again with a companion – it was more than that. For Juniper, apart from the voice with its slight American accent, and the hazel eyes, looked strangely like Ia. And she certainly had the same enquiring mind; there were days when Alice felt exhausted from racking her brains to answer all the queries. Some days it was birds or flowers, another the tides and fish, another the planets.

'I'd like to be buried here, right under this rock,' Juniper said one particularly hot and beautiful day when even the sea seemed to be exhausted from the heat and the water merely lapped the rocks instead of thrashing them.

'What a macabre thing to say,' Alice laughed but a shiver sped down her spine.

'It's so perfect here, that's why.'

'I'll make arrangements for you,' Alice teased and wished the child would stop talking of death. She wondered if sitting by the sea was making Juniper talk and think about death. She had been glad when Juniper first joined her on the rock, hoping it was a sign that her fear of water might be fading. Now she was not so sure.

'How on earth could you have been happy in New York when this was your home?'

Alice looked out over the sea to the familiar craggy bulk of the Brisons rocks. It was a question she had often asked herself, now that she was safely back. 'I used to get dreadfully homesick and then I thought how pointless that was, and I had to get on with my life. I liked America, and the people were always kind and charming to me.'

'What was my real grandfather like?'

'I beg your pardon, Juniper. What do you mean?' Alice spoke sharply to cover her confusion.

'I know about it all, my father told me.'

'He had no right to do that.'

'Oh, no, Grandmother, I think I have every right to know who my true ancestors are.' She shook the glorious mane of long blonde hair – just as Ia used to do, Alice found herself thinking. 'I think he told me in the hopes that I would love Grandpa less. He's very jealous, you know.'

'Yes, you're right. He and your grandfather were very foolish when it came to you . . .' She relaxed now, thinking the girl had forgotten her earlier question. 'Have I told you about the green flash?'

'No, what's that?' She sat up with interest.

'When the sun is just about to slip over the horizon, just as it kisses the sea, they say sometimes you can see a flash of green light. I've watched all my life, but I've never been lucky. But I can't believe it doesn't exist.'

'Perhaps it's something you only see when you're about to die.'

'Juniper! You have such gloomy thoughts!' she admonished.

'We all have to die sometime . . .' she said with the

confidence of the young, convinced they will never die. 'So, what was my real grandfather like?'

One thing Alice had learnt about her granddaughter was that once set on a track, nothing would deviate her. 'Come with me,' she said, standing up and taking the girl's hand.

They walked up the path to the house while Alice told her of Chas Cordell; she was surprised at the amount of detail she could remember. She told her nearly everything – but not the circumstances of his death. It struck her, as she talked, that in telling her she might be damaging her own precious relationship with the girl.

Juniper stopped walking, Alice turned to her to see tears pouring down her face. 'Oh, my poor Grandma, how you must have suffered.' She flung herself into Alice's arms and Alice wondered why on earth she had worried that Juniper might condemn her.

They entered the house, crossing the great hall with the hammer beam roof, and from a niche Alice took a key to open a small oak door and led her up a short flight of steps into a room entirely lined with shelves on which stood large boxes stacked one upon the other. Muted light filtered through a window which was covered in creeper.

'Golly, what on earth are these?' Juniper looked about the musty room with curiosity.

'This is our muniment room.'

'Oh, yes, and what's that?' Juniper said doubtfully.

'It's a grand word for documents and archives. Here,' and she gestured with her hand, 'is the history of your family. All the wills, deeds of settlement, entails, dowries. I've found some going back to the sixteenth century but there might be some earlier than that . . .'

'You don't know?'

'My darling, I only discovered this room myself last year. There was a large piece of furniture in front of the door, it needed treating for woodworm, and when they came to take it away, I found the door and this room. My father never told me of its existence.'

'Why didn't he tell you?'

'I doubt if he was interested in them himself. And there was much my father chose not to tell me,' she said ironically. She crossed to one of the shelves. 'There, you can see the ones I've been sorting through.' She indicated a small pile of boxes which were not covered in the dust of years as the others were.

'These are all clean too.' Juniper had crossed to a shelf by the door.

'Ah, they only arrived a few months ago. When our lawyer in Penzance, Mr Woodley, died, his son requested that I remove some of our deed boxes. But here.' She opened one box, bright red, unlike the others. 'This is mine, I thought I should start putting my papers here too. And this,' she rustled through the contents, 'this is your grandfather.' And she produced a faded sepia photograph which Juniper eagerly snatched from her hand.

'Gee, he's so handsome, but what a funny hat,' she said, laughing with pleasure.

From that day there was no stopping Juniper, the cliff was forgotten, the rock was no longer visited. All she wanted to do was to delve into the boxes. Each morning they would haul a couple out and seat themselves at the long refectory table in the hall and sift and search and attempt to put the papers in some order. They had opened a great ledger to catalogue the contents and entered each document in turn.

Alice had started with the oldest boxes but Juniper would have none of that, she wanted to look at the more recent boxes first and work backwards.

'Well, you're not looking at mine, not until I'm dead and gone,' Alice said emphatically, and Juniper had to content herself with the Woodley boxes.

'Grandma, what category would you put this under? I think it's a letter but it's difficult to tell. It's almost illiterate.' She handed Alice a small scrap of paper, lined, as if it had been torn from a child's exercise book.

Alice read the printed capitals. *'Your Lordship. You'm owe me mam money. You knows that is so. Please help.'* She looked with disbelief at the signature, rounded and immature – *Mary Blewett.* 'Good gracious!'

'What did he owe them money for, do you think?'

'I can't imagine. I knew her, she was my friend Ia's sister.'

'He wouldn't have borrowed from someone like that, would he?'

'There would have been nothing to borrow. They owned nothing. What was it with? What is the next document in the box?'

Juniper picked out the next document, which was a copy of a letter, and read it. 'Oh, how horrible. Look, it's from the lawyer telling them that his Lordship will not be blackmailed and that the police will be informed unless they stop bothering him. Isn't that awful? Threatening them. People like that would have been terrified by the police, wouldn't they? And it's hardly a blackmail note is it?'

'What's the date on Mr Woodley's letter?'

'May 26th, 1881.'

'The month after Oswald drowned, the year Ia was born . . .' She sat with a puzzled expression but deep within her a thought was beginning to take seed, a thought that filled her with enormous excitement.

'Find my father's will,' she ordered as she opened another of the boxes and began to search frantically through the papers.

'I think your father made more wills than anyone else in the world, look at them,' Juniper laughed at the pile of folded documents in front of her.

'His circumstances kept changing, no doubt that's why. Don't read them in detail, just look for the name of Blewett.'

They worked in silence for ten minutes as they rapidly scanned the documents. 'Here. I've found one. *To Ada Blewett the sum of £200* . . . £200 doesn't sound a lot.'

'It was a fortune then. And here look, it's in this will too. The same sum.'

In a subsequent will made five years later, Ada was still a beneficiary. And then there was a change – in 1893, a new will named *Ia Blewett* and that same legacy persisted over the years despite the many changes in the various wills.

'Why does the name change?' Juniper asked.

'Ada is the mother, she died.'

'So Ia got the money in the end.'

'I fear not. When my father died he had no money left to leave to anyone.'

'I wish it said why he wanted her to have it.'

'Oh, so do I, Juniper, so do I.'

That night, alone in her bedroom, Alice took down from the wall the small watercolour of her rock that she had painted from memory all those years ago in New York and which had been returned to her upon Lincoln's death. She crossed to the lamp and studied the face of the young girl seated upon the rock. Ia.

She touched the face gently. It could be Juniper, the likeness was extraordinary. But when they were children people had often said how alike they were, Alice and Ia. They had loved each other like sisters. They had longed to be sisters. Was that what the note and the legacy were telling her? Had she had a sister after all?

5

At the beginning of the following summer Juniper was sulking. She had not wanted to come to the South of France with her parents; she had wanted to return to

Gwenfer, to be with Alice and to sift through the documents. But her contented absence the previous year and her announcement upon her return that she intended to go and live with her grandmother at Gwenfer had put the fear of God into Marshall. He was in no financial position to allow his daughter to live with anyone but himself. Flippy Sigford had been proved wrong: the health spa had collapsed and Marshall had lost every penny which was legitimately his. The only way he could recoup his losses was by milking his daughter's allowance and the allowance made to himself and Grace for Juniper's care. For the one and only time he had raised his voice in anger to his daughter and insisted she join them. Grace needed a holiday, he informed her, and it was selfish of her to refuse to go. Her mother wanted to be with her daughter, needed her, he stormed. Juniper doubted if this was the case but finally gave in.

She was still sulking, for her sacrifice seemed to have been for nothing. Yachting was all the rage and Marshall had insisted on leasing a large motor yacht even though he knew of her terror of the sea. She had refused to set foot on it, at first politely, then sharply, but finally with a hysterical ferocity that frightened everyone round her. So, in addition a villa had to be rented for her and Tommy to stay in while the others cruised. It was a pretty villa, just outside Cannes, on a promontory overlooking the sea. Strangely, as Juniper had discovered in Cornwall, she did not mind the sound and the sight of the sea, it was being on it that terrified her.

Grace was sitting on the deck beneath a striped awning. She wore large dark glasses to shield her eyes from the glare of sunlight on the water and from the blindingly white houses. She had not enjoyed the cruise at all. Most of the time she had been seasick, today was the first day she had not felt ill. Later they were setting sail for Cannes and she had decided to join her daughter there on terra firma.

She fanned herself with a magazine and cursed the heat. She should have refused to come: she hated the heat and always had done. Now that she was fat again she hated it even more. She had showered only half an hour ago and already she could feel the trickle of sweat snaking down her back. Any moment now she knew that she might begin to smell and she delved into her large beach bag for a bottle of perfume which she sprayed into her armpits. She shifted uncomfortably on the cushions of her chaise. Soon, despite the clouds of talcum powder she used, she knew the sweat would begin to chafe the flesh between her thighs making it look like a lump of raw meat. How she longed for England. She felt tired and dejected, she returned to her bag and from it took a small jewelled box and shook out two pills. She poured herself another glass of lemonade, swallowed the pills, and lay back waiting for them to take effect and perk her up before the others returned: where were they? They would be late casting off. She heard the clatter of footsteps on the gangplank and looked up.

'Look who I've found,' Marshall called.

Grace shaded her eyes against the glare, peering to see her husband's companion. Standing with her arm nonchalantly linked through his, dressed in a straight, sharkskin skirt in immaculate white, a smart navy and white striped blouse and a jaunty cap set on her long hair, was Francine Frobisher looking exactly as Grace dreamt of looking.

'Mrs Boscar,' she advanced with her hand outstretched in greeting and with a broad smile. 'So wonderful to see you again.'

'Mrs Frobisher.' Grace took her hand gingerly as though she expected it to hurt her.

'Girls, girls! Such formality. Grace and Francine surely,' Marshall joked, as he organised the steward to bring them drinks.

'We're late casting off,' Grace said anxiously.

'I couldn't abandon Francine. She's been having a dreadful time.'

'Dreadful, Grace,' she gushed. 'Such a dreary house-party – Phillip Treacher, the theatrical entrepreneur. Well, I expected some fun,' she giggled. 'My dear, they all had one foot in the grave – all dreary Shakespearian actors, or people whose books are completely unreadable. God, they took themselves so seriously. Poor me – like a duck out of water,' she pouted prettily. 'Oh, Marshall, decent champagne, you should have tasted the rubbish I've been suffering.' She took a glass and rolled her large green eyes heavenward in appreciation.

'I've invited Francine to join our cruise, Grace. Her maid is packing now. It will only mean a small delay. Is everyone back?'

'The Rickmansworths are but I haven't seen the Marts.'

'You haven't got Freddy Mart on board? Oh, how divine, I just love his films.'

Grace hauled herself up from the low chair, aware that she exposed the roll of fat at the top of her stockings as she did so. 'I'll go and arrange accommodation for Mrs Frobisher,' she said, deliberately remaining formal.

'The steward will see to that, Grace,' Marshall said, offering her a glass of champagne.

'Later. I'd rather see to it myself,' she said over her shoulder, determined to find the smallest, noisiest, hottest cabin for her unwanted guest.

The following morning the party were clustered on the deck beneath the blue and white awning as *The Grafton* slid gracefully into Cannes harbour.

'So,' said Marshall looking particularly handsome, Grace thought, in his white yachting trousers, immaculate blazer and jaunty peaked cap. 'So, what are everyone's plans?'

'I must go to the hairdresser,' Grace announced. 'I usually go to the one in the Carlton, he's very good, if anyone would care to join me.' She smiled shyly at the other women. Penny Mart and Gwendoline Rickmans-worth immediately agreed.

'Mrs Frobisher?' Grace asked.

'Darling, bless you, but I always go to a little salon in Juan les Pins – I've been going there for years. If I might use someone's car?' Francine replied, choosing to ignore Grace's continued formality. She flashed her famous smile and was immediately offered the use of three cars. Grace was relieved. To have spent the day with Francine would have undermined what little self-confidence she still possessed, and with Francine safely on her way to Juan les Pins Grace could leave Marshall without her usual anxiety.

Marshall and the other men decided on a round of golf and it was agreed that they should all meet at the Beau Rivage for lunch at one.

The men were on the second tee when a club servant handed Marshall a telephone message.

'Sorry, partner,' he said to Freddy Mart. 'An urgent appointment – completely slipped my memory.'

He hurriedly left his complaining companions, slid behind the wheel of the white Bugatti and raced down the Corniche to the yacht basin.

'What an elegant strategy!' he said kissing the neck of the woman who was waiting for him in the forward saloon.

'I thought we would never manage to be alone,' Francine replied as she turned with a beguiling smile and slipped into his arms. 'Why have you been avoiding me in London? You are a dreadful man.' She chuckled huskily.

It was a combination of the heat of the day and the intolerable heat of the hair dryer which gave Grace a headache. She was afraid she was about to faint.

'So silly of me,' she said to her companions. 'Please explain to Marshall . . . I've some pills in my cabin. I'll send the car back for you all. If I feel better I'll rejoin you,

282

but don't wait for me.' In the overheated interior of the Rolls Grace felt even worse as she ordered the chauffeur to hurry to the yacht.

She stumbled up the gangplank, fumbled her way along the corridor and opened her stateroom door. She stood there dazed with shock, her head throbbing, as she watched the two lovers who, in the throes of their passion, were unaware of her presence.

Grace wanted to race from the room but her large, puffy feet seemed rooted to the spot.

It was Francine who saw her, gazing wide-eyed over Marshall's shoulder. Then Francine smiled and Grace felt bile spurt into her mouth.

'Oh, Marshall, my darling, I love you,' she heard Francine sigh.

'God, Francine, how I adore you,' her husband replied as he continued to ride the actress's slim, beautiful body.

Francine looked straight at Grace and smiled again, a smile which did not reach her eyes.

Grace clutched her hand over her mouth and lumbered from the room as Marshall roared his climax.

Locked in the lavatory Grace fought to gain control of herself, splashing her face with water, taking deep breaths to quell the nausea. She leant against the basin and tried to rationalise what she had seen, her reaction to it.

She had been certain for some months of Marshall's infidelities. She knew of the chorus girl in St John's Wood, the shop girl from Marshall and Snelgrove, the manicurist. So, was it seeing them making love, instead of imagining it, that had made her sick? There was no difference between Francine and the others; for what was she but a jumped-up chorus girl? She might have a husband who was heir to a barony but she was still a tramp. Surely he would never leave her for someone like that. He would never risk losing Juniper, and he certainly would not abandon Juniper's money for that slut.

Grace sighed at her reflection. Always the money. The

money had caught him in the first place, and Juniper's money was all that bound him to her now.

What an indictment of her life and worth.

She pulled a comb through her hair – hating the new style the hairdresser had bullied her into having, hating herself.

'After all I've done for him . . .' she yanked the comb. 'After all the degradation . . .' yank, yank, yank – she found herself almost enjoying the pain caused by the tortoiseshell teeth as they scraped across her scalp.

She must not panic . . . This would mean nothing to Marshall, just another body to satisfy his overactive libido. But still, he had never, as far as Grace knew, been unfaithful with anyone who might be connected to their set.

Grace stopped dead, the comb poised – wasn't Richard Frobisher an old friend of Marshall's? Surely Marshall would never deceive a friend. But then he had, she had the evidence of her own eyes. Fear clutched at Grace and made her entrails go into spasm.

She must remain calm, behave as if nothing had happened, she would weather this – somehow or other. It would not last, these affairs never did.

Grace snapped her handbag shut, straightened the seams of her stockings and slipped quietly from the boat.

She sat outwardly calm, sipping a cocktail on the terrace of the Beau Rivage with their friends, as they awaited their host and last guest.

Marshall came first. Grace's heart contracted as her husband crossed the terrace towards them, a single red rose in his hand which he presented with a kiss to Grace as their friends applauded the gesture.

Francine arrived minutes later in a dramatic flurry of gushing apologies for her lateness.

'I thought you were going to the hairdresser's?' Gwendoline Rickmansworth said, eyeing Francine carefully. 'They don't seem to have done much.'

'Oh, I didn't go. The day was too divine, I just took off along the coast for a little drive. Do I look dreadfully windswept?' Francine shook her head, the famous Frobisher tresses cascading over her slim shoulders, and she smiled boldly at Marshall.

'You look wonderful, Francine, but you always do.' Marshall smiled carefully back at her as the waiter presented the menus.

In the babble of conversation about what they should eat Grace sat quietly as hatred took root within her.

6

'Tommy, what would you do if your husband was unfaithful to you?' Juniper and Tommy were sitting on the terrace of the villa watching the lights which shone brightly across the bay, even at this late hour. The air was heavy with the smell of jasmine and the crickets' calls of love. They had just returned from an evening with Marshall and his party, they had dined well, had been to a night club and had finished up at the casino. Only Grace was missing, her headache had persisted.

'I haven't got one so I don't know, do I?' Tommy laughed, then yawned and suggested they went to bed.

'But if you had one – would you leave him?' Juniper persisted.

Tommy looked closely at Juniper. 'I think it would depend on how much I loved him and how serious the affair was,' she answered quietly. She knew Juniper well now and realised that the girl rarely asked a question unless there was a good reason.

'What if it was someone so beautiful, far more beautiful than you?'

'Well, that wouldn't be difficult, would it?' Tommy patted her neat hair, smoothed her long plain skirt and peered at Juniper through her spectacles.

'I think you're very pretty.'

'Why, thank you.'

'But it's as if you don't want to be pretty, as if you're hiding it.'

'Juniper, you say such funny things,' Tommy replied, but secretly rather pleased with the girl's assessment.

'You didn't answer my question,' Juniper persisted.

'Beauty shouldn't matter, it's what a person is inside that's important. But, sadly, men seem to be more interested in the externals.' She half smiled.

'My grandfather thought you were beautiful and he loved you very much.'

'Your grandfather was not like other men,' she said dreamily, remembering the unexpected happiness she had found with Lincoln. 'But you weren't supposed to know anything about that, young miss!'

'Bah! You can't keep secrets from me. I was pleased. You were such an improvement on the others.'

'You're too sophisticated for your own good. Just look at you in that dress, you look like a woman already. And what your parents are thinking of, letting you go to night clubs and the casino . . . !'

'You're my trustee. You stop me.' Juniper grinned at her.

'I can just imagine the fuss, and whoever stopped your father doing whatever he wanted? No, I'll just accompany you everywhere, make sure nothing dreadful happens to you.'

'My father likes me to look sophisticated.'

'I know.'

'Oh, Tommy, you sound so disapproving. But you've changed the subject, you're good at that.' She turned to face her. 'Are all men unfaithful?'

'Oh, darling, I don't know, I've no experience of such matters. My parents weren't, and don't think my brother would be unfaithful to his wife, but then . . .'

'But then . . . what?'

'Well, I think the society you move in affects behaviour. It seems to me the richer people are the less constrained their behaviour.'

'What's constrained mean?'

'It means . . . well, it means you can get away with more if you're rich.'

'I'm rich but I don't think I'd want to be unfaithful to my husband. I want to live happily ever after and have dozens of babies.'

'And I'm sure you will, Juniper. But what on earth brought this conversation on?'

'I think Daddy's in love with Francine. I watched them together and he can't take his eyes off her . . . She's very beautiful of course,' Juniper added almost as an after-thought.

'Oh Juniper!' Tommy said, shaking her head. 'You do say some odd things sometimes.'

'I don't want my mother hurt. She loves my father desperately.'

'It's your imagination, I'm sure,' said Tommy firmly.

'But what if I'm right and it's serious between them? What then? I mean . . . my mother always seems to be unhappy – she rarely smiles, have you noticed? He couldn't really love the Frobisher woman, could he? She's lovely but she's so stupid. She's only ever interested in the conversation if people are talking about her.'

'Juniper, I'm sure it isn't "serious" as you call it. Mrs Frobisher's a dreadful flirt and men fall for that sort of behaviour.'

'I think it's more than that. I think they're *lovers*. I know about these things, you know.'

'Really, Juniper. You're imagining things. It's the heat, or something. Try and forget about it,' Tommy spoke sharply and Juniper knew the subject was closed.

But Juniper could not forget. It took her a long time to get to sleep that night. On the one hand she felt sorry for her mother – she knew how much she adored Marshall –

but on the other hand Grace exasperated her – she seemed to have no spirit left in her and she was always so miserable. And Francine was vivacious and beautiful. Juniper doubted if there was a man alive who could resist a woman like that.

Juniper had lied to Tommy: she knew very little about the facts of life, though she had tried to find out often enough. She had asked Tommy who had blushed and said it was not her place. She had asked her father, who told her to ask her mother, and all her mother had said was, 'There's time enough for all that,' which was no answer at all.

Juniper's hands felt her breasts, ran down her slim body until they lay between her legs. She found herself enjoying the familiar warm sensation this gave her – was this what husbands did to their wives?

For a week the yacht had been cruising. Grace had cancelled her plan to join Juniper at the villa and had sailed with them. She kept a tight control on herself as each day she watched her husband become more besotted with Francine.

At first Grace had made certain they were never left alone together. But the dark, intimate looks between the two continued. It was always Marshall who leapt up to light Francine's cigarette, it was always he who insisted on pouring her drink, fetched her wrap, danced attendance upon her.

The yacht returned to Cannes for the Rickmansworths to leave and for four more friends to join them. A short trip along the Italian coast was planned.

Grace changed tactics. Perhaps, if she left them to spend all the time they wanted together, her husband would become bored with this creature.

Grace excused herself. She needed to see her dress-maker and jeweller, she explained. She would join Juniper in the villa and meet up with them in five days' time.

It was a long five days for Grace who barely slept, who walked the villa at night like a giant ghost in her voluminous nightdress. She wrote copiously of her agony in her diary. She longed for her step-father and snapped at her daughter.

She stood, newly coiffed, in a white linen shift whose extreme simplicity had cost a small fortune, and waited for the yacht to dock.

Grace knew as soon as she saw them that her experiment had not worked. She saw that her husband was even more involved with Francine – he looked at her with the eyes of a man whose hunger could never be sated. Grace knew she had lost.

She sat through the long luncheon at the Beau Rivage; she talked, she smiled, but slowly she disintegrated inside.

Grace refused to rejoin the yacht. She could not bear to watch her husband's infatuation. She returned to the villa. There she made a long-distance call: it was the only weapon left to her.

'Richard Frobisher? We met a couple of times – my name is Grace Boscar.'

'Of course, Mrs Boscar, I remember you well.'

'I'm afraid, Mr Frobisher, my husband is having an affair with your wife.' There was a long silence. 'Did you hear me?'

'I'm sorry, Mrs Boscar,' Richard Frobisher replied calmly.

'Shouldn't you come?'

'There would be little point.'

'Don't you care?'

'I'm afraid, Mrs Boscar, I ceased caring about my wife's activities years ago.'

'But, what about me?' Grace's voice was becoming shrill as she realised this last hope of controlling Francine was fading.

'I'm sorry, Mrs Boscar, for any pain that my wife is

causing you. But, you see . . . there's nothing I can do. My wife is a law unto herself.'

'But this is serious, Mr Frobisher. I think they are in love.'

'In which case, Mrs Boscar, there is even less we can do about it, isn't that so?'

Wordlessly Grace replaced the receiver.

The pain that had burnt red hot for the past two weeks seemed to disappear, to be replaced by the cold blackness of despair.

Grace Boscar looked at her future and shuddered. A large tear escaped the pale grey eyes and slid down the red, fat cheek. Grace felt totally alone.

Juniper was starving. She and Tommy had had a marvellous day, taking a picnic to Juan les Pins where, on the beach, Juniper had met the most beautiful boy she had ever seen in her life and remembering how Francine acted with her father she had flirted, extravagantly – and enjoyed it. She liked the sense of power it gave her.

But now, on the villa terrace, at the table set for three she waited impatiently for her mother to join them for dinner.

'Where on earth is she? She's never late for meals.'

'Juniper!' Tommy admonished her half-heartedly, knowing it was true: her mother was usually the first at the table. 'Maybe she's dining in her room. I'll go and see.'

'No, you wait there, I'll go.'

Juniper raced from the terrace, across the large drawing room, up the white marble staircase and knocked on her mother's bedroom door. There was no reply. Juniper tried again. She was probably in the bathroom and could not hear. She pushed open the door.

'Mummy, I'm starving, do come quickly.'

Juniper stopped in the doorway frozen like a statue with horror.

Sprawled across the bed, her head dangling down, the pale grey eyes staring at the ceiling, her mouth open, a trickle of vomit on her chin, lay Grace. In death, Grace Boscar looked truly ugly.

Grace had been buried. She lay in the private chapel of Boscar Manor. Marshall felt guilty about that since she had hated it so, but she had not liked Gwenfer either. He went to bed exhausted.

Juniper was exhausted too but she could not sleep. She wanted her mother. She wanted her in a way she never had when Grace was alive. She wandered downstairs to find some milk. In the hall, still unopened, was their luggage. Not certain why she did it, Juniper began to undo the clasps on one of Grace's trunks. On top of the clothes were laid a collection of vellum-covered books – diaries which went back over the whole of her mother's life. To her frustration the small clips on the side were locked, except one, the last one her mother had kept – unfinished, the last entry made on the day she died.

Juniper scooped up the books and returned to her room. With her nail file she prised the locks open. Through the night she read. She read of her mother's obsessive love. She read of her trip to Switzerland. Paris. She read of the degradation, the perversions and her mother's loathing for what she thought she had to do. And in her heart, which had always been full of love for her father, ice began to form. Hatred took root and a resolve never to be like her mother, never to love as she had done.

In the middle of the night Marshall's dream returned. He woke, his body soaked in sweat and his mind filled with terror – '*Rosemary*,' he muttered. He turned, searching for someone – for Grace, wanting the comfort of her large yielding breasts . . . then he remembered. 'Oh, my God, Grace, I did love you. Why didn't I realise? Why didn't I tell you? Why did you leave me?' he cried into the silence of the night.

In the morning Juniper hid the diaries amongst her possessions, locked the case and put the key in her pocket. She did not stop for breakfast but went straight outside, walking quickly in the direction of the farm. She leant against a gate, the sun shining on her loose hair, a blade of grass in her mouth.

Several farm workers passed by. Some spoke but most looked in silent awe at such an exotic creature in their yard. She ignored them until towards her strode a tall, broad-shouldered youth with a mop of black hair.

'You,' she called out. 'What's this?' she asked, holding out a weed she had picked.

'That's cow parsley. Don't ee know cow parsley?' he grinned.

She laughed with him, tossing her hair, leaning forward towards him, brushing his hand lightly just as she had seen Francine do. She began to tease him, flirt with him, confusing his simple country boy's mind with her seduction.

Suddenly she held her hand out to him and, as if mesmerised, he took it and, stumbling, gauche and unsure of himself, he allowed her to lead him towards the hayrick.

Once they were hidden in the rick, his unsureness disappeared as he grabbed her and with sweaty hands began to pluck at her clothes. Juniper began to feel afraid but it was too late, she could not stop him; it was she who was now unsure. The more she shouted, 'No!' the more excited he became and then drew her back into the hay.

The whole experience for Juniper was loathsome. The heat, the prickly hay, the youth's acrid smell, the fear she felt at not being in control, the power she had unleashed in this man, and the pain as he entered her.

But, as she walked back to the house, picking the last pieces of hay from her dress, she was satisfied with this morning's work. By giving Marshall's 'Princess' to the first man she liked the look of, she felt she was punishing him in the cruellest way she knew.

Chapter Seven

1

It was March. A glorious day, more summer than early spring, was shambling lazily into evening, as if loath to give way to night. Polly, settling her pony, was irritated to be summoned by her mother to the drawing room.

Polly resented her mother's presence at Hurstwood. In the past she had so rarely come that Polly felt Hurstwood belonged to her and her father and that Francine had no place here. But, during the last couple of years Francine had come too frequently for comfort. And here she was for another weekend – probably filling the house with her London friends whose glossy sophistication made Polly feel uncomfortable. She knew she would learn nothing from them for nothing interesting would be said – only London gossip. Whereas when she dined alone with her father they would discuss and argue about politics, literature and art. Polly knew the empty chatter of her mother's friends would annoy him even more than it did herself, and no doubt her parents would argue and her father would become strange and distant, as he did whenever her mother was here. Distant from everyone, including Polly.

Despite the uncertainty of youth Polly was sure of two things. She loved her father and hated her mother.

As Polly entered the drawing room her father rose from his chair. He smiled at her absent-mindedly and resumed his seat, picking up the newspaper he had momentarily discarded.

Just recently her father had started to stand when Polly entered a room. On the one hand she liked this for it made her feel almost grown-up. On the other, it embarrassed her. Perhaps he was embarrassed too which was why he hid himself so quickly behind *The Times* again.

Across the room her mother was fussily draping a swatch of material over the knoll settee. Polly stiffened. Polly had never minded what her mother did to the London flat. She rarely went there and felt the flat had nothing to do with her. But Hurstwood was sacrosanct – surely her father would not let her change as much as a cushion?

'Ah, there you are, child. What took you so long?'

Polly ignored the question as she ignored the greeting. Polly had discovered long ago that by ignoring her, she could in turn annoy her mother.

'What do you think . . . ?' her mother waved her hand at the new chintz.

Polly shrugged her shoulders, the uninterested gesture effectively masking her anger. The girl knew that if she said she disliked the material it would be a guarantee that new covers made from it would be in place within the week.

So worked Polly and Francine.

'Why is it you never have an opinion on anything, child?' The irritation in the comment was masked by Francine's famous smile which Polly knew was as false as the silver blonde of her mother's hair. She had once been naturally blonde but now, nearing forty, the colour was artificial – Polly knew for she'd seen the bottle of bleach in her mother's bathroom. Polly picked up a magazine and leafed through it, all the time alert to her mother's decorative plans. 'Something's got to be done about this dreary room. Just look at it – dull as ditchwater! I can't be expected to live in these surroundings. I shall wilt, positively wilt!' She looked about the room with distaste. 'I'd have that panelling out for a start.' Her arm waved at the offending panelling – bleached pale from centuries of sunlight which poured through the long, latticed casements. 'And that horrid lead on the windows stops the light!'

'I like the house just the way it is, Mother.' Polly's love and fear for the house forced her to declare an opinion.

'You would. You're just as scruffy as the house. Richard, for God's sake put that bloody paper down and tell me what you think.'

Francine was bored and that frightened Polly most of all, for when she was bored her mother's moods were even more unstable.

'Opinion on what?' he asked vaguely, looking over the newspaper.

Francine looked heavenward, widening her green eyes exaggeratedly.

'The material, Richard. This new one I've selected. Though really what we should do is throw this mouldering heap out and get nice new furniture.'

'No!'

Both Francine and Polly jumped at the emphatic tone and loudness of Richard's reply.

'I beg your pardon?' Francine said with deliberate enunciation.

'I forbid it.'

'You forbid me?' Francine laughed a cynical, questioning laugh.

'You are not to touch a thing in this house, Francine, do you understand? Do what you like in London but leave this place alone.'

'But Richard, I only want to make it pretty,' Francine had changed the tone of her voice to that of a wheedling child's lilt. Of all her mother's repertoire of voices this particular one irritated Polly the most. It sounded obscene – a grown woman pretending to be a little girl. 'You know everyone thinks I'm brilliant with interiors. I'm always being told that if I hadn't been such a success on the stage I could have been equally successful as an interior decorator.'

'Maybe, but not here.'

'It's too dreadfully shabby.'

'I like it shabby.'

'It suits the house,' Polly chimed in.

'Shut up, and keep your sodding nose out of things.'

It always shocked Polly when her mother swore in her carefully modulated voice with its beautiful professional tone. It was not that Polly was unused to swearing or disapproved of it, her father often swore and Jim the stable lad was brilliant at it. No, it was different when her mother swore – more vehement, more angry, as if the words were really meant. And it was an indication that at any moment she would lose her temper.

'I don't wish to discuss it further,' her father said, noisily reorganising his newspaper. Polly braced herself for the screaming that would surely start. Her mother paused, the length of material in her hand, and looked with loathing at the newspaper. Abruptly she flung the material on the settee and swung round to face Polly.

'Darling Polly, I've a wonderful surprise for you.'

Polly was caught off guard; she had been waiting for trouble, not a surprise. She waited patiently while her mother went through the elaborate ritual of placing a cigarette into her long ebony holder, each movement over-emphasised, drawing attention to the long elegant hands. Then she waited for someone to light it – as someone always did. Her father rose, proffered his lighter, lit the cigarette and sat down again in one smooth action, perfected from years of practice. Francine slowly inhaled the smoke arching her back slightly as she sensuously let the smoke out of her mouth. Polly waited.

'Such a lovely surprise . . .' she paused dramatically. 'A little friend for you to play with.'

Polly forced herself to look blankly at her mother.

'She'll help amuse you, living in this dreary place. And . . .'

'I don't find Hurstwood dreary, Mother.'

'Of course you find it dreary. Everybody does – except your father.' Francine cast another furious look at the paper. 'If you like each other then maybe she'll invite you to stay in the South of France with her during the beastly, boring summer.'

'I don't find summer boring or beastly.'

'Of course you do. No one enjoys an English summer! There are no good plays. Not a living soul in London. Everyone who's mildly interesting will be on the Côte.' Francine's voice had risen dangerously.

It was odd about the South of France, thought Polly. The year before last her mother had returned earlier than usual and in a filthy temper had lasted for weeks. Then last year she had not gone at all. Polly's grandfather, Basil Frobisher, had died suddenly of a heart attack. Her father had shut himself in the study and had waited for his mother to telephone and summon him. The telephone did not ring. The following day Richard continued his normal routine and did not mention his father again. Polly was sad but it was a sadness caused by knowing she would never know her grandfather now: she could not grieve for someone she did not know. Francine, on the other hand, cancelled her trip to France and, dressed hypocritically in black, rushed to Hurstwood, an atmosphere of excited drama swirling about her. She was happy – a titled lady at last. With unseemly speed Francine had ordered all her linen to be embroidered with a baron's coronet and the Frobisher arms had sprouted everywhere – on firescreens, a plaque on the wall and all the silver and even the plate had been engraved.

What was really odd was the argument she had overheard a few days ago between her parents in which her father had forbidden her mother to travel south this coming summer. That her father should forbid it was astonishing enough, that her mother had appeared to acquiesce was even more so. In the past she had gone every year without fail. Polly had never been able to understand her mother's passion for the South of France. Hurstwood had to be more fun than sitting on boring fat men's yachts, drinking too much and indulging in what she thought of as '*God knows what*'.

Years ago '*God knows what*' had featured frequently in conversations she had overheard between Nanny and the cook. For years Polly had been uncertain what Nanny had meant, but suspected that, whatever it was, it would only make her dislike her mother more. But now, at seventeen, she was beginning to realise the meaning behind the old lady's whisperings. Polly found she was not surprised, she was not even disgusted; she just did not care and hoped her father felt the same way.

Nanny had been her father's nurse and was the only member of his past to have moved with him into his future. Doubly dear old Nanny, for Polly was certain, although nothing was said, that Nanny hated Francine as much as Polly did.

'Who is she?' Polly finally asked, her curiosity getting the better of her. 'How long's she staying?'

'As long as she wants.'

'What if I don't like her?'

'Of course you'll like her.'

'How do you know if I will or won't? You don't know what I'd like, Mother.'

'Good gracious, aren't we being childishly dramatic. I certainly do know what you like. Painfully so. Disgusting, smelly horses, unspeakably scruffy clothes and unsuitable brats from the village.' From the rising shrillness of her voice, Polly knew that any minute now there would be tears. Sure enough, slowly, from the great dark green eyes a tear appeared and slid smoothly down the beautiful cheek. The ease with which her mother could cry never failed to fascinate Polly. She seemed able to do it at will.

'I thought you would be pleased,' Francine said petulantly, wiping her eyes prettily with a lace-edged scrap of a handkerchief. 'Such a dear, sweet friend too. Richard, talk to your daughter, do.'

'She has a point, Francine. She might not like the girl and then what do we do?'

'I only wanted it to be a lovely surprise for her.'

Polly looked at her mother with suspicion – if this girl was coming it was because, for some reason, Francine wanted her to.

'But you hardly know the girl, Francine.'

'We know a lot about her – her background, her parents . . .'

'Exactly,' said Richard in a surprisingly ominous tone of voice. 'Not the best recommendation for a companion for Polly if you ask me.'

'God, Richard, you're vindictive. Don't you ever forget anything?'

'There's quite a lot to forget in this instance.'

'Richard, you can be a beast,' and Francine stamped her foot prettily.

'Who is she?' Polly interrupted, before her mother could unleash another of her histrionic performances.

'Her father's a great friend of your mother's. You'd better ask her.'

'Why do you see evil in everything I do? I felt sorry for the girl, she needs friends, that's all,' Francine screeched.

'But which girl, Francine? Yours or Marshall's? Polly asks a reasonable question. With all their money I can't imagine why on earth she wants to come here. Why, Francine?'

'You always were insanely jealous of the money weren't you, Richard? I often wonder which offended you most . . .'

'You bitch.' To Polly's amazement her father stood, poised it seemed to hit her mother. She was used to her mother's tempers, but her father rarely lost his.

'Name calling, that's all you're good for, Richard.'

Francine shook her head, evidently in her anger forgetting that the famous Francine Frobisher locks had recently been cut and permed into a frivolous bob. 'If you're going to be impossible, I refuse to talk to you.'

Noisily collecting the clutter of her bag, cigarettes, and *Vogue* magazine Francine swept to the door. Daintily holding the door with one hand, she arched her elegant whip-thin body, swayed slightly and half turning the famed profile, did not so much speak as proclaim – 'I tell you one thing, Richard. You may incarcerate me in this Godforsaken hole, but you can never imprison my spirit.' Dramatically she swept from the room with all the style of the West End actress she was.

'I always want to applaud when she does that,' Polly said as brightly as she could. 'I wonder which play that line's from.'

'It could be funny if it wasn't so sad,' her father said wearily.

'I love you, Daddy.' Polly did not know why she suddenly said that. She and her father were not given to saying such things. It was not necessary. But, suddenly, he looked so sad, almost beaten, Polly thought, that the words seemed very necessary.

'I know you do, sausage. I love you, too.'

'I don't love her.'

'Now, Polly. You shouldn't say such things. She probably meant well. It could be fun. Try and make it fun, for me?'

'I'll try. But who is she?'

'Juniper Boscar . . .'

'Juniper . . . ! What a daft name,' Polly burst out, laughing.

'Yes it's unusual but they're an unusual family. Her mother, Grace, died a couple of years back. And her father . . .' he paused and coughed. 'I knew him slightly years ago. As it happens her grandmother is a great friend of my mother.'

Polly leant forward eagerly. He rarely mentioned his family and Polly had met them as a baby, which did not count. Hence, she was hungry for any scraps of information that came her way. Neither parent discussed their past. Polly had once asked her mother about her family and where she had been born. 'Long ago . . .' her mother had said vaguely and changed the subject.

'Best friends?' Polly persisted.

'Well, yes, I think so.'

'I shall enjoy meeting her then.' Polly's mood had changed dramatically. 'Why did mother invite her?'

'She didn't. Juniper invited herself.'

2

The following week Polly waited, with her mother, on the steps of Hurstwood for the guest's arrival. They were not speaking to each other. Her mother had insisted that she change into a blouse and skirt in honour of the guest. Polly had argued for the right to stay in her jodhpurs. Now Polly stood, uncomfortable in linen skirt and blouse, a sullen scowl on her face, her mother in smart crêpe de Chine beside her.

Polly loathed skirts. As soon as she put one on she felt her legs grow another six inches and her feet loom alarmingly large. Her suspenders dug into her, and the silk stockings, borrowed from her mother, made her feel hot and sweaty.

A sleek drophead Lagonda drew up. Out of the car and into Polly's horrified sight stepped an elegant, fashion plate of a young woman. She wasn't a girl, she was an exact replica of her mother's sophisticated friends – from her suit with its slim, daringly slit skirt and shoulders heavily trimmed with fur, to the jaunty hat perched over one eye and the sleek high-heeled shoes.

'Juniper, my dear,' her mother swept down the steps

towards the girl, embracing her, each kissing the air beside the other's face. Disgusting, thought Polly. The girl approached her, smiling, her hand held out.

'Polly, I'm so happy to meet you.' She had a surprisingly low and husky voice, which had the hint of a chuckle in it and a slight American accent that added to its charm. Polly looked at the pristine white glove which was held out to her, and involuntarily wiped her own hand down the side of her skirt before gingerly accepting it.

'Hullo,' she said shyly.

'Lady Frobisher, what a delightful house. It positively reeks of history!'

'It is quite pretty, but compared with your homes, very modest.' To Polly's astonishment her mother giggled almost nervously.

'But I adore little houses. I just adore them!'

Polly fumed inwardly. How could a house of eight bedrooms be considered small? And modest? Hurstwood was a famous Elizabethan manor house. Perfect, a gem, any fool could see that. Moodily Polly kicked at the gravel path.

'Polly, your shoes! Tiresome girl!' It wouldn't have been too bad if her mother had been speaking to her, but, to Polly's mortification, she spoke directly to Juniper.

'Shall we take tea?'

Grudgingly, Polly followed them across the stone-floored, panelled hall. The others walked ahead in animated conversation. So much for Juniper being her friend, thought Polly moodily.

Juniper sat elegantly on the sofa in the drawing room, making Polly feel more clumsy than ever as she helped her mother serve the guest.

'You didn't go South last year, Lady Frobisher?'

'No, I couldn't. My father-in-law died last spring – I was so sad, a dear man – and my husband needed me.'

Polly could hardly believe her ears.

'And this year? Shall you be going?' Juniper asked.

'Sadly, no. My husband decided I needed a rest. I've had a strenuous year, two plays in nine months.'

'Oh yes, Lady Frobisher, I do know. Why, I went to see *Roses, Red Roses* three times. Divine!'

Francine Frobisher preened herself with pleasure at the young girl's obvious admiration. As they discussed, in detail, the plays, Francine's roles in them, and the short-comings of all others taking part, Polly decided she had solved the question of the reason for the visit. The girl was stage-struck and wanted help in getting on the stage. Ridiculous profession, Polly thought, and ceased listening. Only when she heard the subject of the South of France being discussed did she bother to tune in again – that part of France had a morbid fascination for Polly.

'And was last year as much fun on the Côte, Juniper?'

'I didn't go either, Lady Frobisher. In the circumstances, I doubt if I would have found it much "fun" . . .' Juniper replied in a voice which had such a sharp edge to it that Polly was fascinated to see her mother look, for a moment, completely lost for words.

'Oh, dear, how silly of me, how insensitive . . . Of course . . .' and Francine patted Juniper's hand gently, making cooing noises. Juniper removed her hand.

'This year I shall have my season. Maybe one day it will be possible for me to return.' She looked steadily at Francine. 'But I so wanted to come here,' Juniper brightened. 'I'd heard so much about you, I just had to meet you all. Daddy never stops talking about you,' she said archly, almost flirtatiously, to Francine.

Francine's expression was smugly satisfied. 'Oh Juniper, you're teasing me! I'm sure your father doesn't even remember me.'

'But he does, Lady Frobisher, oh he does. You've no idea the effect you had on him . . .' she chuckled, the lowness of it matching her voice exactly.

'Is he there this year?'

'No, he hasn't left Boscar Manor since . . .' Her voice

trailed off as if she couldn't say since what. Polly noticed a flicker of emotion flit over Juniper's face but it was so fast that she did not have time to register what it meant. 'Maybe this summer he'll take a holiday. Perhaps he'll return to the Greek Islands, he liked it there.' Juniper suddenly looked down at her lap and began to straighten her perfect skirt with busy, bird-like, motions of her fingers.

It was sadness, Polly realised, and a very deep sadness she was sure.

'Oh, the Greek Islands, what a dream. Socrates and Jupiter. How I'd love to be there,' Francine trilled.

'Or even Socrates and Zeus, mother!' Polly said in her most scathing voice.

'I've never been to the islands . . .' her mother continued, ignoring Polly's interruption.

'Oh they're pretty, but I think you might find them boring, Lady Frobisher. No night clubs or casinos. Just gnarled men and fish!' Again the chuckling, almost mocking laugh.

Polly sighed audibly. To have to attempt to be friends with someone who'd stood where Homer had stood and found it 'boring' – dear God!

'Poor darling Polly, are we boring you to tears?' Juniper smiled at her, and for the first time Polly was exposed to the full, extraordinary power of Juniper Boscar's smile. It seemed to encompass her, hold her, melt her irritation away.

'No, no, not at all,' she lied, not knowing if she did so out of politeness or because of the charm of that smile.

Within five minutes Juniper had extricated them from the drawing room without annoying her mother – something Polly could not have achieved.

Polly sat cross-legged on the couch in Juniper's room watching as the girl flitted about studying the paintings and porcelain with intense concentration. What a strange mixture she was, thought Polly. She'd seemed empty-headed downstairs, but here her interest appeared genuine. But then she would use some silly word like 'divine' or call Polly 'darling', and Polly would revert to her initial distrust, and mentally distance herself again.

'What a lovely painting, darling. It's like a Zoffany, isn't it?'

'It is one.' Polly replied, trying to introduce a note of boredom into her voice to cover up the fact that she was impressed.

'Good God, is it?' She clapped her hands with pleasure. She smiled that haunting smile at Polly who, disarmed, smiled back. 'Of course, I remember now, your grandmother told me about it.'

'My grandmother? You know my grandmother?' Polly swung her long legs to the floor and sat bolt upright.

'Oh, very well, she's marvellous. But why do you keep such an important painting in a guest bedroom?'

'My mother doesn't like it,' Polly replied, longing for Juniper to return to the subject of her grandmother.

She crossed to the window and Polly, for the first time, was aware of Juniper's remarkable eyes. They were translucent hazel flecked with gold. Her long naturally blonde hair swung unfashionably loose – it was the only unfashionable thing about her. She had fine cheekbones which made natural hollows in her cheeks – she would never have to suck in her cheeks if she wanted to look like Garbo, Polly thought ruefully.

'It's lovely here, isn't it?' Juniper said, leaning her beautiful head on her hand as she studied the view from the window. 'Just look.'

Polly slid from the sofa, crossed to the window and looked out at the view which was so much part of her life that she rarely noticed it.

Her father was a gardener of genius. No matter what the time of year there was always a mass of colour, plants were allowed to grow in haphazard profusion so that the garden looked as if it were nature's doing alone. In truth, as Polly knew, this effect was the result of a constant battle between the gardeners and the moor which lay huddled beyond the granite walls, hungrily waiting to recapture this land stolen by man. As far as the eye could see the moors rose in great green and brown swells like the billowing, coloured sails of a giant ship. The sun was shining, giving the moorland a look of deceptive innocence. Polly loved the moor but she respected it and often at night she would lie in her bed and imagine it as a large wild animal lying out there beyond her home waiting for man to leave, to cease his futile efforts to tame it.

'That village down there is so perfect it looks like a stage set.'

'That's Widecombe.'

'As in the song? Oh, how wonderful. We must go there. I must see it.' She swung round to face Polly, her face aglow with excitement which in a second was changed into an expression of seriousness. 'I can't explain to you how excited I am. It's the timelessness of this place you see, it makes me feel safe and secure. I haven't been able to feel that for ages. And yet, I'm probably explaining this badly – I love this house and the village but I could almost wish they weren't here. Do you know what I mean?'

'Oh yes, I do,' Polly replied, for she'd felt the same often but no one had ever said it before. 'It's as if we are usurpers, as if we've no right here.'

'That land knows more and is wiser than we shall ever be. It's as if it's watching us, don't you think?'

Juniper's eyes were sparkling and Polly suddenly felt as if they had known each other for a long time. But the spell was broken when Juniper's quicksilver attention was caught by a figurine of a girl on a swing which she swept up with a cry of 'Divine'.

'Are you planning to be an antique dealer?' Polly snapped, feeling she had been cheated.

Juniper merely laughed good-naturedly. 'My father said it's essential that a woman should know about such

things. When we lived together in London . . . before . . .' she shook her head. 'He taught me how to look
at things and then I discovered I liked looking at them.
Cigarette?' From her crocodile handbag Juniper took a
heavy gold cigarette case, and matching lighter.

'No, thanks.' Polly virutally backed away from the
offered case.

'Have you ever tried?'

'Yes, the stable boy gave me a Woodbine last year and I
was sick!'

Juniper chuckled and Polly was furious with herself for
confessing – hadn't she made Jim promise on pain of
death not to tell a living soul of her shame?

'My father used to say it's essential for a woman to
know how to smoke, otherwise one can look like a
washerwoman.'

'What else has your father taught you?' Polly said,
irritated at the continual references to him.

Either Juniper did not hear the tone of Polly's voice or
she chose to ignore it. 'He taught me masses of things.
Jewellery, and how to tell a good diamond from a poor
one, and what makes a good sapphire. And horses, and
gambling, I play a good hand of poker,' she announced
proudly. 'About food, wine, clothes too. He taught me to
drive. He knew a lot about clothes. He said you should
always listen to a man when he talks about clothes, never
a woman. I suppose you could say he taught me everything. I used to wish I could marry him. I felt I'd never find
anyone like him.'

Polly sat bolt upright, her eyes wide with astonishment.
How could this strange girl suddenly voice her own
thoughts? And she felt ashamed of her previous irritation,
for Juniper spoke in the past tense. Was her father dead?
But downstairs she had talked as if he were alive?

'Is your father dead?' she asked baldly.

'No. My mother is.' Juniper looked away abruptly.

'Then why do you speak about him in the past tense?'

'Did I? How silly.' And she laughed shortly. 'Look at the pink on this ornament. I'd love a lipstick in that colour.'

Polly scowled.

'Oh Polly, darling, you look so cross, what have I done? I do so want us to be friends,' Juniper said anxiously. 'Please tell me.' Juniper smiled her winning smile.

'It's just . . .' She looked at Juniper with exasperation. Natural politeness held her back but then, she reasoned, if she didn't tell her they would never be friends. 'As soon as you say something interesting, you follow it by something utterly silly. I don't think I understand you.'

Juniper looked contrite. 'I'm sorry if I get on your nerves.'

'You only get on my nerves half the time. I just wish you would be one person and not two.'

'What do you mean?'

'When you were talking to my mother about Greece, for instance.'

'Oh, I didn't mean it, I don't feel like that.'

'Then why say it?'

'Frankly I didn't think your mother would understand how I really felt. Greece is magical. When you are there you feel as if you are part of something vast and mysterious. When I sat by Ariadne's pool, on Naxos, with the sun setting on the Aegean, I thought I would be content to die.'

Polly laughed with delight. 'You were right, Juniper – my mother wouldn't have understood one word of that.'

'So?' Juniper asked quietly. 'So are we to be friends?'

'I don't know. Perhaps,' Polly replied guardedly.

'What does one have to do to be your friend, Polly?'

'Do?' Polly laughed nervously. She had never been asked such a question in her life. 'I don't know. Nothing, I suppose. It happens or it doesn't. Friendship, I mean.'

'So true, Polly, so sadly true. Like falling in love.'

'I wouldn't know about that,' Polly said quickly.

'But I do hope it happens with us, Polly. I so desperately want to be your friend. I need a friend so badly.'

Polly turned away, embarrassed by the intensity in Juniper's voice.

'Do you ride?' she asked suddenly to cover her confusion.

'Adore it!'

'Like to meet my Thistle?'

'Can't think of anything I'd like better.'

'Come on then, we'll be able to get an hour in before we have to change for dinner. There's just one thing, Juniper, please don't call me "darling". I hate it.'

3

Juniper quickly changed into jodhpurs, slipped on her gleaming black leather boots and carefully tied her silk cravat, holding it in place with a diamond stock pin from Cartier. She slipped on her hacking jacket tailored for her by her father's Savile Row tailor, picked up her gold-topped Hermès riding crop and ran down the oak staircase to join Polly.

Juniper stopped dead in her tracks. Below, Polly waited for her, her back turned as she rifled through the mail on the large refectory table in the hall. Polly was dressed in tattered jodhpurs, a check cotton shirt, its tails awry, and small scuffed chukka boots; her hair was tied back with a piece of string. Juniper stood frozen, one foot in midair, then quietly turned and began to tiptoe back up the stairs.

'There you are,' she heard Polly call.

Juniper turned back blushing deeply. 'I'm afraid I'm a bit over-dressed,' she tried to laugh. Polly was surprised, she had not thought Juniper, with all her sophistication, would blush.

'Well, a bit posh. I can't think what Jim and Thistle will make of you.'

'Sorry.'

Juniper looked so dejected that Polly raced up the stairs and put her arm about her. 'You look lovely. I'm sure Thistle will be most impressed,' she said kindly.

Polly led the way to the stables at the back of the house. They entered the yard – deserted except for a fat cat, sitting on the cobbles in the unseasonally warm sunshine, contentedly washing itself. The cat's eyes flicked disinterestedly over them before it continued its preening.

Juniper looked about her at the pine stable doors, stone pots of polyanthus glowing against the grey granite walls, she noted the flicks of straw on the cobbles, the pile of stable sweepings in the corner. She remembered her grandfather Wakefield's stables – as busy as a regiment's, they'd been, doors slickly painted, not a stick of straw in sight – and decided she preferred these. She followed Polly into one of the boxes.

'Jim?' Polly yelled. 'I'm taking Thistle.'

'All right, Miss Polly, but watch Ferdinand, he's got the wind up his arse today make no mistake.' A dark head appeared to accompany the voice. 'He's down in long mead . . .' he stopped in mid-sentence, his mouth hanging open slackly, and looked at a point beyond Polly's shoulder.

'Jim, shut your mouth, you look like a cod,' Polly teased.

Jim blushed a deep red that started at his Adam's apple and rapidly spread across his face like a rising sea of red ink which eventually disappeared into his dark hairline.

'This is Miss Boscar who's come to stay,' Polly said vaguely.

'How do you do, Jim. What well-kept stables . . .' Juniper held out her hand. Jim looked at his own, doubtfully wiped it against the side of his breeches before taking hers.

'Jim! You're blushing!' Polly shrieked with laughter.

She couldn't believe it was happening. To Polly, Jim was a man of the world who, every Saturday night, disappeared into Widecombe and didn't return home until he was roaring drunk. She knew he bedded a farm girl from Southcombe, and he bet money on horses, and was utterly fearless in the saddle. She had presumed that nothing and nobody in the world could make *him* blush. 'Jim, you fool, you've gone all red! What on earth's got into you?'

'I expect it's these bloody stupid clothes . . .' Juniper said and rushed out of the tack room and hurled herself into the pile of straw and sweepings from the stable.

'Juniper! What on earth are you doing?' Polly looked at her anxiously.

Covered in straw, dung and dust, Juniper emerged from the heap.

'Trying to look more like you two,' she replied, grinning at them and picking straw from her hair.

'Still looks bloody beautiful to me,' Polly's astonished ears heard Jim mutter.

'Jim, you're smitten!'

'Please, Miss Polly. Please.' Something in his voice made Polly stop teasing him.

'Come and help me collect Thistle's tack, Jim,' she said more kindly.

In the paddock, Thistle was, for once, on her best behaviour. She came at first call and made no fuss about being saddled. They led her to the jumping paddock.

'Would you like to ride her? She can be a bit stubborn at times, got a mind of her own.'

'We'll see,' said Juniper as she swung effortlessly into the saddle and they were soon gliding over the jumps in perfect harmony.

'She can ride, that one!'

Polly started, unaware that Jim had joined her at the rails. 'Yes, she can. Look how well Thistle's responding, even on that last jump, and she can be sticky with that one – often spooks at it.'

Pony and rider cantered back and Polly changed places with her. She knew that, as well as she rode, she would never be as good as Juniper. When she returned, Juniper and Jim were leaning on the rails, smoking. Juniper threw back her head, laughing at something he said, and shook her long hair from side to side, looking at him with a strange sideways glance. For a moment, Polly felt oddly in the way.

'Super ride, that pony,' Juniper said quickly as she became suddenly aware of Polly's return.

'Yes, he is a darling.'

'Watch out, Polly. You're beginning to sound like me.' Polly laughed good-naturedly at Juniper's teasing.

Together they took the pony back to the stable, rubbed him down, cleaned his tack and put it away, and then walked back to the house.

'Is he anything to do with you?'

'Jim?'

'You know. Is he, well, is he your sweetheart?'

'Jim? Don't be daft!'

'Good,' Juniper said as they arrived at the back door and began to remove their boots. 'Do you have a boyfriend?'

'Don't be silly,' Polly pushed her gently with embarrassment. She could not possibly tell her about Jonathan, not that there was anything to tell. She doubted if Jonathan, nephew of the local vicar, even noticed she existed when he visited his uncle. But Polly, who had known him nearly all her life, was increasingly aware of him. In the past three years every time she saw him her stomach felt most peculiar and her heart raced and, worst of all, she couldn't think of anything to say of any interest to him. He was coming to dinner tonight – suddenly she wished Juniper were not here.

In the hall they met Francine, already changed for dinner in bright red silk. Around her neck she wore several large tortoiseshell bead necklaces and in her ears were matching ear-rings. Several ivory bangles in different sizes clattered on her wrists.

'My dear Juniper, what has happened to you? Did you have a fall?'

'In a manner of speaking, Lady Frobisher.'

'Give your clothes to Emma, the maid. She will get them cleaned and pressed for you.'

'Oh, no thanks, Lady Frobisher, I like them like this.'

'Oh surely not, Juniper. Why, you look nearly as dishevelled as Polly.'

'Good,' called Juniper as she ran up the staircase. As Polly went to follow her, her mother grabbed her by the arm and held her back until Juniper had disappeared along the gallery.

'What on earth do you mean letting the girl get into that state?' she hissed.

'I didn't. She wanted to.'

'Don't lie to me. I can't trust you to do anything properly, can I? Not even entertaining a guest your own age. Just look at you,' angrily she shook Polly. 'Your father's already changing. Go and take a bath and, for God's sake, just for once try and look half human!'

'Yes, Mother,' Polly said with exaggerated politeness. She paused at Juniper's open door to see her surrounded by cases, the contents spilling out on the floor while a flustered Emma endeavoured to comply with the stream of instructions Juniper was giving her.

'I'll wear that one, no, no I won't – the dark grey.' Emma discarded the light grey for the dark. 'No, maybe the black. Oh glory be, I don't know. What are you wearing, Polly?'

Polly laughed. 'I don't have your problems, I only have two frocks. One night I wear the yellow, the next the green.'

'Yes, you'd look real nice in yellow with your black hair – perfect – like a beautiful gypsy.'

'Me?'

'Sure you would. With your height and figure you can wear anything. I'm stuck with duck's disease, which makes dressing hell.'

'But my mother always says I'm too tall and dark.'

'Don't listen to your mother. It's in her interest to let you think you're an ugly duckling.

'I don't understand.'

'That's because you're a sweet precious thing. Think about it. How old are you? Seventeen? How old's your mother?'

'Thirty-nine.'

'Exactly. Need I say more?' she appealed to Emma.

'No, miss,' and the young maid giggled.

'Crikey,' Polly exclaimed, glancing at her watch. 'Look at the time. I'll meet you in the hall in ten minutes.'

'Oh, no, you won't, I need thirty at the least.'

In her own room Polly stood a long time in front of the mirror. She poked her tongue out at her reflection, displeased with what she saw. She wished she were blonde instead of dark. She picked up a strand of her thick, short hair and wished she had not listened to her mother but had kept it long like Juniper's. She hated her eyebrows, which were thick and dark like her hair. She wondered how they would look if she plucked them into a thin line like Juniper's, or if they had grown in that lovely thin arch which gave Juniper's face such an interested and wide-awake look. And why were her eyes a dull brown, just like a puppy's, not hazel flecked with gold like hers? Her father often told her she was lovely, but she didn't believe him. All fathers said that to their daughters surely? Her mother on the other hand sniped incessantly about her appearance, repeating again and again her disappointment at having such a daughter, so dark . . . 'like a man,' she'd said spitefully one day, 'it wouldn't surprise me if you didn't start shaving soon!' Polly had pretended to ignore the remark but, alone in her room, she had taken to studying her face intently for the first sign of hair. With her height how could any man possibly find her attractive?

Her mother had so demoralised her that she was now incapable of looking uncritically at herself. She had no idea how attractive she was. Hers was the face of a strong person, with good bones, fine intelligent eyes, a large and expressive mouth and a pale and perfect complexion. Her dark hair was raven black with a healthy sheen. Her figure was full and firm but the height which bothered her made her tend to walk with a stoop, proclaiming to the world how ashamed of herself she was.

In her unfashionably waisted, yellow dress, Polly ran down the stairs. Her father was looking through the evening mail. She skidded to a halt, and flung her arms about him.

'So, what's she like?' he asked, laughingly disentangling himself from her embrace.

'She's odd. I mean half the time, she's super, and then she says something grotesque, and I can't stand her.'

'Perhaps she's finding it difficult to know how to talk to you.'

'To me? Why?'

'She's a lonely child, from what I hear, and I doubt if she knows many girls her own age. She's led an odd life . . .'

'What do you mean, Daddy?' But the question was never answered. Looking up, Polly saw her father had the same vacant expression on his face as Jim had worn earlier. Polly swung round.

With the glowing confidence of a woman who knows exactly the effect she is having, Juniper descended the stairs. The folds of the flowing silk jersey dress one moment accentuated, the next tantalisingly hid, the outline of her body. The soft muted grey contrasted dramatically with the rich gold of her hair which cascaded about her shoulders. She wore no jewellery and yet there was an iridescent quality about her that fascinated Polly.

'Dad,' she poked her father. 'This is Juniper.'

'Miss Boscar,' he held out is hand in welcome. Richard was not a large man but he made Juniper appear even smaller and very fragile.

'Lord Frobisher, at last we meet,' her voice seemed to sigh the words.

'I hope Polly has been taking good care of you.'

'Yes, thank you, I just know that we are meant to be the greatest friends.'

'Good,' Richard coughed as he realised he was still holding her hand. Taking the elbow of each girl he guided them towards the drawing room where his wife awaited them impatiently.

'At last! I'm dying for a drink!' she exclaimed. Her husband crossed to the drinks tray and poured her a Martini.

'Miss Boscar, Martini for you?'

'I'd rather have a Boxcar if that's possible, Lord Frobisher.'

'Of course. Polly?'

'I'd like a Boxcar too,' said Polly with no idea what it was. But if Juniper was having one she'd no intention of being left out.

'Don't be stupid, child. You're too young for spirits, have a sherry,' her mother interrupted to Polly's mortification, but her father was continuing to mix the two Boxcars. Polly fully expected her mother to expand the incident into a full-scale row. Instead, the woman ignored her husband and patted the settee beside her and invited Juniper to join her. It was a mistake, Polly decided, looking at the two women sitting side by side. For, with the stunning young woman so plainly but so beautifully dressed beside her, for the first time Polly saw her mother look over-dressed and over-painted. It wasn't until this moment that Polly realised for the first time that they never had beautiful women to stay, only women past their prime. That the guest lists to Hurstwood might be manipulated for Francine's benefit had never crossed Polly's mind, not until now, that is.

Jonathan arrived. Polly watched for his reaction as Juniper was introduced. She half expected him to look as smitten as Jim. He didn't, but she wished he hadn't held Juniper's hand quite as long as he did.

To Polly, Jonathan was the most handsome and brilliant man on earth. This assessment was lost on others who, instead, saw a polite young man with a rather serious expression which was enlivened by an occasional infectious grin. He had a shock of mousy-coloured hair. He was very tall and slim but had a permanent stoop caused by years of bending down to hear what others were saying. He had the reputation of being a pleasant fellow and a reliable dinner party guest given that he was a good listener. But, as the vicar's nephew, nothing much was expected of him and little was known about his aspirations. After Oxford, and a year at the Sorbonne, and a spell of teaching it was generally assumed that he too would eventually become a vicar.

He was seven years older than Polly, who had always found talking to him difficult. Juniper did not have this problem. In the shortest possible time Juniper had him telling them of his life as a poor student in Paris, his hopes and ambitions. It was she who drew out of him the information that he was writing a novel – and Polly hadn't even known he wanted to. Inwardly she sighed, resigned to remaining unnoticed by him.

Normally Polly hated to dine with her mother. It always seemed her opportunity to nag Polly constantly about her manners, her deportment, her looks. What conversation there was was monopolised by her mother and the chosen subject was invariably herself.

But this evening, with Juniper and Jonathan there, the conversation flowed back and forth. Polly was fascinated by the way Juniper could talk to both parents on their disparate levels and about things which interested them, and she resented her easy camaraderie with Jonathan. There was a social glossiness about the girl that belied her youth and filled Polly with envy.

Only once did she appear to slip, when Francine asked her if she was going to have her hair bobbed. Juniper shook her head in the way that was becoming familiar to Polly; it reminded her of a beautiful horse shaking its mane.

'Oh, never, my father hates the shingle!' she replied, smiling sweetly at the shingled Francine who patted her own hair jerkily and gave a short nervous laugh.

'Really?'

'He says he's old fashioned and likes women to look like women.'

'For once I agree with him,' Polly's father added, smiling broadly. Jonathan demurred and Juniper chuckled. For a fleeting moment Polly wondered whether Juniper had made a *faux pas* or whether she had intended the conversation to go that way.

The subject moved to talk of Richard Frobisher's family. Not only did Juniper know them but Jonathan had met them too and Polly had not realised. Polly sat forward eager to catch each word, hungry as she was for news. She learnt for the first time that she had an uncle and an aunt who had children – five cousins whom she knew nothing about. She was made aware that the grandmother she longed to meet had once been a suffragette but, not content with the vote, was now an active campaigner for equal rights for women. Each time the talk turned to the Frobishers Francine would moodily begin to pick at the bread on her plate, rearrange her cutlery or quickly interrupt and divert the conversation. She looked simply bored when the conversation turned to horses.

'There's good hunting here, Miss Boscar, if you'd like to come out with us.'

'It's so kind of you, Lord Frobisher, but I never hunt.'

Her wonderful smile lightened Polly's intense disappointment; she had hoped, seeing how well Juniper rode, to take her out at the next meet.

'Would you do me a great favour, Lord Frobisher?'

'If I can, Miss Boscar.'

'Then please call me Juniper. I would so like you to think of me as Juniper,' the husky voice almost pleaded, and Francine Frobisher knocked her wine over.

4

Polly sat on her bed, deep in thought, idly brushing her air. It had been a strange evening. Everything had been going well, she had thought Juniper marvellous in the way she handled her parents. Then, suddenly, even she was aware of an atmosphere; she and Juniper had barely had time to drink their after dinner coffee before both had been unceremoniously sent to bed by her mother like small children. It was humiliating, with Jonathan there: heaven alone knew what Juniper must be thinking.

There was a gentle knocking on the door and Juniper's head appeared.

'Do you think she'll object if we talk?' she asked half laughing.

'She won't know. Come in.' Polly made room on the bed for Juniper who sat at its foot, facing her. 'Cover yourself with the eiderdown, you'll get cold. I thought you'd be packing by now,' she said as she settled the quilt about Juniper's legs. Juniper offered Polly a cigarette. Polly's fingers hesitated over the case.

'Go on, these aren't Woodbines, they're best Turkish, you won't be sick with these.'

Gingerly Polly lit the cigarette. She could just see herself in the mirror opposite and liked the grown-up image of herself smoking. But she still didn't like the taste at all.

'What happened? What went wrong?' Juniper asked. 'I

must have missed it, blinked or something. There we were, nattering away, and suddenly it's all icicles and whoosh we're sent to bed! Gracious, I haven't had that happen for years. And poor you, in front of Jonathan too.'

'What do you mean?' asked Polly, blushing furiously. 'I don't care about him.'

'Sure you do, it's written all over your face.'

'We did talk quite a bit about the Frobishers, Mother wouldn't like that at all,' Polly said, abruptly changing the subject.

'Of course, the feud.'

'What feud?' Polly said, trying to keep her voice as calm as possible for she felt that if Juniper discovered how little she knew, she might, like everyone else, shy away from the subject.

'I suppose it was rather tactless of me but how was I to know the subject of your family was forbidden?'

'Don't blame yourself, Juniper. Father and I were interested. Perhaps it will be better if we talk about them when mother's not around?'

'Yes, far better. What's it like having a "star" for a mother?'

'Ghastly!' Polly smiled whilst her mind raced, desperately, searching for a way to turn the conversation back to the intriguing topic of the feud.

'Men are strange, aren't they? They are so easily swayed by beauty, don't you think? I mean . . .' But she stopped and looked about the room with what Polly thought was a distinctly sheepish expression.

'What do you mean?'

'Nothing.'

'I think you were about to say what an odd mix you think my parents are.'

'It's dreadfully rude of me, but yes, I was.'

'Don't let me stop you.' Polly grinned, not in the least perturbed.

'They seem to have so little in common. What on earth do they find to say to each other when they're alone?'

'Undoubtedly my mother talks about herself, the subject that most interests her,' Polly said cynically.

'Don't you like your mother?'

'Not particularly.'

'I see.'

'Mind you, if my father made an odd choice, so did my mother. What could have attracted her to him?'

'Oh Polly, don't be dense – pots of money and rolling acres. It's amazing how attractive that makes a man to a woman, or some kind of women.'

'But we don't have lots of money, and we only have Hurstwood and that's not very big, is it? Mother says if it wasn't for what she earns on the stage she'd look like a tramp and we'd virtually starve.'

Juniper looked at Polly, her eyes opening wide with surprise.

'You don't know, Polly, do you?'

Polly looked woebegone. 'No, I don't know a thing and it drives me mad. All I get is endless hints. Now you'll clam up too, just like everyone else.'

'Well, it's difficult. I mean it's hardly my place to.'

'Oh Juniper, please. I need to know, don't you understand?'

'It's only gossip.'

'Gossip – anything – just tell me,' Polly banged her hand on the coverlet.

'Oh all right then, gee, how exciting! I'm going to feel so important!' She leapt off the bed and darted towards the door.

'Where are you going?' asked Polly anxiously.

'Supplies. This is going to be a long night!' she said, disappearing with a wave of the hand. When she returned it was with her tooth mug and a bottle of whisky which she flourished in the air. 'My father's number one house party rule – always travel with your own booze supplies, just in case.' While Juniper busied herself pouring the drinks, Polly's heart raced with excitement. 'Right,' Juniper settled a cushion behind her and, tantalisingly, lit another cigarette before beginning.

'Get on with it, please,' Polly begged, beside herself with impatience.

'Right.' She grinned. 'There was once a chorus girl called Blewett – stunningly beautiful, not particularly talented. She had a pleasant voice and what they call stage presence. Gossip says that she was always willing to do private parties for a price – God knows what went on. But, in all fairness and all honesty, I don't know if that is true, a woman in such a profession – the most ludicrous rumours abound, don't they?' Polly sagely nodded her head as if listening to salacious gossip was a normal pastime for her. 'I can't find out how or where they met but meet they did and, hey presto, there you are!'

'There I am what? Who is she?'

Juniper giggled. 'Your mother, of course.'

'Don't be daft. Her name was du Bois before she married my father.'

'Who ever heard of a star with a name like Blewett? No, she changed her name, and then pretended to be French.'

'But my mother doesn't speak French.'

'Exactly.'

'Where was she from?'

'London. And . . . are you sure you want to go on, it's all rather sensational.'

'Please.'

'*Her* mother ran a brothel.'

'A brothel? Good gracious.'

'Isn't it exciting? I do envy you such an interesting background.'

'How did you find out?'

'Most of it I gleaned from Daisy Lavender. You know, at the Eddington.'

'I've never been there.' Polly shook her head, never having heard of either.

'She used to be a great friend of my father's, he took me there to drink champagne. She's a wonderful old girl, full of the most marvellous stories from the past. She knows absolutely everyone who's anyone in London. Then I got into the habit of dropping in on my own. Daisy likes young people.'

'How did she know?'

'She knew Francine's mother, she even had an old creature working for her – one foot in the grave mind – who'd worked in the brothel.'

'Gosh you do know some interesting people. There's no one like that in Ashburton.' Polly giggled excitedly. 'Go on,' she urged her, wide eyed.

'Well, anyway, somehow your father met her. I suppose he must have been a stage door Johnny, my father was. At first your grandparents, the Frobishers, didn't mind, I mean all young men went out with chorus girls, didn't they? But then he wanted to marry her. Your grandmother thinks she tricked him into it by being pregnant. I mean, chorus girls get pregnant all the time but men don't marry them. But your father insisted. I respect him for that, don't you?'

Polly could not speak. She sat stunned, only able to nod her head inanely.

'There was the most awful row,' Juniper rushed on. 'And your grandparents disowned him. Absolutely awful – the houses, the land, everything except his title – of course, there was nothing they could do about that. As my father said, he was bloody mad. He could have paid her off, that's what everybody else would have done. But no, he married her.'

'He must have loved her enormously,' Polly had finally found her voice again.

'He sure as hell must have.'

'I've always thought I wanted to meet my grandmother. I'm not so sure now.'

'Maybe it wasn't her, maybe it was her husband?'

'But my grandfather Frobisher is dead. What's stopping her from getting in contact now?'

'It's a different generation, Polly. I mean, your grandmother is wonderful and I adore her, but she's pretty strict, isn't she?'

'I don't know, Juniper, I've never met her.'

'I'd forgotten. She's the strongest woman I know. When your grandfather died she was devastated – but no one was allowed to know – only her best friend, my grandmother. But your granny is so strict she's the type of person who'd make Queen Victoria seem flighty.'

'She sounds terrifying,' Polly said doubtfully.

'Well, she's awfully stern, but tremendously fair with it. She's got high standards and she cannot forgive people who can't live up to those standards.'

'But surely she should forgive my father. He made a mistake, but, having made it, he did the right thing.'

'Yes, of course, but she was heartbroken. She couldn't forgive him getting involved with such a woman in the first place. Your grandfather just thought him a bloody fool. He doesn't seem to have got much sympathy from any quarter.'

'Poor Daddy.'

'And, of course, once the deed was done, if your mother had been different maybe bridges could have been crossed, and all that, but she wasn't.'

'What happened?'

'Your father brought her to visit. Mine was there, in fact you and I were in the nursery. Did you know we'd met before? Apparently she was made up to the nines, lipstick, rouge, the lot I mean, in those days, imagine! Her skirts were above her ankles and horror of horrors,' Juniper giggled, 'she smoked. Any one of these would have been enough to give your grandmother apoplexy, but something absolutely ghastly happened.'

'What?'

'I can't find out,' Juniper lied. It was one thing to gossip to Polly about a grandmother long dead, quite another to tell her of the scene she learnt about from her father and a reluctant Alice when Francine was caught out with the footman – there were limits, she thought. 'Apparently her attitude was the last straw, your grandmother claims that things might have turned out differently if your mother had made at least some effort.'

'I don't think she'd behave so outrageously now.'

'No, she's obviously learnt a lot. Our generation has no problem accepting someone like her. The "Embassy" is full of actresses these days. But our grandparents can't change their attitudes and we shouldn't expect them to, should we?'

'Well, I suppose not.'

'Anyway, to cut a long story short . . .'

'Please don't cut it short. I want to hear absolutely everything.'

'She was rude and . . .' Juniper paused and Polly wondered what it was she was deciding whether to tell her. 'They quarrelled and she told your grandmother she was a "bleeding 'orrible snob".' Juniper smiled at her own attempt at a Cockney accent. 'Gee, the very idea,' she chuckled, 'You've got to admire her really. I don't think I would have had the courage to speak to your grand-mother like that. And then,' she spluttered through her laughter, 'and then, according to my father, your mother told her where she could put the family estate – quite literally . . .'

'Put it where?'

'Polly, you are an innocent. She told her to stuff it up her arse.'

'Oh cripes,' Polly's hand shot to her mouth in a hope-less attempt to stem her laughter.

'And they swept out of the house and your dad's never been back.'

'He was right, of course. He had to stick by his wife and

it does sound as if they were ghastly to her. One can hardly blame her for lashing out, can one?' Polly felt a kindling of admiration for her mother, but it was to be short-lived. 'But why are she and Daddy so unhappy if he loved her so much once?'

'It's pretty ghastly. Are you sure you want to know?'

'It hasn't been too pleasant so far. No, I want to know everything there is to know.'

'She didn't play fair. Less than a year after the marriage people were already gossiping about her affairs, apparently. It may have been just malicious gossip, of course . . .' Juniper felt as if she might have gone too far.

'I don't think so,' said Polly bleakly. 'I guessed ages ago there was something wrong – there were hints, and she was so often away. And Daddy was always so sad.' A large tear rolled down her cheek. Embarrassed, she briskly rubbed it away and turned her head for fear Juniper might see.

'Oh, Polly, I'm making you cry. I'm sorry, I'll stop.'

'No, no! Juniper, I'm all right really. You've just made me face the facts. It makes me so angry for my father's sake. You know I don't like her. She's not very likeable, my mother. But I never loved her either, and it's worried me because, although I can see you needn't like a parent, you have to love them, don't you? I didn't love her, and now I know why.'

'Oh gosh, maybe I shouldn't have told you. You'll have some ghastly breakdown and it'll be my fault.'

'No, Juniper, I'm just relieved. I don't have to feel guilty now. I mean, if she could do that to my father who is the sweetest, kindest man, then what is there to love? It lets me off the hook. You've done me a favour, Juniper.'

'I'm glad you see it that way. I've probably told you more than I should. But, in any case, this feud is ridiculous. I'm going to tell your grandmother that you're super, that you're my best friend, and that we want to do the season together.'

'The season? I don't know even if I'm to come out. We haven't talked about it.'

'But everybody comes out, and we must, together. It'll be such fun.'

'But the expense. I don't know if Daddy can afford it.'

'Piffle! I can pay for both of us. In any case, once your grandmother meets you she'll want to help.'

'You think so?' Polly asked eagerly.

'I sure do. And we can husband-hunt together.' She lifted her glass and drained the last of the whisky. 'Do you realise, I haven't called you "darling" once,' she said with a triumphant grin.

After Juniper had returned to her room Polly was unable to sleep . . . Wide eyed, she lay grieving for her father, feeling no pity, only anger, for her mother. Polly was still too young to allow herself any gratitude to the woman who had given her life.

Juniper, in her room, was doubtful. She had wanted to hurt Francine – that was why she had engineered this visit and why she had spilled the beans to Polly. Now she feared she might have hurt Polly instead, and that she didn't want to do. She liked her, liked her more than any other girl she had met. She searched in her case and took out one of her mother's diaries and began to read. She smiled; with the diary in her hand she knew she had done the right thing.

5

Several times in the next few days Juniper disappeared at odd times. She never said when she was going or where, but after an hour or two she would reappear and each time Polly felt as if her friend was distant from her – but not for long. Once she found her in the stable yard, where the bonnet of her motor car was up and she and Jim were bending over it, their heads close together, giggling. When

Polly said hullo, she had the same feeling she had had the day of Juniper's arrival – that she was in the way.

She had a suspicion that Juniper and Jim had become sweethearts. If so, she realised, it was none of her business. She was disappointed that Juniper had not confided in her; although she liked Jim she could not understand why Juniper should have chosen him. And, there was something she preferred to try to ignore. She discovered she was jealous, that she resented every moment that Juniper spent away from her. It was an uncomfortable feeling, one she despised, and one she wished would go away.

Juniper also spent a lot of time in the small room that was set aside for the telephone. Not only were there many calls for her but she was always asking permission to make calls herself. She never told Polly whom she was calling nor who called her. Polly began to imagine a whole army of friends who knew Juniper better and whom Juniper preferred to her.

And then one day, at breakfast, Juniper suddenly asked Richard if she might take Polly with her to Gwenfer. She had received several calls from her grandmother, she explained. She was missing her dreadfully and Juniper felt she had to go, she lied effortlessly. Richard was most impressed by such concern in one so young and immediately gave his permission. An hour later, after warm farewells to her father and a more frigid departure from her mother, Polly found herself in Juniper's car heading across the moor to Okehampton. The early spring weather was still holding and with the roof of the car down, the wind in their hair, and the moors looking more beautiful than ever, Polly was in seventh heaven. She so rarely went anywhere apart from her occasional trips to London with her father. Certainly she had never been away by herself with a friend. She was excited at the prospect, and rather proud to be doing something so very adult. She envied Juniper this car: ever since Jim had taught her to drive last year she had longed for a car of her own. They spoke little for the noise of the wind and the roar of the engine made conversation difficult. 'Doesn't your father live near here?' she shouted as they approached Bodmin.

'Over that way,' Juniper pointed vaguely towards the north.

'Don't you want to visit him?'

'No,' was Juniper's short reply.

Polly pulled the motoring rug more closely about her. It was getting chillier but Juniper, wrapped warmly in a fox-fur coat, made no move to stop to raise the canvas hood. Polly thought it best not to suggest it. It was strange that she did not want to visit her father when he was so near, and when she spoke so often of him, Polly thought. They could have stayed the night there instead of motoring the whole way in one day. Polly, remembering the sad look that had flickered over Juniper's face when she spoke of Marshall, wondered if they had quarrelled. As to her mother, Juniper had not mentioned her more than once. Perhaps she was still too grief stricken? They might be friends – why, there was no might about it, she thought – they *were* friends, but all the same Polly felt there were areas of Juniper's life from which she was excluded, and always would be.

It was early evening as the car bounced between the gates of Gwenfer and hurtled down the drive. Polly missed the driveway totally for, seeing its steepness and the drop on one side, she had closed her eyes firmly until she felt the car braking in front of the house. The building was beautiful, the same period as her own home, but larger and much grander. She made sufficient appreciative noises to endear herself to Juniper for life.

From the house a tall and elegant woman appeared, her beautiful face marred by a frown as she hurried towards the car. 'Grandma, meet my best friend Polly.' Juniper leapt from the car, ran around it, hugged her grandmother and opened Polly's door in one continuous flow of movement.

Alice shook Polly's hand, and welcomed her, but with an agitated and distracted air. Polly, convinced the woman wished to speak in private to Juniper, busied herself with unstrapping the cases from the luggage rack.

'This is most presumptuous of you, Juniper.' She could not help but overhear, even though Alice spoke quietly to her granddaughter.

'Of course it isn't, I'm being helpful.'

'It could easily be misunderstood.'

'Oh, piffle, Grandma darling, you worry too much. Look at poor Polly, she looks so embarrassed. She'll think you don't want her here.' Juniper laughed at the ridiculousness of the idea.

'Of course we want you here, Polly. I'm sorry, forgive me.' As Alice smiled the frown disappeared and Polly was struck by her beauty. How like Juniper she looked, except for the eyes: hers were a beautiful clear grey while Juniper's were hazel.

Polly shuffled her feet with embarrassment. She was not used to adults apologising to her, so she grinned rather sheepishly and bent down to fiddle with one of the cases to cover her confusion.

'Leave the cases, Polly. They can be taken in later.'

'I've put you both in the west wing, Juniper, then you can play that infernal machine of yours and not disturb the more civilised elements of society with your music.'

'You're going gaga, Grandma,' Juniper said with a laugh and Polly's mouth dropped open in amazement at such familiarity.

'Yes, I am, and glad of it when I hear the sort of row you call music.'

'She doesn't like jazz,' Juniper explained, linking her arm through Polly's and walking her towards the house.

'I don't think I do much either,' Polly said.

'It's nice to know you have one civilised friend,' Alice

said gently as she ushered them through the front door. 'We shall dine at eight, Polly. We usually meet at seven-thirty for drinks in the small parlour, over there.' She pointed towards a door leading off the great hall. 'Juniper will show you your room.'

Finally left alone, Polly chose the yellow dress because Juniper had complimented her on its colour. She quickly washed, brushed her hair and, since that was the extent of her toilette, she was left with half an hour to wait. She did what visitors to Gwenfer invariably did: she hung out of the window and watched the sea restlessly pounding away at the mouth of the cove. Its vastness and relentlessness reminded her of the moors lurking outside Hurstwood. There the battle was with the land; here she was certain a similar one must be fought with the sea.

When the long hand of her watch was exactly on the half hour she gingerly made her way down the oak staircase, crossed the hall and entered the door which Alice had indicated, apprehensive that she might find the room beyond crowded with other guests. It was almost with relief that she saw only Mrs Wakefield with another woman also in her fifties, judging from the grey of her hair, and a third much younger woman, with a severe hairstyle and large spectacles half covering what should have been a pretty face. She stood uncertainly in the doorway.

'Ah, there you are Polly, come in.' Alice stood as Polly shyly entered. 'Where has that girl got to? Excuse me, I'll have to go and find her.'

'Shall I go and find her, Alice?'

'No thank you, Tommy. You look after Polly.' And Alice appeared almost to bolt from the room leaving Polly standing uncertainly in the middle, unsure what to do now.

'Did Mrs Wakefield say your name was Polly?' asked the woman whom Alice had addressed as Tommy.

'Yes.' Polly smiled tentatively.

'Is it short for Margaret?' the other, older woman asked.

'Oh, no, just Polly. My mother said I was so plain it was best to give me a plain name.'

'How very unkind and how untrue, you're a very attractive young woman. That must have upset you,' the woman said, her voice rich with concern.

'Yes, it did once. But now I like the name and . . .' she shrugged her shoulders, embarrassed at her admission. 'It doesn't matter any more . . .'

The door swung open and Alice entered followed by Juniper carrying a large ice bucket.

'Sorry everyone, I couldn't get the ice out of the trays. American ones are so much better. I must get Charlie Macpherson to send us some.' She swept over to a drinks tray on a table set in front of the open window through which could be heard the boom of the sea. She began, with an expertise of long standing, to measure out the gin.

'Juniper mixes the drinks?' the grey-haired woman said, looking at Alice with marked surprise.

'Marshall taught her some very strange accomplishments,' Alice said briskly.

'Good gracious, we did not even drink when we were their age, did we, Alice?'

'That's because you both lived in the dark ages,' Juniper called out, and again Polly was shocked by a forwardness bordering on rudeness, and astounded that the older woman did not seem to mind.

'And where are you from, my dear?' The stranger smiled at her and Polly was struck by the way in which her smile transformed her rather stern face into one of beauty.

'Devon. But I was born in London.'

'That's a beautiful county,' Tommy said enthusiastically.

'Yes, it is. My favourite.' Polly smiled at her own words – she knew so few places it was silly to say it was her favourite. And then she realised she was staring at the older woman who was dressed as if from a history book. They were all in dinner dresses, but the others were fashionably dressed whereas this woman wore a dress which was beaded and tight, and swathed, and frilled. 'My favourite,' she repeated to cover up her rudeness.

Juniper glided over with the tray of drinks.

'Martinis,' she announced.

'Since when have you been drinking Martinis, Alice?'

'Juniper introduced me to them and most uplifting they are too.'

Suspiciously Alice's friend sipped at her drink. 'Ah, yes, I see what you mean. I should think they could be most uplifting.' And she suddenly hooted with laughter so loudly that Polly jumped with surprise. 'So, Juniper, you've been staying with your friend in Devon?'

'Yes, on Dartmoor, actually,' Juniper said pointedly, and Alice looked nervously about the room.

'Dartmoor?' the woman said sharply, glancing quickly at Alice. 'Then you must hunt if you live there, my dear?'

Polly was aware that the woman was staring at her now, which made her feel better about having stared earlier.

'Whenever I can, yes.'

'I used to love to hunt – that was before the old bones told me it was time to stop.' The loud hoot rang out. 'The longing for it never diminishes, unfortunately. It gets into one's blood, I'm afraid, and the need to be in the saddle on a sunny winter's morning, the sound of the hounds speaking in the valley, carrying miles on the crisp air – it'll never leave me.'

'I hate hunting,' Juniper said defiantly. 'It's cruel. Think of the poor foxes, the poor stags.'

'You've obviously never been in a chicken house when the "poor" fox has been visiting,' Polly said with spirit.

'Stags don't bother chickens,' Juniper said sharply in reply.

'Stags eat crops and life is hard enough on the moors for the farmers. And in any case if they aren't culled, they would overbreed and starve.'

'That's a silly argument, one I'll never agree with. Animals shouldn't be hunted so cruelly, that's all there is to it.'

'Then don't eat meat.'

'But I don't eat foxes,' Juniper said triumphantly.

'No, but you don't mind wearing them,' Polly said with equal triumph.

'Bravo, bravo, Polly,' and the woman was laughing loudly and clapping her hands with glee.

'Thank you, Mrs . . . ?' and Polly paused, confused, realising no one had yet introduced them.

The woman looked at her for what seemed a long time. She was not laughing, nor smiling. 'Gertrude,' she said slowly. 'Gertrude Frobisher.'

Polly jumped to her feet forgetting the glass in her hand. Glass and Martini clattered to the floor and broke into smithereens, the liquid spreading at an alarming rate on the carpet. 'Mrs Wakefield, I'm so sorry,' and red-faced with embarrassment, emotion and fear, Polly knelt and began to pick up the pieces. She heard the swishing of silk and a hand placed on her elbow, lifting her up. She found herself looking into intelligent brown eyes which for a fleeting moment of hope she thought were smiling at her.

'You didn't know I was here?'

'No. No one told me,' she looked down miserably for the smile had gone from the fine brown eyes.

'And whose little idea of fun was this?' Gertie looked angrily from Juniper to Alice.

'Gertie, I didn't know,' Alice said anxiously. 'Juniper phoned last night and she said she was unhappy at Hurstwood and could she come home. She asked if you were here, but then she knew that you were coming today. I knew that Polly was with her only when Juniper phoned when they were an hour from here.'

'We stopped for tea,' Juniper said helpfully.

'I didn't know what to do. I was afraid that, if I told you, you would leave immediately. I didn't want that, my dear.' Alice's face was full of anxiety. Juniper was smiling broadly. Tommy sidled discreetly from the room.

'Polly knew nothing, Lady Gertrude, it was all my doing. I didn't even tell her my grandmother had a friend staying.'

'Why?' The question was asked in a voice of terrifying chilliness. 'What right do you think you have, young woman, to interfere in other people's lives?'

'Because . . .' Even Juniper seemed to be daunted by the severity of voice and expression facing her, for she faltered as if unsure how to continue. 'I did it because Polly is a dear sweet girl and you did not even know she was. And I love you and I thought it was silly and stupid and, yes, if you like, wicked that you did not know each other. Polly's desperate to have family, to know them, it just didn't seem fair.'

'I'm sorry, Grandmother, I really am. I'll leave immediately,' said Polly miserably. At the word 'grandmother' Gertie looked at Polly, an intense look which made everyone in the room stand silent almost as if they were holding their breath. The look seemed to last for ages, Polly wished the floor would open up and swallow her.

'Utter nonsense, of course you won't leave. You were tricked by this, no doubt, well-meaning but extremely presumptuous young woman.' Juniper blushed and had the grace to look long and hard at her feet. 'And what are you sorry for? Sorry for being yourself? You must be proud of who you are – always. Maybe you're sorry for giving me a start? Eh? I'm a tough old trout, don't you worry.' And to everyone's relief they saw that Gertie was smiling.

'Then you're not cross?' Juniper was jigging from one foot to the other.

'I most certainly am cross, Juniper. There's an arrogance to you that I find *most* unattractive in one so young. And I do not take kindly to your taking it upon yourself to interfere in my affairs.' Juniper's blush deepened. 'However, over the years your grandmother has told me that I should meet Polly. I begin to think she might be right. Mind you, it's a pity no one saw fit to tell me before that my granddaughter was such a passionate advocate of hunting – that would have made all the difference.' Gertie hooted. 'Any more of those delicious Martinis, Juniper? I quite understand why people like them so much!'

6

Alice and Gertie sat a long time beside the fire after the young women had gone to bed. Gertie needed to talk and Alice sat and listened patiently as she poured out her anger that she had allowed all those years to go by with such bitterness inside her. She gave herself no quarter, chastising herself verbally for the corrosiveness of that bitterness. She had always thought herself fair-minded, but what could have been more unfair than to punish Polly for her mother's unsuitability and rudeness? It was her own intransigence that had kept the feud going, so it was her fault that Basil had died without knowing this delightful young woman. It was a situation for which she could never forgive herself.

'And what about seeing Richard? Isn't it time?' Alice asked gently.

'I don't know. What a pickle I've made of everything. Maybe he doesn't even want to see me. Look at everything I've deprived him of in the past – his relationship with his whole family, money, land.'

'Maybe, in a strange way, he's grateful. From what Polly has said he seems to be very happy with his life at Hurstwood. Perhaps he would not have enjoyed the responsibility of large estates in Berkshire and Scotland.'

'Do you think so?' Gertie grabbed eagerly at this straw of hope.

'I don't know, of course, but it's a thought.'

'But then I would have to meet that awful woman. I couldn't do that, Alice. I still remember, as if it were yesterday, that fearful scene at Mendbury.' Gertie shuddered. 'No one can expect me to forgive her for that conduct, surely?'

'She's produced a delightful granddaughter for you, perhaps she's not so bad after all.'

'It's very sweet of you, Alice. But I think we have to face the fact that Francine is little better than a whore. You have no idea of the stories I hear about her behaviour. Not just in London, but when she goes to the South of France with those incredibly vulgar people she clatters around with. No, Polly is Richard's doing. I can hear him in her when she speaks. She seems well read and interested in politics – now how many young women do you know who are? She's wonderful, isn't she? So spiritied, and yet very gentle. And attractive too, not pretty, but a strong face, a face full of character – I prefer that.'

'Yes, Gertie, she's wonderful,' Alice chuckled.

'How about us giving them both a season together? What do you think? She could join us next month in London. In fact if she came back with me next week we would have plenty of time to get her a wardrobe. Wouldn't that be such fun?'

'I wonder if they will hate the season as much as we did.'

'It has to be endured whether they want to or not. But times are different, Alice. I was talking to Augusta Portley only the other day, her gal came out last year. She says things are not as rigid as in our day. Do you know, the young go off to clubs and dinners without proper chaperons? They all seem to have the most enormous amount of fun, she says.'

'You wouldn't approve of that for one moment, Gertie. You'd never let Polly out of your sight.'

'I would, I've always been the most forward thinking of the two of us.'

'Oh, really, have you?' Alice chuckled with disbelief.

'The thing is, if we did that and we gave them a ball together, then I'd have to ask Richard first. It would be the most normal thing, wouldn't it? It would be easier in lots of ways to meet that way.' She paused, looking long and hard into the fire. 'But then perhaps he will want to give her the season himself – oh, surely not, not with that woman. She's never been presented at court, you know – probably no one could be found to sponsor her,' she said with a marked degree of satisfaction. 'But then, Richard's never had a lot of money, has he? It would be fearfully expensive for him. And he surely wants the girl to make a good marriage . . . ?'

Alice sat quietly, fully aware that Gertie was really talking to herself, arguing, persuading herself to a course of action. She said nothing, for there was no point. She listened and she allowed herself a smile of satisfaction that Gertie was so enamoured of her granddaughter.

The following week was one of the happiest of Polly's life. Her only regret was that her father was not there to enjoy it too.

She discovered another Juniper. One who would sit as still as a rock for fifteen minutes at a time and watch a hawk hovering above the bracken, its wings barely moving as it kept its height and patiently sought its prey. Juniper would silently will it on, longing for the moment when it would stoop, drooping like a lance into the bracken. And then Polly would see her cry for the mouse or vole dangling helplessly from the hawk's talons.

This was a quieter Juniper. One content to sit by the sea on a rock that she insisted on calling Ia's rock, though Polly never found out why. There was a stillness about her here; the restlessness, the movement that she had seen at Hurstwood had gone. She read constantly, avidly, and she painted for hours at a time, competent watercolours. Even her vocabulary changed. She no longer said, 'divine' and, to Polly's relief, had not once called her 'darling'. The contrast was so great that one day Polly asked her what it was about Gwenfer that had made her change.

'Here I feel I'm part of the place. As if I've sprung from the granite of the land myself. I'm totally at peace here, content and happy,' Juniper replied, looking at Polly almost with surprise that she should ask such an obvious question.

'Maybe your parents gave you life here.'

'What a wonderful idea. Oh, yes, I do hope so, that would explain so much of how strongly I feel about this place. I'm sure I must have been. Oh, Polly, you're so clever.'

If the consolidation of her friendship with Juniper was wonderful, that with her grandmother was marvellous. There seemed to be a conspiracy between the others to leave them alone as much as possible. Polly took long walks with her grandmother, spent hours in the small parlour listening to her tales of family and the past, of her exciting days as a suffragette. After the first couple of days she was invited by Gertie to visit her in her bedroom each morning and evening – which rapidly became a ritual.

Gertie's first impressions of the girl had been right. She liked her enormously but as the days passed she found to her surprise that she was beginning to love her, deeply. At first, despite herself, she would remember the many rumours about Polly's true parentage. But then she found so much in the girl that reminded her of her eldest son that memories of the vicious gossip began to fade. When these had gone, it was so easy to relax and let all the love, dammed up inside her for so many years, flow free.

Gertie had questioned Juniper closely about Polly's parents. Juniper, in her straightforward manner, had told her in no uncertain terms that Richard was 'terrific' and adored Polly whereas Francine was 'ghastly' and horrid to the girl.

Gertie was more than impressed therefore to note how loyally Polly spoke of her mother. Gertie approved of such loyalty – even if, in her opinion, it was grossly misplaced.

Polly was entranced with her grandmother as was everyone who met her. She was impressed with Gertie's original mind, her sense of humour, and her great ability to have fun. And she was proud, too, of the intellect she discovered her grandmother possessed. Gertie did not pry. She asked questions about Polly's parents, but they were interested questions, and not once had she asked for the truth about Francine. Polly was grateful she hadn't for she would have found it difficult not to tell her the truth.

Alice struggled alone with her own particular problem. She pored over her boxes of documents, looking for further clues, but with no luck. If her surmise was correct, that Ia had been her father's illegitimate daughter, then Francine must be Alice's niece and Polly her great-niece. Should she say anything, should she mention it? This was Alice's dilemma. If the truth came out, would it make matters worse for Polly? Weren't there sufficient rumours about her ancestry without adding more which could never be substantiated? And what would be Juniper's reaction? Young women were strange: perhaps she would be jealous that Alice was not hers alone. And finally, it occurred to her that Gertie had had enough shocks for the time being. She put the boxes away and decided the secret might be best left with her, perhaps for ever.

Juniper was most satisfied with the turn of events. She was not surprised for she was used to most aspects of her life turning out to her advantage. When she had first gone to Hurstwood the idea of Polly meeting her grandmother could not have been further from her mind; all she could think of was Francine and revenge for her mother. But the fonder she became of Polly, the more she found she wanted to do something to help her friend to be reunited with her family. Once the notion had taken root she never wavered from the conviction that it was a good idea, never thought that it might be none of her business. She was even more pleased with the dawning realisation that as Polly was united with her grandmother, it was one in the eye for Francine.

But, best of all, was the suggestion from both grandmothers that the girls should share the season. At first Polly was adamant that she did not want to be a debutante, but the three of them cajoled and argued until eventually Polly was persuaded.

If Juniper were totally honest with herself, which she invariably was, the idea of coming out with Polly coincided nicely with her own half-formulated plans.

Chapter Eight

1

They had been in London for nearly two months and Polly had hated every moment of it. Since she did not want to find a husband, she could see no point in the season. She loathed the constant necessity to change her clothes. The endless repetition of luncheons, tea parties, dinners and balls, where the same people were always present holding conversations of depressing familiarity, bored her.

The expense of everything worried her and made her feel guilty – there was too much poverty in the land, too much unemployment, too much misery in Europe for her to be happy about the cost. She was grateful, realising Gertie was lavishing clothes and presents upon her to make up for all their lost years, but all the same, she wished she wouldn't.

Her mother was right – she was too tall. She towered over the other debutantes. No doubt Gertie was as tired of telling her to stand up straight as she was of hearing it. Maybe if she had looked like Juniper she might have felt different. Juniper had created her own individual style. She only ever wore grey or black with touches of white or red. Crêpe de Chine was the rage so Juniper wore satin. Linen was *de rigueur* for day wear so she wore cotton. And whereas the other girls seemed to vie with each other to show as much flesh as possible – with backless dresses which went so low that even the crease of the occasional bottom could be seen – Juniper was always well covered, which seemed to interest the men even more. Short permed hair was the fashion so Juniper wore hers long or piled on top in a severe chignon, a style which made her look even more beautiful. The others flirted, used their eyes, their mouths, stood with hips jutting forward provocatively, and shrieked loudly for attention; they paraded their sex. Juniper did none of these things. She would enter a room, stand still as she surveyed the occupants, and then she would smile and it was as if there was no other young woman there, it was as if a bright light had been switched on. No one could compete, least of all Polly.

Polly dreaded each event. Polly found the whole exercise of husband-hunting demeaning – like a cattle market, she had complained to a laughing Juniper. She seemed to have four feet when it came to dancing, and after falling over twice in the charleston she had refused ever to dance it again. She had not even attempted the tango but danced only a safe waltz or a foxtrot. She didn't even like champagne.

Juniper was always slipping away to the fashionable night clubs but Polly did not like them either. She found them unpleasantly noisy, dark, and smoke filled; the dance floors were crowded, and Juniper's cronies, who all seemed to have remarkably silly names, cracked infantile jokes. Polly was aware she embarrassed the others as much as she did herself.

One dreadful night her mother had been at the Embassy with a group of young, sycophantic men and had swept up to their table, gushing at everyone. The males in their party had been agog that she and Juniper should know the famous Francine but Polly had been mortified – first by her mother's behaviour, and secondly when, as soon as Francine had left, the men in the group, still unaware of their relationship, had made remarks about her mother's morals. Juniper had rushed spiritedly to her defence, the men apologised profusely to Polly, but it was too late: she had heard her called a whore.

There had been funny moments. Polly had thought she

would burst from laughing the night when Juniper and a friend whisked down the stairs at Londonderry House on tin tea trays only to land, bottoms up, at the feet of Lady Cunard who was not amused. And they had both been told off for giggling when they had been presented at Court and Polly's Prince of Wales feathers kept slipping over her eyes so that she looked the worse for drink. And who would not have laughed when the particularly smug Fiona Fitzwilliams was sick from nerves.

Juniper was a constant puzzle to her. Polly regarded her with a mixture of affection and exasperation. She was incapable of being punctual. She was constantly in a flutter, looking for things, for she was so untidy that half a dozen important items went missing daily. She changed her mind a dozen times a day. The fact that Juniper was completely selfish and always wanted her own way in everything was impossible to ignore. She was noisily enthusiastic over whatever took her fancy – for the moment – but her enthusiasms rarely lasted long, whether they were pursuits or people. During their eight weeks in London she had been desperately in love eleven times.

Polly would reach such a point of exasperation, be about to tell her she was leaving, when Juniper would enter the room, smile her dazzling smile, and make Polly feel she was the most important person in London. Juniper would laugh at her own lateness, gushing a thousand apologies and promises that she would reform. She would make fun of her latest exploits – the interest that had held her attention for a day, or the man whom yesterday she loved and today she loathed. She was totally unaware of her own selfishness. If she insisted on something, it was only because she thought it was the best thing for everyone.

Her generosity was legendary. Polly did not dare to admire anything for if she did so, Juniper would give it to her or rush out to buy an identical one for her. It distressed Polly to see how often unscrupulous people worked on this facet of Juniper's character to extract expensive gifts from her – watches, cases of champagne, crocodile handbags, diamond pins, while Juniper appeared blithely unaware of the value of these things. Once she had tried to intervene when Juniper was giving one of their acquaintances a pretty sapphire ring. But Juniper had interpreted this as jealousy on Polly's part and had gone there and then to Garrards to buy her an identical one. How could one ever stay angry with such a person?

And Polly had other worries too. Juniper fell in love too easily – it must, with all her money, make her vulnerable. To Polly's incomprehension she was desperate to find a husband. Polly realised that without one her own future promised a quiet, economical life in Devon, but Juniper had no need to look for a man to provide for her. Finally she had explained to Polly that she must find a husband for only then would all her money be hers to control as she wished.

Polly had a shrewd idea that Juniper had slept with several of her boyfriends. Polly was not censorious, she was concerned. One's virginity was important – there were still men who would demand it in a bride – though its loss was not the end of the world as it would once have been. But talk had started and that was serious. The most valuable asset for any debutante was her reputation and Juniper was at serious risk of losing hers. Polly felt that there was a recklessness in Juniper, a desperation to be loved. Had she been unloved as a child this might have been understandable but, she gathered, Juniper had been adored. It was all very puzzling to Polly. She was bored to death with the season but felt she had to stay if only to look after Juniper.

But unknown to everyone, including Polly, Juniper was playing a charade. Each night, no matter how late the hour, Juniper's routine never varied. She would walk across the thick carpet of her own room unclipping her dress and allowing it to slip to the floor. She stepped out of it and, as she progressed towards the dressing table her slip, her French knickers, her camisole followed until behind her were a line of silken stepping stones. Invariably she slumped on to the dressing table stool and stared moodily at her reflection.

Polly was right, she thought. The season was boring, mind-numbingly so. All the parties and the balls were identical, the same people twirling round and round hysterically looking for pleasure, for love, for lust, for money . . . Once everything had been fun. Once she had enjoyed life to the full, every single moment of every day. Now she felt old – old as the hills. Every day was an effort to be the bright and sparkling '*golden butterfly*' – the title the popular press had given her as the most beautiful and popular debutante of the year. Butterfly? There were days when she felt more like a slug.

She knew the reason. She crossed to the wardrobe and dug deep into the back of the large piece of Edwardian furniture and took out a slim, red, morocco-bound book. She sat cross-legged on the bed, opened and began to read the book she had read and reread so many times – trying to understand.

She looked up at the ceiling, tears pouring down her face. 'Oh, Daddy, how could you? How could you have been so cruel? How could you have deceived me so?' she said aloud, as the tears smudged the pages of her dead mother's diary.

And then at one of the despised balls, everything changed.

Polly sat at one of the side tables with her grandmother and Alice. At every ball and reception she had attended this summer there were the same small marble tables accompanied by the fragile gilt chairs. She sometimes held her breath when corpulent people sat on them fearing they were about to crash to the floor. So ubiquitous were these furnishings that she had begun to wonder if perhaps there was a company which hired them out. It was the same with the flowers, the choice of blooms never varied. Were they rushed from one ball to another? Always the sameness, so that it was often difficult to remember which house she was in and whose ball it was. The same drinks – champagne or fruit punch – served in the same shaped glasses night after night. Identical buffets with lobster, salmon and strawberries and cream; the rich, it seemed, were doomed never to eat anything else. She doubted if she herself, once this was all over, would ever enjoy eating any of them again.

'You're not enjoying yourself at all, Polly, are you?'

'Grandmama, I am. It's just that I'm not very good at dancing.' Polly laughed nervously.

'Doesn't she remind you of someone, Alice?'

'Oh, yes, Gertie, very much so,' Alice leant forward and patted Polly's hand gently.

'Who? Who do I remind you of?' She looked from one to the other.

'Why, us! We were the most reluctant debutantes of our season. I thought I was far too intellectual for such nonsense, didn't I, Alice?'

'Yes, and I was the most desperate disappointment to my stepmother, Daisy Dear.'

'Daisy What?' Polly tried to stifle her laugh.

'You can laugh, Polly, that's what I thought too. Such a silly name, but she insisted. She was a complete social animal, she lived for society. She even managed to get the Prince of Wales to my ball, such a coup . . .' Alice chuckled.

'What happened to her, I haven't met her, have I?' Polly looked along the row of dowagers who, night after night, sat in the same places and with sharp eyes and sharper tongues watched the young to see which matches were to be made this season.

'No. She died in Italy, oh, five or six years ago now. I last saw her when I was eighteen.'

'I'm sorry. What did she die of?' Polly asked politely.

'Exhaustion probably.' Gertie hooted, then, aware of whom she was talking to, quickly switched the conversation. 'In our day things were far worse. Our chaperons were absolute dragons. Why, we were not even allowed to walk in the street alone for fear of being compromised. Now the young marry for love – we married for status. Isn't that so, Alice? I was a social disaster for I was only interested in art and literature and that frightened the men away.'

'It still does,' Polly said ruefully. 'I bored four guards officers rigid last night saying I admired Picasso. You would have thought I had said I was a communist. I must seem so ungrateful, Grandmother, but when people are hungry in this country and when I read such dreadful reports of what is happening in Europe – then I'm sorry but I'm afraid all this . . . seems a waste of time and maybe there isn't much time left . . .' she said seriously, her voice trailing away as she realised how pompous she must sound.

Gertie glowed with approval. 'You don't mind being different?'

'Heavens, no. I shall scuttle home and settle most contentedly to a life in the country. If I'm to marry I think I would be better off looking for a nice uncomplicated farmer.'

'Richard did a good job with you, my gal.'

'Then see him again, Grandmama, please. He does love you, you know.' Polly leant forward, her face eager with hope.

'I did invite him to your ball. I could not invite your mother. I argued with myself long and hard, but I just could not bring myself to be so hypocritical. I don't like her, I never shall, and I could not pretend that I did. One day, one day you will understand.'

Polly put out her hand and touched her grandmother. 'I already do, you know.' She smiled sweetly at her. 'No one gets on with my mother except those silly people who follow her around with adoration.'

'Excuse me, Lady Gertrude. May I ask permission to have the pleasure of this dance with Miss Frobisher?'

Polly looked up with surprise at the tall young man who stood beside them. 'Jonathan!' she exclaimed, knowing she blushed as he gave her a small courtly bow. Polly made a fuss of looking unnecessarily at her ball card – she had only two dances written in, both of them with friends of her grandmother – and then jumped eagerly to her feet. 'Thank you,' she said quickly, fearful that he might change his mind.

Gertie and Alice watched as Polly was led on to the dance floor by the pleasant-looking young man.

'Now, he would be most suitable – I've known the Middlebanks for years, his family live close to Richard's. Unfortunately he has no money, his father's a second son, but then one can't have everything,' Gertie announced.

'*Gertie!* He's only asked her to dance.'

'She's so precious to me, Alice. Did you hear her worrying about the unemployed, about the Nazis? How many of the debutantes here even read a newspaper? And, do you realise, that was the first time I've heard that child say anything remotely against her mother. I wonder why, suddenly.'

'I think it means she's beginning to feel relaxed with you and that you're someone she can trust.'

'Do you really? Oh, how absolutely wonderful.'

Their conversation was interrupted by the arrival of Phillip Whitaker, the eminent and fashionable portrait painter, who asked Alice to dance.

Across the large ballroom a tall man with black hair and eyes of darkest brown, with a serious expression and a sardonic tilt to his mouth held out his hand to Juniper.

Polly meanwhile could not believe that she was dancing with the man whom, since childhood, she had put on a pedestal. She was not to be disappointed in him now: as they danced he talked and it was of the things which interested her. She found she could talk to him as to none of the other young men, and for the first time since the start of this endless season, she relaxed. Even her dancing seemed to improve: was this what was meant by dancing on air, she wondered.

Juniper, however, found conversation with Lord Hal Copton difficult: they seemed to have little in common, but there was a mysteriousness about him, a strength and elegance that made her pulse quicken.

And Alice, who had begun the dance by making polite conversation, suddenly found herself feeling light-hearted and with a strange, dimly remembered sensation close to her heart that she had not experienced for a long time.

2

During the next few weeks Alice felt almost like a young girl again. Common sense told her she was allowing herself to fall in love far too quickly but what hope had sense in the scheme of things when matters of the heart were involved?

She knew she was in love for it had happened to her only once before, long long ago. She was falling in love with the same alarming speed as she had fallen for Chas. She had the same sense of excitement, of elation, that strange feeling that she could hardly breathe. She had never expected to feel like this again. Just once, at the Summer Exhibition where they had gone to view Phillip's submissions, it had occurred to her how ridiculous she was, to feel such emotions at her age. She had confronted this thought face on – and she had rejected it. What did it matter what she did, how she felt? Whom could she hurt? Only herself. Turning to Phillip she had laughed aloud and when he had asked her what was funny, she had promised to tell him – one day. For, strangely, she knew there would be many days in which she could tell him of her thoughts.

It had been only a matter of days before Phillip declared his own feelings. She felt it best not to tell Juniper, not until her season was over and they were both back in Cornwall again. Intuition had told her to delay. Alice could not be sure if Juniper was ready to accept her grandmother with another man. She was also aware that the young tended to regard love as their prerogative. She feared any indications of disgust which Juniper might show for this love she felt for Phillip – Alice did not want her happiness marred in any way. Far better for Juniper to get used to Phillip's presence slowly. Phillip, she had learnt, had a house and studio near Newlyn, close to her home, to which he went each summer. He was leaving next week and Alice was to join him as soon as possible for he wanted to paint her portrait at Gwenfer. But what excuse could she possibly make not to go to Scotland for the rest of the season? She did not wish to hurt Gertie's feelings, and she did not want Juniper to realise what was happening.

She was so involved with her own concerns that, one morning, alone in her room, she realised with a start that for days she had not thought about Juniper. Immediately the worries came flooding back with a vengeance – Juniper's behaviour this season had bordered on madness. Every night she was out until all hours at clubs or driving out into the country in noisy cavalcades to road houses. Alice had never been to a road house in her life, but heard stories of late-night dancing, drinking and swimming in lakes and swimming pools. Nor was she happy with the friends Juniper had made. With its rouged young women and slick men, it appeared a very fast set with which to be involved. Juniper seemed to flit from man to man at an alarming rate – madly in love with one today, replacing him tomorrow. Alice had met some of these men and discovered, to her horror, that most of them were much older than Juniper and far too sophisticated. Her great fear was that Juniper might have behaved stupidly with several of them and that the girl would become pregnant. Alice doubted if Juniper had the maturity to deal with an illegitimate child as she herself had done. Juniper might, with her acute dress sense, look older than her seventeen years but frequently, Alice thought, she behaved more like a child.

Alice was frustrated. Juniper had everything – she was beautiful, charming, intelligent and rich. But she seemed to be bent on a curve of self-destruction. She smoked too much, drank too much, she ate and slept too little, and her enjoyment had an hysterical edge to it.

And then there was the enigma about Marshall. Once the two had been inseparable, but now, Juniper rarely mentioned him, refused to visit him; it was as if he no longer existed in her life. Alice had been to Boscar several times, out of courtesy. With each visit she found her son-in-law's behaviour stranger. Since Grace's death, he had become almost a recluse. He had given up all interest in society and clothes, which he had once so enjoyed. He spent his days reading and writing. On the visit before last she had found him dressed like a monk, in a strange grey costume that looked as if it had been fashioned from an old blanket.

Alice felt he was slipping away from reality and she did not know what to do to help him. He would not tell her what had caused him to behave in this way. She was certain it had to do with Grace's death. It still pained her to think about her daughter; she had not even discussed her grief with Gertie, preferring to conceal it, to fight it alone. So it was with difficulty that she raised the subject with Marshall. He had looked at her with a sad expression, as if she could not possibly understand, and had begun to talk about the vegetables he was growing and the trees he had planted.

She also saw with concern the people with whom he

was surrounding himself. She had met those who claimed to be students of philosophy – though why the study of that subject should involve one in being so unwashed and scruffy escaped her – and a de-frocked monk who, she felt, was nothing better than a confidence trickster, as well as a woman who claimed to be an expert in witchcraft and demonology. Once Juniper's season was over, she was going to have to make a concentrated effort to restore poor Marshall to normality.

When she raised the subject of Marshall, her fears for him, and Juniper's neglect of him, Juniper's mouth would set in a hard line. She would sit, like a coiled spring, waiting for Alice to finish. 'Is that all you want to discuss with me?' she would ask coldly and Alice, invariably at a loss for words, would let her go. If she tried to say anything about her lifestyle, Juniper would merely laugh and tell her she did not understand modern young women.

Alice had always congratulated herself on how normal Juniper appeared despite the avalanche of love and material objects heaped upon her by Lincoln and Marshall. Now Alice wondered if she were witnessing the reaping of the whirlwind.

Alice wished that Tommy were here with them in London. It had seemed the most reasonable thing for Tommy to take a holiday. She had always been dutifully available, ever since Lincoln's death but, with her usual keen sensitivity, Tommy had allowed herself to fade more into the background as Juniper's relationship with her grandmother developed. This summer she had gone to Italy. Alice felt that being nearer to Juniper in age, she might have been able to help to control her. Should she be selfish and send a telegram to ask her to return? No, that would not be fair. Tommy needed the break. She had to try, somehow, to control the girl herself.

Now Alice had Hal Copton to add to her list of worries. He seemed taciturn and permanently depressed, not the type she would have wished for her granddaughter. She could see that he was physically attractive, tall and slim and handsome, with dark, brooding looks. Alice sighed. She did not know why, but she feared for Juniper with that particular man.

A knock on the door interrupted her thoughts, the maid announced that Mr Whitaker awaited her in the drawing room, and with nimble feet Alice ran down to see them. They had much to plan.

Gertie was excited, almost as much as if she had fallen in love herself. She approved wholeheartedly. Phillip was ideal. The right age, prosperous, kind, amusing, a perfect gentleman. Gertie herself could not have chosen anyone more suitable. She was all for telling everyone but respect for Alice sealed her lips. Instead she amused herself with secretly planning Alice's wedding. The fact that Phillip had not yet asked her friend was neither here nor there: Gertie had decided they were to marry.

And then there was Polly to think of. The more Gertie saw of young Jonathan Middlebank the more she approved of him.

Polly too had not been mistaken. Always, she now realised, deep down, first as a girl, then as a young woman, she had sensed that Jonathan was the man for her. Now she knew him well and did not have one smidgin of doubt. The amount they had in common delighted her. He was not enjoying the season either and confided that if he had not met her at the ball he would have escaped weeks ago. Polly was still obliged to attend balls, luncheons and teas, but now she slipped away at the earliest opportunity to join Jonathan. Together they had roamed all the galleries and museums and excitedly discovered they shared the same taste. Politically they were in tune. He had taken her to a soup kitchen in the East End run by friends of his from Oxford and she felt such pride in his social conscience. He had taught her to roller skate, to row on the Serpentine. But the outings she liked best were when, daringly, she went alone to his lodgings in Chelsea and there, sitting on large cushions on the floor, they would drink tea and read poetry to each other – poetry that had new meaning now she was in love.

Daily it amazed her that he should choose to spend time with her. Polly, always insecure in her looks, was unaware of how attractive he found her and how puzzled he was that in all the years he had known her he had been unaware of how lovely she was. His delight was to sit and watch her, her long legs curled elegantly beneath her, her dark eyes intense with emotion as she read a favourite passage to him. At such times he wished he were an artist, instead of a writer, able to capture her natural beauty in paint; meanwhile, unknown to her, he struggled to convey it in words.

She began to make plans. As a writer he'd had several articles published and was working on a novel – he could live anywhere. If he asked her to marry him – and the more she saw him the more she was convinced that this was only a matter of time – she would ask her father if they could have one of the cottages at Hurstwood to live in. Neither of them was interested in society, nor was money important – just enough to survive. Polly spent many happy hours imagining how she would care for him while he wrote the novel of the century. His success, again only a matter of time, would be her reward.

She had not meant to confide her feelings to anyone, she wanted to keep her secret close to her for it was almost too precious to talk about. But when her grandmother suspected that something was afoot, Gertie, with the ease of years spent worming secrets out of people, had persuaded Polly to tell her everything. Gertie had immediately insisted on inviting Jonathan to tea and that day Polly felt sick with apprehension. She need not have worried. Gertie announced that she was happy with Polly's choice, that a man's intellect was far more important than his wallet, and that if her son did not have a suitable cottage there would always be one at Mendbury for them.

But there was Scotland to be endured first: Polly could not let her grandmother down. Jonathan was trying to make arrangements to join them, which would make it all bearable.

Juniper was finding that things were not going as well as she had anticipated. Hal was not like the other men in her life. With them she had only to raise her little finger and they would come running. She had thoughtlessly turned down marriage proposal after proposal, so many she had lost count. It had always been she who had backed out of the relationship. But Hal did not give her the choice – there was no relationship to make a scene about. The rare men who had not done her bidding as quickly as she had required had been easily removed from her thoughts. Not so with Hal: she found she thought about him all her waking hours, she longed for him, wanted him, was becoming obsessed by him.

She never knew when she was going to see him. If he said he would be at a dinner or a ball it was no guarantee that he would arrive. Many were the evenings now when Juniper returned early with Polly, too miserable to go on to a club, after yet another ball where her neck ached from looking through the crowds to see if he were there. If he did come, he might have only one dance with her, making her afraid that she had offended him in some way. And yet, at the next ball, he would insist on every dance. He was the most fascinating and frustrating man she had ever met.

It was as well that Juniper was ignorant of an interview Hal had with his mother two weeks after he had met her.

'American, you say?' Lady Copton asked.

'Yes. From New York, and they have an estate outside.'

'I suppose we should be grateful she's from the East

coast. Sylvia Penshurst's boy has married a very strange girl, vulgarly wealthy, from California, with, would you believe, Irish peasant forebears?' She sniffed, a sniff that encompassed her disdain for new wealth, California, the Irish and any peasantry. 'A pity she's not from Boston, at least there one would have a glimmer of hope for some decent antecedents. New York? God knows where her family's from.' The Dowager Lady Copton shuddered her dislike of all things foreign.

'Her grandmother's English. A Tregowan from Cornwall.'

'Alice Tregowan? Oh dear, her father was a reprobate, a gambler. Her mother went raving mad. She eloped, too – always a weakness of character I feel, eloping. At least on her mother's side this girl's not a peasant.'

'Beggars can't be choosers, Mother.'

'We are hardly beggars, Hal. Your name is one of the proudest, your title one of the oldest.'

'It doesn't alter the fact we've no money, Mother. And Juniper would not be in the least bit impressed by my title.'

'Don't talk such nonsense, Hal. All gals want titles. You might think times have changed but they haven't.'

'She's not a virgin.'

'How rich?'

'Enormously.'

'As far as I can make out virginity becomes a rarer commodity these days. And, with enough money, I'm sure you can overlook her lack of it. I look forward to meeting the young woman then. A pity about her name – Juniper, the Americans never fail to amaze me.'

Hal had not enjoyed this conversation but he had no choice. He did not wish to be married, certainly not to a child like Juniper. He knew he would never enjoy being married. But then he needed an heir. Yesterday the bank had foreclosed on his property in Kent. Six hundred years in his family and with one flourish of his pen it had gone for ever. He hated his father, every day he hated the bastard even more. He only wished he were still alive so that he could tell him just how much he loathed him. Cut off without a penny, just the mouldering house in Kent, and that was his only because it was entailed. All the money had gone to his younger brother Leigh whom, after his father, he hated most of all. What little he and his mother had been left with had gone on a futile court case, a vain attempt to win back his inheritance by challenging his father's will.

In the gloomy house he and his mother had rented for the season, so that Hal could venture out into society and hopefully trade his name for a rich wife, Hal planned his strategy. Unknown to Juniper, from the start of the season he had been following her progress. She was well named the Golden Butterfly; she had flitted from man to man. Her conquests had been too easy, Hal decided. Juniper should have a challenge, he would arrange it so that finally she would beg him to marry her.

A wild storm which had ripped up off the Atlantic and damaged the roof of Gwenfer gave Alice an excuse to return home. She broke her journey at Bodmin and arrived at Boscar to find tragedy. The morning of her arrival Halliday had made the first test run in a new electric motor car he had invented. Mathilda was a willing passenger. Half-way across the park the tiny car, unstable from the weight of the many batteries it required, had hurled out of control and had curled itself around the great Domesday oak in the centre of the park. Both Halliday's and Mathilda's necks were instantly broken.

By the time she arrived, the house was in turmoil. Efficiently Alice took control for there did not seem to be anyone else willing to do so. The bodies were still in the car, Marshall kneeling beside the wreckage, his head in his hands, rocking back and forth, bellowing his despair.

Alice had called for the police, for a doctor, for stretchers to be made and with difficulty persuaded Marshall back into the house while the professionals examined the car and drew their inevitable conclusions.

She did not know what to say to him. She heard herself trot out the platitudes, that it was how Halliday would have liked to go, that Mathilda would not have wanted to live without him, that they were in a better place. And so on, and so on, until she hated the sound of her own voice and wished she could think of something just half-way intelligent to say to comfort Marshall.

A carpenter appeared with coffins, a woman from the estate came to wash the bodies. They were finally laid in state on biers in the great hall. The shutters at the long windows had been closed, the only light from giant candles in sconces on the walls, and in four enormous wooden holders at the four corners of the dais. Mathilda's dogs lay on the floor beside her coffin, on permanent guard, sighing and howling through the night.

The following morning when Alice came down it was to find Marshall standing in the same position she had left him the night before, looking stonily down on to the faces of his dead parents. The keening of the day before had ceased but in a way his stoic silence was even more chilling.

Alice could not get him to make any decisions concerning the burial. If she raised the subject, he closed his eyes as if silently praying and turned his head away from her. These were no circumstances to inflict on Juniper so she delayed sending a telegram.

On the third day she was beside herself with worry. Still he would not speak, he had not eaten, he had had nothing to drink. He would die himself, at this rate. At each mention she made of a funeral Marshall would look at her with the same silent stare. Only once did he speak.

'They hated the dark,' he said in explanation.

On the fifth day, with the temperature rising, something

had to be done. Covering her nose with a lavender-scented handkerchief she entered the hall with a purposeful step.

'Marshall,' she said loudly and sharply. 'This has gone on long enough, you are to come with me.' She put her hand on his arm and pulled him towards her. To her surprise, as docile as a lamb, he shuffled along beside her out of the hall and into the parlour. She pushed him into a chair, poured him a large brandy and said, 'We've got to talk, Marshall.'

'I know.'

'They have to be buried, my dear, we can't keep them in the hall any longer.'

'Yes.'

'This afternoon, don't you think?'

'If you say so, Alice. But you see, Grace is there.'

'In the chapel, yes, Marshall I know.'

'She hated them. How can I let them all lie together? It wouldn't be fair.'

Gently Alice took his hand. 'Grace isn't there, my dear. Her soul has gone, only the husk remains. She won't know.' Her voice broke as she spoke. Since Grace's death Alice had found it difficult to think of her, let alone to talk about her. 'It's your parents' right to lie with their ancestors.'

'I loved Grace, you know. I really did but at the end it was too late . . .'

'Yes, Marshall, I understand.'

'You can't, Alice. No one can understand. I was such a bad husband to her and I did not know how much she loved me until she killed herself for me.'

'Hush, my love. Don't torture yourself. You could not have foreseen what Grace decided to do.'

'No. It was my wickedness which killed her.'

Alice did not know what to say. This did not sound like Marshall speaking. She squeezed his hand in a futile attempt at comfort. She felt tears forming in her eyes as she remembered her poor sad daughter and longed for this conversation to end. 'I thought to send for Juniper,' she said, hoping that the thought of his daughter would help him.

'No,' Marshall shouted and sat bolt upright in the chair. 'No I can't see her. I can never see her.'

'But why not? You were once so close. You loved each other so much.'

'I love her still, but she knows, you see. She knows everything. I can't face her.'

'Knows what?'

Marshall looked straight at her and she felt herself recoil from the despair she saw in his eyes. 'Grace kept a diary. She wrote down everything, she spared nothing. The night she died I stayed up and read them. Stupidly I did not burn or hide them. Instead I packed them away in a trunk. Then at Boscar, after the funeral, I found they were missing. Juniper must have found them. I was too ashamed to ask her and too afraid.'

In the parlour of Boscar Manor, Alice listened with a mounting sense of horror as Marshall told her everything. He told of Grace's disappearance, of the brothel in Paris, the secret apartment in New York, of what together they had done. She felt herself go cold. She was filled with rage, fury, disgust. She wished that he were dead . . . And then, seeing his misery, seeing his hopelessness, she took him in her arms and held him. 'I used to make excuses all the time, Alice. I blamed her, I was so afraid of losing her – at first I admit it was the money but then I did genuinely become fond of her. I thought it was what she wanted, that she would leave me otherwise.'

'Didn't you talk about this with her?'

'I tried, she would never listen. If I said it had to stop, she accused me of having found someone else.'

'And had you ever?'

'No, never – Oh, I had the odd adventures but nothing to signify.'

'Then why did she kill herself, what happened?'

'She found me with Francine Frobisher on the boat. I'd no idea . . .'

'My poor Grace. Did Lincoln know?'

'Yes, he made it his business to find out. That's how he was able to get Juniper so easily – I couldn't risk going to court and Juniper finding out about us – but then she did,' he buried his face in his hands.

'Oh, my God, poor Juniper. I'll try and talk to her, Marshall, try and explain,' she said, wondering already how on earth she was to explain to the girl what she herself was finding inexplicable.

'I can't see her. And I don't want her to be made unhappy. Don't tell her my parents are dead. She's known such unhappiness, let her be happy for the time being. Let her finish her season. Do you promise?'

'I promise.'

She finally persuaded him to eat a bowl of soup and some bread and to sleep for a little while. That afternoon she supported him as both his parents joined his wife in the family vault.

She delayed her return to Gwenfer for a week until she was sure that Marshall was not going to harm himself.

The week before the journey to Scotland Juniper did not see Hal once, it was as if he had disappeared off the face of the earth. Each time the telephone rang she prayed it would be him, but it never was. She despaired of ever seeing him again.

Unusually for her she went, alone, for a walk in St James's Park, hoping by keeping busy she would forget him, and unable, at the moment, to enjoy the chatter and gossip of her friends. She walked, hands in pockets, head down, her mind a jumble of plans and perplexities. Unless he had called her name she would not have noticed him amongst the strolling crowds.

'Jonathan, what a pleasant surprise,' she lied, wishing he had not seen her, wanting to be alone.

He fell into step beside her. As if sensing her mood he walked in silence. They paused by the lake and she looked moodily at the swans.

'Perhaps the press should have christened you the Swan instead of the "Golden Butterfly". An elegant and mysterious creature more like you,' he said.

She swung round to face him, chuckling at the compliment – she could not recall being regarded as mysterious before.

'My neck's too short. Let's have lunch,' she suddenly suggested.

'Why not?' he agreed.

Over the meal he talked incessantly about Polly, plying her with questions about her friend. Juniper soon grew bored with having to listen to his endless praise of Polly. But, she was not simply bored, she was jealous: jealous not only that Polly was loved when she was not, but also because this young man should suddenly have taken the central place in Polly's affections instead of her.

'I'd love to see your room in Chelsea,' she said, taking him by surprise, as she picked up her handbag and stood up with the air of one who was never thwarted.

En route she stopped the taxi and insisted on buying champagne from Fortnums. Once in his rooms, champagne glass in her hand, it was she who took the initiative and seduced him.

3

Polly peered anxiously along the busy platform at Euston. The engine of the overnight sleeper to Inverness was huffing and puffing its imminent departure.

'Polly, get in, it'll go without you.'

'I can't see him, Juniper.'

'He must be somewhere, Polly. He's probably in the restaurant carriage with everyone else.'

'Do you think so?' she asked hopefully as she stepped up into the first-class sleeper compartment.

They made their way with difficulty through the crowded corridor. The grouse shooting would start next week and the season decamped from London to the mist and chill of the Scottish moors. The highlight of the Scottish season was to be the Frobisher Grouse Ball, an event that people would have sold their souls to be invited to, an event of such importance that not to be invited meant certain social death. Most of Juniper's friends were already in the restaurant car, champagne corks popping, glasses topped and a party atmosphere in progress. But there was no Jonathan.

'Juniper, he's missed the train.' She felt her eyes filling with tears.

'He'll fly up. He can hire an aeroplane, it'll find a field to land somewhere near your grandmother's.'

'Don't be silly, he couldn't afford it.' Sometimes Juniper irritated her with her notions that everyone was as rich as she.

'Then perhaps he'll drive up. There must be masses of people coming up by car.'

'No, I don't think he's coming,' Polly found herself saying. She suddenly felt cold inside. Strangely, irrationally, she felt it was all over. 'I don't think I'll see him again.'

'Piffle, don't be so dramatic, just because he's missed the silly train. Come on, I've booked us seats for dinner, let's join the others.'

'No, thanks, I'm not hungry now.'

Polly went to her sleeper. She had been looking forward to this sixteen-hour trip by train – the longest journey in the country – and the novelty of sleeping on board. She undressed and went to bed and when, hours later, Juniper crept in, she pretended to be asleep. She lay wide eyed as, in the blue glow of the little night light, the train thundered its noisy way north, up the spine of England. From England into Scotland, from the flat lands to the high, Polly lay awake and stared at the ceiling.

'Guess what?' Juniper hung down from the upper bunk, her upside-down face looking at Polly, her hair hanging down, brushing the sheets on Polly's bed. 'I've had the most amazing dream.'

'Have you?' Polly said without interest. She was more intent on watching the view from the train window. They were in the mountains now: it was a view she would have liked to share with Jonathan.

'Stop mooning over Jonathan and listen,' Juniper said. 'I dreamt we were in a car going through a gate with large stone pillars with bears on top, bears with big round balls at their feet and the most appealing smiles. We floated up a long, winding drive with rhododendrons on either side, to a huge house with turrets, looking just like a giant wedding cake, overlooking the sea.'

'So?' Polly felt as bored as most people do when others insist on recounting their dreams.

'The door opened . . . no one opened it, it just swung open. And there was this dance going on and, suddenly, you were there and you were laughing fit to bust, and I looked down and we both had rings on our fingers. Isn't that amazing?'

'Not particularly.'

'Gee, you are in a beastly mood. The rings were on our engagement fingers. Don't you see, we're going to get engaged this holiday. You to Jonathan and me, well if I'm lucky, to Hal.'

'You don't really want to marry him, do you? He's so old and he's always so gloomy.'

'No he's not, he's only thirty and he just gets bored with our more juvenile friends. He's the most fascinating and sensuous man I know. He's a mystery, and he's a mystery I'm determined to solve.'

'Poor Hal.' At last Polly laughed, and Juniper threw a pillow at her for her pains.

At Inverness the Frobisher Rolls-Royce was waiting for them. No one had news of Jonathan. As they drove through the splendour of the Northern Highlands, with the mountains purple-tinged in the distance, their caps topped with snow even in the summer sun which glinted on the many lochs they passed, even Polly's spirits lifted a little.

'Polly, look,' excitedly Juniper was pointing out of the window at the great stone bears standing sentinel at the gate of the Frobisher Scottish home. 'See, they've got stone balls between their feet, just like my dream. And they're smiling,' she shrieked with excitement. 'Polly, look! Aren't those rhododendrons?'

'You get those everywhere. You have them at Gwenfer. And bears are common as heraldic devices.'

'How pedestrian you are. It's my dream. We are going to be so happy, you and me,' Juniper said, flopping back on the cushions of the Rolls-Royce. 'The house is exactly as it was in the dream. I tell you it is exact in every detail.'

Polly looked out of the car for her first sight of her family's Scottish home. It did look like a wedding cake, a giant cream one, as terrace after terrace tumbled down to formal gardens beside the Dornoch Firth. The roof proliferated with turrets, the gutterings with gargoyles, and the stone work of each of the hundreds of windows was a swirling confection of the stonemason's skill. The only difference, it appeared, was that the door did not mysteriously open of its own accord. It was opened by a very dour, unfriendly butler who bitterly resented the annual August arrival of his employers and their guests.

All through the day, into the early evening, the house party began to arrive. The house was rapidly filling up. The young for the ball, the elderly and middle-aged for the shooting. The new arrivals were shown their rooms with streamlined efficiency. In each room was a small book full of useful information – the times of meals, of trains, of tides, when the post was collected, church services. There were maps indicating the best walks, the most famous beauty spots. Even information on the flora and fauna. It was more like staying in a hotel than a private home.

Their first evening was fairly quiet with a sedate dinner and a quiet game of charades; everyone was tired from the long journey. Gertie had decreed that all the young women should go early to bed, and who was there willing to argue with Gertie? Her younger son, Charles, and his wife, Fiona, were in residence but not once did Fiona try to take control from her mother-in-law or even appear to want to. As far as hosts and guests were concerned it was Gertie's house and Gertie's ball and no doubt would remain so until the day she died.

Meeting her uncle and aunt, and their five children, was an added bonus for Polly. On this first evening it helped keep her mind off Jonathan from whom there was no letter or telephone message.

The next day the dancing master arrived. All those who did not know how to dance the reels were expected to take a course of lessons. It was not done to make a mistake at the actual ball; to throw everyone into disarray would have been too shaming. Besides, such a faux pas carried with it the risk of Gertie's banning the culprit from ever being invited again.

The novices collected in the huge, marble-walled and echoing ballroom. They huddled in groups clutching their arms about them against the chill draughts that whistled through the vast room. After a short time, Polly found she was enjoying the lessons. This was not like the dancing she had been avoiding all summer. This sort of dancing she could understand. There was a set pattern to follow, a set of rules which, once learnt, were easy to follow. There was a freedom to the dances which she enjoyed and she found a gracefulness which surprised her. Those who were finding it more difficult than she were an endless source of amusement to everyone, including the dancing master and the burly piper who, several times, overcome with laughter, lost his mouthpiece, causing his bagpipes to wail in lament, which only made everyone shriek the louder.

Juniper appeared at the door waving a letter importantly in her direction. 'See, look, he's written. It came on the afternoon train.' She thrust the letter into Polly's hands. Despite breaking up one set Polly raced from the ballroom, ignoring the complaining voices of her partners. Up the stairs she went, racing along the corridor to the safety of her own room and, with thudding heart, tore open the letter.

My darling,
I don't even know where to begin this letter to you. Before I start I want to tell you how much I love you and how much you mean to me. I can't thank you enough for the happiness you have allowed me.

I have decided that it is best if I go away. By the time you get this I will be on my way to Spain. I think I told you that I wanted to go there to write.

I have betrayed you, Polly, and I am finding it difficult to come to terms with what I have done. You gave me your love and trust and I was not worthy of them. You should forget me.

Please try not to think too badly of me but understand that what I am doing is the hardest thing I've ever done. Will I have the courage to post this? Or will I tear it up and follow you to Scotland and lie to you?
Jonathan.

Polly looked at the letter with disbelief. She felt a tear roll down her cheek and did not bother to brush it away. There was a soft knock at the door. 'Go away,' she sobbed. The door opened and Juniper tiptoed in.

'What's it say?' she asked anxiously.

'He's gone to Spain.' An enormous sob racked Polly's body.

'To Spain? What on earth for?'

Unable to answer she picked up the letter and waved it at Juniper, who grabbed it and hurried crossed the room to read it by the light from the window.

'The bastard!' she said, making her voice angry to mask the relief that she had not been named. She swooped across the room and took Polly into her arms. 'How could he hurt you so, a dear sweet thing like you? They're all the same you know, you can't trust any man.'

'He's not like the others,' Polly protested.

'Poor darling Polly. He is, you know. It's better to know now and not when it would have been too late. I heard rumours . . .'

'No, you didn't, you're making that up.'

'I'm not, Polly. He's had affairs with dozens of women. Not all of them nice either,' she lied. 'You must listen to me. You've had a narrow escape. He would have made a disastrous husband. Forget him.' There was after all a certain logic to her argument, she reasoned. He had been unfaithful with her, which meant he was capable of doing the same again with anyone. In a way, by seducing him, she had done Polly a favour – showing her what Jonathan was really like. She had saved her friend, if truth be told.

'I can't forget him. I love him,' Polly shouted with frustration.

'I know, my sweet, you do now, but it will fade. You'll meet someone else, I know you will.'

'Not like him, I won't. Oh, Juniper, what am I to do? I'm so unhappy and yesterday I was so happy.'

Polly's tears soaked into Juniper's blouse as she poured out her grief. Her face averted, Juniper wished Polly would not cry; it made her feel quite guilty.

Three days later, Hal arrived by road. Juniper's excitement at his arrival was short-lived. From Hal's car stepped Christabel Summerton. Christabel was two years older than Juniper, and her complete opposite – dark, soignée and tall. She gave Juniper a look of triumph, an expression which stated blatantly – 'Hal's mine, hands off.' Demoralised, Juniper turned back into the house. She joined in the chatter, the laughter, she helped Gertie serve tea. At the first opportunity she slipped away to her room.

Later Polly found her hanging upside down from her four poster bed.

'What on earth are you doing?'

'Stretching myself. I want to grow another inch. It's not much to ask is it, just another inch?' she said with difficulty.

'Your face is terribly red, are you sure you're all right?'

'I love hanging upside down like a bat, did I never tell you?'

'Then get down, Juniper. You're being silly, you'll hurt yourself. You'd need to stretch at least four inches to be as tall as Christabel and I don't think that's likely, do you?' Polly laughed.

'Don't laugh. It's all right for you. Look at you – five feet eight if you're an inch – I hate you.' She allowed herself to flop down on to the bed.

'No, you don't,' Polly grinned. 'You love me.'

'I do, too.' Juniper grinned back, turned, opened a drawer of the bedside table and rootled about in its chaotic contents, finally finding the nail file she needed. She began to work on her already immaculate nails with long, almost angry sweeps of the silver-handled file. 'What am I to do, Polly? I haven't seen him for over a week and then he ignores me completely. And what made him bring that simpering bitch Christabel?'

'He telephoned Grandma and asked her if he could.'

'Did you see the looks she was giving me? He's all over her, it's disgusting,' she was now buffing her nails angrily.

'I think he's playing games with you. I think he's just pretending to be involved with her.'

'Do you really? What makes you say that?' Juniper sat up with interest and for the moment forgot her manicure.

'He fusses over her but, if you notice, he rarely talks to her. And, when he thinks no one is looking he sneaks looks at you.'

'Honestly? Really? Oh, you are a pet to tell me.'

'What's so different about Hal? You've never been like this over any of the others.'

'Because I've never felt like this before, you silly goose. Just being in the same room as him makes me go peculiar – he makes my insides feel slithery,' she giggled with delight at the thought.

'He treats you differently. The others, they're like pathetic slaves, they race after you. He doesn't. Maybe that's why you're so besotted with him, because he's mysterious and, well, difficult to pin down.'

Juniper threw her nail buffer at her. 'You are so prosaic. That's got nothing to do with it. This is love. I feel different because I'm really in love with him.' She examined the nail of her index finger. 'Something's got to happen. I'm determined. I'll make him sick with jealousy. And if that doesn't work then I've decided that, somehow, I'm going to inveigle him away on the night of the ball and I'm going to ask him to marry me.'

'Juniper! You couldn't!' Polly sat down heavily on the dressing stool.

'I can, and I will. What have I to lose?'

'It's very brave of you. I don't think I could.'

'You would if the man was important enough to you.' She looked across at Polly, looked down at her nails, and then looked at Polly again sharply as if checking something.

'You seem very jolly today?'

'I couldn't sleep again last night but, this morning, I thought, *I am being ridiculous*. Who the hell does Jonathan Middlebank think he is, eh? He was playing games and I only imagined he was serious about me. I can't spend the rest of my life mourning something that did not exist. So, I'm going to enjoy myself for what's left of the season. I've decided to show him I don't care. Then, when he comes back from Spain, I want him to know I wasn't moping around, pining for him.'

'Good, I'm glad to hear it. Three days of misery is enough for any man. Now, please don't take this the wrong way, but if you would just let me do your hair and maybe a little make-up? It'll make all the difference. And what about letting my maid make over your ball dress? It's just the teeny weeniest bit dull.'

'Juniper, you are kind.'

'No I'm not. I want my dream to come true.' She swung from the bed, dispatched Polly to collect her dress, and rang the bell for her maid. With a few deft snips and tucks, the maid began the transformation of Polly's dress for the following night's ball.

4

The final guests arrived in time for dinner. There were now fifty in the house party. Half-way through the meal Polly looked up from her plate to see a man further down the table looking at her with such an intense stare that she found herself blushing and had, hurriedly, to look down at her plate. His look gave her strange butterflies in the stomach, half pleasant and half uncomfortable. As the meal progressed, whenever she looked up it was to find him still staring at her. Eventually she became so confused that she had to spend the remainder of the meal looking down at the table, which made conversation difficult with the men on either side of her. She continued to feel so confused that, at the end of the meal, she made excuses to her grandmother and went to bed.

Juniper, curious as to why Polly had disappeared, and

demoralised by spending yet another evening being ignored by Hal, slipped away too and joined her.

'Have you got a headache?' she asked, popping her head around Polly's door. Their bedrooms were adjoining in the wing set aside for young women. To get there one had to pass Gertie's bedroom door which was always, during a house party, ajar. There was no greater deterrent for any young man who might have dishonourable ideas than the thought of having to tiptoe past that open door, especially since it was common knowledge – from a rumour started by Gertie, years before – that she was an insomniac.

'Come in and sit down.' She patted her eiderdown. 'I had to leave. There was a man at dinner who kept staring at me. It made me feel so uncomfortable.'

'He was probably looking at you with *desire*.' Juniper laughed her delightful husky laugh. 'How exciting. Who was he?'

'I don't know. He was sitting between Fiona and Primrose.'

'No wonder he was gawping at you then, poor soul. Fancy having to endure those two.'

Polly was unsure how to take this remark but before she could think of a reply a scuffling and muffled giggling from the corridor caught her attention.

'What's that?' Polly looked at the door.

'Oh, they're making apple pie beds and other silly things. Honestly, they are so juvenile,' Juniper said dismissively.

'You don't like women very much do you, Juniper?'

'Not at all. Except you, of course.' She smiled brilliantly at Polly.

'May I ask you something very personal?'

'You can try.' Juniper chuckled.

'Have you, you know . . . have you . . . done *it*?'

'Slept with someone? Yes.'

'What was it like? What does he do to you? I know about animals but I don't know a thing about humans.'

'There's not all that much difference, actually. Quite honestly, I can't see what all the fuss is about.'

'Really? It's not awful then?'

'Not after the first time. It's dreadfully messy though, sticky and well, ugh! You keep having to change your knickers afterwards if he didn't use a – you know what.'

'No, I don't know.'

'You should or you could be in trouble. A French letter, that's what. I can't say I've ever enjoyed it. It seems to be an awful lot of effort for nothing. But the men seem to enjoy themselves. They're always so extraordinarily grateful.'

'Maybe you haven't enjoyed it because you haven't really been in love with any of them?'

'I reckon it's always the same, it doesn't matter who you do it with. Haven't you ever wanted to try?'

'No. Though now I begin to wish I had, with Jonathan. It might have been a nice memory to have for the rest of my life,' she said, a sad expression fleetingly crossing her face.

'I doubt it. He's no great shakes.' She was folding the corner of the eiderdown back and forth.

'How would you know?' Polly felt her stomach lurch.

'You just have to look at him. He's cerebral. No, the remotely good ones have a look about them, it's the way they glance at you, and something about the mouth.'

'Oh, thank God, Juniper.' Polly laughed with relief. 'The way you spoke then I thought you had . . . well . . . Jonathan.'

'Don't be silly,' Juniper laughed as she lied. 'You're my friend. But if I had, would it have mattered?' She watched Polly intently from the corner of her eye.

'Not now, I suppose.' Then she shook her head, finding her thoughts confused. 'Actually, I don't know.'

'You haven't got over him.'

'I have. I know I have. No one, no one treats me like that.'

'That's my girl,' Juniper patted her hand. 'Your mystery man sounds as though he's been sent from heaven.'

'I don't think I could do *it* with him. He must be at least thirty – I'd be too scared.' And she giggled.

'Maybe when you take the plunge, you'll enjoy it more than I did.'

'I hope so. It would be awful to be married to a man and have to, and not like it, wouldn't it?'

Back and forth their conversation went in the time-honoured way of young women where one knows and the other doesn't. After Juniper had gone to her own bed, Polly resolved that by the time she returned to Devon she too would have lost her virginity. If she couldn't give it to Jonathan, it didn't really matter whom she gave it to.

The following morning was the Glorious Twelfth. Glorious to everyone, that is, except the grouse.

The men had left early for the damp and misty moors. All morning the distant sound of gunfire could be heard in the house. Polly would have liked to join them but it was considered unladylike to shoot. She wandered about the house, bored, since Juniper had spent the whole of the morning with her head under the pillow trying not to hear the guns, upset about the grouse.

At lunchtime most of the women left with the servants, taking the picnic in horse-drawn wagons up to the moor. Three other large carts were needed to carry all the food, wine, cutlery, silver, tables, chairs and even potted plants. Since Juniper would not go, Polly stayed behind too. She did not mind. When she had seen the supplies being loaded it had not looked the sort of picnic she was used to – more like a formal lunch party.

The ball was three hours old and already a resounding success. Scottish balls, with most of the men in kilts, were more colourful, far noisier, more boisterous than those in London. There was a wildness to the proceedings, too, no doubt fuelled by the day's killing, which added to the general air of excitement.

Polly, on her fifth glass of champagne, was beginning to feel remarkably light-headed but was having a wonderful time, albeit rather hysterically to those who knew her well. She had mastered the reels so skilfully that her dance card was nearly full. The alterations to the dress had made a great improvement to her appearance, and with her hair dressed with flowers, and discreet make-up applied by Juniper, Polly looked lovelier than ever.

'Miss Frobisher?'

She swung round, eyes smiling, to find the gentleman who had taken such an interest in her the night before, immaculate in white tie and tails, bowing to her. 'Yes.'

'I wonder, Miss Frobisher, if I might have the honour of escorting you into supper?' Again he gave a small bow.

'You're French.' She laughed, though at what she hadn't the least idea.

'My poor English has betrayed me.'

'No, no. Your English is excellent. It's the way you bow. I saw Charles Boyer bow like that in a film. Only a Frenchman could bow so beautifully.' She was amazed at herself for being able to talk so easily to this stranger. 'Of course I should be delighted for you to take me into supper, Monsieur . . . ?'

'Michel de Faubert et Bresson, Comte,' again he bowed.

'Oh Monsieur le Comte, you do me an honour.' She sank in a graceful curtsey and on her way back up took her sixth glass of champagne from the tray of a passing footman.

With his hand under her elbow he guided her through the crowds to the supper room. 'This castle belongs to your grandmother?'

'That's right.' She giggled, waving her hand about. Never one to boast, to her astonishment and shame she heard herself busily explaining about the family's various houses and land. And then, red-faced with embarrassment, her hand clapped over her mouth, she suddenly sat down vowing to herself not to say another word.

'So your father is Lord Frobisher?'

'You seem to know a lot about us,' Polly said sharply, her vow of silence short-lived. He apologised charmingly for his curiosity, explaining that he had a passion for genealogy. Elegantly he flicked up his tails, sat down and summoned a waiter with a click of his fingers. Then he smiled at her, softening the rather austere, autocratic expression. His face had been bothering her ever since she had first noticed him. He looked a little like a monkey and should have been ugly, but he wasn't. There was an intensity in his expression which she found flattering. She liked the darkish colour of his skin, so different from the Englishmen she was used to. And she admired his fine high cheek bones. All in all, she thought, she could not imagine what had first made her think he looked like a monkey.

He leant forward as he spoke to her, his dark brown eyes studying her face intently as she replied. She found his concentration on her and her alone very flattering. She liked his voice, which was very deep, and his accent, which like Charles Boyer's sent thrills down her spine. By her seventh glass of champagne she had decided that she preferred him to Jonathan. Jonathan was still a boy; here was a man. And when he invited her to take a stroll with him in the gardens she quickly agreed.

Outside the heated and crowded house it was cold. A sharp wind whipped off the waters of the Firth. Polly began to shiver. Immediately he removed his jacket and slipped it around her shoulders. It smelt wonderful, of musk and sandalwood – more intriguing than Jonathan, who smelt only of tobacco.

She wasn't sure how it happened but suddenly she was in his arms and his mouth was on hers. She stood rigid, her arms hanging loose at her sides, unsure what was expected of her. And then her arms, as if they had a life of their own, rose and put themselves about him and she felt his muscles under the fine linen of his dress shirt – it was a very pleasant sensation. His tongue prised her mouth open, searching the inside of her mouth, probing deep inside her. Jonathan had never kissed like that.

'My darling, I shall marry you,' she heard him whispering huskily into her ear which he then proceeded to lick with short sharp movements that made her insides do a somersault. Had she washed her ears properly, she wondered.

She tried to step back, wide-eyed with surprise.

'Me?'

'Ah, yes, you are everything I've ever wanted in my wife.'

She felt quite giddy at the words, at the accent, or was it the champagne?

'But we've only just met,' she said lamely.

'I always knew that I would know my future wife the moment I met her. And, just as I imagined, it has happened. I love you, Polly, my darling.'

'Oh, Michel, you must stop talking like this.' Feebly she tried to push him away.

'Don't ask me to stop, never . . .'

A second later there was no question of her pushing him away as he passionately held her to him, kisses raining down on her mouth, her eyelids, her hair. When he thrust his hand into the front of her dress she knew she should object but the thrill it gave her made resistance impossible. With a little moan of pleasure she settled deeper into his arms . . . Suddenly he let go of her and stood back looking far out over the water. To her shame she found she felt disappointed as she rearranged her dress.

'Forgive me. I behaved unspeakably. We must return or I shall shame both of us.'

'Michel,' she sighed his name and all thought of Jonathan was banished with these entirely new sensations.

'My dear one. I . . .' He looked at her with such an intensity that involuntarily she shivered. 'Come . . .' abruptly he took her arm and led her back to the ballroom.

Juniper had never looked more beautiful – and she knew it. She knew why too: the excitement bubbling inside her made her eyes sparkle, her cheeks becomingly flushed. She did not dance the reels. Not for her, dancing in a group – Juniper only liked to dance when she could move about the floor in the arms of the best-looking man, both moving as one – as lovemaking should be but never was for her. She had spent the evening flirting with every single man who spoke to her. So extravagant were these flirtations that the ballroom was full of bewildered men. Hal, she had quickly noticed, did not dance either. He had stood for most of the evening watching the dancing with the expression of one who regards such pastimes as mildly ridiculous. This could not have been better for Juniper since he could not but be aware of her progress around the edge of the ballroom as she flitted from man to man.

Between each dance, Christabel returned to him. Her arm would slip through his in a proprietorial way which made Juniper long to scratch her supercilious face.

Her hard work on the other men, however, did not seem to have had the desired effect. Hal had not spoken to her once. She had no choice, she was going to have to take the initiative herself. She waited for the Gay Gordons, for which there was always an encore, thus ensuring Christabel's absence for some time.

'Excuse me, Hal, I wonder if I could talk to you for a moment?' Alarmingly her stomach felt most unstable as she stood in front of him.

'Of course, Juniper.' He leant forward the better to hear her.

'Not here, in private,' she said, shortly, turned on her heel and led the way out of the ballroom, along the cold, stone corridor to the library. She pushed open the large mahogany door. She crossed to a drinks tray and poured two large glasses of whisky.

'I thought you only drank champagne.' He smiled the slightly lopsided, sardonic smile which made her feel weak inside.

'One needs something to warm one in these fearful freezing houses.'

'Of course you poor Americans must suffer greatly,' he said adding another log to the fire.

'I used to get angry with my mother when she complained about the chill in British houses. I forgive her now.' She knew she was talking like a tourist only to delay the fateful moment. 'Please sit down, Hal,' she finally said, taking the seat opposite him.

He looked at her quizzically. 'You wanted to say something to me.'

'Yes. Are you going to ask Christabel to marry you?'

He laughed. 'What a strange question.'

'Are you?'

'Quite honestly, Juniper, I can't see that it's any business of yours.' He sipped his drink, eyeing her over the rim of the glass.

'I want to marry you myself,' she blurted out. This was not at all what she had planned. But having said it, she shook her head defiantly and looked him straight in the eye.

'I'm honoured, Juniper. But I don't think I have ever given you cause to think this way.'

'I know you haven't, that's the problem. At first I was certain you felt something for me but then you began to ignore me. I refuse to be ignored.'

'I'm sorry. But it's out of the question.'

'Why? I love you.' She looked miserably down at her hands. She longed for him to get up, cross the rug and take her in his arms. She could think of a dozen men who would leap at the opportunity. There was a silence broken only by the cracking of logs, the ticking of a clock, and the noise of the ball muted now by the thickness of the door and curtains. As the silence persisted she could no longer resist lifting her head. He sat in the chair completely relaxed, his long legs stretched elegantly in front of him, a strange smile on his face.

'I can't marry you, Juniper.'

She felt as if her heart was tumbling into her dancing slippers. 'Can you tell me why not?' Her voice, normally bubbling with emotion, sounded flat.

At last he stood, crossed the room and sat on the tapestried footstool in front of her. He took one hand in his and with the other gently stroked her face. 'I can't marry you because I have no money.'

'Money isn't important.' She leant forward eagerly.

'It is to me.'

'But I have plenty of money, I'm very rich.' She laughed, relieved at the unimportance of the problem. 'If you need a rich wife then let it be me.'

'Ah, no. I care too much for you, you see.'

'No, I don't see,' her voice was rising with frustration. 'You have to marry for money, I have money. I insist you marry me.'

'I've no home – the bank took my family estate away from me last month. I have no job – I've no skills to sell. I am virtually a bankrupt.'

'I don't care. I can buy us a house, I can give you all the money you want.'

'And have people gossip about me, talking about my living off my wife's money?'

Her mind was racing. 'I could settle money on you in America, then no one need know.'

'I couldn't possibly allow that.'

'But why not? If you were rich and loved me, you wouldn't think twice about marrying me – it wouldn't matter.'

He merely shook his head.

She poured them more drinks. She sat on the footstool

beside him and she talked and argued as she had never done before.

An hour later a radiant Juniper emerged from the library. It had taken all that time to persuade Hal to accept a house, a capital sum and an annual allowance. Juniper hurried to find Polly. Hal telephoned his mother.

The next morning Polly woke with a dreadful headache and, as she sat in bed, she blushed at the memory of the night before. It must have been the drink, she decided – nothing else would have enabled her to behave so stupidly. She would have to find Michel, apologise to him and hope that he would leave a day earlier.

Michel had been waiting for over an hour for her. He had refused to go shooting, not a great sacrifice for Michel was a city man – preferably Paris – and the country held little attraction for him. They walked in the garden and Polly tried to explain to him that last night she had made a dreadful mistake. He silenced her protestations with a kiss, under a beech tree which dripped water down the back of his neck. Alarmingly for Polly, the kiss held as much attraction for her as those of the night before.

As they walked, she found that he was interesting to talk with. And he appeared to find her interesting too. And today he made her laugh. Their conversation was very general and then suddenly he talked of their marriage again as if it were all decided.

Polly, totally perplexed, decided to say nothing. No doubt he would meet someone else at the next house party to which he went. Undoubtedly it was because he was French that he had behaved as he had; no doubt he proposed marriage several times a week. Probably she would never see him again.

Once back in London, Michel began to court Polly in earnest. Daily flowers were delivered to Gertie's house. Not the large bouquets of red roses which suitors normally sent their loves, but one day a single perfect rose, the next a bunch of marguerites, even a potted palm. Frequently chocolates were delivered in boxes so beautiful that she could not bring herself to throw them away. When he called it was always with a small gift – a bottle of scent, a book he thought she might enjoy, an engraving he had found, and once he gave her a china cat for he said she reminded him of a panther – such a compliment reduced Polly to helpless laughter. Soon a pyjama sachet, kept under lock and key, was overflowing with the letters and poems he had written her. They were rather flowery in tone, but nevertheless, she read them several times a day.

She had not intended this relationship to continue but then she had never dreamt of being courted in this way and found she liked it. She was being swept along on a sea of seduction, but seduction was a word not included in her vocabulary. Even had it been, it was doubtful if she would have understood its full meaning.

Nightly she and Juniper went out to dinner with Hal and Michel. If they did not go to a club they would go to a party, for every night they had a choice of several to attend. Fancy dress was all the rage and they had gone dressed as babies, as courtesans, even to one particularly successful one as film stars. She kept telling herself that she despised this empty life. She reminded herself of the unemployed, the hungry. She resolved that it must cease, but once again she would find herself in Juniper's car, hurtling about on a treasure hunt or off to another party or anther country weekend. She found that the busier she kept herself the easier it was to keep at bay all thoughts of Jonathan who, despite her protestations, kept sidling into her mind. It was also fear of being alone, and his taking over her thoughts completely, which stopped her from returning home to Devon.

Hal wanted to ask Marshall formally for Juniper's hand. Juniper refused to allow him to go to Boscar and she refused to tell him why. Instead, Alice was summoned from Gwenfer and Tommy returned from Italy.

Neither Alice nor Tommy was impressed by Hal. It did not take much investigation to discover his serious financial problems. But their concern went deeper: both women observed a coldness about him which made them anxious for Juniper. Both tried to talk to her but she was not in the mood to listen to anyone. She dismissed any criticism of Hal as their inability to understand the young. They talked long into several nights but both came to the reluctant conclusion that there was nothing they could do. Juniper had chosen and, if thwarted, would elope.

Alice telephoned Marshall to inform him of Juniper's intentions. She called out of courtesy only, for it was Tommy and Charlie Macpherson who would have to give their permission. Telegrams were sent to Charlie and after his reply it was a radiant and triumphant Juniper who finally sported her engagement ring – one of the few pieces of the Copton jewel collection left, the rest having long since been sold.

Alice invited Hal's mother to tea at her small house in Chelsea the day before the formal announcement was to be made. The minute that Hortense, the Dowager Lady Copton, arrived in her car, Alice felt her forebodings were justified. The moment she alighted and saw the small, terraced house, she could be overheard loudly telling the chauffeur that there must be some mistake – no one of any consequence would live in such an area. From this point it was obvious that she did not approve of the furnishings, the food and Alice's plain clothes – for Hortense was dressed as if for a palace reception. Alice felt animosity towards this arrogant and utterly charmless woman.

Hortense sat opposite her, rigidly upright. She was tall and lean. Faded blue eyes glanced suspiciously from left to right constantly restless. Her mouth was a thin mean line which seemed incapable of registering mirth.

'And where do you intend to hold the reception, Mrs Wakefield? Not a hotel I trust,' Lady Copton's voice, chill with disapproval at the recent habit of using hotels for receptions and balls, rang out across the tea table.

'I had hoped that Juniper would wish for a country wedding but she says she wants a London wedding. A friend has kindly offered us her house.'

'Of course it must be a London wedding. My son and I shall need to invite at least three hundred. I trust your friend's house is large enough?' Hortense with a lift of the eyebrow, a curl of the lip managed to imply how inferior she regarded the borrowing of a house to be. Since she had had to rent one for the season, Alice could feel herself begin to bristle with righteous anger.

'The house of my friend Lady Frobisher is, as I am sure you know, quite substantial.' Alice's smile was rigid.

'The Frobishers? That makes all the difference.' She patted her thin lips with her napkin. 'The young couple will require a London home,' Hortense continued almost aggressively, leaning forward, her glance flitting quickly from Alice to Juniper and back again.

'That is up to Juniper's trustees of course.'

'I can't foresee any problems, Lady Copton,' Tommy volunteered.

'And what do you know about it, young woman? Are you not Miss Boscar's companion?' Hortense's tone of voice changed to that reserved for servants and those socially beneath her.

'I also happen to be one of her trustees.'

'A governess?' In these two words Hortense Copton distilled doubt, horror and incredulity.

'Miss Randolph was a very close and respected friend of my late husband.'

'Your husband's?' Normally verbose, Hortense suddenly seemed capable only of using two-word sentences but still managed, in her inflection, to convey the doubts and gossip that had rocked Dart Island over Tommy's true relationship with Lincoln.

'My lawyer is the other trustee and he does whatever Tommy and I want, doesn't he, Tommy?' Juniper smiled brightly, as brightly as she could as she began to realise that here was a formidable mother-in-law to be.

'The country?' Hortense asked, apparently still stuck with two words.

'I'm sorry, I don't quite understand?' Alice understood perfectly but contrarily she had decided to be obtuse.

'A country estate will have to be purchased,' she boomed with exasperation.

'We don't need one, Lady Copton. We've got Gwenfer. My grandmother will be overjoyed if we use it, won't you?'

'Of course,' Alice said politely.

'But Cornwall?' Hortense shuddered. 'So far away.'

'It's lovely – it's the most wonderful place in the world,' Juniper said heatedly and was rewarded by a withering glare from Hortense.

'Of course they will have the estate at Dart Island,' Tommy added helpfully.

'There is no question of my son residing abroad. And we should also discuss the settlements. If you would kindly give me the name of Miss Boscar's English lawyer? The sooner everything is official the better, don't you agree?' For the first time she smiled. Large yellowed teeth flashed, and as quickly disappeared, so that everyone wondered if they had imagined the smile.

'What settlements?' Tommy was aware that Juniper was looking everywhere but at her and Alice.

'The capital settlement and allowance arranged between my son and Juniper.'

'That's most kind of Lord Copton, but in the

circumstances I don't think it will be necessary.' Tommy smiled for the first time at Hortense.

'Are you being insolent, young woman?' Hortense's bony chest swelled with indignation.

'No, Lady Copton. I don't wish to be impertinent, but I gather your son is not very wealthy and, since Juniper is well provided for, Hal need not worry himself about a settlement.'

'I was referring to the arrangement that Miss Boscar has promised my son,' Hortense trumpeted. Juniper looked at the floor, Alice the ceiling, and Tommy looked angry.

'What arrangement would that be?' she asked in a deceptively calm voice.

'It was my idea, Tommy. Poor Hal has nothing. I suggested I give him a little something and I'd buy us a house,' Juniper interrupted.

'How much?' Alice asked in a chill voice. Juniper looked down.

'£50,000 and £5,000 income,' she said in a barely audible voice.

'I think you should have consulted your grandmother and me first.'

'I trust there is going to be no difficulty?' Hortense was incapable of keeping silent for long.

'If you must know, Lady Copton, I find it most distasteful. Juniper is not a commodity for sale. Had she spoken to me, I would most certainly have counselled against this . . .'

'But, Tommy, I promised . . .' Juniper wailed, remembering the difficulty she had had in persuading Hal to marry her. 'I've got masses of money. Hal didn't want it, I insisted.'

'I know you have money Juniper, and it appears already to be a problem. This is so undignified. I have never heard of anything so degrading in my life.'

'That's because you are not a European, Miss Randolph.'

'And glad of it, Lady Copton. In the circumstances, Mr Macpherson and I would have accepted that the financial responsibility of this marriage should fall on Juniper. But to make cold-blooded arrangements with lawyers I find appalling and certainly, since Juniper is an American, unacceptable.'

'What if they divorce?' Hortense asked sharply. 'Where would my son be then?'

'Good gracious, they're not even married yet. I find this conversation unspeakably vulgar, Lady Copton.' Tommy, Juniper noticed, was quite red with indignation. She did not like the way the conversation was moving but she could not help herself watching, fascinated. She had never seen Tommy angry before.

'But look what Juniper is gaining from marriage with my son. His title, social standing.'

'We don't give a fig for his title and she has social standing.'

'You Americans understand nothing.'

'We Americans understand everything. I can assure you, Lady Copton, if you continue with this market traders' mentality, there will be no marriage.'

'Oh yes there will.' Juniper stood up, pushing her chair back and flinging her napkin on to the table. 'Thank you for being so concerned for me, Tommy, but I love Hal, I want him to be happy. If you and Charlie Macpherson won't agree then I shall make the settlement after we are married and all my money is mine. Then there's nothing you can do about it.' She sat down breathless from her speech, frightened that she might be about to lose the only man she wanted.

'I fear too much has been said already.' Alice attempted to pour oil on these choppy waters of social sensibilities. 'No doubt, Juniper and Hal are capable of reaching their own decisions and I feel, Lady Copton, that it is none of our business.'

'It's very much my business, Mrs Wakefield.'

'Well, not mine, Lady Copton. Another slice of cake?'
Alice was aware that her hand was shaking as she handed
the plate towards the unpleasant woman. All the hypoc-
risy of English society, which she had hated so much
when she was young, sat opposite her in the form of Hal's
greedy mother. What situation had Juniper wandered
into? Was it just the mother or was Hal a willing party?
The particular horror of the situation was that in the end
there was nothing either she or Tommy could do about it.
Finally Juniper would do as she wanted. She had always
been proud of her granddaughter's generosity. Now she
feared it.

Polly was engaged too. She was somewhat puzzled as to
how it had happened. She could not recall agreeing to
marriage, but one evening Michel had slipped a ring on
her finger and it had all become a *fait accompli*. She knew
she should have taken the ring off, but Michel was so
happy and it seemed churlish to spoil his pleasure. And
there was no doubt that he was kind and attentive. When
she was with him she could easily imagine herself in love –
it was only when away from him that she had doubts.
One day, she thought, she would call the engagement off.

Gertie, with her deep suspicion of anything foreign, was
not impressed. She had immediately contacted her old
friend the British Ambassador in Paris. To her annoyance,
Michel was indeed who he said he was. She was surprised;
in her experience titles of a foreign nature should always
be treated with circumspection. And, while his family was
not enormously wealthy, he would certainly be able to
support Polly in a style far grander than that to which she
was used. She had an uneasy feeling that Polly did not wish
to marry this young man but whenever she tried to discuss
it the young woman retreated into a shell. Perhaps she was
mistaken, Gertie thought. What she did not know was that
Polly was too embarrassed to discuss the problem, since
everyone seemed pleased about the arrangement and she

could not bear to upset her grandmother. Much as Gertie loved Polly she could not understand why Michel had chosen her – he was a continental sophisticate while Polly, though pretty enough, was basically a simple country girl. It was a great puzzle to Gertie but – if it was what Polly wanted – then she would help as much as she could.

Polly had taken Michel to Hurstwood to gain her father's consent. Richard, while not suffering from his mother's xenophobia, was also unimpressed – he did not trust Michel, but because he had no reason for this, merely instinct, his logical mind told him to remain silent. Francine who, for once, had put herself out to be present at the interview was entranced with the charming man and had decided that if the wedding didn't take place, then she would have him herself.

One evening Polly resolved to talk to her father, to tell him about Jonathan, to try to explain how she felt that she was no longer in control of her own life. As she slipped along the corridor to go downstairs to her father's study, Michel appeared in his doorway and took hold of her and kissed her, making her forget everything else.

There was a most uncomfortable interview back in London with Gertie when Michel, having decided that this was where the money lay, asked the size of Polly's dowry.

The explosion of indignation from Gertie could be heard all over the house. The young man was told in no uncertain terms that Gertie's granddaughter wasn't a cow for sale in a market. She would be given an allowance and he would have to make do with that.

It was Polly herself who came closest to making Michel change his mind. Michel suggested that she should take instruction in the Roman Catholic church.

'No. I can't do that. I'm a non-believer and I couldn't be such a hypocrite. We shall marry in a register office.'

'No member of my family has ever married in such a way.'

'Well, we shall be the first. It's a matter of principle, Michel. That or no marriage,' she said firmly.

Noting the opulence of Gertie's house, remembering the luxury and vastness of the estate in Berkshire they had visited last week, and the estate in Scotland, and totally ignorant of English inheritance laws Michel, congratulating himself on his good fortune, agreed.

6

Gertie, thwarted by Polly's register office plans – a bitter disappointment but, where principles were at stake, one she was duty bound to swallow – threw herself instead, with massive enthusiasm, into helping Alice with the arrangements for Juniper's large social wedding.

The press followed Juniper and Hal everywhere. They were on the doorstep first thing in the morning and did not leave until last thing at night. They were determined that the marriage of their 'Golden Butterfly' was to be the wedding of the year. And with a readership hungry for information and pictures of the pair, wherever Juniper went, to the dressmakers, hairdressers, manicurist, she was accompanied by her own personal press corp.

Polly had been chosen to be the chief of the eight bridesmaids, which, much to Michel's annoyance, delayed her own wedding. Plans were well advanced, but still there was no solution to the problem of who was to give Juniper away.

Every time that Marshall's name was mentioned Juniper would go into a silent sulk, a sulk so like those that Grace used to employ, that they made Alice shudder. Gertie's younger son, Charles, was suggested as a suitable substitute and was promptly rejected by Juniper. She wanted Richard, she announced. The thought of Francine gracing the wedding in such an important role sent Gertie herself into a monumental fury. There were days when Alice wished herself away from London, and the fuss, and back at Gwenfer with Phillip. She tentatively suggested that Phillip might be the right person, but a withering look from Juniper silenced Alice. Now was obviously not the right time to tell Juniper of her own plans.

Finally, exasperated by all the delays and with the date advancing rapidly, Juniper announced she would travel to Devon to ask Richard herself. First she telephoned Francine to ask if she would be at Hurstwood the following weekend. She had two reasons for this, first the certainty that if Richard demurred Francine would be a useful ally. She was right, for at the sniff of a thought that she might be invited to the wedding of the year, Francine immediately cancelled the weekend she had planned at Henley with her latest lover. Juniper had a second reason, the details of which were as yet still forming in her mind. Alice was left to persuade Gertie that it was not such a bad idea.

'But why not your own father, Juniper? Of course I'm flattered but I wouldn't want to upset Marshall.' Richard looked at her seriously across the dining table at Hurstwood.

'I don't want him to give me away.'

'But he's your father.'

'He would look ridiculous. He dresses like a monk, you know, prays all the time and lights incense. We would look most peculiar walking down the aisle together both in long frocks, wouldn't we?'

'Maybe he could be persuaded to wear morning dress for the occasion,' Richard tried to keep the amusement out of his voice at the idea of Marshall praying, he was amazed that after all this time the man knew whom to pray to.

'I don't want him persuaded. I don't want him there.'

'But Juniper, darling, weddings are a time of family reconciliations,' Francine interrupted as patiently as she could. She was already planning what she was going to wear.

'No. I can't discuss it further. I don't want my father to give me away. I have my reasons. I want you, Lord Frobisher.'

'Why me?'

'Your mother has been wonderful to me, your daughter is my best friend, and I . . . well, I like you enormously. Please.' She smiled the dazzling smile that all her life had made people give in to her.

Richard sighed the sigh of a man defeated, aware of the effect the smile was having upon him. 'Very well, I shall write to your father. Provided he has no objection, I shall be honoured to be his stand-in.'

Juniper pushed her chair back and ran lightly around the table – like an eager child, Richard thought. She flung her arms about him and kissed him. He laughed, Francine glared. She did not feel that Juniper acted like a child – not a bit. She might not want her husband but, on the other hand, she did not want beautiful young women like Juniper fawning over him.

'Oh, do sit down, Juniper, don't be silly,' Francine heard herself saying sharply. And then, not wishing to upset the plans, changed the subject. 'Isn't Michel divine?' she gushed.

'I'm afraid I don't like him, Lady Frobisher. Everyone can see it's a mismatch, but Polly seems to be in dream and not listening to anyone. And there's something about him – I think it's his intensity – that I find rather creepy.' She shuddered.

'That's because he's French – suppressed emotion.' Francine laughed gaily, glad that Juniper was safely back in her own seat.

'She's trying to get over Jonathan Middlebank, of course, only she won't admit it. That's her problem,' Juniper said sagely.

'She didn't tell me about Jonathan,' Richard frowned.

'She wouldn't. He let her down badly and she won't talk about him even to me. Good riddance to bad rubbish, I say.'

'So he wouldn't have been suitable either in your opinion, Juniper?'

'Not at all, Lord Frobisher. He'd never have been faithful and I think Polly would have looked for that in him.'

'Do you think that Michel is likely to be a faithful husband then?' Francine could not keep the laughter, at such a ridiculous notion, out of her voice.

'I doubt it, but then she doesn't love him as she loved Jonathan so it won't matter so much if he is unfaithful, will it?' she said, pleased with her logic, and carefully cut herself another piece of cheese.

The rest of the evening passed pleasantly enough. The coolness that Francine had shown previously appeared to have gone. Juniper wondered if it was because she was about to be married and thus, in Francine's eyes, safe. After a few games of whist and a brandy, Juniper excused herself.

She lay in bed with an open book in front of her but she was not reading. She marvelled at her self-control with Francine – maybe she should have been an actress herself. No one, she was sure, knew how she hated the woman, how she longed for her to be harmed, preferably dead. She waited for the noises of the house to cease, for everyone to be in bed. Tonight she had decided to put into effect the plan that she had been mulling over in her mind for two years now – the plan she had been unsure how to bring about. In the past her affection for Polly had stopped her. But tonight Polly was not here. At last, all she could sense was the dense, blanket-like silence of a house all of whose occupants, even the cat, were asleep. Juniper slipped out of her bed, put on a silk robe, checked her face in the mirror, sprayed herself with scent and crept quietly from her room, along the landing, and as quietly opened the door to Richard's room.

She tiptoed in. The curtains were pulled back and in the shaft of moonlight cutting across the bed she could see he was asleep. For a moment she looked down on him and then leant over and kissed him full on the mouth. He stirred and without opening his eyes, he put his arms up and pulled her to him. Quickly she slipped out of her robe and slipped naked in beside him. Gently she kissed his face, his neck, his chest and then, sliding down the bed began, with quick darting movements of her tongue, to caress his body. Her hands searched between his legs and she began slowly to massage him. He groaned softly, his body moving rhythmically beneath her, as slowly his senses responded. Still in that warm hinterland that exists just before waking his mouth searched for her breast. To Juniper's surprise she began to moan with genuine pleasure. Gently he pushed her off him and rolled on top of her. Her whole body felt alive with pleasure and a small scream escaped her as she felt his teeth gently nip her breast.

'Richard,' she sighed just as he began to enter her.

He stopped, lifted his head and looked at her wide eyed with shock. 'Juniper!' he exclaimed. 'My God . . . !'

'Don't stop, Richard, please don't,' she begged him.

The door that led to Francine's room flew open, light flooded the room. Francine stood silhouetted in the doorway, for a second.

'You little whore,' she screamed. She leapt across the room and began to drag Richard off Juniper. Demented with rage she was punching and scratching. 'You filthy little bitch, you dirty scheming cow. Get out of my house this instant . . .'

Juniper slid slowly from the bed and stood naked before both of them, her fine body illuminated by the light from the adjoining room. 'With pleasure, Lady Frobisher.' She bent down, and picked up her robe, which had slipped to the floor, and put it on. 'Now perhaps you understand how my poor mother felt.'

'Juniper?' Richard sat up in bed looking from the young woman to his wife, still dazed by sleep, still wondering what was going on and how it had happened. How on earth could he have been making love to her and not known who it was? Or had he? Subconsciously, was that what he had wanted all along? He shook his head in confused amazement.

'I'm sorry to have imposed upon you, Richard.' Again she smiled, amused by her own polite words. She knew full well, from the expression in his eyes, that it had been no imposition. 'It was something I've been needing to do for the past couple of years. And if you don't know why, ask your wife, ask that whore,' and she pointed dramatically at Francine.

'Get rid of her. She's evil,' Francine shrieked.

'But she's right, isn't she? You *are* a whore,' he said in a weary sounding voice and turned away as if there was nothing further to discuss.

Francine leapt across the bed and slapped Richard hard across the face. 'You bastard!' she hissed. Pushing Juniper to one side, she ran from the room, slamming the door violently behind her.

Juniper looked at Richard and shrugged her shoulders. 'I truly am sorry, Richard. You don't mind me calling you that, do you? In the circumstances it seems silly to keep on calling you Lord Frobisher.' She giggled and he saw the young girl she still was. She stopped, looking serious again. 'I had to have my revenge.'

'It won't help you, you know.'

'I feel better already.'

'Because of all this drama and excitement. But, at the end of the day, your poor mother is still dead, and you can't bring her back.'

'She suffered so much because of my father. Francine was the last straw. I did it for her sake. She could never have sought revenge; she wasn't strong or determined enough.'

'It's a very dangerous game you're playing, Juniper. She'll make sure your fiancé hears of this, you know.'

'Maybe, but he'll be so rich if he marries me that he won't even mention it.'

'Such a cynical remark from one so young and beautiful. It makes me sad for you.'

'There's no need. I love Hal, I want to marry him, my money has ensured that I can. My grandfather always said that everything and everyone has a price. But, please don't tell Polly, will you? Francine won't, she's too proud.'

'Of course I won't tell her. But I can hardly give you away now, young woman, can I?'

'That's the price I had to pay.'

'Ask your father, don't be too hard on him. When Francine decides she wants to bed a man there is very little the poor soul can do about it.' He lit a cigarette.

'You don't know the full story.'

'Maybe not, but he is your flesh and blood – that's important. And he loves you.'

'For you, Richard, I'll ask him, but not for anyone else,' and she crossed the room, and kissed him full on the mouth. 'It's a pity really. I've never enjoyed sex but tonight, with you, I think I might have done.' She waved and quietly left the room.

She had packed before she retired, knowing she would not be able to stay. Ten minutes later he heard her car rev up in the courtyard below. He lay, still shocked, but, to his shame, regretful too.

And then the door of Francine's room burst open. She stood posed dramatically.

'Right, you bastard, so you want to know who Polly's father is?' she screeched.

'I've told you, it's irrelevant to me. I no longer care,' he said wearily.

'Don't care? Don't you lie to me, you filthy lecher. I shall enjoy this.' She stepped into the room and he realised from the smell of her breath that she had been drinking, she drank heavily these days. He half closed his eyes in resignation; when Francine wanted to make a scene there was no stopping her.

She stood beside the bed and smiled maliciously down on him. 'Marshall Boscar,' she hissed. 'Your great friend, remember? Marshall, the best man I ever had. All the time you were mooning over me, he was having me – *and* after we were married. Oh the bliss . . .'

He leapt from the bed, grabbing her by the shoulders and shaking her violently. 'Do you have to take everything from me?' He was shouting, his anger immense. Even in her inebriated state he frightened her. She backed away from him towards her own door. There she stopped.

'Marshall.' Her laugh was more of a shriek as she closed the door behind her and locked it firmly.

Richard slumped back on to the bed, as if he had received a physical blow.

Francine stood in the centre of her room shaking. She might not want Richard but no one else was going to have him – certainly not that rich bitch. She crossed to her dressing table upon which stood the azure bowl. She traced the largest of the roses with her finger. Funny old bowl, she thought. What had she achieved since she received it? Fame – she had that in abundance. Money? never enough. Love . . . only once, with Marshall. Angrily she pushed the bowl to one side and poured herself another large brandy.

7

Marshall waited in Gertie's drawing room for the winter bride to appear. He rang the bell but no one appeared. Then he remembered the house was empty, even the staff had left for the service. He crossed to the drinks tray which Gertie had thoughtfully provided. He poured himself a large whisky and looked at the golden liquid for some time before he sipped it – it was over a year now since alcohol had passed his lips. He smiled to himself, how well he remembered the taste, how quickly he felt it speed through his body to relax him. He needed to be relaxed.

He took out his pocket watch and anxiously looked at it. There was still plenty of time. He flipped up the coat tails of his morning suit as he sat down. It seemed strange to be dressed normally again; he had become so used to the comfort of his quasi-monk's outfit.

He could not remember a time when he had felt so anxious. There were many things unnerving him. The thought of facing Juniper again, after nearly two years, and with the knowledge that she had read Grace's diaries. Fear that he would loathe his son-in-law on sight, for how could anyone be good enough for his princess? Being again in society was proving a daunting reality; he spent most of the day alone now at Boscar, reading and meditating. Would he remember how to act, how to make light conversation? Would Francine be there? How would he react? He dreaded the thought that those fires which once had raged so fiercely in him and which, with great self-control he had stifled, might roar up again when he saw her – that witch of a woman who for years had entranced him. So many fears for him, once so fearless . . .

The door opened. He jumped to his feet and, as happens to all fathers of brides, he was taken aback by the radiance of his daughter as she stood there in the doorway. Her dress of cream velvet was of such simplicity that it enhanced her natural beauty dramatically. Around her neck and around the cuffs of the huge sleeves that fell almost to the floor, was a trimming of ermine. The dress trailed behind her in a long fish-tail train, a veil of cream Brussels lace shrouded her hair which she wore loose. She looked so virginal, so vulnerable that he wanted to take her in his arms and rush her away to Boscar and safety.

'Father,' she said formally.

'Juniper, you look more beautiful than ever. Like a lady from King Arthur's court, like a medieval princess – my princess.' He put out his hands to her.

She stood, awkwardly, by the door. She longed to cross the room, the space that divided them, ached to heal the rift between them. Suddenly, desperately, she wanted to feel his arms take hold of her, whirl her in the air, smell him, feel the comfort and security he once had been to her. Instead she looked at the floor.

'Juniper . . .'

'I can't.'

'I understand, my love,' he said softly.

'No you don't, no one understands how I feel,' she said sharply and saw the pain flicker across his face.

'I can imagine. I know it is a lot to ask of you but can you not forgive me? There is another side to the story, you know.'

'What side? What excuses are there? I could understand infidelity, I could even forgive that. But never the degradation she suffered because of you. You might just as well have killed my mother with your own hands. I didn't realise how much she needed my love until she was dead. It was always you I adored. Then you let me down.'

'Don't you think that perhaps you are punishing me because of your own guilt?' he said in a voice full of compassion.

'Don't try to make me feel guilty. Don't make excuses.'

'I don't, my darling. There is no excuse. The tragedy is that your mother and I never talked to each other, never explained ourselves, never knew what the other was thinking and wanting.'

'We know what you wanted,' she spat the words out venomously.

'No, I didn't. Never. It was her imagination. Good God, Juniper, don't you think I suffer, long to turn the clock back? You're not the only one who, too late, discovered that they loved her. How I long to have made everything different. Night after night, I torture myself about what happened.' He looked at her with eyes bleak with despair and in that moment she knew he spoke the truth. For a second she wavered, her longing for him to be part of her life again threatening to drown all thoughts of revenge, of bitterness.

'I beg forgiveness,' he said in almost a whisper.

She took one step towards him and then, never far from the surface, the memory of her mother's dead body floated into her mind.

'Forgive you, never!' She shook her head defiantly. 'And, what is more, I've decided that I no longer wish to support you at Boscar. In less than an hour I shall be a married woman and then my money is my own. I've decided you are not to get another penny from me. My grandfather would have done this and I feel it is my duty to do the same.'

'I quite understand, Juniper,' Marshall said with quiet dignity. 'Am I no longer to live at Boscar?'

She frowned, she had not thought about the house, she never regarded it as anything to do with her. 'You may stay there,' she said relenting a little. 'You can do what you like with it.'

'Thank you, Juniper. I'm grateful for that.'

'You don't seem very upset,' she said, a shade petulantly, for she was deeply disappointed by his calm reaction. It was as if he had expected this to happen, as if he almost welcomed it.

'I need to be punished.'

'Oh, I see,' she said, though she didn't, and she felt angry, as if he had won in the end and she had lost.

The bridesmaids were in dark green velvet – dark as the leaf of the holly. St Margaret's, Westminster, was full. Captains of industry, newspaper barons, half the cabinet – most of the establishment and their wives were present.

The Prince of Wales stood bored and waiting. Every society lady of any consequence was in her pew; necks swivelled back and forth like exotic birds in brightly plumed hats, as they checked who was present, who had not been invited, who had been placed where, and who had been dressed by whom. And all were agog that, although Polly was chief bridesmaid, and the reception was to be at the Frobishers, there was disappointingly no sign of Richard and Francine. There was no reverential mumbling in this church. The shrill gossip echoed off the ancient walls, new acquaintances were noisily greeted. English society deferred to no one, not even God.

An hour later the church bells peeled out, the pavement was seething with shop girls, typists, maids, all come to see the 'Golden Butterfly' wed. A mob of cameramen pushed and jostled for prime positions to photograph their protégée. Juniper, now the twelfth Baron's wife, stood proudly on the arm of her handsome husband and smiled at the world. The smile told how much she loved, how sweet was revenge, how she would live happily ever after.

'But, Juniper, I'd arranged our honeymoon – the bride-groom usually does, you know,' Hal said, exasperated, as Juniper ordered the chauffeur to drive, and he silently cursed the waste of his money on the tickets.

'I've arranged something better.'

'You don't know what I had decided upon so how do you know it's better?'

'What was your plan?'

'A booking to New York, we would still have time to catch the boat.'

'Oh, piffle, who wants to go there? We can go there any time. My surprise is much more exciting.'

As the Rolls-Royce bowled along the empty roads out of London it was obvious they were making for Kent. Europe, he decided. How boring, he had wanted to go to

New York, he wanted to meet this Charlie Macpherson. Now Juniper had total control of her financial empire he very much wanted to talk with him. There was nothing he could do about it, though. Better to let her have her own way this time.

'Close your eyes,' she ordered as they approached Sevenoaks.

For nearly half an hour, with much complaining, he sat with eyes closed. It was unnecessary since it was pitch dark and he had no idea where they were. But nothing could have prepared him for the sight which confronted him when she ordered him to open them again.

The car had drawn up in front of Summercourt, his ancestral home. The fine black-and-white timbered building was ablaze with light. The door opened and two dogs hurled themselves down the steps and gave him an hysterical welcome.

'Flint, Slipper.' He patted the prize retrievers he had sold last month. 'What are you rascals doing here?'

'For you, my darling, my wedding present to you.' Juniper was smiling broadly though her eyes glistened dangerously with tears.

'It's a dream!' He turned to face her, his face for once animated with pleasure. 'You've borrowed it for our honeymoon?'

'Better than that, Hal, my darling. I've bought it for you, look.' She picked up an attaché case that had been at her feet throughout the journey. She flipped it open. 'See, the deeds, and all in your name again!'

'Juniper!' He stood virtually speechless with surprise.

'Yes, and there's more,' she said excitedly. Dragging him by the hand, she raced up the steps and through the open door. 'You see,' she twirled around in the hall, her hand indicating the furniture, the pictures, the tapestries, the suits of armour.

'All my things!' he said amazed, looking about him at the objects which had stood in those selfsame positions for hundreds of years until he'd been forced to send them for sale. And then he saw his servants lined up in greeting, all of whom he had sacked when the house had had to go. 'It's unbelievable.'

'Yes, it was difficult. I felt like a detective. I've had agents scouring the country ever since we became engaged, tracking down every item that was sold at auction. And keeping it secret was hard. Are you pleased?' She looked at him, eyes shining with happiness.

'My darling,' he swept her into his arms.

'You never called me darling before.'

'You never gave me anything like this before.' He laughed as he lifted her into his arms and held her tight.

Juniper thought she knew men and was certain that she knew herself. Juniper had slept with many men, had never enjoyed herself, and was convinced that this side of married life was going to be difficult to endure. But that night, Juniper was in the hands of a consummate lover. A lover who seemed to know what she wanted before she knew it herself. A man who seemed able to melt her ice-maiden's body. Each time he made love to her, she vowed she loved him more and more. Juniper thought she had found perfect happiness.

8

By contrast, Polly's wedding was a sad affair.

While the talk had been of Juniper's wedding, and during the excitement of the preparations, Polly did not have time to think about herself. But as she watched Juniper walking up the aisle on Hal's arm she realised it was her turn next and, as time crept inexorably towards that day, she began again to wonder what she was doing.

Too often she found herself thinking about Jonathan. Comparing him with Michel, she found her new relationship wanting. She had to accept the truth that she was with Michel because of the hurt and loneliness Jonathan had inflicted upon her – the dreaded rebound, hinted at by everyone and which she had vehemently denied, even to herself. She knew she should admit this openly, she knew she should have the courage to stand up and say she was wrong. She was too proud; she could not bring herself to do it.

Juniper had postponed a trip across the Atlantic, a delayed honeymoon, so as to attend Polly's wedding. She had insisted on arranging a luncheon for the bride. Her plan had been to invite a large number but Polly asked that it be just the two of them. She sat in the Savoy waiting for Juniper who had undertaken to drive her to the register office at Caxton Hall. Not that Polly wanted lunch, she felt so tense she knew she would never swallow a thing. She had been waiting for half an hour but she was not unduly worried. Juniper was always late.

'Polly, forgive me, we had to go to see a house in Belgrave Square.'

'You haven't yet found one then?'

'No. Each one I like seems to be leasehold and Hal insists we have freehold.'

'What's the difference?'

'I haven't the vaguest idea. Whatever it is, it's a bloody nuisance. I leave all the boring legal things to Hal to sort out, he seems to wallow in them.' She summoned a waiter and ordered a bottle of champagne.

'Not for me, Juniper, I couldn't drink a thing.'

'Don't be silly, of course you must have bubbly on this of all days.'

'You're happy, aren't you?' Polly asked suddenly with pleased surprise.

'Delirious. Six weeks and it's perfection.'

'I'm so pleased for you. I was always afraid . . .' and then realising what she was about to say she stopped, embarrassed.

'Don't be upset, that's what everyone thought, that I'd

made a disastrous choice. Me? I *knew* he would be perfection for me. We live in bed, it's divine.'

'And out of bed?'

'Oh, that's fine too. Guess what, don't tell a living soul for I haven't even mentioned this to Hal, but, I think I might be pregnant – just.'

'Juniper, that's marvellous. Did you want a baby so soon?'

'Hal is crazy to have an heir, it's all he talks about so it will make him delirious. Ah, at last, the champagne.'

They waited for the waiter to pour their wine.

'To you, my dear friend.' Juniper lifted her flute to Polly.

'And you too, it seems,' Polly toasted her friend. 'What about the dreaded Hortense?'

Juniper pulled a face. 'Well, she is obtrusive, there's no good saying she isn't. I've suggested that we buy her a house to get her out of my hair. She's dreadfully expensive to maintain – corsets, she gets through dozens of them – and her hair, it's tinted, you know.'

'You don't pay for her too, do you?' Polly asked anxiously.

'I have to. It transpires that her late husband loathed her so much he left her only the tiniest allowance. I can't say I blame him. Still, it keeps Hal happy and that's all I want.'

'Have you met his brother since the wedding? He looked rather nice.'

'Leigh? Once. He is nice. I don't understand why Hal loathes him so – sibling rivalry I suppose. His wife is d-r-e-a-r-y, did you meet her? Caroline. How she got someone as divinely handsome as Leigh, I shall never know. I do hope I am going to have a baby, she can't, and Hal will be over the moon – one up on his brother.'

'They sound a very unpleasant family.'

'Oh, they are, but it's massively amusing. Have you met any of Michel's lot?'

'No, and they won't be at the wedding – it's not *comme il faut*, you see, simply a register office *and* my not being a Catholic.'

'Polly, forgive me asking but you don't think Michel is marrying you because he thinks you're rich?'

'I hope not. He's in for a fearful shock if he does.' She laughed as she accepted a second glass from Juniper. 'Good Lord, you don't really think so, do you?'

'Well, Gertie is so obviously rich – and your uncle too.'

'Heavens, Juniper, I never gave it a thought.'

'Well, my friend, whatever happens you have me, never forget that.'

They were well into their third glass of champagne when the waiter came to tell them their table was ready.

The bottle of Chablis seemed to go in a twinkling and then they were enjoying a particularly good bottle of Château Lafite.

'You're not sure you want to go through with this, are you?' Juniper looked anxiously at her friend.

'No, I'm not. I know I like him but equally I know I don't love him.'

'He is shorter than you.'

'Oh, Juniper, be serious. As if being short has anything to do with it.' Polly laughed.

'I think how he looks is very important. After all, you are going to wake up beside him for years and years.' She leant across the table conspiratorially. 'Have you ever thought that he looks just a little bit like a monkey?'

'Well, yes,' Polly said rather ashamed of her disloyalty. Juniper shrieked so loudly that the people at the next table looked at her with disapproval.

'I'm so glad you agreed – does he like bananas?' She shrieked again and the next table asked to be moved.

'What am I doing here, Juniper?'

'Looking frightfully pretty and getting rapidly drunk with your best friend in the whole world.' Juniper unsteadily poured them each another glass, waving the waiter away. 'Now, listen to me seriously. You don't have to marry him, Polly. No one can make you. It's not as if you're pregnant or anything, is it?'

'I haven't even slept with him,' Polly confessed miserably.

'I didn't for one moment think you had, a good girl like you, not like bad old Juniper here.' She chuckled huskily. 'What if he's disgusting in bed, then what do you do?'

'Oh, Juniper, don't even think about it.' Polly looked miserably at her wine glass.

'I don't think you should go ahead with it, honestly.'

'But what do I tell everyone?'

'I'll tell them for you.'

'Would you?'

'What are friends for but to sort out muddles like this? It would give me the most enormous pleasure.' She bowed solemnly and ordered two large brandies. 'It's Jonathan, isn't it? He keeps getting in the way.'

'Yes,' Polly said softly.

'He's a bad lot, Polly. You were too good for him.'

'I think I could forgive him now, Juniper.'

'Polly, I've got to tell you something. It's been bothering me for ages. Now it looks as if there's a possibility you might get back together – he's sure to tell you.'

'Who will what?'

'Jonathan, he's the honourable sort who opens his mouth too wide – they're dangerous.'

Polly looked at her, perplexed.

'It was me.'

'It was you what?'

'It was me he was unfaithful with. We got drunk, a bit like this, and one thing just led to another. I'd never have breathed a word, but he's the type to do the honourable thing. He will confess. So silly . . . You do forgive me, don't you? I am awfully sorry, if only I could turn the clock back.' Juniper's fine eyes filled up with tears.

'Oh, Juniper . . .'

It was this information and the effects of the alcohol which made Polly insist, immediately, on being driven to the register office to become Michel's wife.

It was late when they finally arrived in Paris. They took a taxi from the Gare du Nord to Michel's house. The concierge was still up and opened the outer gate, glaring unpleasantly in response to Polly's thanks. Michel led her into the inner courtyard and through the main door.

His mother was in bed. Polly was relieved. It had been a dreadful day. The ceremony had passed in a miserable blur because of the effects of the wine and the knowledge that Juniper, her friend, had also deceived her. Her grandmother had carried out her threat not to attend if Francine was present. She might just as well have come for Francine, Polly never found out why, was delayed and did not turn up at all. Only Juniper, Alice, Tommy, Phillip and her father were witnesses. Half-way through the ceremony Polly had burst into tears, from emotion thought everyone except Juniper who, shamefaced, wished she had not got so drunk. She vowed to herself never again to get drunk or sleep with a friend's man.

A maid showed Polly to her room and wearily she bathed and undressed. She slipped into a fine silk night-dress – one of the many presents that Juniper had showered on her. As the silk caressed her body she wished it was Jonathan for whom she was waiting.

The door opened and Michel entered dressed in a long, black hand-embroidered dressing gown. He had ordered the room to be lit by candles. As he paused in the doorway, the flickering light of the candle made his shadow loom large on the ceiling above her. He did not smile but looked seriously at her as if preserving this moment. There was an aura about him, a dark aura of power, and she felt herself shiver and clutch the silk of her nightgown close to her.

'My darling,' he said quietly, crossing the room

towards her. He took her into his arms and kissed her. As always at his kiss she felt her body come alive, felt pleasure rippling from nerve to nerve. She laughed at her previous fantasy and put it down to the light. He lifted her effortlessly and carried her towards the large bed in the centre of the room. He laid her on it. Quickly he cast his dressing gown aside revealing his naked body, a firm, muscular and hairy body. He stood awhile, his hands on hips, his legs astride as if allowing her to admire him. She looked away embarrassed. He put out his hand, she thought to caress her; instead, he took hold of her night-dress and ripped it from her.

What followed changed Polly for ever. Her innocence had made her anxious about what was to happen between them. But this unease was countered by dreams of love and tenderness, of excitement of the unknown. Her soul, fed by poems and sonnets, was not prepared for the violence, the sadism unleashed upon her.

That night not only did Michel abuse her body, he raped her mind.

Chapter Nine

1

The day after Polly's wedding Alice invited Juniper and Hal to dinner. Alice had intended speaking to her after the short reception, but Juniper had behaved most oddly, and Alice had reached the unpleasant conclusion that she was the worse for drink. Now she waited nervously for their arrival.

She was nervous because she dreaded telling Juniper of her own wedding plans. She felt instinctively that Juniper would not approve. She knew it was this that had made her not only delay telling Juniper but delay the wedding as well. Phillip had been patient long enough. At their age, feeling as they did, there was no point in a long engagement.

At last she heard the car draw up outside her small Chelsea house. The maid opened the door and she listened to the bustle of people divesting themselves of their outdoor clothes. Phillip smiled at her encouragingly. She had said nothing to him of her fears but realised that he had probably guessed that all was not well.

Juniper swept into the room. Alice looked at her with pride. Since her marriage she had become even more beautiful, she had the glow of a well-loved woman. In the close fitting, black dinner gown she wore, Alice thought she looked as if she had put on weight – a sure sign of happiness. She hugged Alice, shook hands formally with Phillip and demanded a cocktail – 'or she would die'.

'Phillip and I are not very knowledgeable about cocktails. Perhaps you would do the honours, Hal?' She smiled at him. She felt guilty about her previous doubts. He appeared to be making Juniper extremely happy and for that she would always be grateful to him.

'I'd quite expected to find Tommy here. She rushed off like the wind after Polly's wedding.' Juniper accepted the pretty green-coloured drink from Hal; Alice looked at hers doubtfully, but when she sipped it, found it very pleasant.

'She's gone back to Italy. She was rushing for her train.'

'She didn't say so,' Juniper frowned.

'Now you are married she probably thought you would not be interested in what she was up to.'

'Not interested? Of course I'm interested,' Juniper said sharply.

'We've managed to get tickets for the maiden voyage of the *Queen Mary*,' Hal said, smoothing over the awkward pause.

'I hope it doesn't sink like the *Titanic*.' Juniper laughed and picked at the material of her skirt.

'Unlikely. The ship builders must have learnt from their mistakes, and no one is boasting about unsinkability this time. And surely there will be no icebergs in May?' Phillip said encouragingly, feeling that Juniper's laugh was one of nervousness, that in truth she was afraid of the planned trip.

'I haven't the vaguest idea but if it sinks I'm not letting Hal be a hero and a gentleman by staying on board, he's too precious to me, aren't you, my darling?' She trailed her hand along the back of the sofa and tickled the back of his neck. 'But you didn't finish telling me about Tommy and why she scuttled off without a by-your-leave.'

'She hasn't said anything, but I think she might have an interest there,' Alice said, clutching at her pearls, a Christmas present from Phillip.

'An interest? What does that mean? You're being very coy, Grandmother.' Juniper laughed gaily.

413

Reassured by the gaiety of the laugh Alice plunged on. 'I think she has found a man.'

Juniper carefully placed her glass on a side table and turned slowly to face Alice.

'Did I hear correctly? You said Tommy had found a man?'

'I said I think so.'

'How ridiculous. Hal, darling, could I have another of these delicious drinks?'

'What's ridiculous about it, Juniper?' Phillip looked at her closely.

'At her age I think it's ludicrous. And what if I need her? A lot of good she'll be to me stuck in Italy. I assume he's some awful foreigner?'

'But you're married now, Juniper,' Phillip continued, relentlessly it seemed to Alice. 'You have your husband to turn to, don't you?'

'Of course, but I've had Tommy for ages, it will be most odd not to have her to rely on.'

'But she has her own life to lead now. You don't need her any more.' Phillip persisted.

'Who said I don't need her?' Juniper said, her face going pink.

'I've a new cook, I'm hoping dinner will be excellent,' Alice interrupted, still playing with her pearls.

'We've other news for you, Juniper,' Phillip continued.

'Oh, Phillip, I think . . .' Alice's voice wavered.

'No, Alice. Enough time has passed,' he said firmly.

'What are you two being so mysterious about?' Juniper said, smiling quizzically up at Phillip.

'Your grandmother and I are getting married. Next month in fact, at Gwenfer, in plenty of time before you sail to America.'

The smile slid from Juniper's face like melting snow. She jumped up from the chair, spilling her drink but totally oblivious of it. She looked wildly from one to the other. 'You can't,' she said sharply. 'I won't let you.'

'Juniper, don't be silly.' Alice fluttered towards her, while Hal crossed the small room and put his arm around Juniper's shoulder.

'I'm not being silly. Tommy was bad enough, this is truly ridiculous. You're my grandmother,' she said, her voice rising shrilly.

'I'm sorry if you think it's ridiculous, but I don't. Phillip is a wonderful man and I know he will make me happy.'

'But you belong to me.'

'Your grandmother doesn't belong to anyone, Juniper. She is a free spirit and can do as she wishes,' Phillip interceded and Alice sensed that he was a man rapidly losing patience.

'You'll get no money from me.'

'Oh, Juniper, how could you say such a thing? When have I ever asked you for money? That remark does you no justice and causes me great pain.'

'The money you have is my grandfather's, so therefore it's really mine. I shall talk to Charlie Macpherson about this when I see him in New York.'

'That money was left to your grandmother by your grandfather. It has nothing to do with you, Juniper. Your lawyer will tell you exactly that,' Phillip said sternly.

'Morally it is mine. Of course you're happy about it, you can live off my money.'

'Juniper, apologise, that's unforgivable.' Alice felt as shocked by her granddaughter's words as though Juniper had attacked her physically.

'I won't apologise. It's the truth.'

'In fact, young woman, it's a long way from the truth. I have sufficient money of my own, thank you, to care for Alice. Money I have worked for, might I add, not merely inherited.' Phillip was angry now, a pulse on his forehead began to pound. His colour was rising. Alice put her hand out to try to stop him saying any more but he brushed it away. 'How dare you upset Alice in this way. What right do you think you have? Do you really think your money

415

impresses me? It doesn't. I don't like drones and I never have done.'

At this Juniper let out a wail and slid back on to her chair, her shoulders heaving, tears pouring from the beautiful hazel eyes.

Hal fussed over her. 'Come, my darling, calm down, do. As for you, sir,' he looked up at Phillip. 'How dare you speak to my wife like that.'

'Why not? Is she the only one allowed to bandy insults?'

'Phillip, please,' Alice looked pleadingly at Phillip and knelt on the floor in front of the sobbing Juniper. 'My darling, why are you so upset? I thought you would be happy for me. I had no idea that you would react in this manner.' Her gentle face was marred by a deep, worried frown.

'What will I do if you marry him?' She gave Phillip a venomous look.

'But you have Hal now, you don't need me any longer, a grown-up married woman . . .'

'I do need you, I'll always need you.' She looked at Alice, her lovely face tear-stained.

'And I shall always be here for you if you do,' Alice replied gently.

'No you won't. You're leaving me again, aren't you? Just like you left Grandpapa and me. You don't care about me, you only care about yourself.'

'Juniper, that's not fair. You know I never wanted to leave you, I had no choice.'

'That's what you say, but you've never explained to me why you ran away as you did. Why you couldn't even give Grandpapa time to find you, you left that night, that very same night.'

Alice slumped back on her heels. She could never explain, she could never fully defend herself. 'I had good reason to leave. I promise you. Let me just say this. Had I stayed, your grandfather would have had me killed.'

Juniper let out a shrill shriek. 'Rubbish! How can you

say such things? My grandfather? He was the kindest man on earth, he loved you, he never stopped loving you.'

'The truth is, young woman . . .' Phillip began, but hurriedly Alice took hold of his hand.

'No, Phillip, I forbid you . . .'

'Forbid him what?' Juniper demanded.

'Something I don't wish you to know, ever.'

'But he's allowed to know.' She pointed angrily at Phillip.

'He knows because I wanted him to know everything about me. There is no point in your knowing. Trust me to know what is best for both of us. I love you, Juniper, I've always loved you and always shall. You are not losing me, you're . . .'

'Don't say it,' Juniper screamed, clapping her hands over her ears. 'I had a grandfather, no one, no one on this earth can ever take his place.'

'Please try and understand, Juniper. I am so alone now, I need Phillip, I love him.'

'Love?' she shrieked. 'Love? You and him? You were sixty last month, for God's sake – you disgust me.' She jumped to her feet. 'You've let me down again, Grandmama. You are deserting me just as you did before. Get married, I don't care, but I promise you one thing, you'll never see me again – ever.' With which, and without a backwards glance, she swept from the room. Hal turned to Alice with a bemused look and shrugged his shoulders. Then he followed his wife from the room and a second later the front door slammed.

Alice slumped down on the sofa and at last allowed herself to cry. Phillip put his arms about her but she was past being comforted. He allowed her to cry, stroking her hair and trying at the same time to control his own anger.

'It was just a tantrum, my darling, a spoilt child's rage. She'll come back,' he said eventually when the sobbing had subsided a little.

'I don't think she will, Phillip. She really believes I am deserting her.'

'I think it was one of the most unpleasant scenes I've ever had the misfortune to witness. There, I'm afraid, my sweet, we see the result of all those years of indulgence from Marshall and Lincoln.'

Alice looked at Phillip, her eyes still brimming with tears, 'Oh, no, Phillip. That has nothing to do with it. Can't you see? That child has been so hurt in her life, all those she loves have let her down, have left her – all, that is, except Lincoln.'

'You should have let me tell her what that bastard did.'

'No, I could never allow that. Take from her the memory of the one person she feels was always true to her? No, Phillip, I love her too much for that. I just pray that she and Hal remain happy. If not, whom has she got? She refuses to speak to Marshall, her mother and Lincoln are dead. In her eyes, Tommy has left her; and now me. Oh, the poor child.'

Phillip held her close, all the while making comforting noises, at the same time thinking that a good slap on the bottom was what that spoilt child needed.

2

Since their marriage, of all the gifts that Juniper had showered upon Hal – the settlement, the large allowance, the house and its contents, a brilliant white Hispano Suiza, a race horse, a new wardrobe, many items of personal jewellery – there was nothing that gave her so much pleasure as telling him that he was to become a father. His reaction and excitement were just as Juniper had imagined they would be. And because a baby was the one thing that her money could not buy it was a doubly precious gift.

If she had one complaint it was that he now treated her

too protectively. The doctor had suggested she smoke only five cigarettes a day; Hal had banned them entirely. She was allowed only one glass of champagne daily and that only when she had complained to her gynaecologist that she would go mad without her favourite drink. She was made to rest each day, her shopping trips were seriously curtailed and any sport was out of the question. And dancing, her favourite pastime, was totally banned. This enforced idleness for one so active was irksome: there were days her body screamed for activity.

But there was worse. Hal had moved out of her bedroom into one of his own. He had vowed he would not touch her again until the baby was born. She tried every way she knew to interest him. She spent a fortune on new and exciting negligées, she bathed herself in different scents, she fed him oysters by the barrel and she used all her feminine wiles, but he was adamant – he would do nothing to harm his child. Having at last discovered a sexual relationship which gave her pleasure it was inevitable that Juniper was racked with frustration. And a thought took root, slowly at first, but then mushrooming with alarming speed until her mind was obsessed with it. If he wasn't sleeping with her, who was he sleeping with?

She, who had never had cause to mistrust any suitor – why should she, for they were all crazed with love for her and frightened to offend her in any way – now found herself tortured with doubt and suspicion. Since he insisted she must lead a quiet life he frequently went out in the evening without her despite her objections. He would leave her with his mother for company. The two women had nothing in common, apart from a mutual dislike which daily grew stronger. The first time he left her with Hortense she made such a scene that she made herself sick and the doctor was called. Hal's fury with her was so great that she was afraid she had lost him. She had had to apologise and acquiesce to being left behind –

it was only for a few months, she told herself, then they'd have fun together again. So to escape Hortense, Juniper usually retired early. She would toss and turn in her beautiful room, a room which was fast becoming a prison, convinced that he was meeting Christabel Summerton again.

Eventually she could stand it no more and hired detectives to follow him everywhere. But their reports did nothing to help her. They claimed that they followed him nightly to illegal gaming houses. This she knew to be rubbish – Hal did not gamble. There was only one conclusion: he had discovered he was being watched and had bribed the inquiry agents to lie to her. She dismissed them from her service and was left with the canker of her worries.

He wanted to cancel their trip to America in May but over that, Juniper dug in her heels. Her life in England was becoming intolerably boring, the interference of her mother-in-law was insupportable. At least if she were travelling she would feel she was doing something. At least in America there would be no Christabel.

She had to assert herself again when Hal suggested that his mother come too. She had never been to America and it was her dearest wish to see New York, he explained. Juniper did not care if the interfering woman never saw the country – she was not coming with them. A compromise was finally reached: Juniper would pay for a stateroom for Lady Copton and a cabin for her maid on a much later sailing of the *Queen Mary*.

So desperate was her need to get away and to be active again that she had forced from her mind her fear of the sea. She stood on the deck of the great ship. The brass band was playing, she was surrounded by happy people waving and shrieking with excitement at their friends far below on the docks. Streamers were being hurled from ship to shore so that the line from stem to stern was wreathed in brightly coloured ribbons. Champagne corks were popping like miniature cannons and Juniper felt the old nervousness return. The same clammy feeling, the dizziness, the same feeling of panic and impending doom. As soon as the fussy tugs, which had been escorting the great liner through the Solent like stunted ugly sisters, had dropped their lines, Juniper's terror increased alarmingly. By the time the ship finally reached the open sea and the great waves took hold of her like a toy boat in the vastness of the ocean, all Juniper wanted to do was to cower in her bed, feeling sick and wretched.

Hal, appalled by her white, strained face had summoned the ship's doctor. He jovially informed them that it was merely an attack of seasickness which would disappear as soon as she had found her sea legs. He assured them that no harm would come to the baby. Thereafter Juniper saw little of Hal. Early in the morning he was off to the gymnasium or the swimming pool, in the afternoon he napped, and in the evening he was quickly out of their stateroom and away to dinner and whatever entertainment was available.

But the sickness did not pass. The further out into the Atlantic they steamed, the more frightened she became. Alone in her cabin with only her maid in attendance, Juniper missed seeing the shipload of famous and interesting people. She missed the Captain's cocktail party, the balls, the food, the champagne, and the pervading atmosphere of one large, never-ending party.

She tried to explain to Hal what she was feeling. She even told him of the dreadful day her grandfather had drowned and she had failed to help him. She was afraid, she needed him. But Hal laughed at her notions and told her not to be so silly: beneath her was over eighty-one thousand tons of ship, there were over a thousand crew to look after her, and there was a particularly good party that evening which he had no intention of missing.

She often cried herself to sleep, feeling lonely and neglected. She knew that she could never be happy now without him and yet he seemed happy enough without her. Juniper had convinced herself that Hal loved her, even if he never said so. Now she was not so sure. Everything had been perfect until she had told him about the baby. Before that she had been the centre of his world; now it was as if she was of no importance except for the child within her. Racked with frustration, she found herself wishing there was to be no baby.

At least she would no longer be ill, she thought, as they walked down the gangplank at New York, at least she would be able to spend more time with Hal here in her city. Maybe here, alone with him, without his omnipresent mother, they would recapture their old happiness.

Hal approved of the large apartment that was hers in the Wakefield building but he liked none of the furnishings. Neither did she, now, remembering that everything had been chosen by her father. They set to with enthusiasm to have the whole apartment redesigned. In the first week they chose decorators and spent happy hours visiting shops, choosing new furnishings, for the apartment was to be as modern in every way as the expensive decorators and New York's shops would allow.

Juniper had forgotten the shops. She had left America as a young girl; now returning as a rich woman she went on a shopping orgy. Ignoring the fact that she was pregnant and that the clothes she bought would no longer fit in a month or two, she continued to spend. And there was never a day when she did not return with a gift for Hal. Now that she was her old self again he was attentive to her. Coming to America, she thought, was the best thing they could have done.

As soon as she could Juniper went to see Charlie Macpherson. She had invited Hal to accompany her but he had declined, saying he had no interest in boring talk of money. She wished her grandmother and Tommy had heard him. She knew they thought his only interest was her money and here he was proving he didn't give a jot for it.

It *was* boring. Even more so when Charlie explained to her that there was nothing she could do over her grandmother's allowance. Her head ached at the pages she was supposed to read, the information she had to digest, the pile of documents which needed her signature seemed endless.

After three such visits to her lawyer her complaints were vociferous.

'Shall I go with you next time? Maybe I'll understand a little better,' Hal asked, taking her hand in his. 'Maybe I can help you.'

'Would you? Oh, Hal, how kind of you,' she kissed him gratefully.

The two men appeared to like each other on sight. She explained to Charlie that, as her husband, Hal wanted to help her understand her money. She wanted him to inspect her books and, smiling charmingly, she said, 'I know you won't mind?'

'Of course not, Juniper. It's good and right that your husband should take an interest. I'm glad, I've had the responsibility too long on my own.'

'That good. Then I can leave you two to burrow away.' She turned towards the door.

'There's just one thing, Juniper. You should be thinking of making a will,' Charlie called out.

'A will? Whatever for? I've no intention of dying,' her husky laugh rippled out.

'But, what if you had an accident?'

'What would happen if I didn't make a will?'

'Everything would go to your next of kin – your husband.'

'That's all right then, isn't it? I'd have left everything to him anyway,' she announced gaily. 'I'll never make a will. If I did, I'd be sure to die.' Juniper happily tripped out to find lampshades for the new décor.

For a month she escorted Hal about the city, pointing out the haunts of her childhood, taking him to the best restaurants, showing off the glories of her home town. It had changed in her five years away. The buildings were even taller and the Empire State Building was now complete and soared at an unbelievable height above the other skyscrapers. When she left there had still been horse-drawn vehicles on the wide avenues which cut a swathe through the canyons of buildings – now, apart from the tourist carriages in Central Park, there were hardly any horses, only motor vehicles. Noisy the city had always been, now it seemed even noisier. Had she been too young when she lived here to be aware of the exciting atmosphere of the city, or was it something new? Whatever it was, she grabbed at that sense of exhilaration, of being keenly alive, and began to toy with the idea of not returning to England.

And then Hal suggested they should visit Dart Island.

'I don't want to go there,' she said, her eyes large with alarm.

'But you must, darling. You must inspect your properties, see that they are being well looked after.'

'You go and check it, I'll stay here.'

'But I don't know the place. Of course you must come. I suggest we stay for a month. Charlie has given me a lot of your paperwork to study. Maybe I shouldn't have volunteered to help,' he laughed. 'It will be more pleasant to do it in the country – this city is getting intolerably warm. You'll be better off, too, out of the heat.'

Though she would never confess it to a living soul, Juniper rather liked it when Hal was domineering. She liked not always getting her own way – it was a novelty to her, and made her feel very feminine and cherished. Placidly she ordered her maid to pack for a month at Dart Island.

Juniper left the city in good spirits. They had decided to take the car, rather than the train, in order to drive upstate at a leisurely pace, stopping for lunch on the way. It was a glorious July day and as they reached the suburbs the heat and dust of the city left them as though they were stripping off a fusty coat. Juniper took off her hat and let her hair flow free, kicked off her shoes and felt the excitement of a child off to the seaside. Even Hal, always the epitome of elegance, removed his hat and loosened his tie.

He was in a good mood, singing ragtime as the car hurtled along the roads, which became more deserted the further they went from the city. Juniper felt happy and content and began to wish they had left the city weeks ago. She could not imagine why she had not suggested it before.

The nausea started twelve miles from Dart Island. She shivered, pulled on her coat, put her hat back on and slipped her shoes on to her feet. Reflecting her change in mood the sun disappeared behind a large and threatening cloud. As they crossed the wooden bridge that connected the island with the mainland she began to shiver. Hal looked at her concernedly, and asked if she was unwell.

'It's the heat, it's made me feel a bit peculiar.'

'But you're shivering.' He braked and stopped the car. Gently he took her hand. 'What is it, my sweet? You're so pale.'

'I'm frightened, Hal. I'm scared of this place.'

'Of course it has bad memories for you but they can only be conquered if you face them squarely. You've got me, I won't let any ghosts get you.' He smiled and she managed a weak smile in return. He put the car in gear and relentlessly, it seemed to Juniper, it slid along the driveway. At the approach of the last bend before the house, she felt her heart pounding, her skin damp with sweat.

The house stood in its serene whiteness, rising from the luxuriant acres of green grass like a pillared, canopied liner on the ocean. The sun reappeared, rippling along the colonnade, settling in pools on the wide veranda. Even as she did so, she knew it was illogical, but she looked for her grandfather to appear. She was fearful that he might be there, she was disappointed when he wasn't.

The whole staff were lined up on the steps in welcome. Septimus, her father's old butler, bent double with age, his limbs deformed with arthritis, stepped slowly forward, his face alight with pleasure. His rheumy eyes were bright with emotion that at last she had come. Hal hurried her past him, past the ranks of footmen, of maids, of cooks, of gardeners, calling for iced water for Lady Copton. Leaning heavily upon him she directed him towards the long salon. He led her to a couch, opened the windows wide and picking up a handy magazine began to fan her.

'Are you sure it's just the heat? I mean, it's warm but not that warm.'

'I knew I shouldn't have come. It's my grandfather. He's here, I can sense him. This very room is full of him and so many memories.'

'What nonsense you do talk, Juniper.' Hal barked a short laugh. 'You must stop such thoughts, in your condition. Your grandfather is long dead, he can't harm you.'

'I know it's silly. He would never have harmed me in life, why should I think he will harm me in death?'

'He can't, it's a simple as that. The only person who can harm you is yourself. Think of the baby. Ah, here's the water,' he took the glass from the maid. 'I suggest we have some tea, and get the butler to put a little brandy in it,' he told the maid.

Juniper leant her head back on the cushion. She did not understand Hal; one minute he could be so kind and solicitous, the next quite brusque. The wind lifted the white muslin curtains and swept across her face. She opened her eyes and looked out of the window at what had once been such a familiar scene to her, the wide lawns, the large Italianate fountain, and in the distance the sea, oh God, that sea. She shuddered. She felt such a sense of foreboding that it now seemed inconceivable that she could ever have been happy in this place.

'It is truly an extraordinary house,' Hal said, leaning out of the window the better to see the façade.

'What do you mean?' She forced herself to take an interest.

'Well, this house is such a hotch potch of styles it looks as if it was designed by a committee who could not agree,' he said with a laugh. 'It must have cost a fortune to build. What a waste. Your grandfather may have been many things, my sweet, but a man of taste he certainly wasn't. It needs altering drastically.' She felt herself begin to bristle with annoyance. Who was he to talk about her grandfather in such a way? – he could not even keep his own house, let alone build a huge mansion such as this.

'And did you notice the number of staff lined up to greet us? There must have been at least thirty of them,' he continued, pacing up and down the room, inspecting the paintings and ornaments. 'What do they do, for goodness sake? They must just sit around twiddling their thumbs eating and drinking their heads off. How many years has this been going on?'

'The last five years. Since my grandfather died. We left the day of his funeral. None of us ever came back.'

'Good God, and no one thought to sack the majority of the staff? Why wasn't a skeleton staff organised just to maintain the house and grounds?'

'Why should we? It's not their fault none of us comes here, is it? Why should they lose their jobs because of us?' She was beginning to feel angry.

'I've never heard of anything so ludicrous. That's one of

the first things I shall have to see to. For a start there's the butler, he's so old he can hardly stand, let alone buttle. Why, he'd never be able to pour a drink without spilling it.'

'That's Septimus, he worked for my grandfather all his life from a young boy, they came to New York together. He's not to be given notice. He stays until he dies or he wants to go.' She was sitting up now, her nausea completely gone. 'And what did you mean when you said this house needs "altering"?'

'It's too big for modern days. You must admit, Juniper, the styles are such a pickle. If we knocked down both wings, we would still have a large house and one that would look more beautiful. The centre part appears to be original. I presume it's a colonial attempt to reproduce an English country home,' he said with a smug expression.

'No,' she almost shouted. 'You won't touch a brick of it. Do you understand, Hal, I want it left as it is. I love it as it stands.'

'You didn't even want to come here yesterday.' Hal laughed cynically.

'It's how my grandfather saw it, it's his house, it was his dream and it stays. He built this for my grandmother. It may not be as old as your precious Summercourt, but I'll tell you something, it was built with love. I wouldn't dream of touching a thing at Summercourt. You must respect how I feel about my family home.'

'But you told me he wasn't even your real grandfather, and your grandmother ended up loathing him. He sounds an awkward old bounder from what I can make out.'

She stood up abruptly and faced him. 'Don't you speak about him in that way. He was more than a grandfather to me. He loved me.'

'And I don't?'

'No, I don't think you do. In fact I don't think you ever have. You've not once told me you do.'

He crossed the room and took her hand. 'I'm an

Englishman, my dear – we're not good at expressing emotion. I'm sorry, I've been insensitive. Of course you love this house and respect his memory. I'm sorry . . . You've had a dreadful time coming here with such a tragedy hanging over the house. I shouldn't have insisted.'

She sat down again on the couch. 'No, I'm sorry, Hal, I over-reacted. I must be turning into an old shrew.' She smiled weakly at him. He approached the couch; she thought he was going to kiss her, to tell her he really did love her. Instead, he poured her a cup of tea.

Tea was not a drink she normally enjoyed but with brandy she thought it one of the best beverages she had ever drunk.

Juniper had hoped that, with Charlie still safely in the city, she would see more of Hal. She was to be sadly disappointed. In London and New York he was never up before ten and his dressing took so long that he was rarely out of the house before noon. But here, in the country, he was up early in the morning inspecting every inch of the estate with an almost professional thoroughness. He found wastage on an appalling level, all of which he reported back to Juniper, usually over dinner in the evening.

'I don't mind if the staff have a large beer bill. Poor darlings, they must get very bored with no one to look after. I can afford it after all,' was the reply he got for his pains and to his exasperation. Neither did she object that her idle staff had steak to eat and out-of-season fruit, and that the wine cellar looked suspiciously depleted. Nor that the stables were full of horses as if carriages were still the order of the day.

'The horses stay and die here, I can't risk their being sold to bad homes. They were my grandfather's.'

The fact that there was a seamstress living in the attics, who had long since finished mending everything there was to mend, did not appear to interest her at all. In fact, unknown to Hal, the next morning she climbed to the attics to assure the woman her future was secure. This she did with all her staff.

Each economy that Hal suggested she airily brushed aside. As soon as she mentioned her grandfather, Hal had learnt that the battle was lost. Juniper could see no point in explaining to him that she wanted things kept as they were because, in a strange and illogical way, she felt that if nothing were changed, she might wake up one magical day and find Lincoln here and his death a dream. Hal would never have understood, would no doubt have thought she was going mad. Better, she thought, that he should put it down to the whim of a rich and extravagant woman.

They would dine together but as soon as the meal was over Hal would disappear into Lincoln's study to pore over the account books and financial statements Charlie had lent him. Far from being bored by financial matters, Hal enjoyed working with figures and the more he worked the more excited he became. Charlie was a clever man, the discrepancies were hard to find, but Hal was cleverer. He kept his findings to himself. If his empty-headed wife cared so little about money, he was not going to bother to tell her.

Each day Juniper walked in the grounds but never to the sea, she was not ready for that yet. She spent hours looking at the large photo albums her grandmother had kept and she found herself longing for that lost childhood. The constant feeling that her grandfather was still here began to affect her more noticeably. She could feel him in every room, at the stables, in the gardens. Her inability to see him, to speak to him, to smell him, to hug him began to make her depressed. She longed for him to appear and yet was terrified by the prospect.

Night after night she had nightmares. Always the same dream. Herself in the sea searching for her grandfather – but this time she found him. But when she grabbed him her hand would slide through his flesh, flesh which was soft as lard. And from the gash in his arm an army of crabs emerged. He had no eyes, his nose had been nibbled away. But she knew it was he. And he would open his mouth to speak to her and from the gaping hole great eels slithered and swayed. Night after night she woke screaming and bathed in sweat but there was no one to turn to.

When she told Hal of the horrific dream he suggested she stop eating cheese. She begged him to sleep with her – he refused. She began to fear sleep and would read until her eyes ached, until the book slipped from her fingers. When the dreaded sleep came it was followed quickly by the nightmare. She began to look ill.

One morning she smelt cigarette tobacco on her maid's breath. The maid, terrified that she was about to be dismissed, began to tremble. Juniper laughed until her sides ached.

'Don't be silly, Ella, I want one, that's all,' she told the astonished girl.

At first it was the occasional cigarette. Then she got Ella to buy her a packet, then two, then three, and finally a carton. These she smoked in a little-used sitting room with the windows wide open and a giggling Ella posted as lookout. Together with the carton of cigarettes she ordered her to buy her a bottle of brandy, and one of rum: both were delicious in tea.

Now she had tea laced with either for breakfast, for lunch, for tea and dinner as her husband nodded his approval for the dutiful wife she had turned out to be.

4

'So, Mr Macpherson, how clever you thought you were.' Hal stretched his long legs out in front of him and lazily blew cigar smoke in the direction of Charlie's large mahogany desk.

'I've done my best for your wife, Lord Copton.'

'I didn't mean that, Mr Macpherson. Oh no. I meant you thought you were so clever that no one would find out what you've been up to since the old man died. And long before that for all I know.'

'I don't understand what you mean.'

'I think you do, Mr Macpherson. I feel quite sorry for you, it was a work of genius but unfortunately for you, I have always had a passion for figures and am, it appears, even more of a genius.' Hal smiled pleasantly. All the time his dark eyes, glittering with intelligence and sardonic humour, never stopped studying Charlie's face. Charlie sat down heavily on the thickly padded leather chair. He stretched his hand out to the humidor and as he took a cigar he was aware how badly his hand shook.

'Of course, Mr Macpherson, I've only the books you lent me to work on. From the figures I've uncovered, if you multiply that by Juniper's holdings, in the past few years I would say that, at a conservative estimate, you have embezzled in the region of $2,000,000 – a tidy sum, wouldn't you agree?' Charlie sat silent, his mind racing, trying to find a way out, a lie to tell, a plausible explanation. The fear oozed out of his pores in acrid-smelling sweat. 'But then these figures do not take into account any commissions or bribes that you have, no doubt, negotiated. So,' he pursed his lips, 'the final sum makes it look as if you're going to retire a very rich man. And where were you thinking of going? After all, you could hardly stay here with new lawyers and accountants delving about in the books, could you? Mexico? South America? I'm really interested.' The reasonableness of his tone sent bolts of fear through Charlie, making his gut twist painfully. Still smiling, Hal stood up and crossed the large room to a cabinet full of drinks. 'A brandy might help, Mr Macpherson,' he said as he poured two large measures.

'What are you going to do?' Charlie mopped his sweating brow.

'Nothing.'

'Nothing?' Charlie repeated with disbelief.

'For the time being.' Hal was enjoying himself. For the past few years men like Charlie Macpherson, in banks and money institutions, had made his life hell, had mortified him, stripped him of everything. Now, he felt that he was having his revenge on them all in the shape of this overweight, greedy American.

'Am I to presume that you intend to blackmail me, Lord Copton?'

'Nothing so vulgar, my dear chap. Presumably you've been silencing any awkward interest from Tommy and Juniper's father and grandmother by being reasonable in meeting demands, especially from my father-in-law. I bet you had a nasty moment when my wife cut off all his allowances. I suppose you thought he would come whining to you, but luckily he appears to have acquired a large dose of religion.' Hal made a steeple of his fingers and studied them closely, pretending to reach a decision. How often he had sat sweating in financiers' offices and watched their hands, tried to read their thoughts as Charlie was doing now. 'No, I think it's only fair that I should share in your machiavellian pastimes, don't you?'

'And Juniper?'

'She need not know, she would take no interest in any case.'

'Not a very pleasant husband, are you?'

'No. But then you're not a particularly pleasant advisor and lawyer, are you?' Hal asked good naturedly, totally unperturbed by Charlie's opinion. 'In fact, I think I've found one or two other areas where we could, perhaps, benefit ourselves.' He flipped open the great ledgers on Charlie's desk and pointed out his findings. After several brandies and much discussion, the two men ended their session with a healthy respect for each other and on Christian name terms. They arranged to meet the following day to arrange where Hal's share was to be banked safely and discreetly.

Juniper was furious with Hal for not taking her with him. He had been frustratingly mysterious as to why he was going. She could not see any valid reason why she could not accompany him; if he had business to attend, she could have shopped.

'You are looking tired, my sweet.'

'I'm as fit as a fiddle. I'm bored with doing nothing. You can't expect me to live like a nun for the next four and a half months.'

'Yes I can. The welfare of the baby is the paramount thing. I want nothing to go wrong.'

'What can go wrong, for God's sake? I'm young and fit. You're suffocating me with all this caring. What if I were a working woman? I'd be up early, scrubbing and cleaning, they don't get mollycoddled like this.'

'But then you're not a working woman, are you, my dear? You're very special, with an extremely special baby inside you.' He bent down and kissed her on the cheek. 'I shall probably be back tonight. Take care and rest,' he said as he shut the door behind him.

Juniper sat slumped against the pillows of her bed and looked moodily out of the window. It was a beautiful July day, the sun had been beating down since early morning. Her grandmother's rose garden was a riot of colour, the sea was glinting azure blue at the edge of the gardens. Juniper suddenly remembered Gwenfer and the memory filled her with such longing that she had to turn her head away from the view. She buried her face in the pillow, conscious that she longed to cry. Why did she always think of Gwenfer when she was unhappy? And why was she thinking of it so often recently? She longed for Alice too. She closed her eyes and in her mind a picture of her grandmother appeared, emerging from the doorway of Gwenfer, her arms outstretched. At this memory Juniper began to cry. She missed her grandmother more than she

434

would ever admit to anyone. She regretted the way she had lost her temper, the hurtful things she had said. She regretted losing the one person she could always trust. And still, after all these months, she was uncertain why she had reacted as she had. She did not dislike Phillip; logically she knew that he was good for her grandmother, that she should be relieved that Alice had someone to love and care for her. But even as she reasoned, she felt the uncomfortable worm of jealousy. She wanted her grandmother to love only her.

She rang for her maid, took a leisurely bath and spent as long as possible in dressing. She did her nails. But still the day stretched endlessly ahead of her.

She wandered about the house for a bit, picking up books, putting them down. She began to write a letter and then could think of no one to write to, so doodled instead.

Finally she decided to take a walk. She walked towards the stables and then, suddenly, strode off the path across the lawns towards the sea. It was time, she decided, time to lay some ghosts. Time to get rid of that fearful dream for she knew if she did not soon begin to sleep healthily she would become ill.

She approached the shore as warily as a wild animal. Her heart was racing, each step forward took every ounce of her willpower. By the time she reached the beach she felt weak and sank exhausted to the sand. She sat waiting for she knew not what, but nothing happened. She edged a few feet further down the sand. She sat silent and waited. The sea was lapping lazily against the sand, seagulls swooped and dived against a clear blue sky. She felt calmer now, strangely so, and she edged forward foot by foot until she was by the water and she allowed it to cover her feet.

She sat hunched on the sand, gazing far out to the horizon, and found she was enjoying the feel of the sea on her feet, the light breeze that seemed to be embracing her. She realised her pulse was normal as was her breathing.

She felt totally at peace – her grandfather was here, but it was as if he were holding her, as if he were the wind. As if he was caressing her and calming her.

As she sat on the beach, watching the sea lapping lazily at the shore, the water looked so harmless that she wondered how she had ever allowed her fears to dominate her for so long. She made herself think of that day, to go over in her mind the whole sequence of events. She could understand the child she had been, blaming herself for her grandfather's death. Now, as a woman, and one about to become a mother, she could see how hard she had been on herself. For the first time since her arrival she began to think of her grandfather calmly. The longing for him was still as great but she could face that; it was the strength of his character which made the memory of him so strong. She began to remember with affection and gratitude the wonderful person he had been. She was no longer afraid.

To her surprise she found that two hours had passed and it was early afternoon. She made her way back to the house, found she was past wanting lunch and went to her room. There she poured herself a large brandy, foregoing the tea, lit a cigarette, and settled herself on the chaise, conscious that she was happier than she had been for some time.

Her hours in the sun had made her sleepy and by the time she awoke it was time to change for Hal's return. How pleased he would be that on her own she had managed to face the sea, to rationalise her fear. The telephone rang.

'Juniper, it's Hal. I'm staying another night.'

'Hal, no! I've missed you terribly. Please come home.'

'No, I've important business to attend to tomorrow. I'll return early evening.'

'Hal . . .' she wailed.

'Don't be tiresome, Juniper. Pull yourself together.' And the phone went dead. Juniper kicked the telephone table with anger, knocking the instrument flying. She picked it up, it was dead.

'Arrogant bastard.' She flung the telephone on the floor. She crossed to her dressing room, took from its hiding place her bottle of brandy and poured herself a large glass. Then she rang the bell for Ella and ordered a light supper in her room with a bottle of white wine.

By nine Juniper had drunk the whole bottle of wine and was now enjoying her third brandy. In the distance, the sound muffled by the thick door, she could hear the telephone ringing. She picked up the extension, from the floor, forgetting she had broken it. Exasperated she hurled it away from her, ran from the room and raced down the stairs to the ringing telephone. She was convinced it was Hal telephoning to apologise. She was half-way down the stairs when her slipper caught in the hem of her gown. She screamed as she lost her balance and lunged for the banister to steady herself, but she slipped and her slight form, unbalanced by her swelling belly, hurtled down the steps and she lay sprawled unconscious on the marble floor.

During the next two hours she fluctuated between the velvet blackness of unconsciousness and wakefulness; but a fearful wakefulness when her body seemed to be being torn apart and she screamed in agony. She was aware of people fussing about her, mopping her brow, holding her hand, making encouraging and comforting noises at her. She could not register who they were. For some strange reason she did not want to open her eyes. If she opened them she would see reality, if she kept them closed she could pretend that this was all a nightmare.

One dreadful pain tortured her, flamed up her body and back down again. The intense agony lasted minutes before, with unbelievable relief, it stopped as quickly as it had started and she allowed herself to slip down into comforting blackness.

*

'You stupid, irresponsible bitch!' She awoke to Hal shouting at her.

'Hal,' she croaked. She put her hand up limply towards him, her gesture one of entreaty. 'Hal, thank God you've come. I'm sorry. I'm so sorry . . .' and she began to cry.

'You're useless, you can't even have a baby.'

'It was an accident, Hal. I tripped. I was rushing to the telephone, I thought it was you. I was so lonely without you,' she sobbed.

'Don't lie to me. You were drunk. No need to deny it, the doctor told me, you were paralytic. He had a job saving you, how I wish he had failed.'

'Don't talk to me like this. I need comfort. I'm so unhappy. Forgive me,' she shrieked.

'I shall never forgive you.'

'We'll have another baby and I promise you I'll do everything you say,' she was wheedling now.

'If you can.'

'What do you mean?' she asked with horror.

'It remains to be seen if you are capable of having a child now.'

'We'll see specialists, there are wonderful doctors in New York.'

'We shall go home to London. This place is bad for you.'

'I want to stay here. This is my home.'

'Your home is where I am and you will come to England and see the doctors there. I'm going back to the city.'

'No, Hal, don't leave me, please.'

'Madam, I'm finding it difficult to be in the same room with you,' he said, his face rigid with anger. He walked from the room impervious to her white-faced entreaty.

It was a very subdued Juniper who came back from America. Gone was the happy, carefree girl who had set off in the *Queen Mary*. It was a deeply depressed, lost and lonely woman who returned.

She understood Hal's initial anger. His bitter disappointment had made him unreasonable. But she had expected him eventually to understand her feelings, her anger with herself, her sense of failure. She had assumed that their grief would bring them closer together. Nothing was further from the truth. What she could not grasp, what depressed her deeply, was the hatred he obviously felt for her. She was hurt and confused by the complete injustice of his attitude. It was as if he thought she had planned her miscarriage, as if she had wanted it.

He hadn't said he hated her, but he did not need to: it was there in the looks he gave her, in the way he avoided her, in the long silences if they happened to be in the same room. In company he was at least polite to her. She should, therefore, have searched out company, instead she avoided it – she was too morose to be able to go out into society.

She was no longer the Golden Butterfly, the darling of the press. She had lost a lot of weight, her skin and hair were dull, she could not find the energy to go to the beautician or hairdresser, she had not the interest to summon them to come to her.

Her loneliness was the hardest to bear. Hortense wasn't even there to annoy her: while they had been away, she had found her own home, purchased for her by Juniper. She longed for her grandmother and for Polly. Often she would get as far as picking up the telephone to call Alice, but each time the shame of her behaviour forced her to replace the receiver on its cradle. Many times she began to write to her friend but each time the letter ended in the wastepaper basket. There seemed little point in struggling with a letter, she doubted if Polly would answer. She would probably never be able to forgive her. Had she forgiven Jonathan or would her hurt always be reserved for Juniper? Because of what she had done to Polly she did not even feel she could contact Gertie, she was too frightened of Gertie's wrath if Polly had hinted at what she had done.

And then, on top of everything, guilt began to filter into her mind. She realised she did not mourn the child as she should. Her concern was only for Hal and her relationship with him. Now she remembered how she had begun to wish the baby away so that she and Hal could once again be happy with each other. She realised that the baby had, in her mind, become the cause of her unhappiness on the boat, on Dart Island. Had she at that moment begun to reject the child? Had she intended to fall down the stairs and kill it? She no longer knew – she feared it might be so, in which case Hal's hatred of her came to seem reasonable. Once again she could find excuses for his behaviour. And she began to wonder if she wasn't as other women. She had never found pleasure in sex before she met Hal; perhaps she was also incapable of maternal love?

She spent more and more time alone in her room staring vacantly out of the window. She, who all her life had been surrounded by people, now lived a solitary life.

As soon as she arrived in England she had intended seeing her doctor to find out if she might now be barren, as Hal had suggested, but she kept postponing the visit. Hearing the worst would destroy that one glimmer of optimism to which she clung. The key to Hal's love seemed to be in presenting him with a child. Without consulting a doctor, she had little chance of finding out if she could conceive since Hal never visited her room at night. In fact, when he returned from wherever he'd been, he was frequently too drunk to have found his way there.

Juniper did not know what to do; she had no one to turn to for advice.

One king abdicated, another was proclaimed, Christmas passed followed by New Year, her nineteenth birthday came and went with no celebration. Juniper showed no interest in the world outside. She found pleasure only in brandy, which she took from the moment she awoke until she went to bed alone at night. By nightfall, she had often drunk a whole bottle.

She sat at her bedroom window idly watching the traffic and people passing by in Belgrave Square. They had searched a long time to find this house and she had begun to have it redecorated but when Hal hadn't even commented on the new drawing room she had scrapped all the plans. It might annoy him, might make him notice her. The previous owners' dark and old-fashioned wall-paper still hung on most of the walls. And since she could not be bothered to go shopping, the rooms remained sparsely furnished. It had the atmosphere of an empty house even though two people and their staff lived in it.

'Come in,' she said to the soft knock at the door.

'M'Lady, there's a lady to see you.'

'Who?'

'She didn't say, M'Lady.'

'Walters, how many times have I told you to ask people's names?' she said, irritated.

'I did, M'Lady, she refused to give it.'

'I'm not at home to anyone,' Juniper said without interest, and turning back to the window, idly picked up a book and flicked the pages, not even registering the words.

There was no knock. The door flew open and Gertie Frobisher strode formidably into the room, Juniper's maid fluttering impotently behind her like a pilot fish following a whale.

'I'm sorry, M'Lady, she pushed past. She wouldn't listen.'

'Out, young woman.' Gertie pointed with her umbrella at the door and the maid, not waiting for a second bidding, scuttled out.

'Now, what have we here?' Gertie crossed to Juniper, put her hand under her chin and turned her face to the light. 'Young woman, you look dreadful. What has happened, my poor dear? Who has done this to you?'

The love and concern in Gertie's voice was too much for Juniper who stood up, flung her arms about the older woman and began to sob uncontrollably. Gertie held her to her ample bosom and allowed her to cry herself dry. The sobs began to subside. Gertie let go of her, crossed to the bathroom, soaked a flannel in cold water and gently, as if bathing a baby, wiped Juniper's face with the cool water. Juniper, her face devoid of make-up, her eyes pink from weeping, looked more like nine than nineteen. Gertie pulled up a chair and sat opposite her.

'Now, I want to know everything.'

Juniper told her. She told her of how Hal had been kind and caring one moment, the next freezing her out. She told of her fear of the sea and of Dart Island, of the strange thoughts she had had about her grandfather, of her nightmare. She told of her drinking that fateful night, her fall, the loss of the baby, her fears that she was barren and Hal's attitude to her since the accident.

'Do you still love him?' Gertie finally asked when Juniper appeared to have nothing more to say.

'Yes, I do. I can't live like this, with him ignoring me. Sometimes I wonder why I bother to continue.'

'Stuff and nonsense! What good would that do? I've no time for such talk.'

'But he's never here.'

'Can you blame him? Just look about you, Juniper. This house is a disgrace. It's certainly not a home, such dreary decoration and this room . . .' She tutted as she looked about the bedroom which, apart from the bed, contained only a small table and the two chairs they sat on.

'There doesn't seem any point in doing it. He wouldn't notice, he doesn't care.'

'Rats! Now stop feeling sorry for yourself. I'll concede that your husband is obviously a very insensitive man. Only a fool would not have realised the strain on you of returning to the scene of your poor grandfather's death. You should never have been left alone in your condition. Men are insensitive, you know, my dear. There's no point in hoping that you will find the sensitivity that you find in a woman, because you won't. If such a man exists, I've never met him,' she hooted loudly. 'But that's no excuse for all this self-pity. How much are you drinking now?' The question was shot at Juniper so unexpectedly that she did not have time to parry it.

'Several brandies a day.' She looked guiltily away.

'How much, I asked? I've no time for lies. And don't for one moment think you can get away with lying to me, because you can't.'

'Sometimes a whole bottle.'

'That's no solution, Juniper. Apart from destroying your looks, it'll soften your brain and make you no good for anyone. Now which doctor has told you you are barren?'

'No one, Hal said it was likely.'

'Who's your doctor?' Gertie crossed the room to the telephone.

'I can't see him, I'm too afraid.'

'You're afraid because you don't know the truth. In the unlikelihood of your being barren you will have the courage to cope. You're Alice's grandchild after all.'

'Why do you say the unlikelihood?'

'Juniper, women have miscarriages all the time. Is Hal a doctor? What does he know about it?'

'Then why did he say it?'

'Anger, and to make you feel even guiltier I should think. Now, come, the doctor's name and number.'

Within the hour, at Gertie's imperious command, the doctor had called, examined Juniper, and declared there was no reason why she should not have a dozen children if she wanted. The change in Juniper was instantaneous. The doctor was hardly out of the front door before she was flinging open her wardrobe doors and asking Gertie's advice on what she should wear tonight when she gave Hal the good news.

Gertie helped the young woman decide on which frock to wear, elicited from her the promise that if she were unhappy again she was to contact her immediately, made her promise not to drink, suggested she should write to Alice, invited Hal and Juniper to dinner the following week and, in the same breath it seemed, bade her goodbye and swept from the room.

The minute Gertie reached home she was on the telephone to Alice. She told her everything, but more, she told Alice she was concerned for Juniper. She felt Hal was behaving most strangely, that there was something more behind the loss of this baby than met the eye. She became exasperated when Alice refused to telephone Juniper.

'She has to contact me herself.'

'Rats! Pride, my friend, that's what you're allowing to get in the way.'

'You weren't there. You didn't hear what she had to say, you didn't see the look of hatred in her face. Gertie, I'm happy with Phillip. I cannot cope with any more drama in my life.'

'Poppycock! You are allowing your principles to stand in the way. She needs you.'

'Then she will have to ask, Gertie. And, if you don't mind my saying so, you've no room to talk,' she found herself snapping at her old friend.

'Yes, and look what a stupid pickle that got me into. Learn from my mistakes, Alice, for goodness sake do.'

Gertie had left at four. By seven, Juniper was waiting downstairs in the drawing room, her hair washed and dressed with pearls and diamonds and piled up in a becoming top knot, make-up covering the ravages of the past weeks, her slim figure pretty in a soft grey, chiffon dinner dress.

Hal did not come back for dinner but she did not fret, he often came home late. She ate little herself but tonight she sat and waited with only barley water to drink – she'd never drink again, she had resolved.

It was past midnight before she heard his key in the lock. Shyly she went to the door and called his name. He entered, stood in the doorway, surprise on his face to see her up and dressed becomingly. He had become used to finding her always in her room in a dressing gown, sullen and uninterested.

'Hal. I know it's difficult for you but I beg you once again to forgive me.' He looked at her with distaste and began to turn. She ran quickly across the room and caught hold of his arm. 'Listen, I love you.' In answer he shook her hand off his sleeve. 'I've seen the doctor . . .' He turned back into the room and faced her. 'There's nothing wrong with me. I can have dozens of babies,' she was smiling at him, and frowning, and her lip was trembling. 'Hal, I love you . . .' But she did not finish the sentence for, to her overjoyed astonishment, he took her into his arms and kissed her, and it was as if the nightmare of the past eight months had never happened.

6

The September sun blazed down on the park at Summercourt as if determined not to let summer pass. The gardens were ablaze with colour from the flowers and the beautiful women in their gaily patterned summer dresses. None was more beautiful than Juniper who skipped about making sure that her guests' glasses of champagne cock-tails were continually topped up, that no one was lonely, that everyone was having fun. Fun was the order of the day at Summercourt weekends and Juniper was the most expert and thoughtful hostess.

Since March everything in Juniper's life seemed perfect once more. Hal was considerate and kind just as he had been when they first married. If he went out in the evening, it was with her. Now, there were no long lonely evenings spent wondering when he would be back, whether he would be drunk or sober. And now there was no question of her having to sleep alone.

Juniper had once tried to discuss the lost baby but the expression of anger on Hal's face had so frightened her that she had never touched on the subject again. She often wondered why it was that she could think about it so dispassionately. She regretted the distress she had caused Hal, but for herself she felt nothing.

Even Hortense had been banned. Hal had finally accepted that his mother's interference in their lives was no help. She lived in her London house where Hal visited her weekly for tea. Juniper had also bought her a small country house at Sevenoaks – so that she could see her old friends – but far enough away from Summercourt. Juniper was astonished that Hortense had any friends to enter-tain. Undoubtedly she spent her time with them black-ening Juniper's name, but Juniper did not care. All her expenses were Juniper's – she did not mind, what was money for but to make her husband happy? The know-ledge that his mother wanted for nothing was, she knew, a great relief to Hal.

Making Hal happy was the whole of her existence. She was determined he would never ignore her again but of one thing she was aware. Because of his past neglect she had emerged even more dependent on him. He had only to say he was interested in something and she would buy it for him. If there was someone he particularly wanted to meet, she immediately made the arrangements. Should a guest appear to be boring him, the offender was never invited again. A meal he had not enjoyed was never served again. Only the drinks and wine that he preferred were brought up from the cellars. If a curtain displeased, or a cushion dismayed, they were banished from sight. Her reward was his smile and the disappearance of his silent, morose moods.

The London house had been decorated from attic to cellar. The house was now famous throughout London for the exquisiteness of its furnishing, for its innovation – black and white throughout, with beautiful lacquered Japanese screens and tables, fine hand-painted wall coverings, lavishly swathed curtains and pelmets. Juniper's table was as famous as her house. She had found a French chef who delighted in surprising her guests with new food, each meal seeming more delicious than the one before. She chose her guests with one proviso, that they must be intelligent and amusing – who they were, their families, their background, were of no interest to her whatsoever. She had, in a few short months, become a society hostess of charm, care and fame.

The introspection had gone, the laughter had returned. She rarely thought of Alice or Polly and missed neither. Juniper thought she was happy.

She had arranged drinks and a light salad lunch for her guests by the swimming pool she had had installed. She sat on one of the brightly striped garden chaises scattered about the edge of the pool and watched her friends in the water.

She picked up a magazine to make certain they knew she intended not to swim, for Juniper had a secret: she was almost sure she was pregnant again. But this time, she had decided not to say anything to Hal until it was necessary. This time she was determined not to have him leave her bed. As it was, they seemed to be celebrating a constant honeymoon. And the prospect of all those months with no

447

champagne or cigarettes was too daunting, she thought, as she picked up her champagne cocktail, sipped it and then lit a cigarette.

By December, her pregnancy, long confirmed by the doctor, was still her secret. She had been lucky. She had felt no sickness, no nausea, it had been easy to keep the secret. But now it was getting more difficult: dresses this year were a problem. Although draping around the hips helped cover her stomach, everyone was sporting a tiny waist. She had managed this for the first three months but now, well into her fourth month, it was no longer possible. She dressed for dinner in a dress that disguised her thickening waist and resigned herself to the fact that Hal must notice any day now. He did that evening, in bed.

'Juniper, are you keeping something from me?' He was leaning on his hand, his elbow propping him up as he looked down at her.

'What on earth do you mean?' she asked innocently.

He outlined her stomach with a finger. She chuckled, 'You're tickling me.'

Then, sitting straight he put one hand one side of her waist and one the other. 'I can't even begin to get my hands round now. Either you are getting disgustingly fat or there's something you haven't told me.'

'I didn't want to spoil everything.'

'What do you mean, spoil everything?'

'The way things are now. The fun we have. Last time you stopped making love to me and became a tyrant.'

'Then you are expecting my baby.'

'Yes.' She smiled at him coyly, looking at him from under her eyelashes trying to gauge if he would be angry with her for keeping it secret.

'You should have told me.'

'I've explained why I didn't. I've spoken to the doctor and there's no reason why we have to sleep separately. The dangerous period is over.'

448

'And you risked it?' He frowned.

'Don't be silly, the time I was most at risk was when I didn't know I was pregnant.'

'You know what this means, Juniper, don't you?'

She nodded dutifully, as she knew what he expected, but gleefully congratulating herself on her foresight in hiding away some brandy, champagne and a cache of cigarettes in her dressing room weeks ago. She did not feel guilty about this. She was determined not to be as silly as last time but she had checked with friends who had had babies, she had checked with her doctor – moderation seemed to be the order of the day.

'Then I can't tell you how pleased and proud of you I am.' Gently he kissed her, and she put up her arms, as always eager for him, but he patted her, covered her with the blanket, and switched the light out. Juniper lay in the dark wide-eyed. Things were going to be just the same, she knew it. Why did a baby have to spoil everything?

She met her sister-in-law quite by chance. Hal would have neither his brother nor his wife in the house. Juniper had met Caroline once at a large party and at her own wedding – even Hal could not refuse to invite his only brother to that. She had assumed that Caroline was dull simply because Hal had told her she was. But, at the inaugural committee meeting for a charity ball to be held the following summer, she was surprised to find Caroline also a member.

The two women eyed each other suspiciously. Aware of Caroline's eyes on her stomach Juniper pushed it out further as if saying '. . . look at me, I'm pregnant . . .' Caroline smiled at her.

'I didn't know, congratulations.'

'Thank you,' Juniper answered, caught off-guard by the warmth of the smile. 'You mean the old hag didn't tell you?'

'Hortense?' Caroline laughed a delightful open laugh.

'No, and I doubt it was out of tact. I don't think she knows.'

'Really?'

'Hal is probably protecting you from her.'

'Do you think so? How sweet. You don't get on with her either, then?'

'Does anyone?' Caroline sighed.

From this beginning it was only natural that after the meeting they should go to the Ritz together for tea, and a friendship began to develop. They often met for lunch. Caroline was far from dull, she was highly intelligent, fun to be with and, of course, they were united in their loathing of Hortense Copton.

'Why don't Hal and Leigh get on?' she asked one day as she toyed with a grilled sole and green salad at the Caprice.

'It's not Leigh's wish, I promise you. It goes back a long way. I gather that Hal was the hag's favourite and Leigh was their father's. Old Lord Copton was a patient man but Hal tried him to the core. He bailed him out time and again over his gambling debts . . .'

'His gambling debts?' Juniper repeated raising her eyebrows in surprise. 'But Hal doesn't gamble.'

'Doesn't he?' Caroline said, a hint of cynicism in her voice and then, as if conscious of Juniper's condition, added hurriedly, 'I'm glad to hear it. But he used to, like a madman. His grandfather left him a fortune, his father settled money on him and he got through the lot, it was only because of Leigh and a few friends that he did not end up a bankrupt.' Juniper had stopped eating, had even stopped toying with the fish, so riveted was she by this tale. 'So, the old man saw only one way out: he cut Hal out of his will. He would have prevented him having Summercourt, if he could have done so, but it was entailed. He left everything else to Leigh – the house in London, the estate in Scotland and the money.'

'Poor Leigh.'

'What makes you say that?' Caroline asked with interest.

'He seems, on the two occasions I met him, to be a fair and very pleasant fellow. The sort who would hate this kind of drama.'

'He is, he loathes it, but he realises his father had no choice. There really would be nothing left now. Remember how we nearly lost Summercourt? It was only your galloping to the rescue that saved it. Leigh was beside himself when Hal put it up for sale. He wanted to buy it himself, you see. He tried to raise the money, but he couldn't afford the house, let alone the contents.'

'Well Hal seems to be reformed now. I've never seen him gamble once, not even on a game of snap,' she said gaily. 'Poor Hal, he must have been so ashamed. Still he's happy now with the baby coming. He's certain it's a boy.'

'I'm sure he's counting on it. The will is useless if it's a girl.'

'What will?'

'Old Lord Copton's. Everything is in trust, you see. He didn't leave it entirely to Leigh, he cut Hal out but he left it that, if Hal has a son, everything reverts to him.'

'To Hal?'

'No, the baby. It's fearfully complicated. But put simply, the London house and the money would be the baby's. He left Leigh the Scottish estate outright. If Hal has only girls, then we stay put and it goes to Leigh's heirs.'

'But Hal couldn't touch it?'

'In theory, no. In practice the child's custodian takes responsibility for the money so, as the child's father, Hal would have a big say in how it was invested and spent.'

'Oh dear, how will you manage?'

'With difficulty.' Caroline laughed which, in the circumstances, impressed Juniper enormously. 'I've some money, but we shall just have to make the Scottish estate pay in some way or other. We couldn't afford a London home. And, if you don't mind, I'll pray you have a girl.'

The full meaning of what Caroline was saying began to take shape in Juniper's mind. This was no joke. The child within her could make this couple desperate for money. The child within her could make Hal secure for life . . .

'Are you all right, Juniper?'

Juniper looked at her with dazed eyes. 'He never told me about the will. He's been longing for this baby and I thought it was because he wanted our child, I thought he was so desperate because he loved me. Stupid of me.'

'My poor Juniper, I should never have told you. But it's common knowledge around London, you'd have found out sooner or later from someone.'

'This explains so much.'

'Lord, I wish I hadn't told you now. You look as if you're going to faint.'

'No, Caroline, I'm not going to faint. I'm glad to know, I always like to know the truth. Then I know what I'm up against. I'll tell you one thing, though, I hope it's a girl too.'

Juniper let herself into the house and crossed the marbled hall to the drawing room. She poured herself a large brandy and nursed her anger. The distasteful conclusion was that Hal was using her. How dare he!

Over the months she had begun to realise just how important her money was to Hal – she would have been a fool not to realise how much he spent, how much he enjoyed the style her money gave them. Just recently she had begun to wonder if, that evening in Scotland when she had begged him to marry her, she wasn't acting a part that he had already ordained for her, a scenario he had already planned. But this was much more disturbing. He should have told her, should have explained; she would have understood. Now she felt like a brood mare. And if the baby was a girl, what then? Did she have to have another and another until a boy was born? Never, she vowed.

It was all so senseless too. He had Summercourt, they had a London home and all her money, so why deprive Leigh? What on earth did they need more money for? Unless . . . She opened her handbag and took out a cigarette. She did not care if Hal walked in and found her smoking.

What if, once a boy was born, Hal had no more use for her? Would he lead his own life again? Would he seek to divorce her? Reluctantly she admitted to herself that she still loved him and needed him. She stubbed the cigarette out and quickly opened the window. There was no point in making him angry. If this marriage was to survive she would have to move carefully.

7

It was a boy.

Juniper lay in her bed in the nursing home in Portland Place, aching from head to toe and vowing never, ever, to go through such an experience again. The pain, the indignity, had been appalling. And for what? As she had feared, when the nurse gave her the baby to hold, she had looked at it and knew she was incapable of loving the poor thing as it should, and deserved to, be loved.

Every spare space was covered in vases of flowers. Elaborate baskets of blooms stood on the floor. The room was filled with a dozen different scents. None of them gave her pleasure, she felt as though she were in a funeral parlour and that the flowers were for her dead youth. What was she to do, how was she to manage, feeling as she did? She was twenty, to others she appeared a sophisticated woman but Juniper knew herself – deep inside she was still a child, a child who longed for love and attention. Yet now she would be expected to be an adult and bear responsibility for a son whom she did not love, and doubted if she ever would. Was it simply her own childishness which was to blame, she wondered? All her childhood she had been the centre of attention. Was she now loath to give up centre stage?

She looked moodily out of the window at the tiny space of blue sky above the buildings opposite and wished her grandmother were here. She would tell her what to do, she would love the baby for her.

The door opened and the matron walked in with another bouquet.

'This is the advantage of a May baby,' she said brightly. 'Such lovely flowers.'

'It must be the only advantage.'

'Oh dear, Lady Copton, are we feeling a little bit depressed?'

'Enormously depressed, Matron.'

'It's early days for that, but then it's quite usual. Nothing to worry about. Have you fed the little chap yet?'

'I'm not breast-feeding him, you'll have to get him a bottle or something, whatever you do with babies.' She was sitting up, an alarmed expression on her face. She could think of nothing she wanted less than to feed the baby herself.

The matron looked at her with a patient smile. How often she had heard that same reaction from young women – it never lasted. Give them the child and all the resentment, all the memory of the pain, faded. She looked at this patient with admiration. The baby was barely six hours old and yet she looked beautiful – a strange naïve, almost childlike, innocence about her – unusual in the patients in this fashionable clinic.

'Many of our mummies feed their babies.'

'Well, Matron, I'm one who won't, I can assure you.'

'Dear, dear, we are in a bad mood, aren't we,' she smiled over-brightly. There was a tap at the door. 'And who have we here?' Her starched uniform rustled as she crossed to the door and opened it. 'Why, Lady Copton, Daddy's here, perhaps he can persuade you.'

Hal was only half visible behind a large bunch of roses as he moved with a stealthy step into the room and looked about sheepishly, as men tend to do in maternity hospitals.

'Persuade you to do what?' He laid the flowers on the bed and kissed her gingerly on the cheek. 'You look tired, Juniper,' he said unnecessarily.

'I am tired. It's not a particularly relaxing pastime giving birth,' she snapped.

'I think our mummy looks very beautiful, Lord Copton,' Matron chided him gently, aware that she must not offend, not with the high expenses her patients were charged. 'I'm afraid we're rather fractious this morning, Lord Copton. Your wife says she doesn't want to feed the little fellow.'

'Juniper, you must. All the doctors say it's the best thing for the baby.' He looked down anxiously at her.

'It's not the best thing for me,' she said petulantly.

'I'll leave you two alone,' the Matron said archly, 'I expect you're longing to see your son, Lord Copton.' The starch-clad figure crackled out of the room.

'Does she always talk to you as if you're an idiot?' he asked quizzically. She shrugged.

'I'm so proud,' he went on.

'Of yourself? Of him? Or of me?'

'Why, all three, of course. But call him Harry, that's his name.'

'We haven't discussed his name.'

'All the Copton firstborns are called Henry. I'm Hal so we'll call him Harry.'

'I wanted to call him Lincoln.'

'An English child? It might be hard on him at Eton – imagine the jokes about going to the theatre. He has to be called Henry.'

He opened his mouth as if to continue his argument and

then shrugged his shoulders. 'Very well, Henry Lincoln Copton. I don't mind. You don't seem very happy, Juniper.'

'I'm not. Everyone expects me to be delirious with joy, and I'm not.'

'The doctor tells me you had a bad time, that you were incredibly brave. It'll be easier, next time.'

Juniper looked at him with disbelief. Slowly she said, 'I'm not sure there will be a next time. I did what I had to, it's a boy.'

'We'll discuss it again, later, when you're fully recovered.'

Juniper slumped back on to her pillows and watched as he circled the room inspecting the flowers, reading the cards. He should be the one person to whom she could talk about how she felt, how she feared she could not love the child. Yet he was the last to whom she could voice her thoughts.

'Lovely flowers.' He sat on the chair beside the bed and looked trapped as if he did not know what to say. She slid her hand tentatively across the sheet towards him.

'Hal, I want it to be as it was before, just you and me. It was so perfect. I don't want anything to spoil it,' she suddenly burst out, feeling she wanted to cry. She wanted him to take her in his arms, tell her nothing had changed, and to tell her he loved her.

'Too late for that, Juniper. There's the three of us now . . . Ah, here he is.' He leapt to his feet with apparent relief.

He opened the door for Matron who entered carrying the carefully wrapped baby. Reverently she placed the child in Juniper's arms and discreetly left the room. Hal looked down at his son with an expression of wonder on his face. Gently he touched the baby's cheek, gingerly he took his hand. 'Juniper look, he's holding my finger. He's so strong. Harry, my boy, my God, I love you . . .' he burst out.

'Here,' she said, thrusting the child at him. 'Here he is, your heir, what you've always wanted.' And she turned her face away from him and with breaking heart looked at the wall.

Juniper's attitude did not improve. Her feelings towards the baby were now fuelled by jealousy. He husband had said he loved the child; not once had he ever said he loved her.

It seemed she could never please Hal. She began to think she must have imagined that they were ever happy together, ever meant for each other. Finally, she had had enough. In the past she allowed his behaviour to make her depressed; she was determined not to go the same way again. She had known jealousy; now she would make him jealous. This time it would be Hal who begged her to love him.

She dutifully visited the nursery with Hal, she played with the child, cooed over him, fed him his bottle. If Hal was not there she did not go near the place and left his entire care to the nanny. She loathed children, she decided, and wanted no more. If she wasn't maternal, so be it – she had tried and failed to change her spots. Now she resolved to be herself.

Soon after she returned from the hospital Hal again took to going out alone in the evening without saying where he went. Now she fought back. She held as many dinner parties and cocktail parties as possible and arranged trips to the theatre with friends. If he were present, fine; if not she would still have fun – helped by the wine and brandy which she now drank constantly. She accepted invitations even if he were not able to escort her. And she flirted – how she flirted, just as she had in the past. She felt confused and she felt bitter but no one was to know.

Hal had always been prone to moods but recently these had become more frequent, darker. He could sit for hours at a time, a drink in his hand, gazing morosely into space.

She did not know what to do when he was like this and found she could not pierce his depression no matter how witty and gay she attempted to be. So, often, after trying and failing to cheer him, she would flounce out of the house. His moods began to irritate her.

But one thing had not changed. He was determined to have a second son. Unknown to him, she had visited her doctor and had arranged her own contraception to make this well-nigh impossible. If she could not love one son, how on earth could she love the second? Each night before she went to her bed, she fitted her dutch cap neatly into place, in case tonight was to be one of those nights. If he came, she enjoyed the pleasure he always gave her.

Christmas gave her the opportunity to contact Alice. She had a copy of a photograph of herself with Harry, which was to appear in *The Tatler*, framed in silver. She put in a short note, wrapped it up in brown paper, addressed it and then put it in a drawer unable to bring herself to post it.

She refused to make the mistake of allowing her looks to suffer, as she had after losing the first child. She quickly recovered her figure and spent a small fortune on a completely new wardrobe. She had her long hair cut and permed. She had kept it long only because that was how her father had liked it. Since he had ceased to exist for her, this no longer mattered.

Her friends were delighted that Juniper was back in their circle, not only was she good fun but she invariably insisted on picking up the bill.

One night on such an excursion, she met her husband. Her heart had nearly stopped when someone recognised Hal across the dining room with a party. She looked up fearful of seeing him with a woman, the mistress whom she feared he had. With relief she saw him in a party of young men, and could wave at him quite cheerfully.

She longed to be able to arrange house parties at

Summercourt again, as a distraction. When she had been pregnant, and because it was the winter, she had embarked on a massive redecoration of the country house. She had more bathrooms put in to suit her American standards, paintings were cleaned and restored, books rebound, new curtains and covers ordered. The work had taken longer to complete than she had anticipated. She was frustrated by the inability of workmen to work faster.

But it was not finished until early July. She set to like a demon to arrange her weekend parties. Ideal guests, wonderful food and fun, endless fun. But secretly, Juniper was drinking heavily again.

8

'Juniper, I think it's about time you increased my allowance,' Hal said matter-of-factly one morning in her dressing room at Summercourt.

'Increase it? Whatever for?'

'Because I need more money, that's why,' he smiled sardonically at her as she brushed her hair in preparation for the arrival of another large house party.

'But you have everything you need.'

'I don't like to be short. I thought it was about time you gave my allowance a boost.'

Slowly she replaced her brush on the dressing table and appeared to study her face in the looking glass. She wasn't; she was wondering why he should require more money.

'I don't think so, Hal. If you need anything, you have only to ask.'

'I just have.'

'You know what I mean.'

'It's so undignified for me to have to ask you for money, like a child.'

'I'm very generous to you already,' she said angrily, picking up the brush again and attacking her hair with abrupt strokes.

'I never thought you would be like this, Juniper.'

'Probably not, but there's much in life that I hadn't expected either.'

'Such as?'

'It seems a strange marriage we have, Hal. The only way I can be sure of seeing you is to invite other people here – then you deign to appear. Why should I give you more money to enable you to avoid me even more?'

'Don't be silly, Juniper. I'm here, aren't I? Most weekends I come here for your house parties.'

'That's why I prefer the summer. I hardly saw you last winter. God only knows what you get up to.'

'You were pregnant then, remember? You could hardly go gadding about as you like, it wouldn't have been appropriate.'

'As you like. I wasn't pregnant for most of May, June and July, was I?'

'Good God, woman, we've been married for two and a half years now, you can't expect the honeymoon to go on for ever, can you?'

'What do you need the money for anyway?' she asked abruptly, forcing herself to stay calm. Twice now he had missed weekends at Summercourt. There had been no phone call, no explanation.

'I need £2,000.'

'What for?'

'Not a woman, if that's what's worrying you. Just a little debt I've run up.'

'A debt?' she said sharply, remembering her conversation with Caroline.

'I'm too generous in the presents I give you,' he said with a rare laugh.

She picked up her lipstick, relief and guilt over her suspicions flooding through her. So that was it. The bracelet he had given her for her birthday, the pendant when Harry was born. Of course, that was it, they must have cost him dear. How could she, who was always so carefree about money, find herself being so petty? Guilt made her expansive.

'You're sure that's enough?' she asked as she opened her handbag and took out her cheque book.

'Well, £3,000 would make me a lot more solvent,' he replied.

She wrote the cheque and he kissed her cheek as he took it. Then quietly he let himself out of the room.

In September he was asking for more.

'I thought I'd like a little flat in town – just a pied-à-tierre.'

'What on earth for? We've got a perfectly adequate house,' she snapped, alarmed at his request.

'I think it would be good for us if I had a little place of my own that I could use when you're at Summercourt. So stupid to keep this house open when we are not here. It will be an economy.'

'It's silly, the staff is here.'

'Yes, but don't you see we need not duplicate them in both houses? When you go to Summercourt most of the staff could go with you, instead of sitting idle here.'

'Hal, you are funny the way you are obsessed with the servants' working hours.'

'I like to look after your money well, for you,' he said persuasively and smiled the lop-sided smile which still had the power to charm her.

Even as she wrote the cheque she knew she did so for the wrong reason. She blotted the cheque had handed it to him: she knew she was making a last attempt to buy his love and she despised herself.

Flower lay on the chaise beside Juniper, by the pool. Idly they sipped their champagne cocktails.

'You're an amazing woman, Juniper. Aren't you ever jealous?' Flower lisped.

'Me? Of what?'

'Hal, of course.'

Juniper's heart lurched. What did Flower know? 'I don't know what you're talking about.' She managed a bleak smile.

'Well, that for a start,' and Flower nodded to the other side of the pool. Juniper looked across to where Hal was arm wrestling energetically with Robin Dorchester, a young actor friend, who had been a frequent visitor to Summercourt on those weekends when Hal chose to appear. Juniper smiled broadly.

'A man should have friends of his own,' she said.

'Amazing,' said Flower, turning over to tan her other side.

It was November. Everyone was exhausted. There had been a frenetic atmosphere to the past season. At the start all the talk had been of war in Europe. Those who could remember the last war were filled with fear, those who had been too young were filled with excitement at the possibility of the unknown. Consequently, the season had been treated as if it were to be the last. Not until September when Chamberlain returned with the letter from Munich did the hysteria subside and life return almost to normal.

All this autumn Juniper had not felt well. She had caught a chill in late September which she was finding difficulty in shaking off. Her spirits were low too. Once the summer was over Hal had reverted to what she regarded as his London self – the one who seemed to have a life apart from her and to which she was not welcome. It was worse now he had his flat. Now he sometimes went for days without coming home, and when he did so she was sure it was to see Harry and not her.

In the past fortnight on the few occasions she had seen him he had seemed deeply depressed. She knew there was no point in asking him why.

Her maid entered with her breakfast tray, the newspapers and her post. She picked up the papers first as she always did. She never read them but turned immediately to the gossip pages and the court circular. The world could be collapsing and Juniper would never know. She never bothered with her mail until she had finished eating. There was always so much of it, bills and invitations, that she liked the bed clear before dealing with it. She picked up her large engagement diary from the bedside table and began the task of sorting which invitations to accept.

The sixth envelope she opened made her feel sick. It contained a note: '*I thought this might interest you, Lady Copton*,' signed, '*A well wisher*.' Accompanying the note was a photograph of her husband with his arms about Robin Dorchester.

She fought to keep down the toast and tea she had just consumed. She began to sweat. Pushing back the covers she raced to the bathroom. Five minutes later she emerged, white-faced and shaking.

She got back on the bed and made herself pick up the note and the photograph. She forced herself to study them. So, she reasoned, Robin was a great friend of his, she'd often seen him put his arm about him. She'd even seen Robin plant a kiss on her husband's cheek once. It meant nothing, he was an actor, they were more demonstrative. She tore both note and photograph up and flung them into the waste-paper basket. Then she tried to concentrate on the rest of her mail.

That evening she attended a large dinner with Hal. His mood was still dark, but the company was good and he even managed once or twice to laugh. Later in his arms, in bed, she resolved to say nothing.

Three weeks later her Christmas mail contained another photograph and this time the note was more threatening. Unless she paid £1,000 the photograph would be sent to the newspapers. She followed the instructions and paid. She did not intend to let such a sum of money spoil their Christmas together, Harry's first, and long planned by Hal with a tree and presents galore for their son.

By early February she had paid £3,000. She began to worry. Was she being stupid, panicking and paying out on an innocent photograph, as she thought, or was it all true? But how could she even think such a thing, when he was such a consummate lover? The only time she ever felt secure with him was when they were in bed together. Should she go to the police? But the suspicion planted by the blackmailer would not let go. What would happen, if it were true? She risked her husband being arrested, the disgrace of a court case, his possible imprisonment and the blight on her son's future. In her distress she was not even aware that she had for once shown concern for her son.

Pulling herself together she telephoned Caroline who, she knew, was down from Scotland, packing up their London home at Hal's insistence. She arranged to meet her for lunch at the Savoy Grill.

As soon as they were settled and had given their order to the waiter she came straight to the point.

'Caroline, do you know if Hal's a homosexual?'

Caroline slowly sipped her wine and looked closely at Juniper. 'Why do you ask?'

'Then it's true,' she sat back in her seat and found, to her astonishment, that she felt nothing. She had often in the past weeks anticipated how she would feel – angry, sick, humiliated. She had not expected this void of emotion.

'I didn't say it was,' Caroline said anxiously.

'You didn't need to. If it weren't true, you would have ridiculed the idea, not asked why I wanted to know,' she said calmly. Too calmly, Caroline thought.

'I'm sorry, Juniper. I had hoped you wouldn't find out.'

'I don't know how to deal with this, Caroline. I don't know what to do. I feel nothing, I feel numb.' She looked at Caroline with dawning panic.

'What woman would?' Caroline put her hand out and gently took Juniper's in hers. 'Come on, we don't want to eat, not after this. Let's go to the river and walk.'

She allowed Caroline to lead her from the restaurant and across the road to the Embankment. Slowly, they paced along beside the river, their fur coats wrapped about them against the chill breeze that scudded up the river, making the sluggish water ripple as if it too were shivering with cold. Neither said anything, for neither knew what to say – Juniper from mounting shock, Caroline from mute concern.

'How did you find out?' It was Caroline who finally broke the silence.

'I'm being blackmailed. Since November.'

'And you've said nothing to Hal?'

'I didn't want to face the truth,' she said bitterly.

'Oh, Juniper, what can I say?'

'Nothing.' She leant against the stonework of the Embankment and looked across the river but even as she looked she saw nothing. And as she stared vacantly anger began to grow inside her, great black, bleak waves of anger. She began to shake uncontrollably.

Caroline put her arm about her in a futile gesture of comfort. 'Juniper, I'm so sorry.'

'I feel I'm nothing. Imagine, Caroline, him in my bed, taking me in his arms when all the time he'd have preferred . . .' she shuddered, unable to put her thoughts into words.

'You can't *know* that.'

'I know.'

'But for your own sanity, you must think he loved you, wanted you.'

'I feel sickened . . . used.' She rubbed her hands frantically up and down her arms as if washing herself.

'It's always me who gives you the bad news, isn't it? First the gambling and now this.'

'He's gambling too, then?' she said in a hard little voice.

'Yes, Leigh heard that last year he lost over £100,000. Being such a huge sum, we assumed that you knew. I mean where would Hal get the money from?'

'That much?' she said with disbelief. 'I don't know, Caroline, he didn't get it from me. Someone must be financing him, some rich lover presumably. Oh, my God, what on earth am I to do?' She was speaking to the air not to Caroline. 'What do I do?' she kept repeating as if unaware that her friend stood beside her, so lost was she in her despair.

'Would you like me to come back with you? Stay with you?' Caroline's voice was rich with concern. Juniper looked at her blankly and then with an expression of surprise that she was still there.

'No, I don't want you there. I don't want anyone with me, I don't want anyone to hear . . .'

'Juniper, there's something else, you see. Something you ought to know.'

'I don't think I want to know anything else.'

'Very well. I understand. Are you sure you don't want me to come?'

'What else?' she said in a steely voice, now wanting to know, yet afraid of what else she was to hear. 'Taxi!' she yelled, almost pushing Caroline to one side as one drew up at the kerb. 'What else?' she asked through the open window.

'Look in *The Times*. Call me . . .' Caroline called as the cab drew away.

Back at her house she went straight to the library where the papers were neatly folded. With shaking fingers she picked up the paper and scoured it quickly, fearful that one of the photographs might be there. She could find nothing. Then she went through the newspaper a second time, more slowly, reading the headlines. Still nothing. What did Caroline mean? And then she saw it – amongst the advertisements of properties for sale. The largest advertisement was for Summercourt and its contents on the instructions of The Right Honourable The Lord Copton.

Her legs felt weak, she slithered to the floor. The present she had given him, the present she had given with so much love . . . You couldn't give presents away – never! Perhaps in time she could have come to terms with his need for Robin. She might have been able to forgive, but this – never.

She crawled across to the phone and flicked through her address book. Quickly she dialled a number.

'Robin? It's Juniper, may I speak to Hal,' she asked, forcing herself to sound calm.

There was a pause. 'Juniper?' She heard the familiar voice.

'Get over here, you bastard, this minute.'

9

Juniper did not waste time. She knew Hal, he hurried for no one. She probably had a good hour to do what she had to do.

She rang for the butler and ordered him to get Hal's valet and a footman to pack all of her husband's possessions and to have the trunks in the front hall within the hour. She rang the Savoy and booked a suite and then raced upstairs to the nursery to tell the nanny and nursery maid to pack Harry's toys and clothes, their own clothes, and to go immediately, within three quarters of an hour, to the Savoy. Then she telephoned Caroline.

'Caroline? Thank God you're in.'

'Are you all right, Juniper?'

'I'm fine, demoralised but fighting fit.' She managed to laugh. 'I saw the advert. Thank you for warning me.'

'I'm sorry about Summercourt. I telephoned Leigh, he reckons Hal's in debt again and is doing it to shock you into giving him more money.'

'It's too late for that. He's gone too far. The house was a present. As my grandfather told me many years ago – funnily enough over another house – you can't give presents away. It's unforgivable.'

'Maybe it's just a manoeuvre to get more money. He adores Summercourt. I'm sure he doesn't really intend selling it.'

'If you're right, the game he's playing his misfired. But that isn't why I'm phoning. I've booked a suite for you and Harry at the Savoy. He'll be there within the hour. Would you and Leigh take care of him for me and take him to Scotland as quickly as possible? I'll pay all his expenses, of course.'

'Juniper, you mustn't rush into anything and do something you might regret later. Of course, if you want, if it will help. I'll take Harry to Scotland tomorrow and look after him until things calm down.'

'No, Caroline, I mean for you and Leigh to have him for ever.'

'That's silly, Juniper. You're in a dreadful muddle at the moment. You're suffering from shock. You'll think differently when everything is sorted out with Hal.'

'I won't. This is what I want. This is the best thing for Harry. I want him to have a real home, a decent home. I can't give him what he needs and you will.'

'We'll discuss it later.'

'I shan't change my mind.'

'What will Hal say? He'll be furious.'

'I don't care what he has to say. He's given up any rights he might have had. I don't think he has a leg to stand on, do you? The courts wouldn't like what we know. No, it will be most amusing to see what the lawyers make of this one. If Leigh has custody of my son, then presumably the Copton money goes with the boy.'

'Juniper, you couldn't!'

'Oh, yes, I can, Caroline. This will hurt Hal like nothing else could.'

'But Harry, the poor little scrap?'

'You'll be a far better mother than I could ever be. Let's be honest, I'm not very good at it. I just don't seem to have the right feelings. All I can give the boy, it seems, is money. That I will do, I promise you.'

'Don't be so hard on yourself, Juniper. It seems to me that you care very much for your son: his welfare is the first thing you've thought of . . .'

'Caroline, I don't wish to sound rude but I've a lot to see to here. Please get him to Scotland quickly. I'll talk to my lawyers as soon as possible. I'll be in touch.'

Juniper then changed, did her make-up with especial care, but could not relax until the nanny brought Harry to her. She kissed the baby goodbye. As she did so, to her astonishment, she suddenly felt immeasurably sad. She took him from the nanny and hugged him tight. 'Bye, Harry,' she whispered to him. 'Forgive me. It's better this way,' and quickly she thrust him back into the nurse-maid's arms before she changed her mind.

She had been wrong: it was two hours before she heard Hal's key in the lock. She waited in the upstairs drawing room, a large brandy beside her and, although she was not aware of it, more beautiful, in her fury, than ever. She listened by the door. With satisfaction she heard him pause by the cases. Heard him ask the butler what they were doing there, heard the enigmatic reply that, 'it was her Ladyship's instructions'. By the time he entered the room she was sitting calmly in a chair leafing through the latest *Illustrated London News*.

'What are my cases doing in the hall?' he demanded.

'You're leaving.'

'Don't be silly, Juniper.'

'I'm not being silly. I'm throwing you out. If you won't go quietly then I shall call the police.'

'You saw the advertisement?'

'Yes. I saw it. I didn't realise how little you thought of my present and how little you thought of me and my feelings.'

'Juniper, I was at my wits' end. I needed money desperately. I didn't know what else to do. I hate asking you for money, as you know. The house is, after all, the only thing I possess.' He crossed to the drinks tray and calmly poured himself a whisky. She watched him through her lashes, her anger barely controlled. With a blinding flash of intuition she realised that, once again, she was in a scenario of his making.

'It must have been a shock for you,' he said. 'I do apologise. I've been trying to think of the best way to tell you.'

'Gambling is it, or blackmail?'

He swung round. 'What do you mean?'

'Oh, come on, Hal. I know everything. I even know how much you lost last year.'

'I've been a fool, Juniper, a bloody fool. It's difficult to explain to someone who does not gamble, but it's like a drug. I promise it will stop.'

'You mean, if I pay your debts, you won't have to sell Summercourt?'

'Exactly. You are a brick, Juniper. I knew you would see sense. Maybe I should have come to you straight away. Confessed I'd been a bad boy.' His smile evaporated when he saw Juniper's stony expression. 'You can be angry with me now, I deserve it.'

'Whether you continue to gamble or not is of no interest to me whatsoever. Do as you please.'

'Juniper, I knew you'd understand.'

She saw the relief in his eyes, noted the way his shoulder muscles relaxed, watched as, at last, he could sip his drink with pleasure.

'No, Hal, it's you who does not understand,' she said after a long pause. 'It's of no interest to me because *you* are no longer of any interest to me. Do what you will with your life, I shan't be part of it.'

Quickly he placed his glass on a side table and advanced towards the chair where she sat, apparently, in total serenity.

'You can't mean this, Juniper. You love me. You've told me yourself that I'm the only man who can satisfy you. You couldn't survive without me.'

'Yes I can. I've let my love for you blind me to what you really are – a cold, selfish opportunist. I've been stupid and weak.'

'Yes, you are weak, you'll always be weak, that comes of being spoilt all your life.'

'Yes, I've been spoilt by money. But don't forget, Hal, that money gives me the power to cut you out of my life and hurt you where you need me most, my cheque book. I want a divorce.'

'My gambling, my being forced to sell the house, aren't grounds enough.'

'No, but Robin would be, wouldn't he? Imagine what the courts would think of the poor wife being duped into buying that little love nest for you.'

'What on earth do you mean by that? Robin's a friend, nothing else.'

'Then what about the photographs, what about the blackmailer?'

'The photographs proved nothing.'

'Ah, you've seen them, have you? Have you been blackmailed too? Or did you send them yourself?' She studied him closely but he did not react.

'What on earth are you talking about?'

'I think that's the truth. I think you sent the photographs to get more money out of me.'

'I've never heard such rubbish in my life. Why should I risk my marriage for money that I could get anyway?'

'But could you? It would depend on how much you needed, wouldn't it? Even I might balk at the sort of sums you've been losing. Maybe you were desperate. I hear that the people who run these gambling houses are not very particular how they get their money. But that's not the point. I know about you, Hal. I know everything.'

'From one photograph?' He snorted but she noticed he was sweating. 'I've explained that we're good friends.'

'Stop denying it, Hal,' she said wearily. 'I know, people have told me, people who really know you.'

'Who's been slandering me?'

'How can it be slander when it's the truth? Now if you wouldn't mind removing your possessions . . .'

'I'm not going anywhere.' He crossed the room and poured himself another drink. 'This is my home, I'm staying. You have nothing on me, Juniper.'

'But I will have, Hal. You will book into a hotel, with a woman, and my detective will find you. Simple as that. The alternative is that I bring into court evidence of your homosexuality.'

'You can't prove it.'

'I can. That, Hal, is the advantage of money. I can buy the evidence.'

'But what about Harry? He'd suffer. For God's sake think of him.'

'Far better to do it my way, don't you think?' she said coolly.

He looked at her in silence for what seemed an age. Despite her racing heart, despite the dreadful nausea she felt, she looked back at him calmly, with an icy stare he had never seen on her face before.

'I couldn't lose Harry.'

'Always Harry with you, isn't it, Hal? I gather that, apart from my money, that's why you married me, to get Harry, to get your inheritance. It's a shame for you that you love him as much as you do for I shall make certain you don't get custody of your son. I shall fight you

472

through every court to ensure that you don't. I almost feel sorry for you, you're about to lose everything again, Hal.'

He moved so quickly across the room that it took her by surprise. He grabbed her arm and twisted it painfully. 'You wouldn't do that.' He was shouting at her. 'You filthy rich bitch, you'd use your own son.'

'You should have thought about that before,' she shouted back oblivious in her anger to the pain. 'He's gone already. Fight for him if you can,' and she brought her knee up sharply and with cold precision aimed it between his knees.

He crumpled to the floor clutching his crotch. 'I hate you, Juniper. You'll never know how much those nights in bed with you disgusted me,' he roared.

'Thank you for that, Hal. You've made everything so much easier for me.' And she swept from the room.

In her own bedroom she stood in the centre of the room and shook from head to toe. She would never know how she had remained so calm. Long, long ago her grandmother had told her that she thought of herself as a daughter of a granite land which had given her the courage to survive. Maybe she was one too, after all.

She heard the front door slam. Quickly she packed an overnight bag and hurried from the house and to her car. She turned it towards the west.

It was six in the morning before she turned through the gates of Gwenfer. It was dark, the darkness of winter far darker in the country than in the town. Below her she could hear the sea pounding on the rocks and as she climbed from her car the wind from the Atlantic gusted about her so that she had to fight the wind to reach the front door. She thundered on the door with both fists, screaming her grandmother's name, which the wind gleefully scooped up and bore away. The door opened, Phillip stood there, a shotgun in his hand. Behind him on the oak staircase stood Alice, her hand at her neck in agitation.

'Grandmama,' Juniper cried, and raced past Phillip, across the great hall, and into her grandmother's arms. 'Please forgive me, please take me back. Please let this be my home again.'

'My poor darling, of course I'll take you back. This has always been your home. What has happened?' She gently led her towards the small parlour signalling to her husband to bring brandy.

Juniper told her story to her grandmother's and Phillip's shocked ears. She spoke in a dull monotone in a voice that did not sound like her.

'He doesn't love me, Grandmama. He has never loved me.'

Chapter Ten

1

Polly frequently went to the Café Maurice. In winter she would sit inside by the antiquated stove, which creaked and groaned alarmingly but which heated the old café to the temperature of a hothouse. In spring and summer she would while away the hours sitting at a marble-topped pavement table, sipping her coffee or her *citron* or very occasionally a glass of wine, and just watch the bustle of everyday life in the square.

But it was a Polly who her old friends would have had difficulty recognising. She had become an elegant woman, tall and slim, who held herself proudly, showing off her clothes to the best advantage. And what clothes. Schiaparelli, Worth, Chanel, she patronised all of them and they were pleased to dress this young Englishwoman who, despite her nationality, was nonetheless a good advertisement for their skills. Her hair was cropped into a thick, sleek and shining black skull cap of hair. Her make-up was pale, her lips painted bright red, her fine brown eyes ringed by eyelashes thick and black with mascara. Many turned their heads to take a closer look, to make sure that they had really seen such elegance sitting in the old café in this unfashionable quarter of Paris.

The regulars were used to her now and many passed the time of day with her. But still, after two years of her patronage, none could say they knew her. When she left, frequently there was speculation as to who she was, and why such an obviously chic and rich young woman should choose this particular café. For while they loved their café they acknowledged that it was shabby and dull compared to those one would have expected her to patronise in the grander *arrondissements*. There were a few tradesmen but for the most part they were writers, as yet unsuccessful, students who had perfected the art of making one *pression* last a whole session while they argued and impressed each other. All of them, to a man or woman, were existentialist from the tops of their black berets to the tips of their black shoes. Not bourgeoisie or people of wealth, certainly no women in couture clothes normally entered the Café Maurice.

Why did she come, how had she found it? It was chance really. Every afternoon after his hour-long siesta – never a minute less or a minute more – Michel would leave the house. His tailor, shirt-maker, boot-maker, glove-maker, his hatter, his jeweller, the apothecary for his perfumes, oils and unguents were all visited on a regular basis. Each visit took hours as the experts were consulted with the reverence and respect more fitting a consultation with a pope or a cardinal, so fervent was his pursuit of excellence in his attire. As the skeleton clock in the great salon chimed eight he would return to change for dinner which was at nine. His routine never varied and so Polly, lonely and bored, had after six months taken to exploring the city.

Her excursions had led to much tutting from her mother-in-law and her companion, Mademoiselle Marguerite, a thin, dried husk of a woman, a poor relation, embittered by her poverty and her permanent virginal state. She was dependent on Madame la Comtesse for everything in her life, and was, as most people were, terrified of her cousin, sounding like an echo as she agreed, wholeheartedly, with everything her *patronne* said. Michel had not been happy either but, having followed her at a distance a couple of times and finding that she was walking in the parks, visiting the Louvre, studying the churches just as she had said she was, had left her to her own devices and scuttled back to his temples of toilette.

She loved Paris. It had been a case of love at first sight. It did not matter to her what time of year it was. She adored the spring when the horse chestnut trees, bound round by iron railings like grand Edwardian ladies encased in whalebone stays, burst into improbable pink and white candles of blossom; when from the flower-sellers' baskets great clouds of mimosa spread across the pavements; when the young women with pretty hats on their heads sashayed up and down the boulevards like birds of different breeds, searching for their mates.

Much to Michel's distaste, she even liked the summer when the dust swirled through the plane trees, the heat soared from the pavements, and all of Paris left the city to the tourists and those who had to work. She resented having to leave for the Loire and the family château, beautiful, austere and sparsely furnished compared with the English country houses she was used to. It was not country as she knew, understood and loved it. There were no light-hearted picnics, no fishing, riding was a sedate promenade. Life in the country for this family was only an equally formal extension of their life in the city. No one in the vicinity was deemed suitable to entertain and so night after night there was only Michel, Madame la Comtesse, her companion and the ever present Père Jean, the family's confessor and spiritual advisor. The whole group never gave up on the pursuit of Polly's heathen soul and she knew that in the eyes of Michel's family her marriage was no marriage. The country bored the family to distraction. The atmosphere in the great château was leaden as they waited restlessly for the summer to pass and for autumn and release to the city.

Back in Paris she spent hours walking in the parks, absorbed in the beauty of the leaves in a last defiant, glorious, burst of colour before death claimed them. She took pleasure in the children playing with their hoops, scuffling for conkers, and wondered why, after all this time and suffering, she had not been blessed with one. She laughed at small hysterical lap dogs, normally so pompous and well behaved, who seemed beset with an autumnal madness as they chased the scudding leaves. Always the air was full of the smell of the roasting chestnuts. But perhaps, of all the seasons, she preferred the winter when fog swirled about the city, masking the beautiful buildings so that one moment you saw them, the next you didn't, as if the city was a flirtatious woman hiding her beauty with a greyish yellow chiffon scarf.

There was nothing about the city she disliked. She loved the smell of it, the bread, the coffee, the Gauloises, even the strange acrid smell of the *pissoir* – all combined to form a special smell that seemed to seep into her soul. She enjoyed the arrogance, the frequent rudeness of the Parisians, admired their confidence in their own importance for having been born in the one city, the one country, that mattered in the whole of the world.

For over a year she had been exploring Paris and one spring afternoon she had found the café. She knew the moment that she saw it that it was the one, the dull maroon paintwork, the M of the Maurice slightly lopsided, the large plane tree in the square with the rough round bench encircling it where the women sat and chatted, the proximity of the *charcuterie* with the lifesize wooden pig on the pavement outside, a pig with one eye closed in a saucy wink; the *pâtisserie* run by a huge woman with a red jolly face. He had described it all perfectly. It had to be his café. And when she entered and saw the patron with his large moustache and the scar over one eye and his hennaed wife with the large breasts, she was certain. This was Jonathan's café, the one in which he had spent long hours in winter as a poor student who could not afford to heat his attic. She sat here because he had sat here, the explanation was simple.

Jonathan. It was a rare day when she did not think about him and long for him. She must, over the past three years, have gone over and over in her mind the conversations they had had, the arguments, the endless discussions of politics and literature. She had learnt, too late, that he had been the love of her life and that her hurt pride had allowed him to leave her.

She worried about him constantly. He would have been in Spain at the start of the civil war. With his views and principles it was inevitable that he would have joined the other young men from England and America who flocked to Spain in their hundreds to fight for liberty against fascism. Daily she bought several newspapers, French, English and American, all so that she could follow the fighting in detail, fearful always that there would come a day when she would read his name as one of the young foreigners who had died in a cause that had moved them beyond consideration for country, for personal safety. Brave men, fine men, men not concerned with the turn of a cuff, the recipe for a pomade, the exact set of a suit . . .

In secret she had even begun to write about him and her feelings for him, that fleeting love, lovely in its innocence, destroyed by an unfaithful friend. Her fear for him, her melancholy thoughts, her loneliness, her pain had made her large brown eyes deep pools of sorrow, so at odds with the youthfulness of her face. The patron's wife would have liked to talk to her and to help her, but there was an air of isolation, of dignified reserve, which made approach on an intimate basis impossible.

Her French, after three years, was perfect. So she could sit for several hours, as she did now, listening with pleasure to the chatter about her. She particularly liked the talk of the writers as they argued about the latest book published, held forth on their own great opuses, discussed the problems of characterisation, plot, the use of their language.

She spent hours here, she knew, in the vague hope that one day the creaking door would open just one more time and he might enter. She knew he would not recognise her, not the smart painted doll she had become, she doubted if she would have the courage to speak to him, or even if she should. She just wanted to look at him again, to be in the same room if only for a moment, to breathe the same air . . .

She looked at the gold Cartier watch on her wrist. It was nearly six-thirty. Time to go home, time to change, time to look as perfect as possible for yet another interminable evening of rigid formality.

The old concierge at the outer gate of Michel's family home still did not speak to her, did not even acknowledge her as she let her in. But always she managed to imply the annoyance it caused her to interrupt her tasks in order to open the gate to someone as inferior as this foreigner who had dared to marry her master.

Polly could be quite happy roaming this city but as soon as the great wrought iron gate swung to behind her, her mood would helter-skelter into a constant mild depression. Even her step changed as she crossed the courtyard with its ancient cobbles, the large tubs of geraniums scenting the air, the great chestnut tree set in the middle, surrounded entirely by the paving stones so that it seemed a miracle it could grow so large. It was a courtyard that, had she glimpsed it as a stranger passing by, would have given her enormous pleasure. Instead it was the forecourt to her own personal prison.

She always let herself in silently and crept up the stone stairs which led to the first floor where all the main rooms were situated. She dreaded the high-pitched screech from the main salon which announced that her mother-in-law had heard her. She did not like to be alone with the old Countess, who frightened and demoralised her; she needed the buffer of Michel and other guests between them.

In the daytime her room was her refuge. Here she kept her books, her attempts at writing, her diary, her sewing. Here she spent many hours alone just thinking. Its long shuttered windows opened on to the street and she never tired of watching the comings and goings below.

At night-time this same room was a room of fear. Would he come tonight? The thought would ruin her dinner, would ruin all conversation, spoil any pleasure she might have found in the guests. The only blessing was that now, into the fourth year of their marriage, he did not want her as frequently. If she was lucky a whole week would go by without her husband demanding to abuse her body.

2

'Polly?' The harsh voice rang out and made her freeze where she stood on the stairs about to go up to her room. With a resigned expression Polly turned, descended the stairs and entered the salon.

Despite her loathing for it, she was the first to admit that this was a beautiful house in which to live. The great salon in particular was magnificent. The room stretched the whole width of the back of the house, overlooking gardens rather than the busy street as did her bedroom. Long windows looked on to a balcony and when open the fine white lawn curtains billowed in the breeze, making the room a cool place when the weather was hot. It was painted in grey, that special French colour more blue than grey. The mouldings were picked out in gold and white, as was the beading on the tall, double doors. The furniture was a priceless collection of Louis Quatorze, spindly, elegant, beautifully carved and gilded. Elegant, beautiful and, as she knew to her cost, uncomfortable. There was not one armchair or sofa in the whole house into which one could collapse and relax. The furniture here was made as if to ensure that one sat up, that one's back was straight, that guests did not sit long and overstay their welcome. Large vases of valuable Sèvres porcelain were permanently filled with flowers; Madame la Comtesse had a particular liking for large madonna lilies and tuberoses and the room was always heavily scented. In winter flowers were flown up from the South of France so that there was mimosa here long before it appeared on the streets. Despite the heavy scent of the flowers, before guests arrived Mademoiselle Marguerite's task was to burn, in a miniature brazier, small sachets of a musky perfume. The sickly laden atmosphere often made Polly sneeze.

'Madame?' she said politely as she entered the room.

'I want you to meet a great friend of mine, La Princesse de Galierre.'

Polly crossed the room to where a slim, attractive woman sat. Nicole de Galierre was fashionably dressed, her make-up perfect. She was, Polly estimated, in her forties, but she always found the guessing of French-women's ages so difficult. They were not like English women who, past a certain age, no longer bothered with make-up and fashion but seemed to settle into a dow-ager's uniform of scrubbed face and unfashionable com-fort. French women battled relentlessly against the onset of age, and never gave up the fight until death ended the struggle. The woman smiled at her charmingly and at the same time quickly looked her up and down, assessing her clothes, her shoes, who had made them and what they had cost. This did not offend Polly, she had become used to it; all French women did it to her, and each other. But it was a habit that her own upbringing would never allow her to copy even if she had had the inclination.

'Madame, at last we meet. I've heard so much about you,' she said as she took hold of Polly's hand. She spoke English with barely a trace of accent and Polly was pleased to hear her language spoken. Her mother-in-law also spoke perfect English but since Polly had entered the house had not been heard to utter one word of that language. She also stolidly refused to accept that Polly's French was good. Doubtless she was fully aware, but it amused her to speak always about her in front of her, voicing her criticisms openly as if Polly did not understand one word.

'Madame la Princesse,' she replied, puzzled as to why the woman should want to meet her and how she knew so much about her.

'I've been in England with my husband, at the Embassy. I met an old friend of yours and she asked me to look you up. Lady Copton.'

At hearing Juniper's name, Polly froze. 'Oh, really?' she said, injecting a tone of cool disinterest into her voice. Both older women, with senses honed over years of social experience, sensing her distress leant forward eagerly at what might transpire to be a morsel of gossip. 'I haven't seen her for years.'

'No, and it distresses her very much. She said she did not like to write but that perhaps you might honour her with a letter.'

Polly stood silent.

'And who is Lady Copton? I knew a Lady Copton once but I could not imagine her being desperate to meet Polly.' Madame la Comtesse, speaking in French, managed to imply her surprise that anybody should.

The Princess looked at Polly, but seeing that she was determined to remain silent, launched into an explanation. 'A very rich American heiress, she married Hortense Copton's eldest son. It's been a disaster.' She looked up slyly at Polly to see her reaction, Polly's face remained impassive. 'They are to divorce.'

'*Mon dieu!*' Polly's mother-in-law fanned herself with the small mother-of-pearl and feather fan she always held. 'Poor Hortense.'

'It has been *the* scandal. All of London talked of nothing else for months. It transpired that the noble lord was a victim of . . .' she paused, and certain that she had everyone's attention, lowering her voice, and arching her brows announced – '*le vice anglais.*'

'And she is divorcing him for that? Good gracious, then the whole of English society should be divorcing.' Madame la Comtesse shrieked with laughter, Marguerite's chuckle followed a split second later. Polly felt herself bridling. She had no idea what this '*vice*' was, obviously something unpleasant, but still she managed to contain herself.

'Well, of course, he is a gentleman, despite his habits and he has done the honourable thing and given her grounds of adultery. She had to leave London, of course. She went to her grandmother – there's bad blood in that family, you know, the grandmother eloped to America with one American and married another, a vulgar manufacturer. Her father, Lord Tregowan, killed himself.' The whole conversation had finally settled into French.

'The poor man, who could blame him, the shame of his daughter marrying . . . a manufacturer, you said?' The fan moved agitatedly. 'Appalling.'

'Mrs Wakefield is a charming woman.' Polly could not let such criticism of Alice pass. Her mother-in-law waved her hand at her with irritation for interrupting such an interesting flow of gossip.

'She's no longer called Wakefield, her new name is Whitaker. Did you not know, madame? She married an artist.'

'An artist! A manufacturer *and* an artist. The English never fail to amaze me.' Madame la Comtesse glanced at Polly, deliberately goading her.

'An artist!' said Mademoiselle.

'No, I did not know,' Polly said simply. It was strange that she did not. Her grandmother wrote to her, admittedly fairly spasmodically, and must have forgotten to mention it or else thought she knew. She wrote to her father but no doubt he assumed she would receive news from Juniper. She was glad that kind, gentle Alice had found happiness with Phillip. It would be happiness, Polly was certain. He had seemed the ideal man for Alice.

'The young Lady Copton came back to London about two months ago, behaving outrageously of course – drink, men. It would have been far more dignified, in my opinion, if she had stayed quietly in the country.'

Polly felt momentarily sorry for her old friend. But then she remembered Jonathan and closed her mind to pity.

'Worse still, she gave her son away.'

'Her son . . . !'

'Her son . . . !' Mademoiselle echoed.

'Juniper wouldn't do that,' Polly burst out.

'She did. To her brother-in-law.'

'Then she must have had a reason,' Polly said staunchly.

'Scandalous behaviour. Abnormal – everyone said so,' the Princess said with evident enjoyment.

'Then I hardly think she is a suitable person for you to know, Polly. I'm surprised you received her, my dear Nicole.'

'She is rich,' the Princess replied with all the pragmatism of the French.

Polly was often homesick but this news from London intensified her unhappiness so that she longed to be home, even longed to see Juniper, to learn the truth. She realised there was no point in asking Michel if she could return for a visit. He hated England, found it barbaric and lacking in style with dreadful weather and food. He would not let her go without him. Homesickness was something she had to learn to live with. Perhaps she would bury her pride and write.

She was alone in her room, the dinner had been long and formal as always, with three friends of her mother-in-law and two of Michel's. As always it included no friends of hers, but then that was not surprising for she did not have any. All the people she met were older than herself, and society here was too rigid for warm friendship to blossom. Their guests had known each other all their lives and in most cases were related; in turn the only houses she visited belonged to these same people so that, although she lived in a teeming city, Polly knew no one. In Paris there was only a small handful of people one was allowed to know.

She brushed her hair and studied her face in the mirror. She did not like what she saw, she never did – it did not look like her. She hated the make-up that Michel insisted she wore and had experts teach her to apply. She liked this moment of the day best of all, the time when she could remove it. She did not like her smart clothes either. It was Michel who accompanied her to the fashion houses, it was he who chose everything. He had impeccable taste, she knew. But sometimes she longed just to wear a simple blouse and skirt or, better still, her old jodhpurs. He had arranged lessons in deportment, and taught her to be proud of her height and not to slouch in an attempt to hide it. She was like a toy to him, she realised. He was proud of the smart woman he had created.

He puzzled her. Sometimes she even felt guilty about him. He was generous to a fault, she wanted for nothing. Her cupboards were full of expensive clothes and furs, he showered jewellery upon her, everything she wanted, except freedom. He loved her. She knew that now. He really had fallen in love with her that first night. She was exactly what he had been looking for, a simple, innocent girl whom he could mould exactly as he wanted. And he had done so, outwardly. The problem was that Polly remained the same inside. She did not want to be a fashion plate, she hated the rigidness of her life, the exaggerated politeness of Parisian society where everyone moved as though in an ornate minuet. His passion was genealogy – his own. She could take no interest in it, she found it absurd. He spent hours with Père Jean, closeted in his study, poring over documents and books, endlessly charting his relationship with this duke, that count, that royal house. His enormous pride in his descent from Charlemagne bemused her. And now he burrowed daily into her own family tree with equal enthusiasm.

She knew she had proved to be a great disappointment. Despite his mother's and Père Jean's constant assaults on her lack of faith, she resolutely refused to take instruction in the Church. She went to church, frequently, but that was because she loved the music, the panoply, the buildings. She could not bring herself to espouse the faith.

And, of course, she had not produced an heir. Every month she longed to find she was pregnant. It wasn't that she wanted a child particularly; it was just that she hoped, if she gave him a son, Michel might leave her alone at night. If she did not have to sleep with him, perhaps she could grow to love him too. Hers was a dismal failure that reverberated monthly through the ancient house. She knew how queens of old must have felt. How, she had no idea, but her mother-in-law mysteriously appeared to know that she was menstruating almost as soon as she found out herself. Then, to her embarrassment, it seemed as if the whole house knew, from the chef to the priest, to the hateful simpering Mademoiselle.

Polly blamed herself. In her innocence she was sure that a child could not be conceived without love. She did not love Michel and she hated what he did to her. His pleasure was to give her pain, his satisfaction came only when she cried. She had learnt early to cry quickly

She heard his footsteps. Her heart lurched as it always did and she dutifully climbed into the large and hated bed.

The Princess became a regular visitor and was soon quickly established as Madame la Comtesse's greatest friend and confidante. Polly was not sure when it began, but after a few months she was convinced that Michel had taken a mistress and she was fairly certain, from the occasional glance between them, that it was Princess Nicole.

She supposed she should have minded; in fact she was grateful. Each day, in that hour the French call 'blue' when husbands never appear in their own homes but visit others, she was certain Michel was in Nicole's bed. Now he only required her in the middle of the month, the time, he explained, she was most likely to conceive. It was a measure of freedom.

3

The air in the Café Maurice was thick with smoke and the foetid smell of damp and none-too-clean clothes. Polly had not meant to come today, it was unseasonably chill for April, and had been raining off and on all morning. It was an argument with her mother-in-law which had forced her out for a walk to what she regarded as her second home. A quarrel between them was a rarity, Polly had long ago decided it was simpler to ignore the woman and her constant jibes. But at lunch, her mother-in-law had questioned the courage of the English in the event of a war, which was too much even for Polly's equanimity. But the conversation had given her room for thought. The talk for the past year had been about war, of Hitler, of invasion. There were those who thought that it was imminent, and those sure that such madness would never occur again. The horror of fascism, just as Jonathan had predicted, was sweeping across Europe. Czechoslovakia had been invaded, Poland was threatened, Franco had won in Spain. If there was to be a war, where did she belong? If France fell, should she and her husband escape to England? Try as she might she could not imagine Michel fighting, or wanting to stay behind to do so. She loved France but if the worst happened she felt she wanted to be with her own people.

The door opened and the wind slipped cunningly in making the lamps swing and the residents curse and order whoever it was to shut the door quickly. But the door did not close and the muttering rose in a crescendo. It was a young man whose large rucksack, like a huge deformity on his back, had become wedged. The patron waddled to the rescue.

Even before the man had been sorted out, before the door was shut, Polly knew it was him. She closed her eyes, afraid to look, fearful she might be wrong. She heard his voice first, apologising profusely to the customers for causing them inconvenience. Then he was recognised by the regulars and fully welcomed. He looked what he was, a defeated warrior returned from Spain. As such, space was made for him, drinks were ordered, a hero's welcome was given him and she watched with pride.

It was Jonathan and it wasn't. He looked bigger, the fitness that war had thrust upon him had made his body firmer, the muscles larger. He had a beard and he looked older.

He looked across at her, no doubt feeling her intense gaze. She looked down at the glass on the table in front of her. She was nervous but she was certain he could not recognise her, not as she looked now. She had thought she would not speak to him, now she had to fight to stop her mouth forming his name.

'Polly? Is it you?'

He was standing over her, so close she had only to put out her hand to touch him again. It would have been so easy to lie, speak her perfect French, forgive him for mistaking her for that child from long ago.

'Jonathan,' she heard herself reply.

He tore his hat off his head, threw it in the air and, with a great yelp, jumped with joy. He grabbed her hand dragging her to her feet, and, in front of everyone, hugged her to him as if he would never let her go. She buried her face in his jacket and she could smell him, the smell she had never forgotten, tobacco and sweat, no hint of pomade. The customers cheered, the patron appeared with champagne.

'What on earth are you doing here? You're like a

dream.' He was finally sitting down opposite her, grinning from ear to ear.

'Waiting for you, I suppose. I come here often and think about you.'

'Oh, Polly,' he put his hand out across the stained marble-topped table and took hold of hers. 'Oh, my darling Polly, you'll never know how often I've thought of you, dreamt of you, longed for you.'

Abruptly she removed her hand from his. 'It's too late, Jonathan. I'm married.' She looked away, afraid she might begin to cry.

He touched her face, gently forcing her to look at him.

'But not happily?'

'No.' It was a whisper more than a word.

'Do you love him?'

'No.'

'Did you ever?'

'No.'

'Then why?'

She could not look at him. 'Because . . .' but she could not finish.

'Because of me and what I did? Or am I being dreadfully arrogant?'

She still could not speak but looked at him, and in her eyes he saw the pain of those years ago.

'My poor Polly. Why was I such a coward? Why didn't I have the guts to face you and tell you instead of writing that pathetic letter? God, how weak I was, how stupid. It meant nothing, my darling. I got drunk, stupidly drunk and after weeks of longing for your body, it was just so easy for me to take that other woman's. I hated myself. I knew immediately what I had done. But I loved you so much, I couldn't lie to you, couldn't begin a life with you with a lie between us. I ran away. Now we both have to live with my weakness.'

'My pride too. That got in the way. If I knew what I

know now, I'd have forgiven you, I'd even have forgiven Juniper.'

'You know? Who told you? Do you see her?'

'No, not since the day I got married, that's when she told me. I lost you both.'

'Juniper would miss you far more than you her. She needed you, a friend she could trust. She's a butterfly, the way she plays with life, with men, with others' emotions. It meant absolutely nothing to her, too, you realise. She was miserable that afternoon, she wanted Hal, so she chose me.'

'She's getting divorced.'

'From Hal? Why?'

'Do you know what *le vice anglais* is?'

'Yes.'

'He's got it.'

For the first time since his arrival he laughed. 'He's got what, Polly?' he spluttered.

'That, whatever it is. Can't you tell me what it is?'

'It means he prefers men to women.'

'I still don't understand, prefers them for what?'

'My dear, innocent married lady . . .' And to her wide-eyed astonishment he explained.

'Poor Juniper. She loved Hal. Imagine how humiliated she must feel,' Polly said quietly.

Jonathan was silent for a moment. Suddenly he said, 'Come back to London with me, Polly. I need you. I've never stopped wanting you . . .'

'Please, Jonathan, it's not possible.'

'Then tell me why you look so unhappy, why there is such pain in your eyes?'

But she could not tell him, for all she knew all men were like Michel. She might still be in love with Jonathan but, if she committed the sin of going to bed with him, there was just as much chance that he too would hurt her as Michel had done. She told him she did not wish to speak about herself, she wanted to know what had happened to him.

She wanted to know about Spain. She listened with horror to his story, she longed to hold him, to make the pain of memory go away.

She looked at her watch. It was nine.

'My God, the time. I'll be in such trouble.'

'Come here tomorrow, promise . . .' he begged as he helped her on with her coat.

'I'll try.'

They had nearly a month together before his money ran out and he told her he had to return to England. She had her allowance from Gertie which she begged him to take but he refused. In any case, he explained, with the worsening situation in Europe it was his duty to return to be prepared to fight. He had experience which would be valuable. She cried out at this; surely he had suffered enough in Spain. Let others go, not him. He begged her again to come with him, to desert her life of unhappiness for one of happiness with him. Somehow they would survive, somehow they would sort out the problem of her marriage. He argued that since there had been no religious ceremony, she had made no vows.

'I made a promise,' she said bleakly.

'I'll be back, I'll keep coming back until you agree to leave him and come with me.'

It had been a magical month and Polly knew she would remember every single second of it. He had allowed her to read the book that he had finally written. In reading it she learnt to know him better, to love him more. Often they had come close to consummating their love, but each time her fear drew her back from the brink.

The day he left, she cried until she felt there were no more tears left in her.

The day he left, she left Michel. She was surprised by the suddenness of her decision. She had returned from the station after watching Jonathan's train depart. She had flung herself on her bed and wept. And when there were no more tears she found she had decided there was no point in her staying. She was unhappy, she had known she was. But the weeks with Jonathan had proved to her the depth of that unhappiness. She was twenty-one and she did not wish, doubted if she could endure, to be as sad as this for the rest of her life.

She did not tell Michel. She left a note wishing him well with the Princess, packed a small bag and left the expensive clothes and the jewellery.

She could have caught the next train and followed Jonathan. Her pride would not let her. She had to allow him to be free. If he came back for her it would not be out of pity or guilt. If she followed him, he would have no choice.

She found a small room in a pension close to the Café Maurice since that was an area she now knew well. But she stopped going to the café. If she kept going then, if he did not return, she would know. By not going she could always pretend he had come and they had missed each other. Dreams were kinder than reality, she thought.

She found herself a job in a bookshop for she was aware that the allowance from her grandmother might stop. Once Gertie, with her strong principles, discovered the truth, she might be angry.

The day she left she also acquired a cat. She had found him in the gutter outside the pension. A small, half-starved and frightened cat. He no longer had the energy to plead with her to take him in but just looked at her with a sad and beaten expression. He was not even a beautiful cat but one whose fur was mismarked so that he looked as if a painter had wiped his brushes on his coat – a mixture of black, brown, white and ginger. She scooped him up and took him to her room and called him Hurstwood after the home she longed for.

In her tiny room in the eaves of the pension, the rooftops of Paris stretched out beneath her, with her cat, her job and her books, Polly found at last a degree of happiness.

4

Juniper had given up society. It had happened quite suddenly. Not because of censorious glances which were cast her way, nor the whispering that followed her, nor being cut dead by some, for Juniper did not care one iota what people thought of her. No, one day she had looked at her life, the repetition of each summer, the same people, food, drink, music, conversation and had decided there must be more of interest – somewhere. So she was never seen at the Embassy, the Savoy or the Coconut Grove as in the old days. She had decided on two things. One was that she wanted to educate herself. Her governesses had had an uphill task with her education. Her time at Miss Lambert's school had been too short. Now she set to with typical enthusiasm to repair the lack of it. She spent a whole morning in consultation with the manager of Hatchards bookshop and ordered a trunkload of books on subjects from Greek civilisation to modern art, with a hefty pile of literature and poetry.

Secondly, she had decided to eliminate her immediate past. Anything that had to do with Hal, or reminded her of him, was to be removed. Consequently the large house in Belgrave Square was put on the market together with its contents. All the staff were given notice with large cash settlements and glowing references. Even the cars had to be changed. She toyed with the idea of reverting to her maiden name but then decided she liked being a Lady and having people bowing and scraping to her – it fuelled her sense of the ridiculous. She had dual nationality and, since her American passport was in the name of Boscar, she could flit from one persona to the other as it suited her.

The day she left Belgrave Square she felt a great sense of

relief. Since Hal had moved out she had found herself night after night returning to her house with a crowd of people, most of whom she barely knew, whose friendship bordered on sycophancy and whom she finally rejected.

She had found a large imposing Victorian house with a plethora of turrets overlooking Hampstead Heath, complete with ballroom and panelled library. But what had attracted her to it were the vast grounds, full of trees and bushes overgrown from neglect which, with the adjacent heath, made her feel that she was in the countryside. She immediately filled it with a collection of motley dogs – four borzois who regarded themselves as very superior dogs, three snuffling pugs and two mongrels of indeterminate ancestry. She filled the conservatory with exotic birds, the pond in the garden with golden carp. Six peacocks noisily patrolled the grounds thus ruining any chance of her forming friendships with her neighbours, and she was awaiting the arrival of two Persian cats. She rapidly settled in with her books and animals. This turn of events had come as a great relief to Alice. The beginning of the season had been a time of great worry to her. It seemed that her granddaughter had lost her reason. She had appeared with a different man on her arm each evening, and frequently not the most suitable of men at that. She had stayed up all night and slept most of the day. She had rarely eaten, drank far too much, and was seldom seen without a cigarette in a long black ebony holder. She appeared bent on shocking people and Alice had had a difficult time following in her wake attempting to salve offended feelings. Her only worry now was that this phase would not last. Juniper, she had decided, had very short-lived enthusiasms.

Alice was in London because Phillip, as a Fellow of the Royal Academy, had several works in the Summer Exhibition. He also had several commissions to execute. He had never enjoyed being a fashionable society painter and would have liked to concentrate on the landscapes he was now doing. But society women paid more handsomely for his skills and, determined never to rely on one penny from Alice, he needed the annual injections of money into his coffers.

In the past Alice had not enjoyed London, but with Phillip she did. With him, she had found a society where people were allowed to be themselves without playing social games. Women were listened to as individuals whose opinions mattered. Unknown to Phillip, this year Alice had herself submitted, under a *nom de plume*, a small oil painting, which had been accepted. Life for Alice was perfect. Late in life she had found total contentment. She was in love and loved, but best of all she had found the ideal companion. Daily, at Gwenfer, they would stand side by side at their easels and paint. Her small talent, under Phillip's tutelage, was blossoming.

Marshall hated summer for it reminded him even more of Grace. And he was ill. Boscar was full of people, men like himself, disillusioned, wounded or fleeing from life, all intent on finding themselves, on understanding the meaning of everything. So intent were they in their searches and their pursuit of their own salvation that none had the time or inclination to see that Marshall was losing his own salvation and with it his sanity. It was something he was aware of but chose to do nothing about, he did not seek advice, treatment or comfort, for he no longer had any interest in himself or what was to come.

It was a rare night now that the dreams did not come, but just recently matters had got worse. He had become the man in the shell hole, it was his head which was half missing, the physical agony was his, it was he who screamed '*Rosemary*', and sometimes he screamed '*Grace*'.

And then, last week, the dream had come in the daytime as he worked in the vegetable garden. He had stood in the sun, on his ancestors' land surrounded by the trees he had known since childhood, by the same sounds he had always known, but he was back on the Somme and everywhere he looked men were being blasted into little pieces. Shells were falling, guns were rattling and men were cursing, begging, pleading. And he was one of them, screaming for *Rosemary*, screaming for *Grace* until he collapsed and as he fell he prayed he was dying.

But he didn't. He regained consciousness, and he was back at Boscar in the garden, the hoe still in his hand.

The next time it happened he was crossing the great hall, the third he was motoring up the drive after a trip to Bodmin. He had woken up in a ditch, the car on top of him. Now he was afraid to sleep, but equally he was afraid to be awake. He felt like an animal in a trap from which there was no escape. Except that there was . . .

He was found, late at night, his service revolver at his side, half his head blown away and his mouth open as if screaming his way into eternity.

At one o'clock in the morning Alice received the news by telephone. She and Phillip hurriedly dressed and took a taxi to Hampstead. Alice was nervous, she did not like to arrive at Juniper's house unannounced, afraid of what she might find. There was a wildness in her granddaughter which Alice preferred not to dwell upon for fear of what she might discover.

She need not have worried. Juniper was alone having spent the evening engrossed in Thackeray and it was she who answered the door, her maid having long since gone to bed. She peered around it anxiously, her face devoid of make-up and looking like a little girl's instead of that of a woman of twenty-one. The moment she saw her grandmother her eyes registered fear. What was the bad news? Why else should she and Phillip be here at this time of night?

'What's wrong?' she asked immediately.

'Can we come in first, Juniper?' Phillip pushed the door further open for Alice to enter.

'Something must be dreadfully wrong, what is it?' she asked, backing in front of them into the drawing room where her collection of dogs rose up in welcome. It took several minutes to calm them all and get them seated during which Phillip crossed to the drinks tray and poured them all large brandies.

'Juniper, I'm sorry, it's your father,' Alice said, taking hold of her hand. She thought it best to get straight to the point.

'Is he ill?'

'No, darling, I'm sorry. He's dead.'

'Don't say that . . . how can you . . .' Juniper backed away from Alice. She put her hands up in front of her as if warding the words away.

'Have this drink, Juniper, it will help you,' Phillip held the glass out to her. With one wide swipe of her hand Juniper knocked the glass out of Phillip's hand. It bounced across the floor and the pugs slithered under the piano.

'I don't want a drink. I don't want to hear all this. Go away,' she was shouting.

'Juniper, please. We can't leave you alone, upset like this. We have to stay, you must understand.'

'No.'

'We've come to collect you and we'll all go together to Boscar. You need not travel alone,' Phillip said as kindly as he could.

'No!' she screamed.

'We must go, Juniper, there are things to do.' Alice's hand fluttered about her neck searching for the pearls which, in her haste, she had not put on.

'You go, I don't want to go, I never want to see the place ever again. I hate it . . .'

'But the funeral . . .'

'I won't go to any funeral, you can't make me. I can't go, not again.'

Alice looked helplessly across the room at Phillip. He shook his head as perplexed as Alice. Alice sat down.

Phillip picked up the glass. The pugs came out from under the piano. Juniper was studying herself in the mirror; suddenly she swung round.

'I've treated him badly, Grandmother. I stopped his money, you know. I tried to hate him, you see. Oh, why do we do such things? Then it's too late to say sorry.' She slumped down on to the foot stool, speaking calmly now but looking immeasurably sad. 'I always meant to see him again, one day . . .'

'I know, my love. I'm sorry things were as they were but you must not blame yourself, you had too much to comprehend for one so young.'

'I do blame myself and I always will. Was he ill for long? Was he ill and alone?'

Again Alice looked anxiously at her husband. She looked back at Juniper, her mind racing, weighing up the pros and cons of telling her. She would have to know eventually. Perhaps it would be best to get it over and done with all at the same time.

'I'm sorry, Juniper. He shot himself.'

'No!' The one short word was a long wail. 'No,' she repeated and again and again. It was not a word, it was a cry of pain. The dogs retreated.

Alice knelt beside her on the floor and put her arms about her.

'What hope is there for me, answer me that? Both my great-grandparents, both my parents – how long before it's me, before I kill myself?' she sobbed.

'Oh, Juniper don't talk in such a way. You wouldn't do anything like that, I know you. Our family has known great misfortune, but it's not an illness that passes from generation to generation, I'm sure.' Alice stroked Juniper's hair. 'Now, get your coat, we'll use your big car and motor through the night. Wake your maid and get her to pack your bag for you.'

'Oh, no, I'm not going. I can't see him. I've got to forget him.' She jumped abruptly to her feet. 'You go, you sort everything out, you bury him for me.' And covering her face with her hands she ran from the room, out of the door and into her car. Alice and Phillip sat helplessly as they heard the car roar out of the drive.

She went straight to the Embassy Club. The last person she expected to see there was Jonathan, looking uncomfortably out of place with a noisy group of young blades about town. He looked relieved to see her, she was amused to note. He got up and came across to her table. But once there he seemed at a loss for words.

'Jonathan, how wonderful to see you, for God's sake, don't just stand there, get me a drink.' She flopped on to one of the settees, clicked open her handbag and with shaking fingers lit a cigarette.

'Champagne?' he asked, his mind sinking at the thought of the expense.

'No, brandy. A large one, and then another.'

'Are you all right, Juniper? You look dreadfully pale.'

'I've just had some beastly news, nothing important,' she shook her head as if shaking the thoughts away. She could not face what had happened – perhaps she never would. Jonathan signalled to a waiter.

'I've got some bad news too. Maybe it ought to wait.'

'What? Tell me, I insist.'

'It's Polly.'

'You've seen Polly? Where is she? I must see her.' She jumped to her feet.

'You can sit down again, Juniper.' He smiled at her enthusiasm. 'She's in Paris. I saw her on my return from Spain. She's desperately unhappy, though. She admitted as much to me but I couldn't get any details out of her. She had a heartbreaking look in her eyes, Juniper – almost like a young animal that's been maltreated. Do you know what I mean? It may sound melodramatic, but that look sent shivers down my spine. Perhaps she'd tell you though . . .'

'I doubt if she's forgiven me.'

'Polly could never hate anyone for long. She was concerned about you and Hal.'

Juniper picked up her bag, drank her large brandy in one swig. 'Come on then,' she said, eager to be on the move and not to have to think.

'Where?'

'Paris, of course, you fool. If we leave now we can go to Croydon and catch the first flight in the morning.'

'But we've no clothes with us.'

'Don't be so prosaic, Jonathan. We can buy them there.'

'But . . .' he looked away embarrassed.

'What's the matter?'

'I'm sorry, Juniper, I can't come. That's why I haven't gone back to her. I can't afford the fare.'

'Don't be silly. I'll pay. Come on, let's go and find dear, darling Polly.'

5

Polly was in the bookshop window, on all fours. The owner, Claude Fabris, was getting rather arthritic these days and was glad to have a young assistant able to crawl about the display window for him, dusting the books, arranging the new publications. There wasn't a day went by that Polly did not thank her lucky stars for leading her to the shop. Claude was a kind and considerate boss, only too happy to teach her all he knew about the business, and Polly was hungry to learn. Already, in her mind, was sown the idea that this was what she liked to do most, that one day she would have a shop of her own.

Above the shop was his flat where Chantal, his wife, cooked and cleaned all day with no interest in books whatsoever. Polly was thus a joy to him with her love of books and reading, and her insatiable curiosity. She loved the feel of the new books, and her greatest delight was to take the large sharp silver paper-knife and slit the uncut pages and smell the scent of the clean paper, the printer's ink.

After a week in the shop she had been invited to take lunch with them and this had now become a daily occurrence. Chantal had a passion for cooking and, for the first time, Polly was introduced to the delicious pleasures of French provincial cuisine rather than the elaborate, complicated dishes that had been normal at Michel's house. Chantal was from Normandy and so her liberal use of butter and cream made certain that Polly soon put on a little weight. It was just as well she had left her elegant and expensive wardrobe behind, she thought. She felt more like her old self. The razor-slim person she used to be had been an artificial creation. Her appetite pleased Chantal who glowed with pride as Polly's figure rounded out. Not caring what she ate underlined her determination never to go back to her life with Michel.

A large, white, open touring motor car glided slowly past the shop. She called out and she raised her hand to bang on the glass in welcome as she saw Jonathan, in full evening dress, at the wheel. As quickly she lowered her hand, bent her head and slithered from the window – beside Jonathan in the open car, her head thrown back in laughter, looking more beautiful than ever, was Juniper.

Polly had known many bleak moments in her young life but none was as bleak as that instant when she realised he was not alone. That she should have been deceived a second time into thinking him kind and sensitive, into loving him, was too much. How could he come back with Juniper, just as if he were gloating, as if he were punishing her?

She sidled into the back of the shop and peered around one of the bookcases to see out of the side window. The car had stopped further along the street at the opening into the square. She hurriedly took the money from a customer, her heart thumping as she did so in case they should already know where she worked and were, this very moment, walking back to the shop. She scuttled into the back room where Claude was patiently sorting through a box of secondhand books he had just purchased.

'Monsieur, please don't ask me to explain but if two English people should come into the shop asking for me, would you please say you never saw me?'

'That would be difficult, madame,' he said, smiling over his dust-laden spectacles.

'I have to leave . . .'

'You are unwell?'

'No, I mean I must go from here, from this district. And forgive me, I shouldn't ask you to lie, just say I left your employ, you need not say when.'

'Madame, is there something I can do? These people, why should you run from them?' His voice was brimming with concern.

Polly was hurriedly pushing her arms into her linen jacket. 'Monsieur, I can't explain, not now. I'll write, I promise. Please give my apologies to madame . . .' she looked over her shoulder with an expression of panic at the street.

'Madame, I can't let you leave in such distress.'

'Don't stop me, please. I will explain but not now.' And she grabbed her bag, let herself out of the back of the shop and raced through the labyrinth of alleyways to her room.

She owned so little that within the hour her bag was packed, her cat was in a box with holes cut in the top, her geranium in its pot was in a brown paper bag, her books were tied into two bundles with string. She paid her astonished landlady what she owed, ordered a taxi and was on her way out of the district.

It took only another hour to find a room in a pension and to settle her things. She sat on the edge of the bed in her new room and watched the cat exploring his new surroundings. Why had she bolted like that? What had made her panic so? Was she afraid she would make a scene, would she have burst into tears? She wasn't sure, she just knew it was the best thing to do, she knew that she could never see them together. The pain would be too much to endure, it would make her hate them and she didn't want to hate.

'This is a bizarre café, Jonathan.' Juniper looked around her, incongruously dressed in her silk lamé dress of the night before.

'The best in Paris, Juniper. Poor souls like you, with too much money, never know the joys of simple living. I tell you, the cassoulet in this café is the best in France.'

'I've never had cassoulet.'

'You see, you've never lived,' he said with a laugh.

'Now what do we do?' she asked after the patron had served their drinks.

'We wait. Polly will come. She always came in the afternoon, when her husband was visiting his mistress, to sit here, hoping I'd come. And then, one day, I did.'

'It's so deliciously romantic. Did she mind her husband having a lover?'

'No, that's the odd thing. She didn't. I got the impression she was relieved.'

'Ah . . .' said Juniper and sipped her pernod.

By five o'clock Jonathan was agitated, by six he was depressed.

'Maybe she'll come tomorrow,' Juniper said helpfully.

'I've only got today and tomorrow, I have to be back in London on Friday. I join my regiment then.'

'I could always wait for her, if you like. I've nothing else to do . . .' Juniper looked across the square as she spoke and bit her lip hard, then turned her face and smiled. 'I should like to help, it will make amends for all the trouble I've caused you two in the past.'

Finally he did what he should have done the moment they arrived had he not been so convinced that Polly would come – he asked the patron if he had seen Polly. He was devastated to be told the last time she had been here was with him. He was about to turn away, unsure what to do, when the patron told him that she worked in a shop fifty yards down the road and lived in the Pension Phillibert close by. Jonathan gave the portly man an enormous hug and with Juniper in tow raced out of the café. They reached the shop just as Claude was putting up the shutters. His elation turned again to disappointment to be told she had left his employ. But armed with directions to the pension his spirits rose again as he dragged Juniper after him, complaining about her long skirt and her high heels on the uneven pavement.

'I don't believe it! Where has she gone and why?' He was sitting on the steps of the pension, his head in his hands. Juniper stood watching him, swinging her handbag and unsure what to say.

'Maybe she saw us. Or rather she saw me with you and jumped to the wrong conclusion. You could hardly blame her, could you?'

'Would it help to go and see her bastard of a husband? I know where they live.'

'He's probably in the country, you know the French all rush from the city like lemmings when summer comes.'

'It's only June.'

'Maybe he doesn't like June. No, he won't know anything. She's unlikely to let him, of all people, know where she is – he'd probably make scenes and try to get her back. We're just going to have to look for her, we'll find a detective in the morning. Come on, let's find the Ritz and book in.'

'Juniper I can't, and don't say you'll pay, I can't let you. You take the car and go there. I'll get a room at the Café Maurice.'

'Then I shall come with you. You can't be left alone.'

By midnight, after what Juniper acknowledged as one of the best meals she had ever eaten, they were sitting in the café with their third bottle of wine. Jonathan had done most of the talking and, suddenly aware that he had been monopolising the conversation, he apologised.

'You needed to,' she laughed.

'You're really a very kind woman, Juniper.'

'Not many people think that.' She snorted and stared moodily into her glass.

'How's your grandmother?' Jonathan asked, for something to say.

'She's remarried, a very nice man. You know, Phillip Whitaker, the artist.'

'Did she bring you up? Did your parents die?' he asked, realising that, even though he counted her a friend, even though they had shared a bed, he knew next to nothing about her beyond the strong willed, slightly wild, social façade.

'Yes,' she looked away from him, tears filling her eyes. He put his hand out to her; she had not turned away in time.

'What's the matter, Juniper, why are you crying? What have I said?'

'I'm not crying,' she protested, fighting back the longing to cry. 'It's nothing you said.' She took a deep breath looking wildly about her. 'It's my father, he died yesterday.' She had said the words, now it was real.

'My God, Juniper, I am sorry. But what are you doing here? Why aren't you with your grandmother?'

'I didn't want to be there. I was glad of the excuse to come here with you. I haven't seen him for years, he's almost a stranger.' Her voice as she spoke did not sound like her, it was tight and hard, the voice of someone who was having difficulty in controlling it, Jonathan thought. 'The last time I saw him was the day I married. I didn't want to see him and yet, now . . . I wish to God I had.'

'Juniper, you must go home, you must be there when they bury him.'

'I can't. I'm too confused. I don't think I'm brave enough to face that.'

'Yes, you are. You've the courage of a lion.' He held her hand tightly. 'For your own sake you must say farewell to him properly.'

'Do you think so?' She looked up at him and in her eyes he saw the same look of bleak despair he had seen in Polly's. He wished he could take her in his arms and comfort her, and then chided himself for even thinking of it.

'I do, Juniper. I've seen a lot of death in the past few years. Those who managed best were those who allowed themselves to grieve.'

'You see, Jonathan, all day I've been obsessed with one thought: what if I died and because of what I've done my son Harry refused to come to my funeral?'

'All the more reason for you to be there. Honestly, Juniper, if you don't you'll be haunted by this for life.'

'What about Polly? We can't just leave her.'

'I've been thinking about that. We need help to find her. The police won't take any notice of us, they won't look for her just for a couple of friends. I think we should tell her father and grandmother. The authorities might act for them.'

'You're right. Come on.' She had jumped to her feet.

'Where are you going?'

'To catch the plane.'

'Don't be silly, Juniper. There won't be one till the morning. It's just past midnight. We'll be better off getting a good night's sleep. In any case I think we should telephone about the availability of tickets. What if we get all the way out to the airport and there are no seats left?'

'Then we hire our own little aeroplane, of course.'

'So money solves everything?'

'To tell you the truth, Jonathan, money is a mixed blessing,' she said sagely, and seeing her sway on her feet he led her to her room. He returned for a nightcap with the patron and then made his way to his own room.

6

They arrived at the aerodrome with less than ten minutes to spare to board the London flight. They nearly missed it when Juniper disappeared to make a telephone call. Jonathan paced up and down becoming more and more agitated. It took all his charm and a lot of fast talking to delay the departure for a few minutes until they saw Juniper hurtling out of the waiting room. Jonathan was rather short with her as he bundled her aboard the aircraft. She was very quiet; she did not say whom she had called and he did not like to ask. He was relieved that she seemed not to want to talk since he suddenly felt so tired that he could have slept on the wing let alone in the cramped, cold and noisy aeroplane. Throughout the bumpy flight Juniper sat silent, staring out of the small window, apparently not even noticing the silver water of the Channel beneath them.

Juniper's plan to buy clothes in Paris had not materialised and so they were now very dishevelled, their evening clothes looking crumpled and incongruous, and they both longed for leisurely baths. In London they went their separate ways – Jonathan to his small flat in Chelsea and Juniper to her mansion. They arranged for Jonathan to come to Juniper's house as soon as possible and that she, meantime, would telephone Gertie Frobisher to arrange a meeting.

When Jonathan arrived, an appointment had been made. Unfortunately Gertie was at her estate in Berkshire, not London as they had hoped, so they ate a light lunch before setting off in Juniper's Lagonda.

Gertie was waiting for them in the drawing room. Since receiving Juniper's telephone call, Gertie had spent an uncomfortable few hours wondering why on earth the girl had invited herself to tea. Unless, perhaps, she wanted to talk about her father. Many chose Gertie as a confidante, but then, if that was the case, why was she bringing the young man, Jonathan, with her? She could think of no other reason why they should travel out from London. It left Gertie with a distinct feeling of foreboding which her logical mind told her was ridiculous. Not even the cross-word puzzle in *The Times*, which normally made all irritating worries disappear, helped. In fact, she could only complete half of it, an unheard-of event.

She rose quickly to her feet the moment the young couple entered the room and, putting her stupid notions to the back of her mind, Gertie swept towards them, her hands outstretched in ebullient greeting.

'My dear Juniper, I was so sorry to hear about poor Marshall. Such a sad business, Alice told me.'

'Yes.' Juniper hung her head, unable to meet Gertie's eye, knowing full well that her grandmother would undoubtedly have told Gertie of her behaviour upon receiving the news of Marshall's death.

'Of course you are going to the funeral.' It was not a question but a statement and, if any doubts remained in Juniper's mind, the matter-of-fact presumption by Gertie dispelled them immediately.

'Yes, Lady Gertie. I behaved badly. It was the shock, I suppose.'

'That's what I told Alice. What could she expect, turning up in the small hours with dreadful news such as that? Of course it was shock. I knew you would come to your senses and behave properly eventually. And Mr Middlebank, so pleasant to meet you again.'

'Lady Gertie,' he too bowed his head in embarrassment, unsure how much this indomitable woman knew about himself and Polly.

'This is a pleasant surprise, Juniper. It's months since I last saw you, what have you been doing?'

'Getting divorced, Lady Gertie,' Juniper said flippantly, much to Jonathan's surprise.

'I was sorry to hear about that, my dear. Such a tragedy. The man should be horsewhipped. I don't mind him being a catamite, these things happen, but he should never have married you. Too inconsiderate of him. Society will be cruel to you, you realise? They will ostracise you but you should ignore them. At times like this society can be unspeakably stupid. It's a ridiculous notion that a gal should have to live in misery for life. I'm sure the good Lord will forgive you, undoubtedly he was unaware of your husband's proclivities when he heard your vows. Indian or China?'

'China, please,' they spoke in unison. For a few minutes they were all involved in handing each other plates and napkins and helping themselves to cucumber sandwiches. Then Juniper looked at Jonathan and realised he was as nervous as she was herself. To come here had seemed the right and only thing to do but now, in Gertie's formidable presence, they both feared that she might resent interference in her family's affairs. Since it appeared that Jonathan was not going to speak first but instead was busily helping himself to another pile of cucumber sandwiches and had begun to speak of the weather as if this was just a social visit, Juniper took a deep breath and . . .

'Lady Gertie, Jonathan and I are worried. We were not sure what to do so we decided to come and speak to you.'

'If I can be of help.' Gertie beamed with approval.

'It's Polly.'

'Polly, my Polly?' There was an edge to her voice – her strange feeling of premonition was coming true, but still she sat regally still.

'Yes. Jonathan saw her in Paris and there's something very wrong with her, she's not like Polly, he says, but dreadfully unhappy. And now she's disappeared, and we thought you would be in a better position than us to find her. We didn't think the authorities would take any notice of us. Jonathan knows more about it than I do, I haven't seen her,' Juniper finished in a rush.

Gertie moved her upright figure slowly round until she was facing Jonathan and waited for him to speak. The only indication of her irritation at his slowness to explain was the slight drumming of her fingers on the arm of her chair.

'I don't know exactly what to say. She admitted she was unhappy but she would not tell me why. You see, Lady Gertrude, this might sound stupid to you, but I sensed more than she told. I fear for her, her sadness is very deep, it's in her eyes . . .' He looked at the floor, aware that his voice was shaking at the memory of Polly's face and his inability to help her.

Gertie put out her hand and gently touched his arm. 'Young man, I don't think what you say is stupid. I would expect someone as sensitive as you to have an intuitive feel about things.'

Jonathan looked at her with gratitude. He coughed and continued. 'When I last saw her, about six weeks ago, she was still living with her husband. But she has now left him and has been working in a bookshop. She was no longer at the address we were given.'

It would seem impossible that Gertie could sit more upright but she did as she absorbed this information.

'He's a sadist, Lady Gertie. He is beastly cruel to her. Everyone knows it,' Juniper suddenly burst out.

Jonathan jumped to his feet, his plate clattering on to the carpet. 'A sadist? How do you know that? You didn't tell me,' he demanded. 'I'll kill him. I'll go back . . .' He was stalking up and down the carpet, avoiding the sandwiches.

'Killing Michel will not help Polly, Jonathan. Now sit down, pull yourself together and listen,' Gertie ordered and Jonathan slumped back on to his chair. Silent and shamefaced like a little boy he bent down and picked up the sandwiches.

'I telephoned a friend of mine, from the aerodrome, don't know why I didn't have the sense to do it while we were still in the city. She's French, she knows everyone in Paris including Michel and his family. She told me. Everyone in Parisian circles knows what he's like.'

'That could be merely gossip, Juniper,' Gertie said, sagely.

'I don't think so, Lady Gertie. You see, before he married he had a mistress who was not very discreet and she told various people what he was like. She enjoyed what he did, you see.' Juniper looked away embarrassed to be speaking of such matters in front of someone of Gertie's age.

'This is dreadful,' Gertie announced. 'This comes of marrying a foreigner, of course. I tried to warn her, they're not as we are, you know. I've heard of all manner of perversions in my time.'

'No, I mean yes, Lady Gertie,' Juniper could not help but smile. Gertie had forgotten completely that she too was a foreigner. But somehow it seemed strange and wrong for her grandmother's best friend to know about such matters.

'Well, something has got to be done about this. I shall go to France, find her, and bring her home if necessary – if that's what she wants. Personally I've never regarded it as a proper wedding, a register office, how can it be? Some cake?'

Jonathan and Juniper relaxed with relief. 'Tell me, Juniper, are you motoring to Boscar?'

'Yes, Jonathan is catching the train back to London, he joins his regiment tomorrow. I'm going straight on to Cornwall.'

'Then would you allow me to accompany you as far as Hurstwood, if that's not too far out of your way? You could stay the night, I'm sure.'

'It would be a pleasure, Lady Gertie,' Juniper answered politely, hoping she did not sound as shocked as she felt.

What if Francine were there? How could she possibly sleep under the same roof with her? With Francine moving in theatrical circles they rarely ran into each other.

'How long will it take us, I assume you drive like the wind?'

'She drives like a demon, Lady Gertrude, I should warn you.'

'Good, I enjoy speed and excitement.'

'Between four and five hours.'

'It's four o'clock, if we leave in half an hour then we shall be there in time for dinner. I shall go and instruct my maid to pack my bag. I can't begin to tell you both how grateful I am that you came to confide in me. If you will forgive me, Mr Middlebank?' And she swept from the room.

'It'll be all right now, Jonathan. There's nothing and no one that Gertie can't sort out, I'm sure even Genghis Khan would have been afraid of her.' She crossed the room and kissed him lightly on the cheek. To his shame he found he would have liked to kiss her on the mouth.

Richard was perplexed and a little annoyed. He did not like surprises and it would seem that was what the young were up to. At teatime he had received a telephone call from a Jonathan Middlebank, the name rang a bell but for the life of him he could not remember who he was. The man had been very unhelpful, giving him no hint of who he was, and Richard was far too polite to ask. To his astonishment the young man told him that Juniper was on her way with another guest and could they dine and could they stay the night? He had never expected to see Juniper in his house again and wondered why she was coming, he felt it must be something of importance to bring her back. But what? He could not say he was sorry she was coming. The last time he had seen her was at Polly's sad little wedding where she had been slightly drunk and, if possible, even more beautiful. He had often thought of the night she had crawled into his bed and still, after all this time, felt a secret regret that his wife had been there. As to the identity of the other guest the young man was infuriatingly vague and refused to say. Richard had been quite abrupt and had eventually hung up. What he did not know was that Gertie had left Jonathan with strict instructions that he was not to tell Richard that it was his mother who was on her way. She feared if Richard knew she were coming after all this time, after all the bitterness, he might refuse to receive her. If he did she wouldn't blame him. If he did she would continue on to Boscar with Juniper.

The car slid to a halt outside Hurstwood shortly before nine. Juniper was quickly out of the car, waving gaily at him as she ran around to open the passenger door.

'Mother!' Richard stood on the steps of the house, his mouth gaping with astonishment.

'Richard.' Gertie hesitated on the driveway, almost shyly. 'I apologise for this inconvenience.'

'My dear mother, it's no inconvenience, it's a joy to me.' He quickly ran down the steps and across the forecourt towards her. In front of her he paused. 'Oh, Mother, welcome.'

Gertie stepped forward, arms held wide in greeting and he gladly slipped into her embrace. He felt the comfort of his mother's arms and he was no longer a lonely, middle-aged man, but a boy again.

'You still smell of carnations,' he said laughing at the childhood memory of his mother's scent. Ever since he had never been able to smell that particular flower without remembering her.

'Some things never change, my son.'

'And Juniper? I'm so sorry. Forgive me . . . It's lovely to see you again.' He meant what he was saying.

Juniper had been watching the reunion with a lump in her throat. That's what she should have done with her father. How she wished she were going to Boscar for just such a reunion rather than on this sad journey. 'Don't apologise, Richard. You must be very excited.' She smiled at them both. 'I'm so happy for you.'

'Come in, come in . . .' He began to usher them towards the open front door.

'If you both would forgive me, I think I'll press on. I can get to Boscar by midnight if I do.'

'Of course, your father . . .' and then he did not know what to say and fought with himself for common courtesy. 'I'm sorry,' he managed eventually.

Juniper ducked into the car. She did not know what to say either, and when people said how sorry they were she feared she was about to cry. So instead she concentrated on switching on the motor and putting the car into gear; with a wave she left mother and son.

'Is your wife here?'

'No, Mother, luckily not. In fact, Francine is rarely here, I read more about her in the papers than I hear from her direct.' He led her across the hall and into the drawing room.

'Remarkable,' she said. 'It's exactly as I remember it when I visited your great aunt here as a young woman.'

'I refuse to change a thing. I love it as it is.'

'You must be bitter about not having the other houses.'

He smiled at her. 'You know, Mother, I'm grateful not to have them. I love Hurstwood. It's small, manageable, and I have a good life here.'

'Alice said you might feel that way. She's so often right about things.'

'I'm sure she says the same about you. A sherry?'

'A very large, very dry Martini, if you don't mind.'

'Martini?' He looked surprised. 'I never thought to hear you ask for a drink like that.'

'Just because I'm in my sixties it doesn't mean I can't be modern too.' She smiled at him. 'We have to talk, Richard.' She settled herself on the knoll settee.

During that long evening, over dinner and wine followed by several large Scotches, they planned what they were to do about Polly. And, that settled, they began to talk, really talk, as they used to all those years ago before Francine had driven them apart. Her heart ached for her son as he told her of his marriage and of his isolation. He told her of Francine's drinking and her indiscretions. Then he told her who Polly's father really was. She felt the anger she always felt at mention of her daughter-in-law. She felt pain for him. But by the end of the evening, mother and son had reaffirmed their love for each other.

7

'Grandmama, I seem to spend my life apologising, saying I'm sorry to you.' Juniper had arrived at midnight to a surprised but warm welcome from Alice and a rather cooler reception from Phillip. She said little until Phillip had gone to bed leaving the two women alone. They were in the small parlour at Boscar. She was tired and was certain she had never felt so demoralised in her whole life. 'Will you forgive me for everything?'

'Of course I forgive you, my darling. At least you are one of those rare people who can admit they might have been wrong.'

'Why do I always hurt you, though? The one person who has only ever been good and kind to me.'

'Maybe because you know how much I love you and that whatever you do I shall always forgive you – mind you, that's not an invitation,' she added.

'I presume a lot on your love,' Juniper said seriously.

'Ah well, there's always a down side as well as an up to everything in life.'

Juniper sat silent again as if, it seemed to Alice, she was absorbing what she had said and was thinking about it, a rare thing for Juniper to do. Alice also felt that Juniper wanted to talk to her and was perhaps weighing up what to say, so she too sat silent, waiting, the clock in the corner and the sibilant whisper of the wind at the windows the only sounds.

'I feel so confused about my father.' She finally spoke but with an odd urgency in her voice. 'I still can't forgive him for what he did to my mother, but at the same time, I loved him, I should have been here. I should have come to him when I finished with Hal, not to Gwenfer.'

'My dear Juniper. I think your father was lost to all of us some time ago. I don't think he would have appreciated your being here, you know. He had his own life, it was one that I don't understand but it seemed to suit him. He knew you loved him, I'm sure of that. He understood you very well, you know. In many ways, you're like him.'

'Do you think happiness exists?'

'That is most definitely the sort of question that one only asks after midnight.' She smiled kindly at her granddaughter, sensing her confusion, hoping she could help. 'I know it does, Juniper. Of course, it's far easier to be happy when you have someone you love, with whom to share your life, as I have with Phillip. But I was happy when I did not know him. Happiness comes from within. Only you can make yourself happy.'

'I feel better since I stopped rushing about so much. There isn't much to satisfy one in society, I've decided.'

'I'm glad to hear it. I felt the same.' Alice waited expectantly for Juniper to say more. She sat gazing into the fire, which was burning, despite it being July, for it had been a chill day. Juniper seemed to be thinking and then speaking her thoughts in short sharp bursts.

'Sometimes, I think I should move back to Gwenfer. I was always very happy there.'

'You would be most welcome. But I don't think it's a good idea. When I was young I always dreamt of just living there all my life. As it was, I lived a very interesting life in America which made me the person I am now – the one who is content to live an isolated life at Gwenfer. It's not time for you to do that, my darling. You have to live.'

'I should like to come back with you to Gwenfer, though, after the . . . after Daddy . . .' But the words 'funeral' and 'buried' would not come.

'Of course.' Alice waited expectantly, wondering if the conversation was finished, if she could suggest they go to bed.

'I'd really like to do something with my life. Everything has always been so easy for me.'

'I would hardly call Hal an easy experience,' Alice said softly.

'No, I mean, materially. You know, I often wonder what it would be like to have nothing, to be poor. If I were, maybe I'd be a happier, a better, person.'

'Poverty does not make one happier or better, I promise you that. There's no romance in being poor. Perhaps if you found an interest outside yourself, it might help you at the moment . . . But it looks, my darling, as though you and your generation are to be tested anyway, and the empty life will not continue for much longer.'

'War you mean? Things look bad, don't they?'

'Very.'

'I saw the air raid shelters being built in London. The streets are already full of sandbags. The army is everywhere – digging up the parks, God knows what for. It could be interesting.' She brightened up.

'Oh, yes, I'm sure, very interesting.'

The clock ticked. 'Do you see much of Harry?' Alice asked the question that frequently bothered her.

'No.'

'Is that wise?'

'I can't.'

'Why not, my dear?' Alice asked kindly.

'I don't love him as I should. He's better off with Leigh and Caroline.'

'Are you sure you're not blaming the child for the unhappiness Hal caused you?'

'No. It's not like that. I don't want to talk about him, Grandmama.' She did not see the child but it did not stop thoughts of him creeping into her mind – thoughts which she fought against. She was trying to forget him but was finding it harder than she had imagined.

'Juniper, it's two o'clock. If you don't need sleep, I do.' Alice stood up and collected her book and spectacles, knowing that she would have to try another day to talk to Juniper about her son – now was not the time.

'I love you, Grandmama.'

'I love you, too, Juniper.'

'Hal never said that to me.'

Alice quickly put her arms about her and held her close. 'Poor Juniper. Someone will come to love you, I'm sure,' she said as she led the exhausted young woman to bed and, worried, made her way to her own.

Marshall's funeral was as different as his life had been. He had left meticulous instructions in a letter addressed to Alice, the one person he knew who, no matter what difficulties, would fulfil his wishes to the letter.

There had been no question of Juniper having to go through the ordeal of seeing her father in his coffin, which, in the circumstances, with only half his head to see, was just as well. He wanted his body washed in water from the river Fowey which flowed through Boscar. He was then to be dressed in his monk's robes and to be cremated and by the time that Juniper arrived his remains had been sent away, by train, to the crematorium at Woking – it was the arrival of his ashes they awaited at Boscar.

On a glorious July morning Alice, Phillip and Juniper followed on foot the motley collection of Marshall's companions. His ashes were in a beautiful urn a friend from India had given him. The men chanted a strange chant, it could have been Indian, Chinese or of their own composition as far as the family were concerned. They stopped four times. First at the river where some of the ashes were cast on the water and one by one his friends read from a selection of poetry, parts of novels he'd enjoyed, mystics, philosophers – all chosen by Marshall, all of relevance to life, reincarnation and water, all shouted triumphantly over the sound of the rushing river. Juniper had expected to be unhappy, to cry, instead she found herself enjoying the ceremony, the words. Everything spoke of hope and rebirth. She felt Marshall was happy.

Then to the wood and the ceremony was repeated. And Marshall's ashes were strewn on the ground which in spring was a carpet of bluebells. From there they climbed the highest hill and handfuls of ashes were thrown into the wind and then finally, in the great hall of Boscar the last were scattered on the huge log fire. And Marshall was finally laid to rest.

Phillip had pointed out to Juniper that she would have to make decisions about Boscar. Since her arrival she was aware that Marshall's companions – she did not know what else to call them – were eyeing her suspiciously, and when she approached their voices dropped and they tended to sidle away. She wanted to know more about them and her father's work but to find out she had finally to call a meeting in the great hall, when all twenty of them shuffled in, faces downcast.

It took little time to discover that their elusiveness was born of fear of her and her intentions. She soon found they were gentle people. Their stories were of sadness and courage against all manner of problems and, she discovered, all but the youngest had been soldiers in the Great War, warriors who had not returned in triumph but as mere husks of the men they had been. Their nerves, their intelligence and often their abilities had been shattered by the shell-shock from which many still suffered.

Boscar was virtually self-sufficient. If any had money

they pooled it for the community's needs. In the spirit of the old religious orders no one was ever turned away from their door and many were the poor in the district who had cause to bless them. Her father, it seemed, had been studying the old medicines with the help of Helga, a self-proclaimed witch who knew the name of every herb and plant that grew at Boscar. Her father, she learnt, was loved by every one of them.

Before she left for Gwenfer she told them they could stay. She had decided to set up a foundation for the study of alternative religions and holistic medicine in the name of her father. She packed and left with Alice for Gwenfer. She knew she would never come back – there was no role for her here nor any happy memories to pull her back. Boscar was Marshall's, it should remain so in death.

Gwenfer, as always, helped restore her, helped give her peace. She grieved here, for Marshall, for Grace and Lincoln – all those she had loved and who had died. And here she discovered that, unknown to herself, she had been mourning the futile love she had given Hal. Whatever he had done, whatever he was, she had once loved him more than she had loved any man – that could never be denied. Now she found she did not wish to deny it. She had wanted to hate him, had even begun to do so, but here, by the sea and the cliffs, within the walls of the old house that always made her feel it was holding her safe, all such ugly emotions began to fade. Peace came to her. She telephoned her English lawyer and instructed him to make Hal a monthly allowance. Without her help, she was certain he would starve.

They had been at Gwenfer two days when a telegram arrived from Gertie, requesting, if she was not imposing on their grief, to visit. Both Alice and Juniper agreed that Gertie, of all people, was the one person they wanted with them. Alice telegraphed back their welcome and by the following morning Gertie had arrived. The moment she stepped from the car Alice sensed that something was wrong even though Gertie was bubbling over with excitement at her reconciliation with Richard.

Richard had left that morning for Paris by aeroplane. Gertie explained she would have liked to go with him – as he had suggested. Not only would she have liked to spend more time with him but she had never flown and felt she would rather enjoy it. However—

'In the end I thought it best he went alone. It's more suitable that he sort everything out with Polly by himself, don't you think?'

'Sort what out?' asked Alice vaguely as she concentrated on tacking together the blackout blinds that despite Juniper's jeers, she thought prudent to make. When Gertie did not answer she looked up to see her pleating the material of her skirt with restless fingers, and staring out of the window with a faraway lost look in her eyes. She laid down her needle and thread. 'What's the matter, Gertie?' she asked, her voice rich with concern. Gertie's fine brown eyes focused upon her as if she suddenly realised Alice was there, while her fingers continued to toy with the fabric of her skirt. 'My dear friend . . . let me help . . . Tell me . . .'

Abruptly Gertie stood, straightened her skirt as if angry with it and picked up her large handbag.

'It's up to Richard and Polly . . .' she crossed to the window. 'Such a lovely day, I shall take a walk.' With a purposeful stride she left the room. Alice in turn looked out at the garden – it was misty and damp and far from being a lovely day. A moment later Gertie trudged past the window and down the steps which lead to the valley, her shoulders were slumped, her heels dragged – not like Gertie at all, Alice worried.

Another telegram arrived mid-afternoon. It was addressed to Gertie but Alice, with a sense of foreboding, opened it herself. It was from Gertie's younger son Charles to say that he and Fiona were travelling immediately to Gwenfer.

Alice stood in the great hall tapping her cheek with the orange envelope and wondering what to do. She tipped the telegraph boy threepence, asked after his mother and upon closing the door leant upon it, thinking.

Charles had never been to Gwenfer before. Why on earth should he come now? Why had he not telephoned? He was a courteous man who would never have put all courtesy aside and just presumed that he and his wife would be welcomed unless there was very good reason . . .

Something had happened, something so dreadful that he felt he had to come in person, she was convinced as she slipped the telegram into her pocket and resolved not to mention it to Gertie. There would be no point in the two of them worrying. There was no way Charles would be here before midnight and by then Gertie would be in bed. Alice would wait up for them.

Gertie was in fine form that evening – an evening which to Alice seemed interminable.

'Everyone should have a rock like yours, Alice. It's a good place to sit and put everything into perspective.'

'Ia's rock?' Alice said. She would have liked to ask what it was Gertie needed to put into perspective. Instead she talked about her love of the rock and the peace she found there – no doubt Gertie would tell her in her own good time.

'Maybe Richard's already found Polly. What do you think? Perhaps we should celebrate?'

'Champagne?' Juniper jumped up eager to fetch it.

'Perhaps we should wait until we know for sure before celebrating,' Alice said, her anxiety increasing as each hour of the clock passed.

'Oh, don't be so stuffy, Grandma. Champagne's a super idea.' And Juniper was across the room and racing for the cellar.

Alice could not drink but watched alarmed as Juniper and Gertie finished the bottle. Ten passed and eleven – Gertie made no move to go to bed.

To Juniper's surprised delight, Gertie was singing old music hall songs which she accompanied badly on the out of tune piano, when Alice's sharp ears heard the throb of a motor descending the steep drive. Silently she left the room.

She opened the hall door as the car came to a halt. Charles looked ashen with shock and fatigue as he entered the door, a red-eyed Fiona closely behind him.

'Richard?' was all she said.

'Over the Channel,' he could barely reply.

'I didn't say you were coming. She's had such a happy evening.' She took their coats and led the way across the hall towards the parlour, from which Gertie's strong voice, half-way through 'Nellie Dean', issued forth. Charles stopped in his steps, his face creased with anguish. Alice took his hand and opened the door.

'. . . seemed to whisper sweet and . . .'

Gertie did not finish the line, her voice trailed into nothing. She looked at Charles then Fiona and back at Charles. Her hands slipped from the piano keys on to her lap.

'Oh, no,' she said, barely audible.

Alice motioned to Juniper to come with her. They were half-way across the hall when a loud moan stopped them. They stood like statues as an icy chill filled both of them and they clung together for comfort.

Strong, powerful Gertie became a husk of her former self.

When Basil, her husband, had died everyone had said how wonderful she was, how courageous. Gertie had buried her grief for him deep inside her, conscious of her responsibilities to their large staff, to her family. She had never wept for Basil. But now away from those selfsame responsibilities and obligations, alone with her son and her greatest friend, the grieving for Richard unleashed her grief for Basil too.

The wreckage of Richard's plane had been found in

mid-Channel but not his body. That sad fact, thought Alice, made everything crueller. For days poor Gertie hoped he would be found. But as each day passed and that hope faded the loss of hope seemed to fuel her despair. No one else had hoped as she had; they had accepted the experts' finding that the aeroplane had exploded in midair and that survival would have been impossible.

Charles and Fiona left – the house in Berkshire was to be requisitioned by the army and there was much to do there. Everyone insisted Gertie stay with Alice. They had expected she would argue, insist she must return with them to supervise the packing up of her home. Instead, she acquiesced without a murmur. Alice did what she could as Gertie remained alone in her room barely eating or drinking.

A week had passed and Alice once again was about to toil over the blackout curtains which even as she sewed them she prayed she would never need. She moved her material into the little-used library where the large table would make cutting out far easier. She looked up as the door opened to see Gertie, a much thinner Gertie, standing in the doorway.

'I feel like one of Juniper's wonderful Martinis,' she announced.

Alice hurriedly prepared the drink for Gertie and, although it was only eleven in the morning, one for herself since she sensed that the moment had come when Gertie wanted to unburden herself.

'Alice, I must apologise for my behaviour this past week. I'm ashamed of myself.'

'My dear friend . . .' Alice patted her hand consolingly.

'It was as if a dam had opened in me and I lost control. Most unlike me . . .' she fretted.

'I do understand.'

'There's something I need to confide in you, Alice. It's been tormenting me.'

Alice sat and listened with astonishment and disbelief as Gertie told her that the rumours from all those years ago had been true. That Marshall was Polly's father, that Richard had known for some time and had long ago accepted the situation. She explained that nothing had altered his feelings of love for the girl. It was why he was en route for Paris. He wanted to find and tell Polly himself for he feared that Francine, who had begun to drink heavily, was vicious enough to tell her in a fit of pique.

'I can't believe that, Gertie. Dear Polly is so unlike Marshall.'

'But she hasn't my red hair.'

'Don't be ridiculous, Gertie – Basil's family were dark, she need not be a redhead.'

'I do so want her to be my granddaughter.'

'Then she probably is. I've never heard such nonsense, no wonder you got into a state.'

'But if it's true, it means she's Juniper's half-sister. Should we not tell them as Richard wanted?'

'In my experience these matters are best left untold,' Alice said firmly.

'But what about Francine?'

'She's said nothing so far, so why should she now? Let's keep it a secret, Gertie.'

'Too late . . .' Juniper's voice rose from the depths of the knoll settee where she had been curled up with a book. She had meant to let them know she was there but when the conversation became so interesting . . . 'Sorry.' She grinned as her head appeared over the back of the huge piece of furniture.

'Juniper! What unspeakable behaviour. How dare you listen to other people's conversations.' Alice was furious.

'I didn't mean to. You rarely come in here after all. You started talking before I could let you know I was here.'

'I'm glad she knows, Alice. It's as if it was intended she should know.'

'I'm going to find Polly,' Juniper leapt to her feet.

'Juniper you can't, there's going to be a war. You can't go to France now, you could be trapped there for the duration – you could be killed.'

'All the more reason to go and find her. It means Polly's in danger and she could never manage on her own.'

'Juniper, I beg you, don't go,' Alice pleaded.

'I shan't die, Grandmama. I have to go, don't you see? I would have gone anyway but now she's my sister, I have no choice.'

'Let her go, Alice. All this talk of war is too defeatist for words. There won't be any war, I'm sure dear Mr Chamberlain will see to that. I'll stay here with you, if you'll have me, now the wretched army have stolen my house – goodness knows what damage they'll do, imagine their boots on the marble floors.'

'Of course you can stay, Gertie.'

'So stop worrying Alice, it doesn't suit you. And in a home this size you're going to need help with all this blackout material.' Once again Gertie took charge.

Chapter Eleven

1

Juniper had been in France for over a month when war with Germany was finally declared. Not that she was initially aware of the fact. Her French had always been poor and since she had never taken any interest in current affairs she never bothered to read a paper. So it was two days before a friend told her the momentous news. But even as he told her she showed little interest for it was is if it had nothing to do with her, an American.

At the beginning of her journey her intention had been to go straight to Paris in her quest for Polly, but early on she had been seduced from her task by two events.

The first delay had been caused by a house.

Upon arriving at Le Havre she had immediately bought herself a new motor car and, since she was in France, she had chosen a Citroën. Juniper had always enjoyed driving and with her natural curiosity decided to make her way towards Paris by wending her leisurely way along the minor roads. This was a part of France she did not know. Her father's preference had been for the South and that was the area she knew best. And, she had reasoned, a delay of a few days would make little difference to Polly.

The weather was hot and the whole country was steeped in that lethargy which is August in France. In England the talk everywhere was of impending war but here, bowling along the dusty roads, through scenery which had not changed in a thousand years, the very idea seemed to be too ludicrous to even contemplate.

The tyres of the Citroën complained loudly as Juniper slammed on the brakes. Across a field, nestling in a copse of trees, seen through an avenue of orchards which in spring would be a sea of apple blossom, stood a small, ancient manor house. Two of the gables swept to the ground in graceful thatched arcs. The walls were pale cream, the exposed timbering the colour of milk chocolate, colours which gave a softness to the house which would have been lacking in a similar timbered English building. Attached to the side of the house was a small round turret and in the garden she could see the outline of an equally old *pigeonnier*. Such a gem would normally have intrigued her, made her pause, but what made her swing the car up the unmade driveway was the atmosphere of neglect and emptiness about the place.

She called out but could find no one to ask who owned the house and what was its history. But, from peering into the dirty latticed windows, she thought it was uninhabited. The furniture was covered with a fine film of dust and ghostly swags of cobwebs hung everywhere. The garden was everything that Juniper demanded in a garden – wild and unkempt. Roses and honeysuckle grew untamed, snaking over walls, fences, and across the paths. The grass about the house was covered in buttercups so that the lawns were more golden than green. At the front was a large pond, choked with weeds and rushes and surrounded by a sea of marsh buttercups, wild iris and, she was certain, wild orchids. The stables at the back were virtually falling down but the cobble stones in the yard were bleached almost white from the sun and everywhere was the heady smell of geraniums which, left to their own devices, had grown enormously, more like bushes than potted plants.

Juniper immediately fell in love with the house.

She headed for the village and, in the local café, over a lunch of bread and cheese, coffee and cognac, with her schoolroom French elicited the information that the house was, as she had hoped, empty and '*peut-être*' for sale. She had to be content with the 'perhaps' since the explanation was too fast and complex for her poor grasp of the language. But she was given the address of the notary in the next town who would help with her enquiries.

Fortunately for her the lawyer spoke passable English and could confirm that the house was certainly for sale with its entire contents. Inevitably, French law was incapable of moving fast enough for Juniper. She wanted it and she wanted it now. The lawyer promised to contact his clients that same evening and Juniper spent a restless night in the hotel after she had revisited her house. Seeing it again, in the moonlight, she knew she must have it. She felt destiny had brought her here. For what, she did not know, but was certain she would soon find out.

For a week the negotiations moved relentlessly slowly. Exasperated by the delays Juniper begged the keys from the notary who, knowing he should not give them to her was, nonetheless, completely won over by Juniper's smile. From the village she found half a dozen women and with her small army of helpers descended on the house to clean it.

The interior was as perfect as the outside. Great armoires that smelt of lavender and the past stood in every room. The large oak table was indented with the marks of a thousand meals. The range in the kitchen, black as soot and decorated with brass, was soon gleaming. The copper pots shone blindingly. The tiled floors glowed red with new polish and from the garden she filled vases full of wild flowers. The village women thought she was mad and decided she was even madder when they counted the money she had paid them in wages.

Concerned by her youth and her insistent demand that she own the house *now*, the notary, against his own advantage counselled caution. The house had stood empty for five years, God alone knew what structural damage there was. If she acted too hastily she might regret it. Did she not know that there was to be a war? What would she do then so far from home? And if she returned to England or America, what would there be left to return to after the fighting?

The absent owners, at long distance, sensing they had a desperate purchaser prevaricated about the price and not until she had paid three times its value was she able to move into Le Manoir de la Renoncule des Champs.

Her first night there she slept in the round room of the turret which she had chosen for herself. With the rooms sweet smelling from their cleaning, the heavy scent of flowers as yet unidentified wafting through the open window, listening to the bark of a fox, the hooting of the owls, Juniper felt completely content. More at peace and in a strange way, happy for the first time in months. She never wanted to leave here: that was her decision as she fell asleep.

And then she fell in love again which was the second reason for her delay.

Christian Fôret owned an antique shop in the local market town. Looking for some tapestries to hang on the walls she entered his shop. Christian was one of those lean Frenchmen whose bodies seem to be coiled like springs with suppressed and secret emotions. His long black eyelashes guarded eyes of the darkest brown, his skin was pale against the black of his hair, his mouth was full with a heavy lower lip which, the moment Juniper saw it, she wanted to kiss. All the time they discussed the tapestries in his shop she felt herself wanting to touch him. Had he leapt upon her there and then she knew she would not have resisted. The tapestries decided upon, she turned her attention to some chairs, and then an old coffer, anything to delay leaving the shop. Oddly she did not flirt with him, unusual for her. She felt too shy and, even odder, fearful that he might reject her. She hurried back to her manor, quickly bathed and changed, and restlessly awaited him.

The furniture placed, the tapestries hung, the seduction

which followed was slow, elegant and tortuous. So tortuous that Juniper was eventually begging Christian to take her. He would kiss her, gently touch her, all the time softly whispering to her words that had no meaning for her but which required no understanding. And then he would stop and lean back and smile his dark and lazy smile and she longed for him to undo the buttons of her dress, to feel his hands, his mouth on her breasts. Instead, he would kiss her again, gently touch her, whisper incomprehensible words to her.

Beside herself with frustration, Juniper jumped to her feet and with feverish hands she tore at her own blouse ripping the buttons off in her haste. She threw aside her silk chemise, slipped quickly out of her skirt, tore off her stockings and suspender belt until she stood naked before him.

'Please,' she begged. And laughing, he obliged. He took her in his arms and lowered her gently on to the floor and slowly he entered her.

Every day and every night for over a month they made love. Juniper felt she had exorcised Hal's ghost for here was a man who could give her as much pleasure as he had, pleasure she had thought she would never find again. And then one day Christian did not appear.

At first she had not worried unduly, presuming he was delayed with business – it had happened a couple of times before. But, by the early evening, when he still had not arrived and had not telephoned, she got into her car and travelled into town where she drove past his shop which was in total darkness.

She slept little that night for she was worried and perplexed. And because her body, with its seemingly insatiable need for him, wouldn't let her.

The following morning she laughed at her fears of the night when a letter from him arrived. Impatiently she tore the envelope open. He explained that he had had to go to Brittany and looked forward to seeing her upon his return from collecting his wife and children from their annual holiday. A wife and children she had not known existed.

That day Juniper packed her bags, loaded the car, locked the door of her 'house of buttercups', and took the car down the drive without a backwards glance. But something in her had been destroyed; she drove away with a hardened heart.

Paris was ablaze with September sunshine, the trees in their mantle of autumn, and just the slightest hint of the chill to come in the early morning air. The boulevards were full of people going about their daily tasks and when there was talk of the war it was to reject the very idea that the Germans would ever come to Paris. The Maginot line would hold; they would be safe. Troops were sent to the front but the casualties were so light as to be almost insignificant, the occasional death, a few wounded. The Parisians continued in their normal search for excellence and pleasure. Much hot air was expended but little action was taken.

Juniper booked into a suite at the Ritz. She had not allowed herself to think of Christian on her journey from Normandy, but now, alone in the city, she thought of him and despised herself.

Men were untrustworthy and once more she had been a fool, she thought. She would learn to hate them and to use them just as they used her.

She bathed and dressed and sauntered down to the bar intent on finding a man to destroy.

2

Unlike Juniper, Polly knew all about the war. Prior to September she had read several newspapers each day voraciously. And one of her first purchases had been a wireless so that she could listen every evening to the BBC.

She had spent many hours wondering if perhaps she should return to England for there was nothing to keep her here. But she did not go. For one thing, she had grown to love this country and for another she was too ashamed to return. She continued to write regularly to her father and grandmother, but she still gave Michel's address for she had assumed, rightly, that he would be far too proud to announce her sudden departure. There were days when she longed for news of her family and she had once even gone so far as to approach Michel's house to collect her mail. But as she stood in the street, looking through the ironwork of the gates she had found herself shuddering at the memories the beautiful house held for her. That, and fear of Michel's mother, held her back from ringing the bell to summon the concierge. She had turned on her heel and with head down had walked rapidly away from the familiar district. She was waiting, she realised, waiting for her stupid pride and hurt to heal – then maybe, she might return to her own country.

Apart from this occasional homesickness, she was content. She had a small flat in a thin, tall house that seemed to have been built to fill the empty narrow space between the larger houses on either side. There was only space for one room on each floor so that her apartment took up three storeys at the very top of the house. Behind her front door was the kitchen, the walls of which she had decorated with laboriously cut out flowers from magazines. She had handsewn gingham curtains and a matching tablecloth; and, each month when she received her pay, she placed on the shelf on the wall a different pretty plate which she found in the flea market. She had eight plates now, one for each month which had passed since she had seen Jonathan with Juniper, and had had her heart broken a second time. Outside the window, prevented from falling by ornate ironwork on the sill, stood her window box in which she grew herbs. For her stay with Madame Fabris had inspired her to learn how to cook.

A small pine staircase led from the room to her sitting room, bigger than the kitchen since the communal stairs finished on that floor. The boards were bare with one rug, Indian she thought, purchased like the plates from the market. She had made bookcases from bricks and boards and, each month, after she had bought her plate she would buy books from the secondhand bookshops. She had been given an old and rather rickety gramophone that, no matter how tightly she wound it up, always needed rewinding half-way through a record. With any spare money she would, after great thought, buy another record for her growing collection. She had two chairs and had made large cushions in bright-coloured fabric on which her guests, when they came, would loll as they drank their wine, smoked their Gauloises, argued about the meaning of life, and put the world to rights. On the walls hung several paintings, all abstracts, given her by friends in return for her rabbit casserole and her company.

An even narrower stair led to her bedroom in the very eaves of the house. Her bed was a mattress, over which at first she had allowed herself some self-pity, until, that is, she had discovered how well she slept on it. Now she doubted if she would ever enjoy a conventional bed again. This mattress, in daytime, was covered with cushions all of which she had worked herself. Hurstwood her cat – now called Hursty for short – slept in a basket by her side. A curtain in the corner screened off her wash basin and bidet, she frequently regretted the lack of a bath. The long window opened directly on to the rooftops, so that when she looked out it was as if she could have walked across the roofs of Paris. Here were her potted plants and Hursty's exclusive front door.

Polly loved her flat and each night when she returned to it she felt safe and secure.

At first she had spent many hours thinking about Jonathan – wasted hours she had finally decided. He loved Juniper, there was nothing she could do about it. She would forget him. The pain of his deception was less now but she had not forgotten him as she had promised. There was no one else in her life, which in many ways was a relief, for Jonathan had destroyed her trust in love and men.

She had had several jobs. First in a couple of bookshops and then as a translator but now she worked on a small arts magazine with a circulation so low that it was spoken of in whispers.

She knew this could not last. Soldiers were getting killed on the front and the wounded needed help. She realised that the production of an esoteric magazine was of little importance at such a time.

That first January of the war she had reluctantly given in her notice, dreading the reaction of the editor who was a close friend. She need not have feared. With paper and ink shortages imminent he too had decided that perhaps he would be better off finding other employment and had only delayed doing so because of her.

She had read in the papers of the Colis de Trianon founded by Lady Mendl to supply comforts to the troops. Often she read their appeals for warm clothing, soap and cigarettes and drivers. She presented herself but under the assumed name of Liz Somerset – with the English aristocracy involved she did not want anyone to recognise her name and thus her. She was welcomed with open arms as someone who could drive and spoke fluent French. There was one bad moment when she asked how much they could pay her – everyone else was a volunteer. But Lady Mendl, taking pity on her, arranged for a small wage to cover her rent and her food.

For a time she was happy knowing she was helping, knowing she was doing good. But soon the social banter of the other women, with whom she had nothing in common, began to pall. She started to feel as if she had wandered into an exclusive club of which she was not a member. Dressed as she was in relentless black, bright red lipstick and kohl-blackened eyes, she certainly did not look a member. Her appearance worked to her advantage since none of the women ever asked who she was, presuming from her bohemian style that she could not be from the same world as they. Soon the packing of gift boxes was not enough and she longed to be more active. It was the appearance, one day, of a friend of her grandmother's from the Embassy which galvanised her. She had ducked out of the room before the woman noticed her and had never gone back.

She approached the French Red Cross. Within days she had more action than she had imagined possible and there were moments when she wondered if she had been mad to leave the safety of the Colis de Trianon's office.

Her job was to motor, several times a week, to the front, with the large car she had been assigned, loaded with plasma, dressings and linen for the field hospitals. In Paris, apart from wild rumour, and the false air-raid alarms which had become so frequent that no one took any notice of them, the war was a distant thing. But, hurtling along the narrow country roads, seriously pock-marked from stray shells, her car often forced off the road by the convoys of army lorries and occasionally strafed by enemy aeroplanes, the sound of gun fire unpleasantly close – the war became a very real and fearsome thing, and Paris seemed a million miles away.

At the field hospitals, after she had made her deliveries and collected all the paperwork that French bureaucracy dictated, she would visit the wounded. She comforted, as best she could, young men no older than herself who were maimed and frightened. For many it was their first time away from their homes and their mothers. She would read to them and help them write letters, and each time would leave feeling totally inadequate at the little she could do to help.

'Excuse me, Miss Somerset, isn't it?'

She wound down the window of the car. 'Yes?' She could react easily to her assumed name these days but it had not always been so easy.

'Would you do me a huge favour? I'm here with the British Expeditionary Force. I've a weekend leave and wonder if you could give me a lift back to Paris – no point in spending it here.' He smiled and she was struck by how white his teeth were in a face tanned from hours in the open.

'With pleasure.' She leant over and opened the other door of the car. He picked up his case and walked round the bonnet and leapt in.

'Andrew Slater.' Formally he shook her hand. 'This is most kind.'

'I shall enjoy the company.' She put the car into gear.

'This is a lonely and dangerous job for a young girl like you.'

'It was worse in the winter – it was icy and dark – and I think the French army consider all the roads belong exclusively to them. I was always landing up in a ditch. But I'm not always alone. They send us in pairs if they can.'

She put her foot down and the large heavy car surged forward. She noticed the young officer grab at the handle of the door, his knuckles white.

'Sorry about the speed. It's best to go fast here, the planes often strafe near the front – despite the red crosses on the roof. It's safer ten kilometres further on.'

'Even if you drive this fast they can still get you.' He attempted to laugh.

'Oh, I realise that. It's just that it's more comforting to get out as soon as possible. As if I am doing something to control my own destiny.' She laughed at the irony.

'Would you have dinner with me tonight?' he suddenly asked.

She did not know why but she found herself blushing as she accepted.

'Somewhere really splendid, filthy expensive. You recommend it.'

'The Duke of Windsor goes to the Grand Véfour. But it really is frightfully expensive.'

'That's the place then.' He leant back in the seat, relaxed now that she had slowed her breakneck pace.

'How long do you think before the Germans break through?' She asked the question that everyone was asking of everyone else mainly, she realised, to hear the comfort of someone saying 'never'.

'I don't understand why they haven't already. The French seem to have an almost mystical faith in that flaming Maginot line, they're convinced the Ardennes will hold them too. Neither will. It's hopeless up there, the anti-tank traps are a joke . . . But please, dear Miss Somerset, no talk of war, not for this weekend at least.' He smiled at her and she swerved as she noticed for the first time just how handsome he was, with his blond hair and blue eyes. How nice too, after all this time, to be speaking her own language with a man only a little older than her twenty-two years.

Paris was full and though they drove from one hotel to another Andrew could not find a room.

'You had better come back to my place. It's not very grand and I'm afraid it's a bed of cushions on the floor.'

'It sounds like paradise,' he said with a grin.

They clattered up the long flight of steps, past the other apartments, the smell of cooking heavy in the air. Odd she'd never noticed that before – the very pervasive smell of garlic. At the top, outside her door, sitting despondently on the stairs was Pierre with Simone, Auguste, Jean and Marie-Louise – all friends she had made in the past year through the magazine. Each held a bottle of wine, Marie-Louise a large melon and Simone a bowl of salad.

'I think we can forget the Grand Véfour,' she said in English. 'I hope you don't mind?'

'Not at all, this looks fun.' With relief she heard him enthusiastically introducing himself in passable French.

Hursty welcomed them graciously, checked that Polly put the gas on beneath the casserole and then, slinking up the stairs in front of them all led the way to the sitting room and purred his welcome to them one by one, rubbing his body against their legs before settling down to continue his interrupted sleep.

It was three in the morning before the others made their way drunkenly and noisily down the steep stairs.

'Why do they call you Polly?'

'They like it.'

'You're more a Liz than a Polly,' he said. 'Are they always that intense?' he asked, draining the last of the wine into a glass and grimacing at the bitter taste.

'Yes.'

'And so depressed by everything. Don't they ever laugh?'

'I don't think any of them find much to laugh about.'

'But you laugh.'

'But then I'm not a French intellectual.'

'Do they always wear black?'

'Of course, it's the existentialists' uniform.' She laughed as she plumped up the cushions for his bed.

'And you, are you an existentialist?' he asked anxiously, since all evening he had felt deeply out of his depth.

'No, not at all. I dress like this because it makes me feel anonymous.'

'And do you want to be anonymous?'

'Yes.'

'But why? Most people want to be noticed.'

'It depends on what they have to hide.'

'And what are you hiding?'

'My past.' She looked away from him, she wished she had not said that. Now he would pry and she did not want to tell him she had a husband, who she was. She did not know why but it seemed suddenly important that he should not know.

'Then I shan't ask,' he said gently. 'Come here,' he held out his hand to her and pulled her down on to his cushion. She found she let him, easily. He took her face in his hands and looked at her long and hard. 'You're very beautiful,' there was a husky tone to his voice, one she recognised, one that made her shudder. He leant forward and he was kissing her. She wanted him too, she realised. No man had touched her since Jonathan and now his lips on hers gave her that old, familiar thrill. She leant away from him.

'Sorry, I shouldn't have done that.' He busied himself opening his cigarette case.

'I wanted you to. But, it's not fair on you, you see. Because I couldn't let it go any further.'

'That past?'

'Yes, something in my past.'

'Liz, can I sleep with you? I won't touch you, I promise, I just want to feel close to someone in the night.'

It was the expression in his eyes that told her she would be safe with him.

'I understand that, I'd like that,' she replied and taking him by the hand, with Hursty in attendance, she led him up the stairs to her room.

3

April has always been the month that peculiarly belongs to Paris. But this April of 1940, Paris surpassed itself as if in defiant gesture to the endless threats upon her. The weather was perfect, the blossoms on the trees more abundant, more colourful than anyone could remember. Even the graceful buildings had taken on a special spring face and the stones gleamed warmly. The boulevards and pavement cafés were bustling as everyone seemed to want to be out on the streets at every available opportunity.

Shortages were beginning to bite, real coffee was hard to find and petrol was in short supply but there was plenty of wine to sit and sip as the people of Paris, in all their elegance, strolled by.

Polly had known Andrew for six weeks and in that time miraculously, it seemed to her, she had almost forgotten Jonathan. Every moment Andrew could get away from his duties they spent together and they were six of the happiest weeks in Polly's life. He made her laugh, he never probed, he had kept his promise and had never forced himself upon her even though they slept together each night he could arrange to be in Paris.

After a month she had confessed her true identity to him and the fact that she was married. Her instinct not to tell him when they met had been right. He confessed he would have run a mile. The last thing he needed, he joked, was an irate husband chasing him. But now he loved her and it did not matter, for, he was determined, once this mess was over, they would marry. But one thing he could not alter – he still called her Liz.

There had been times when Polly felt that tonight she would do it. Tonight she would allow his kisses and caresses to reach their natural conclusion. She was fully aware that it was not fair to expect him to lie night after night beside her and not possess her. But each time she reached this decision, each time she was about to tell him she was ready, then, the horror of her nights with Michel would return to her and she would shrink from closer contact. She was happy, she loved him, she could not allow it all to be ruined by pain and degradation.

They spent many hours wandering about the city she had grown to know so well. In these now familiar surroundings it was impossible to grasp that already coastal towns were being bombed, that English people were dying. Here there was little to indicate the horror that was breaking across Europe. Admittedly there were more men in uniform and many of her Jewish friends had left for England and America but, to Polly, the most poignant indication she had seen that things were not really as they appeared, was the grass in the city parks, normally so svelte and smooth, grown waist high from neglect like a field of corn as more men were called to serve.

She continued her work with the Red Cross. The front line held. For the time being the Germans were otherwise occupied and a shiver of fear went through the city at the news that Denmark and Norway had fallen. Only the most optimistic now felt that the war would not spread, that France would not be invaded.

Juniper was frustrated in her search for Polly. She had worked her way through four private detective agencies, none of whom had been able to find her. Juniper ranted and raged at them, finding it unbelievable that they could not trace one English girl in this city. She accused them all roundly of Gallic incompetence.

Although she found the idea of meeting Michel repugnant, finally she had no choice. Eventually she visited Michel at his home – just in time, it transpired. She arrived to a scene of chaos. The family were packing to flee to their château in the country. Michel was not only convinced that the Germans would invade, he expected it by the hour. Each morning his listened at his window, convinced that in the night they had come and that he would hear their boots tramping down the Champs Elysées. He had no intention of allowing any of his valuables, including himself, to fall into their hands. Chandeliers weighing half a ton lay like great stranded crystal animals on the priceless carpets. Packing cases littered the floor while a small army of men packed the Sèvres, the Meissen, the Lalique, the library of first editions, the great parchment charts of family trees and all his relevant research books and notes. All was supervised by a perspiring and fussing Michel who, with such a task to be completed as quickly as possible, received Juniper with scarcely concealed ill-grace.

He was useless to her. He had no idea where his wife was and even less interest.

'So you're running away with no concern for her?'

'Lady Copton, I am not running away, as you put it. I am making sensible arrangements for my mother. I shall serve – if called upon.' At the unthinkable thought he took a large white handkerchief from his immaculate jacket to mop his sweating brow.

'Have you made no attempt to find her?'

'I saw her once from the window, in the street, looking up at the house.'

'And you didn't go out and speak to her? Ask her if she wanted for anything?'

'My wife chose to leave me. I didn't make her go.'

'And we know why, don't we?' she said coldly. 'The whole of Paris knows.'

'I don't know what you mean. I suggest you leave, immediately.' He spoke with cheeks and chest puffed up with indignation and he appeared to be standing on tiptoe in anger, as if to give himself more authoritative height.

'With pleasure, Monsieur. There's just one thing,' Juniper paused at the door. 'I haven't been the least bit frightened here in Paris. But if you're the sort of person the French army are going to be forced to rely on – then I think it's about time I was petrified.' And she slammed the door with a satisfying bang behind her.

Frustrated by others' attempts to find Polly, Juniper had begun to drive about the city for hours looking for her herself. Logically, given the size of the city, she knew this was a futile task. But Juniper had a strong feeling that this was exactly how, one day, she would find her – walking down a street, sitting at a café. Buoyed up by this conviction, armed with a street map, this was how most of her days were spent.

In the evenings she frequently received long impassioned telephone calls from her grandmother. When begging her to leave before it was too late had no effect, Alice would read her frightening reports from newspaper pundits. When that did not work she resorted to the wild rumours that were flying about England like a plague. But Juniper's response was always the same – she wasn't leaving without Polly and as an American, with that country's passport, she was safe. This wasn't her war.

Her social life could not have been busier. As a beautiful rich American woman alone in Paris it was inevitable that she was inundated with invitations – to dinners, parties, receptions at the various embassies. It was a rare night that she did not have an escort to take her to Bricktops or the Boeuf sur le Toit and occasionally Casanova. Soon she was well known in all of them for her gaiety and her generosity. Juniper was one of those people who, when she entered a room, seemed to galvanise everyone within it to enjoyment. She had completely forgotten her declaration of a few months ago that social life was not for her and that it was 'empty'. Juniper was having a great deal of fun.

These days she did not look for love, she searched for conquests. In the six months she had been here she had had six serious affairs. These affairs did not take into account the handful of lesser ones, for to Juniper an affair was only serious if, after a week, she could remember the man's name. A month was her limit. During that time she spoilt her men, flattered them, gave them whatever they wanted, showered them with gifts and then, once they had declared their love and she was convinced of their sincerity, she would tell them she was sorry but she could not see them any more. Each time she saw the pain on their faces, each time she listened to their pleading she gained a measure of satisfaction and allowed herself to imagine that it was Hal or Christian at her feet begging for her love.

She made few mistakes, only once did she meet a man

who had awoken in her the same response as those two who had ruined her ability to love.

She was in the bar of the Ritz where she had arranged to meet her escort for the evening – a diplomat from the American embassy. She was early and the bar, as usual, was crowded. She turned round and literally bumped into a young man. As they fussed over spilt drinks she noticed his blond good looks and began to talk to him.

They ordered more drinks and he invited her to dine. Glancing at her watch and seeing that her escort was five minutes late, she accepted – no man kept Juniper waiting. She was impressed that he took her to the Grand Véfour and even more impressed that he insisted on picking up the bill. Juniper had years ago become accustomed to people expecting her to pay the bill.

He was miserable at the start of the evening as he explained that his regular girlfriend had been called out for extra duties motoring plasma up to the field hospitals. But she soon cheered him up. When they returned to the Ritz she invited him to her suite for a night cap knowing very well that she intended taking him to bed.

He made love superbly. She found herself responding to him. Once more she had found a man who could arouse her to real passion, she allowed herself to think that the loneliness of the empty affairs might be over. Then suddenly he had shouted '*Liz!*' and she had felt herself freeze inside. She did not arrange to see him again.

People were beginning to leave the city. Those with country homes were going to them, those with relatives invited themselves to stay. It was May and Holland had fallen, the Germans had broken through the French front line and by the 21st they were only sixty miles from Paris. Belgium fell and the Allied army was cut off at the coast. Even Juniper began to realise how serious the situation was.

The casualties were heavy now, and Polly's car,

changed now for a cumbersome station wagon, sped hither and thither so laden with supplies that frequently the axles grated and she always carried a spare exhaust. The back seats had been removed and often now she returned with wounded, for the pressure on the ambulances and trains was becoming colossal. It was not just the wounded she tended now, she was often called upon to comfort the dying.

Her constant worry was Andrew. Each day she felt sick with terror for him, certain that he would be killed. Guiltily she found she sometimes wished he would be wounded – just so that he would be safe. They grabbed what time they could.

She knew she loved him deeply. She loved him even more the night he had confessed his infidelity with a girl he had picked up in a bar. She had silenced his confession with a kiss and took the blame for it herself. If she could not give herself to him then he had every right to seek his comfort elsewhere. Reasonable words, quickly spoken, and ones she meant – she thought, until she felt the discomfort of jealousy for that girl worming away inside her.

And then came a night when at last her love for him was greater than her fear and she gave herself to him. To her astonishment he was gentle and kind to her as he possessed her and she could have wept with gratitude had she not been so happy.

Wearily Polly drove the battered station wagon through the bright June sunshine back into Paris. She swung into a narrow street and found the way blocked by a slow-moving line of cars. Impatiently she drummed on the steering wheel with her fingers. At this rate she would be late and she had a feeling that tonight Andrew would come. They had not seen each other for nearly two weeks, he must get away soon. She must be there should he arrive. She wound down the window and poked her head out. What could be the problem? The traffic in Paris these days was usually light: with so many having left, and petrol hard to come by, a traffic jam was becoming a rare thing. There was a car broken down in the middle of the road. A beautiful woman was standing grandly directing the traffic while a mechanic burrowed into the inside of the engine. Polly noted the immaculate white gloves waving the traffic on, and saw the smart grey suit with a scarlet blouse and matching hat. She still remembered enough from her years with Michel to recognise a Jacques Fath outfit when she saw one . . .

'Juniper!' Polly shouted with surprise as she drew nearer. 'Juniper,' she yelled over the noise of the motors, her excitement at seeing her old friend making all bitterness fade, all memories disappear. 'What the hell are you doing here?' She hung out of the window.

'Blown a gasket, what else?' Juniper laughed at her as if she had seen Polly only yesterday.

Polly had to keep moving. As soon as she could stop without holding up the traffic further, she parked the car and raced back.

'Oh, Polly, I've been looking for you for months.' Juniper shook her almost crossly. 'Where have you been?'

'Here and there.' Polly grinned.

'Oh, my dear friend . . .' And to a chorus of enraged motorists' car horns they hugged each other.

4

Polly had gone straight to the shops. Tonight she bought chicken instead of her ubiquitous rabbit. She found a pâtisserie and bought a tart and returned to the apartment with armfuls of flowers.

As soon as she entered she regretted insisting Juniper visit her flat. For the first time she saw its shabbiness, the makeshift air about it. What on earth would Juniper think of it after the luxury she was used to? Juniper had suggested Polly drive to the Ritz and she would take them out to dinner but Polly had declined. She could not possibly go if there was a chance Andrew might get away to see her. Instead she had invited Juniper to dinner.

When the casserole was in the oven she ran up to her bedroom and looked at the clothes which hung about the room on the picture rail, for lack of a cupboard. At first she took down one of the two flower-patterned frocks made of cotton, all she could afford, which she had bought at Andrew's insistence. He had complained about her customary funereal black. He said the sight of her in it always made him feel intellectually inadequate.

She chose the blue one with sprigs of red flowers and a white Peter Pan collar and then immediately hung it back and selected a pair of black slacks and a jumper. If she put on the dress he wouldn't come. She had learnt that. Nights she had sat in her cotton frocks and there was no ring on the bell. But then, if she wore her black frequently he surprised her. To liven up the outfit a little, just in case he came, she slung a long, chiffon scarf of emerald green about her neck.

'What a dear little place you have, Polly. Just like a boat,' Juniper swept into the sitting room, dressed in a grey-and-red silk evening dress – Balenciaga, Polly was sure. She clicked open the Hermès crocodile handbag with solid gold chain and taking out a bottle of Ma Griffe unnecessarily patted some on her wrist. Unnecessary since she was already enveloped in a cloud of the scent. She swooped on the cat, who hissed at her, and then admired the view, studied the paintings, talked non-stop, and then plopped down on to one of the large cushions – a black one Polly noticed, with amusement, which made her dress look even more stunning. She suddenly realised that Juniper was nervous. She selected a cushion and dragged it across the floor to sit opposite her. 'I was sorry to hear about Hal.'

Juniper shrugged. 'An expensive lesson.'

'And your son, how is he?'

'I don't know, I rarely see him.'

'Oh, Juniper!' There was a hint of admonishment in Polly's voice.

'Can't,' she said simply and looked away from her, not, Polly realised with a shock, from shame but from her own form of grief.

'And Jonathan, do you see him?' With great effort Polly managed to sound merely polite.

'Not for ages, not since we were in Paris.' She opened her handbag and noisily rootled about in it. Polly felt a wave of anger at her barefaced nerve in admitting she had been here with Jonathan. Still, it didn't matter now she had Andrew. And Juniper, it was obvious, was far from happy – she was too edgy, too nervous. She must try and forget the past and her friend's betrayal, there was no point in harping upon it. 'I left immediately after we got . . .' Juniper continued as she nervously lit a cigarette. 'I've been in France since last August looking for you. Well, that's not strictly true, I did get delayed in Normandy. I bought the most spectacular house – you will love it. And there was a man, of course – well, there's always a man, isn't there?' She chuckled in her deep throaty way. 'We should go to my Manor of the Buttercups – lovely name isn't it?'

'I think you should go home now you've found me. It won't be safe here shortly.'

'I'm not going without you. I promised everyone I wouldn't return without you – glory be, I virtually swore on the family Bible. And a few Germans stomping around aren't going to frighten me.'

'It's not like that, Juniper. It's not a game. I've seen hell in the past weeks driving for the Red Cross.'

'Yes, but once they get what they want they'll stop shooting people and then we can all be friends. I like the Germans, the men are so delicious.'

'Juniper, you're impossible.'

'So, shall we leave tomorrow or tonight?'

'I can't go with you, Juniper. I've someone here . . .' She looked down at her hands, aware she was blushing.

'Who, tell me who?' Juniper looked up with a marked interest.

'He's English, in the army, he's been here since the beginning of the war. I love him, I couldn't leave him. We see so little of each other as it is.'

'But Polly, every day the army is getting pushed back, he'll be the other side of Paris within a day or two. You know that,' Juniper was leaning forward, a serious expression on her face. 'We have to get out soon or we shall be trapped.'

'Then you are taking it all seriously.'

'Of course. I'm terrified, like everyone else. I just refuse to show it.'

'I'll see what he says. I promise.'

'If you don't think I'm being dreadfully rude?' Juniper arched her brows questioningly and delved into her handbag and produced a silver hip flask which she waved at Polly. 'Emergency supplies.' She smiled and took a swig of brandy. 'I saw your loathsome husband.'

Polly sat up warily. 'How is he?'

'Pathetic. Running around packing his little possessions like a demented rabbit. They're off to the country.'

Polly laughed. 'They'll hate that more than the Germans I should think.'

'Why did you stay with him so long?'

'Ignorance really. He could be kind. It was only . . .'

'I know about that. A friend told me of his reputation.'

'I felt it was all my fault. I didn't have to marry him but having done it, I thought I should stay, even though I didn't make any vows in church. And, well, I was so innocent, I thought what he did was normal, that all men were like that. I've learnt since.' She allowed herself a small private smile.

'He looks to me as if he would be very irritating to live with.'

'Yes, he was in the end. All he cares about is his family history. Do you know, he was absolutely disgusted that we only go back to William the Conqueror?'

'Who does he go back to? Caligula?' She lit another cigarette. 'Why did you hide yourself so well, why did you not come home?'

'Pride. And I didn't want to worry my father – he has enough problems in his own life. Also, I didn't want to face my grandmother with my failure – you know how principled she is.'

'Polly, there's something I've got to tell you and it's not pleasant.'

Polly looked at her and felt her stomach lurch. It was rare to hear Juniper speak in such a serious tone and she was not smiling.

'It's about your father.' She took an extra large gulp of her brandy. And there in the little apartment that had always meant safety and security to Polly both vanished simultaneously as Juniper's tale unfolded.

'I killed him,' she said, stunned for this moment beyond grief.

'As your grandmother would say, that's silly talk. It was Richard's decision to come here, no one made him. You mustn't think such thoughts . . .'

'My mother?' Polly did not know why she asked after the woman to whom she never gave a thought these days, but it was as if she could watch Juniper talking and was not able to understand what she was saying.

'Drinking like a fish, lovers by the cartload but still, it's a mystery to me, tremendously successful.'

'Hurstwood?'

Juniper looked at her friend with undisguised surprise and disapproval at what, in the circumstances, seemed an almost heartless question.

'Your father left it to you.'

'Ah, of course,' Polly slumped back on to the cushion. Her face was very white but apart from that she looked very calm – too calm. Juniper got to her feet.

'I'm going out to buy some brandy. Will you be all right for five minutes?' She looked anxiously at her friend. She had anticipated tears, anger, guilt – not calm questions about who owned what. This was a dangerous reaction, Juniper decided; brandy would be called upon before the night was out she was sure.

'Take my key,' Polly said matter-of-factly calling Hursty over to her and burrowing her face in his fur as he settled on her lap.

Half an hour later Juniper let herself back into the flat. From above the kitchen she heard the sound of voices. Collecting glasses from a shelf in the kitchen she mounted the stairs.

'Masses of bubbly, that's what I got. Took me ages to find some well enough chilled,' she announced gaily as she entered the room and placed the bag with the bottles on the floor. 'I . . .' but she never finished the sentence.

'Juniper!' Andrew said with surprise and immediately swung round to face Polly. 'I didn't know . . .' And he began to blush. A slow, bright red tide mounted from his neck and rose up his face so that he appeared to be drowning, from inside, in his own blood.

Polly looked from one to the other. 'It was you!'

'Me, what? I don't understand.' Juniper blustered.

'You slept with Andrew. You filthy bitch!' she spat out viciously.

'I know Andrew, certainly. There's nothing between us.'

'Oh, yes there is, he told me. It was her, wasn't it?' She swung angrily round to face her lover.

'Yes.' Andrew looked at his boots, shame etched on his face.

'Oh God preserve me from honourable men,' Juniper sighed, rolling her eyes to the ceiling. Polly leapt across the room and slapped Juniper first on one cheek and then on the other.

'Don't make jokes, you evil bitch. I was so happy to see you. Wasn't Jonathan enough for you? You had to have Andrew too?' She slapped her again, harder this time, and Juniper reeled back from the force of the blow.

'Polly, for God's sake listen to reason.' Juniper put up her hand to fend off further attack. 'I didn't know you even knew Andrew. It's not my fault. Why don't you bloody well blame him? Why does it always have to be me? He didn't have to make love to me.' She spoke in as calm a voice as she could muster which completely camouflaged what she was feeling. She felt abused and appalled by Polly's attack.

'No man's safe with you around. I don't know why you're not honest and go professional.'

'Polly. That's not fair . . .' Andrew stepped towards her.

'Get out. I never want to see you again,' she screamed at Juniper, and picking up the bag of champagne bottles from the floor hurled them at her. They exploded with the impact.

'What a waste, they were vintage too,' Juniper said calmly as she retrieved her handbag. 'I'm at the Ritz for the next two days, Polly – when you've come to your senses.'

'Get out!' she screamed and once Juniper had gone down the stairs she slumped to the floor and began to sob. 'How could you both? The only people I have left in the world to love. How could you?'

And Andrew tried to comfort the uncontrollable grief which burst forth, unaware of whom and what she was really grieving for.

Polly walked across the city. It was a strange experience. In the last two days the Germans had advanced to thirty miles beyond the city boundary; it would be a day or two at the most before they marched in. The heat was intense, for the second week in June, and Paris was virtually deserted. It was like walking through a city where most of the inhabitants had mysteriously disappeared as if hit by some unseen catastrophe. There were no buses, no taxis, the few cars for the most part contained army officers rushing hither and thither with serious faces and sheafs of papers as if they knew what they were doing. The cafés were closed, the boulevards empty. Despite the warmth, the windows of buildings were shut, the shutters closed tight as though the houses themselves did not wish to see what was now inevitable. Only those who needed to be here, or who could not afford to escape, had remained. The only cats and dogs to be seen were the strays, the pets had long gone or were carefully barricaded into their homes. In the distance, instead of the noise of a busy city was the relentless booming of guns.

The Ritz was busy, the entrance hall a seething mass of people. Army personnel who had been billeted there were checking out. Staff were packing away everything that was movable and the last remaining guests were making frantic efforts to leave, noisily refusing to believe that the hall porter could not arrange transport and tickets for them. Round one table in the bar, like an oasis of calm in the panic surrounding them, sat a group of newspaper journalists with hard faces watching the chaos with a strange air of detachment as if the war were of no great importance but just another story to be superseded by yet another tomorrow.

Polly approached the desk nervously. She feared that Juniper might have left already. When she was told

Juniper had not yet booked out, she felt another and different kind of fear, wondering if Juniper would be angry with her, refuse to help her.

She tapped on the door of the suite and upon hearing Juniper's voice paused, still unsure what she was going to say. She opened the door and entered.

'I'm sorry.' She stood in the doorway and knew she was about to cry again as she had done almost non-stop for the past two days.

'My friend,' Juniper looked up from her packing and smiled broadly at her as she crossed the room with arms held wide in greeting. 'I'm sorry, too,' she said as she took Polly's hands in hers and led her into the room.

'I'd no idea you knew Andrew, you know.'

'I realise. I was overreacting – it was on top of everything else, I suppose. Andrew made me see sense. The last of his unit has left. He wants me to leave with you. He thinks we will be safer together.' She blew her nose hard into her handkerchief. 'God, I wish I could stop crying.'

'You will, I promise. Andrew's a sensible man.' She took out her own handkerchief and gently wiped a tear from Polly's cheek. 'Now,' she said briskly. 'To business. We're too late for the trains, I'm afraid. My maid went this morning to arrange tickets and it's total bedlam there. Not a hope in hell of even getting close enough to an official to bribe. I managed to get her into a friend's car to take her home to Switzerland. I thought of going there, but if we did we could be trapped for ages. So, with no chance of a train, we'll have to go by road. Look . . .' She spread out a large map of France on to the table. 'I'd initially planned to go to my new house to wait to see what was going to happen. But a friend in the French army advised me not to. That's where the worst of the fighting will be, he says. He suggested we should make for the South and then, if the unthinkable happens and France falls, we can always pop into Spain or Portugal and get home from there. With both of us driving it should only take a couple of days, three at the most. If we go by Tours and . . .' She looked up to see Polly standing clutching her hanky and shaking from head to toe. She obviously hadn't heard one word she had been saying. Juniper dropped the map and bundled Polly into her arms and let her lean against her and cry.

'You won't want me with you if I go on like this . . .' Polly eventually said between sobs. 'It's just that every so often I realise what's happened, and when I think of my father . . .'

'I understand. Good Lord, you'll be reeling from shock for days, weeks maybe. You need a drink. I do too.' She smiled as she poured two large brandies.

'Not for me, it's too early.'

'Drink,' Juniper ordered. 'It's never too early.' She chuckled and at the familiar sound Polly smiled. 'However, there is one thing more, and I think we should get it out in the open straight away. Then if you hate me after that, we both know where we stand.'

'What, for God's sake?' Polly felt sick with apprehension.

'You're not exactly alone any more. I'm your sister,' Juniper announced with a huge grin on her face.

Polly sat down with a bump. 'Is this a joke, Juniper? If so, I don't find it funny.'

'No joke, I'm being serious. We have my dreadful father and your dreadful mother to blame. It seems they got up to some hanky-panky and . . .'

'But *my* father?'

'Richard was on his way to tell you himself, he didn't want you to hear it from anyone else. Apparently he feared that your mother . . . That's why I'm spilling the beans now. If he wanted you to know then I think you should.'

To Juniper's surprise Polly burst into further floods of tears. She felt a slight tinge of annoyance: she had expected Polly to be as happy as she was with the news.

She had told her to cheer her up, not to make her cry again.

'Sorry you think it's sad news,' she said a shade petulantly.

'It's all too much to take in on top of everything else, and . . . well I feel I've lost my father all over again. Twice in forty-eight hours.'

'Stupid me, I didn't think. I should have waited but I've been bursting to tell you. That's why we made such instant friends, I'm sure,' she said brightly.

But Polly did not look as if she was in the mood for brightness or to be cheered up. 'Come on then, let's go,' Juniper said in a more serious voice, picking up her handbag and a small attaché case.

'Where?'

'Escaping, of course. Exciting isn't it?'

'But all this . . .' Polly waved her hand around the room filled with half-packed cases.

'I shall have to abandon it, I'm afraid. When you're an escapee, you've got to travel light. We'll drive over and pick up your stuff.' And she ushered Polly briskly from the room.

Juniper had not been telling the whole truth. In her car, already stowed away, were two large cases and on the back seat two fur coats on which stood boxes of canned food, a crate of champagne, a crate of mineral water and a large basket of crystallised fruit.

'Travelling light?' At last Polly smiled.

'For me, madame, that is exceptionally light.'

At the apartment, to Juniper's relief, Polly managed to keep herself under control but it was hard after the shocks of the past few days. Ideally she wanted to lock the door and hide away here from everyone, to grieve in private in the safety of her little flat, not to abandon it in this heartless way. At least her luggage was small. Her few clothes fitted into one case. She began to pack her books and her plates but, realising that she would need neither on the journey and the less they had the better, she reluctantly left them. She paused in the doorway, giving one last look about her home, saying goodbye to the cosy familiarity. Purposefully she turned, slammed the door shut and ran down the stairs to Juniper's car.

'I thought this might come in handy,' she indicated her small radio.

'A very good idea. What's in the box?'

'Hursty, my cat. I couldn't leave him.'

'Well, I hope he likes caviar, we've no fish,' Juniper said as she put the car into gear. The cat mewed in protest. 'The poor darling can't travel in a box, he can't see out, he'll be bored to smithereens. We must find him a basket.'

As the guns boomed, as the great German army moved inexorably closer by the minute, the two motored about, Polly insisting Hursty would be fine, stopping at every likely shop and banging frantically on the door demanding service. It was over an hour before they found one owner willing to open up for them and Juniper emerged triumphantly with a fine cat basket. Finally, with Hursty inquisitively peering out of the basket, they sped quickly through the empty streets.

Although Paris was empty, the roads leading away from it were jammed. As far as the eye could see stretched a long trail of cars, carts, bicycles, overladen prams – anything with wheels – moving in inches rather than feet. In the heat tempers were frayed, engines overheated and cars stalled, all adding to the chaos.

Four hours later they had travelled less than twelve miles. But in that four hours they had talked themselves almost dry as they went over the past, and Jonathan, and Andrew again, and their own new relationship.

'My poor father.'

Juniper said nothing, guiltily hoping Polly would never find out that she had attempted to seduce him and had so nearly succeeded – there were limits after all, she thought to herself. 'But he had known since you were the tiniest thing and had always loved you. I think that's nicer than a real father. I mean a real father feels he's got to love you. You can never be sure if he does so only out of duty. But yours really did love you and just because you are you.'

It was this fragment of conversation that more than any other helped Polly, enabled her to accept this new situation and calmed her.

There was no question of pulling over to the side of the road to eat a picnic, they doubted if the other cars would ever have let them back into line. So, sitting in the car while Juniper moved forward whenever she could, they ate a meal of *coeur de palmiers*, ham, caviar and candied fruit washed down by champagne.

'Escaping could be fun . . .' Polly giggled after her unaccustomed third glass of champagne. 'Where on earth did you get all this?'

'From the chef of the Ritz, of course. Finish the bottle, it'll go flat otherwise . . .'

Juniper did not finish the sentence for, as if from nowhere, a plane appeared, flying towards them up the column of stationary cars. It looked so beautiful and in the heat haze seemed to hover over them like giant hawk. Neither of them realised that the spray which burst from its wings were bullets that hit the tarmac in dusty spurts, ripping through metal, causing the screams that eventually brought them to their senses.

'Get out. The ditch . . .' Juniper shouted and pushed Polly ahead of her.

'Hursty!' she wailed.

'Bugger Hursty, he's got nine lives,' Juniper yelled back, pushing Polly unceremoniously in front of her into the safety of the ditch.

The ditch was crowded with a great huddle of people. The noise was intolerable as some cried from wounds already inflicted, and others screamed out the names of loved ones from whom they'd been separated. A woman beside them, a baby in her arms, two small children crouched beside her, rocked back and forth in mute despair.

The aeroplane had swept up the column and heads began to appear over the grass verge only to pop back down again rapidly. The plane had banked and turned beyond the end of the column and was now making its way back firing indiscriminately.

'Heads down,' shouted Juniper in a voice that sounded to Polly almost as if she were enjoying herself.

'Michelle . . . !' It was a scream from the woman beside them. 'Michelle? *Où es-tu?*' she cried.

'Oh, my God, look . . .' Polly pointed. In the stubble of the field a small child was wandering, picking up stones and examining them as death rained out of the sky.

'Is that your child?' Juniper thumped a man on the back to attract his attention and pointed to the child.

'*Non, non,*' the man looked sheepishly away.

'What about you?' She looked belligerently at a young man crouching on the other side of them.

'*Merde!*' He spat a huge gob of phlegm in their direction.

'Well, that's one word of French I do know. Men!' she said, exasperated, and hitching up her skirt began to scramble up the side of the ditch.

'Juniper, no!' Polly grabbed at her skirt but Juniper shook her hand away. She lay for a moment on top of the ditch watching until the plane was furthest from them. She leapt up and ran twisting and turning across the field towards the child. The plane turned and swooped nearer, the bullets making a metallic *ping ping ping* as they strafed the column. Juniper scooped the toddler into her arms. She stood upright in the field in the bright sunshine.

'You son of a bitch, you bloody bastard!' she screamed, waving her fist at the plane which was circling above her, watching her. And suddenly the wings of the plane tilted as if saluting her and with a graceful arc flew away from the column of cars.

Juniper returned to tumultuous applause and Michelle to a big slap from her mother.

'Stop that,' Juniper pushed the woman. 'I didn't risk my neck for you to beat the brat up. Stop this minute. Polly, you tell her.'

Angrily the mother pushed at Juniper who stepped forward as if to begin a fight.

'Juniper, leave her, she's upset.'

'I'm upset, too.'

'I know, I know. But look . . .' She pointed to where the mother was now smothering the child with kisses.

'She didn't even say thank you, ungrateful bitch.' Juniper turned towards her car.

'Don't you ever do anything like that again,' Polly ordered, following her. 'I've never been so frightened in my life.'

'What was I supposed to do, let the little scrap get shot?'

'They wouldn't have shot a child.'

'Oh, no. Then what's that?' A few feet further along, sprawled on the road as if asleep in the sun lay the bodies of two small boys, their mother dead beside them.

'Oh, dear God, the butchers.' Her hand shot to her mouth as she felt the bile of nausea rising. 'I've seen dead soldiers, but children . . .' She stood stock still, white-faced with shock and began to shiver. Juniper took her firmly by the hand and bundled her into the car.

'This convoy is a sitting duck. Look on the map and find out where the next side road leads to. I think we should take it and try to get South by secondary roads.' Juniper thrust the map at Polly to give her something to do. 'Don't you?' she added quickly, as if suddenly realising how bossy she sounded.

They were, unfortunately, not alone in this decision and the secondary roads, if not as congested, were still busy. But they consoled themselves that they now moved ahead in feet rather than inches.

At each village and town they were stopped at barri-
cades and their documents were demanded. Never patient,
Juniper found these endless checks intolerable but speaking sharply only delayed them further. Eventually it was
Polly who handled the documents, cajoled the officials,
calming Juniper. Finding petrol was an almost impossible
task until Juniper opened her attaché case and pulled out a
fistful of dollars. The car was filled up instantly and two
spare cans provided. Despite the presence of the petrol in
the boot, Juniper insisted on smoking and Polly sat waiting
at any moment to be blown into little pieces.

As they waited at one village Juniper got out her
handbag mirror.

'My God, what a wreck. It seems impossible that I was
out dining the night before last. Look at me . . .' She
picked up a lump of her skirt stained with grass and filthy.
'And just look at my stockings. God, I want a bath.'

Evening was approaching but every inn and hotel they
stopped at was full. They tried several farms but either
they were full or the young women were made to feel most
unwelcome. They tried a barn but both took fright at the
unpleasant stares of the men who had already take up
positions for the night.

'I suggest we motor through the night, one sleeping one
driving. I've friends who live near Tours. If we can get
there tomorrow, they'll put us up for the night.'

'If we can get there tomorrow,' Polly said cynically,
very much doubting it.

But many chose not to travel through the night since the
use of headlamps was forbidden at risk of being shot. This
was where Polly's time with the Red Cross came into its
own. She was used now to driving through France with no
lights.

It was nearly midnight, but midnight of five days later,
when they arrived at the château of Juniper's friends.

Every door of the château was locked, each window firmly shuttered. High in the roof they saw a chink of light and they hammered on the door, yelling and shouting until they were nearly voiceless, their cries startling the roosting birds and waking every dog in the area. Eventually a disgruntled retainer unbolted the front door and in a surly manner told them to clear off. It took Juniper's address book with the names of his employers in it to convince him they were respectable. Grudgingly he opened the door and let them into the kitchen. He stood to one side, arms folded, sucking his teeth noisily and watchful of every fork and plate. He relaxed a little at Polly's excellent French and unbent sufficiently to say that the Duc had left for his estate in the South of France two weeks before. The sniff with which he imparted this information speaking louder than words his true feelings for his master, he then lapsed into sullen silence.

'Do you think he intends to stand there all night? He's like a Cerberus fallen on hard times,' said Juniper while continuing to smile in his direction.

'He's only doing his job, he doesn't know us from Adam,' Polly replied, conscious of how rude it was for them to be speaking English in front of him.

'Eve, more like, judging by the look in his eye. He's not as old as he looks, you know. See if he'll rustle up some food for us.'

But at the mention of food and hot water he seemed to have become momentarily deaf. Until that is, Juniper's attaché case appeared and dollars changed hands and he shuffled away into the back of the house.

'How clever of you to bring the money.'

'Never travel without money and especially dollars. That's what my grandfather always said.'

'But so much?'

'Who knows what lies ahead and how much we shall need?'

Juniper had just begun to voice her doubts that they were ever likely to see the servant again when he reappeared with bread, cheese and some eggs. Without being asked, he lit the range, muttering continuously in a patois that was beyond Polly's capabilities. He hauled two large pans of water on to it and then disappeared to return with a tin hip bath which unceremoniously he plonked before the range.

'How kind.' Juniper rewarded him with one of her most beguiling smiles and was rewarded by a black-stump toothed one in return. 'Quick, Polly before he reverts, ask him about some beds.'

Polly asked. He lit a candle.

'The blackout,' he said, putting his finger to his mouth as if it were a secret. He beckoned them to follow and led them through the great empty building, their footsteps echoing as they passed through rooms where the furniture was covered in white sheeting, making the rooms look as if they were inhabited by malformed, crouching ghosts. On a bend in the stairs the candle flickered.

'I hope it stays alight otherwise we shall lose him in this warren,' Polly whispered.

'No problem.' Juniper chuckled, feeling no need to whisper herself. 'We'll just follow his pong.'

They stopped in a long corridor and with an expansive gesture of his arms he indicated they could choose any of the rooms. They chose two side-by-side with an inter-connecting door. They returned to the kitchen where it was apparent that he did not wish to leave them alone. It took another dollar bill to get rid of him.

Polly cooked them omelettes, while Juniper sat drinking champagne, smoking and watching Hursty slither about the kitchen, nervously exploring every nook and cranny. That omelette, they both agreed, was the best they had ever tasted. And the baths they subsequently took, their knees hunched up to fit into the hip bath, warmed by the fire from the open doors of the range, were the most luxurious ever. They brought in Polly's radio which they plugged in and it was only then, after a lengthy twiddling of the knobs, they discovered that Pétain had signed an armistice. France had truly fallen.

They sat stunned, either side of the pine table, totally unable to comprehend what they had heard. If the events of the past few days had been serious, this was a catastrophe. Both felt frightened and isolated but neither felt they could confide her thoughts to the other. Juniper tried to joke and failed and Polly tried to laugh at the joke and failed also. Both had to face the fact that they might not be able to return, might even die. And for Polly there was the added worry of what was happening to Andrew. And then both found themselves thinking of other houses, other times – Juniper found herself longing for Gwenfer and Polly longed for the safety of her home, Hurstwood. And both wished that Gertie were here.

When they were so tired that even fear could not keep them awake they made their way by candlelight to bed. But they rejected separate rooms and chose to sleep with each other – more from comfort than anything else – with Hursty wound round the top of Polly's head.

They stayed at the château for two days, resting and planning, listening desperately to the radio for any good news. There was none. They learnt that they had escaped from Paris just in time, that the Germans had entered the following day. They learnt that the great Allied army had been beaten, forced to evacuate ignominiously back across the Channel. This news made them feel even more isolated than before. They had to get to Portugal, that was obvious now. Nowhere in France was going to be safe. So they reloaded the car, presented the radio to the astonished servant, and sped off to the South.

It had been difficult on the road before but now it was almost impossible. Each town and village was bursting with refugees from the north and there was little fresh food to buy. Not unreasonably the shop-keepers were reserving what they had for the local townspeople. Sometimes, though, they were lucky and Juniper's dollars persuaded a recalcitrant shopkeeper to find a loaf of bread and some cheese for them. They now realised they must ration their tins of food and Hursty who, at the beginning, had loudly proclaimed he did not like caviar, conceded and they reserved the remaining tins for him.

Upon arriving at a town they would immediately try the best hotel – if they were unlucky there it was unlikely they would get a bed for the night anywhere else, for the best hotel filled up last. Juniper who had never slept anywhere in her life that did not boast five stars had now learnt to accept a bed in a peasant's cottage as if it were a luxury – and frequently the cost was the same, she would comment ironically. They had become used to sleeping with each other – and frequently with strangers – and many were the nights they slept in the car. Juniper's address book was a marvel to Polly, no matter where they were, it seemed, Juniper had an address of a friend or acquaintance.

'Isn't anyone in this country prepared to stay and fight?' she said bitterly as she turned once more from the house of a friend she had assured Polly would be there.

'You can't blame them. If the government has given in what is there to stay for?' Polly said.

'You always were so damned reasonable,' Juniper snapped and then realising she was being unpleasant, smiled. 'Just as well one of us is, I suppose.' And she laughed, all bad humour gone for she appeared incapable of staying cross about anything for any length of time.

For a week they had been pressing on southwards through Limoges, past Périgueux, Bergerac. Polly had always wanted to see more of France and she was now getting her wish. The vastness and beauty of this great country stunned her. Each area she saw she longed to live in. She fell in love with the Loire valley with its great ribbon of a river looking like a wide strip of mercury as it slid, lazily and slowly, towards the sea past the huge noble châteax which she prayed the Germans would not harm.

Lying in a field after a picnic near the banks of the Dordogne, with the wind rippling through the dense trees on the steep banks, and the crystal clear water gurgling over the rocks, she could easily imagine herself back in Devon and she felt an ache for her own beleaguered country. At such times she would have liked to suggest to Juniper that they stayed and took their chance in this other England but she knew she could not, that they must press on, and she remained silent.

There were times when she would slip away and walk for an hour or two. She needed to be alone because she found she had become used to solitude, and although grateful for Juniper's company, it was necessary for her. Juniper found this difficult to understand, to her solitude meant loneliness, and loneliness meant silence and a time to examine oneself, not an occupation that Juniper found particularly comfortable. If Polly went for a walk, Juniper would search out other people to talk to and if none were available she would bury her head in a book, anything rather than think. But Polly needed time to think. If she could concentrate on Andrew strongly enough she felt she might in some way be keeping him safe. She would spend this time thinking of those magic hours with him, and sometimes she would hurl herself on to the grass and ache with longing for him. And, also, she had to think of her father and this new father Juniper had given her. She could not believe it, try as she might. How could Richard, with all his love for her, not have been her father? She felt he was, she grieved for him as a father, she wanted no other. She rejected Marshall from her mind but she could not bring herself to tell Juniper, who was so happy to have her as a sister, and she could not hurt her, not now, not yet.

Each day Polly felt more bedraggled and the bath in the château was now a cherished memory. In even the best hotels the water for bathing was so severely rationed it could never be called a true bath. Often the waiting time for a bath was so long they would wash in the basin in their room. They had become experts in washing thoroughly in a minimum of water.

But Juniper never looked bedraggled. She always looked smart, her hair well-groomed, her make-up perfect. It was a continuing mystery to Polly how this was managed. Even in the humblest hotel Juniper would insist on changing for dinner, or what passed for dinner. And she seemed to have an inexhaustible supply of white kid gloves, for as soon as a mark appeared on one pair they would be replaced by another.

Without Juniper Polly knew she would have given up, but nothing seemed to impair Juniper's spirit and humour. Polly would have forgiven her if, after her pampered life, she had been disgruntled and petulant – but she never was. She managed to convey the idea to everyone they met that this was adventure and she was enjoying it enormously. Maybe she was, Polly thought. For, although their friendship had been renewed and deepened, she knew she did not really know her friend. Although she had learnt more about Juniper, she began to realise that still there was a part of her she would never know. For sometimes conversations would abruptly stop as if Juniper had decided she had gone far enough, that it was leading to a subject she did not wish to pursue further. It was as if Juniper's life was lived in a series of boxes to which she was not prepared to give Polly every key.

They began to acquire obsessions. Finding fresh bread was one – if they could buy a fresh loaf then they would get a bed for the night. If they saw three Rolls-Royces in one day then the war would end – they never did. The biggest obsession was the collecting of petrol. They had not once run out and they had spare cans in the back but at the merest hint of available petrol they would make a detour, as much as twenty miles, to try and buy some – if they never ran out a boat would be waiting for them.

Juniper's dollars were accepted in preference to French francs offered by others, a situation that embarrassed Polly more than she cared to admit. Juniper merely felt others were to blame for not having seen what was going to happen and for failing to get themselves some dollars in reserve. However, those selfsame dollars had also led them into trouble.

On one occasion the garage owner had indicated that it would be better if Juniper negotiated with him inside his house for he did not want his regulars witnessing the transaction. Two minutes later she reappeared in a hurry, red-faced with indignation and with no petrol.

'What happened?' Polly asked as she switched the ignition on.

'Dirty bastard. He didn't want my dollars, he wanted me! Imagine, a filthy old man like that,' she said angrily as she changed her gloves.

'Oh, Juniper, how awful. What did you do?'

'Kicked him where it hurts a man most – how he howled! Come on, let's get out before he recovers and comes racing after me.' She was laughing now, all anger gone.

Juniper had learnt to be discreet in her negotiations with garage owners but frequently the murmurs that greeted their good fortune were threatening and they would have to get away quickly before anyone took it upon themselves to steal their petrol. After one garage stop it appeared their luck had completely run out.

As always, they drove away at speed. Four miles outside the town, deciding they were now safe, they slowed down as they passed through a pretty wood.

They felt happy, they had managed to buy two cans of petrol; with what was left in the tank they felt confident they would reach Biarritz.

They were singing 'Greensleeves' in harmony and feeling very pleased with themselves when suddenly, less than a hundred yards further on, a car appeared and swerved across the narrow road, completely blocking it. Juniper stopped their car. Two men got out and began walking up the road towards them. The blocking of the road was ominous but their slow measured step, the constant stare that never wavered from their car was horribly menacing.

'They were at that last garage,' Polly gasped. 'I remember thinking how rough they looked. They look as if they're up to no good,' she added lamely.

'Well, they need not think they're getting our juice. I'll see to that.' Juniper clutched hold of the steering wheel as if for support. Then one of the men bent down and picked up a large piece of wood. 'You're right, Polly, they're after us. Hold on to your hat!' And with a loud 'Oh boy!', Juniper put her foot on the accelerator and aimed the car directly at them. The two men stood firm but Juniper did not falter, she drove straight for them. At the last moment the men leapt for their lives but not before one had hurled the wood, shattering the windscreen. Covered in glass, Juniper put her foot further down and the large car hurtled towards the bonnet of the other car blocking their way. Polly ducked. There was a shattering of glass and metal, their car rocked alarmingly from side to side. The other car was flung to the side, rolled over and burst into flames.

'So much for civilisation!' Juniper laughed loudly. 'Gee, wasn't that fun?'

'No. I was terrified witless. What if we'd turned over?'

'Of course we wouldn't have. I'm not that daft. This car is much heavier. I knew we'd win,' she said. 'Well, I hoped we would.' She grinned sheepishly at Polly.

Dusk was falling as they entered a small market town. They parked in the main square and sat for a good ten minutes picking the glass out of each other's hair, both giggling uncontrollably when Juniper pointed out they must look like monkeys grooming each other. With a broken windscreen the car and its contents were vulnerable. But they were hungry and still shaky from their adventure and needed to search for food. They would have to leave the car and hope the citizens were honest. They removed the attaché case and Hursty's basket – their two most precious possessions.

They found a small bistro which was open and miraculously had plenty of food to sell. They had two large bowls of soup and two plates of casserole the contents of which neither was capable of identifying. However, both had reached the point where they didn't care. After the meal, washed down with a large carafe of red wine, they returned to their car feeling quite elated. Everything was exactly as they had left it, but then they realised that it was now too late to find a bed for the night. Gone were the days when French towns were awake half the night. As soon as darkness fell the streets were deserted.

'Serves us right for taking so long over our meal,' Polly said as she fed Hursty the scraps she had saved, wrapped up in a paper napkin. She was not having much success since Hursty's palate was obviously more discerning than their own.

Juniper sat dejectedly on the running board. 'Another night in the car, I'm afraid.'

A man approached and having ascertained they had nowhere to sleep, offered to help. They both looked at him suspiciously at which he assured them he was the mayor of this town. Reassured by such credentials and dreading another night of discomfort, they followed him across the square, through large iron gates and into a building that smelt unmistakably of disinfectant. He led

the way up a long flight of stairs. '*Voilà*,' he said with the
air of a magician as he flung open a door. Before them was
a long ward of empty beds. 'Take your pick, my dear
young ladies.'

'A hospital?'

'The maternity ward. But you are lucky tonight, we
have no babies.'

That night they had a bath and a bed each for no one
else turned up to join them and no babies arrived. Hursty
tried every bed in the ward before finally ending up with
Polly.

One of the greatest problems that plagued them was that
rumours ran like wildfire and they very much regretted
having given the radio away. At every town and village, in
every café and garage, there were prophets of doom
spreading fear and despondency. Both had made a pact
not to listen to any of it. But some rumours they could not
ignore. They were told that England had fallen, London
was destroyed and that the Germans were eating babies.
They both knew too many Germans from the embassy in
London to believe the baby stories. And it was beyond
belief that the British would have given in without a fight,
thought Polly. And a London without a Mayfair, without
the clubs, without her favourite restaurants, without
Harrods and Harvey Nichols was impossible for Juniper
to imagine.

The rumours of the impossibility of getting visas for
Spain and Portugal began to haunt them the nearer they
got to Biarritz. Shifty-eyed men with cigarettes dangling
from their mouths who spoke in whispers behind cupped
hands began to proliferate. £20 it would cost them, said
one. £50 claimed another. And one, assessing the car and
the furs in the back, expected £100 each. Each of these
men claimed to have relations in any embassy or consulate they cared to mention, and each claimed he needed
their passports – no need for them to bother their pretty

selves. Always their passports, never themselves. But they were wiser now and both realised that without their passports they would be stranded. They would smile their thanks and drive on alone, often with the curses of their 'saviours' ringing in their ears.

But, on the whole however, they trusted the French – too much.

Mid-afternoon, finding a café open with real coffee and pastries for sale, they stopped. Hursty was curled up in his basket fast asleep so they decided to leave both car and cat.

Half an hour later, when they returned, congratulating themselves on finding such excellent coffee – a commodity becoming more and more difficult to track down – it was to find that the car, with Hursty in it, had gone. Slumping on to the side of the kerb Polly burst into tears.

'Oh, really Polly, pull yourself together, do. Crying won't get him back.' Juniper was aware she spoke too sharply but she could not help herself, she could feel panic rising in her – with no car, no clothes, no extra food or drink the situation was serious.

'Why are you often so hard?' Polly spluttered at her through her tears.

'I'm not being hard, I'm being practical. It's still miles to Biarritz. We've lost almost everything. I'm sorry about the cat, I really am, but I can't worry about it for the moment – don't you see?' She bent down and picked up her attaché case from the pavement. 'At least the bastards didn't get our dollars. Come on Polly, try and cheer up. Let's go back to the café to see if they can help.'

Everyone in the café was sympathetic. The patron poured them both large brandies and refused payment. Juniper asked where the nearest police station was but the assembled company were unanimous that they would be wasting their time. Not only were the local gendarmes fools who could not find a cabbage in a cabbage patch, they were told, but with a war on the last thing in which the police would be interested would be a stolen car. The patron, a large man with skin like lard and a pock-marked nose, poured them two more brandies. As he did so he smiled, but it emerged as more of a leer than a smile, thought Juniper.

Before they drank their brandies she ushered Polly into the evil-smelling lavatory at the back of the building.

'I'm not peeing here,' Polly said wrinkling her nose. 'It's foul.'

'I'm not asking you to. Take these,' from her case she handed Polly a pile of dollar bills. 'Stuff them in your knickers or somewhere. If we get separated, at least we've both got money.'

'Juniper, don't even say such a thing.' Polly looked horrified. Maybe Juniper was fed up with her. She certainly had snapped at her over Hursty. Perhaps she thought she would be faster on her own. Once Polly had not minded being on her own but now, after all the things that had happened, she could not face the prospect.

'The case is safe with you.'

'We didn't think we'd lose the car, did we? It looks to me as if anything is possible and I can't face the responsibility of losing you and knowing you've no money. Careful, that money is slipping out.' She pointed to the cascade of bills falling out of Polly's pants.

Polly transferred some of the notes to her suspender belt, a few she carefully placed in her shoes. Juniper did the same, leaving a third of the dollars in the case.

They returned to the café and the brandy. Juniper, turning one of her most winning smiles on the patron, asked Polly to beg him for some bread and cheese since they had lost all their money.

'But that isn't true,' Polly protested.

'Oh, really,' Juniper rolled her eyes in exasperation. 'Sometimes Polly . . . These are exceptional circumstances. And the way everything is going at the moment, if they think we are loaded with dollars we won't get out of here alive.'

Polly, feeling stupid, did as she was asked. To her surprise, the man acquiesced and handed them a baguette and a large slab of cheese. They made their farewells and slipped out into the heat of the late afternoon.

'What a kind man,' Polly said.

'Um . . .' Juniper replied. 'I don't like the way he looked at us. Let's get moving.'

They set out along the road, their progress impeded by Juniper's high heels. A lorry stopped, and a farmer offered them a lift. Both wondered if this was wise but the sudden appearance of a small boy hanging out of the window made up their mind for them. They were disappointed that the lift was only for four miles, but at least it was four miles less.

Both were tired and it would soon be dusk so they left the road and cut across a field towards a wood where they intended to camp. They walked for a good ten minutes into the wood, grateful for the coolness that the trees afforded. They heard the trickle of water and following the sound found a small river, the water cascading crystal clear through a steep wooded valley. At least they had water to drink and at least they would be able to wash.

They gathered moss and clumps of grass and made themselves a bed in between the large gnarled roots of an oak.

'Like the babes in the wood,' Juniper laughed. And then, seeing the irritated expression on Polly's face, stopped. 'Polly, don't be such a misery – cheer up.'

'What have I to be happy about? My boyfriend is God knows where. My father's dead, or rather the man I've spent the whole of my life thinking of and loving as my father is dead,' she snapped, her voice shrill with emotion she was unable to control. 'I've lost my cat – the one creature who was constant to me. I'm tired and I'm hungry and you tell me to *cheer up*?'

'I was only trying to help.'

'You're not helping, you're making everything worse.'

'We'll find Hursty.'

'Don't talk to me as if I were a child. Of course we won't find him, where would we begin to look?'

'You mustn't give up hope.'

'Shut up! God, you get on my nerves. You're stupid, Juniper.' Polly looked at her angrily and having started found she wanted to continue. 'Stupid, with your endless cheerfulness and asinine remarks. Hope? What the hell have either of us got to hope for? We're never going to make it now.'

'Polly, I'm sorry . . .'

'No you're not. You've always caused me trouble and now is no exception. I hate you. Just get out of my sight. Leave me alone . . .' She turned her head into the sweet-smelling grass. She had never known such bleakness in her life, she burrowed into the grassy nest longing to cry, longing for her cat.

Juniper stood for a moment looking down on her, surprised. This was so unlike Polly. Surely she didn't really hate her? Impotently she kicked at the root of the tree, turned abruptly and walked off along the bank of the river.

She had not meant to upset Polly, she had only been cheerful because by joking she covered her guilt, and jokes could hide the real fear she was beginning to feel. It was all her fault Hursty had gone. Polly had insisted on carrying him everywhere with her and Juniper had too often been irritated by the cat's wailing in the various cafés and restaurants – no one loved animals more than Juniper but she felt strongly they should be excluded from places where one ate and slept. When she had seen the cat asleep it had been her idea not to disturb it – 'Don't wake the dear little thing . . .' she had said. And it was due to her carelessness in leaving the keys in the ignition, that the car had gone. It was hardly surprising

Polly was furious with her . . . She really could not blame her.

A noise on the other side of the steep bank caught her attention. It was dark now as she crept up the bank and peered through the trees.

What she saw made her dizzy. In a clearing, by the light of a bonfire, she saw a group of men in uniform. To the side was a row of vehicles neatly parked along the wide path that led out of the wood. On each vehicle was painted the unmistakable sign of the swastika.

She ducked down and began, stealthily to slide down the bank. All this time they had thought themselves safe and miles ahead of the Germans, yet here they were. She must return to Polly . . .

As she turned to head back, an arm from behind grabbed her tightly around her waist. A large hand smelling of oil and petrol was clamped over her mouth – the fumes so strong she thought she would be sick. She fought the nausea, fearful that she might choke. Her terrified eyes saw the cuff of a German uniform.

Unceremoniously the soldier pushed her along the river bank for about a hundred yards. He then pushed and dragged her up the bank and back into the wood. She felt her knees grazed, cursed him for the loss of her silk stockings. They stopped and, turning her around, he pushed her against a tree. With his hand still over her mouth, he began, roughly, to pluck at her dress. Juniper stood rigid with terror. Then panic spurred her to action and she began to struggle to get away, which only made him hold her harder.

The dollars! He must not find the dollars. She could think only of the money. The thought of losing the money made her mind razor sharp as she planned what she could do. She stopped fighting him.

He relaxed and began to unbutton his trousers, his hand more loosely clamped over her mouth. She had only to move her head to one side and it was free. She smiled at him. At her smile he exclaimed, stopped fumbling with his trousers and stood gazing at her with an amazed expression. He was tall and blond, the kind of man she would normally have taken a distinct interest in.

'Slowly,' she said in her husky voice. 'You must not rush things so.' She leant back against the tree and again smiled at him, wishing she knew some German, hoping he understood. He did. The tone of her voice, in any language, was unmistakable. He smiled back.

She began to undress herself, slowly, fearful of revealing the money if she moved too quickly. She folded her clothes neatly and stood back, naked, her arms up in welcome. With a groan of delight the soldier was upon her, kissing her, whispering incomprehensibly to her.

He dragged her on to the ground and was upon her. Her hands slid the length of his body and at his waistband found what she had hoped would be there – a knife. With agonising slowness she removed the knife from its sheath, all the time sighing and groaning as if she were enjoying what he was doing to her. He rose slightly and her hand moved quickly, stabbing him with all her strength beneath his ribcage.

He made no sound but looked at her with blank astonishment as his eyes glazed and he slumped on top of her. She struggled to free herself from him, frantically pushing at him, wriggling from beneath him, feeling he was suffocating her with his weight. At last she was free. She looked down at him with loathing. She looked at her body and she began to shake – she was covered in his blood. She grabbed her clothes and clutching them to her ran headlong into the wood, oblivious of the twigs that thrashed her naked body, heedless of the roots of trees over which she stumbled.

She stopped. She stood panting, the air rasping through her lungs. She held her breath to listen. Faintly to the right she heard the sound of running water. She made her way to the river and followed it, more slowly now, aware that by panicking she could so easily have lost her way.

With a relief that made her shoulders slump she recognised in the moonlight the spot where Polly lay sleeping.

'Polly, wake up.' She shook her urgently.

'Go away.'

'Polly, something dreadful's happened. Please wake up.'

'What's happened?' Polly sat up rubbing her eyes, stretching her stiffened body.

'I've killed a German soldier.'

'Oh, don't be silly.' Polly lay back on the grass as if about to go back to sleep.

'But I have. Wake up, for God's sake, we've got to get out of here before the others find him.'

Again Polly sat up, wide awake now from the urgency in Juniper's voice. 'There are no Germans in this part of France, they're up in the north, miles away.'

'No, they're not, they're about a mile up this river and . . .'

But she did not finish for at that moment in the light from the moon Polly saw the blood on her friend's body. 'Oh, my God, Juniper! What happened?'

'The filthy bastard was going to rape me. No one takes me – or my dollars – unless I want them to. I tricked him, I killed him,' and she began to shake, violent tremors which ripped through her body. Her teeth began to chatter as though they would never stop.

Polly leapt to her feet. She took Juniper in her arms and tried to comfort her.

'Look at me . . . just look at me . . .' Juniper began plucking at her skin as if she could pluck away the blood.

'Come, my darling. Shush, come with Polly.' Gently Polly led her towards the water. 'Let the river wash it all away. You'll feel better when it's gone. Come.' And using her hands she cupped the water from the river and gently washed her friend. As the blood disappeared Juniper began to calm down. Using Juniper's petticoat, Polly dried her as best she could and helped her back into her dress which, because she had run with it pressed to her body, was also stained with blood.

Juniper looked down at the dress and Polly feared it would make her shake again.

'Bastard, and this was by Molyneaux,' she said, angrily.

'Oh Juniper, I love you,' Polly said almost laughing with relief.

Quickly Polly scattered the moss and grass she had been sleeping on. She picked up the soaking petticoat, wrung it out, and decided it would be safer to take it with them than leave any evidence. When she had done all she could, she took Juniper's hand and led her back through the wood towards the road and, hopefully, the south.

8

They found the road. With troops about it would be too dangerous to walk on it, so they stayed in the fields as close to the road as they dared.

'Are you sure we're going in the right direction?' Juniper said suddenly, the first words she had spoken since they had left the wood.

'I think so. Look there's the north star,' Polly pointed behind her – to the south.

'You are clever. I wouldn't know one star from another.'

'Neither do I, to be honest. But it looks the brightest. Are you all right?' she asked with concern.

'Yes. I'm fine,' she lied. In fact she felt sick to the bottom of her soul. She would never have thought she could be capable of the dreadful thing she had just done, she who could not bear to see anything suffer, who could never hunt, hid from the sound of guns at a game shoot – she had killed a man.

'He deserved it, Juniper,' Polly said as if reading her mind. 'He might have killed you once he had finished with you. In fact I'm sure he would have, he would have had to – you might talk, report him and then, no doubt they would have shot him.'

'Do you really think so?' Juniper's voice was brimming with relief. 'But I'd hardly go to the Germans, would I?'

'Why not? You're an American, this war has nothing to do with you, you're a free agent in this country. He was not to know what nationality you were – so . . .' expressively she drew her finger across her throat. 'No more, Juniper.'

'It seems a lifetime ago that all I had to worry about was which place to dine, what to wear. All that's another world, isn't it?'

'Yes, and I wonder if it will ever be the same again. Come on, Juniper, we're slowing down, if we don't hurry we'll never get back to England to find out.'

They marched on in silence. Juniper had taken off her shoes several miles back and she walked barefoot, holding them firmly in her hand.

It was just past four, they had been walking for a good three hours and already there was a pink tinge in the sky to the right of them. Juniper stopped dead.

'Polly, the sun rises in the east.'

'Yes, of course it does.'

'Then if we're going south, why is the sun to our right? It should be to our left.'

Polly stopped and looked, puzzled, at the sky. 'Oh my God, Juniper, you're right, we're retracing our steps north. I'm so sorry. It's my fault entirely. We'll just have to go back the way we came.'

'Look,' Juniper pointed over the hedge at a small village ahead of them. 'Isn't that the village where we lost the car?'

'So it is. Oh, wonderful, that kind man in the café, he'll help us.'

'No, Polly, I think that's too dangerous. He might turn us in to the Germans. Why should he risk his neck over strangers?'

'Oh, Lord, you're probably right. What do we do? I'm exhausted.'

'I think it's too risky for us to travel in the daytime. Just look at me, with these blood stains on my dress the French will arrest me, let alone the Germans. We should find a barn or something and sleep until the evening.'

'A farmer might use his barn in the daytime and find us.'

'There was a large one behind the café, I saw it when we went to the loo. He probably just uses it for storage. What do you think?'

Polly thought a moment. 'Let's risk it. In any case, there might be food there and I'm starving.'

They skirted the village, freezing like statues each time a dog barked or a rat rustled. It seemed to take them longer to get into the village than it did to walk from the wood and each minute the sky was getting brighter. Juniper was finally frustrated by the slowness of their progress. 'Come on, Polly, we'll be doing this all day at this rate,' she whispered and broke into a run. With Polly close behind she raced down a lane, past the war memorial, and slipped by the side of the café, across the yard to the barn – and not one dog barked. She grinned triumphantly at Polly. 'I enjoyed that.' And Polly, to her immense relief, saw that Juniper was laughing.

The large doors of the barn were bolted from the inside. The side door was locked. They were about to give up when Juniper noticed a small window slightly ajar. For once she did not complain of her smallness as she wriggled through leaving the larger Polly to wait for her to open the door. It seemed an age before the side door opened.

'Close your eyes,' Juniper instructed.

'What for? Don't be silly, let me in, before people get up.'

'Close your eyes. I've got a surprise for you.'

Sighing with irritation, Polly closed her eyes and allowed Juniper to lead her into the barn. 'You can open them now.'

'I don't believe it!' Polly exclaimed. There in the centre of the dusty barn stood their car. 'Hursty?' she asked, her voice fearful.

'In the back, and furious,' Juniper replied.

'Are the keys there?'

'No, but it doesn't matter. I've a spare set. The way I lose things I always travel with two sets. Come on, let's get changed.'

'Is it all there?'

'Everything except the last of the champagne and my two furs.' Juniper said as she undid her case and quickly stripped and changed into clean clothes. She left the bloodstained clothes in a pile on the barn floor.

'What are you going to do with them?' Polly asked, pointing at the offending clothes.

'Leave them there and hope the Germans find them and then our dear, kind patron will have some explaining to do, won't he? That'll teach him to steal my car.'

It was remarkable how much better they felt with clean clothes and brushed hair. They would both have liked to wash their hands and face but there was no water.

'Hang on.' Juniper disappeared into the back of the barn and returned with two bottles of champagne. 'It's not my vintage, but it will do.' Expertly she knocked the bottles against a stone slab, slicing off the tops. 'Here you are, ever wanted to wash in champagne?' She laughed with delight, the horror of the night having faded with the excitement of the day.

As quietly as they could they opened the barn doors and with superhuman effort rolled the heavy car out into the yard and as quietly closed the doors behind them. They slipped into the car.

'Ready? Hold on,' Juniper said as she pressed the starter sending up a prayer that it would fire first time. It did. She quickly slipped into gear and with her foot hard down they shot like a bullet out of the yard, rocked alarmingly as she swung the wheel tight to corner into the main road through the village, and they headed for the south at speed.

Hursty was beside himself with fury at their gross neglect of him. For over an hour he berated them in no uncertain terms, told them what he thought of them for leaving him with no food and water for so long. So vociferous was his wailing that they eventually had to risk pulling into a side road to feed him his caviar and give him water from the last bottle of Evian. With peace restored and after a hug from Polly, they were forgiven, and Hursty settled back into his basket to sleep.

They bowled along, Juniper joking and almost in a holiday mood. But Polly was concerned, she felt that Juniper was laughing too much, that beneath her apparent gaiety lurked hysteria.

'Glory be, look, I'd swear those are Germans,' Juniper exclaimed. Ahead of them was a road block manned by the French police but with two large blond men in black leather coats which gave them a sinister air. 'We can't go back,' she said looking at Polly with the wide-eyed terrified look of a trapped animal.

'Drive up slowly, keep calm,' Polly ordered as if she spent her life giving orders. She took Juniper's handbag and removed both passports.

A policeman stood in the middle of the road and waved them down. As the car slowed, the two men in black leather stepped forward. Polly opened her door and leapt out, clutching their papers. She smiled at the men who spoke in halting French. Polly replied in fluent German and a long conversation ensued. After a few minutes she got back into the car, smiling triumphantly.

'Drive on,' she said, 'Smile at them as we go by.'

With difficulty Juniper did as she said. 'What did you tell him?'

'The truth. That you are an American trying to get home and that since you do not speak French I had volunteered to help you. Then I lied, I said I had to go back to Paris, good French woman that I am, to my husband. Little did he know,' she snorted.

'But I didn't even know you spoke German.'

'I never told you. One thing for which I shall always be grateful to my father is the education he gave me.'

'Me too . . .' Juniper said with feeling.

They never stopped being grateful for the reliability of their motor car. When they thought of all the things that could have gone wrong they would shudder. Luckily the good weather held and they continued on their way despite having no windscreen.

At last they arrived in Biarritz. There was just one address in Juniper's book, a friend of her father's who would be willing to help them. Juniper climbed the steps of the imposing white villa resigned, after their experience so far, for no one to be in. She could hardly believe their luck when she heard footsteps approaching the door and she jumped excitedly from one foot to the other.

As Frank Howard opened the door, there was a large bang and from the radiator of the Citroën a large plume of steam rose into the air and the car seemed to settle on to the road as if telling them it wasn't going any further. Polly leapt from the car startled by the ominous noises coming from the engine. She grabbed Hursty.

'I think that's it, Polly. It's died.' Juniper began to laugh and found she could not stop, she laughed so much her sides began to ache. She hardly knew Frank but it did not stop her flinging her arms around him with relief and kissing him soundly on the mouth.

After long, luxurious baths, a change of clothes and

over gin and tonics they at last acquired information they could believe in. London had certainly not been destroyed, Britain was still in the war though everyone was mystified as to why Hitler had not invaded. Frank explained they were lucky to have caught him; he was travelling to Portugal in the morning to a trade fair in which his firm was taking part.

'Can we come with you?' Juniper asked ingenuously.

'I'm afraid not, Juniper. Visas are essential and they can take a week or two to get and I shan't be coming back. I go straight on to England with the navy.'

It was this information that finally broke Juniper. She began to cry and it was as if she would never stop. Her shoulders began to shake and then her whole body. She tried to sip her drink and spilled it, attempting through her tears to apologise.

'My dear, what is the matter?' Frank stood up looking helplessly at her.

Polly, horrified at seeing Juniper of all people so distressed, hurriedly explained to Frank about the German.

'You poor child,' he said. 'Juniper, listen to me. You did the right thing. This is war and what we believed in in the past no longer applies. He was the enemy. You did what was right, what any sane person would do.'

'I never killed anything in my life, Frank. Nothing.'

'I understand, Juniper. I really do. I was seventeen when I had to kill – on the Somme. But it was no different to what you had to do. Don't you realise, it was either him or you.'

'That's what I told her,' Polly said.

'I'm going to call the doctor, you need a good night's sleep. And all is not lost – I've heard there's a boat leaving tomorrow from Bayonne. If you get up very early, you should be lucky.'

The next morning the two young women thought they had stepped into hell. The dock at Bayonne was a heaving mass of fighting, arguing, desperate people. Rumour, which can transform the most calm and practical people into demented opposites of their true selves, was firmly at work. Each scrap of information, no matter how innocuous, became news of terrifying consequence by the time it had passed through the frenzied crowd.

Everyone seemed to be fighting everyone else in their efforts to get on the ship. People were screaming, crying, cursing, and pleading. Several young men jumped into the oily, murky, water and swam round to the far side of the boat in a last desperate bid for freedom. There, they were picked up out of the water by the sailors and unceremoniously dumped back on the shore. The officials stood in dazed huddles, their faces creased with fear, congregating together for comfort of a sort. Unable to control the mass hysteria and incapable of doing anything, they watched, impotent.

'Juniper!'

They swung round, over the crowd a hand was waving at them, 'Over here.' They struggled through the crowd.

'Willy Durban! What on earth are you doing here?' Juniper flung her arms round a portly young man whom, with sinking heart, Polly recognised as one of her clique from London.

'Diplomatic service,' he announced pompously. 'I was with the consulate in Nice. I'm supposed to be seeing an important person off. The only trouble is, I appear to have lost her.' He guffawed.

'Is this really the last boat?'

'Probably, Juniper. The Channel is becoming a decidedly unhealthy place to be.'

'Oh, my God. Willy, do you think you can get us on? We can pay.'

'Leave it to me, Juniper, old sport. Give me your passports and wait here.'

They waited an anxious half hour feeling, without their precious passports, very vulnerable. Willy returned waving two boarding passes at them. 'You're in luck, my old friend. Met a fellow who owes me a favour. Mind you, looking at that lot they seem to have given up official passes. You're going to have to fight your way through. I'd like to help but I've just seen the old trout I'm supposed to be looking after. Good luck.' He waved, and Polly could only feel relief that he had gone. Comforting as a solid male companion might have been, she had never liked Juniper's London friends enough to welcome one now.

'Got the cat?'

'Yes. But I don't think I can manage this case as well.'

'Dump it then.'

'The cat? I'm not leaving the cat.'

'No, daft thing, the case. I'll buy you masses of clothes when we get back to London.'

Polly clutching Hursty's basket, and Juniper her attaché case, they moved back into the crowd. At first they said 'excuse me' and 'I'm sorry' and 'forgive me'. Five minutes later they were pushing and shoving with the rest. It took them nearly an hour to reach the gangplank. Here the situation was desperate and people were falling into the water between the ship and dock. It was only a matter of time before someone was killed. Seeing their pretty faces, and hearing their English, the seaman at the bottom of the gangplank grabbed their hands and pulled them through.

'You're lucky. No more after you two, or we'll capsize.' A burly seaman grinned at them.

'Pleeze . . . me British . . . me British citizen . . .' They were both nearly knocked sideways into the water by a rough push from behind.

589

'Best stand on the gangplank, miss, or you'll be overboard. Ain't much in good manners round here. Cor look at them. British? I bet!' He snorted. 'Sorry, guv, these ladies were first. No more. Full up. Scarper,' he shouted.

From the safety of the gangplank Juniper and Polly saw behind them an old man clutching hold of an equally aged wife in whose arms was a child, watching the chaos around him with large and soulful eyes. From his clothes, his accent, his air of desperation they and the seaman doubted if his papers were anything but forgeries. But from both their faces it was easy to see why his fine eyes wore such a look of total terror and why, at the realisation that the boat was full, tears slid down the lined and frightened face of his wife.

Polly looked at Juniper questioningly.

'I heard such dreadful tales of what the Germans are doing to Jews. We'd never be able to live with ourselves, Juniper.'

'You're right, of course. Oh boy, why do I have to be travelling with someone like you – all conscience? All right.' She turned and led the way back down the gangplank.

'Not coming then, miss? Last boat to Blighty, you know.'

'We know. It's my friend here, she's a girl guide,' Juniper laughed. 'Here you are then, sir. You'd better have these for good measure.' And Juniper gave the old man their boarding passes. Polly gently touched his arm as she passed and both slipped back into the pushing throng before he had time to express his gratitude.

'What do we do now? Frank will have left,' Polly asked clutching only the cat basket for the case she had dropped had completely disappeared.

'We shall go and acquire visas for Spain. What else is there to do?' Juniper said airily and led the way.

It was easier said than done. The consulate was nearly as crowded and frenzied as the docks. There they learnt that they could not get a visa without having first acquired one for Portugal which, as all their new-found experts in the untidy queue informed them, was impossible.

'What now?' Polly said.

'We shall go to the Hôtel du Palais, book in and have the best possible lunch available. I hear the food is very good there.' Juniper set off with Polly trailing along behind her.

At the hotel there were no rooms available. People were even sleeping in the baths, they were told. However, the food was good. They ate until they thought they would burst. Polly looked at Juniper with admiration. Despite their fatigue and the heat, she was as always looking immaculate, whereas Polly felt she looked like an old sack of potatoes. Today Juniper was her old self again. It was as if the drug-induced sleep of last night had removed from her mind the horror of her experience – she had not mentioned it once. They sat over their coffee and cognacs, the cat basket secure under the table, and wondered what next to do.

'Lady Copton, isn't it?'

In unison they both looked up to see a tall dark-haired man standing over them bowing elegantly.

'Don Brisighello! What a pleasant surprise.' Juniper held out her hand which he kissed elegantly and reverently. Polly hoped he didn't want to kiss her hands. Her nails, she knew, weren't up to close scrutiny.

Juniper introduced the man as a Portuguese friend of her father's. It seemed to Polly that the whole of Europe must have known the man who, if Juniper had her way, she was supposed to think of as her own father.

'And how is your wife, Donna Salete, isn't it?'

'How clever of you to remember, Lady Copton. She is well but at home.'

'Oh, please, call me Juniper. When I'm called "lady" it makes me feel indescribably old.' She smiled blindingly at him. This was news to Polly who had never noticed any previous reluctance on Juniper's part to use her title at every opportunity. 'Why, I remember your visit to the villa as if it were only yesterday.' The smile flashed again and for a moment Polly felt she was back at home in Devon, experiencing the feeling she had had when she introduced Juniper to Jimmy. Stable lad or Portuguese grandee they all reacted in the same way to Juniper's smile.

Juniper invited him to join them and he sat down with alacrity and ordered champagne. After ten minutes Polly felt distinctly uncomfortable as the other two flirted shamelessly. She excused herself saying she felt like a walk.

She wandered aimlessly around for a couple of hours and then made her way back to the hotel. There was no sign of Juniper or her Portuguese friend. Only Hursty waited for her. She sat in the lounge of the hotel with her cat basket and had read every magazine available by the time a porter came to tell her that her room was ready for her now. Mystified she followed him.

She assumed that somehow Juniper had managed to get them a small room somewhere. She did not expect the large, airy and beautifully furnished suite into which she was shown. She took a long and leisurely bath in a tub where the hot water gushed from the taps. She had planned to try and find Juniper but, exhausted from the day, Polly fell deeply asleep.

She was awoken in the morning by Juniper banging on her door.

'Wake up, Polly. I've got our visas – Spanish and Portuguese,' she shouted through the keyhole.

She unlocked the door to find a jubilant Juniper flourishing the precious papers.

'But you didn't have my passport.'

'Oh yes, I did, when you went out for your walk, I took it, just in case.'

'But how . . . ?'

'Never ask, my dear little one, then I need not lie.'

That afternoon Juniper led her to a large black limousine waiting for them outside the hotel. It returned them to their own car outside Frank's villa to collect the rest of Juniper's luggage. Ignoring the remaining tins of food they transferred her cases and then Juniper, apologising profusely for the broken windscreen, handed the keys of the Citroën and its papers to the astonished and grateful chauffeur.

The road to the border with Spain was dense with traffic all, like them, fleeing. The other traffic edged laboriously towards safety in the intense heat, red-faced and frustrated drivers at the wheel. But their impressive car was waved on by the police. At the frontier a huge queue of cars waited in line. Polly sat back on the cushions, resigned for a long wait; the last three weeks had been nothing but long waits. Three weeks, was that all it was? It seemed more like three months, she thought. It was all going too smoothly, Polly decided, now they would be stopped for some reason or other. But there was to be no wait; the large car swept past the line of vehicles to the customs post. Evidently Juniper's Portuguese gentleman was as important as he looked for within minutes they were across the border and by early evening they were in San Sebastián and a suite at the best hotel – where else, thought Polly, amused at Juniper's style of travelling.

The world was normal again – people were strolling about laughing and unconcerned, no one was pushing, there was no air of desperation. The shops were full, the lights blazed. The first thing Juniper insisted on doing was taking Polly to shop for some clothes. From clothes they moved on to shoes, and from shoes to hats and gloves. Then they visited a perfumier and stocked up with bath oils and perfumes – or rather Juniper selected them and pressed them upon Polly who tried impotently to refuse.

'I'll never be able to pay you back for all this, you realise?' Polly said guiltily over dinner.

'Don't be silly, I don't expect you to. I've masses of money, you know I have.' Juniper looked anxiously about the dining room. 'Where's Pedro got to? He said he would be here by now. If he's been held up then we have a problem. I asked the concierge and he says the trains for Lisbon are booked for three weeks in advance – our visa to stay here is only for three days.'

'Perhaps another of your father's friends will turn up,' Polly giggled.

'Our father,' Juniper said quite sharply. 'I do hope not. They're so old,' and she shuddered.

Polly looked at her horrified. Did the shudder mean what she thought? 'Juniper, you didn't? You mean you got our visas by . . . Oh, how dreadful.' She covered her face with her hands.

'There was nothing else to do, my sweet. Don't worry. It didn't bother me unduly.'

'Oh, but it does me. I would rather have stayed in France than have you do something like that for me.'

'Don't be so pompous. Of course you wouldn't have preferred to stay there facing God knows what. And don't for one moment think I did it for you, I'd have done the same if I'd been on my own. This is war and normal behaviour no long exists,' she said pragmatically. 'It really isn't important. It doesn't bother me as it would someone like you. I'm different.'

'No woman's that different.'

'Aren't they? I feel I am. Now, in the absence of Pedro, let's see who's here and who could possibly help us.' Juniper walked half-way up the sweeping staircase the better to survey the crowds in the hallway below.

Polly followed behind her racked with worry and guilt at what she saw as a sacrifice on Juniper's part. But as the evening wore on and she watched her friend laughing and flirting, without a care in the world, she wondered if perhaps Juniper, so different from everyone else in so many ways, was different also where making love was concerned. It did not seem to mean the same to her. Or had what had happened to her in France changed irrevocably her attitude to men?

But it wasn't Juniper who rescued them this time, it was Polly. She had bought a small dog collar and lead and, leaving Juniper in the bar surrounded by an adoring audience of men, she took Hursty for a walk. A young man fascinated by a cat being walked like a dog, and certain that only an English person would do such a thing, fell into step beside her, introduced himself, and they began to talk. Two hours later it was a triumphant Polly who returned to the hotel with the news that she had made arrangements for two Wagons-Lits for them on the train to Lisbon in the morning.

'Polly, you didn't!' Juniper admonished angrily. 'How could you?'

'Good heavens, you're a fine one to talk! But, no I didn't as a matter of fact. I met this young man and we talked about cats and England if you want to know. But . . .' she began to giggle. 'But, you'll never believe this . . . his father is a member of the government and it only took one phone call, and, guess what? – his father was a friend of Marshall's!'

They stood on the platform of Lisbon station but no friends of Marshall's magically materialised.

'I'm disappointed in him, Juniper. I thought he'd become our guardian angel,' Polly said.

'We're not home yet but I'm sure the system won't let us down.'

'What system?'

'Didn't you realise? The world is just one big club created by the English.' Juniper shrugged and scanned the crowds. 'Look!' She pointed excitedly to a large crowd of people who, from their easy manner and noisy confidence, had to be English. They made their way across to where the group were enthusiastically welcoming a beautiful, sophisticated woman off their own train. She paused at the top of the steps and smiled down at them.

'Good gracious, it's Polly Frobisher, Polly . . .' the woman waved enthusiastically.

'Who is she?' Juniper asked out of the side of her mouth.

'I don't know,' Polly replied through her teeth.

'Then wave back, pretend you know her,' Juniper ordered urgently.

The two were immediately taken up by the group and bundled into their cars. Polly sat beside the strange woman and had the nightmare experience of having a conversation about herself and her family with someone she did not recognise from Adam. It was the number of people which saved her from further embarrassment, for everyone wanted to know what adventures they and the other woman, called Rosamund, had had.

There was not one bed free in Lisbon that night and it was nearly midnight when someone suggested that they drop Juniper and Polly at the British Caledonian Club where they could sleep on the sofas – no one would mind.

They were ravenous now. Around them was the debris of a cocktail party which had been held earlier in the evening, for the Duke of Kent the waiter told them, inviting them to help themselves. So with plates of canapés and some flat champagne, they settled down to sleep on the sofas in the club's drawing room.

The next morning Polly felt she had become a character in *Alice in Wonderland* as their new-found friends reappeared and, bundling them into their cars, bore them off to the International Exhibition which was the reason why Lisbon was so full.

At the exhibition all nations were represented. And there, with the German contingent, was a friend who had been with the London Embassy before the war had started. They were soon involved in sipping champagne, joking and making small talk with the others of his party –

and yet only days ago these were the very people they had been running away from, who had been inhabiting their nightmares. Polly felt she should hate them and when she found she could not, she felt guilty, as if she were letting Andrew down or being disloyal to Juniper. Andrew was one thing, Juniper another, for there she was joking and laughing as if nothing untoward had ever happened to her. Then when, with a smile, she thanked a heel-clicking, blond-haired young German for filling her glass it made everything that was happening seem even more night-marish than before.

Don Pedro had not let them down. He had alerted the British Embassy and the following day they were told that berths were available for them on a ship sailing for Britain in two days' time.

Polly was content to wait on the ship, reading, and at last with the time to write down what had happened to them. But such activity was not for Juniper. She rushed on and off the ship like a whirlwind, a luncheon appointment here, cocktails there and dinner with a 'divine' Frenchman she had met at the exhibition. Polly was glad he was French; it would have been difficult if Juniper had embarked on an adventure with a German. They had been charming to them at the exhibition but on the ship, hearing tales from the crew of ships being bombed and the horror of Dunkirk, they were the enemy again.

10

It was late at night, three days later, when the ship slipped into Greenock. Three days of fear. Three nights of terror.

The passengers crowded on to the deck too dazed to weep or cheer, all feeling disbelief that they had arrived and were alive. Alive despite the submarine which like an evil black fish of death had lurked beneath them, appearing and disappearing, as if playing games with them as it terrorised the ill-armed ship. Alive despite the planes which had bombed them, first to port then to starboard causing great plumes of water to gush impressively into the sky, bombs which could have hit them full on, if the pilot had chosen. Fear had stalked that ship at every moment of the day and night.

It was wet and miserable. Not a light was to be seen in the town which they assumed lay beyond the docks, the blackout shrouded everything.

'You had better cover Hursty's basket with this blanket I've "borrowed".'

'Why?'

'So the customs men don't see him. Don't forget you'll have to put him into quarantine otherwise.'

'Juniper!' Polly said, shocked to the core. 'I can't smuggle him in. I don't want to lose him for six months but if it's the law, I have to.'

'You amaze me. You spend hours telling me it's all right that I killed a young German – which, let's face it, was hardly lawful. Now you're telling me you won't break one tiny little law to get your precious cat into the country?'

'Yes, that's what I'm telling you. It doesn't matter that there's a war on, the law is the law.'

'Sometimes I don't think I'll ever understand you English, and especially you, Polly, my dear.'

With the other passengers they shuffled down the gangplank. Juniper and Polly stood on the quay guarding their cases.

'Welcome home, Polly.' Juniper grinned. 'I said I wouldn't come back without you.'

'I could never have got back without you, Juniper.'

'Of course you would, don't talk such rot.' She lit a cigarette and from the gloom someone shouted at her to 'put that bloody light out!' She clicked her lighter shut.

'God, do you think we can't even smoke now? I can't go through a war without smoking!'

Polly, seeing the shadowy figure of a man, dashed over to ask where the customs men were, to be told there were none. There had been so many ships in the last few days and this one had not been expected until the morning.

'But I've got a cat to declare,' she said anxiously.

'I shouldn't let a little thing like that bother you, love,' the official said with a smile.

'Honestly?'

'Well, I ain't seen no cat.'

Polly raced back to Juniper bursting with this information, wondering what to do.

'At least you tried to be law-abiding. It's hardly your fault if there's no one here, is it?' She looked about her. 'Do you think there's such a thing as a taxi? Oh, look, Polly, look at those car headlamps: those little slits make them look like cats' eyes, how sweet.'

Polly looked at the headlamps taped over with black paper, only the merest glimmer of light to guide the way. They looked ominous to her and she pulled her coat closer around her. 'Isn't it all sad-looking, after Lisbon?'

'Bet it's always dreary here,' Juniper sniffed.

'I wonder what's ahead of us, Juniper? Will I see Andrew again? What are we going to find? What's London like, what have they been suffering?'

'God knows. Best not to think about it. Look there's a taxi,' Juniper ran across the docks towards it, beating the other stampeding passengers by a whisker as she triumphantly grabbed the door handle. She and Polly bundled into the back and asked to be taken to 'the best hotel'.

'Did you ever remember who that woman Rosamund was?' Juniper asked as she fumbled in her handbag in the gloom.

'No idea at all, though I've racked my brains.' She smiled slyly at Juniper. 'Mind you I did wonder if she's another sister.'

Juniper chuckled. 'No, I'm the only one, I'm sure. In any case, I shan't let you have any others.'

Polly peered out of the window at the darkened streets, the windows of the houses shrouded in blackout, the panes of glass criss-crossed with sticky paper, like lattices, against the blast. No people walked the streets, there was no laughter or music from the pubs. She felt so sad and defeated – to be returning to an England where there was no Richard was more than she could bear to think about.

'Oh, Juniper, it's all so dark and defeated-looking.'

Juniper, finally finding her cigarette case, lit a cigarette and in its glow Polly caught sight of her lovely smile. 'I'll tell you one thing, Polly. I've really enjoyed myself these past few weeks. It's been so exciting – I've felt totally alive. Do you know, provided I don't have to kill anyone else, I think this war might turn out to be quite good fun.'